I0760993

THE PARALLEL SOCIETY COLLECTION

VOLUME 2

STUART JAFFE

The Parallel Society: Volume 2 is a work of fiction. Names, characters, places, and incidents either are the product of the author's imagination or are used fictitiously, and any resemblance to any persons, living or dead, business establishments, events, or locales is entirely coincidental.

THE PARALLEL SOCIETY: VOLUME 2

Cover art by Deranged Doctor Design

ISBN: 978-1-963517-16-3

First Edition: March, 2024
First Hardcover Edition: March, 2024

This compilation includes the following three novels:

LOST TIME

Cover art by Deranged Doctor Design

PAGES OF GLASS

Cover art by Deranged Doctor Design

THE BOLD WARRIOR

Cover art by Deranged Doctor Design

CITY OF INFINITY

Cover art by Deranged Doctor Design

For Glory and Gabe,
of course

Also by Stuart Jaffe

Max Porter Paranormal Mysteries

Southern Bound
Southern Charm
Southern Belle
Southern Gothic
Southern Haunts
Southern Curses
Southern Rites
Southern Craft
Southern Spirit
Southern Flames
Southern Fury
Southern Souls
Southern Blood
Southern Graves
Southern Dead
Southern Hexes
Southern Hart

Nathan K Thrillers

Immortal Killers
Killing Machine
The Cardinal
Yukon Massacre
The First Battle
Immortal Darkness
A Spy for Eternity
Prisoner
Desert Takedown
Lone Star Standoff
The Puppeteer
Blowback
Prime

The Ridnight Mysteries

The Water Blade
The Waters of Taladoro
Waterfire

The Parallel Society
The Infinity Caverns
Book on the Isle
Rift Angel
Lost Time
Pages of Glass
The Bold Warrior
City of Infinity

The Malja Chronicles
The Way of the Black Beast
The Way of the Sword and Gun
The Way of the Brother Gods
The Way of the Blade
The Way of the Power
The Way of the Soul

Gillian Boone novels
A Glimpse of Her Soul
Pathway to Spirit

Stand Alone Novels
After The Crash
Real Magic
Founders

Short Story Collection
10 Bits of My Brain
10 More Bits of My Brain
The Bluesman
The Marshall Drummond Case Files: Cabinet 1
The Marshall Drummond Case Files: Cabinet 2
The Marshall Drummond Case Files: Cabinet 3

Non-Fiction
How to Write Magical Words: A Writer's Companion
For more information, please visit ***www.stuartjaffe.com***

CONTENTS

INTRODUCTION

When I came up with the idea for *The Parallel Society,* I had planned the series to last six books. Each of the first three would focus on each of the elderly superheroes of the group. The last three books would introduce the new team. In that way, the entire series would represent a changing of the guard and offered a bit of symmetry.

But plans never go the way they are, well, planned.

By the end of Book 2, I had realized there needed to be one more book. When envisioning the overall series, way back at the start, I did not know all the little details of Roni and her life. The whole idea of her Lost Time did not come into existence until I started writing Book 1. But as I ventured further into the stories, I knew I had to deal with that aspect of her life before she could truly grow enough to become a strong leader. Thus Book 4, *Lost Time,* became part of the series making the whole thing seven books long.

Every book in this series presented great challenges, and no more than Book 7, *City of Infinity*. Ending a series is always a difficult thing to do. Ending a series well is even harder. A big part of the reason behind that is we authors don't get much practice at it. Starting a series? Sure. We do that far more than end them. Oftentimes, ending a series is a business decision by the publisher and out of our hands. We may not even know the book we're writing is the last one. So, when we can consciously end a series, we tend to be in uncharted territory.

For me, ending *The Parallel Society* was only the second time I had concluded a long-running series (the first being *The Malja Chronicles*, a six-book post-apocalyptic fantasy). I knew I had to finish things with Yal-hara, finally have Roni achieve her leadership role, and close out the loose ends that needed closing — all in a book that did not run too much longer than the average for the series and still deliver a good story that stood on its own. Yikes.

I won't say whether or not I succeeded. That's for you to judge. But I do feel I managed to address all the goals I had set out. I also know that Roni and the whole gang don't plague my dreams with unfinished business, so I must have done something right.

Anyway, sit back, dig in, and have fun. Happy reading!

— North Carolina, 2024

THE PARALLEL SOCIETY BOOK 4

CHAPTER 1

Before she opened her eyes, a man's voice called Roni's name. It started as a craggy sound in the distance but soon altered into a rich tone that reverberated in her ears. Her face scrunched tight. She smelled dampness in the air and her skin prickled. A rough thudding pulsated in her head as if her heart had decided it would be fun to repeatedly inflate her skull with sudden flushes of blood.

When she managed to open her eyes, she saw only white. She coughed and the white fluttered askew — a cloth had veiled her face. She reached up to remove it, causing thick aches to roll along her muscles. She groaned.

Pulling the cloth away, she gazed at the uneven ceiling of a large cave. It oscillated as if hundreds of creatures clung above. But as her eyes focused, she saw that they were chains. Thick, heavy chains. And what appeared to be books. Chained books bumping against the ceiling like abandoned balloons.

In a limp voice, she said, "What the hell is going on?"

A second later, Elliot's comforting face looked down upon her. His dark, wrinkled skin and his broad, caring smile enveloped her like a favorite blanket. He put out his hand and helped her sit up. "We are happy to see you alive," he said, his deep and precise way of speaking like a pleasant song.

Massaging her temples, Roni surveyed her surroundings. They were in a cave large enough to house at least a city block. Maybe more. Darkness shrouded the far end. Books littered the ground, some in tatters, some covered in dirt. A campfire crackled in front of her — its rich, burnt aroma rising into the air. Nearby, she saw stalagmites and stalactites reaching toward each other in massive columns while holes pockmarked the ground — some with half-buried bits of chains snaking out. Drips of water echoed in the distance.

From the fact that she had seen the chained books, she thought it safe to assume she was in the caverns below the family bookshop. Technically, not really below since the caverns existed in their own universe, but the access point sat beneath the bookshop, *In The Bind,* and that worked enough for Roni's struggling mind.

She turned her head with deliberate care so as not to cause a headrush. Squatting off to the side, a black woman stared back. This woman looked strong, had short hair, and determination blazing in her eyes. Her outfit struck Roni as a cross between pragmatic, American denim and the colorful, African robes of Senegal.

Further back, standing near one of several exits, Roni spotted a short man wearing slacks and a simple button-down shirt. The man kept his eyes on the tunnel leading away. With his arms crossed and his body bent forward, he allowed the shadows to hide much of his face. Still, he reminded Roni of Sully, the Parallel Society's leader, except this man was far younger and had a hue to his skin as if he spent too much time in a tanning bed.

She turned to Elliot, and the white cloth that had covered her face fell into her lap. "What is all this? Who are these people? Where's Gram and Sully?"

"We are deep in the caverns. The woman over there is Teanna. We met her on our way. And the one by the door is a golem Sully prepared for us."

Lifting the white cloth, Roni said, "And this?"

Elliot's eyes glistened. "Covering the face of the dead is a sign of respect."

"I died?"

"I thought you might. But, happily enough, you pulled yourself back."

Teanna stood — not as tall as Roni had expected — and gestured towards the exit. When she spoke, her voice had a melodic, articulated accent unlike any Roni had ever heard. Teanna said, "She is clearly going to be fine. Can we go now?"

"Slow down," Elliot said. "She has been through a lot."

He raised his old, gnarled cane and proscribed a special motion over Roni's head. Moments later, she felt warmth cover her body as Elliot's healing magic took form.

"The longer we wait," Teanna said, "the greater our chances of losing her. If she escapes —"

Shaking his head while continuing to cast his healing, Elliot said, "That thing looked as confused as Roni. It has suffered as well, and it will require rest, too. We have time."

Roni grabbed Elliot's hand. "Please, tell me what's happened? I don't understand how we even got here."

Elliot gazed upon her with pity that reached into her core like a twisting blade. "What's the last thing you remember?"

She closed her eyes and thought back. Her stomach dropped. Her brow tightened as she fought the fear mounting inside her. But then she smiled. She remembered. "This morning. I had breakfast with you and Sully in your apartment. I had toast with raspberry jam. Sully had a bagel and coffee. And you went with only a cup of tea. After, Sully and I took the elevator down to the bookstore, and you said you'd be down after a morning shower. Gram was getting ready to open up. She wanted me to run the register for an hour around lunch so she could have a break, and I said that I'd planned to spend the whole day in the Grand Library catching up on work, so yeah, I'd do it."

Elliot placed a hand on her shoulder. "That was days ago."

"What?" The word echoed from deep within. From her core. From her past. From a little girl learning that her mother had died in a car accident and her father had lost his mind with grief, yet she had no memory of it happening. Gram assumed the duties of raising her and called it Lost Time. But to Roni, it was a dark gap in her life — and not the only one.

Her body shivered, and Elliot returned to his healing motions. A scream gurgled up her throat, but she wrestled it back. Something bad had happened, and if she wanted to stop things from getting worse, she needed to be clear-headed. Besides, no way would she let herself fall apart in front of a stranger.

She eyed Teanna before leaning closer to Elliot. "This can't be happening again," she whispered.

"This is different," he said. "You'll see. I'm here to aid you before the Lost Time can swipe everything." He glanced back at the large, empty cavern. "Maybe it can't ever do it again. Doesn't matter. Give it a chance and I feel confident your memories will return."

"I know what Lost Time feels like. This is exactly it, and I know what it'll do to me." The panic rose up her chest. She clenched her muscles until it relaxed back into the pit of her stomach like a lump of mud.

"This isn't like what happened with your parents."

"Why? What's so different?"

He gestured to the echoing space around them, the books on the ceiling, and those on the floor. "This is all that's left of the Cave of Lost Time."

CHAPTER 2

Roni opened her eyes and saw only white. A piece of paper had settled on her face. She pulled it off, and as she lifted her head from her worktable in the Grand Library, she swooned. Reaching for the edge to steady herself, Roni paused long enough to regain her equilibrium.

After several seconds, she grumbled as she picked up the papers that had dropped to the floor. She had never passed out like that before — just going along and then suddenly faceplanted into the wood. At least, never without a hefty amount to drink.

Maybe she had been working too hard. Not looking after herself. But that didn't seem right. Ever since returning from Ireland, she had started to exercise and made sure to eat breakfast with Elliot and Sully at least every other morning. Although, the exercise mostly consisted of finding excuses to avoid the gym, and she couldn't really call a breakfast of toast with raspberry jam good nutrition.

"Okay," she told the empty library. "Message received."

She would have to do better. After all, what was the point of going through all her hard work restoring the Library, if she only fell down dead the moment she could finally make use of it?

The Grand Library had become a treasure to Roni. Originally, Gram appeared to have used the place as a way to keep Roni out of trouble and limit her involvement. Let her join the Parallel Society but stick her in the Grand Library organizing for a few years. Even after Sully took over the leadership role, the job still felt like a way to sideline her. And with all that had happened in Ireland, it should have felt like a punishment.

Except, for Roni, the Library had transformed her as much as she had transformed it. Most of the texts were old diaries and journals of those who had been in the Society before her. Far too much to read for one person, but the act of sorting through it all had revealed plenty of exciting tidbits.

Like Benjamin Zepke's 1924 descriptions of a universe with people that made the Lilliputians sound like giants. Or the 1872 account by Margaret Carnicero of a mermaid-esque creature that fell into the Atlantic Ocean and caused a lot of trouble with British sailors. And, of course, the rather flamboyant journals of Sasha Grace who spent more time discussing her desire to bed various men from various universes than actually detailing how she succeeded in her missions.

Roni glanced across the beautiful woodwork to the far corner where she kept her growing map of the caverns. It had been a project that consumed her from the start — combing through the drawings and sketches and anecdotes and descriptions of the caverns to compose a single, reliable map. Since much of the exploration had been done long ago, back when they knew far less about the dangers of traveling through the caverns, much of the information lacked an accurate scale. But Roni persevered.

All because of the one section labeled *Lost Time*.

The area had no known direct connection to the rest of the caverns, leaving Roni to resort to an educated guess as to its placement on the map, but over the last two years of work, she grew more confident that she could find it. In fact, she had moved its location three times — always a little closer, a little clearer, a little surer that she would one day step foot in the large cave. There were two clear gaps from the cave to the rest of her map. Somewhere in all the books of the Library, somebody had to have put the answer to paper. After all, somebody already found the Cave of Lost Time once before.

She glanced at her laptop's clock. She had promised Gram that she would mind the bookstore at lunchtime and did not want to be late. Gram's need for punctuality had worsened recently.

"Not just recently," she said as she sat at the table.

When they had returned from Ireland, Gram became stricter, if that was possible. Roni tried to be understanding. The woman had spent decades mourning the loss of her daughter, and Roni's actions at the Abbey had brought a lot of the secrets concerning that loss to the surface.

But Roni's patience had begun to wear thin. Yes, Gram went through losing her daughter all over again, but that same daughter was Roni's mother. An echo of her, at least. Losing the mother she barely remembered ripped through her whenever she thought of it. And as much as she had promised herself that she would ease back on the search for the truth of what had happened to her and her parents — her Lost Time, as Gram would say — Roni had pushed ahead with greater urgency.

Rubbing her face, she sighed. She could hear Sully in her head. *Books are great, wonderful things but you still need people.* Closing her laptop, she thought about going out later that night. Maybe drive into Philly and bar hop for a bit. Probably not what Sully had in mind, but she could use the break and the release.

"Besides," she said. But she never finished the sentence.

The blast struck in the center of her head. It burst outward like a migraine volcano erupting throughout her brain. She cried out. Her knees buckled. As she crumpled to the floor, warm blood dribbled from her nose.

That warmth spread. Not in blood, though. When the initial shock to her system waned, the pleasant warmth that took hold reminded her of days spent under the sun in the Poconos.

And that thought brought to mind her father. Lawrence Rider. Before the death of his wife, Roni's father was a vibrant man, truly full of life. She could see him standing on the shore of Lake Wallenpaupack, his thin but well-defined body golden and shining. He waved for her to follow him into the water. She was scared. Maybe only six- or seven-years-old. The lake was big. Maybe a few billion years old. It would gobble her whole.

Her concern rippled across her skin, and another painful blast in her head spun her world. She found herself sitting in the visiting area of Belmont Behavioral Hospital waiting to see her father. She was an adult again. And he was lost again. His gaunt and vacant eyes, his wasting body, his labored breaths — how could this be the same man?

He had leaned toward her that day. She had told him that she knew about the Parallel Society, and he inclined his head with the same water-gobbling fear she felt so long ago. "More will be coming." His warning. His prophecy.

"Come on, Roni," he said, his voice young and comforting.

She looked over her shoulder, back at her mother standing by a cooler filled with water, soda, and beer. Her mother, Maria, pointed toward the lake and smiled with rare sobriety. "Go on," she said. "Daddy will be with you."

Roni toddled across the stones and pebble-strewn shore until she reached the edge of the water. Her father stood knee deep and smiling.

Children screeched and chased each other while adults waded in and out of the dark waters.

Dark. That's how her mind felt most often. Lost Time.

Her father's voice reached out to her from the same place the migraine had begun. "Gram called it that for a reason," he said. It was his voice now, old and cracking, yet the tone held the potency of his life before.

"Daddy?" she said, her own voice a mixture of her adult and child selves as if only a thin membrane separated the different vibrations.

"Come out to me," he said, standing in the lake, his arms wide open and welcoming. "Come out to me." He stood in a hallway of the hospital, his eyes wide open and lost.

"Daddy?"

His call returned weaker, quieter, as if somebody faded down the volume control in her mind. She thrust her arms out, trying to snatch anything that might bring her father back. But as his voice swept out into the emptiness from where it had come, a new wave crashed over her — pain.

Gripping her skull, she rolled onto her side, her back banging against the Library worktable, and she screamed. The blood running from her nose trickled into her mouth, bitter and metallic. Tears welled in her eyes, leaking out of her tightly-closed lids, and her brain continued its painful pounding.

Then nothing.

Quiet.

She heard only her own breathing.

The pain dissipated. The pounding flowed away. Though her heart thrummed against her ribs and her muscles juddered when used, she managed to pull back up to the table. Gazing around the Library, she sought any sign that what happened had actually happened.

"Of course, it happened," she said, the sound of her voice — her adult voice — easing her mind. "I can still taste the blood."

What had happened was an entirely different question. She had experienced a flash of memory, a glimpse of her Lost Time. That much was clear. But what of the rest of it?

Ever since joining the Parallel Society, experiencing weird occurrences no longer jarred her as much, but that didn't mean she accepted it all with ease. Or pain free, for that matter. But it did mean that she would not deny the experience. She had seen her father in the hospital standing in a hallway, beckoning her to come. He saw her, recognized her. It felt real.

This could not be a misfire in her brain. She refused to entertain the idea. Though a small whisper in the back of her mind suggested that she should see a doctor, check for a tumor, make sure nothing bled where it shouldn't. After all, she had stepped into other universes. She had been exposed to alien environments and alien germs. The possibility that such exposure might cause a change in her physical chemistry — in her brain chemistry — could not be denied.

No. No. She could not allow those thoughts. It would be the cruelest irony for the universe to ruin her mind just as she had begun to find her place. She refused to accept that she might end up in a straightjacket, banging her head against a padded cell. If she went to the Belmont Behavioral Hospital, she would go as a regular visitor, not as a new patient.

"Then I'm going," she said. That would settle it. She simply had to climb upstairs, get in her car, and drive out to the hospital. She would visit her father, and in doing so, she would learn the truth. Either he would tell her why (and how) he had called upon her, or she would sit with him in silence until he fell asleep. Then she would make an appointment for a brain scan.

Roni remained sitting at her worktable for another five minutes. She opened her laptop but did not hear or see. Her mind relived the strange experience that melded with her oceanside memory as she sought a crack in its armor — a confirmation that would settle the debate inside her. But with a sigh, she closed the laptop. Procrastination would not solve anything.

When she stepped out of the elevator onto the main floor of the bookstore, she noticed the lack of customers. According to her phone — 11:47 am. Usually, the store had at least a few browsers by this time. Plus, they had some regulars who spent their lunch break walking up and down the narrow aisles and occasionally buying a book or two.

"Gram?" Roni said but received no answer. She walked to the front. Gram was not there. The front door was locked and the CLOSED sign hung in the glass.

Part of her thought to go up to the fifth floor where the Old Gang lived and check on her grandmother. But Elliot and Sully were around. If something important had happened, they would have told her. More likely, Gram decided to close shop rather than trust her granddaughter to arrive on time.

Don't be like that, she thought. Gram had been a lot better lately.

Stricter but better about her assumptions. Besides, Roni had to admit that she had given Gram plenty of reasons over the years to doubt.

It didn't matter at the moment. Gram had closed the store, so Roni no longer needed permission to skip minding the front desk. She could visit her father and avoid an onslaught of pointed questions which she had no way of answering.

Not yet, anyway. Soon, though. Soon she would know. Even if it meant she was losing her sanity. Even if that whispering voice grew louder in her head. Even if it proved to be right.

CHAPTER 3

Elliot halted his cane above Roni's head. His brow narrowed as he observed her. "Are you okay?"

"Why do I get the feeling you're going to ask me that question about seven hundred more times today?" She tossed a stone into the dark end of the cavern and listened to its small clicks as it bounced along.

He chuckled. "I think it better that you have somebody asking than nobody asking at all."

Teanna stood against one bumpy section of cavern wall, her arms folded tight, and watched Roni whip another stone into the dark. A tremendous number of questions battered Roni's mind about this woman — though *woman* might be the wrong word. Elliot had said they met Teanna on the way here which meant that she came from somewhere else, from a different universe. Beneath those robes, she could be a millipede or have an extra head.

Elliot resumed casting with his cane. "Tell me what happened just now. You closed your eyes, you coughed, and then I saw you startle."

"I remembered something. From that last morning. Something strange happened in my head. I was in the Grand Library, and I made a connection with my father. At least, I think that's what happened. It was confusing. And worrying. So, I went to see him."

"And?"

"Nothing. That's all." She threw another stone — this time with enough force to rattle other stones loose when it hit the ground.

"Why are you angry? This is good."

"Good?" She hocked the word out like a vile clump of mucus lodge in her throat. "I've already spent my life with one large chunk of my memory stolen. How is going through it again *Good?* You think I should be praying for my entire mind to become part of Lost Time?"

"Praying?" His face opened wide with mock concern. "Did you forget you're an atheist?"

"Very funny," she said, but even her annoyance could not hold. She snickered and he laughed.

Teanna swirled her robes as she spun toward them. "If you two can make jokes, then you two can walk. We need to go."

Before Roni could snap a reply, Elliot put his hand out between them. "Roni's healing is not done. She has already started to remember. If we wait longer, the benefits to her and us will be better than rushing off now."

"If we wait longer, it'll be that much harder to find that thing. Do you want me to lose her trail?"

Roni scrunched her face as she looked at Elliot. "Trail? Now there's a thing leaving a trail?"

With all the firm kindness of a concerned uncle, Elliot pressed his hand on her shoulder. "You must calm yourself. You have been through an ordeal that has left your mind jumbled. I know you want answers, and they will come. I believe it. But you must have patience. The connections in your brain that make up, store, and access all of your memories were not created in an instant. But the Cave of Lost Time swiped them nearly that fast. That is why you suffered."

"Is that what happened in the Grand Library? Did I lose more memories then?"

"No. That was a very different phenomenon."

Teanna said, "At least go a touch faster. Not so much that you burn away her mind, but I know my job, and I can tell you —"

With a sharp swing of his cane, Elliot said, "If I were to hasten the restorative patterns I'm using, I could end up worsening her condition. She might forget more even as she gains what she has lost."

Roni reached out towards him. "But it sounds like we don't have time."

"I trust the golem more than this woman, and he doesn't seem anxious at my slower approach."

Indeed, the golem continued its vigil by the tunnel exit, never once bothering to look in their direction; however, Roni sensed that it listened closely to them. If Sully had given this golem powerful hearing or a similar ability, then Elliot's faith in the creature made sense. It could hear whatever Teanna feared might escape.

Roni snatched another stone from the ground, but before she threw it off with a huff, her eye caught its smooth shape and the speckles of green glistening off the firelight. Here she sat in the Cave of Lost Time, a place she had sought for years, yet she tossed it away without a thought. While she believed in Elliot's intentions, she had lived with Lost Time for decades. If he succeeded in restoring her memories, great. But she would be a fool to rely on those gaps ever fully returning. She placed the stone in her pocket.

Glowering at Teanna, Elliot pointed at the fire. "You want us to move quicker, please get some more wood. I won't be able to help Roni as well when I can barely see."

"It's good, it's good," she said, throwing her arms above her head. "Just get back to it, you slow old man. I'll get the wood. I need the light, too. I've got to look over my maps — again."

Elliot scowled, but he began turning his cane once more. Roni reached up to stop him. His shock shifted to defeated concern. "You are going to demand that we leave now."

Sheepish, she said, "We have to."

"Teanna is wrong."

"You said it took us days to get here. If we don't start after that thing —"

"But you can't know —"

Teanna said, "Nobody can know. The only thing for certain is that the Keeper is moving away from us."

Putting her hand over Elliot's, Roni said, "We'll go slow. We'll take breaks for you to heal me. But we are going."

Elliot held her stare before nodding. Teanna launched into packing up. "Thank you," she said.

Roni kept quiet. Her gut told her she had made the right decision. The rest of her wasn't so sure.

CHAPTER 4

Roni parked in the Belmont Behavioral Hospital lot and idled. How many times had she done this? No matter her mood, no matter if she came to provide news or simply keep him company, no matter her age or her hopes or how long it had been since her last visit, whenever she came to see her father, she started out by sitting in her car and staring at the cold, brick building.

It was not ritual. At least, she didn't think it was. Though she suspected that after so many years, her mind had ritualized some of it. But no, in her heart, she knew the real reason — fear.

As a girl, she feared seeing her father turning into a madman. As a teen, she feared that he would never get better, never return to the man she barely remembered. As an adult, she feared that she had given up on him by accepting that he would always be this shell of his former self.

This time, however, her fears were not the troubles of a loving daughter struggling to deal with the loss of her father's mind. That always scared her, but this visit, if she wanted to be honest, she feared for her own mind.

Worse than that, I'm more scared that I'm sane. At least if she were going crazy, she could discount everything and drift away into a madwoman's bliss.

Cloud-covered sky shrouded the area in gray, plastering her with its pall. A rainstorm had passed by hours earlier, and the world remained damp and grim.

"Get moving," she said, letting her voice bounce back in the car. "This won't get any easier by sitting still."

As she headed toward the main lobby, she caught her reflection in a wide puddle. Her ragged eyes gazed back at her like a woman walking straight into the place she belonged. With a firm step, she disrupted the water, shattering the image, and marched onwards.

"Ms. Rider, I'm so glad you're here," the desk nurse said with uncommon exuberance. The hospital brought together the worst aspects of a medical facility and a library — murmured, tense quiet with an antiseptic atmosphere. But this nurse nicked through that with her strong voice. "We were going to call you in."

Roni's pace slowed. "Is something wrong?"

"No, no. Good news." As another nurse walked by, the desk nurse snapped her fingers. "Jennie, come here. This is Ms. Rider. She goes by Roni. Roni, this is Jennie. She started a few weeks ago and she's the one who found out."

"Found out what?" Roni sprang her attention to Jennie — mostly for information, but partly to gloss over not recalling the head nurse's name. "Somebody tell me what's happened to my father."

Jennie had the bubbling enthusiasm of somebody new to a career. "Oh, you're the daughter? Great to meet you. Your father is having a wonderful day today. Really perked up all of a sudden. First thing out of his mouth was that he wanted to see you."

"When was this?" Roni curled her lip at the desk nurse. "Because nobody contacted me."

"Not long ago," Jennie said, but Roni couldn't tell if the woman was covering for the hospital or simply excited at Mr. Rider's improvement. Splashing her bright smile, Jennie went on, "Come with me to the Day Room, and I'll have Mr. Rider brought out. See for yourself. He looks fantastic."

Roni knew the way but allowed Jennie to lead. Once in the Day Room, she waited alone. The room had plenty of chairs and tables for patients to spend their days playing games or working on puzzles or watching television. Large windows allowed the world outside to bathe the room. Even on a gray day. At the moment, the room stood empty — probably mealtime or naptime or some other scheduled control of the patients' lives.

She wondered if she might be the one to be wheeled around soon — maybe by Jennie — or if the thought of mealtime or naptime would become the height of the day. From the hall, Jennie's voice bounced its way into the room. "Yes, yes, Mr. Rider. Your daughter is here. She's waiting for you."

Roni had seen her father wheeled into the Day Room so many times over the years that she could see it before it happened. His feet would lead the way, poking ahead of the chair like bumpers on an old car, and the rest of him would arrive, slumped to the side, head lolling as his unfocused eyes trailed off at whatever played out in his mind. On a bad day, drool might be swinging free from his lip or his fingers would never stop pilling the blanket over his legs.

But from Jennie's energized attitude, Roni expected an alert version of her father. Perhaps she would even hear a coherent word or two. Certainly no drool. With any luck, he would answer her questions, confirm her fears, or dispel them.

Perhaps I'm fooling myself.

Lawrence Rider pushed the door open with his hand and strode into the Day Room with all the pride of a conqueror. His tattered, maroon bathrobe fluttered like a cape, and his rail-thin body puffed as he approached. Even his unkempt hair and unshaven face added a touch of grizzled warrior to his image.

However, when he turned back to Jennie and squeezed her shoulders, the idea of a heroic figure fled with his manic, crazed voice. "Thank you, thank you. The universe thanks you and it doesn't know it yet, but one day, it might. The universe is fickle that way. But you — you're incredible. I mean it." His fervor challenged Jennie's joyful demeanor.

She laughed, not too convincingly, and removed herself from his grasp. "You can see your daughter is here. Just like you wanted. Go be with her." Before he could launch into more praise, she nodded at Roni and hastened an exit.

Lawrence rushed across the room and embraced her with surprising strength. "My sweet, sweet daughter. Oh, the things you have had to go through. So unfair. But it's all going to be different now. We've finally heard the call."

He spoke like a racehorse held in the gate for so long that when the door finally snapped open, he could only move with a full-on gallop. Stepping back, he gazed upon his daughter, and she squirmed under his appraisal. His eyes watered up.

"Chairs!" He lunged across the room, grabbed two chairs, and swung them in the air, nearly cracking the legs across a sofa, and settled in an open space by one of the windows. Waving her over like a child anxious for a cookie, he sat and crossed his legs.

Roni tried to hide the trepidation in her steps, but her nerves vibrated at every end. "You seem to be feeling better."

"Of course, I am. Don't you feel it? After what we both

experienced, I should think you'd be bouncing off the walls, too. How can you not? Well, of course, you don't know, don't see, it's all new to you. But it happened. She reached out to us. Connected us. As I always hoped and waited for. But after so long, I thought for sure I had been duped. I mean, we're talking about Chak, after all. What if I had believed in a lie, and in the end, I had gone mad for nothing but a dream which would never become true?" He peered out the window, smiling at the gray clouds as if they warmed his face. "But here we are. I have to be careful. If I allow myself to lie to myself, then there might not be enough of myself when the time comes. Your mother always said I go too far ahead of what needs to be done now. Patience, she would tell me. And she was right." He let his head roll back, and he laughed. "She was right. Despite all her own impulsiveness and impatience, she was right."

Roni wondered if she had suffered another mental blast. No migraine, though. The world around her had not jumped anywhere. In fact, the longer she remained seated with her father and nothing changed, the deeper her heart sunk until she could feel it in her shoes.

With great care, she said, "Do you understand where you are?"

"Yes, yes. I'm in the Belmont Behavioral Hospital."

"That's right. And do you understand that in all the years you've been here —"

"Stop it," he said with a chuckle. "I'm fine. Better than ever. I know how this must look. After all, if you're standing still while the world around you spins out of all sense and control, if everybody to your left and right are screaming mad yet you stand serene and confident, then of course, you are the one that looks crazy, but I assure you, I am the sane one." He jumped to his feet, rushed across the room, and passed his hand along the wall. "Look how solid this is. When we go, we'll need to remember that not all solids are solid."

If he had been rambling from the confines of his wheelchair, Roni would not have listened to a word or given him much thought at all. But he stood. He jumped around like a teenager. He moved with such living fluidity that she could not deny something had happened. And since it came on the heels of her own odd experience, her insides twisted at the implications.

Wincing at her thoughts, she said, "Is it possible that, for a short time today, earlier in the morning, that maybe we were somehow mentally connected?"

"Isn't that why you're here? I called out to you, told you to come here."

"You caused that to happen?"

"No, no, not the cause. That's the reason we have to go." He hurried back to the chair. "I merely recognized what was happening and took advantage of it. Tried to, at least. Been waiting for so long. But I kept my faith and she delivered."

Roni's skin prickled. Some remnant from the mental blast, this connection her father rambled about, some part of it flashed an image in her mind. "You said *she delivered.* Do you mean Mom? But Mom died in the car accident."

Breathing hard, Roni's father paused. His jaw dropped an inch, and pity filled his eyes. "I'm sure Gram meant well, she always means well, but you should know better than to trust her words at face value."

Roni's chin quivered. "What are you saying? Is Mom alive?"

"I wish that were true. Maybe it is. But not like you mean. Never like that." With visible effort, Lawrence tried to slow down. "There was no car crash. Not a crash that took her away from me. I wish it had been. That would've been easy to accept. Well, I'd have been devastated, but still far easier than reality."

Grabbing his bouncing knees, she said, "Stop it. Please, just answer me straight."

But he was gone again. "Not a straight line. Or maybe it is and I can no longer see it."

"You're saying there was no accident. Then what happened to her? Why are you in here? If this is true, then I never had Lost Time over the accident because it never happened. But I do have Lost Time, so why?"

"No car. No accident. Your mother died for the Parallel Society. Well, no that's not accurate, but it was because they exist, because of the caverns."

Roni's thoughts cascaded over each other as fast as her heart raced blood through her veins. Gram always told her of the car accident. She always insisted that Roni's mother had wanted nothing to do with the Society. She always said that she had never lied. Once again in her life, Roni found the opposite to be true. Except she had doubted Gram before — sometimes with disastrous results. And her father was a raving madman.

Before her mind could rationalize away her doubts, her father scurried to the door that led back to the patient rooms. He opened it a fraction and peeked out. Bent over as if he could somehow be camouflaged against the wall, he rolled his head at her.

"Come, come," he whispered, keeping one eye on the nurses. "I've got to show you the truth."

"I won't sign you out of here," she said. "I don't think I can anymore. About ten years ago you were legally committed. It would probably take a court order and —"

"My room. Come with me to my room. You need to see what I've been working on since we were touched. Then you'll know. You'll see and you'll know and you'll have no doubts that I'm speaking the truth."

He slid the door further open, crouched even lower, and swept off down the hall. With an impatient sigh, Roni rose and followed. She made no effort at secrecy — the nurses didn't care if she visited her father's room — but her mind swirled at the thought of Gram's secrecy. Or if she betrayed Gram by so easily swaying to her father's viewpoint. If only they weren't family. Her father, her grandmother — if they were two strangers Roni had been asked to judge, she could make a decision with ease. This one spoke true. That one lied. But with family, everything became muddled.

However, when she entered her father's room, the world narrowed into sharp lines. Little more than a glorified dorm room, her father's place bore little to signify the individual who lived there. Except for the drawings — on clean paper, on used paper, directly on the walls.

Roni's father had drawn the same image over and over. To the nurses, the drawings must have looked like the abstract scribbles of an abstract mind. A rabbling set of lines that never intersected. They resembled the edges of rivers or segments of a maze, at best. But most of them showed nothing that an average viewer could point to and understand as meaningful.

Roni understood right away. Over the past few years, she had seen countless examples of similar sketches. Maps.

Her heart quickened again, only this time fear did not plague her. She moved closer to the ragged lines on the wall, her fingers shaking as she touched the cool surface. Picturing the maps she had seen in the Grand Library books, picturing the gaps between pieces, she tried to orient her father's work with what she knew.

And it clicked into place.

"The Cave of Lost Time," she whispered.

Arching back and reaching his hands toward the sky, her father let out a boisterous howl. "Yes, yes, yes! The Cave of Lost Time."

"You know how to get there?"

"Do I? Oh, I see. You still don't see. I see but you see not."

Grabbing her father's face in her hands, she narrowed her focus to his eyes. "Do you know how to get there?"

"I know my part, of course. Just as you know yours. And now that you know that I know and I know that you know, we can know together. We can go. We must go. We have to see the Keeper."

"The Keeper?"

"You poor thing. Gram has kept you in the dark for so long. Unless she never knew, either. Probably she didn't. If she knew, she would never have sent your mother. I would never have followed. None of this would have ever happened." He broke free of her grasp and checked the hall. "Don't blame Gram. She tried her best. Though she did lie some. I suppose you can blame her for that."

"Dad," Roni said, the snap in her voice pulling his attention. "This Keeper in the Cave of Lost Time — can it help me —"

"My sweet, sweet daughter. The Keeper will help us all. Why do you think we've been called?"

"That brain thing? That was the Keeper calling us?"

"That was so much more. But we must go see. Now. It's the only way to set things right. The only way to stop what you've already started."

Roni looked back at the marks on the wall. She had to consult her maps at the Library, had to make sure. But if this checked out, if her father spoke the truth … she quashed those thoughts fast. After decades of thinking that every glimmer in the eyes or twitch of the face signified a spark of life in her father, she dared not hope that this massive change could be counted on.

Yet still, she hoped.

CHAPTER 5

Swirling her finger in a pouch of instant oatmeal, Roni wondered why Elliot had not packed a spoon. She would have to ask him when he finished his rest. The healing and the hiking had taken its toll. They had halted in the middle of a passageway with water trickling streams down one smooth wall.

The golem continued sentry duty whenever they stopped, sneaking furtive glances in her direction. Of course, a golem lacked the subtlety to go unnoticed. The mass of sculpted clay seemed to want to talk with her, but it did not move, unwilling to abandon its post.

The moment Elliot closed his eyes, Teanna announced she wanted to scout ahead and left. Roni wondered if the woman would ever come back. For that matter, why did she stay with them at all?

Digging her heels into the dirt and stones, Roni clenched her jaw. On an intellectual level, she understood why Elliot had refused to rush ahead with her memory. She had experienced the dangers firsthand. With every bit of information he had restored, she felt gut-punched and wary. And worried.

After all, the bits of memory she had reclaimed coupled with the fact that she had awoken in the Cave of Lost Time implied that she had used her father's maps to come out here. The fact that they had a golem suggested that Sully knew where she was. But what of Gram? What of her dad? What of the million other questions pinging her brain?

She finished the oatmeal — pasty and cold but at least her stomach no longer rumbled — and she waited for Elliot to wake up. Those minutes lasted an eternity. Yet when he finally stirred, the eternity disappeared, and she hustled over to his side.

"Feel better?" she asked.

Elliot grinned. "I should be asking you that."

"Teanna is scouting. If you're up for it, we can start another healing session."

"Give me a moment."

She helped him up. "I was thinking about things you can tell me that wouldn't cause problems."

With a suspicious eye, he said, "Oh? What is it you have in mind?"

"Don't sound like that. I won't ask you about my father or about how we got out here or why or any of that."

"But?"

"But you could tell me about Teanna. Not her history with us, but just who she is. Heck, what is she? That kind of thing."

"We have to be so careful with the way the brain works."

"Not knowing is a torture in itself. And we're in the caverns right now. You and Gram and Sully have made sure that I've learned to respect the threats inherent in this place. Just sitting here healing is not enough. How can I decide what to do when I know so little?"

She babbled any argument she could think of, and Elliot endured each one. She did not stop until she saw the change on his face — a look he often had when Sully talked him into doing something he resisted.

"I suppose," he said, each word strained, "that I could provide some basic facts about Teanna."

"Thank you."

"But you must not ask specific questions. Be satisfied with what I provide."

"Yes, yes. Anything is appreciated."

Elliot crossed his legs and set his cane upon his knees. "Teanna is human. At least, from all I've heard, I think the universe she comes from is similar enough that we can consider her human. She's a member of her version of the Parallel Society which is what brought her out here into the caverns." He paused, bumping his head from side to side as he considered what else he could divulge. "She's a tracker for her team, probably because she has an ability to detect relics."

"She's got a power?" Roni shook her head. "Am I the only one without powers?"

As the corners of Elliot's mouth lifted, his shoulders eased off some of their tension. "You have far more power than you ever give yourself credit for."

She leaned into him, letting her head drop to his shoulder. "This last memory that you brought back — Dad said I needed to come out here to find the Keeper. Do you know who or what the Keeper is?"

Elliot's body tightened. "Please. No questions."

"But I'm not asking about something I don't know. Dad told me about the Keeper."

"Then you must be satisfied with what you recall he said."

"Fine. What about the books back at the Cave? I saw them already. Can we talk about them?"

Elliot groaned as he clambered to his feet. "Perhaps it's best to wait on this subject as well."

Unable to leash the fire inside, she flailed her hands out. "Good Lord, this is getting cruel." She pointed at the golem. "Will you at least tell me about that thing? Why is it here and not Sully?"

Elliot's stubborn stare broke. His eyes glistened. Turning away, he rubbed his palms against his cheeks and they came away wet.

"What is it?" she asked, her anger dissipating into guilty concern. "What did I say?"

Elliot required a moment to pull himself together — an endless moment as far as Roni could tell. Her feet tapped away, and her shivering exhalations did nothing to calm her. By the point that she wanted to whirl Elliot around, scream at him, and demand answers, he faced her with a sense of broken peace.

"When you felt that pain in your head, when you made some type of link with your father, the two of you were not the only ones who were struck."

"Sully?"

"He was finishing a snack before coming downstairs, and he started shaking. Violent shaking. His eyes rolled up, and he called out your name. When the whole thing ended, he told me that he had been connected to you and Lawrence. I thought it was over. But then ..."

"What? Is he okay? What happened?"

"He had a heart attack. He's not here with us because he had a heart attack and is recovering at a hospital."

Roni's emotions twirled through her. "But he is recovering? He's going to be okay?"

"I don't know. I'm here with you."

CHAPTER 6

The odor permeating the hospital left Roni with a turned stomach. At least, she tried to convince herself that the sour smell caused her discomfort. But she knew better.

When she returned to the bookstore after visiting her father, Roni received a text from Gram that Sully had suffered a heart attack. Immediately, Roni bolted back to her car and sped off for the hospital. Her mind locked in a rotation of *No, no, no* and *Hold on, hold on, hold on.*

Navigating through the maze of corridors, and with the help of a few nurses, she finally found Sully's room — a two-bed affair with a curtained partition. Thankfully, the second bed remained unoccupied. Roni swept right by Gram and up to Sully.

"Are you okay? What happened to you? Do you need to rest? I can kick Gram out if she's bugging you."

Sully's lips lifted. The exertion weakened him. Yet with great effort, he lifted his left hand and patted Roni's arm. Tubes ran under his nose and a clip on his finger kept a machine recording his pulse.

Stepping back, she took a good look at him. Sully had always been a small man, but he had shrunk noticeably since that morning's breakfast. His glasses sat askew on his nose, and as Gram adjusted them, Roni noticed how thin Sully's legs looked under the blanket — like bones without muscle. She knew a heart attack could seriously damage a person, but she did not understand how it could have so drastically changed him in mere hours.

"Where have you been?" Gram said. "We were worried about you." Her calm tone did not trick Roni. The sharp bite hunted right under the surface like a prowling shark.

Roni knew how to play this game, though. She and Gram had dueled words for too many years. "You should have texted me earlier. I would've dropped everything."

"I was a little busy keeping Sully alive. When I came downstairs to wait for the ambulance, I expected to find you at the desk — you said you were going to watch the store for me so I could eat lunch. But you weren't there. Thank the Lord Elliot was there with me. I don't know what I would have done on my own."

Gram lifted the small crucifix resting on the shelf of her bosom and kissed it. She shifted to one hip and sighed along with her chair. Never a small woman, she had put on weight recently and that worried Roni. Gram was younger than Sully, but not by much. She had to take better care of her health.

In an effort to defuse any fuss, Roni said, "I'm sorry. Something happened, and I needed to run out. I intended to be back as soon as possible, but then things changed."

"That's your excuse? A bunch of vague words and *things changed?* Listen to me, young lady, if seeing poor Sully here doesn't get it through to your head, I don't know what will. We are not going to live forever. You will be taking over the Society, and judging by dear Sully, it might happen sooner than we all think. You cannot lead the next generation based on *things changed.* We have to be able to rely on you."

"Are you really going to bring up this old argument? I thought we were beyond that."

Gram's lips clenched. "I thought so, too, but then you pull a stunt like this when I most needed you."

"I didn't know Sully was going to have a heart attack today," Roni said, her voice rising. "Next time one of you plans to rush off to the damn hospital, I'll be sure to read all of your minds and schedule accordingly."

"Watch your language."

Elliot entered the room carrying a tray with two coffee cups. He smiled at Roni before reading the scowling faces. "If the two of you insist on behaving abominably, at least have the courtesy to do so outside of Sully's recovery room."

He set the coffee on Sully's rolling table and sat on the side of the bed. Adjusting Sully's blanket, he inclined his head toward his cane. "I'm sorry I could not have been quicker. Had I reached you sooner, I might have mitigated the heart attack altogether."

Sully waved his hand and shook his head, but Elliot clasped that hand, holding it still. The two had been friends as long as Roni could remember. Certainly longer than she had been alive. As they had aged and lost those close to them, they turned towards each other to lean on. It warmed Roni to see such a strong friendship.

"When Sully comes back to the bookstore," she said, "can't you use your cane to heal him properly?"

Keeping his eyes on Sully, Elliot said, "I will try, of course, but a heart attack is not a broken bone or a deep laceration. It is not often brought on by an assault from without. It is the body striking at itself. Had I reached him sooner, I might have slowed things enough for Sully to settle, recalibrate, let go of the battle on his system. But this — I can't reverse the damage of age. I can't stop what Nature demands."

Gram walked over and squeezed Elliot's shoulders. "This is not your fault."

Roni could not tell if that was another passive-aggressive swipe at her, so she kept silent.

Patting Elliot's hand, Sully gestured to Gram. With a wisp of a voice, he said, "I need to speak with Roni alone. Please."

"Of course," Elliot said and stood to leave. Gram remained in her spot, but a sharp look from Elliot forced her to nod.

Roni released a held breath. She did not know which shocked her most — that Elliot would give Gram such a look or that Gram would acquiesce. Even as the two exited the room, Roni stared at them like exotic animals brought to a new exhibit at the Philly Zoo.

"Come," Sully said, his voice stronger. "Sit."

She obeyed as she watched him with care. He pressed the button to raise his bed and closed his eyes for a moment. Roni thought he might fall asleep, but then he snapped awake as he looked around the room.

"Do you need something?" she asked.

"A few more years would be nice. Oh, don't get all gooey in the eyes. Let an old man joke. Well, sort of joke." His soft smile dropped into a serious line. "Earlier today, you were assaulted. Mentally."

All her warm feelings splintered under a cold weight. "How did you know about that?"

"It happened to me, too. That's what caused my heart attack. I was connected to you and your father. I tried to call out to you, but my connection was weaker. Or perhaps the one between you and Lawrence was so much stronger. But I felt it all."

Roni rolled back her shoulders and took a deep breath. Her stomach wanted to empty all over the floor, but she managed to keep her throat from letting loose. Unable to fully believe the words coming out of her mouth, she said, "Is everything my father told me true? My mother didn't die in a car accident? Did she really work for the Parallel Society?"

"Not exactly."

"Don't play semantics. The only thing keeping me from boiling into a rage is that you're lying in a hospital bed after having had a heart attack. So please, for once, could everybody just tell me the truth?"

"If getting the truth were that easy, we wouldn't need entire court rooms and juries and lawyers and all of it. The truth is based on semantics. It's based on how people see things."

"It doesn't matter if you believe in gravity or not. If you even understand it or not. You jump off a building, you're going to fall. That's the truth. That's a fact. So give me some facts. The car accident — did it happen?"

Sully's head bobbed as if he might lose consciousness. Roni did not want to bully him or even cause more distress, but she had to have answers. At length, he said, "No. There was no car accident. That much truth is easy. But her relationship with Gram and the Parallel Society was more complicated."

Roni inched back. Her fingers dug into her knees. "My father? He spent all that time in a mental hospital. Is he sane? Have you all been keeping him there like a prisoner?"

"This is why the truth is so difficult to understand. We get little facts and jump to conclusions. Most of the time, we're wrong."

"Last warning. No more word games."

"It's not a game. Far from it. Your father lost his mind when he lost his love. I never thought he was as insane as he made himself seem, but he was not completely in his right mind, either. Did he belong in that hospital? Who can say? Sometimes, yes. Other times, perhaps not. But he has been there. That much is true. And after this shared mental attack between us, it appears he may have had other reasons besides being distraught to hide out in that place."

The rollercoaster ride Roni's stomach had been experiencing dropped yet again. "Are you saying that someone is after my father?"

"Only your father knows that answer. But something coordinated that attack on all three of us. It wanted more than just your father."

"Why? And why you? I mean, I'm his daughter — there might be some logic to going after me as well, but what do you have to do with this?"

Taking sudden interest in straightening his blanket, Sully said, "When you've lived as long as I have, you get plenty of time to build up regrets. When things happen, you ride it like a wave, trying to hold tight. But now I can look back and see a clear roadmap that led me here."

"Map? Could this be because he knows the missing part of the map?"

Sully pushed his glasses up his nose. "What map?"

Words gushed out of Roni as she explained what had occurred during the recent visit with her father. When she finished, breathing hard and noticing the smell of evening meals being served down the hall, she watched Sully for his reaction.

Bobbing his head again, only this time with a clear nod, he said, "Please get Gram and Elliot back in. I'm still the leader of the Parallel Society, and I have some orders to give."

When Roni stepped into the hall to call Elliot and Gram, she locked eyes with Gram. Over their time together, the two women had glowered at each other countless times — especially during Roni's teenage years — but Gram's sharp look pierced into Roni in a way unlike any of their previous battles. In the past, Roni interpreted these to be a warning that she should rethink her position on whatever stood between them. This time, however, she felt as if Gram threatened her.

Roni wanted to be understanding. After all, one of Gram's closest friends recuperated after suffering a heart attack. Her overprotective nature accounted for much of her attitude, but the idea that she thought Roni would do anything to put Sully in danger was insulting.

"He wants to speak to us all," Roni said and returned to the room without waiting.

Once the group had assembled around Sully's bed like some mini-cult, he took hold of Roni's hand — an act which brought a childish reaction from both Gram and Elliot. Roni bit back her thoughts. No good would come from her pointing out that they all wanted to hold Sully's hand, that they all cared about him equally, and that her role in the Society would not be diminished because Gram or Elliot felt they had seniority over her.

Clearing his throat, Sully said, "Roni and I have been contacted by an old and dangerous creature of the caverns. Roni has a frightening path to follow. She will need all of our help to see her through." He let go of Roni's hand and took hold of Gram's. He raised his free hand to hold Elliot's as well. "We have been through so much together. More than anybody would ever believe. But it will mean nothing if we fail in our task ahead."

Gram raised an eyebrow at Roni. "What have you gotten yourself into?"

"None of this is her fault. You and I and Elliot are the ones behind all of this. That is why we are going to support Roni in any way that she needs. Beginning right here and now. The first step is to help her free Lawrence from the mental hospital."

"Lawrence?" Gram patted her crucifix as she backed up a step. "Why would we want to get her father out of the hospital?"

"Because he needs to join her in the caverns. They have to go to the Cave of Lost Time."

Gram's mouth dropped. "This heart attack has clearly impaired your judgment. The Cave of Lost Time? You keep talking like that and you'll be the one stuck in a mental hospital."

Elliot said, "Calm down. We need to approach this in a peaceful and thoughtful manner."

"Easy for you to say. It's not your granddaughter that's being sent off to her death."

"Roni is every bit as important to me and Sully as she is to you. And Sully's right — we're the ones who created this situation long ago, so if the time had come to fix it, then it is our responsibility to help."

"If you think that I am —"

Elliot raised his hand. "You are panicking. It is understandable but not helpful. Now, while it is true that we need to be the ones to help Roni, it is also true that we are limited in what help we can provide. The fact is that none of us knows how to get to the Cave of Lost Time. That secret died out long ago."

Sully pointed his shaking finger at Roni. "She knows. She and her father. You can argue all you want, but it will not change my decision. And it is my decision. I am the leader of this group, and the only person that's in line to take over should I die or become incapacitated is Roni."

Thumping the end of his cane onto the floor, Elliot bowed his head in a fast motion. All arguing died off as they watched him. "You are right," he said, his soothing tones drawing their attention as much as his words. "We have an obligation to Roni, and more importantly, we still have our duties as members of the Parallel Society. I will follow your command and see that Roni's father is freed from his imprisonment. You have my word that I will make sure they are safely brought to the Cave of Lost Time."

As Elliot left the room, Roni leaned over and kissed Sully's forehead. "Thank you."

Sully clamped tight onto Roni's wrist. "Make sure he comes back in one piece."

"Of course." A chill cut through to her bones. "Always."

As she stepped outside, she heard Sully say to Gram, "Stay a moment. There's something I need you to do."

CHAPTER 7

Trudging through the caverns, Roni silently argued with herself. Their last healing session only ticked her off more. The fact that they had made it to the Cave meant that they had succeeded in getting her father out of the mental hospital. Yet he was not there with them. Roni doubted they could have found the Cave without him. Why wasn't he with them? Was he dead? Is that what they tried to hide from her?

Elliot dabbed the sweat off his forehead. From all she could tell, the intensity of her memories had a direct effect to the intensity of the healing process upon him. Relying on his cane more than usual, he did his best to keep up with Teanna's pace.

As if suddenly clairvoyant, Elliot came alongside Roni and said, "I hope you understand that I can't answer many of your questions. Not won't — can't. I don't know everything that happened."

"That only makes me more curious. And worried."

Elliot planted his feet firm on the ground and passed his cane from one hand to the other. As Teanna hiked onward without them, he said, "You must know that you are a granddaughter to all of us. Sully and I love you every bit as much as Gram."

"Of course, I know that."

"Then know that I will never take unnecessary risks with your life."

Before Roni could answer, Teanna pushed by the golem as she rushed back. "The caverns are starting to change."

Roni looked from Teanna to Elliot with a dumbfounded scowl on her face. As if she had stepped in a pile of animal droppings, she said, "Well, that's great. The caverns are changing. I didn't even know they could do that."

Teanna nodded like a child unable to read the social cues of the room. "Not all of the caverns, but a section like this that has its substance tied to a figure like the Keeper — well, we can't expect things to stay the same without her."

"I should say not," Roni said, her mocking tone speeding by Teanna's confusion.

Ever the voice of reason, Elliot said, "Roni, Teanna, please listen to each other. This is no time for —"

"Losing my head? That's already happened. And you, Teanna, who are you? Why are you here? You clearly want to run off after this Keeper, but you don't go. What's stopping you? Go if you want to."

Though Teanna had missed Roni's sarcasm, she understood anger quite well. Her nostrils flared as she pulled her head high back. "I have answered all of your questions before. I won't go through it again."

"Before what?"

"Before you went against everybody's good advice and acted like a stupid youngling. I told you not to trust the Keeper."

"Does that have something to do with why you're still here? Did you join our team? Or did you have something to do with the reason my dad is missing?"

Teanna moved her hands in an unusual yet clearly aggressive manner. "Don't you dare suggest that I would have harmed Lawrence in any manner."

"Lawrence?" Roni swiveled towards Elliot. "Why does she know my father's name?"

With deliberate steps and playing up the use of his cane, Elliot moved between the two women. "The cavern is changing?"

Teanna lowered her hands. "That's correct."

"How fast?"

"I don't know. I've only ever read about such things. This is the first time I've seen it. But it is happening."

He shifted his body so that he faced Roni full on. "You have a decision to make. The caverns are changing which means our way back is changing as well. We can stay here, and I will do as in-depth a session as I can. It's risky and it is not the way I wish to bring your mind back to its complete self, but I will do it. However, chances are it will still take too long and we will be forced to find a new path home — if we can find one at all. Or we continue to follow our path back. When we get home, I'll try my best to complete the healing, but the gap in sessions may cause gaps in your mind. Meaning more Lost Time."

Teanna said, "We must follow wherever the Keeper goes."

Over his shoulder, Elliot said, "The Keeper called Roni in the first place. That's still the strongest connection at the moment, and that connects to our world. That is where the Keeper is headed."

"And if you're wrong?"

"Then we will gather reinforcements and head back into these caverns. You're the tracker, right? You'll track for us." To Roni, he added, "I will honor whatever choice you make."

Roni's fingers curled into tight fists. Her eyes darted from Elliot's earnest face to Teanna's harsh glower to the golem in the distance, standing like the statue it could become. A heavy grinding noise rumbled and the ground trembled. It lasted only seconds, but it gave some proof to Teanna's claim.

Reaching in her pocket, Roni fished out the flat rock with green speckles. After running her thumb over it several times, she hurled it back through the tunnel. "Sully made me promise to bring you back in one piece. That's what we're going to do."

To her surprise, Roni saw Teanna jump into action, eager to please. The golem shouldered one of Elliot's bags and followed down the path. Roni watched everybody as she stood there like a supervisor. A dark thought slithered into her head — *Am I the leader of this group?*

CHAPTER 8

Two in the morning. Rain tap-tap-tapped on the car roof. Trapped inside with Gram in the passenger seat and Elliot in the back, Roni waited. They monitored the Belmont Behavioral Hospital from across the street and tried to ignore that somebody in the car had passed gas. Or maybe Gram and Elliot's sense of smell had gone away with age and Roni suffered alone.

"How long are we going to sit here doing nothing?" Roni asked.

Gram watched the hospital like a cat stalking a mouse. "Until our chances for success are the best they'll be."

"You're obviously waiting for something. Tell me what we're looking for."

"Some sign that the place is as shutdown for the night as it will ever get."

"The lights are out in the all the rooms. Only activity seems to be in the lobby and that's just some cleaning. You think there's anything else going on this late at night?"

"I don't know. That's why we're sitting here. In the past, when we've done things like this —"

"Hold on. You've done this before?"

Elliot snickered. "Surely by now you realize that we've been involved in many things that the average seventy-year-old has never done."

"I know that," Roni said, shifting in her seat but unable to find a comfortable position. "I'm used to hearing about your battles and such, but breaking people out of hospitals is another thing."

"Jail, too. Remember that one?"

As Gram nodded, the streetlights cut lines across her face. "They should never have arrested Sully in the first place. But we're going to stay focused here. I don't want to find myself trying to break one of you out of jail because you got sloppy. Since we've had no time to prepare, to adequately case the area, make a thoughtful plan, anything useful really — well, we're going to have to rely on each other. Can we do that?"

"This is not breaking into a high security facility," Roni said. "The plan is pretty straightforward."

Gram turned her head toward Roni. "Can we rely on you?"

"Of course. No need to be nasty."

The few lights on the bottom floor went dark. Gram patted her chest before opening the car door.

Roni glanced back at Elliot. "Guess it's time."

If she had younger teammates, Roni would have expected to scurry low along the outside of the building, duck out of the rain fast, and pick a lock to get inside. With Gram and Elliot, they walked at a steady but measured pace, and the rain soaked them long before they reached the hospital grounds. But Roni knew better than to underestimate these two. Even if they had been using walkers and wheelchairs, she would not assume they were weak or capable of failure. Certainly, nobody would see them and think they stood on the precipice of a crime.

Roni led them around to the back of the building. Counting windows from the far end, she stopped at her father's room. Like all the windows on the first three floors, this one had iron bars across it.

"You're sure this is the right room?" Gram said.

"I've been visiting my father for years."

"Things change over time."

"I was in this damn place seven hours ago."

Gram stopped. "You have got to clean up your language. Lord, it's getting worse all the time."

"Fine, fine. Can we keep moving?"

"It's not fine. People judge you by the way you speak. I shudder to think what they might say if they heard you."

"Shudder for what they think of me or you?"

"Both of us."

Elliot nudged them with his cane. "Ladies, we have a job to do, and this cold rain is bothering my arthritis."

Gram clasped Elliot's hands and blew warm air on them. "I'm sorry. I suppose we never stop worrying for our children and our grandchildren. It seems it's our duty to guide them even this late in life." She turned toward the hospital window. "Now, to work."

Flicking her wrist, a metal chain descended from her sleeve. Roni never asked where these chains came from — did they emerge from the arms? did they materialize from another universe? were they even chains or were they something more organic in nature? — and she had decided she never wanted to know. Any answer would be disturbing.

With short motions, Gram twirled the chain at her side. Water flung off the links as she narrowed her eyes upon the barred window. A car rolled by, splashing through a puddle, and honked its horn twice. Roni startled only to hear the driver hooting at a young woman hiding under an umbrella as she walked her terrier. *Who walks their dog at two in the morning?* Roni wanted to comment, but Gram never even flinched at the sounds.

Moments later, the car drove away and the woman guided her terrier into an apartment building. Though Gram did not take her focus off the window, she somehow knew when all possible witnesses had left. She let the chain loose.

It whizzed through the rain and wrapped around the first two bars. The chain locked around itself like a living creature biting into its own flesh. For any other person, Roni would have been impressed with the feat. For Gram, Roni knew the old woman could do better — she should have lassoed the center bar for an even pull.

"Come here," Gram said, indicating for Roni to grab onto the chain. "This particular chain will act like a pulley system, taking our small bit of strength and amplifying it. But it doesn't last long. You, too, Elliot. All hands on deck."

"Give me the end," he said.

Gram reached up her sleeve and detached the chain. Elliot rolled the end around his cane seven times.

"Ready?" Gram said, readjusting her grip. "Pull."

Roni had expected to dig in as if playing tug-o-war against the entire building. But on their first try, she heard the metal whine. The second pull crumbled bits of the brick wall. On the third pull, the entire thing ripped straight out, clanging to the ground.

Checking the area, Roni expected to see numerous lights pop on, but the street remained dark and quiet. Elliot walked over to the wall and tapped against the window. The pane rose and Roni's father, Lawrence, poked his head out.

He frowned at Elliot, but when his gaze drifted over to Gram, his brow dropped low. "Go away."

"Dad," Roni said, hurrying up to the window. "We're busting you out."

"Roni? Get in here. You'll catch a cold in all that rain."

"You need to come out. Quick, before the staff checks to see what's going on."

Elliot set his cane firmly on the ground and placed one hand atop it. Closing his eyes, he started a series of motions with his other hand.

Lawrence shook his fist at Gram. "I am not going anywhere with her."

"Oh, for Heaven's sake," Gram said. "You cannot keep blaming me for your failings. Or Maria's, for that matter. Look at Roni. I've done a remarkable job raising her into a fine, young woman. Where have you been? Relaxing in this self-imposed prison."

"If I had voluntarily put myself in here —"

"You did."

"I mean afterward. If I had chosen to stay, there wouldn't be bars on the windows and you wouldn't have to be here breaking me out." He crouched over the window ledge toward Roni. "You see? That woman will twist anything to her advantage. Even my mental health."

A soft hiss followed by a pop announced that Elliot had put a shield over them. The rain ceased to patter on Roni's head, and she suspected anyone outside the shield would not hear them. Or at worst, would only hear a muted version.

Roni said, "This isn't about Gram. This is about you and me."

"It is?"

"Don't you remember me visiting earlier today?"

Closing his eyes, Lawrence appeared to be concentrating on finding that visit. Gram cleared her throat, and when Roni peeked over, she saw lights come on near the lobby end of the building.

"Maybe," he said. "Did I ask you to get me out of here? I don't think I did. I shouldn't. I have to be careful."

"The time for careful is gone. Don't you remember? You and I and Sully — we were contacted by something. The Keeper."

His eyes widened. "You shouldn't know about her." To Gram, he yelled, "Why did you tell Roni about the Keeper? It was your job to stay silent about that. I knew I couldn't trust you. Knew it the day I met you. You don't care about me or Roni or Maria."

"Watch yourself." Gram crossed her arms. "And you can trust that you're going to get caught if you keep shouting. Elliot's protection only goes so far."

"Forget about Gram," Roni said. "Forget all of that. Listen to me.

The Keeper knows about me. She contacted us, and you started drawing a map that will help get to the Cave of Lost Time. That's why we're here. We have to go into the caverns."

Her father cocked his head. A broad smile overcame his features. "Roni? My sweet, sweet daughter? You're here. You came." He heard a noise from inside the building. "We have to get out of here. If they stop me, we'll never get to the Cave."

"Then quit yapping," Gram said. "Let's go."

He looked at her as if only noticing her presence for the first time. "What's she doing here?"

Roni reached up to assist him out the window. "I'll explain when we're not trying to escape."

He hopped down, gave Roni a hug, and patted Elliot on the shoulder. Elliot let his shield down, and the cold rain soaked into them all once again. By the time they squished into the car and Roni pulled away, the hospital had lit up with activity. With any luck, when the hospital finally notified the police and a larger search took place, Roni and her father would already be underground.

Forty minutes later, they parked a block down from the *In The Bind* bookstore and made their way to the back entrance. As they settled around the big table on the main floor, Gram brought some food out of the small kitchen off to the side. Roni wriggled off her sopping wet jacket and set it on a chair. Her hair clung to the back of her neck. Her father slumped at the table while Elliot put a kettle on the stove for hot tea.

From the outside looking in, Roni thought everything must have appeared so normal. Just a family gathering around a table. They looked tired, perhaps a bit tense, but nothing out of the ordinary. Peel back that thin veneer and a group of oddities sat together, plotting toward an unknown enemy.

Massaging her temples, she watched her father scarf down the cheese sandwich Gram had provided. Roni only had a few memories of him outside the mental hospital and none of him sitting at the big table in the bookstore. Seeing him now loosened her tense muscles and brought a sense of peace over her body.

"This is like the Poconos," her father said. "You and your mother and I would rent a little place up there. We'd eat sandwiches and drink cocoa."

"You'd drink, alright," Gram said, "but I doubt it was cocoa."

As Elliot set a cup of steaming tea in front of Lawrence, Gram walked around the table toward Roni. "Let your father gain his strength. Where you're going, he'll need all he can get."

Searching for the fight but not finding it, Roni said, "You say that like you're not coming."

Gram paused. "Let Elliot take care of your father. I need you to come with me."

She climbed up two flights of stairs, entered the room used for restoring old books, and opened a hidden door. Roni followed. They entered Sully's workshop — a large loft with several high tables like those found in a university lab as well as plenty of open floor space for the construction of golems.

Before flicking on the lights, Gram faced Roni, her hands pressing into each other. "Lawrence seems agitated. Are you sure he's ready for this?"

"He was fine when I saw him earlier. Bouncing around, excited. He only got upset because of you. I'm not trying to pick a fight. But that's what happened."

"I was there. I heard him, saw the look on his face. He never liked me much. Never was outright rude, but he clearly tolerated me. That's probably something your mother loved about him." She glanced into the dark workshop. "You think he's stable enough to go with you into the caverns? That he can really help you find the Keeper?"

"Isn't that why we're here? Look, I appreciate your concern, but it'll be fine. Is that why you aren't coming with us? Because of him?"

"Lord, no. I'd never let Lawrence dictate where I go."

"Then what is it?"

"Sully, of course. The man had a heart attack. He's lucky to be alive. I won't risk leaving him alone right now. You'll have Elliot. And I suppose Lawrence might come in handy, too. But this'll be your first time on your own like this."

"Oh," Roni said, the word dropping sharp. "I see. You don't think I can handle it."

"That's not true."

"After going to Ireland, after going into another universe with Elliot, after dealing with the hellspiders and everything else we've faced, you still think I'm not capable. Not only that, but you doubt me even when Elliot and my dad are going to be there, too. What is the problem?"

Gram pulled Roni into a hug. "Stop assuming you know what I'm thinking. I love you, and I worry about you. Not your capabilities but your safety. Your well-being. A lot is going to change in the next few days. Change is hard under any circumstances, but not being able to be there with you, to help you through it all, that's worse."

Roni stepped back. The odd mixture of sadness and pride that crossed Gram's face reminded Roni of when she left home. Gram knew the time had come for her to move out, but letting go had proved difficult.

With a guilty sniffle, Roni said, "You have to stay for Sully."

"I do."

Forcing confidence, she said, "Don't worry. Whatever happens, I'll be careful. I know how serious the caverns are. I'm as ready as I can be. All that old arrogance of mine is gone."

"I doubt that."

"Mostly gone, then."

Gram flicked on the light. In the middle of Sully's workshop, a sheet covered an object — presumably, a golem. "Sully wants you to have this on your journey."

She whipped off the sheet and revealed a five-foot statue made of clay, stone, and metal. The golem had a fully-realized face with carefully sculpted lips, ears, eyes, and even nostrils. It had thick hair carved into its head and well-defined musculature on its chest, arms, and legs. Though it lacked reproductive organs, its proportions clearly indicated male.

Roni had never seen such a detailed golem before. "He's amazing."

"Sully's been working on this for almost a year. He didn't tell any of us because, well, this golem is meant to proxy for him. That's his word, but I think he meant more like a replacement for after he dies."

"But he's okay, right? He didn't —"

"He's fine. As much as he can be for having had a heart attack at his age. He won't return to us the same. That's certain. That's why he told me about the golem. Not only did he work long at designing this thing, he also wrote detailed instructions for it. Come here."

On the side of the golem's neck, Gram slid a small door open. Inside, Roni could see several pieces of paper forming a tiny stack. In the past, she had seen Sully use a simple slip of paper with some Hebrew jotted down in miniature script. That was enough to animate a golem with a modicum of brain power. This thing had a tiny book inside — it would probably be able to solve math problems or drive a car.

Roni paused. "Doesn't Sully have to whisper something to the golems to get them alive?"

"He already did. Before we left for the hospital, he insisted on coming in here. I could tell by his face that he'd rather die fighting me to get in here than listen to common sense, and I figured whatever he needed, better to get it done fast and rush him to the hospital than to waste time arguing. Lord knows, we've done enough of the latter in our life." She winked. "I try to learn when the Lord provides a lesson."

"So, Sully came in here and whispered this thing alive?" She stepped closer to the golem. "Why's he just standing there doing nothing?"

"He's waiting for you."

"Me?"

Gram moved in behind Roni. "According to Sully, the golem won't react until you've named him."

Roni held back a barking laugh. Sully had made a private golem for her. Amazing. "Well, he's a golem. And he's from Sully. Golem and Sully — Gully."

"Are you serious?"

"Yup. You hear that, Gully? That's your name."

CHAPTER 9

"Hold on, hold on," Roni said, stopping in the middle of a narrow tunnel and setting her hand against the soft moss growing on the cavern wall.

Leading the way, Teanna turned back, her eyes searching for the problem. Elliot also showed concern, but his fear surrounded the stability of Roni's head.

"Are you dizzy?" he asked. "How do you feel?"

"I just had a memory return."

"Without my aid? That's a good sign. Very good."

She turned around to face the golem. "You. You're Gully?"

The golem lifted his head, smiling broadly. "Yes. Oh, yes. You finally remembered old Gully."

Roni held back her laughter — the golem sounded like a raspy version of an old Jewish man. She wouldn't go so far as to say that Gully had Sully's voice, but the imitation came awfully close. Then the reality of the moment hit her. "You can talk?"

"Of course. I wouldn't be of much use without a voice. I'm not just a dumb golem like a pack mule. I've got skills and talents that you've found quite useful up to this point. Isn't that right, Mr. Elliot?"

Elliot grinned — as polite and non-committal as Roni had ever seen him.

"If you can talk, why haven't you said anything until now?" Roni asked.

"Because you told me not to." Gully scratched the top of his head.

She didn't think he could feel anything, let alone have an itch, but clearly Sully had outdone himself with this golem's instructions. Like a far-future android, Gully must have been programmed to mimic human behavior.

"I told you not to speak?" Roni said.

"Right before."

"Before what?"

Gully looked to Elliot and then Teanna.

Roni tapped her fingers at her side. "Gully, do I need to order you to tell me what happened to me? Is that how this works?"

Lowering his head as he shifted from foot to foot, he said, "Please, don't do that. I'm not sure how I'll react."

Elliot nudged Roni's shoulder. "Before you took a risky action, one that you had no idea of the consequences, you ordered Gully not to respond to you until you spoke his name. You then told him to obey me until you could resume your leadership."

"I did this?"

"As a precaution. I further ordered him not to divulge anything about the past days until I assured him that your mind could safely handle it. Since we do not know the extent of Sully's instructions to the golem, we cannot be sure what will happen if you give Gully conflicting orders. So, please, respect your own word."

Roni did not utter a sound. Not only did she have Elliot blocking her from restoring her memories right away, she had herself doing it, too. Her mind reeled, and she wanted to sit on the ground.

Teanna said, "The air is cooler up ahead."

"The ice lake?" Elliot asked.

"As long as the caverns haven't altered too much, then yes, the ice lake should be around the next turn."

To Roni, Elliot said, "We must keep moving. Will you be okay?"

"No," she said. "But I'll keep moving anyway."

They soldiered onward. When they neared the lake, Roni could see her breath. Any wetness on the walls froze into majestic icicles. The temperature had dropped fast. They must have crossed a threshold from one universe into another — many sections of the caverns belonged to different universes. Or different universes gave up parts of themselves to be utilized by the caverns. Roni had a fuzzy understanding of the whole thing, but the overall concept remained clear enough — strange crap happened in the caverns because they did not exist in any single universe.

So, stepping from a mildly-cool, cramped tunnel with moss and fungus hanging off the ceiling into a frosty, cavernous area with an enormous lake chock full of ice sheets did not strike Roni as odd. Well, not entirely odd. After all, her companions were a magic-healing

Muslim, a tracker from another universe, and a golem named Gully. Why should sudden winter weather bother her?

"There," Teanna said, pointing across the lake. "The Keeper went that way."

Roni peered out over the choppy waters that stretched farther than she could see on the sides — more like a river than a lake. On the opposite shore, distinct marks in the gravelly sands indicated where a creature had been. Lots of distinct marks. As if the Keeper had stomped around in circles for an hour or two.

Poking at a bobbing piece of ice with his cane, Elliot said, "Looks like Gully slowed her down a little."

"Gully did?" Roni said. "How?"

Though his face could not change color, Gully appeared to blush. "An accident I had on our way here."

"So, we crossed this lake already?"

"Yes, yes, and I had an accident. Must we continue to recount my failures?"

Roni stared at Gully. Could he really be upset? A golem? Take out Sully's instructions and the whole thing would return to being clay and stone. Yet she found herself worrying she had offended the poor thing.

"I was only trying to be sure that this is the same lake."

"It is," Teanna said. "My people mapped this lake a long time ago. There isn't another like it for days. Except when you crossed, it was solid. And if I had been with you, I would have made sure we had a way back. Your home is on the other side."

"Can we swim across?"

"This is the first time I've seen it. Don't know how deep it is or what might be living beneath the surface. But I do know that you'll freeze to death long before you make it across."

"But the Keeper swam across."

Teanna's eyes scanned the cavern. "I doubt that."

Elliot said, "It doesn't matter. At my age, that cold will definitely kill me, and Gully can't go in at all. The water will dissolve the clay parts of his body. He wouldn't survive."

"We can't stand here twiddling our thumbs." Roni shivered. "If the way across is no good, we should at least head back where it's warmer. Find a path around."

With a graceful motion, Teanna slid off one of her robes and draped it over Elliot's shoulders. "We will get across here."

Roni moved closer to Elliot and tried to ignore the sensation of jealousy wriggling within. "What about your cane? You've created protective domes around us before. Maybe you can create a big dome or a bubble or something, and we can walk across."

Elliot cocked his head as if he would ask a question, but he swallowed back whatever words he wanted to utter. "I'm willing to try," he finally said. "However, it will take a lot of time. I have used most of my energy healing you. I'll need to rest first. The casting will take some time as well, since the dome will have to prevent water from coming in but not air — it's easier to build a shield against large creatures yet leave enough gaps for tiny particles. Like a mesh filter. But water is a different thing entirely. And then, when we actually cross, we will all need to put muscle into moving the dome because we'll be displacing a large amount of water. It won't go easily. Especially if the lake is deeper than we think."

"A simple *no* would have sufficed."

"It is possible. I can do it."

"Possible but not practical. Teanna has made it clear that we can't let the Keeper get too far away from us. We probably don't have the time for you to regain your strength enough to create that dome. And the idea might not work anyway."

Teanna gave Roni a respectful nod. "Thank you for finally grasping the seriousness of our situation."

"Sure. Anytime. Maybe we should go back to the Cave of Lost Time and try one of the other tunnels."

Elliot shook his head. "The path back is gone. The caverns are changing."

"So how do we get back to the Cave?"

"We don't. Probably not ever again."

Roni's stomach quivered. She tried to convince herself it was due to the cold.

Shaking her hand at one wall, Teanna rushed over to Gully. She turned the golem around and rifled through one of the bags he carried. With a triumphant cheer, she pulled out two long coils of rope. "We will be fine here." She spun Gully back. "Mr. Golem, I will need your assistance."

Gully rubbed his hands together. "If it means getting out of this icebox, I'm all for whatever you're thinking."

She climbed a small hill of rocks and stalagmites with Gully following. At the top, she reached up to touch the tip of a massive stalactite. Nodding, she tied the end of one rope around herself and the other around Gully. Once she appeared confident the knots would hold, she brought out the second rope and repeated the process.

"You stay here. Feed these ropes as I go. Don't let them get tangled and don't let them snag anything. Understand?"

Gully snapped his fingers and pointed at her. "Clear as can be."

She hesitated but then shrugged. Testing the knots around her waist once more, she positioned underneath the stalactite. With a grunt, Teanna sprang upward. Her hands locked onto the bumpy stone, and she climbed toward the cavern ceiling as if she had been born there.

"Be careful," Elliot said, as the shadows engulfed her.

For the next several minutes, Roni stood at Elliot's side and stared up at the ceiling. They could not see Teanna, but they could hear a series of grunts and the scrabbling of her efforts. The two ropes hung from the dark, leading back to Gully, and they swung and wiggled as Teanna moved from one stalactite to another. It was the only measure of her progress that Roni could see, so it became the focus. Those two thin lines shimmying over the lake — their lifeline home.

As the ropes crossed over the shoreline, Teanna lowered on another long stalactite. With a whoop, she let go and dropped to the shore. Laughing, she waved back.

Roni cupped her hands and yelled, "Good job. Now what?"

Shouting back, Teanna said, "Mr. Golem, tie your ends the same as I do. Watch."

As the strange woman searched her side of the lake, Gully paid close attention. After a moment, she tied one rope near the top of a stalagmite that nearly kissed the stalactite above it. She then pointed to Gully and waited.

"Your turn," Roni said, and the golem nodded.

"Make it tight," Teanna called out.

Gully obeyed and searched out a similar formation nearby. When he finished, she climbed atop the rope and bounced twice. Satisfied, she then reached up to the stalactite above and secured the second rope. Gully did the same.

"I'm coming back to test it," Teanna said, her voice echoing but still clear. "All of you watch carefully how I move."

She stepped on the bottom rope and reached above to the top. Spreading her limbs to form a narrow X, she moved in a sideways motion. Slow and smooth, never crossing her arms or legs over the other. Clearly, she had done this before.

As Roni observed the procedure, she said to Elliot, "Are you going to be okay to do that?"

"Hopefully, it's like riding a bike. You never forget."

"You've done that before?"

"I've done a lot of things before."

When Teanna hopped off the rope, she gave Gully a firm smack on the shoulder. "You tied those ropes like a pro."

Gully said, "I try my best."

Teanna stepped over to Roni and Elliot. She took her robe back. "This will only cause you trouble. If you want, I'll carry your cane, too."

He clutched the cane against his chest. "I'll manage with this."

"The ropes won't be easy."

Roni said, "He'll be fine. He's done this before."

Chilled air wafted off the icy waters like an evil tongue sneaking a taste of its next meal. Elliot rolled his shoulders back and approached the ropes. With Gully's help, the old man set his feet in place and hoisted up. Being the tallest of the group, Elliot had no trouble reaching the top rope. Gully handed up the cane which Elliot slid down the back of his shirt and tucked the end through his belt.

He winked at Roni. "Just like I remember."

Though he moved slowly, she watched every step. Her heart raced for him. At her side, she noticed Gully also riveted. Maybe Sully had given the golem instructions to worry about Elliot, too.

When Elliot's foot slipped, both Roni and Gully gasped. Teanna put her leg against the bottom rope to steady it, but otherwise, she showed no concern. When Elliot finally touched the shore, he waved back and gave a thumbs up.

Roni snorted a laugh. The gesture looked quite wrong on his dignified hands.

Teanna tapped Gully. "You go next. Best to have one of us on each side."

"That's true," Gully said, climbing onto the ropes. "I probably should have gone first. Or you should have stayed."

"I needed to test the ropes — that's why I came back. And, yes, you should have gone before Mr. Elliot, but I had expected our leader to speak up before he went off."

Refusing to take the bait, Roni motioned to Gully. "Go on. The sooner we get across, the sooner we can all warm up."

Once she had spoken, Gully launched into action. He moved with fearless abandon, crossing one hand over the other, traveling with sure speed and perfect balance. Halfway across, Roni understood that Gully felt no fear because Sully had not instructed him to fear anything. The golem simply crossed the lake as if strolling over a bridge.

Teanna said, "Now you."

Roni set her foot down on the rope and thrust up to grab the other rope. Her heart froze. The others had made it look easy, yet every tiny movement of her foot or hands sent the rope wobbling. Or maybe her nerves caused the vibrations and the rope held firm. The distance stretched across the lake, growing further with each chilly breath.

"I know how it looks," Teanna said. "The first time is always a bit scary, but you can do it. Just slide your front foot out and bring the other to join it. Do the same with your hands. Go slow, take your time, and you'll make it across."

"The rope feels weird, that's all."

Thankfully, Teanna did not call Roni out on her lie. She didn't even chuckle. With simple patience, she waited until Roni took a tentative slide outward.

"Good," Teanna said. "That's exactly right. You do it like that and you'll have no troubles."

Roni tried to control her breath from giving away how hard her pulse beat through her body. "Sorry this'll take so long."

"It is always more important that the team live than that they rush into a fight."

"As long as I don't screw this up, I guess we'll live, then."

"Keep going. You're doing everything right. If you do feel your balance leaving you, remember the most important thing — don't let go. Lock your hands on that rope. Your feet can dangle for days, but if you lose your grip, you'll be dunked in ice water before you even know what happened."

Trying to blot out Teanna's final words, Roni shoved all her focus into her hands and feet. Slide the front foot out. Slide the front hand out. Bring the back foot and hand in. Out and in. Repeat.

Sweat tickled her sides. Her thigh muscles complained and a headache throbbed low, near her neck. When she dared peek ahead — expecting to see she had maybe reached the halfway point — Elliot's hands grabbed hold of her.

"You can let go now," he said, calm and pleasant. "You've made it. You're safe."

When her feet touched solid ground again, she let out a held breath and grinned. "I'm okay," she shouted across the water.

Teanna bounded up onto the ropes. Making quick work of the crossing, she had shimmied three-quarters of the way when then ground quaked. A loud rumble bounced through the air like thunder from an unseen storm. Gripping the rope tight, Teanna held still as the moving caverns swayed her to and fro. Rocks dropped from above, splashing into the water and shattering bits of floating ice.

A crack loud enough that Roni covered her ears ripped into the air. The massive stalactite that held the far end of the rope hit the ground and fell over like a sawn tree. With it, the rope Teanna held became slack and useless. She tried to balance like a circus performer on a tightrope, but in seconds, her arms pinwheeled and she toppled into the water.

Roni rushed to the edge, kicked off her shoes, and waded into the lake. She heard Elliot and Gully calling her back, but their voices seemed distant and inconsequential. Partly because she focused on getting Teanna to safety. Mostly because the moment she hit the water, its frigid temperature turned her blood into ice shards coursing through her body.

"Holy sh-sh-sh—" Her teeth chattered so fast, she gave up on swearing. *Keep going.* If she lingered, she would never get moving again and death would claim her fast.

Ignoring the warnings blasting in her mind, she dove forward and kicked hard as she plunged toward Teanna. She wanted to scream but her lungs would not expand enough to make such a sound. The world disappeared around her. She saw only Teanna's dark figure against the white frothing water and ice.

Teanna had managed to latch her arm around a block of ice large enough to help keep her floating above water. But like the water, the ice would only sap what little heat she had remaining. Roni held out a hand as she neared the block.

"G-Grab me," she said. "We've got to go." Roni's head dropped under, but she fought back to the surface. Sputtering, she splashed closer toward Teanna. The cavern echoed the sounds of struggle back upon them, making each movement louder and more powerful, but also amplifying their flailing fear, too. "Damnit, grab my hand."

Teanna shoved off the ice and wrapped her arms around Roni like a girl clinging to her mother at a public pool. "M-M-My legs won't kick well. Too cold."

"Can you get on my back?" Roni wouldn't be able to work her own legs and arms well enough with another woman glued to her chest.

"I don't know. If I let go — I just can't move well — so cold —"

"Just hold on. I'll make it work."

The woman's body pressed tight against Roni, and what shreds of warmth remained gave Roni the push to keep swimming. Elliot stood at the water's edge, urging her onwards. Gully stood several feet behind, acting concerned and afraid. They seemed so far off.

Through her shivering voice, Teanna kept repeating, "You can do this, you can do this, you can do this."

Elliot leaned out over the water, reaching out farther with his cane. "Grab hold," he yelled. "We'll pull you in."

Gully stood behind Elliot, ready to yank the old man off his feet and drive them all to shore.

But each stroke required more from her muscles and each breath provided less strength. Her head felt numb. Teanna's weight grew heavier. Something at her feet — something pulling her down — or maybe not — maybe only her legs had stopped moving and she heard all the shouting voices drift away and she felt her lips pressed against each other but refused to move again and she had trouble thinking how to keep breathing.

And the water covered her head.

CHAPTER 10

Every time Roni set foot into the caverns had been distinct from every other time. Her reasons for being there, the emotions smashing through her head, the physical sensations of her body, of the air, even of her mood — each journey might as well have been the first. This time proved no different.

Of course, she travelled with her father this time and that alone made it singular. His jittery presence hung over the entire party like a winter blanket made of silk — soft and comforting, yet odd and out-of-place. Gully also brought a sense of strangeness to the group. He behaved like many other golems Roni had worked with, but the extra directions Sully had provided turned this golem into something more. Even the way Gully walked had a quality both human and golem. In the middle of it all, Elliot brought the sturdiness to bind the group together. With barely a word, he instilled a sense of competency in this goofy outfit, a sense that they had every reason to be optimistic towards the outcome.

Roni led the way. She had the maps in her bag but no need to consult them. Not yet. Eventually, they would reach the point that they needed to rely on her father's knowledge, but she figured the less taxing the journey on him until then, the better.

As they hiked along familiar paths with books chained to the walls and lighting from various eras of the Parallel Society illuminating the way, Roni kept a close watch on her father. His eyes hardly blinked as he went from one amazing grouping of books to another. Brushing his lips with his fingers, he tripped twice from keeping his attention locked on the walls.

"Did you capture all of these universes?" he asked.

"Some," Roni said. "Most are the work of Gram and the boys. And, of course, the majority beyond that belong to previous incarnations of the Society."

"These walls were so bare when I walked through here last." He placed a hand on his chest and raised an eyebrow toward Elliot. "You all sure were busy."

Elliot's face tightened. "We did what needed to be done."

"I have no doubt. You always were able to do that. No matter what."

The two men grew silent, and Roni had the sudden urge to blurt out anything that might move minds to some other topic. Not that she had any clue what the friction in their words had meant, but it sure scraped her teeth. Unfortunately, no words would come to her.

They traveled on in uneasy silence.

After a long and quiet hour, they reached a point where two tunnels branched off to the left and a third went to the right. As she headed toward the first on the left, her father flagged his hands in the air.

"No, no," he said. "To the right. That's the way to go. That's the route."

"I'm fairly certain it's to the left."

"Right, right, right, it's right. Listen to me. I'm the one with the knowledge unlocked from my head. Not your noggin, my noggin. And I know it's to the right."

Gully said, "The two of you and your bickering. Why argue? You're wearing a simple solution to this all."

Roni had to admit the golem had a point. She set her bag down to get out the map she had taken from the Library.

"Your map is wrong." Lawrence wrapped an arm around a rock the size of a large child. "I know. I've been down here before. After all I went through, I promised I could never forget. Even if I wanted to, the Keeper won't let me. She's calling, and I can still hear her. Can't you? Listen to that tunnel. It's practically singing for us."

Roni glanced at Elliot, but he only shrugged. She inched toward the tunnel on the right and listened. Nothing. Not a sound beyond those of any cavern. She could not tell if that pleased her or worried her.

Lawrence pushed her aside and pressed his ear against the cool stones. "It's so clear. We must go this way. Your way will take days longer. Did you not see the drawings I made? This way is better, and we'll reach the Cave in one or two days at the most."

"But the map —"

"You broke me out of a hospital because I know the way. So, let me do my part."

Despite his agitation, Roni thought her father sounded quite clear-headed at the moment. He lacked any doubt. As long as she paid attention to every turn they made, she would be able to backtrack to this point again. If they lost a day, what did it matter? She would gain further trust of her father, map out a little more of the caverns, and know whether to believe the things rattling in his brain.

"Okay," she said. "I guess you lead the way now."

Gully rubbed the back of his neck. "This doesn't make sense. Just check your map."

"Sometimes you have to trust people more than a piece of paper." She started off to the right tunnel but hesitated. "Of course, pay attention to where we go. In case we need to get back here." Better to have two working the problem. She noticed Elliot digging a mark in the ground with his cane. Three, then.

After a few hours, Lawrence halted. "Listen."

Roni closed her eyes. She heard a gentle hum like a new refrigerator.

"Won't be long," he said and resumed walking.

Four minutes later, the tunnel opened up to a wide corridor bisected with a transparent wall. It reached floor to ceiling and ran the full-length to the end. On the other side of the wall, the corridor appeared similar. The wall itself looked like colored glass — a salmon-pink hue — yet it also glistened like a sheet of water.

Roni extended her hand, but Gully pushed her arm down. He said, "Certainly, Gram taught you not to touch things you don't understand."

"You know what that is?"

"Not a clue. But I don't have nerve-endings. Allow me."

Gully extended his index finger and touched the wall. With a sound of static and the smell of a kiln, his body stiffened for a breath before a jolt sent him tumbling backwards. He did not move.

Rushing to his side, Roni patted his clay face. She urged Elliot over. And her father — she looked up to see him racing down the far end of the corridor. He howled, and Roni saw where an old cave-in blocked their path.

"That did not feel good," Gully said, rolling his head in a gentle circle.

"You said you couldn't feel anything."

"I said I didn't have nerve-endings. At least, I didn't think I had any. Apparently, I was wrong. But I have less than you. If you had touched that wall, I don't think you'd have survived."

Roni gazed over at the shimmering pink. To Elliot, she said, "Is it like one of your protection domes?"

"I've never seen it before. From your father's reaction, I'd say he also is surprised by it."

Gully said, "It is a remarkable oddity. When I touched it, I both felt it and pressed through slightly. It was there and not there. Like Schrodinger's cat."

Returning to the group, Lawrence scowled at the wall. "That thing caused the collapse up ahead and it's blocking the other way through. You can see a tunnel on the other side and that route is clear. It's taunting us, isn't it?"

"It's a wall," Roni said. "Walls don't taunt."

"Not in our universe. Don't be so sure about anything when you're in the caverns, though. A sentient wall would be the least of possibilities around here. There's that humming again. Listen to it. Oh, I'm a fool. I thought for sure it was the Keeper humming a path to follow, but she never spoke to us so softly. Right? When we connected before, it wasn't a gentle, pleasant experience. Gave Sully a heart attack. Nearly killed him. This hum — it's the wall."

As Elliot assisted Gully to his feet, Roni came alongside her father. She closed her eyes, and in that instant, the hum burst into life. A single note rang out with harmonics waving throughout it like the light shimmering on the wall itself. She opened her eyes. The sound ceased. *Both there and not there.*

Elliot stood next to her. He held his cane out towards the wall but did not let it touch. "I can feel vibrations."

"I hear the hum, but I don't see how any of that helps. I mean, this thing is strange and interesting and all, but we're not here to play with a wall. Wouldn't it make more sense to backtrack and find another route?"

"No," Lawrence said, whirling on her with his eyes wide open. "This is the path and only this. All other paths lead to false paths which never reach this path and only this path. Through the wall."

"Okay, okay. Let's stay calm, so we can figure out how to get through this humming wall."

In a lower voice meant only for Roni, Elliot said, "If it were as easy as going a different route, the way to the Cave of Lost Time would never have been so hard to find. But don't worry. I have an idea."

With his cane in one hand and his arms parted as if he acted in a

Biblical movie, Elliot let his deep voice boom a long, low tone. Ripples crossed the wall — short, fast, and gone the instant Elliot ran out of breath, but ripples nonetheless. He tested the sound again, and as before, the wall rippled like a liquid.

Dropping his arms, he turned to the group. "Roughly ten years ago, Gram and Sully and I had a mission in Adelaide, Australia. It seemed simple at first. Gram made her book, we pinpointed the universe — luckily, no relics had slipped into our world — and she tried to lock it away. Only each time she opened her book, nothing happened."

"Amusing story." Lawrence paced in front of the wall. "But Gram isn't here and this is not another universe. And I'm hungry. I sure would like a cobbler right now. Maybe cherry. Not a lot good I can say about the Belmont Behavioral Hospital, but they make a cobbler at least once a week, and I love it. Cherry's the best, but even peach is good and I don't like peaches. I wonder if they'll serve cobbler today. Hey, Roni, stay a bit longer today and you can have a piece of cobbler, too."

Before Roni could address her father's slip from reality, Elliot said, "I will jump to the end of the story since it appears to be bothering Lawrence. Sully solved our problem. From various clues, he realized that the key was sound. The properties of that particular universe had a frequency which Sully matched with a unique golem. The sympathetic vibrations gave the universe enough solidity that Gram captured it and we accomplished our mission.

"I am going to attempt making a dome around us like my protective shields. However, if I succeed, the dome will resonate with the frequency of a single note. Once I find the correct note to sync with the wall, I think we can achieve a similar effect — only the opposite. Instead of forming a more solid structure, we should hopefully loosen it enough that we will pass through without being hurt."

Roni placed a calming arm around her father and urged him to sit. "Sounds like the best idea we have."

Gully said, "Especially because we don't have any others."

Without further discussion, Elliot positioned near the wall and got to work.

Roni noticed the glow of salmon-pink against his dark skin, the way it seemed to cut him out of reality like the lights on a dance floor. For a moment, they existed not in a cavern but in a pinkish room overflowing with energy and possibility. Roni half-expected music to pump through the air while a trove of dancers gyrated into view.

But then Elliot held his cane in both hands and raised it overhead. He hummed a single note. With a flourish, he brought the cane down, planting the tip into the floor near the wall. Leaning over, he placed his neck against the cane and hummed the note again. A miniature dome appeared around the cane's tip — this one pearl-white — and spread far enough to touch the wall. A sharp hiss like water snuffing out fire, a puff of gray smoke, and the shield evaporated.

Elliot grinned. "I didn't think it would work on the first try. But it would have been nice." He reset the cane above his head and hummed a different note.

The dance floor image shattered as Elliot continued his work. It had been no more than a passing thought, a rambling of Roni's mind, yet it left her wondering — why were only certain memories taken by Lost Time and not others? She had thought about this before, but never in this context. Her dance floor pondering had created a rich, atmospheric moment. Surely, that had more unique substance than a commonplace memory of growing up with a mother and father. Why did Lost Time exist at all?

With a huff, Elliot reset his cane. "Not that one," he said, and sang a lower note.

Shucking her shoulder against her father, Roni said, "This might take a while."

"I've always trusted Elliot to do well," Lawrence said, his breathing erratic but his eyes finally blinking again. "You're lucky to have him on your side."

"It's *our* side. We all do our part. Including you — we couldn't have made it this far without you. I never noticed the humming wall until you heard it. And, of course, without you, we wouldn't know how to get to the Cave."

"Maybe I make it easier, but I probably make it harder, too. Besides, if I were dead, I'm sure the Keeper would have reached out to you anyway. When she wants something, she knows how to get it."

Roni angled her head closer toward him. "Is that what happened with Mom? Did the two of you fight the Keeper or something?"

"Your mother?" When his gaze fell on her, his face scrunched as if he struggled to understand what girl sat next to him. It lasted only seconds, but Roni caught the look. His eyes brightened, and he patted her knee. "My sweet, sweet daughter. You've been through so much. Too much. And now you have to deal with so much more. Be brave with what I'm about to tell you."

Swallowing against a hard lump, Roni nodded. "I can handle it."

"Such a courageous girl. I hate that I have to be the one to tell you this, but you see, there was an accident last night. A car accident. I'm afraid your mother didn't survive."

Roni opened her mouth but held back from speaking. Nobody at Belmont ever suggested that her father had shown signs of Alzheimer's, so perhaps his confusion was another effect of the mental blast — like Sully's heart attack.

Elliot grunted as his next attempt fizzled into more gray smoke. He paused long enough to take a deep breath before raising the cane to start once more.

Stepping away from the men, Roni strolled to the back of the corridor. Gully stood with his hands on his hips, looking over the pile of rubble blocking their way. When he noticed her, he gestured to the pile. "I had thought maybe I could dig through all of this. Then Elliot wouldn't have to strain himself searching for the correct frequency and your father might snap back. But it appears I am not as strong as other golems my creator has made."

Grateful for any distraction, Roni said, "He made you weaker?"

"There is always a tradeoff when constructing a golem. In order to make me smarter, he had to sacrifice something. He could have taken away a limb or two, but he wisely decided I would need them all. He could have made me less articulate in vocal capability or physical appearance. The former he discounted fast because what would be the use of having me if I could not communicate. The latter, well, I suppose I could have done with a less-defined face, but I shudder to think what you would have thought if you found me hard to look at."

"Less-defined does not mean ugly."

"Perhaps so, but I like the way I look."

"I didn't know a golem could have an opinion."

"I'm not like other golems."

Roni laughed. "Of that, I'm certain."

The ragged scuffle of Roni's father announced his approach. "He's got it! Elliot's got the way in!"

Roni and Gully hastened back along the corridor. As they reached the end, Elliot stood tall with both hands clamped around the neck of his cane. Sweat trickled tributaries down his cheeks to form larger streams along his jaw and neck like liquid cracks against his skin.

"Hurry, hurry," he said, his voice barely above a grunt. "Can't hold this long."

Roni saw a canary-yellow dome about seven feet high cutting through the salmon-pink wall. Wherever it made contact, static crackled and smoke rose into the air. It smelled like burning plastic.

Gully pushed aside Lawrence and stepped through first. Roni understood — Gully wanted to test the world on the other side before allowing her to enter. Even as that thought flashed in her mind, the golem returned.

"Breathable and pleasant air, though there is an unusual pinkish haze everywhere," he said.

Elliot rocked forward, but his cane provided the stability to avoid falling over. This time. Roni pushed into her father's back. "Go, go," she said.

They hustled through the opening provided by Elliot's dome. She had been under his protective magic before — her skin prickled by its energy, but otherwise, she felt nothing. Elliot followed behind and let the dome sizzle away. They all stood in the light haze of another section of the caverns. Another universe.

Roni walked over to her father. "Where to next?" she asked, but the last word choked. Her father stared off at the end of the corridor, and tears wet his face.

He sniffled, grinned, and nodded as if responding to another speaker. Finally, he whispered, "Don't worry. I'll be there, my love. My Maria."

CHAPTER 11

The campfire ringed with stones warmed Roni and Teanna's shivering bodies. Elliot stood behind them, weaving his cane through the air above their heads. No memory restoration this time — just straight healing to fight off hypothermia and any other damage the icy waters of the lake had inflicted.

They sat in a circular alcove off of the main cavern path. Elliot and Gully had rushed them out of the lake area until they reached this point which existed in a different section of the caverns. Different section implied different universe — one that operated at a mild temperature. That coupled with the campfire and Elliot's healing meant both women travelled on a road toward remarkably fast recovery. But until they reached the end of that road, Roni's body continued to shake, and she could hear Teanna's quivering breaths.

"S-S-Sorry," Teanna managed.

Roni tightened the towel on her bare shoulders. Their clothes had been draped on a cooking spit above the fire to dry out. "N-N-Not your f-fault. The cavern shifted. What c-could you do?"

Gully stood guard at the mouth of the alcove. Roni tried not to stare, but her eyes drifted down to his legs. They no longer had the fine, detailed craftsmanship of Sully's practiced hand. Instead, they had been deformed by the lake water — now rumpled blobs that held the shape of legs but no more. Though neither Gully nor Elliot said anything, Roni knew the golem had been the one to wade into the lake and save her. And he had paid a terrible price.

With a sigh, Elliot broke off his magic and stumbled back. He slid against the wall, gently to the ground, and coughed hard as if he had pneumonia. "Oh," he said, dabbing a handkerchief across his sweating brow. "I have not cast so many spells in such a short time in ages."

"Sorry about that," Roni said.

"No need for an apology. Sometimes a mission calls upon one of us more than another. It's been many years since I've been taxed so greatly. My turn had to come up eventually. But let me rest for a bit while the fire warms you. Up ahead is a barrier which will require me to create a harmonic dome in order for us to pass. I need to gather my strength for that."

"Do what you have to." Roni looked to Teanna. "I know the Keeper is getting away, but it's pointless to confront that creature if we're all too exhausted to do anything once we get there."

"My father would say the same thing." Teanna adjusted her towel as she scooted closer to the fire. "He always told me I was too impatient and that my pushing on things would one day cause me trouble. Well, look at us now. He was right."

"You can't keep blaming yourself for this setback. Without you, we would never have made it across that lake at all."

"If I had shown true patience, I would never have needed to cross in the first place. I wouldn't even be here with you."

Choosing her words, Roni said, "If you can't answer this, I understand, but I'm still going to ask — what happened that you ended up with us?"

Teanna checked over at Elliot. He already snored. "I have not told any of you this, so it will not infringe upon Mr. Elliot's work. However, as much as I want to hurry just like you, I'm starting to believe Mr. Elliot is right. Please, don't tell him I said that."

"Don't worry. My group goes out of its way to deflate each other's egos. The last thing we want to do is tell somebody they're right."

As if this gave her all the answer she needed, Teanna hugged her knees and stared into the flames. "You have your group — the Parallel Society. Where I'm from, we call ourselves the Protectors. Our team is always comprised of five people — a tracker, a healer, a fighter, a bookmaker, and a craftsman. Those five are the active Protectors. Each one comes from five families. Each family trains generation after generation to fulfill this sacred duty. This way, we always have somebody ready to become an active Protector when the need arises."

"I take it your family is the trackers."

"My generation is the trackers. It varies because nobody knows what powers a particular family will produce. But all of that family's generation will be the same. So my little brother is also a tracker. You see?"

"Not your father, then? Or your mother?"

"No. Not my father." Teanna said the words like a teenager learning an awful truth. "His generation produced fighters."

"Oh. Was he disappointed you weren't a fighter?"

"Why would he be? No generation is the same as that before it."

"Sorry. The way you were talking, I thought —"

"Perhaps if you stopped interrupting to hear your own voice and listened, you'd understand better."

Roni fought back the urge to throw out a comment about sounding like Gram. In the end, she knew Teanna would not comprehend the reference, and despite the desire for Teanna to be wrong, Roni knew otherwise. "Sorry," Roni said. "Please, keep going."

"My father is a great fighter. He's helped defeat countless intruders into our universe. He was the one who brought up the idea of going into these caverns to stop the intruders before they ever reached our home. Until my father, the Protectors always remained in our own universe. We knew the way into the caverns but never took it. He changed that. He's the reason I'm out here.

"I became an active Protector only a short time ago. This is my fifth mission and only my second time in the caverns. We have scholars back home that take the notes we make and turn them into maps. That's what we were doing in here this time. Taking notes on the layout of the caverns to improve our maps.

"But then we heard movement. Wallum heard it first, and she suggested we hold quiet until we were sure whatever made the noise had gone. Then we could note its presence for the scholars." With a bitter laugh, she added, "What good are all those maps now? The cavern has changed. All that hard work was useless. We knew parts of the caverns could change — at least, that was what the legends told us, but somehow we convinced ourselves that we knew better."

Roni wanted to offer some consoling words but decided it would be much safer to keep her mouth shut.

"My father led the way." Teanna spoke in a rigid manner yet managed a tinge of warmth, too. Like a military commander fighting hard against showing emotion — but some of it seeped through anyway. "That's part of the fighter's job. He always enters a room first, throws the first punch, and defends to the last person. This time, we found ourselves in the Cave of Lost Time."

"What? You just stumbled into the Cave?" Roni wanted to scream about wrongness and unfairness and how it felt like a slap in the face after all she had been through to find the same location, but she snapped her lips closed.

"We didn't know anything about Lost Time or the Keeper or the Cave. None of my people had ever been there before, and of course, none of us had ever mapped it. But I know now that we did not *stumble* upon that terrible place. The Keeper lured us there. She made it happen. Just as she sent you and your father a mental attack to bring you here."

"She also struck Sully, but that didn't work out as she planned."

"Are you sure?"

Roni felt a chill that did not arise from her recent plunge into the ice lake. "You think she wanted Sully in the hospital?"

"I think if she wanted Mr. Sully here, he would be here. From what Mr. Elliot has told me and from what I see in Mr. Golem, it seems to me that your Sully is a brave, intelligent, and loyal leader. Also, a bit of a complainer but an all-around *mensch* — if I understand that word correctly."

"Admirable and worth following? Yeah, that's him."

Teanna tested her clothes. "Dry enough. We should dress and get moving."

"But what happened with the Keeper? Where's the rest of your team?"

Tossing Roni her shirt, Teanna said, "You'll remember eventually."

Though Roni got dressed — her clothes still had damp spots but were overall dry enough — she scowled inwardly. However, Teanna had given away a bit more than intended. A few times she slipped into the past tense when talking about her father. And mentioning how the Keeper may have targeted Sully because Sully would have been the equivalent of a fighter on Teanna's team — brave, first to go in, the leader — suggested that Teanna's father also became the target of the Keeper.

Thrusting on her pants with aggressive motions, Roni forced her thoughts away from such speculations. They would do her no good and only filled her heart with anxiety. She had enough direct problems to deal with. And as Teanna had pointed out — Roni would remember eventually. A strange question popped in her mind — did she really want to know?

It was not lost on Roni that her father was not with them. In the memories that had returned, he certainly came into the caverns with them. Where was he now? Or did he not survive?

She shoved away these thoughts with more aggression. He was alive. He had to be. If he had died, she would have felt something. No amount of Lost Time could take that bond away.

While her mind fought for something better to think on, she noticed a marking on the alcove wall near the edge. A circle with a staggered line running down the middle and branching off numerous times. Running her fingers along the lines, a dark thought pushed aside all the others.

Did I make this?

They had to have hiked by this alcove on their way in, so perhaps she had drawn this mark. But why? If she had made it, then shouldn't it mean something to her now?

She glanced down at Elliot. After so many years trusting him, it hurt to doubt. But she could not deny the sense that he held back less from fear of brain damage and more from fear of what she might do.

He roused a moment later as if he could feel her attentions. Gathering himself together, he said, "Are you both warm enough? I can offer more healing."

"We're fine," Roni said. "It's time to go. We've got a Keeper to catch."

CHAPTER 12

A somber silence overcame the group as they sat around a campfire set in a circle of stones. Roni's father had led them to this alcove off the main corridor and suggested they rest. He promised there would be plenty ahead that required energy, and Roni thought it sounded more like a threat than a promise. Elliot, however, did not hesitate. Before Roni had dropped her backpack, he had curled against the alcove wall and fallen asleep. Lawrence put the fire together and Gully, of course, stood guard.

Roni enjoyed the fire's warmth, though she did not need it — this section of the cavern maintained a mild temperature. The smoky aroma and the soft crackle of burning wood turned the cramped space into a luxurious comfort — tolerable, anyway. She closed her eyes and let the sensation roll across her. With so few opportunities to enjoy her life lately, she thought it best to grab them when they arrived.

"I've been here before," her father said, his voice cutting a jagged line through the peace.

Roni's eyes snapped open. Her mind flooded with questions, but years of practice kept her from bursting every thought upon him. If she threw out too much at once, he would either close up or his manic side would take control. The trick was to keep him talking, keep him going down the road towards the answers she wanted, but at a pace that did not break him.

At least, that had always been the way in the past. But back then, they sat in the Day Room of a mental hospital. Back then, he had been administered medications and she tried to determine if he had any shred of sanity left. Back then, she sought answers about the car accident that had claimed her mother's life. Only that never happened. And while his sanity still remained in question, he had enough presence of mind to guide them this far through the caverns. Enough that Sully thought it wise to put them all in this situation.

Lawrence poked a small branch into the fire as he thought. When he pulled it out, he pointed its blackened tip in Elliot's direction. "Your mother and I cuddled over there. I remember trying to kiss her — just a kiss, not trying to start anything — but she refused even a kiss. Didn't want to show any physical affection in front of Gram. Maybe not in front of any of them."

"They were all here?" Roni asked, forcing her voice to sound calm and casual.

"Gram sat where you are. Sully and Elliot were over here. I think Sully cooked something for us to eat. I can remember him going on about being prepared. I teased him. Called him our Boy Scout." With an ache behind his eyes, he looked at the spot where Elliot now slept. "I wonder if she would have let me have that kiss, if she had known it would be our last."

"It's so strange to hear any of that. Gram always told me that you and Mom wanted nothing to do with the Society."

"That's true. Your mother rebelled against everything Gram stood for."

"Then how did you end up here?"

He sighed. "Ask yourself that question. You didn't set out to be in the Society, either. You didn't even know about it. Yet here you are. The fact is that being in your family means you'll end up in the Society. No matter how hard you fight against it — and your mother put up a hellish fight — but the Society always wins. Even if you somehow manage not to actually join them, you can't unlearn the truth of the universes and the relics and all of it. Once that's part of your life, there's no going back to normal. For me, well, where Maria went, I went. I loved her. Still do."

Roni tried to memorize each word, each inflection, each facial tick of her father as he spoke. Later, she would want to replay it on a loop in her mind, analyze it until she broke through the surface and drained every bit of truth she could from below. But she also needed to be present and aware so as not miss signs of her father losing touch. Like coaching a gymnast on a balance beam, she had to keep her father from falling off.

"I'm sorry that you got pulled into all of this," she said, hoping to sound soothing.

"I suspect your mother thought she had managed to escape it all.

She fell in love with me, married me, had you — and it was only natural that she wanted to share herself completely. So, one night, she told me all of it." He lowered his head and chuckled. "I thought she was crazy, that she needed time with a therapist, that she might even end up in a place like Belmont. But she insisted I come to the bookstore and see the magic caverns underneath. Being a loving husband, I agreed. After all, I didn't know what was going on in her head, and I wanted to see the extent of her delusion. Of course, I soon learned that I was the delusional one."

Grinding his teeth, Roni's father watched the smoke drift up from the tip of his burning stick. She had seen him slip away from reality many times. Never before had he looked so ready to lash out. Short of making fists, his fingers wrapped around the branch as if choking the life from some unseen foe.

"I believe you," Roni said, hearing the slight tremble in her voice. "Tell me the rest. Tell me the truth."

With a short gasp, he appeared to pull himself together. "Yes, the truth."

Roni blocked the half-dozen questions that threatened to rip out. She let a soft pause create quiet around them.

Her father poked the stick into the fire once more. "Everything changed after I went in the caverns. The world did not exist like before. It was as if I had been behind a pane of glass and your mother's reality smashed through it with a sledgehammer."

"Yeah. I've been through that feeling, too."

"The hardest thing for me was that she wanted nothing to do with that world. I loved her, so I accepted. But that didn't get the things I had seen out of my head. So, one evening, your mother decided she would take me into the caverns for a little excursion — a controlled sort of thing that she hoped would be adventure enough for me. I think she thought it would get the whole curiosity out of my system. And it did. We had a great time while Gram took care of you, and that felt like the end of it."

"But?"

"But then Sully learned about the book referencing the Cave of Lost Time. Gram, Elliot, and Sully all came to us one night. See, there was this living relic stuck in our world. You know about living relics?"

"I do."

"There was this one, and Gram had decided that instead of banishing this living relic into another universe, trapping it in a book, that they were going to help this creature find its way to its own universe. I could tell that Sully and Elliot were not necessarily onboard with the idea, but Gram led the group, and what she said was the way things were going to be."

"Are you sure? I can't imagine Elliot or Sully not wanting to help another being."

"Let me finish. You see, this relic did not remember where it came from. According to it, the Keeper at the Cave of Lost Time had swiped that memory from its head. The group had spent a couple years searching for this mythic place. They came up empty. Until Sully found a book with evidence of its existence. So, Gram decided they were going to try to help this living relic. By the way, now is the part where you interrupt to ask what any of this has to do with me or your mother."

Roni cringed. She had been thinking that exact question. But also, she wondered if this story was about the living relic Yal-hara. Roni had met that relic — well, she had met the relic's proxy, Kenneth Bay — over a year ago. After a moment, it became clear that her father would not continue until she spoke, so she said, "Well?" It was enough.

"This book that Sully discovered passages about the Cave in — it came from your mother."

"Mom wrote the book?"

"What? No. When she and I went on our little trip through the caverns, she first noticed it. I was too caught up in the caverns themselves to notice anything like a specific book, but to her, there was something about it. Days later, she snuck back in and snatched the book. At some point, she showed it to Sully. Well, when Gram got all of this information, she separated us into two rooms and interrogated us as if we were criminals. In the end, they concluded that we did not know how we found that book but that your mother had felt drawn toward it. Of course, later we would understand that the Keeper had called your mother toward the Cave."

"Gram wanted you to lead the group to the Cave for them?"

"Not me. Your mother. But exactly right. They brought the relic along and we made our way through the tunnels connecting up with this path."

"Did it work? Did you get the living relic back where it belonged?"

Lawrence yanked the stick out of the fire and jumped to his feet. With the smoking charred end, he stepped over to the alcove wall and drew a symbol — a circle with a jagged, branching line cutting through it.

"What does it mean?" Roni asked, every cell in her body craving an answer yet hoping to hear only crazed babble.

Lawrence turned back to face her. He panted like a wounded beast. In his eyes, Roni saw enough madness to convince her, yet her skin still prickled, her heart still raced. If it had ended there, she could have believed any lie her mind conjured. She would continue their mission and all the uncertainty and uneasiness her father's behavior formed would vanish.

But then Elliot spoke.

He sent his cane on the ground with a loud thud. Roni whirled at the noise and saw him standing tall and strong. "Enough of this," he said. "Gather your things. We leave now."

As Lawrence packed up, Elliot moved toward Roni. "Your father does not know reality from the fictions of his mind."

"You were eavesdropping?"

"How am I going to sleep in this tiny alcove with the two of you jabbering away?"

She glanced at her father. "You're denying what he said happened?"

"I am telling you that it did not happen quite as he recalls. Memories, especially traumatic memories, can be unreliable things. I cannot prove to you that I am more truthful than he is, but I can tell you this — I have never been in these parts of the caverns before. I have never been in this alcove."

"It's all just him raving?"

"Not all. Gram, Sully, and I have been searching for the Cave. There was a living relic that we wanted to save, and we did try to use this mission to recruit your mother. But we never got the chance. The night she died — none of us were with her. As far as I know, it was just your mother and father. Together. Alone."

Roni knew it would be mind-wrenching to figure out which story to believe. The pain shimmering beneath the surface of Elliot's face told her how much he understood her dilemma. That didn't make it any easier to handle, but it suggested that the answer probably rested between the two tales. That was not the kind of truth she wanted it to be.

Chapter 13

As they entered the corridor, Roni finally had some expectations. Enough of her memories had returned that she knew there would be a transparent, salmon-pink wall that required Elliot's magic to step through. She would see the pinkish haze in the air. At the far end of the opposite corridor, she would spot the cave-in that blocked their way several days earlier. Once they crossed through the shimmering wall, they would be back on familiar ground. Not far then to the path that led home.

Except the wall had been shattered.

Jagged shards lay scattered on the cavern floor. They looked like glass but still flickered light. Blood-red goo dripped from the ceiling where the wall had once been. The pinkish haze had disappeared as well. Peering through the clear air, Roni thought that the cave-in had remained. So, at least one expectation had panned out.

Toeing the shards, Teanna said, "I think it is clear that the Keeper came this way."

"The strength of this thing," Elliot said, nudging another shard with his shoe.

While Gully jogged over to the other corridor to stand guard, Roni stared at the destroyed room, unable to sync this place with the memory she held. If not for Elliot's stunned reaction, she would have doubted the memory that returned to her. Everything had changed — except the cave-in, but looking closer, she suspected it had worsened with the shifting of the caverns.

She leaned against Elliot. "You okay?"

"I had no idea she could be like this."

Clenching her jaw, Roni said, "From what I do remember, we're getting awfully close to the bookstore. Don't you think I should be prepared before we face this thing?"

"Enough already." Elliot turned away but not fast enough to hide the deep scowl on his brow. "If you had ever shown me that you actually learned from your mistakes, I might be inclined to listen to you. But always when you want something, you pick and push and prod. You won't let up until you get your way."

"Sorry. I didn't mean —"

"You did. You just don't like being called out on it." He pointed his cane at her. "Do you really believe I would ever put your life in more danger than necessary in this line of work? Do you honestly think I would hold back on you when our lives and our universe could be in danger?"

"Of course not."

"You are remembering enough on your own. You do not need my assistance anymore. Until your memory is fully restored, Teanna and I will remember enough for us all."

Roni closed her eyes. "Then I guess I have no choice but to walk blindly into whatever this thing is."

"You are ridiculous," Teanna said. "And I thought you complained a lot before you lost your memories."

"You do not want to get in the middle of this."

"I think I'll … what? What are you looking at?"

Roni had opened her eyes and stared at a small puddle on the ground. The dark liquid did not move like the pieces of wall sprinkled about the cavern floor. It did not resemble the thick liquid dripping from the wounds in the ceiling. But something about it caused Roni's stomach to twist.

"Is that blood?" she said, knowing the answer already. "Is that the Keeper's blood?"

Teanna rushed over, dropped to her knees, and brought her nose in close to the puddle. She inhaled deeply. "The Keeper has been wounded. We must find her. She cannot be allowed to die."

"Why not?" Roni looked to Elliot for support. "I mean I'm all for convincing the Keeper to turn back in peace, but isn't killing her better than letting her loose in our world? That's where she's going, right? This path is heading straight back home."

Teanna stepped in front of Roni. "Until the Keeper returns my father, she cannot die."

"Don't be a fool. I've lived my whole life waiting to get back my Lost Time, and clearly, that won't ever happen. From what I can tell, the Keeper took my mother. Since you and Elliot are cagey about it, I'm guessing I won't be seeing my father anytime soon, too. When those words truly set into me, it'll rip me apart. Nothing I can do about that. But you have choice — you don't have to let the Keeper's crap destroy you. Trust me. Don't let her cruelty define your life. It's not a good life to have."

Teanna tightened her fists. "My father will return."

"I'm sorry, but if killing the Keeper is the only way to protect my world, I won't hesitate."

"You have no right."

"I have a universe to protect."

Teanna threw a hard punch. Roni winced, expecting a painful blast to her jaw. Nothing. No pain. No jolt to her head. Peeking, she saw Gully with his hand locked around Teanna's wrist.

"Let go," Teanna grunted.

Gully wrenched her arm, forcing her to stumble backward. "Perhaps I lack instructions enough to understand, but it seems to my golem brain that all three of you are behaving a tad counter-productive." He squeezed Teanna's wrist tighter before releasing her. "I will never allow you to harm Roni. Now, if I may throw a little wisdom your way, according to Rabbi Joshua ben Avrahim, we must never put the value of one above the whole nor the whole above the one."

Rubbing her wrist, Teanna said, "That makes no sense."

"Yeah, I don't get it, either," Roni said. "What are you trying to say?"

"We all agree," Elliot said. "Your rabbinical paraphrase is not helpful."

"No?" Gully said. "Well, it seems to be you all are finally agreeing on something."

Roni couldn't stop herself. She burst into laughter. Elliot soon followed, and despite her efforts to hold back, Teanna laughed, too.

"We need to get moving," Roni finally said. "Let's catch up with the Keeper and see what happens."

"I won't let you kill her," Teanna said.

"I won't let her kill my universe. But there's a large distance between those two statements. We'll figure something out."

Teanna glanced at the puddle of blood. "Okay."

They headed off. All four moved with solemn appreciation for the sudden truce. But that did not stop Roni's muscles from tensing.

CHAPTER 14

As the air grew colder, Roni suspected they had traversed into another universe. She thought it strange how she could now tell by mere shifts in the air. A year ago, she would have had no inkling that she had crossed universes. A few years before that, she would have had no clue that more than one universe even existed.

Yet here she walked.

If only what lay ahead could be as easy. After her short time with the Parallel Society, she had learned to be comfortable with the unknown — well, if not comfortable, at least cautiously accepting. But at some point soon, provided her father did not lead them in circles, they would reach the Cave and the Keeper and the source of her Lost Time. The unknown would become no more than a memory.

As long as they kept moving, she could focus on the next step and the next. She could force herself into a myopic trance that ignored the endgame. Life became nothing but another step forward.

Except the growing anxiety in her father refused to be misconstrued. They were getting close. He felt it and it showed. If she would be honest, she felt it, too. An electricity charged the air. More than the shift to another universe. And if she let her honesty dig down into her core, she quaked with fear.

When her father finally said, "We're here," that fear threatened to rise up her throat.

They had entered a large cave dominated by a lake covered solid in ice. "This is the Cave of Lost Time?" she asked.

"What? No. This is an ice lake."

"But you just said —"

"The ice lake is the last universe we have to go through. We get to the other side and we'll reach our goal." He scratched his ear. "I think."

Elliot opened one of their bags and pulled out a coil of rope. He handed one end to Roni's father and waited. After tying the rope around his waist, Lawrence and Elliot wrapped the rope around Roni and finally did the same for Elliot. Once Elliot secured the rope, he handed it to Gully.

"We'll need you in the anchor position," he said.

Gully inspected the rope, placing it in one hand and then the other. He seemed confused. Considering how much intelligence Sully had given the golem, Roni thought it odd that this would be a difficult task to comprehend. She gazed across the lake in case she had missed an easier path, but she saw nothing. Crossing the ice was it.

With boyish curiosity, Gully said, "Have you given any thought to my weight? Clay, stone, and metal are quite heavy and not a good combination for walking out on the ice. If I'm tied to all of you, I'll be dragging the whole team under before you know what's happened. You call it an anchor position? I'd be anchoring you to your grave."

Though Roni had to agree with the golem, she could not stop smiling at the way he expressed himself. Her eyes teared up, wishing she could be at Sully's bedside, helping Gram nurse the old rascal back onto his feet. She felt both closer to him and further away.

Lawrence tugged on his end of the rope. "Then I guess you stay behind. You've been a good golem to us, but we must keep going."

"I can't do that. It's my job to protect Roni and this group. If I remain behind, how am I to perform my main purpose?"

"Don't know what to tell you about that one, but my main purpose is to get to the Cave. I like you as far as a golem goes, but I ain't turning back for you. I doubt Roni will be turning back, either."

Gully faced Roni. "Is that right? Do you intend to abandon me here rather than find a solution? Sully made me for you, and you'll just throw me aside because things are a little inconvenient now?"

Great. Sully had infused guilt trips into this thing. Roni said, "Nobody's abandoning you. If you can't cross, then you'll have to wait. But we will come back. You'll stick with us all the way home."

"But not any further. You're okay with making me stand here while the three of you go on?"

"It's not a matter of being okay with it. The fact is that this is the only way we know to get to the Cave. That's our goal. I wish you could come with us, but you wouldn't ask us to abandon our whole reason for being here because you're not capable of crossing the ice, would you?" Two could play at the guilt game.

Ever the mediator, Elliot said, "Perhaps the three of us should cross first. We can see the state of the ice and judge whether you'll be safe on it."

Gully said, "I cannot let you do that."

"What's this now?" Lawrence said. "You don't get a say."

"I won't let Roni risk her life crossing this lake without knowing the risks she's taking. And I refuse to abandon my post at her side. I will test the ice first. At least, then, if I break through and die, the rest of you will remain safe."

Before anyone could respond, Gully broke into a thumping run across the ice.

"Oh, crap," Roni said.

Gully stormed along the lake. Every footfall sprayed frozen mist into the air and left behind divots in the ice. Roni, Elliot, and Lawrence stood on the shore's edge as if watching a battle-crazed soldier dancing through a minefield.

When the golem hopped onto the opposite shore and happily waved them across, Elliot snickered. "I guess it's safe."

A low and heavy sound broke through from below the ice like an enormous ship snapping apart. Roni's father pointed to the length of rope hanging on the ground. "Pick that up. We've got to run for it."

Roni said, "That ice is cracking."

"Exactly. We go now or we never go."

Elliot said, "I'm sure we can find another route."

"No time." Lawrence started out, yanking Roni along.

Her pulse jacked into action as Elliot looped the loose end of rope around his shoulder. A thunderous boom rose from the depths. One of the divots left by Gully's crossing exploded upward like a brief, icy geyser. An instant later, frozen shards fell onto the lake top.

"Go, go," Lawrence said, leading out onto the ice.

But he truly attempted to run. Three steps and his feet slipped out beneath him. Roni tried to keep him from going down but that only sent her into a wobble. As the two of them crashed to the hard surface, the rope tying them altogether brought Elliot flailing atop them.

Another divot blew into the air.

"Get up," Lawrence said, his voice rising an octave. He squirmed out from under them and scrambled to his feet. He tried to hurry forward, but Roni and Elliot still struggled to get their balance. The whole group dropped again.

"Stop it," Roni said, massaging her sore backside. "We have to take it slow."

"We slow down, we'll die."

Elliot pressed against his cane to steady himself. "Pay attention to your daughter. She's smarter than you, and she's right."

They started across once more, moving with caution, making sure each one maintained their balance. Roni focused on the next step, the next step, the next step. The explosions of ice went off behind them, but she ignored the violent sounds. If she allowed their existence to enter her awareness, she would act like her father, panic, and down they would go.

A hefty blast split into the air. From the corner of her eye, Roni spied a dark, jagged line bolting out from one of Gully's divots. Her hands tightened around the rope.

"Steady," Elliot said. "Just keep moving ahead. We're halfway there."

Like a chain of firecrackers, the clatter of one break in the ice after another snapped off around them. A rain of fine crystals sprinkled their heads. Roni felt a chilly dusting fall down her back. No word was spoken, yet all three quickened their pace.

A single boom shook the surface, and Elliot slipped hard onto his back, pulling Roni and Lawrence with him. "Get up! Get up!" Lawrence said, rising to his feet only to slip back down.

If not for the threat of a frozen grave, Roni would have laughed. The three of them flailed about the ice like children testing out skates for the first time. But near the shoreline behind them, Roni spotted chunks of ice bobbing on deadly cold waters. Her heart froze.

Through shaking lips, she said, "We're not going to make it." Nobody responded, and she hoped that neither man had heard the words slip out.

Elliot managed to stand, once more using his cane to maintain stability, and he warned Lawrence to wait, to let Roni rise first. But Roni's father only heard the continued crash of ice sheet against ice sheet.

"We're out of time," he said, bolting to his feet.

The jarring action spun the rope around Roni's waist, twisting her off-balance. As she flopped onto the ice, Elliot collapsed on top of her legs, and the rope yanked Lawrence backwards. He smacked his cheek on the hard surface only a foot away.

"Hold on!" Gully said, thumping over the ice toward them.

Roni lifted one hand to halt the golem, but Elliot stopped her. He said, "We won't get there on our own. Not like this."

Gully's heavy steps created new divots in the frozen surface, ones that sent visible fissures shooting out toward other cracks several feet below. Lawrence had managed to get on his knees and held out his hand. Like a professional skater, Gully slid in, grabbed Lawrence's hand, and dragged the entire roped gang.

The ice behind them spit into the air as if struck by heavy mortars. Larger gaps formed, each one filling with water. Roni twirled left then right, the rope around her waist digging into her skin as the uneven surface scratched her underside. When she spun to face backwards, she saw some of the fill water freezing over, but she doubted it could become solid fast enough to save them.

Huffing, Gully pressed on. "Not to worry. We're going to be fine."

Roni wondered why the golem continued to show human aspects like breathing hard when he never actually breathed.

Without warning, they smacked into the pebble-strewn shore. They wasted no time in getting out of the ropes and clambering further inland. Roni only stopped when she had no fear of the ice sweeping away the solid ground beneath her.

"Thank you," she said to Gully.

He nodded as he bent over his knees and coughed. Two more loud cracks echoed off the ice lake. Pointing at them, Gully said, "I don't think we'll be able to cross back this way."

"That's certain," Elliot said, leaning a bit heavier on his cane. "If it doesn't shatter into a thousand pieces in the next few minutes, that lake will be a tripwire waiting for the next person to set foot on it."

"Don't worry," Lawrence said. "When the time comes, we'll find our way across."

"Overconfidence is never a good quality to have."

"The Keeper called us out here. Surely, she knows what we would have to deal with to get to her. Which means that she knows how we get back."

Roni said, "Unless she doesn't intend for us to get back."

But her father only waved off the comment. "Have some faith in me. I would never go out this way, if I didn't have a plan back."

"Then what's your plan?"

"I don't know yet. But it'll come to me." He spoke as if his words made perfect sense.

Roni swallowed back the scream mounting in her throat. If given the chance, her mind would have spiraled off with one question after another, all of them focused on the insanity of her father and her blind willingness to follow him. Except she wasn't blind. She understood the situation exactly.

She also noticed the change in her father. His speech had become less erratic, less frantic. Even when panicking across the lake, he sounded more like a normal man. No matter his tone, however, the words that came out of his mouth still swam in half-sane thoughts. Yet the lure of the Cave hung before her, skimming the surface of her mind, promising answers, promising to fill the voids. Turning away would never be a serious option.

Perhaps that's why Sully sent his proxy golem. Perhaps he knew she would be unable to decline the opportunity of meeting the Keeper, so he wanted her to have the best chances for success. If she ever survived this, she owed that old man a giant hug and the finest cup of coffee she could find.

"Come, come," Lawrence said, hustling toward a tunnel as if the past few minutes had not occurred. With his next words, however, Roni felt the same way. "The Cave is up ahead. We're practically there."

Chapter 15

The familiar sections of the cavern came into view. While this usually brought with it a sense of comfort, like flying into Philadelphia or driving up her home street, this time Roni only sensed threat. Even the smell of moss and wet stone drew only the fear that these comforts and the universe which sat behind them could easily be destroyed.

A high-pitched bark like a choking dog echoed back at them followed by the dull sound of muscle against metal. Gully halted and angled his clay ear toward the noise. "Stay here. I'll check ahead." He did not wait for a response.

Teanna pushed Roni aside, clearly intent on following Gully. Roni said, "You stay here with us."

"What's the point? We know it's the Keeper."

"But we don't know what the Keeper is doing, and we don't know what she has done to the area surrounding the door to our universe. We know she totally destroyed the room with the pink wall. We know she fell into the ice lake. We know she's bleeding. She's angry and rushing as fast as she can manage. We'd be idiots to rush into a battle when we can take our time and go in fully informed."

Teanna moved in close enough that Roni felt the woman's hot breath. She had an earthy smell — pleasant enough but also a tinge of something foreign underneath, something from another universe. With only inches between them, Roni knew Teanna could lash out faster than she could react, but she refused to back down.

Teanna said, "We agreed not to kill the Keeper unless absolutely necessary. Until she breaks into your universe, it's not necessary."

"We never agreed to anything. But if you want to take a moment to talk this out, I'm more than willing."

Elliot's cane cut down between them. "Ladies, this is not the time.

Teanna, Roni is relying on us to have the answers that fill in the gaps in her memory. You and I both know that the Keeper is not a creature to be underestimated. I truly hope we can help you. I told you before that we need to work for each other, to help each other — it's the only way. You have my word that we will do everything in our power to bring your father back. However, you must believe Roni that we will not let our universe fall to that thing. Roni, you need to be more understanding towards Teanna. You know exactly what it is like to lose a parent to this thing. She's lost more than that. Far more."

Roni looked at the two of them. "I suppose that references something I still don't remember."

"It does."

A howl floated down from the tunnel — not the same terrible barking of the Keeper. A pained sound like an old man being tortured by merciless thugs. Gully.

"Do you think he's hurt?" Roni asked Elliot.

Teanna tossed her robes over one shoulder and pulled two small hand axes from behind her back. "People don't cry like that when everything's fine." She took off down the tunnel.

Roni shook her middle finger at Teanna's back. "Great talk. Glad we worked it all out." Over her shoulder, she said to Elliot, "Come on. If she's determined to run in there blind, the least we can do is back her up."

Roni dashed along the tunnels and pathways she had come to know well. The books chained to the walls grew numerous the closer she came to the bookstore. They blurred by Roni as she heard a vile mixture of howling and high-pitched barking.

The path curved around a large stalagmite and opened into a small area Roni thought of as the foyer. At the top of the stone ramp, Teanna blocked the way through the door to Roni's universe. Gully knelt on the floor, hunched over and cradling his right arm. His clay hand, now inanimate, sat on a rock ten feet away. In the middle of it all — the Keeper.

Elliot came short of barreling down Roni as they both stuttered to a halt. During all their travels back, Roni had never settled in her mind what she thought the Keeper might look like. A lizard-skinned monster, a gooey blob, a chimera of lion, hawk, and shark — nothing seemed right in her head. But now she understood that no matter what she had envisioned, she would have been wrong.

The Keeper had pale, saggy skin that hung on its enormous, bony body as if she were an elderly giant. Even with her back curved at the spine, her bald and goblin-ish head scratched the cavern ceiling fifteen feet above. She had a freakish neck — straight like a metal pole and wiry hairs poked out the top. Her torso extended more than seemed natural and sprouted eight knobby arms — long things with bristling hairs protruding out of veiny skin. A narrow section, a strip of flesh covering mostly spine, reached down to a pelvic bone no more than six feet off the ground. Four gargantuan legs — all bone and gangly — shot upward to knees that brushed the creature's shoulders before angling back down and finishing in wide, oversized feet. Though everyone had referred to the Keeper as female, Roni saw no evidence to suggest any actual gender.

The Keeper's head swiveled toward Roni, her eyes widening to reveal a kaleidoscope of color. Blood dripped from a gash on her shoulder. When she opened her mouth to bark, Roni saw blocks of teeth, each one filled with tiny jagged lines — perfect for grinding and gnashing.

Licking her lips, the Keeper did not let loose an animalistic or high-pitched barking. Instead, she spoke. In a hissing, pain-soaked voice as if her throat had been damaged. "Thought you would trick me. Thought you'd make your deals and double-cross me. You're no better than a stupid, whining little whelp. A girl crying for her lost mum. What are you going to do now that I have chewed up Daddy, too?"

Roni's vision blurred as she glanced back at Elliot. She felt the tears dripping down her cheeks. "Is my father dead?"

CHAPTER 16

Twice, Lawrence rushed far enough ahead that Roni worried they would lose him. He picked up speed with every step, calling back in growing excitement — *just up ahead! just around this turn! almost there!*

The last time proved to be true. Roni felt the change in the air first. A shift into warmth like a perfect spring morning. She could practically smell the flowers and fresh dew.

Gully insisted on walking beside her to make sure none of her injuries worsened. He refused to understand her explanation on how bruising worked. But he slowed a couple steps behind, mesmerized by the wonderful aroma. It occurred to Roni that most every sensation would be a new one for the golem. At least, this one was pleasant.

Turning a sharp right in the dark tunnel, Elliot halted. Bright yellows, ambers, and reds danced across his gawking face.

"What is it?" Roni said, ducking under his arm.

Then she froze, too.

The tunnel opened into a vast space surrounded by stalactite and stalagmite teeth. However, before all else, Roni saw the books. They floated like balloons trying to escape, but chains attached to their spines extended downward, burying into stalagmites, heavy stones, and in some cases, the ground. The books strained against these chains, creating strange chimes that blended with the wet drips echoing throughout the cavern. Most of the books had spread open, and an array of colors burst upward. Violet, periwinkle, emerald, ruby, amber, brass, rust, silver, gold — the makers of crayons could spend a lifetime naming all the colors, their light playing against the ceiling in a dazzling display.

The air smelled fresh. Nothing strange about that in the caverns — even regular caverns throughout the world smelled of Nature-washed stone and fresh moss. But this cave had a fresher aroma. Each breath cleared out Roni's lungs and reawakened her senses. It acted opposite to a drug trip — instead of fogging one's brain into euphoria, the caverns cleared the mind to create an experience of greater sensitivity.

With his hands clasped on his head, Lawrence spun and danced and jumped around. "I told you," he said, laughing the words. "I told you I knew the way. Look at this place."

Regaining his senses, Elliot said, "We should not let him get too far ahead of us."

Roni managed a nod and moved further in. It was difficult to watch where she walked when her eyes continuously wanted to gaze upward. She noticed several books had chains that wrapped around the covers to prevent them from opening. Those books she understood — ones that might depressurize the room or open a pathway for horrible things to enter this space. But these others ...

"Are all of these books like the ones we deal with?" she asked.

"Yes and no," Elliot said. "From what I've read and from what Sully has told me, these are entrances into other universes, only in a sense, but each one is a trapped memory or a moment of history."

"Are you saying these are the Lost Time? My Lost Time is somewhere in these? Just a floating book?"

"I don't know for certain. But that's my understanding."

The ground sloped downward and the path curved in a random pattern like the flow of a lazy river. Chained books bobbed on all sides, poking out between the rocky terrain. From ahead, Lawrence called out, "Roni, come here."

Gully grabbed her arm, hard enough to hold her back but gentle enough to cause no pain. "Allow me to lead."

He walked in front with Roni and Elliot following close behind. As they came around the bend, they found Lawrence standing in a cleared circle. The remains of an old campfire marked the center. Sitting on the far end, Roni saw a young, black woman wearing colorful, flowing robes and a strong, cold glower.

Roni stared at this woman trying to fathom how such a small, young thing could have caused her so much torment. She wanted to cry. She wanted to rage. She only managed to open her mouth slightly and say, "So, you're the Keeper."

The woman snorted a bitter scoff. "You really don't know what you're looking for."

Lawrence stomped in a small circle. "Why would you think she's the

Keeper?" He offered his hand to the woman. "Hi, there. I'm Lawrence."

The woman stared at the hand, unsure how to take the gesture. Standing, she thrust her chest forward like a king, and said, "I am Teanna Rowl, tracker of the Protectors and daughter of Atura Rowl, leader of the Protectors."

"Pleased to meet you, Teanna. This is my daughter Roni, our friend Elliot, and that thing is Gully. He's a golem."

Pulling herself together, Roni stepped forward. "We're from a group called the Parallel Society. We protect our universe from —"

"The dangers of other universes encroaching upon yours," Teanna said as a new sense of certainty broke through the thin front she had displayed. "The Protectors are a similar group from my universe."

"I like your name better. Ours is a bit misleading."

"Have you dealt with the Keeper before? Can you help me?"

Clearing his throat, Elliot said, "Anybody drawn to this place needs all the help they can get."

"Then we help each other?"

"It's the only way."

Clapping his hands like a clown at a birthday party, Lawrence said, "Isn't that nice boys and girls? We're learning to get along. And now, do you know what time it is? That's right. It's time to see the Keeper." Dropping his voice and the act, he said, "Where is she?"

Teanna swung her robe over one shoulder and reached behind her back. Even without the glower on her face, Roni could tell Teanna did not like Lawrence.

"Forget it," he said. "I know where to find her."

"You do?" Roni said.

"Of course. Just follow the brown, dirt road." Slightly off-key, he sauntered away singing *follow the brown, dirt road follow the brown, dirt road.*

Roni glanced at Teanna. With a defeated nod, Teanna made it clear that Lawrence went the correct way. As Roni turned to follow, Teanna said, "Be careful. That thing is not a creature to trust. She can steal who you are."

"I know."

They weaved around one set of books after another, following the path as it took them around large rock formations and small. So many books. Each one a moment in time ripped from some poor soul. Each one straining against its chains, yearning to be free.

Gully halted. "There's something you don't see every day."

As Roni came up, she spotted a thick tangle of chains waving like seaweed reaching toward the surface of an ocean. At the bottom, her father dropped to his knees and gazed upward. About halfway up, the Keeper clung to the chains with the dexterity of a monkey and the limbs of a spider.

The Keeper had four thick legs that spread outward from beneath a long cloth like a tunic or a strangely slit dress. Her strong torso defined with muscle could be seen through her tightly fitting shirt — designed with sleeves for all eight limbs. Dark hair like a horse's mane — long, straight, and hanging to one side of her endless neck — heightened her smooth face. She was a beautiful creature albeit a bizarre one. She moved with such careful precision, such artistic grace, that Roni wondered if she watched a performance rather than a creature handling the chains of stolen memories.

"Keeper," Lawrence said with as much energy as he had ever spoken a word. "I have returned. We have heard your call and we have all returned."

The Keeper paused and looked off into the distance as if attempting to identify the source of an unwelcome sound. Gliding from one set of chains to another, she gently lowered to the ground. She turned her head downward and grinned a set of blocky, sharp teeth. "I knew you would come." Her focus shifted to Roni, Elliot, and Gully. "But you are more of a surprise. A pleasant one. Veronica Rider. I have so enjoyed getting to know your mother over the years. I almost feel like I know you."

As she stepped over Lawrence and moved in closer, her footsteps thunk hard on the ground betraying her size and strength. Roni clenched her fingers into fists, tensed all her muscles, and forced her legs to remain still. Gully folded his arms and blocked Roni from view. Elliot moved next to the golem and raised his cane.

"Gentlemen," the Keeper said, her melodic voice soothing as if casting a spell, "I only want to talk. How about it, Roni? Shall we talk about your mother?"

Chapter 17

Strands of spittle hung from the Keeper's mouth as she hissed at Teanna. "Move aside or be destroyed."

"You will not go through this door," Teanna said, crossing her axes in front of her like a shield. "We won't allow it. This universe doesn't belong to you."

"They are all mine. Move aside or you'll end up like your father and your friends." Each word showered the ground with more saliva.

Elliot swished along the path, picked up Gully's clay hand, and then assisted the golem to his feet. The two hurried back. Once Elliot had Gully settled out of the way, he pressed the clay wrist against the clay stump and repeatedly circled the connection with his cane.

During all of this, Roni did not move. She wanted to be useful, but no matter what her brain commanded, her body refused to budge. The Keeper had shown interest in her for a moment, blaming her for some betrayal, but when Roni remained frozen in her shock, the Keeper's lips curled with disdain. She turned her horrid body to Teanna and the bookstore door.

"Please," Teanna said, "I don't want to hurt you. I only want my father back, my fellow Protectors. Return them, and I'll let you be."

"Ah," the Keeper said, arching overhead enough to force Teanna's back against the door. "You have no care for protecting anything but your own interests. Your father is what you care about. Your fellow Protectors, too. But the universe behind that door — that's nothing to you. Just leverage."

The words swirled around Roni's head like speedboats racing. Teanna had no interest in helping. She only cared about her father. And why was this surprising? Roni had no interest in Teanna's problems except to solve her own.

But no — Elliot had been right. They had to help each other. Looking out for oneself rarely ended well. In the short-term, it would seem like a win, but over the length of a lifetime, self-interest paid diminishing returns — and often demanded retribution.

She knew all that. She had a sense that Teanna knew it, too. So why did she doubt the woman?

The words spun faster. Roni heard them over and over, and she noticed that the Keeper had spoken well. Better than before. But even as the thought entered her head, it slipped away. Pulled from her mind as it formed. Lost to her.

"Stop," she said, the force behind the declaration demanding everybody's attention. The words stopped moving, too — and puffed away into the air.

Roni noticed that Elliot continued healing Gully's hand even as he stared at her. The circling cane made her think of the Keeper's circling words. Of course. Elliot wouldn't be the only person in all existence to wield magic through motion. The Keeper's words had encircled Roni, and in doing so, the Keeper tried to control her thoughts. Or steal them.

"I don't know what happened to change you into this broken thing," she said, and the Keeper did not react. Why should she? She knew exactly what memories had been taken from Roni. This thought gave Roni the strength to step forward. "But we won't allow you to enter that door — or any door. You will not hurt another person or steal another life. And you will return Teanna's father and friends."

A gravel-filled noise scratched out of the Keeper's throat. "There's the fire in you."

Moving faster than Roni expected from such a large creature, the Keeper swept away from Teanna. One of her eight arms flashed out and grabbed Roni by the jaw. The skeletal fingers dug into her cheeks, and if Roni could have opened her mouth, she would have screamed. Instead, a pathetic whine locked in her throat.

The Keeper lowered her head, blocking everything but her shifting, colorful eyes from Roni's view. In a second that stretched into timelessness, Roni caught a shiver in those eyes. Not nervousness. Not fear. But struggle. The Keeper wanted to crush Roni's jaw — Roni could feel the pressure increase in those boney fingers — yet something stopped the creature.

"Such fight in you," the Keeper said. "Even when you hurt yourself."

Roni shoved down her mounting fear and let herself become lost in those fantastical eyes. Something about them — something familiar. Had she looked into the Keeper like this before?

But before an answer could form, she heard Teanna roar. "Let her go!"

The Keeper cried out and dropped Roni. Looking between the Keeper's tree trunk legs, Roni saw Teanna attacking with her axes. But the Keeper swatted her aside. Teanna tumbled on the hard ground and smacked into a large rock.

Roni struggled up and searched for a weapon. Gully bolted to his feet. Elliot tried to continue his healing, but the golem darted after the Keeper. With one hand flapping uselessly at the wrist, Gully lowered his shoulder and slammed into one of the creature's legs.

She spun away from Teanna to face this new annoyance. "What is the matter with your brains? Do you actually think you can stop me?"

She raised her foot over Gully's head. Roni leapt forward and wrapped herself over the golem. The Keeper's foot clapped hard onto the stones next to them. Shattered rock blasted in all directions.

"Go back to your cave," Elliot said. He held his cane at an angle like a biblical prophet. "Go back and tend your fallen world. You will not take ours."

The Keeper's horrid mouth widened. "You're no longer entertaining. None of you are."

Shrieking a series of her high-pitched barks, the Keeper snatched away Elliot's cane in one hand and grabbed him by the shoulder with another. A third hand shot behind and picked up Teanna by the ankle. Two more hands separated Gully and Roni. With a final bellow, she tossed the entire team in different directions.

Roni lost all sense of balance as her body flipped through the air. Only the cold cavern wall stopped her, and that brought hot pain across her hip and shoulder. Her legs folded overhead — she had landed upside-down — which dug her neck against a sharp rock.

Even as she managed to get her body situated, even as she shook off the muddled dizziness, she heard the door to the bookstore open. "No," Roni said, but the word barely reached her own ears.

She lurched to her feet. Elliot, Gully, and Teanna all tottered in their own efforts to stay standing. None of them could stop the Keeper.

Chapter 18

At the age of seven, Roni spent two weeks in bed with the flu. Once the initial vomiting and fever had settled, she merely suffered with aching bones and a constant headache. Watching television would worsen the pain. Same for being on the internet. She lacked the concentration to read, but she could listen to an audiobook. With few choices and needing something to help her granddaughter pass the time, Gram bought every audiobook Roni would agree to hear.

She listened to classics, epic fantasies, a few mysteries, and some non-fiction history. But a set of twelve books on riddles and puzzles grabbed her interest and refused to let go. Even when she knew all the answers, she still listened to the books, trying to learn how the author crafted the clues with such precision and care.

Sitting around a campfire with her group, with Teanna, and with the Keeper, Roni felt drawn back to that protracted two weeks of illness. Every word from the Keeper's mouth sounded as well-chosen and full of double-meanings as those of the riddle books.

"Your mother had such grand energy within her. Usually, my calls land a few confused younglings or those too close to death." Looking comical in an effort to fit into the small space allotted her, the Keeper used three hands to gesture at Teanna. "Your father has a lot of strength, but the rest of your group is either too young like you or about to die. The wrinkly one — he is quite ill."

Teanna covered her mouth. "Freture? But he just had a child."

"Good that he got that in before it was too late. His body rots from the inside. His colors are muted and bland to the taste. Like so many around here."

Lawrence snatched a branch from the fire and poked it at the glowing embers. "Don't torment the poor woman. I know you get off on our pain, but after all you've done to my family, I've got enough for you to feast for decades."

"I've tasted you before. A bit wanting, I think."

"You called me here. You wanted me back."

"We both know that isn't true. I want her." The Keeper leaned closer toward Roni, and Gully put a protective arm in front of her. "Relax, golem. I won't harm her unless the books demand it." She sniffed the air above Roni. "And I don't believe they will demand it."

Elliot said, "Then why are we here? If the books didn't want us, and you only obey the books, then what is the reason for calling us?"

Weighing all that had been said, Roni gazed up at the floating books. "They want something else. Or she does."

"Or someone else does," the Keeper said.

Roni stood, forcing the Keeper to back up or clunk heads. "Which is it? You're called the Keeper which implies that you look after these books. Do you control them, or do they control you?"

The Keeper reared back, lifting her body to its full fifteen-foot height. "I do not answer to anybody or anything. When I call, I call. When I feed, I feed. If I obey the demands of the books, it is by my choice and no other."

"That's it?" Roni said, her voice quivering. A thin film floated between her hopes and the truth. As she put the Keeper's words together with all the events of her life, she saw that film split apart. "This is about you feeding?"

Teanna jumped to her feet. "You ate my father?"

"No, she didn't. Not exactly." Roni let her eyes fall upon the books once more. "It's mutual. The books in here act different than any I've ever seen. Other books contain universes, but these hold lives. Well, memories of lives. They need memories to exist. Or life force or something like that. And the Keeper — you feed off the books. You're like a bee pollinating these cursed flowers. Is that it? Did you kill my mother and swipe my memories just so you can have a meal?"

Lawrence raised a fist. "You foul beast. It's coming back to me. You tricked Maria, you stole her, but I fought you. I remember that well. Floating in your books and fighting for my sanity."

The Keeper snickered. "I think you lost that one."

"Hold on," Roni said. "My mother is in one of these books? I thought she died."

"She is dead," her father said, burying his head in his arms.

Teanna pulled him close to her and petted his hair. "Do not cry,

Lawrence. I took care of my father through many challenges. I can help you, too."

Roni wanted to slap Teanna away from her father, but she saw how Teanna's attention calmed the man. At the moment, that made Roni's job easier. One less factor to worry about.

With a snort, the Keeper said, "Maria Rider is far from dead. Perhaps you'd like to find her."

"There is a book in this cave, one that holds her memories and my Lost Time. Right? That's why you called us. Right?" She turned to Elliot. "My parents came here because they heard the call — it's like a fishing lure. It's a worm wriggling on a hook. That's why we never could find this place since. You can't just come here. You had to be called. You had to be given the path."

The Keeper said, "You are a smart one."

"But you haven't eaten well lately. You said you're tired of the too young and too old. The books are getting dull. *Muted,* you said. I'm amazed by their colors, but they must be incredible when fully charged. Then Teanna shows up with her father. That tasted good. That brought memories back to you — days of good feeding. You decided to call my father and me. Hoped to grab hold of some strong energy. We're just here to feed you. Is that right? It feels right. Like an itch of my own memories coming back to me."

Stepping away from the campfire, the Keeper said, "Smart, but not smart enough. Look at the size of me. Do you really believe your puny energy is enough to fill my belly? If that were all true, why would I allow this woman to live?"

Teanna lifted her chin. "We fought you."

"You are not that strong. I let you live."

Roni perked up. "The books. They wanted her alive. They told you to leave her alone."

"You are guessing, and not very well."

"Then explain it to us. You obviously want something. Tell us. Show us. Why did you destroy my mother, my family? Why are you doing the same thing to Teanna?"

The Keeper turned and walked away. Two of her arms gestured back. "Follow me. I think you're ready. Isn't that right, Lawrence?"

"Damn right," he said, dropping the burnt stick as he walked after her.

Teanna rested her chin on her knees. "Don't go. You won't come back."

"What?" Roni asked.

Lawrence tugged on her sleeve. "Ignore her. We need to follow the Keeper before she gets too far ahead."

Roni crouched next to Teanna. "Do you know where she's taking us? Do you know how to get the Lost Time without her?"

With a sharp spit at the ground, Teanna said, "This is exactly what happened to my father. We came here and met the Keeper and she talked in circles until my father led the Protectors after her. Down that same path. But I didn't trust the Keeper, so I refused to go. Made my father very angry."

"Roni," her father barked. "We have to go now."

"See? She's already got your father's head twisted around. Maybe she's got yours, too. Don't trust a thing she says. She is a liar at all times."

"We've come so far to be here. I can't turn back."

"You go that way, you don't come back."

Roni looked towards her father, Elliot, and Gully. They all walked after the Keeper like soldiers marching off to battle. She shook her head, but she didn't disagree with them. Or Teanna. Maybe she only wanted to feel movement of some kind to remind her where she stood.

"My father has been through this before, and he made it back home alive." *Maybe not entirely sane but alive.* "I have to know what happened, and maybe that knowledge will help you, too. You don't want to spend the rest of your life with a hole in your memory. It's maddening."

As Roni stepped away, she glanced down. Her father had drawn a circle in the dirt. A circle with a jagged line that branched out toward the bottom.

They followed the Keeper, passing one thicket of chained books after another. The soft clinking of the metal links sang the tune of Roni's nerves. The strange colors bouncing off the ceiling and the occasional birdlike flutter of pages from above reminded her that she had faced several bizarre and dangerous creatures before. The Parallel Society knew how to deal with these things. She would be okay.

The lump in her throat argued otherwise.

They reached a point where a small stream cut across the stony ground. The Keeper stepped over it before turning back and putting all her hands up flat like a crossing guard. "Only those willing to see this through may pass. I have no doubt Roni and her father will step over these waters, but the golem and the healer — think carefully before you make your choice."

With a shrug as if to say there was no choice, Gully moved forward. But Elliot's cane snapped out to block his way.

"This is not our journey," he said, his sorrowful grimace as chilling as the tune Roni continued to hear. "We will wait for you with Teanna."

Gully said, "I have to go with her. It's my duty to protect her."

"You cannot protect her where she's going. We tried in the past with her mother, and look where we've ended up."

Roni stepped over the stream. She looked back at Gully. "I'll be okay. Wait with Elliot. I'll be fine. You have my permission."

"But my instructions are —"

"Your instructions are to obey me, right? I think I know where we're headed, and Elliot is correct — you cannot come with me. This is only for my father and I. So, I order you, Gully, not to respond to me until I speak your name again. It'll be like when we first met. Except you don't have to stop existing. You can obey Elliot until I get back. That's it. Follow Elliot, obey him. He's in charge of you now until I return and say your name. Okay?"

Before Gully could muster any form of argument, Lawrence hopped over the stream and gestured to the Keeper. "Just us two. Let's go."

They headed off, and Roni forced her eyes to remain forward. She did not want to see the look on either man or golem's face. A look that nonetheless scratched at her back and yelled in her mind that she might not return.

Though the Keeper moved in languid, graceful motions, Roni struggled to keep up. For every solid, slow step the Keeper took, Roni had to hustle four or five steps. This section of the cave lacked any defined pathway, and Roni found it necessary to serpentine through the numerous chains blocking her path. The Keeper, however, soon lifted off the ground using her numerous limbs to climb and swing through the chains.

All along, Lawrence followed the unmarked trail as if he knew it from years of previous experience. The awe on his face widened his mouth and eyes, sped up his breathing, and left his fingers trembling. A brainwashed cultist could not have shown more anticipation and faith.

He mumbled to himself. Twice, Roni thought she heard him say, *I'll be with you soon.*

"Stop here," the Keeper said as she climbed higher toward the ceiling.

When she reached the top of several chains, the Keeper plunged her head into several books, one after the other, like a hummingbird sucking nectar from the best flowers. But Roni reminded herself — it was all a mirage. This image of a gentle, graceful creature that took care of these books and their contents like some noble librarian barely hid the truth. She was a stained-glass window in front of a cesspool. Roni could see through the colorful glass with ease, and behind remained the ugliness — the Keeper was a monster.

Whatever her reasons, whatever her excuses — Roni didn't care. The Keeper had taken too much from her. But Roni could not allow herself to wallow in the mire of vengeful thoughts. She had not come here for vengeance. Answers and the restoration of her Lost Time — that's what mattered.

"Here it is," the Keeper said, crawling from chain to chain until she reached one particular book — one blooming a lovely shade of soft blue.

With a gentle motion, the Keeper closed the book and stuck it under one of her arms. Bending all four legs, she lowered as best she could in the cramped bed of chained books. The chain connected to the selected book gave way, clinking as it piled on the ground.

"I know you have come here burdened with many questions. Whether you realize it or not, you will go home with many still unanswered. Perhaps your father can one day explain." She gave Lawrence a sidelong glance. "Perhaps not."

Roni lifted her hand but held back from touching the book. "Is that it? My mother's book?"

"Your mother? She has no book here."

Roni's throat caught twice before she could utter a word. "But I thought —"

"These books are not universes. And no single book belongs to any single soul. I know in your head you see them like flowers. Many visitors do. That's good. Because like all plants, there is more underneath than above."

Roni looked at the ground between her feet. Part of her wanted to lunge forward and pummel whatever part of the Keeper she could lay her hands upon. Part of her wanted to drop to her knees and dig, dig, dig. She banged her fists on her thighs. "What do you want from us? Why do you hate us so much?"

"Hate you? You're going to be my salvation." She swung her head toward Lawrence. "Isn't that right? You escaped that first time. Waited like a good pet to be summoned back, and then when I wasn't looking, you vanished. Stayed hidden from me for so long. I suspect your old friends had something to do with that. I have rarely failed the books, and I refused to fail with you. So, I searched. Every chance I had, every free moment, I've searched for you."

Lawrence pressed up against Roni's back and placed his hands on her shoulders. "I had hoped you called us here to fix things. Free those who need freeing."

"Don't lie to yourself. You know exactly why you're here."

"I guess I was a fool. But I'm still ready."

A satisfied smirk crossed the Keeper's lips. Three of her arms reached down and picked up the chain piled on the ground. A fourth arm worked the end out of the book's spine while the other hands lifted the section of chain to the Keeper's mouth. She opened wide and chomped down on the links.

The grinding of metal under teeth continued long after Roni's fascination had waned. She had never heard such a sound before and hoped never to again. If it had only been a mechanical sound like the enormous machines designed to crush old cars, she wouldn't have minded. But it was the hungry sounds that churned her stomach. The pleasure-filled groans and the wet-mouthed enjoyment that soured the thought of eating ever again.

When the chain severed, the long end slurped into the ground like a snake escaping into a hidden burrow. The short end hung limply in the Keeper's hands. She coiled it with care before slipping it into one of her many pockets.

Two other hands presented the book to Lawrence with reverence, and he even received a solemn bow of her head. From the ground, the books appeared to be normal in size, but now that the Keeper brought this one in close, Roni observed how absurdly large they were — nearly as tall as her father. She also spotted the symbol emblazoned on the cover. Her heart leapt even as it sunk into her nauseated stomach. The symbol — a circle with a jagged line coming off the top and branching out like horrid roots. Her father licked his lips as he placed one hand on the book.

"I cannot force you," the Keeper said. "I have never forced anyone into a book."

"I know," he said.

"Not even your beloved."

"I know."

"You won't find her in there. Your plan won't work. None of it will be how you think."

"I know."

"You should turn back now. Go away from here."

"Still struggling with the truth, I see."

The Keeper curled her lip. "Then the time has finally come."

Propping the book onto the ground, the Keeper used a free hand to pull open the cover. The wonderful aroma of molding paper wafted out. It smelled so much like an old bookstore that Roni could not stop herself from inhaling deeply. And the color — baby blue like a Spring morning.

Roni laced her fingers with her father's, hoping to find an extra bout of strength in his grip. "I'm ready."

He gazed down at her. The confusion on his face worried her that his madness had returned. But in a flash, the look passed into paternal regret. "Sweet, sweet daughter. You're not going."

"What?" The word bit hard even with its distressed undercurrent. "I have to go. Everything we've been through — you really think I'd let you go in alone? You really think I'd sit back and wait? No way. I'm going."

As her father shifted to face her, the Keeper shifted her head away, taking a polite interest in the walls. That small courtesy angered Roni more than anything her father might say. She wanted to slam that book closed and stomp it under the Keeper. Tell that beast her games would not work on them. Tell her that acting humble and courteous meant nothing when she lived to destroy others.

She could attack the Keeper. Throw everything else aside and strike while the creature had her back to them. But that was only fantasy. Roni lacked the skill to take on a fifteen-foot, eight-armed creature with the power to wipe her memory away. If physical violence could have solved this, it would have been done long ago.

"Look at me. Please." Lawrence hugged Roni and whispered against the side of her head. "You have to stay behind. In case — in case I don't return. You have to survive."

"I can't just do nothing."

"It'll be harder than you think. Enough to drive you crazy."

She pulled back. "You? You stayed here when Mom jumped into that book?"

"I wanted to go in with her. Like you, the thought of staying behind

… but she refused. She shoved me onto the ground and ran inside before I could stand back up. The book shut behind her, and that was it. Don't make me do the same to you. Stay behind by choice. Please, trust me. It'll be far better that way."

She uttered a crackling noise somewhere lost between a cry and a groan. "This is wrong."

"It's the way it must be."

"This Keeper called us out here, lured us with promises of my Lost Time and Mom, yet everything out of her mouth is nonsense and lies."

"Maybe. But there's more to her than you understand."

She pouted and crossed her arms. "I won't let you do this."

"Don't be bratty."

"You think I should sit back here and wait when that turned out so well last time? Mom went in there and never came back. You waited and lost your damn mind. I wasn't even here, I was just a kid, yet I still had parts of my memory taken away. How is it a good idea to go through that again?"

Her father's prickly gray stubble captured bits of color off the book, lending him an ethereal visage. He rubbed her chin with his thumb. "You've had to deal with too much of this already. I promise that I'll take care of it all. You don't have to worry about me. And you don't have to wait. Go back to Elliot and the golem. Let Teanna return to our universe with you. Take care of her."

"Shut up."

"You know better than anybody that she won't ever see her father again. Won't ever be part of her team. If the Keeper has a say, she might not even make it to her home. But with you, she'll have some hope. Just like my nutty ol' presence gave you hope all these years."

She slapped his chest. "Stop saying goodbye."

He kissed the top of her head before easing back. Offering a somber grin, he turned away and stepped toward the book.

Wiping her eyes, Roni looked upward to avoid seeing her father disappear. The Keeper watched them with a lustful, greed-soaked lick of her teeth. The idea that this creature wanted things to happen this way, wanted Lawrence alone in that book, set off a bomb in Roni's chest.

"Fuck that," she said, and charged forward.

The Keeper hissed, and Lawrence turned around, startled at the sight of his daughter blitzing ahead. Roni put out her arms — not to embrace but to tackle. She dropped low and seized her father at the waist. Her momentum thrust them both into the book, and for a breath, her entire world became a gentle, baby blue haze.

CHAPTER 19

Walking out of the caverns and into Gram's private office in the bookstore should have brought warm comfort. But this time, witnessing the destruction wrought by the Keeper left Roni hollow and frightened. Even with Elliot and Gully behind her, even with Teanna's shocked gasps echoing in the rear, Roni walked along the tiled floor like a veteran home from war — lonely, numb, struggling to make sense of a changed world. But of course, she knew the change had more to do with her than the world around her.

The room should have been a well-kept repository for old leather-bound volumes which Gram cherished — nothing like the books she created to hold universes; just beloved stories from long ago. They should have lined the metal shelves set in rows like a palette of literary delights served up to the reader fortunate enough to find this special selection. Fluorescent lighting should have followed the rows above, their stark illumination turning the room into less of a private sanctuary and more of a government office for cataloging forgotten books.

It should have been.

But the room Roni entered looked as if a subway train had run off its tracks and slammed through the bookstore basement. The metal shelves curled away like roadside safety rails after a horrific accident. Yellowed pages were strewn across the floor. Fluorescent tubes hung at odd angles, flickering light in uneven rhythms. Holes punctured the walls where fierce fists broke through.

It wasn't just the damage, though, that kicked Roni in the gut. It was the rage. Despite the Keeper's size, she could have easily smashed her way through the room and left much of it untouched. She chose to destroy the room. She wanted to inflict pain upon Roni's world.

What happened in that book of Lost Time? The memories that had returned told her much, but the difference between the Keeper before and the Keeper now — something terrible must have occurred. Something the Keeper blamed Roni for. It had to have happened with her father in that book.

She wanted to rush over to Elliot, hug him, and beg his forgiveness. She had been harsh to him, demanding he restore her memory, despising his stubborn refusals, blaming him quietly as she sulked about. But now she understood. If he had blasted her brain with the memories she now possessed — not even including those yet to return — it would have been impossible for her to handle. How could any mind sort out the two versions of the Keeper let alone the Keeper itself? How to place Teanna or the Cave or the journeys that brought them together? Two versions of nearly everything existed and her mind would have labored to process it all simultaneously.

"It's okay," Elliot said, setting his hand against the back of her head. "Now you know all that I know." Standing in the middle of the ruined room, he chuckled at her confused frown. "No spell here. I simply see on your face that your memories have all returned."

"Not all of them. After you and Gully went back from the stream to Teanna, I went into one of the books with my father."

"I know. We waited for several hours and then you dropped from above. You were unconscious, injured, and breathing shallow. I thought you were dying."

"That's what happened when I came back. I don't know what happened in there. In the book. I don't know how we got to this point."

"You will. Until you do, there is no sense in worrying about it. Come now. Let's see what's left of our bookstore."

The door leading to the main part of the basement — heavy and normally padlocked — leaned against the far wall, split in two. The worktables had been thrown aside, boxes containing decades of old magazines like TIME and CRICKET had been overturned. The ceiling bore the scrapings of an angry beast forcing her way through a space not designed for her size.

Roni led the group upstairs. They had to hug the sides to climb over the numerous steps smashed by the Keeper's heavy feet. Roni cringed at the thought of what the main floor would look like. In her head, she heard a warning ring out — *it'll be worse, it'll be worse.* The warning undersold it.

The word *apocalyptic* sprang into Roni's mind. It looked as if the

Keeper had stood in the middle of the room, spread all eight arms and spun at high velocity. The old wood stacks had become splintered kindling. Piles of books lay like corpses of a fallen army. Like Gully on the ice lake, the Keeper had left divots in the wood floor. But worst of all, the entire front of the store had been blown apart.

Glass and brick spread across the sidewalk and into the street. Wires hung like old vines — torn from low-hanging fixtures that must have caught on the tangle of the Keeper's arms as she barreled through the wall. Turned out the warning in Roni's head came from several car alarms blaring away. Nobody had claimed them yet, but based on the late-night darkness, someone would wake up soon and shut off the noise.

"At least, she didn't go down to the Grand Library," Gully said, "or climb upstairs to the apartments."

Elliot prodded several books with his cane. "This old store has been through worse. We'll put up the *Closed for Renovations* sign, and in a few months, everything will return to normal."

Teanna stuck her head out the window frame and gawked at a small-town Pennsylvania street. "What a strange world."

Out of habit, Roni looked at the clock near the old table — but the clock had been torn from the wall and dashed upon the wood. A rough-toothed line cut down the middle of its face. It read 4:42.

She spun back to the group. "Here's what we're going to do. Elliot, I want you to take Teanna and go to the hospital. Get Gram back here."

"It's not a good idea to split us up," Elliot said.

"Relax. I'm not going after the Keeper alone."

Teanna said, "Wonderful, you're no longer rash and reckless. But the Keeper is loose. Do we really have time to go find your friend?"

"She's my grandmother, and we need her. We need all the muscle we can get. So, go find Gram and bring her back. The Keeper is smart. She's not going to make a big scene that'll only draw the wrong kind of attention."

Elliot gestured to the front of the bookstore and its bombed-out appearance.

"She was angry," Roni said. "But I'm sure after a block or two, she came to her senses. If she hadn't, we'd be hearing sirens by now. So, she's probably searching for a place to hole up until she can assess her next move. She's been injured several times in her effort to get here, and she knows we'll be following close. She's smart. She'll take a little time to heal up. We have to strengthen up, too. Figure out what that next move of hers is going to be. So, we need Gram. Go get her. Gully, the police and maybe even the fire department are going to be here soon. They don't know about the Keeper, but they'll certainly find out about an explosion that blew out this wall. You can't be seen when they arrive."

"Everybody wants the golem out of the way until the trouble starts. Then it's a lot of *Save us, Gully! Help us! We need you, Gully! You're the best golem we've ever worked with!*" He paused, and when nobody offered a word, he slouched. "Fine. I'll go up to Sully's workshop and wait there."

"Thank you."

Teanna said, "What about you?"

Pulling out her phone, Roni said, "I've got my own errand to run. Be back here by dawn."

The Olburg Chestnut. The quintessential blue-collar diner. Also open twenty-four hours a day.

As Roni waited in a corner booth and heard the electronic two-tone bell, she inhaled the sizzling bacon and bitter coffee aromas. Though not as busy as it would be in a few hours, the place still catered to enough late-night truckers, early-rise sanitation workers, and never-sleep hard cases that the waitresses kept a steady hustle. Like the rest of the Chestnut's daily clientele, these people made the town run. They stayed local and worked hard for themselves and those around them. So, when a man like Kenneth Bay entered — tailored suit, fine watch, and a mustache more at home in the 1920s — they did not hide their sneers.

Though noisy with a handful of conversations and the music of utensils clinking against plates, the diner clung to the subdued quality of sound often harbored in the dark hours. Kenneth Bay's perfect shoes tapped against the cheap floor with every step as he approached.

A bulky man wearing a green Eagles cap tossed some cash onto the counter and stepped back, blocking Mr. Bay's progress. "Good night, Suzie," the man said as he hiked up his pants and walked out.

"Drive safe, Carl," the waitress said from the far end of the counter.

When Kenneth finally reached Roni's booth, he offered a slight bow of his head. "I have to admit that I did not expect to receive a call from you so soon after our last meeting."

"It's been nearly two years," Roni said.

As Kenneth settled opposite her, sitting stiff and wrinkling his nose at some unseen offense, Roni gave herself a pat on the back for having the foresight to clean up at her apartment earlier. Days of cavern dirt caked on her face coupled with clothes that smelled of sweat and old lake would not have made this go smoother.

Kenneth said, "When you are the personal representative of a being like Yal-hara, two years is quite a short time. Your Parallel Society disparages her with the term *relic,* but I assure you, she is far more vibrant than you realize. After all, she's been alive for over a century that I'm aware of and my family has served her for several generations."

"And keeping her that way, keeping Yal-hara alive, that's a big part of your job."

"Of course. If the public ever discovered her existence, a lynch mob would be the best she could hope for. More likely, government experiments would become her lot. Or worse, the Parallel Society could find out that they had failed to get rid of her the first time. I trust, by the fact that she remains safe, you have honored our agreement and not shared your knowledge of her with your Society."

"That's why I asked you here — our agreement."

The waitress, Suzie, approached the booth carrying a pot of coffee. "Evening, folks. Or morning, depending." The way she waited for a chuckle, this line must have been a big winner lately.

Roni forced a small grin. "Just coffee."

As that puny order evaporated Suzie's hope for a decent tip, she forced a grin of her own, poured the coffee, and returned to the customers who actually wanted to buy some food.

Kenneth drummed his fingers on the table. In a softer voice, though no less precise, he said, "Yal-hara does not renegotiate. I expected something far more important to be disturbed at this hour."

"Don't get yourself in a twist. Your boss will want to hear this." Roni took a slow sip of her coffee. She preferred Kenneth to think she had all the time in the world, even as a countdown tick-tick-ticked in her head. Another slow sip — this one because as the hot, strong caffeine hit, her senses awoke from the long hours in the caverns. She indulged one last sip to buy a little thinking time.

At length, Kenneth said, "Please, ma'am, I wish to conclude this meeting as soon as possible. There is still a chance I might get a bit more sleep before Yal-hara begins her day."

"The deal I have with her is that I'm helping her acquire things she needs in order to create her own access point out of here. Get her back to her universe. In exchange, she's going to help me get to the Cave of Lost Time."

"Perhaps you do not understand the words *as soon as possible*. You have accidentally omitted them. I know the agreement you have word-for-word, and reiterating it only means less time for me to sleep."

"Thing is, I just got back from the Cave."

Kenneth's smugness vanished. "Excuse me?"

"Not only that, but the Keeper is no longer there. In fact, she's here — in our universe. I can see by the loss of color in your face that you understand everything I'm saying. So, here's the problem for you — Yal-hara can no longer provide the thing I was after. Getting me to the Cave is pointless now. If she wants me to continue secretly finding items for her, then she'll need to help me. Tonight. Because I don't know how you feel about it, but I have no desire to let the Keeper play around in our universe."

Sliding out of the booth, Kenneth Bay raised one index finger. "Give me a moment. I'll make a call." He walked toward the exit, fishing a cell phone from his coat pocket.

Roni finished off her coffee and flagged the waitress for more. She did not want anything slowing her down. Sure, she had to think clearly, plan, be ready to attack, but beyond that she couldn't afford a quiet moment. That would lead to pondering. Too much of that and she would recognize how impossible defeating the Keeper would be.

They had already fought her once, and she destroyed them within seconds. The bruises on Roni's back served as an aching reminder. But to let her thoughts flow down that stream, to acknowledge how futile their task appeared, would only petrify her into doing nothing. That was not the Roni she would allow herself to be.

So, keep things moving. Keep on the attack. No rest until we finish the job.

And where the heck was Kenneth Bay? If he took any longer, she would fail to stop her spiraling thoughts and the whole mess would be lost before it started.

She edged toward the end of the booth, ready to go search for the man, when she spied his well-groomed attire enter the diner once more. He did not look happy. Not that he ever looked happy, but he appeared particularly unhappy at the moment. When he sat at the booth, he moved stiffer than before, more like a displeased mannequin.

"Good news?" Roni said, wishing her voice sounded light but

unable to cast out the dread.

A flare of his nostrils marked the limit of acknowledging her words. "When two parties enter a contract, it is expected that both will honor not only the word but the intent of the agreement. This is called *good faith.* At the most basic level, both parties should be able to trust that neither will attempt to subvert the contract. Particularly, at the outset."

"I did not go seeking the Cave of Lost Time. In fact, after an incident in Ireland, I had come to terms with the idea that I should stop dwelling on this hole in my past and get on with living in the present. But the Keeper reached out to me. Psychically — oh, that sounds nuts. Look, the why of it all doesn't matter. I never intended to break my word. I mean I'd be lying if I said I didn't want to find the Cave, that's what the whole deal with Yal-hara was about for me, but it's not like I signed my name to an actual contract."

"Yal-hara does not see it that way. A verbal contract is every bit as binding in her eyes. Under many circumstances, the laws of Pennsylvania would back her up, too. Regardless of the technical and legal truths, the fact is that you not only betrayed the spirit of the agreement, you damaged Yal-hara in a far more serious way."

"By going to see the Keeper? How did that damage her?"

"Visiting the Cave and the Keeper did not harm Yal-hara. Destroying the Cave and setting the Keeper loose in our universe did. If you simply had honored the contract, simply shown some patience and restraint, Yal-hara would have gathered the necessary components, and we would have all traveled to the Cave together. From there, she would have negotiated properly with the Keeper to restore your memories. More important to Yal-hara, she would have been able to utilize the Keeper and the Cave for her own return. Finally."

Roni cringed. "I screwed that up for her."

"Yet again, the Parallel Society has cheated her and torn apart her hopes of leaving this universe."

"I'm sorry." She would have to worry about the fallout from this mistake later. Roni had the Keeper to deal with, and clearly, Yal-hara would not be helping. Still, she could not stop the regret slicing through her veins. "I'll leave. Please, let her know this was never meant to harm her. It was never about her. Whatever happened with the Keeper — Yal-hara was collateral damage. I hate that term, but it's right in this case."

Before she could stand, Kenneth said, "Despite all the evidence you have seen, you continually underestimate the brilliance of Yal-hara.

Even from my own poorly delivered description of your events, Yal-hara gleaned all you have said and more. She then ordered me to relay to you the following, and though I think she is being far too generous, I will do as she asks — not only because it is my duty to her but because I do not underestimate her brilliance. If Yal-hara thinks it wise to deliver a message, then I shall deliver it."

A flash fire ignited inside Roni's chest. "Are you ever going to get around to it? Or should I expect you to sit here for another hour telling me what an awful human being I am?"

Kenneth paused. "I've never understood how you can shift your emotions so quickly. A moment ago, you felt guilty towards what you had done to Yal-hara. Yet now, you spit venom at me, her representative, as I prepare to share with you a message from her."

"I do feel guilty. If that makes you or her happy, go ahead and relay that message. But I do not like being lectured to by somebody who doesn't have to deal with what I'm facing. Heck, I don't like being lectured to at all."

"I see. You respond in kind to whatever comes your way."

"What? No. What I do is … it doesn't matter. We're wasting time here. What is it Yal-hara wants me to know?"

"First and foremost, you have broken your contract with her. This will not be forgotten. She gave you a chance to make amends for the wrongs done by your organization, for failing to help her leave this universe, for threatening her life as if she were merely a bug that slipped through an opening. She considers you an enemy now. You should never call upon me for help again. You will not receive it."

The desire to argue or plead or say anything to repair the relationship surged through Roni, but she tamped it down. She would have time later to figure out why she cared about Yal-hara and what to do about this situation, but only if she survived to have a *later*. For now, she simply said, "And second?"

"The Keeper at the Cave of Lost Time has always been a cursed creature. A trapped creature. The Keeper never wanted to be the Keeper but chose to be nonetheless. She is echoes upon echoes. The cycle began ages ago and has endured through endless Keepers, some male, some female, some other. The one you know, that you now hunt, is not the first — though, she may end up the last — and may not even be the Keeper you met." With that, Kenneth Bay stood, adjusted his tie, smoothed his mustache, and offered a curt bow — barely more than a nod.

"That's it? How's that going to help me?"

"Every leader learns that only when you truly understand your enemy will you win the war."

"Then maybe you should be less cryptic and tell me what you're trying to tell me about the Keeper."

"I have given you far more than you deserve. We are no longer allies, and I warn you — Yal-hara understands you more than you do yourself. She will win the war you have started."

"But I didn't start —"

"Good day, Miss Rider."

As Yal-hara's human representative turned on his heel and walked out of the diner, Roni's eyes trailed after him. A commotion at the counter pulled her attention away. Two burly fellows and Suzie the waitress all stared up at an ancient television set.

The local morning program ran a piece with the words BREAKING NEWS flashing below. Apparently, in the hours before dawn several strange animal attacks had been witnessed across town. *A large, ugly looking thing,* one resident said. *Must a been a starvin' bear it was so thin,* another reported. *Didn't get a good look but it stomped right through my car. Caved the roof straight in,* a third said.

Roni dropped a few dollars on the table and left. Time was up.

CHAPTER 20

A pop in the ears. A lurch in the gut. As Roni's body recalibrated to the sudden pressure changes of no longer being in the same universe, she rolled onto her back and opened her eyes.

Her father groaned as he pushed to his knees. He sat at her side, but her attention went beyond him. She noticed the walls — large fixed stones pasted together by gravelly mortar. Rusty, metal rungs had been bolted to the stone. The floor was made of polished wood planks, and as Roni rose to her feet, she had the distinct impression of clashing cultures — a bare Japanese floor mixed with a medieval European dungeon. But both of those oddities paled in comparison to the ceiling.

A thin, baby blue haze filled the top of the room. Gazing upward, Roni saw another room above her. According to that room, however, she looked down from above. Another person stood there, arching back and gazing at Roni. But it was not a mirror image. Not her staring back at herself. They occupied two separate rooms, both sharing the same misty ceiling, both seeing the mist as the top of their room.

"Why did you do that?" Lawrence said, shaking his bowed head.

Roni walked over to one wall and placed a tentative finger upon it. She half-expected the wall to send her a shock or fall apart like an illusion, but the stones were solid, cold, and real. "No point in getting mad at me now. I'm already here, so you might as well deal with it."

"You don't know what you've done."

"And you do? Because if you had answers all this time, you're the stupid one for never having clued me in."

"I only know what happened the first time. And I told you — I waited outside. I survived because of that. Now, I have no idea if you'll get out of here alive."

Roni turned back. The concern flowing through her body, however, was not for herself. "You never thought you'd come back? You walked with the Keeper like you knew where you were going, yet you had no intention of returning? This is a suicide run for you."

Lawrence picked at his thumbnail before exhaling a sad breath. He stood, sniffled, and turned his damp eyes upon his daughter. "I have never stopped loving your mother. Never. Not once. No matter how sane or mad I became, each day I saw her face and the way she smiled at me right before — before she walked into the Keeper's book. Such confidence that she would be back. Although, as I stared at you before going into this book, it occurred to me that perhaps your mother knew all along there would be no return."

"We can't be stuck here forever. I don't believe it."

"That's the stubborn thing about reality. It doesn't care what you believe. It's still going to be what it is."

Roni walked along the wall patting it with her hand. There were no windows or doors, but there had to be some way in — after all, they were there — so, there also had to be a way out. "I've learned a lot of things about universes in my short time with the Society, and one thing is that universes all follow rules. The physics will change in each world, the rules will change, but they all do exist. No universe is without strict guides that you can learn, follow, and use. We just have to figure out the rules for this universe, and from there, we can find our way out."

"Ane that's your first mistake right there. You're not in another universe. It doesn't seem to matter how many times you hear it, you don't want to grasp that these books are not universes — they're Lost Time. They're memories or bits of souls or something like that."

Roni continued tapping the walls. "I understand that, but there still has to be rules. This book we went through, the Keeper brought us to this one specifically. I have to assume that it is either my Lost Time or yours or Mom's. Otherwise, why bring us here?"

"This place doesn't work like that."

Roni stormed over to Lawrence and shoved him. "Then tell me how it works. You clearly know something. I am so sick of you and Elliot and everybody thinking that they know best. I'm not some fragile piece of glass you have to handle with care. I won't shatter under a little stress. So, either help me or shut up. Because worse than you keeping secrets is your pessimism. I don't need you telling me how nothing is ever going to work and we're stuck forever."

"Look around you. Does this look like a normal memory you would have had? Or me or your mother?"

"How should I know? It was taken from my head. I just have an emptiness in there now."

With a frustrated huff, Lawrence put up his hands. "Okay. Fine. You want to hear this? You got it. These are not our memories. These are not any single person's memories. The books in the Cave of Lost Time are not individual universes or memories or souls or whatever you want to think of them. It's not like Gram's books chained to the walls elsewhere in the caverns. You have to think of these books like a living entity. Like a single plant growing up out of the ground. On top of the grass, you see a whole field of beautiful flowers, but underneath imagine all those twisting roots going off in all different directions, and in fact, they connect to each other. It's not a field of little bits and pieces of flower but rather a single giant entity, one single plant."

"You're saying the Lost Time books are a fungus? Like mushrooms growing up out of the ground, it's actually a big thing underneath?"

"Except underneath the Cave, I don't know what it looks like. Maybe all those chains could create one big chain. Maybe there are no chains and no books and it's simply the way it appears to our eyes. Perhaps if creatures from other universes come in and see the Cave, they would witness some other manifestation of this thing. I don't know."

Roni wanted to deny everything he said, but an intuitive part of her agreed. The strange room, the stranger ceiling, and strangest of all — the room connected above — did not belong to any memory she could imagine one of her family having. Rather it looked like an amalgam of thoughts and feelings slammed together. "How do you know this? You didn't go into the books before."

Lawrence hesitated. "When the Keeper called us, she did more than simply show me the missing map. When she opened my head to place back the memory she had taken, when she returned my mind enough so that I could find my way to the Cave, she gave me more than I knew."

"That's why she was talking about you being ready to go in. She brought you here for another reason. Which means you are once again holding a secret."

"Don't look at me like that."

"Do you know the way out of this room? Out of this book? Do you know where we can find my Lost Time? Or Mom's?"

Grasping his hair, he shook his head, wincing as if her words lashed against his back. "No, no, no. It's not like that. I swear."

"I don't believe you. At least, I don't believe that you are stuck in this room. The Keeper would not have gone through all this trouble to bring you here only to make you sit forever in a prison cell. Even if you don't know anything else, you know how to open the door out of this place."

His shoulders sagged. "I do. At least, I know how to open a door for me. You weren't supposed to be in here. Like you said, there are rules. But I don't know how they work."

"Then let's find out together. Do whatever you have to and open the door."

They grew silent.

They stared at each other like statues trapped in a face-off. The urge to press harder filled Roni's chest like a deep rush of air, but she held back. Her father seemed to be thinking things over, and she wanted to learn from her mistakes of the past. Let him consider, let him think, let him come to the right conclusions on his own.

At length, he licked his lips and stepped back against the wall. "Do you trust me?"

Roni tried to hide her disappointment. "Are we really back to that? How many times have we been through these trust games? I broke you out of a mental hospital, I followed you into the caverns without knowing if you actually could find where you were going, I even jumped into this place with you."

"You forced your way in here."

"Semantics. I've shown you a million ways that I trust you."

"No. You've shown me a million ways that you trust me when you desire the outcome. That's not the kind of trust I'm asking about. I need to know if you can trust me the way you trust Elliot or Sully or even Gram. The kind of trust where if I tell you to do something that seems the opposite of what you want, you'll still do it — you'll trust that I know what I'm doing, know what I'm saying, know what will be the best way to achieve what you want. Do you have that kind of trust for me?"

Roni considered lying for an instant, but they were beyond that. His stubbled, craggy face told her that he already knew the answer. "I want to. You're my father. I want to feel that way towards you. I know that I'm supposed to, that I should have a deep, instinctual love that creates the kind of trust you want, but it's not there. Not yet."

He let those words flow between them. "Maybe someday."

"There won't be a someday if we don't get out of here."

Pushing off the wall, he reached back and placed his hand on one of the metal rungs. "Then someday needs to be right now. I'm going to open the door, and I'm going to leave. You need to stay here. I know you don't want that, but I need you to find it within yourself — some nugget of the trust we're talking about. Let me go do what I'm here to do, and I guarantee you will leave this place. All you have to do is let me walk out the door and wait. Another door will open and lead you right back to the cavern, or you'll fall asleep and wake up there, or a hole will form in the floor and you'll jump through. Or something else. I'm not entirely sure how it will manifest, but it will happen."

"You expect me to sit here and wait, and in the end, I'll be whisked back to the caverns — but nothing has changed. I'll still be missing my Lost Time."

"I'm not sure the Keeper ever intended on giving it back. I don't even know if she can. But, if there's any chance, I'll find it."

"Then let me come with you. Let me help."

Without turning his back to her, he pulled down on the rung. Part of the wall behind him dissolved into an open door. Lawrence backed out of the room, always keeping his eyes on Roni. If she tried to rush him this time, he would be ready.

"Trust me," he said. With a hop, he left the room.

Roni lunged across, but the door became a wall before she could get her hand near the opening.

Fighting back the typhoon of emotions swirling within her, she yanked down on the rung. Nothing happened. Growling, she circled the room pulling down on every rung. Nothing worked. When she came around to where she had started, she kicked the wall. Pain shot from her toe up through her leg, and she unleashed a torrent of swears that would have impressed the most effusive sailor. She slid to the floor.

If a door opened now, or a hole appeared in the floor, she thought she would refuse to use it. What was the point of leaving if she had to leave empty-handed? But in the next breath, she saw Elliot's face and Sully's and Gram's and even Gully's.

Why does it have to be so hard? She looked up toward the sky.

The figure up there, the one in the other room that shared the ceiling, it stared right at her. Its eyes shined like a cat. But its skin had a more leathery, lizard-like quality. It raised a hand, and shifted it from side to side. Roni's skin prickled. It was waving at her.

With a slow motion, she waved back. "Hello?"

"You see me? You hear me?" the lizard-thing said.

"Yeah, I can hear you. Like you're right next to me, in fact."

"And you understand me? You speak *Attxil* well."

Roni stood. "I do understand you, but I don't speak your language. Something in here must make it work for us."

The lizard scratched the back of its neck. "The other one with you — I heard you say he was your father — he left. Why didn't you go with him?"

"I don't want to get into it."

"Would you like to follow him? It seemed like you wanted to follow him."

Roni's skin prickled again for a very different reason. "You know how to open the doors?"

"I do. But we have to do it together. In that way, we both get out."

Roni smiled.

CHAPTER 21

From her earliest childhood memories, sitting at the big table in the bookstore had always been a comforting thing for Roni. The enormous, thick slab of wood had survived every calamity that fell upon the bookstore, including the arrival of the Keeper, and though Roni did not realize the fact until recently, part of the table's comfort came from this incredible stability. No matter what else happened, this table would endure.

Teanna and Gully sat on the side opposite Roni. Behind them, the dawn cast golden light across the remains of the bookstore. Gram stood at one end of the table, her eyes often returning to size up Teanna once more. Loose papers from destroyed books fluttered in a gentle, morning breeze. Sitting at the far end, Elliot finished detailing their entire experience, his deep voice blending with the sounds of Olburg waking in the distance.

When he stopped speaking and eased back in his chair, Gram pursed her lips in a thoughtful frown. Placing her fingertips together, one step away from full-on prayer hands, she turned her attention toward Roni. "You're sure you don't remember anything else?"

"I think Elliot hit all the important bits." She had no intention of sharing the weirdness of being inside the Lost Time book. Not yet. Not until she knew more of what it meant.

"Think. Any little piece may give us the clues we need to find the Keeper."

Not this time. With her parents gone, nobody existed that could understand what she had experienced in there. In fact, if Roni tried to explain any of it, she would have sounded insane. Gram would assume that being in the book had ruined Roni's mind the same way it had done to Lawrence. They would placate Roni until they finished dealing with the Keeper. But in the end, after a lot of tears and prayers, Gram would have no choice but to institutionalize her granddaughter. Probably at Belmont. Heck, Roni might get her father's old room.

But more than her fears of being jailed in a glorified asylum, Roni did not want to share her experiences in the book because she needed to sift through that information first. She needed to process it not only from a personal stance but as the team leader.

She paused. *Is that what I am?* She looked up at Gram. With Sully in the hospital and the devastation at the bookstore, Gram had immediately called this meeting upon her return. They needed to regroup and formulate a plan of action. She had slipped right into her old role.

So what? Let her. Roni never wanted to be the leader of this group, anyway. Then again, she had been the one to force Gram to step down.

"Roni?" Gram said, an edge to her voice.

That sound — Gram growing impatient — scraped against Roni's spine. She refused to be reduced to a teenager again, to allow things to devolve back to what they had been years ago. Besides, if she wanted to avoid a rubber room in Belmont, then running the show made the most sense. Nobody sent their leader away no matter how crazy things got.

Roni pushed back her chair, pressing into it to create a loud noise. She stood firm, holding her mouth in a stiff, straight line. Gram held her ground. Nobody spoke a word. Nobody dared. Not even the eternal peacekeeper, Elliot.

To Roni's surprise, possibly everyone's surprise, Gram rolled her lips into an uncomfortable grin and said, "I'm sorry. Old habits and all. With Sully no longer able to lead, I naturally thought — but that was wrong. I guess your little jaunt into the caverns has changed things a bit. Well, good. Lord knows it's about time you stand up."

As she sat, Gram patted the cross on her chest like a flustered churchmarm. Roni let the final jab go. No need to pick a fight, and no time, either.

"Okay," Roni said, thinking the problem through as she spoke. "As I see it, we have two things that need be done immediately. We have to find the Keeper, and we have to send her some place safe. The Cave of Lost Time is gone. The books were an interconnected thing, practically a living being of its own, but it's no more now."

Gram said, "I can always prepare a book that'll put the Keeper in a universe where she can't harm anybody."

"Good. Unless we have another idea, I think that's the way to go."

"You understand that without the Keeper, you can't get your Lost Time back."

Teanna said, "If you send her away, then all chances for me are lost, too."

With a soft incline of her head, Roni said, "There are no chances for either of us. I think you already know that. The moment I woke up in the Cave and saw you looking up at those books bouncing dead on the ceiling, I think you knew. That's why you came with us. I'm sorry, but your father, your friends, and my parents are all gone. We don't get them back."

Elliot reached over and put his hand on Teanna's shoulder. "I know it hurts, but know that you are welcome here."

Holding a stern look, Teanna said, "The Keeper called us to the Cave, and once we were there, our path home vanished. I have no idea how to get back to my universe. In a few months, after we have not returned, our families will mourn our deaths and they will repopulate the Protectors. I suppose I have no choice but to stay."

"If you want to get back to your home, we will do everything we can to help you find that path."

"Even if we succeeded, what would I do? Somebody else will have my job. I can't ask that person to step down because I happen to show up. But it's all I've been trained for. I have no other skills to offer my family."

Roni said, "You can put your training to good use for us. Right now. The Keeper is out there and we need a tracker. Gram, get us one of those old Pennsylvania road maps."

Without argument, Gram scurried toward the back section of the bookstore untouched by the damage. Several years ago, after an elderly man's death, his children dumped several boxes of books on the doorstep of the store. Just left them there with a note asking Gram to find the books a good home. In one of the boxes, Gram found numerous AAA road maps from all over the country. Apparently, people liked to collect anything. Gram returned with the Pennsylvania map and spread it open on the table.

Teanna's eyes widened. "This is a map? What kind of world lives with such a mess of roads and boundaries and whatever that symbol is?"

"That's an airport," Roni said. "Don't worry about any of that. This dot here — that's Olburg. That's where we are. Am I correct that your whole specialty is tracking relics?"

"It's not like tracking an animal. I can do that, too, but not as well. This is different. Tracking relics — I can sense their presence and follow it like hearing a song in the distance."

"Oh. Okay. So, what do you hear?"

Teanna walked into the center of the store, what was left of the store, and closed her eyes. Like a ballerina preparing for rehearsal, she let her arms hang loose and rolled her shoulders back, straightening her body and lifting her head. Her ears perked up as she cocked her head to the side. Slowly, leading with her chin, her head oscillated to the other side and back. Listening, listening, but never quite settling in any direction.

After a moment, she looked back at the group. "There are so many relics here."

Gram stiffened. "We've done the best we could."

"It's so loud. Usually there are only a handful of weak sounds and the real threats, the ones we'd be looking for, those would stand out like a huge horn blaring over a soft hum. But you have more than one horn playing around here. It's loud."

Roni thought of Yal-hara and tried to keep her face blank. "Can you isolate the Keeper's, um, horn from the others?"

"I will try, but it'll be quite difficult with so much interference. If we start to get closer to the Keeper, her tone will become clearer and easier to follow. But right here, there are too many sounds from too many relics."

"This is ridiculous," Gram said, smacking the table. "This woman has no right to come in here and tell us we've done a terrible job. Even if we have kept a relic or two sitting around this world, we've never left anything dangerous. You're the ones that brought the Keeper in here."

Teanna said, "I'm not blaming anybody. I'm only telling you what I can and cannot hear."

"Then clean your ears."

"Stop it," Roni said. "Being bitchy won't help anything."

"Watch your language."

"And you watch your attitude."

Both Gram and Roni froze at the shock of Roni's words. It wasn't so much that she had talked back to Gram — during her teen years, she had mouthed-off plenty — but rather, it was Roni's authoritative tone. She hadn't simply spit venom out of anger. She had shut down the bickering with all the power of a leader.

At least, Roni saw it that way. The fiery flush reddening Gram's face suggested the elder took matters quite differently. To Roni's surprise, Gully rescued them from turning down alleys she did not want to venture.

He started by rising to his feet. That alone drew everyone's attention. He slid two fingers up the bridge of his nose. Though he lacked Sully's glasses, he apparently still behaved like his creator at times.

"The Keeper had to have come here for a reason. She could have gone anywhere in the caverns, could have opened countless doors or books to other universes. But she chose this one. I know I don't have the brains that you all do, but doesn't that mean something?"

Roni imagined the entire group stared at Gully like cartoon characters — jaws stretching to the ground as their eyes multiplied out of their heads, each time getting bigger and bigger. In reality, they simply watched the golem in dumbfounded silence.

Elliot broke the quiet. Rapping his knuckles on the edge of the table, he said, "An excellent point. One that suggests the Keeper is here because of something related to Roni or her parents."

Or Yal-hara, Roni thought. But no, if that had been true, the Keeper could have called out to the Earth's eldest living relic instead of calling upon the Rider family. But something Kenneth Bay had said popped into Roni's mind.

"Everyone stay here," she said. "Gram, call the hospital and check on Sully. Teanna, keep trying to single out the Keeper's sound, and the rest of you either help her or get out of her way. I'll be right back."

"Where are you going?" Gram said, unable to hide the disapproval from her voice.

As Roni headed toward the elevator, she said, "The Grand Library. You wanted me to be the Parallel Society's librarian, and that's what I've done. There's something I want to check, something I remember reading, and it should help us."

"Let us come with you, then. We can find books, too."

Roni stepped into the elevator and pressed the button for the Library. As the doors shut, she looked straight at Gram. With a clear voice of command, she said, "Follow the orders I've given you."

Feeling her legs shiver, she wondered if she could blame the elevator's vibrations or if she had to admit it was nerves. It didn't matter. She had to stay focused, keep everyone on task, and let the rest fall wherever it fell. Because she had those final words of Kenneth Bay

— the message from Yal-hara. *The Keeper never wanted to be the Keeper but chose to be nonetheless. She is echoes upon echoes. The cycle began ages ago and has endured through endless Keepers, some male, some female, some other. The one you know, that you now hunt, is not the first — though, she may end up the last — and may not even be the Keeper you met.* To Roni, those words had started to make some sense.

The second the elevator opened, she darted back toward her makeshift map of the caverns. On the table in front, all of her research spread out upon every available space. In particular, the only two volumes she had found detailing the travels of previous Society members who had encountered the Cave of Lost Time directly.

In both cases, the men who entered the Cave had little to report back. It seemed clear to Roni that their memories had been scrubbed of the incidents. A little Lost Time gift from the Keeper.

However, the first gentleman, Phillip Carstone, had managed a faint recollection. Perhaps the Keeper did not recognize the threat of letting humans know too much. Roni found Carstone's journal and flipped through the pages.

Too fast — she had to be careful. The book dated back to 1801. The pages would be ruined if she did not show more care.

There. July 22, 1802. Carstone wrote:

> *The gap in my memory can only be connected to my travels in the caverns. I have clear and precise recall of the many days prior to entering, and I continue to have no failure of memory since my return. Much of our experiences within the caverns are also quite clear and unencumbered to me. All of this, when summed carefully, leads me to the inescapable conclusion that some terrible incident befell us during our journey. While, to some, particularly those not well-initiated into the lives of those in the Parallel Society, this may seem like a fanciful conclusion, I submit that not only is it perfectly reasonable, considering our fantastical duties in the Society, but also because of the recurring horror I see in my slumber. The creature strikes at me in a manner that can only be ripped from my memories. It knows me. It thinks like me. But, thank all that is holy in all the universes, it is far from a mirror gazing back.*

Either from fear or propriety, Carstone refused to describe his nightmares. But nearly a century later, Harold Greenbaum, a Society member who fell into a similar situation, did not feel the same sense of decorum. After detailing his team's cavern expedition and the experience of Lost Time he had incurred, he wrote:

> *This monster visits me every night since our return. Its caterwauling alone is enough to drive sleep from me, but its visage haunts me far worse. Too many limbs to make sense. Too gargantuan to fit in anywhere but our prehistoric times. Too much like myself in the way it spoke and thought.*

Roni re-read both entries. She had no way to know if Carstone or Greenbaum had actually entered one of the Lost Time books, but they certainly had made contact with the Keeper. And through that contact, perhaps through the process of taking their memories, the Keeper siphoned some of the men's thoughts into herself. Contact with them seemed to have changed her to some degree.

She is echoes upon echoes.

Roni and her father were the last to have contact with the Keeper. If her father still lived, if he never left the book, then his contact with her continued even now. If not — she swallowed down the lump in her chest — if not, then the Keeper's last contact would be Roni. Either way, the answer sat right there.

As she rushed back upstairs and approached the group at the big table, she said, "The Keeper probably needs some place quiet and safe to heal. If we're wrong about that, then she's looking for a place from which she can operate without getting noticed — in other words, the same kind of place. From what I can tell, the Keeper changes with every memory it steals. It changes physically — sometimes even altering its gender — and it changes mentally. All it knows of our modern world comes from her interactions with me and my parents. So, if she's looking for a safe place, she's going to base that off of what we think is safe."

"Yes," Elliot said. "Someplace safe and someplace you care about. Because I've been thinking about what Gully said — that the Keeper chose to come here for a reason."

If Gully had a tail, it would have been wagging hard. "I was right? I helped?"

"Absolutely. Whatever happened in those books, Roni came out of it having had a hand in destroying the Cave. Right before she woke, the Keeper swooped out of the chains, walked right by us, and out the tunnel. That's when the chains fell. The books flew upward to the cavern ceiling, and the chains seemed to wither away until the ground reclaimed them. After Roni was awake, we followed the Keeper. It was easy — she left behind a trail of destruction and she even attacked us. Why? I think it's simple revenge."

Roni said, "I destroyed her home, so she'll destroy mine?"

"I fear so. But if we accept my thoughts and add them to what you have learned, then you can tell us exactly where she's going. It will be a place you remember as safe, loving, filled with happiness, the kind of place she would want to rip apart with all her personal rage aimed directly at you."

Roni lifted her eyes to Gram. "Then we both know where she's going."

"We do?" Gram said, but then her mouth lifted into a knowing smile. "Oh, yes, we do."

Teanna said, "Will one of you care to tell us?"

Roni and Gram both answered. "The cabin in the Poconos."

CHAPTER 22

Roni stood outside the doorless room with Chak, her new lizard-ish friend. Leaving the room turned out to be rather easy. Chak talked her through a series of rung pulls on one wall, then another series on another wall, and without fanfare, a door appeared near where her father had manifested one earlier. When she set foot outside, Chak walked out through a door to her right — as if their rooms had been side-by-side and not set on top of one another.

"Quite a sight, huh?" he said (Roni had decided Chak was male). "I never get tired of seeing this place."

Chains filled a baby blue sky — crisscrossing, hanging, drooping, all like an aged and broken spiderweb. Most of the chains brought to mind those used to anchor a battleship or a luxury cruise liner. Massive, thick links. Some so large a small house would fit on them with ease. Or a bizarre, doorless room.

Roni looked at the metal beneath her feet. Painted brown with chips from use spotting along the side, she marveled that vertigo did not strike and send her plummeting through the haze of whatever this existence was. A warm breeze sent the smaller chains swaying and the air filled with their soft music.

She turned back, but the doorless room no longer stood behind them. Nothing but chains now. Not even another room somewhere.

"I thought the rooms were the books," she said. "That there would be tons of them around here with all the trapped memories of this thing's victims."

"They are not victims. They chose to be here."

"My memories are here somewhere. They were stolen. I had no say in the matter. Are you saying you chose to be here?"

"You are a unique case. I suppose so am I," he said, moving closer to Roni.

Seeing him next to her, Roni learned that he had a rather human face, albeit covered in lizard skin, and when he breathed, he made little guttural noises like a soft snore. He smelled like flowers but not any kind Roni could identify — simply a rich, pleasant floral fragrance. He wore pants similar to jeans except they had a buttoned pocket on each knee, and his shirt hung in strips that seemed both decorative and practical. He certainly could move with ease in the thing.

"Were you stolen, too? Are you like my memory here? A bit of the real Chak stuck here forever?"

"Perhaps I am nothing but a memory," Chak said. "But I don't feel that way. There are real memories in here. You have to leave them behind in order to leave the books. I'm not willing to give anything of myself away, and in my case, if I did give myself away, there'd be nothing left to go anywhere."

Despite feeling as if she talked with her father during his most disconnected moments, Roni kept her face neutral. "So where is everybody? All those memories?"

"Few ever agree to enter these books. Some of what's here is Lost Time stolen from people. Most is given in deals made with the Keeper. Almost all of that Lost Time is gone now, eaten up. Once, not too long ago, there were all kinds of rooms and bubbles and drips and drops of memories. After a war or a plague, there would be so many memories to gobble up. Everywhere I looked, I could see a feast. But no more."

Roni had been so preoccupied taking in the vast and endless chains that her mind required a few extra seconds to process all of what Chak had said. "Hold on. You're the creature?"

"I'm no creature. I'm me. I'm Chak."

"I mean, you're this — the thing that all the chains and books connect into. You're the one that needs all the Lost Time."

"Maybe. How could I know? I've always been here and I've always been me. It's hard to say what I am when I have nothing out there to compare me to."

"You have the Keeper."

Chak stuck out his tongue. "I don't like that word. If she's the Keeper, doesn't that make me the Kept? I don't like that at all."

"I didn't name her."

"Neither did I."

"But you used the name before I ever said anything." Roni wondered if she had been knocked unconscious when she tackled her father into the book. Perhaps this all was simply —

"A dream?" Chak said. "No. You are awake."

Did that thing just read —

"Your mind?" Chak said. "Not exactly. But I connect to memories, remember? By the time you've registered a thought into your conscious mind, it is already a memory of sorts. That's when I have access to it."

"Then why are we bothering —"

"With a conversation?"

"Stop that!" Roni fought the urge to storm off — especially when a misstep might send her nosediving into an abyss of baby blue mist and chains. "If you know what I'm going to ask before I do, why not save us both the trouble and tell me what I need to know?"

Chak frowned. "You really don't understand? The Keeper should have explained things clearly before allowing you in here. Before you even got close to the books. That's part of her job. Otherwise, there's no deal to be made."

Roni had no idea what any of that meant, but she did glean one thing — Chak could not read everything in her mind. Otherwise, he wouldn't be confused.

Clasping his hands overhead in a gesture that might have been triumph or just as easily could have suggested solidarity, Chak said, "I suppose it's up to me. Never was like this before. But then life flowed smoothly before. This Keeper — she doesn't follow through the way the others did. She doesn't make proper deals. She's ruining it all. But then, all things end. I suppose I must end, too."

"You're dying?"

"Everything is in a constant state of dying. Don't let that trouble you. When you get your answers, you'll have more than enough troubling you that I won't matter."

Roni strained to hold back the fire that leapt within her. "Stop doing that. Either tell me what you can or take me where the answers are."

"My apologies. In all the years I've been alive, and that is a lot of years, I have rarely been in the position of disseminating information. I will try to be concise."

"Thank you."

Chak concentrated, his mouth moving silently as he planned out what to say. "Years ago, your mother and father entered one of my books. Your mother procured a deal with the Keeper. The same deal all who enter make with the Keeper — give up your memories to the books and you may take over for the Keeper. Your father betrayed the deal and wanted out. But the price for such a thing was the memories of his daughter. He sacrificed you for his own freedom. Was that concise enough?"

Roni staggered to her knees. Gasping for breath, she managed, "What?"

"I said that years ago, your mother and father entered one of my books. Your mother —"

"No. Shut up." With her hands grinding into her thighs, she said, "My father said he didn't go into the book."

"He lied. Probably he did not wish to admit the selfish and terrible thing he did to you. Am I still being concise enough?"

"My mother — why would she ever agree to that? It's not even a deal. She didn't get anything out of it."

"Of course, she did. She freed the Keeper. Every Keeper must stay and tend the books, must bring in new memories to consume. If the Keeper leaves, it dies. So, the Keeper stays. If the Keeper finds a new mind to inhabit it, then the old Keeper goes on to wherever Keepers go when they are done with me and haven't died."

"So, my mother agreed to jump into one of your books, agreed to sacrifice herself in order to free the Keeper, and then she became the Keeper?"

"You do understand. Charming."

"Then my father was supposed to jump in with her, but he chickened out?"

"He did enter the books. I think they hoped to have him follow your mother's lead, which would have set her free. Of course, he would then become the Keeper."

With her throat aching as she spoke, Roni said, "But if he was to become the Keeper, why didn't he just go inside himself then? Why even bother with my mother?"

"I've never fully grasped the Keeper's reasons for doing things. It keeps me alive, so I keep it alive. That's how we work. Most of the time, I do not pay any attention to the way the Keeper is doing its job. But, if I were to guess based on recent and past events, I would think the Keeper saw an opportunity to finally be free of me. I am not so arrogant as to believe all Keepers value the relationship that I have with them. Some of them feel imprisoned. Some Keepers have been less forthright in explaining the true deal before allowing visitors to enter the books. I believe they find the haggling of the deal distasteful and wish to—"

"Concise, remember?'

Chak's lips fluttered as he sighed. "Yes. Concise. I believe the Keeper tricked your parents into the books with the idea that one of them would sacrifice to free the other. Failing that, they could both give up memories enough to free themselves, and the Keeper and I would gain vitality."

"This doesn't make sense. My mother was not the kind for sacrifice."

"Unless the Keeper said the memories would be of you. What mother would willingly give up all memory of her daughter? Your father suggests the scheme of your mother taking over as the Keeper and then he would follow, freeing your mother to return to you."

"But he lied to her?"

"Or his resolve weakened when faced with actually following through on his promise. The Keeper did not trust your father to honor the deal. Which proved true by the fact that he betrayed you and your mother."

"So, the Keeper now is my mother?"

"Partially. Perhaps. More likely, a bit of the old and the new. Yes. That sounds right. I had not given her much thought, I rarely think about the Keeper, but I see that she is both. That's why I'm ill."

"What now?"

"When your father refused to follow through and become the Keeper, the old Keeper fought your mother for control. The Keeper must honor her deals, and the deal was for both mother and father. So, both old and new Keepers now inhabit the same body. The Keeper must have demanded a surrogate for your father's memories, since he refused to give his own, and your father thought of you. The Keeper sent out her agent, swiped some of your memories, and released the father. I don't know what he told the rest of your people, but I doubt it was the truth."

"This can't be right."

"I could be mistaken. Paying attention to the minor drivel going on with this section of my existence has never been a priority to me."

Swallowing back the bile burning up her throat, Roni shook her head. As much as she wanted to deny all that she had heard, the missing pieces within her opened to the idea. As if this snippet of her father's story fit within them perfectly.

"Follow me," Chak said. "We'll set this right."

"Where are we going?"

"To see Lawrence Rider, of course. He has returned to fulfill his end of things. We have to reach him before he closes his final deal with the Keeper and the Kept."

"I thought you were the Kept."

"Not all of it. I'm merely a piece created to talk with you. Come now. If we're late, you'll be stuck with whatever deal he makes, and if I were you, I would not trust him on that part. You could be stuck here forever. And don't think I'll be here to entertain you for that eternity." With limber movement, Chak hopped from one link to another. Roni tried to keep up, but her fear of falling wobbled her balance, slowing her down. Chak glanced back. "Stop worrying and get hurrying."

"It won't matter, if I fall and die before I get there."

"You can't die. Well, not from falling, at least. It isn't exactly real. It isn't exactly unreal, either." He clapped his hands overhead again. "You're a genius. Superbly brilliant. We don't need to climb the chains. We can fly down."

Roni peered over the chains into the endless drop. "I know I'm only grasping every fourth word you say, but I don't have wings. Flying is not an option for me."

As she sat back, Chak placed a hand on her shoulder and she startled. How did he get back there? He inched his head close to her. "Hold my hand and we can fly. I promise."

Her head grew fuzzy as she tried to fit any pieces of this puzzle together. Even her dreams made more sense than this. But the sentences that did hold meaning screamed out at her — Chak could take her to see her father, time to leave this place ticked away, all her answers awaited her. She did not want to give Chak any real trust, certainly not with her life, but looking around at the surreal landscape pressed upon her shoulders. There wasn't another soul around. Either trust Chak or be stuck here.

Not much of a choice. She took his hand.

"Good," he said, his leathery fingers wrapping around hers. "I'm sorry things have been so difficult for you. The Keeper this time is no good, and she has forced me into this. You'll see. Now, take a breath and try not to scream. I find that shrieking noise people make to be very distracting when I fly."

Before she could say a word, he leapt off the chain, pulling her with him, and dropped into the blue.

CHAPTER 23

Jolting in the backseat of the mini-van, Roni let out a short gasp. To the right, Teanna stared out the window at the passing evergreens, marveling at the new world around her, while Gully sat at Roni's left, his face showing too much concern. Up front, Elliot drove and Gram twisted around to look back.

"Nightmare?" Gram asked. "When you were little, you would always get them if you fell asleep during a drive."

Peeking in the rearview mirror, Elliot said, "Or perhaps you've had more of your memory restored."

"Is that it, dear? Did you remember something?"

Roni thought she would need about ten years of therapy before she could address that question. Turning her gaze out the side window, she tried to put some of her returned memories into place. Her parents going into the caverns alone, stumbling upon the Cave of Lost Time, entering the books without knowing what they were doing — all of that she could believe. But then came the hard part. The idea that her parents would agree to a crazy and convoluted plan of escape, the idea that Roni's father would ever betray her mother, and the idea that he would offer Roni's memories in exchange — it all seemed so farfetched.

Except it also seemed plausible. Especially when Roni factored in the period of her life right after she woke with her Lost Time. Back then, Gram acted perpetually aggressive toward Roni's father. That anger would have been justified, if she knew he had left Maria trapped in the Keeper's body. Later, when Lawrence was admitted to Belmont, Gram refused to visit him, and over the years, she cautioned Roni against forming too strong an attachment to the man.

Driving for hours into the Pennsylvania mountains left Roni with too much time. She wanted to ask Gram about all of it. How much did Gram really know? How much had she willfully forgotten? But that would open up wounds they could not deal with at the moment. Not when they had to worry about a living relic that might be at war with itself.

Thinking of living relics brought to mind Yal-hara and her message delivered via Kenneth Bay. *The Keeper at the Cave of Lost Time has always been a cursed creature. A trapped creature.*

"Slower, please," Teanna said, pressing her hands on the window in an attempt to slide it down.

Elliot decelerated. "Off the glass, please. I'll take care of it."

Gram alleviated Teanna's confusion by gently pushing her back. As Teanna leaned away and Elliot lowered the automatic window, Roni bounced her knee hard enough that Gully placed a hand on her leg. They stopped on the side of the road. Everyone grew quiet. They all watched Teanna.

Roni kept expecting some big moment. A flash of colorful light or Teanna grabbing her head and fainting as a nosebleed formed under one nostril. Anything to indicate that she had performed a special, magical task and found the Keeper. Instead, Teanna simply pointed up the road on the left.

"There," she said. "Can you make this thing go in there?"

"Through the woods?" Elliot chuckled. "Sorry. Cars pretty much stay on the road."

"Then we will have to walk."

After a few minutes of exiting the car, stretching limbs, and rubbing aches, Gram nodded to Roni that they were ready. Roni led the way with Teanna at her side. They weaved through the trees and climbed along the mountains. Twice, they had to reroute because of a sheer rockface that dropped too far. But eventually, they found their way back and Teanna had no trouble picking up the trail. When they reached a tree line that opened on a wide swath of flat boulders, Roni called a break.

"A river once flowed through here," Teanna said. "It must have been quite beautiful."

"Remind you of your home?" Gram asked.

"A little. The universe I lived in — the people have more harmony with the world than you do. We don't fight our environment. We use it, but we also let it breathe. We exist within it. You seem to want to dominate it."

Gram bristled. "The Lord put this world here for us to use. Besides, when you create cars capable of high speeds, you need roads that can handle them. When you construct buildings that touch the sky, you need a solid foundation or the whole thing collapses and everybody dies."

"We have tall buildings, too. Their strength to stand is by building with the strongest trees as part of the structure. A thick, strong tree that has lived for hundreds of years can be trusted to root a building in place. As for your cars — I am not certain they are worth boasting about. They do move fast, but they are noisy and smell awful."

As the two continued to compare worlds, Roni walked away with a smirk. She stretched her arms and settled next to Elliot. "You holding up okay?"

Sweat beaded across his forehead. "I'll be fine. But I'll be glad when this is over and I can rest for a few days. My lower-back is killing me."

They all looked tired. All except Gully. He stood upon a flat boulder the size of a mattress, his eyes roving up and down the tree line and the riverbed. If the Keeper or anything else decided to pay a visit, he would be ready.

"When this is over and you're in blissful sleep, remind me to thank Sully for his golem. I'm starting to really like that guy."

Elliot uncapped a canteen and guzzled some water. "You're on your own for that. I will not be waking up to remind you of anything. And don't try to order me, either. After these last days, I have no problem showing insubordination, if it means a restful sleep."

Roni grinned. "Maybe I'll sleep for a few days, too. Then I'll worry about sending out Thank You notes."

They listened to the breeze rustling branches and leaves, mimicking the flowing waters of the river that no longer existed. Each silent minute that ticked by made Roni more uncomfortable. She wanted to ask Elliot what he knew about her parents — not the stories he had told in the past, but whatever he truly believed had happened. But to do so would bring up times of guilt and shame. He had some hand in this, all of the Parallel Society did, and even if she forgave them, he would not forgive himself lightly.

The leader in her reminded the non-leader that this was not the state of mind her team should be in right before facing the Keeper. Yet the other part of her, the non-leader, the daughter of a man who may have betrayed her, that part forced her mouth open, forced her to face Elliot, forced her to speak his name.

"Yes?" he said, pure and innocent and unsuspecting of what would come from her mouth.

The words would not form. Her throat closed up as if the thoughts of the words would cause an allergic reaction. How much did she really want to know? *All of it,* part of her demanded. But another part, a quieter but no less powerful part, pointed out that the more truth she learned right now, the harder it would be to do what they had come here for.

The Keeper posed a threat to all on Earth and possibly their entire universe. The fact that Roni's mother may still be inside that creature, tussling with the previous Keeper, hoping to control the creature — well, Roni could not allow that to matter. It was a ridiculous idea, anyway. If two Keepers had existed in that singular body, that had happened close to thirty years ago. They would not still be fighting. And if her mother had won long ago, none of the current situation would be going on.

Which meant that the old Keeper fought off Roni's mother. Yet the Keeper had hesitated before, had shown some recognition of Roni. Unless Roni read too much into a pause. Possible, she had to admit. Too much depended on the Parallel Society fulfilling their duties to allow thin, hopeful guesses to hold sway — even at the expense of a life.

Except she shuddered at the thought of giving up on her mother.

"Roni?" Elliot asked. "I'm still here."

He had such kind eyes. She wanted to curl under his protective arm and tell him everything that had happened. She wanted him to know that she was sad and angry and hurt but that she knew he would never hurt her through malice, that he deserved her understanding, and that in time, she would truly forgive him.

But a few feet away, Teanna bolted straight up and Gully narrowed his eyes upon a section of woods to the west. The sound of a large animal moving fast — snapping branches and smashing through the ground. It grew louder.

"Is it her?" Roni asked, squinting into the distance.

"It's definitely a living relic," Teanna said.

Gram scowled. "Then it's her. We may have a lot of relics in our world, but living relics — there's just her."

Roni ignored the lie and focused on the thundering stampede. Just one creature, but it sounded like a herd. With her heart hammering, Roni closed off thoughts of her parents and Elliot and everything Chak had said. She needed to be the leader of the Parallel Society. Otherwise, they would fail like they did at the cavern entrance.

She walked tall and strong into the middle of the riverbed. Keeping her eyes on the tree line, she said, "Elliot, make a protection dome. Be ready to help anybody in need. Gram, books and chains. Gully, Teanna — you're with me. We're going to have to maintain strong and steady pressure on the Keeper. Try to corral her once Gram is ready."

Teanna said, "You want to throw the Keeper into another universe?"

"An empty universe."

"But my father and my team."

"They're dead."

"You can't know that. You came back from the books. They could, too."

Roni stomped over to Teanna. She saw the glisten in Teanna's eyes, the blind wish that the truth would not be the truth. Roni kissed Teanna's cheek, startling the young woman.

"Whatever was left of them is gone," Roni said, willing the words to hold true for her mother, too. "The Cave is no more, and the Keeper is only a maddened beast, lost and confused and attempting to lash out. We have to protect this world now. It's our home. And it will be your home, too."

Teanna swallowed Roni's words with three sharp sniffs — each stronger than the previous one. She stepped back and tossed her robe over her shoulder. With a sorrowful, hard glower, she pulled out her axes and faced the trees.

Roni checked back at Elliot and Gram. They had begun their preparations. Gully, of course, stood at the ready, never wavering.

The sounds of a stampede diminished. The Keeper must have slowed on her approach. Roni searched the tree line for any movement, but the rippling leaves and swaying branches obscured everything beyond. Floating on the breeze, a luxurious smell of evergreens and rich earth jarred Roni's rising tensions. Not enough to ease her, but enough to narrow her mind into focus. Only the present moment, the present surroundings mattered. Get through that, and she could worry about the rest.

Lumbering into the open like a mutated dinosaur, the Keeper appeared further up the riverbed. But this was no herbivore munching on tree leaves. This creature hissed and barked with anger as she reached down with all eight hands and picked up eight large rocks.

Despite her injuries and her ill appearance, she lifted the heavy stones with effortless grace.

Teanna puffed her chest. "I am Teanna Rowl, tracker of the Protectors and daughter of Atura Rowl, leader of the Protectors. Your presence in this world is an abomination and a danger to all. Agree to go back to the caverns in peace and we promise you will not be harmed. Resist, and I will gladly return the pain you have thrown upon me and my people."

As far as speeches went, Roni thought Teanna knocked it out of the park. Certainly far better than anything she would have said, and certainly strange enough that the Keeper paused. Any extra time they could give Elliot to cast his dome was invaluable.

When the Keeper took two thumping steps forward, Roni decided she would toss out a speech of her own. But the Keeper never gave her the chance. With one loud bark, the Keeper hurled all eight stones into the air.

CHAPTER 24

Plunging through an endless baby blue fog, Roni's insides shifted and floated and flipped. Behind her, Chak held her waist, and though his grip felt light, he kept her close as he guided them through swooping maneuvers and wide, steep turns. The exhilaration of flying diminished, however, whenever she saw another doorless room in the distance.

From the outside, some of the rooms appeared similar to the one she had occupied. But others took on varied and unusual shapes. She spotted cones, pyramids, and even a few octagons. Twice, they glided by spiral-shaped mounds hanging beneath the chains like humongous beehives. Still others reminded her of abstract art.

Many of the rooms acted as vessels for Lost Time memories. Some housed people themselves. People like Roni. People that would never agree to give away their thoughts, feelings, and cherished moments.

"Not much longer," Chak said, shouting his words to be heard over the strong winds of their flight.

She shivered. Not from the wind, though. The wind had been surprisingly warm. Rather, part of her clung to the idea of simply flying — enjoying the freedom of it. Better than any dream of flight, the raw sensation of wind buoying her aloft the air dazzled her mind. When they landed, she would have to deal with the ugliness that awaited her. Until that moment, though, she could be a bird, skimming the surface of the sky, never paying attention to how easy it would be to fall through to the other side.

Immediately, a dark guilt snaked up her throat. This was not a place of joyous freedom.

The deeper they dove, the tighter the chains became. Whereas before they drooped like dusty cobwebs in a forgotten haunted house, they now held firm to whatever direction they had been strung. Many links reached gargantuan proportions — large enough to hold a city block. Some even bigger. As Roni marveled at the sight, she noticed that Chak had shifted them towards one of the massive links — one with a section carved into a deep, circular area like an unpainted, helicopter landing pad, only for giants.

When they touched ground, Chak expelled a warm breath onto the back of her neck and released her waist. Roni's legs wobbled as the sturdiness of the surface beneath became reality. Her mind needed a few hefty stomps before it believed that the floating chains she had seen in the air would actually hold her.

"Are you feeling okay?" Chak asked. "This place can be disorienting when you're not accustomed to it."

"I'll be fine." Her head felt all the dizziness of being drunk with none of the pleasure. "Let's keep going."

"It won't take long."

Chak walked ahead. From the air, the spot dug out of the link looked no bigger than a large house. But at the surface level, Roni could barely make out the end.

"How far are we going?"

"Not far. I promise."

"Why don't we just fly over there?"

"Never," Chak said, with a strange laugh as if he did not know whether that was the appropriate response. "The Keeper is up ahead — well, my connection to the Keeper — and we never display our strengths in front of each other. It would be rude. Sacrilege."

Roni had a few choice responses to that but opted for silence. Besides, she feared she might throw up all over his nice floor, and that truly would be rude.

Gesturing with his lizard hand, Chak urged her to follow. The ground reminded her of the caverns — rocky on the sides but a well-worn path in the middle. Of course, unlike the caverns this place had no ceiling. Instead, open skies dominated her view — well, blue haze crossed with chains.

Each step further along the path, her mind cleared. The discomfort of a drunken brain vanished, and her unsteady gait strengthened.

"I think I'm feeling better. Much better," she said.

Chak nodded without looking back. "We're nearing the clip point — where this existence ceases and your universes begin. It tends to sober cognitive ability. Unclutters the mind and returns thoughts. Other things, too."

"Like what?"

Roni's entire body seized. Her muscles clenched, her eyes locked open, and her throat constricted out a tiny gurgle. Chak continued ahead, muttering something to her, never noticing that she had stopped following. With all her will, she tried to force her mouth to work. But nothing happened. She was paralyzed but completely aware.

A sudden, prickling rush covered her skin. The world around melted away.

She was eight. In bed. Two in the morning. And even as she thought about the way Rick Bower threatened if she didn't kiss him, he would tell all the boys that she had lice, even as she worried that some might believe such a lie, that it might get around the school and cause her endless amounts of trouble, Roni the adult recognized this moment. It was a memory. A memory that shined with incredible brilliance because it had not been able to shine for so many years.

This was it. Her mouth dried as her instinct guaranteed the truth. This was the core of everything.

Her Lost Time.

The bedroom door creaked open. Her child heart raced at the sound. She lifted her head to investigate, but her head would not move. Nor her arms or legs. She was paralyzed.

A dream? she wondered. But no. She was awake and aware yet unable to do anything. She tried to call for Gram, but no sound came out.

Her parents had been gone for a week, and Gram had been acting odd the entire time. More bossy. Quicker to correct bad behavior. Sully and Elliot, too. Usually they doted on Roni, supplying her with all sorts of sweets, but over the last few days, they had been avoiding her.

Spindle-thin legs appeared at the foot of her bed. Her eyes blurred with tears — the only part of her that still worked. What stole out of the dark convinced her that no matter how real it seemed, she had to be dreaming. A nightmare, of course, but no more real than a pleasant dream. Because the thing she witnessed simply made no sense at all.

Despite having only four limbs, it moved like a spider — a spider the size of a small, eight-year-old girl. Its torso had a bulbous section, and a stalk-like neck poked out the front. As the monster crept up her body, she wondered how she could not be throwing up. Everything in her mind urged her to vomit, yet the creature continued to move and she continued to stay motionless.

It weighed no more than a cat, barely making an indent on the mattress. As its disgusting, boney legs settled on her chest, she wondered if she would throw up or pee. She had read that fear caused those reactions in people, but her body refused to do anything.

Blinking three bug-like eyes, the monster lowered its twisted face close. Gray skin could be seen through patches of short, dark hairs. Roni managed a soft whimper.

Though she could not see the creature's mouth, Roni heard its voice when it spoke — soft, gentle, motherly. Roni could not imagine anything worse.

"Don't be afraid," it said. "I'm only here to collect what your father has paid. A memory. You must give up a memory. I will take it from you, and I will take tonight away, too. You'll never have to be troubled by thoughts of me again."

Adult-Roni wanted to jab a fist into the creature's jaw, roll the thing onto the floor, and pin it down. She would tie it to a chair, rush to the bookstore, grab any book from the caverns, and send this thing to another universe. But she could only observe as if she sat in an empty movie theater during a horror film.

"I'm sure this is confusing," the creature said, "but you needn't worry. You don't have to understand. All you must do is pick a memory that you'll never miss. Something you don't care to remember ever again, and I'll take it from you. There will be no pain, I promise. Not a single ouchy. Surely, there's some nugget of time in your short life that you wish would go away?"

Child-Roni discovered she could move her head. Only enough to nod.

"Tell me," the creature said with a hungry sound. Lowering its torso onto her chest so that its face came so close Roni could smell it — like vinegar. The creature tapped her forehead with the end of one stick of a leg. "No, no. Not with your mouth. Think it. Remember the moment. It will be the last time."

Adult-Roni stood by, helpless to change events, helpless to even comfort this small version of herself. The poor little girl lay on that bed, terrified, petrified. Her mind threatening to split into pieces. In a weird way, she only survived the encounter sane because this disgusting creature swiped these moments away. Without any memory of the thing, she had nothing to drive away her sanity.

In fact, Roni always recalled the next morning when she told Gram that she had the worst nightmare of her life but couldn't remember a moment of it. All she had left was the foul feeling that remained in her chest. Gram said it was probably better that way.

"Come now," the monster said, extending one of it legs to touch the side of her head. "Just think a tiny bit. Just one awful moment of your life that you'd rather forget."

The little girl sounded like a wounded cat as she wrinkled her forehead.

"Done," the creature said. It pulled its legs off of Child-Roni's head, and with it came a tissue-thin mist of pale yellow. Several small patches of other colors slipped alongside — mint green, muddy brown, and soft pink. "Oh, dear. That's unfortunate. Sorry, young one. I told you to focus on a single moment, but you children always have to mix things together. It's your own fault, really. Nothing to do about it now, though. Go back to sleep. When you awake, you'll know you had a bad dream and that's it. The rest will be gone. Lost to the Keeper. Good night."

With that, the creature ambled off the bed and disappeared into the dark. Control over Roni's body returned slowly like waking a limb that had gone to sleep. She even felt the pins and needles. Even in her ears and up her nose. And as her eyes grew heavy, as her thoughts of what had happened faded, never to be remembered, she had a flash of what had been taken.

Her mother.

Right before her parents went off and dumped her with Gram for a week, Roni had a typical screaming match with her mother. It had been about what age she could start wearing make-up. Hardly worth all the throat-burn the argument had caused. But it had been the moment that popped in her head when the creature asked for something to forget.

Of course, as the creature had pointed out, thoughts of an argument with her mother connected with many other memories of her parents. Adult-Roni understood. This was how it began. This was how she ended up with so many holes in her life.

She opened her eyes. Chak stood over her. "You stopped," he said.

Brushing tears off her cheek, Roni realized her body could move again. She clambered to her feet and slapped the dirt from her pants.

"I see," Chak said. "Your Lost Time has returned. Well, I suppose that was inevitable. We can talk about such things later. We'll have plenty of opportunities. But first, I promised you a chance to see your father. Don't make a liar out of me. Get moving. He's right around the turn."

Chak led Roni around a large formation of uncut chain. As they entered this new area, Roni relaxed a tiny bit. Chak had kept his word. Lawrence Rider stood only twenty feet away.

But so did the Keeper.

Chapter 25

"Take cover!" Roni watched eight gigantic stones hurling through the air. She intended to dive toward the tree line, but Gully dropped on top of her, shielding her with his clay back.

The heavy rocks blasted against the riverbed — some shaking the ground, some shattering into shrapnel upon impact. Little shards peppered around them like hail. When the sounds of tumbling stones ceased, Roni squirmed out from beneath Gully.

Teanna bolted into view, emerging from a nearby log, twirling her axes as she found her rhythm for fighting. Off to the side, Elliot held his dome over Gram — a pile of stones on the outside. For her part, Gram released two of her chains, each one dropping from her sleeve as she stretched her neck from side to side, ready to join the fray.

Roni turned to Gully. "Can you fight?"

Gully straightened, his body deformed by the abuse it had suffered recently, but he winked. "Are you kidding? What do you think Sully made me for? I'm not going to sit around eating bagels and chopped liver all day. Let's go."

As they dashed ahead, the Keeper bent down to grab more rocks. But Teanna had already arrived. Roni never saw how the tracker had managed to move so fast, but she zipped between the Keeper's legs and double-chopped her axes across one of the creature's wrists.

With a raging howl, the Keeper reared to her full height. She jerked her hand up to inspect it, and the hand fell limp as only a swatch of skin attached it at the wrist. Blood rained onto the stones below.

Teanna scampered away, but the Keeper spotted her. Hunching over to keep her target in view, the Keeper stomped at the woman as if trying to squash a roach. The voice-cracked barks synched with each strike, but Teanna dodged the blows. Rolling to one side, leaping to another, she managed to avoid all the Keeper could muster.

But nobody could evade forever. Roni and Gully continued their run to help. This needed to end fast. The longer it went on, the more tired Roni's team would become. She suspected the Keeper could outlast them on that front, and tired people made stupid mistakes.

"Get me up there," she yelled at Gully as they rounded behind the Keeper.

Whether by design or by dumb luck, Teanna had pulled the Keeper's attention away. She never saw the others approach. Gully sprinted ahead toward one of the Keeper's back legs, and Roni snatched a glance to the side. Elliot held strong, and Gram twirled her chain — always like a cowboy with a lasso. She was ready.

"Now, Gully! Now!"

The golem planted into the stone, his clay feet widening as they spread their surface area for maximum stability, and he pressed his hands together to create a perfect step. Roni hurdled off the ground, onto Gully's step, and into the air. He thrust upward, tossing her high enough to grab onto the Keeper.

If she stopped to think about her plan, she would never have done it. But it was the idea that hit at the moment, and she could not turn back now. Climbing up the creature's flank, she expected to be swatted off. A few seconds later, she wished it had been that easy.

The Keeper's head snapped back. She hissed and bared her grinding teeth. But none of her seven working hands plucked at Roni — the limbs could not reach her any better than a person could pluck a bug from the middle of their back. Two arms twisted at an awkward angle, trying to move in on Roni, but two others shoved them off. The Keeper hissed louder and gave her head a strong shake.

Roni wanted to climb all the way onto the Keeper's back, have Gram toss up one end of a chain, and get busy tying this beast into submission. But holding on seemed the limit of her abilities. Each time she thought about releasing a hand to grab higher, the Keeper's body shifted enough to remind Roni that to let go meant falling.

Teanna and Gully continued to harass the Keeper from below. The Keeper kept her hands away from Teanna, and when the woman launched toward the feet, the Keeper hopped aside. The jolting motion thrashed Roni about, threatening to fling her for a short, painful trip into the woods.

The Keeper kicked into the ground, sending a shower of rocks like mortar fire. While Elliot protected Gram, Teanna dodged a large stone but took a smaller one across the legs. She cried out and somersaulted back onto her feet. Gully stood his ground. Dozens of small projectiles punctured his clay body, cratering his skin like a horrid case of acne.

Roni thought she had a break — the Keeper paused to see the damage she had inflicted. Roni climbed upward. But the movement brought the Keeper's attention back to the annoying bug on its side. She had already tried swatting and plucking Roni away with no success. She paused to gaze at the riverbed. At the same moment that the Keeper made a decision on how to deal with the problem, Roni realized what that decision would be. The Keeper dropped to the ground, exposing her flank to the stones below, hoping to pulverize Roni in the process.

Whether from bravery, fear, stupidity, or some wild combination of them all, Roni watched the smooth, enormous stones — boulders, really — coming at her fast. She watched, waited, and thought she could enact some sense of timing. At the moment her brain deemed it best, she shoved off as the Keeper bashed into the rocks.

With a resounding crash, the Keeper thudded against the ground. Roni attempted an athletic forward roll like Teanna but ended up somewhere between a sloppy tumble and skin-shredding skid. She cried out, trying to keep her head up so she wouldn't crack her skull open. Dust billowed around them as shattered pebbles sprinkled the air.

"Take advantage," Gram said and rushed across the stones. More of a hustling waddle than a sprint, but at her age, it was impressive. She whipped one of her chains through the air. It slapped around a waving forearm. Yanking back, Gram roared. Elliot stepped in front to protect any attack while Gully took the chain and wrapped it around his waist.

Teanna tore ahead and leapt across the Keeper, slicing through a second wrist. As Roni pushed aside her pain and reached her feet, she saw Gram lasso another one of the Keeper's arms with a new chain. Success twinkled in the distance, and Roni dared to grin.

But the Keeper refused to give in. She twisted her body, snapping the chains loose, and kicked out, tossing more rocks at dangerous speeds. In one quick and vicious motion, she rose. The momentum sent the chains around her soaring, and Gully flew with them. She snorted, continuing to spin like a carnival ride of nightmares.

Distracted by the sight, Teanna missed seeing the Keeper's one low arm. It swung in and clipped Teanna hard. The hit sent her several feet away, dazing her with sheer force. The Keeper followed up by pounding three fists into the boulders directly in front of Gram and Elliot. He held his cane tight as the rocks walloped the glowing dome. The quake the Keeper created did more damage, sending both fighters to the ground.

Two heavy stomps, and the Keeper swung back to loom over Roni. The hot stink of animal sweat wafted with her movement. Roni gagged.

As she coughed, she saw between the many limbs of the Keeper like watching a scene from behind several trees. Her team had been ruined. Bruised, exhausted, defeated.

They had been foolish. No. Roni had been foolish. She had become so comfortable with the chase that she forgot to plan an actual way to capture the Keeper. Gram would never have been so careless. Sully would have had four plans.

Curling her nose as if Roni smelled worse, the Keeper brought her face in close. She opened her mouth wide. Roni cringed. She had expected brutal retaliation — it never occurred to her that Keeper might try to eat her.

The Keeper hesitated. Shook her head as if trying to rid herself of an odd buzzing. She winced, and her face lengthened as her expression softened.

In a voice that held more lower tones than Roni had heard before, the Keeper said, "My sweet, sweet daughter."

Everything in Roni stopped. With a whimper that reminded her of the little girl paralyzed in her bed, she said, "Daddy?"

CHAPTER 26

Edging away with a low bow, Chak gestured toward Lawrence and the Keeper. Roni held still next to the large piece of chain that formed a wall. The back half of the area did not resemble the rest of the carved-out chain she and Chak had been walking through. Instead, it had old wood planks on the floor and walls, a bearskin rug, and a stone fireplace at the side with a deer head trophy over the mantel. It looked like the sitcom television set of a hunting lodge.

However, where a door should have been, an opening existed like a ripped circle in a piece of paper. On the one side stood Roni's father, a grizzled man in his lodge, and on the other side, the Keeper peered in as she clung to vertical chains that ended in open books shining various colors. Roni blanched — the Keeper was back at the Cave of Lost Time. This was an exit.

"As promised," Chak said. His beady eyes turned toward Lawrence. "I've told your daughter everything."

"I doubt that," Lawrence said.

"The whole truth."

"I doubt that even more."

"She's even had some of her Lost Time return."

"The first thing you've said I can believe. Don't lie anymore. If you thought I'd be the mad version of me that has lived all these decades locked away, you'll be disappointed. My real mind is back. Returned to me just like Roni's Lost Time."

"Wonderful. Perhaps you'll continue to be the idiot you've been since before I met you."

Scrunching his brow, Lawrence checked on Roni. "How are you?"

In that little question, the crushing weight of the past few days dropped onto her. Her knees trembled. Tears carved a pathway through the dirt on her face. She wanted to hide but dared not look away — she needed to see his eyes when she spoke. If she could speak. The idea that she could form words ever again seemed implausible.

Her first attempt resulted in a high-pitched squeak. Hearing the pitiful noise sent a shudder through her body. Her legs weakened, and she gulped air in an effort to regain her composure. Her father stepped toward her, but she snapped out her hand. "No. Stay there," she managed.

He had the decency to listen and dropped his eyes to ponder the floor. "I'm sorry. I never meant for you to be so hurt."

"It's true, then? You gave up my memories and left Mom to rot inside the Keeper?"

"What? No." He looked from the Keeper to Chak. "You liars. What did you say to her?"

Chak lifted his chin with aristocratic pride. "I never lie."

"You bend the truth until it practically snaps."

"Did your wife not jump through and enter the Keeper? Was not the plan for you to follow? For you to kick her free so that she might raise little Roni? Did you not back out and offer up Roni's memories in order to escape? I did not lie."

Lawrence rushed over to Roni, but she retreated as if from a rabid dog. She could not hold back her tears, but at least, she could maintain a safe distance from him.

As she attempted to keep her voice steady, to avoid any blubbering noises, she said, "You." But the word choked in her throat. A few trembling breaths, and she tried again. "You betrayed me. You betrayed Mom."

"We've all been betrayed — by these two, not by me. I've been loyal to you and your mother. Always."

"More lies," Chak said, standing tall as if posing for a portrait. However, he remained pressed against the metal wall, and Roni caught him peeking at the Keeper but never for long. Flapping out one hand, he continued, "You and your wife were made an offer and you accepted. You are the ones who wanted to break the deal."

"You changed the deal."

"Never," the Keeper hissed from the Cave.

"You were supposed to let Maria become the new Keeper. You were supposed to leave that body to her. The moment you fought back, you changed the deal."

"I did not make that deal with you, now did I?"

Chak crossed his arms with an indignant huff. "Don't blame me. We both make deals for us. It's a joint effort."

Lawrence turned away and focused on Roni. "Please, listen to me. Just this little bit and if you never want to hear from me again," he glanced at the Keeper, "well, that won't be hard."

Wiping her nose on her sleeve, Roni said, "Why did you do it? I thought you loved Mom. I thought you went crazy after she was gone because you loved her so much."

"I did. I do. Here's the truth — your mother and I were rowdy, drunken idiots who always thought we knew better than Gram or anybody. Sound familiar? We rushed through the caverns one night — your mother was convinced she had been called, that her true purpose in life had finally been revealed, but I thought she had smoked too much weed on top of the cheap vodka we'd been drinking. When we found our way to the Cave and the Keeper, when we dropped through the books and into this terrible place, we didn't know what we were doing. I didn't even believe the things I was seeing. Thought I was hallucinating. But we sobered up fast.

"See, these two are like parasites on each other, but they need new blood, too. Chak feeds off the Keeper and the Keeper feeds off the Lost Time. But while the Keeper's body goes on and on, the mind is a different matter. In the end, they always need a new mind to fill that body. And there we were. The deal was simple enough. The old Keeper wanted to be free of her prison and we wanted to be free of Chak. We wanted to get back home. To you. So, your mother thought she would agree to become the next Keeper and then right after, I would do the same. She would be free to return to you."

Roni said, "And you would so bravely sacrifice yourself? I'm supposed to believe that after what you actually did?"

"I was not brave. I cried. I cried because I had to say goodbye to you and to her. The loves of my life. But I would do anything for you two."

"You want me to see you as noble?"

"Not noble, either, or anything like that. I love you, but I cried for myself, too. Your mother had it all figured out. Once I knocked her out of the Keeper, she would run back to the bookstore and get Gram and the others. The Parallel Society would come to my rescue. Figure something out. But Gram never liked me, and I didn't think she would really work that hard to help me."

Roni snapped a sharp glare at him. "Gram isn't like that. Even if she's mad or disappointed or even if she hates you, she will still do the right thing."

"I was counting on it." He sneered at Chak. "But then the little details these two neglected to tell us became our problem."

Chak crossed his arms. "It is not our fault that you were too arrogant to ask questions. I never lied, and I never would have."

"You just twist things and hide things and never explain the most important parts of what you offer."

From the Cave, the Keeper said, "Get on with it. We don't like staring into him."

"Yeah," Lawrence said. "I know the feeling." He turned back to Roni. "We really thought we had a good plan to get back to you. Risky, but we hoped it would work."

"Then you chickened out," Roni said, but with less force.

"Not me. The Keeper. She had spent so long connected to this creature, Chak — centuries, at least — and she feared she would not be able to live on her own. Sometimes prisoners become so accustomed to the prison that they can't function without it. When your mother stepped through that hole in the wall behind me, the Keeper refused to leave her body. She fought back. And since your mother was new to the body, new to the experience, and did not know the first thing about what to do, the Keeper had an easy time of staying in control.

"I was about to jump through, too. I wanted to kick out the both of them and stick to our plan. But then the Keeper looked back at me, a lot like she's doing now, and she spoke in your mother's voice. She had gained a tiny bit of control of the Keeper's body, just long enough to tell me that I had to get back to you, that she would continue to fight the Keeper, that it would take time, but when she won — and she was such a fiery force to deal with, I knew she would win — when that happened, she would contact me and call me back to finish our plan."

Roni watched her father's eyes as he spoke. She knew that face so well, had seen him in the throes of madness, had seen him calm and at peace. Every wrinkle, every whisker, every tic and twitch — he spoke the truth. "That's why we're here? You came back for her?"

"I did. That's why we were called."

"But why did I have to lose my memories? Why did you and Gram lie to me about all of this?"

He put out his hand and smiled when she took it. "Chak told the truth about that. The only way they would let me leave was to sacrifice a piece of your memory. They like being cruel."

Chak said, "There is no cruelty in Nature — only what is. I did not create my existence, and I did not create the rules that govern me. Are you cruel when you slaughter an animal so you can eat?"

Lawrence never looked away from Roni. "I had to give them something precious to me, and nothing has ever been more precious than you. It wasn't supposed to be much, though. Just a single moment."

"Something went wrong," she said. "I know that now."

"When I returned and ever since, I haven't been completely in my right mind. I wanted to tell you the truth, all of it, but Gram refused. She had lost her daughter, and she was determined to protect you from the Parallel Society."

Roni thought about their recent experiences in Ireland, about discovering that Gram's daughter had been split — part of Maria locked in another universe, part of her to be raised by a guilty and grieving mother. "It was more than that. I'm all that she had left."

"I couldn't cope. Checked into Belmont and waited. The longer it went on, the years passing by, I had to face the fact that I had failed. That your mother might be trapped forever and it was my fault. My madness spiraled. The only thing tethering me to reality was you. Yet even that made me think I had lost everything. Many times, when you'd visit and I'd see the pity in your eyes and the hollowness in your thoughts, I knew that you'd never forgive all we had taken from you. Taken and never returned. Then, a few days ago, I finally heard from her. You and I both heard from her."

Roni stepped onto the wood floor and stared out at the Keeper. "Mom?"

The face staring back warped between the vile hatred of the old Keeper and the fierce love of a missing mother. Roni burst into tears, dropped to floor, howling at all the years lost to this monstrosity. Living with gaps in her memory had always been painful, but now a hole burned through her heart. So much anger and bitterness had filled the hollow within her, and all of it had redirected to fighting her teachers, her friends, the world, Gram.

Chak walked forward. "Oh, I do not like this part. Too much wailing. Yes, yes, it's very sad, but there are joyful things ahead for us all. If your father had stayed here like I hoped he would, he would never have lost his mind. He would have had a wonderful life. We would have played games and discussed philosophy and anything we could dream up, it would have been our reality for a time. I have had to endure for so many years while these two Keepers battled each other. Quite annoying, I don't mind telling you. But, thankfully, that time has come to an end."

Roni looked up at her father. "What's he talking about?"

Lawrence helped her up. "The reason I'm back here — it's time to finish all of this. I'm going through. I'm going to push your mother free and become the Keeper. Like I should have done all along."

"And what? You'll be stuck here? For centuries? Just talking with Chak?"

"This isn't about me."

Roni dried her eyes as she turned to Chak. "What happens to my mother?"

"She'll return to her body, of course," Chak said. "What would you expect?"

"But there isn't a body anymore. It's long gone."

"Oh. Well, then, I suppose she'll be done. Whatever part of her exists in the Keeper will go on to whatever awaits all upon death. Huh. I wonder if that's why the Keepers always fight so hard to stay around."

Lawrence pulled her around to face him again. "Don't think about that. Your mother died back when you were little. Not a car crash like we told you, but she died nonetheless. I'm here now to free her soul. You understand?"

With a thoughtful nod, she said, "When you step into the Keeper, then you'll die, too."

"Sorry about that. But I can't let your mother suffer any longer. It's my turn."

"But maybe if we —"

He brought her into a tight embrace and pressed his mouth against her ear. Whispering, he said, "When your mother called us, she put more in my head than a map to get here. She had plenty of years to work this out, and she told me what to do. Chak and the Keeper need each other to live. When I free your mother, the old Keeper will try to continue the fight with me. But I'm going to take control, and I'm going to break free from the Cave. I'll fight that thing non-stop until I sever the connection with Chak. It'll kill Chak. Kill him so that this never happens again to anybody. Then I simply have to find a safe place to die and end the Keeper forever. Your mother showed me how to do it all. So, please, let me make this right."

She tightened her arms around him. He managed a strained noise that somehow felt more personal, closer, as if the noise were spoken by his heart directly.

"Lawrence, please," the Keeper said.

Roni's father pushed away. "Your mother can't hold on forever. And Chak wants a friend for the next few centuries."

"I certainly do." Chak took an eager step closer.

"Good bye, my sweet, sweet daughter. All of my love is for you." To Chak, Lawrence said, "I'm ready. Send Roni out of here. Back to her body in the Cave. Once you do that, I'll step through."

"Consider it done."

A thousand questions and emotions flooded Roni, but Chak snapped his fingers with a dramatic flourish. And all went dark.

CHAPTER 27

The Keeper leaned closer to Roni and contorted its lips into an approximation of a fatherly smile. "Yes, my sweet, sweet daughter. You remember now?"

She shivered. Turned out that Elliot had been right — more than he knew. Because even letting her Lost Time return at its own pace, she still suffered. The memories pierced through any defenses remaining and split into her emotions. She needed to cry and scream and rage. She needed to hold Gram close and wordlessly love her. Elliot and Sully, too. Poor Sully.

If the Keeper had not spoken then, Roni's mind would have rocketed off into an abyss of love and regret. But the Keeper said, "I've done all I can. There's no more fight in me."

Roni stroked the Keeper's cheek. "You've done a great job. Chak is gone. Dead. And you've held back the old Keeper long enough."

"I think she knows it's over, too. She's not fighting me as hard."

"You shouldn't have to struggle."

Behind the Keeper, Roni spotted Gram and Elliot taking a position not too far away. Gram lugged the large book she had created and angled it toward the Keeper.

"We tried," the Keeper said. "Your mother and I tried our best to look after you. But we were always too reckless. None of this would have happened if we had been smarter about it all. I know I keep saying it, but I'm sorry."

"It's okay."

"Far from it. I'm glad you know what really happened. You can stop blaming yourself or Gram or whoever you shake a fist at. The fault was your parents. When it comes to your Lost Time — that blame belongs on me."

Teanna and Gully had moved behind Gram. With a swift motion of his cane, Elliot lowered the dome and sidestepped away. They all looked to Roni.

With a voice that sounded more like her father than ever, the Keeper said, "It's time, isn't it? I see it on your face. They're all ready to get rid of me. Well, I guess I'm ready, too. I hope it doesn't hurt."

Roni tried to offer some comforting words, but the sentiment stuck in her throat. Her eyes darted to the group and back to the Keeper. She had to signal Gram — they waited for her to do so — but her body refused to move.

The Keeper said, "Don't worry. I've got this." Lifting its head back, it said, "Okay, Gram. Have at it."

Gram looked straight at Roni with those eyes that always meant it was time for Roni to do what was right. Whether it involved fessing up to something she had done as a child, standing up for another as a teen, or making the hardest call of her life, Roni knew Gram would never back off with that look. Clearing her eyes, Roni straightened her back and returned Gram's steady gaze. She clasped the trunk of a nearby tree, and with a firm motion, she nodded.

Gram opened the book.

A whoosh of wind. A shake in the ground. And the book vacuumed in the air.

Roni felt the draw on her skin, but the Keeper's massive body blocked the brunt of the pulling air. The Keeper watched Roni as it slipped closer toward the book. A solemn acceptance on its face.

She had never seen a living relic enter a book with such ease. Usually, the creatures would claw and scrabble against the forces dragging them away. But her father's acceptance, his insistence on ending the Keeper, meant he practically walked into the book.

Until part of him — the old Keeper part — awoke. She hungered to stay, to remain as long as possible. Each step toward the open book required a strain of muscle fighting against muscle. Easy for one step. Struggling for the next.

Roni witnessed the battle on the Keeper's face. At moments, she watched her father's grim, determined smile as he progressed toward the book. An instant later, the old Keeper's dark scowl covered its face as she dug her feet into the riverbed, trying to push back toward Roni.

"Goodbye," Roni whispered.

With a final shriek, the old Keeper leapt forward. Two of its arms thrust out and one hand snagged hold of Roni's shirt. Roni's shocked cry vanished into the rising winds of the book.

Snarling, the old Keeper said, "If I die, then you'll die, too."

Roni leaned away, feeling the seams of her sleeve rip. The Keeper growled. The shirt ripped more, each tear like crinkling paper, but the Keeper latched onto Roni's shoulder with a second hand.

Roni gripped the rough bark of the tree trunk. She peeked over at Gram. Elliot flailed his arm as he yelled at her, but Gram kept the book open, kept her focus on the Keeper. Roni actually felt a slice of pride — Gram trusted Roni, trusted the team, to end this well.

Indeed, Gully and Teanna raced forward from either side of the Keeper. Gully arrived first, his feet flattening around the stones to keep from falling into the open book. When he reached the tree, his clay hands morphed around the Keeper's fingers that locked a knot in Roni' shirt. He tried to pry them loose but they wouldn't budge.

Teanna sprinted over, wielding her axes and uttering a proud war cry. She dashed from tree to tree, keeping the thick trunks between herself and the vortex of air pulling into another universe. When she arrived, she lifted her axes high. Three strong swings and she hacked off the hand holding Roni's shoulder. As Roni fell against the tree trunk, long shreds of her shirt tore away. Teanna clasped Roni's arm, and the two wrapped around the tree together, holding each other in place.

The Keeper stumbled backward like an awkward toddler. The book wrenched her in. Gully stood firm, his clay feet locked to the rocks, and watched Roni closely, ready to catch her should she accidentally slip loose.

Seconds later, the howling winds and the unnatural depressurization ceased. Gram had closed the book. All became still.

Quiet.

A bird warbled a tentative tune. Seconds later, another. A few more birds joined in. Soon, insects and frogs and all of the woodland creatures returned to their normal ruckus.

As Roni willed herself to let go of the tree, she saw Gram wrapping the book with chains. Teanna hopped over to Gully, and the two hurried to join Gram and Elliot. With the book secured, they all waited for Roni. They clearly wanted to give her some space, a private moment to deal with the immediate feelings of watching her father — or a thing that was partly her father — leave her world forever.

But Roni walked toward them with her head up and her arms open and welcome. "Don't look so shocked. I've been dealing with this my whole life. Finally, it's over. You know what? Feels damn good."

Gram frowned and softly said, "Language."

CHAPTER 28

When she managed to open her eyes, she saw only white. She coughed and the white fluttered askew — a cloth had veiled her face. She reached up to remove it causing thick aches to roll along her muscles. She groaned.

Pulling the cloth away, she gazed at the uneven ceiling of a large cave. It oscillated as if hundreds of creatures clung above. But as her eyes focused, she saw that they were chains. Thick, heavy chains. And what appeared to be books. Chained books bumping against the ceiling like abandoned balloons.

In a limp voice, she said, "What the hell is going on?"

A second later, Elliot's comforting face looked down at her. His dark, wrinkled skin and his broad, careful smile enveloped her like a favorite blanket. He put out his hand and helped her sit up. "We are happy to see you alive," he said, his deep and precise way of speaking like a pleasant song.

CHAPTER 29

Sitting in Sully's hospital room, listening to the murmurs of nurses as they walked the halls, Roni closed her eyes and thought about that first moment waking in the Cave. She had insisted, threatened, bullied, tried so hard to push Elliot into rushing her memories back. Even when she finally agreed to back off, she still wanted to press forward. Well, she would have to get him a big Thank You gift. Had he relented, she would never have believed everything that happened. Or worse, Elliot's predictions might have proved true and she would have lost her sanity.

The rest of her memories had returned — at least, she thought the rest had. Each hour brought moments in her life that felt both new and as if they had always been there. A birthday cake her mom had worked too hard on. Curling up with her mom for a bedtime story. Crying about a bully at school and listening to her mom's comforting words.

Her mother had risen from an empty grave, and though Roni knew that someday these memories would simply be the way things were, for the time being, they were as close to a living moment as she could hope for.

"I'm so very proud of you," Sully's weak voice said.

Roni sat closer and clasped his thin hand. "I don't know what for. Seems like most of the decisions I made were the wrong ones."

"But you made a decision. That's half the job. The other is learning to listen to your team, but that takes time."

She thought of Elliot. "I'm learning that one, too. Maybe someday I'll be ready for all this."

Sully pushed his glasses up his nose — they looked enormous on his shrunken face. "No *someday* about it. You're ready."

"No, no. You'll be released in a day or two. We'll see that you get plenty of rest, but the Parallel Society needs you."

"You did fine with a golem that only had a quarter of my mind. I'm not quitting the Society, but I'm not going to fool myself into thinking I can still lead. That would be selfish. And dangerous, too, for the rest of you."

He reached towards his bedside table, but his hand fumbled about without any clear control. Roni leaned over and helped. When he nodded at a small piece of paper, she handed it to him. But he pushed it back towards her.

Glancing at the page, Roni saw tiny, handwritten Hebrew. "Another golem?"

"Same one. Now, what did you name my alter-ego?"

"Gully."

The old man rubbed his ear and cocked his head closer to her. "You had the chance to name him anything, and you just switched the letter of my first name with a G? For Golem? Oy. You did not put much effort into that, did you?"

Roni chuckled. "We were under a bit of pressure at the time. You know — trying to stop the Keeper."

"Fine, fine. I made the golem for you, and you have the right to name him whatever you want. Who am I to say otherwise? Anyway, take that page, and you put that into this poorly-named Gully, but don't remove the instructions he already has. Over the next few weeks, once I'm done repairing all the damage that poor fellow has taken, I'll keep adding more instructions into his brain. We have to make sure he's ready to help you no matter what happens to me."

"Don't talk like that."

"What? Should I deny reality just because it's uncomfortable? Nonsense. We're the Parallel Society. We fight to preserve our entire universe. You think I should be afraid to talk about my death? At my age? And after I had a heart attack? Don't be silly. That would be letting down all I've fought for most of my life."

Roni folded the paper and stuck it in her pocket. "Fine. I'll make sure all of your golem instructions get put into Gully."

"Thank you."

"But you have to promise not to give up. Like you said, we face down all sorts of dangers to save our universe. Quitting is never an option for us. Right?"

"You've got that right." Sully smiled, and it warmed Roni's soul. "So, together we'll get Gully in shape, and you will accept that you are now the leader of the group. Which leaves two matters, both highly important."

Part of Roni wanted to postpone any further serious discussions. She would rather cuddle with her Uncle Sully, watch some television, and let him rest. But he would never relax until they dealt with everything on his mental agenda. "Okay. What else?"

"First, there's the new girl, Teanna."

"Hardly a girl."

"You have to do more than lead the team with her. She's lost everything and is in an entirely new universe. Ease her into it all."

"I will. And the second thing?"

Sully's friendly smile drew down. "Now that you know the truth, I want to tell you something about the time you lost your memories."

Roni tensed but remained quiet.

"This is between the two of us," he went on. "Elliot doesn't know my suspicions, and the one time I tried to discuss it with Gram, she stopped listening. She didn't want to hear me because, if I'm right, then we are partially to blame."

"My father traded my memories. Not you."

"Don't interrupt. Now, you know there are relics in our universe. There are relics in all universes, probably. But what you don't know is that there is a living relic here, too."

Roni's stomach flipped.

Sully said, "This creature goes by the name of Yal-hara and she's very dangerous. Gram and I should have gotten rid of her long ago, but we made poor decisions."

Though he continued to talk, Roni did not hear a single word. She didn't need to. The spindle-legged creature that swiped her memories, the horrid creature that botched the job and hurt her well beyond the price her father had agreed to pay, that creature was Yal-hara.

While Sully rambled on, the coals of Roni's anger heated up. Yal-hara and her prick of a representative, Kenneth Bay, dared to threaten her, tell her she had made an enemy of them. Yet all this time, they knew what they had done to her. Well, Yal-hara had one thing right. They were enemies now.

An hour later, she returned to the bookstore. A large plastic sheet had been taped across the open wall and it fluttered with every car that sped by. Gram said she had two contractors coming in the morning to give her bids. Elliot and Gully had created two large piles of books — those salvageable and those damaged beyond hope.

Roni settled next to Teanna at the big table. Teanna had spent hours on the internet learning all she could about the world she now inhabited. For the last few nights, she had been sleeping on the store's office couch, waking bleary-eyed and achy from late-night googling sessions, but nobody thought that would be a good permanent solution.

"You holding up?" Roni asked.

Teanna shrugged. "Apparently, people with dark skin like mine are called *black people* or in this country, *African-Americans*. They don't seem to be treated very well."

"Yeah. That's a long, ugly story. But a lot of people are trying to fix that. More important for you, right now, is how we're going to fix your living situation. I was thinking you could move in with me. I have an apartment a few blocks away. And since I'm now the Society's leader, it might be good for us both to spend more time together. Get to know each other's strengths."

"Makes sense." Teanna closed the laptop. "One thing, though. If I'm going to become part of your Parallel Society, then I need to know you'll do everything you can to help me."

"You have my word. If we can find a way to get you back to your universe, we'll do it."

"Thank you, but that's not what I meant. Not entirely."

"What then?"

"I was raised to fulfill one task — I'm a tracker. My life as a Protector is gone. But as part of the Parallel Society, I could be of great value, if you'll let me."

"Isn't that what we're talking about?"

"I mean if you'll let me continue as a tracker. I'm trained to find relics. This universe has too many. I need your word that you'll stop letting these things slip by, that we'll clean them up and send them away. I need your word that we'll hunt down all the relics, including the living ones, and take care of them, too."

Roni took Teanna by the hand. "I couldn't agree more. And I know just the living relic we need to start with."

PAGES OF GLASS

THE PARALLEL SOCIETY BOOK 5

Chapter 1

The wild thumping bass reverberated throughout the club as colorful lights swirled with hypnotic intensity. Roni swirled, too. Spinning on the dancefloor, her dress pinwheeling with the motion, she let her head fall back and her mouth hang open. Off to the right, Teanna jiggled a move of her own creation.

"I like clubbing," Teanna shouted above the music. For a woman from another universe, she had adapted to Earth quite fast. She loved the hodgepodge of cultures clashing together and the vibrant mixtures that grew out of it. And the food — Teanna could not get enough of the variety of tastes available. "You live like royalty," she had said the first time they drove into Philly to go dancing.

Roni had laughed that time. Even when her thoughts turned to the uglier sides of existence, she found that her new friend — and roommate — had a fresh perspective that brightened things. Teanna had not been raised in a life that punished her for having dark skin or a vibrant personality. To Roni, it meant the world did not have to be stagnant.

"I'm going to the restroom," Teanna said and disappeared into the throngs of dancing bodies.

She was tough. Roni would never go to the restrooms alone in a place like this, but Teanna had been taught from an early age to stand her ground. After all, she had been raised with the expectation that, should she be called upon, she would be ready to fight off the creatures that might invade her universe from the others.

Roni spun again as the music dropped before thumping even louder. It had been nearly a year since venturing into the Caverns to find the Keeper, nearly a year since meeting Teanna there and having her join the Parallel Society, nearly a year since Roni's missing memories — her *Lost Time* — had been restored. Before that, Roni would have been jealous at the thought of someone like Teanna benefiting from such an upbringing. Roni's early life had been obscured from the truth — from the Parallel Society and all her family's connections to it.

Not anymore, though. She finally felt free. And real. As if the girl she had been before could never become a full person. But now she had a chance to understand her true nature, to see if her past might shape her thoughts, and maybe to let it influence her future. Coupled with Teanna's exuberance for this new world, the two acted like college co-eds finally unleashed from a strict family yoke. Any free night, they drove into Philly. They drank and danced, filling their time with overly-enthusiastic giggling and feeling a growing bond.

Teanna returned with two shot glasses of sloshing liquid. She picked up dancing next to Roni right with the beat. Roni whipped her body around and let the music gratify. She hadn't worried that Teanna would be unable to find her in this wall of people. After all, Teanna was a gifted tracker — one of the reasons she brought value to the Society.

But even with Teanna's ability to track relics from other universes trapped on Earth, work had been sluggish of late. They had come across nothing which Roni would call exciting. Gram said that when they did their jobs right, things often grew quiet and uneventful. *Be glad for it,* she had said. Roni tried. Every night that she and Teanna went clubbing, she tried.

Two men in expensive sports coats and cheap T-shirts kept looking in Roni's direction. Dancing as they approached, drinks in hand, they split to encircle the ladies. The one in front of Roni — tall, blond, cute — moved in rhythm with her, managing to hold his attention on her face despite her low neckline. A glance behind, Roni saw a shorter man — though still taller than Teanna. He had a richer complexion and a more urgent gleam in his eye.

Roni had tried to explain flirting on several occasions, but Teanna merely laughed. "Why do your people play such games? Is it fun?"

"Not usually. Even when you both like each other, it's often confusing."

"In my world, if I want a man, I tell him so. Simple as that."

"And if he says *No?*"

Teanna mocked surprise. "What man would say *No* to me?"

Less than a year on Earth, and Teanna's attitude had blossomed into grand arrogance. "You might be more American than you ever knew,"

Roni had said before returning to the problems of flirting.

But no matter how many times they went over it, she could not get Teanna to be more cautious with the signals she sent. Teanna listened. She wanted to understand. She even tried. Yet in the moment, she just couldn't see what a gentle look over the shoulder might signify.

Her dance partner clearly thought otherwise. When he moved in close, placing one hand on Teanna's hip, he raised his lips into a wolfish grin. She slipped a hand around his neck and pushed in for a kiss. Roni took over. She smiled at the men, thanked them for the dance, grabbed Teanna, and headed for the door.

"What are you doing?" Teanna asked, as she tottered in her heels. "I liked that one."

"I could tell." She burst out onto the sidewalk, letting the night air cool them down, clear their heads. "It's only been a few months of dancing, and you've never shown the guys much interest."

"Most of your men don't glow with such inner-strength."

"We're going to have a little talk about birth control. Then you can enjoy all the glowing strength you want. But not before that. No way do you want to explain to Gram that you're pregnant. And as leader, I'll take even more of the blame."

Under the rapid fire of their heels against the pavement, they crossed the parking lot toward Roni's dirty, dented car. As she pulled out her keys, she heard the sturdy footsteps approaching.

"Hey girls," Blondie said as he and Mr. Hands moved in. "Why'd you leave us? I thought we were having a good time."

"Sorry," Roni said. "We've got work in the morning."

"That's a shame," Mr. Hands said, leaning one arm on the car as he pressed closer to Teanna. "I thought you and I had a real connection going."

Blondie stepped in front of Roni, blocking her exits. "And we barely got started. But I could tell by your dancing that you were raring to go. That's why we came out here. Right, Nick?"

Nick's hand went to Teanna's waist. "Yeah, we knew you were the kind of girls who wanted to have a real party."

"Ain't that right?" Blondie asked Roni. "Let's have a party."

"No," she said. "We're not interested. And if you don't back off —"

"What? You really think you can get away with that? Move like that on the dance floor, getting guys like me all worked up, and you think you can then just walk away? That's not very nice."

Roni clutched her hands tight to keep them from shaking. "Don't do this. I'm warning you."

Blondie laughed and Nick followed. "Guess we won't be playing the nice way."

He slapped Roni, pulled his hand back for a second strike but never got the chance. Roni barely had time to touch her stinging cheek when Teanna had kneed Nick in the groin, spun aside to elbow Blondie in the back at the kidneys, wrenched open the car door, and pulled out her favorite weapons — two hatchets. With one of the mini-axes pointed at each man, she sneered.

If Roni's heart had not been pounding, she would have laughed as the men scurried off, muttering about *insane bitches* until they were far enough away that they felt safe. Then Blondie gave them the finger, and the men hastened back into the club.

"Are you okay?" Teanna asked.

Roni nodded. "Let's go home. I think I've had enough dancing for a bit. I could use some peace."

She reached for the car door when she saw a strange flash from down an alley. Like green-tinted lightning. Like something from the Caverns.

"What's wrong?" Teanna asked, following her gaze. "Oh."

Without a further word, they walked toward the alley. In each step, Roni felt the world pressing closer, promising that her life would never be simple or normal or even practical. There might be moments when she could spend the night dancing, when she could forget her job and its grave responsibilities, but always, her reality would return. Always, she would have to lead the Parallel Society in its fight against other universes.

Yet I can't even go dancing without having Teanna save me.

They moved with great caution, Roni at the front and Teanna behind, brandishing her hatchets. Probably should be the other way around, but Roni expected to see what most rifts looked like — a gash in the air, a wound in the world that strobed light and gusted wind from a different world. However, about halfway down the alley, the green lightning flashed around an upcoming corner, and they heard a man cry out for help.

Teanna pushed ahead of Roni, moving faster down the rest of the alley. Roni glanced back. If those bastards from the club returned and tried to corner them, she would have to convince them to run away — she'd rather convince them to jump into the rift, but being a jerk did not deserve a death sentence. Roni and Teanna pressed on.

When they turned the corner, they stood in a wide service street lined with loading docks, beaten dumpsters, and a few parked trucks. In the center of this street, Roni saw a Hispanic man, early-forties, on his back and shimmying toward them. Further down, a glowing green centipede reared back like a cobra — a six-foot tall cobra — and let out a chittering that jangled along Roni's spine.

So much for getting home in peace.

CHAPTER 2

Teanna launched ahead with a war cry that pulled the creature's attention. She kicked off her heels as she moved up onto the nearest loading dock. In a non-stop, graceful motion, she sprinted to the end, leapt into the air, and landed on the giant centipede's side, digging in with her hatchets.

"Over here," Roni said to the man on the ground while the creature shrieked.

Like a terrified rabbit knowing it was surrounded by predators, the man's head darted from one direction to another. When he finally settled on Roni, he squinted as if he couldn't understand why a woman dressed for dancing was waving for him to follow.

"Hurry," she snapped.

Something in her voice must have clicked with him. He scrambled across the street toward her. Behind him, the centipede whipped its body about but could not dislodge Teanna. Not yet. Roni had no doubt that given enough time, it would win that bronco ride.

Taking the man's hand, she hustled him back down the alley. She heard his strained breathing and prayed that he didn't have a heart attack. Calling an ambulance would slow her down and risk Teanna's life.

"You okay?" she asked, trying to see if he could think or talk.

The man nodded. "Eddie Garcia. Just call me Garcia. Thank you for helping me. I don't know how that happened." He bent over, putting his hands on his knees. After one long breath, he popped straight back. "Your friend. We can't leave her."

Maybe he could think too much. "I'm not leaving her," Roni said, guiding Garcia to her car. Finally able to take a look at him, she saw a sturdy man shaken by what he had witnessed. Tall, a little paunch, graying at the temples, and wearing a sweat-soaked white button-down and a tan sport coat — he may have been a college professor fallen on hard times or an aimless soul gearing up for another job interview.

She opened the trunk, kicked off her heels, and slipped on a pair of sneakers. "You've had a fright. But it's over now. You need to leave. Go home."

"That thing —"

She dug around the trunk, pushing aside greasy fast-food bags, a chipped tire iron, and an aluminum baseball bat. Pulling out a small book with a thin chain around it, she said, "We'll handle that thing. Besides, by the time you get to wherever you live, you'll realize that none of what you saw makes any sense. It couldn't possibly have happened. Maybe you drank too much tonight."

"But —"

"Heck, I probably don't exist. Do you really think you were attacked by a glowing centipede and saved by two women in high heels? Goodnight, Garcia." She slammed the trunk shut and dashed back down the alley.

When Roni reached the service road, she spotted Teanna forward-rolling across the pavement toward her — a trail of green centipede blood following along. The creature shot after Teanna, but the well-trained warrior shifted to the side, letting the beast pass right by. Cool move, but it meant the centipede headed closer to Roni. A stream of its blood rushed down its side.

"Anytime would be good," Teanna said, the clipped pronunciation of her mother tongue slipping through.

Roni ripped off Gram's chain and turned the book towards the centipede. "Get behind me," she shouted.

Teanna took another chunk of flesh from the beast's side, distracting and confusing its tiny brain. As it looped back on itself, spraying blood across one loading dock like green graffiti, Teanna raced straight for Roni. The chittering noise intensified as the creature reoriented. With a sharp jab, it lunged for them both.

Roni widened her stance and held the book firm as if she aimed a handgun. Her pulse quickened. Her concentration narrowed. For a breath, the world ceased to exist — all but Teanna and the monster barreling upon them. As Teanna glided by, Roni opened the book.

Though small — the size of a trade paperback — the book connected to a stormy world at a high altitude. The difference in pressure sucked in the air like a high-powered vacuum. She saw the change in the centipede's beady eyes. Those tiny black dots grew enough to tell her — the thing knew it was screwed.

It tried to scramble off to the side. It tried to latch onto the metal posts that stopped trucks from backing across the docks. It tried. But wherever it moved, Roni merely had to shift her arms to keep the creature within range of the book. And though this beast was far larger than the book itself, the book was far stronger.

As it slipped closer, its body stretched out — longer, thinner. By the time the book's vortex claimed it, the centipede had become a sinewy line that sucked into the book like a child slurping up spaghetti. A bit jagged for spaghetti, perhaps, but as Roni slammed the book shut and wrapped the chain around it once more, she figured her mind could use whatever metaphors it needed to make sense of what she had experienced.

"That went well enough," she said, turning back toward Teanna.

But her stomach dropped. Garcia stood, his mouth agape. With a torn dress and cuts on her arms, Teanna glanced from him to Roni and back. She shrugged, waiting for Roni to say something.

Indeed, Roni wanted to say something, some lie that would help Garcia dismiss any bit of what he had glimpsed. But the man's trembling chin suggested he would have a hard time accepting the usual excuses. If he could accept any at all.

Forcing a relaxed grin, Roni approached. "I'm sure you're a bit confused right now."

But Garcia rushed ahead, gingerly stepping over the leftover gore on the street, and picked up a small, rectangular object no bigger than a pillbox. Pocketing the box, he turned back to Roni and his mouth raised at the corners. His eyes lifted, too. He let out a whoop. "I knew it. Finally! You're really them. I can't believe it. You're the Parallel Society."

Roni stuttered back a step. *Oh, shit.*

CHAPTER 3

Over the next several hours, Roni felt trapped in a whirlwind of phone calls, driving, and strange silence. The calls went back and forth with Gram to explain what little they knew of Garcia and what very little they could do about him. Though Roni led the team, she stood on unfamiliar ground, so she deferred to Gram's experience.

"Bring him back to Olburg. We'll set up a place to meet and evaluate him from there." Gram's tone betrayed her concerns. Roni had hoped to hear a nonchalant response that suggested all of this was normal, had happened before, and they could follow a simple time-tested procedure. Not so, apparently.

The drive back, with Garcia following in his sleek (and clean) Prius Prime, was quiet. Teanna, usually a bubble of chatter after a night dancing, said nothing as she tapped her fist against the passenger window. Philly traffic was light leaving the city, and as they neared Olburg, Gram texted that they would meet in the Ol' Olburg Gallery — a local art gallery not far from the family bookstore.

And so, shortly after, Roni stood in the main hall of the old gallery, the same one Elliot had taken her to when she had first learned of the Parallel Society. She had not been back since, yet it looked the same. Walls covered in paintings by local artists and a few sculptures haphazardly placed at different sections of the floorspace. Some of the art was good. Some very bad. Possibly the gallery showcased the same paintings as were here years ago. Not a lot of art connoisseurs in Olburg.

She understood the reason for picking an offsite location. With the Caverns underneath the bookstore, Gram did not want to risk bringing in a stranger who knew about their real purpose until she had vetted him. The Ol' Olburg Gallery was a known place for privacy, a place which Elliot's magic could easily unlock the doors, and it wasn't too far from the bookstore — a big consideration now that Sully was stuck in a wheelchair.

When the Old Gang arrived, Roni smiled — they had brought Gully along, too. The golem wore a trench coat and a red ski hat to hide his features. While Sully had made him closer to human than any golem ever before, he still looked like a golem. The clay and stone used to shape him, the carved features that would never age, the way he appeared young yet spoke like an old, Jewish man — he would draw attention when out in public if he didn't disguise a bit.

He was the pride of his creator. Normally, Sully brought a golem to life by lodging a slip of paper into his design with instructions written in Hebrew. Nothing complicated. Enough to get the job done, whatever that job may be. He then whispered into the golem and the creature came to life.

But with Gully, the old man had outdone himself. He had built a surrogate Sully and over the last year had continued to add more and more instructions. A novella's worth at this point. All of which altered Gully into something greater than a mere golem — even if not quite human.

"Don't worry about the golem being here," Gram said, pulling Roni in for a thick hug. Roni hadn't been worried, but she should have been. Gully was their vigilant sentry. Her first thought should have been concern for the Caverns. And having Gram point that out only served to remind Roni that she had yet to truly become a good leader.

As she let those words lump in her stomach, Gram said, "Elliot has cast a spell on the bookstore to alarm us if anybody tries to get in. We've got it all covered."

Elliot stood tall, melding with the shadows, and he gestured back toward the street with his old, gnarled cane. "Once we finish all the renovations, then we'll put in place a more traditional security system."

A year since the bookstore had been demolished by an enormous (and enormously angry) creature, yet they still had more work to do. Hard to pay for repairs when you can't open the store to make money. Of course, the Parallel Society had plenty of coffers filled from centuries of work protecting the world, but they still had to make it look like they were struggling to pay for everything or people might get suspicious.

Garcia rushed up to Elliot and shook hands. "It's an honor to meet you. *Mi madre* would never believe me if I told her that I stood before you fine people. The great spellcaster who can heal the broken." He bent over Gram's hand and kissed the back of it. "Does it hurt when you make the chains that bind the books?" He even shook Gully's hand. "You are real. Of course, I knew Mr. Sully could make such things as yourself, but to see it firsthand — remarkable."

Gram sat on the cushioned bench meant for observing a large painting of Amish farmers raising a barn, adjusted her necklace so the crucifix rested on the shelf of her bosom, and let out a long sigh. She folded her hands in her lap. With a stern appraisal, she said, "Well, Mr. Garcia, I think you better start explaining yourself."

Standing straighter, Garcia adjusted his coat. "Yes, I think so. Um, where should I begin?"

"Wherever will explain who you are, where you're from, and how you know about us."

"Sure. That makes sense. Sorry, I'm a bit nervous. It's not usual that you get to meet people as important as you."

Gram waved away the flattery. "Get on with it now. It's late, and we're old."

With a shaky nod, he said, "My name is Edward Olmos Garcia. My mother was big fan of the actor. But I go by Eddie. Well, actually, most friends call me Garcia and that's what I prefer. My father is from Honduras and my mother is from Florida. They met in Paris, if you can believe that. Both were exchange students in college. They fell in love, got married, and had me. My father taught English literature at Florida State and my mother worked at a medical lab testing facility in Tallahassee. So, that's where I'm from."

Sully chuckled. "You could've just said *Florida*."

His voice rasped, and the little joke appeared to exhaust him. Roni wanted to rush over and wrap her arms around the old man, but she held back. While Sully would be happy for the gesture, he would be ticked off at the timing. Right now was about Garcia and the Parallel Society. Sully only meant to help ease Garcia with the joke, not elicit sympathy.

Clearing his throat, Garcia went on. "My upbringing was about as normal as you can get as a Hispanic man in America. Better than most. My parents earned well, so I lived a solid middle-class life. All quite normal."

Elliot said, "It cannot be entirely normal since you are aware of our existence."

"That would be my grandpa's fault. He had lived in the same small village in Honduras that he was born in. Same one he raised my father in. I visited several times, but mostly, he traveled to Florida to visit us. I think he liked to see America the same way most of us like to visit Disneyworld. In those times when I saw him, he would tell me all the old fables and legends. Some like *la mula herrada* — the Iron Mule — were known to all children from Central American countries. But others were specific to him and his village. So, when he first told me the truth about the Parallel Society, I assumed it was a story unique to his home."

"What changed?" Gram asked.

"He did. The older he got, the more he focused on you. All the other stories drifted away and the only thing he would talk to me about was the Parallel Society. Shortly before he died, he confided in me that once, when he was a boy, he saw you by the beach. He saw the chains come from your sleeves, one of the books, and even a little golem made of sand and stone. I didn't think much of it. I figured he saw something as a kid that stayed with him, but monster-fighting universe protectors? That didn't sound likely. He must have been able to read the doubt on my face because he grabbed me, and I'll never forget how he had such strength even as he neared death. He said that it was all true and he could prove it. In his bedroom in Honduras, he still held the proof."

Roni made sure to observe how each member of the Society reacted. Sully and Elliot listened with careful consideration. Gram had crossed her arms — a sure sign of skepticism. Teanna stood against the back wall, arms at her sides, ready for action as she watched every slight move Garcia made. And Gully — well, he had no physical expressions. He was a golem. But Roni grinned inwardly at the idea that she had looked his way. He was a member of the team. Always.

"At this point," Garcia continued, "I still didn't believe. But I can't say I disbelieved, either. I loved my grandpa, and when he told me that he had proof, he spoke with such clarity, such conviction, that I couldn't dismiss his words entirely. After he passed, I went to Honduras for the funeral and made sure to visit his home. What I found slipped beneath his mattress was a sliver of paper with Hebrew writing on it. I didn't need to have it translated, though later I would do so, because I knew it right then — this was one of Sully's instruction papers for a golem.

"With that, I started a long journey to find you. At the same time, I studied the one thing Grandpa begged me to study — potions."

"Potions?" Roni said. To Gram: "Is that a thing?"

She nodded. "Rare. But yes. It's real."

Garcia went on, "Grandpa taught me the basic concepts when I was little. I didn't pay much attention back then, but I did recall that the most knowledgeable potion-makers could be found in Egypt. I cashed in everything I had and headed for Cairo. That's a whole long story of its own and as you've pointed out, it's late and you're all tired. Suffice it to say that I found one of the last potion-makers alive, and she taught me what she could. I've been learning on my own ever since. I also started travelling to wherever I heard about strange happenings or the tiniest hint that you might be in a location. While in Japan, I found this." He produced the palm-sized, rectangular box swiped at the loading docks. "At the time, it had a lid — almost like a miniature sarcophagus. The writing on it is in no known language that I can find, so I suspected it might be from another universe. An artifact that got stuck in ours."

"We call them *relics*," Gram said.

"It's a good term. Well, this relic took me to Rome when I still hoped somebody might decipher the writing. I thought it might be some dead language a member of the Vatican could translate. No such luck, of course, but while I was there, rumors ran around about strange events surrounding an abbey in Ireland that sounded exactly like what I wanted. That was the closest I'd ever been to you all, and I have spent the last couple years working off all the clues I could find there. Eventually, I traced you back to the States and, after a little more legwork, to the Philadelphia area."

Roni said, "Then showing up at the club — that wasn't an accident."

"Not at all. I had strong suspicions you were involved with the Society."

"And that living relic which attacked you? How did you set that up?"

"I didn't. Not exactly, anyway. I had thought the existence of a relic might get your attention. At that point, I knew you had been to the Abbey, so I planned to approach you when you left the club that night. But I only wanted to show you the box. I didn't know about what was inside it, or that there was anything inside it at all. As I waited, the relic box began to glow. I didn't know what was happening or if it might be dangerous. I thought it might be like a bomb. I ran back to the loading docks and set it on the street. That giant creature burst out of it. I certainly didn't intend for that. You see —"

"Didn't intend? You were drawing us out and risking lives to do it. What if you were wrong about us? That thing could have killed a lot of people."

Garcia's face tightened, but instead of yelling back, he exhaled slowly. Then: "I have trained for years. I have searched for years. I know a lot about the Society, its goals, its purpose. I sought you with the hope that I might join you and help prevent the loss of life in our world."

"You were reckless and foolish. As leader of this group, I have to watch out for our safety as well as those of the rest of the world. I'm sorry, but you are clearly not right for this work. The answer is no."

Gram sniffed sharply to pull their attention. "Well, that's one answer. I, for one, think Mr. Garcia should stay. What do the rest of you think?"

Roni felt the fire race up her neck as she sprang to her feet. "What the heck is going on here?"

CHAPTER 4

"I'm the leader," Roni said, trying hard not to shout.

"But not a dictator." Gram reclined in her seat as if taking in some of the artwork. "If you recall, when I was leader, I did not want you to be part of all this. Yet here you are." She raised her index finger. "This is how it's really done. How it should have been done with you. We all must work together, so we all must get a say in this sort of matter."

"I'm not saying you shouldn't have your voices heard, but in the end, the decision is mine."

"No, dear. When it comes to Parallel Society membership, it is always a team decision. You'd know that if you paid more attention."

"How could I when you hid everything from me?"

Garcia raised his hand like a schoolboy afraid to interrupt his teacher. "Perhaps I should wait outside. This all sounds rather personal."

"Sit," both women said together.

Garcia sat. He took a chair situated to view a sculpture of a sleeping cat. Or maybe a rat. The artist's skill was questionable.

Roni turned back towards Gram, ready to further their argument, when Elliot stepped forward. He leaned on his cane and allowed his long features to quell the room before he spoke.

"The history of the Parallel Society's teams is well-documented in our Grand Library, and since Roni is the caretaker of that room, she could dig out the information to verify what I say; however, I trust that you will all accept my word, even if I fumble with the specific details a pinch."

"Of course," Gram said. "We all have our flaws, but lying is not one of yours."

Roni also agreed, so Elliot said, "Thank you. Because the Society stretches back hundreds of years, we have had numerous incarnations. The groups have never been smaller than two people and usually were around four. On one occasion, in the late-1700s, there were fifteen. It was a temporary matter that involved a living relic which could split into more than one part and mimic others, but for a short time, there existed a large team of Society members. Usually, though, the team is kept rather small except in times of transition, where the old team is still active as the newer team is still learning how things are done. That is where we find ourselves today."

"He's right," Sully chimed in — well, creaked and grated, but he did speak. "And don't forget — it's been ages since there's been a real potion maker in the Society."

"Very true. No single person can perform all the roles necessary for a good, functional team. A potion maker would be a great addition, an asset to you all." He raised an eyebrow at Garcia. "I assume you know how to create mixtures that aid the healing process."

"First thing I was ever taught. Potions take time to make. It's not like it's a sword I can just whip out and start attacking with. They're better used for building strength, protecting areas, and healing bodies. In fact, if given the right ingredients and enough time —"

Elliot put out his hand to stop Garcia. Clearly, the man's enthusiasm for both the Society and his potions would have sent him spiraling into one lecture after another on either subject. To Roni, Elliot said, "I won't live forever. Here is a solution to filling my space as a healer. You see?"

With a wheezing cough, Sully said, "Still, we must be cautious. This man will have to prove his skills." A wince and another cough. "We can't blindly trust. Especially, with Yal-hara active again."

"Active?" Gram said. "Nonsense. She hasn't made a move in decades."

Roni held back the urge to lash out about Yal-hara stealing her memories when she was a child, about Yal-hara sending a man to infiltrate the bookstore and access the Caverns, about Yal-hara's surrogate, Kenneth Bay, trying to bribe and coerce Roni into spying on the Society — it went on from there. Gram knew it all. So did the rest of the team. While Yal-hara had not been seen in the flesh that whole time, the creature certainly made herself known.

Elliot pointed his cane at Teanna. "We haven't heard from our newest member. What is your opinion on this matter?"

All turned to face the young tracker. Teanna squirmed under their eyes, and her mouth twisted under their expectations. Or perhaps only Roni's. She knew Teanna had come to see her as more of a big sister than a leader. The fact that Teanna hesitated told Roni everything — the woman was stuck between wanting to please her big sister and wanting to do what she thought best for the Society. And Roni had no illusions regarding Teanna's inner-strength — she would not let herself become a pawn in somebody else's power struggle.

With her chin up and her eyes blazing, Teanna said, "We would be fools to throw away any asset to our mission."

"I agree," Elliot said.

"But we would be bigger fools to accept this man at his word."

Roni made an affirmative noise.

"When preparing me for my duties as a tracker, my father taught me to never trust the stranger's depth of evil but never doubt the possibilities for good. I think we should allow this man, Garcia, into our Society, but only on a probationary period. Until we can determine where the truth is, he cannot be a full member." She pulled out one hatchet and took a step closer to Garcia. "Should you be lying to us, I'll see that you never speak another lie again."

Though he paled, Garcia said, "I've wanted to meet you all, be a part of this for so long, why would I lie?"

Gram said, "Then I guess this is settled."

"Not quite," a rough voice said from the back — Gully. "I noticed that nobody asked for my opinion."

Roni shared a grin with Sully as Gram cocked her head to the side. "Your opinion?"

"I am a member of the team. Or do golems not count?"

Gram pointed a stern finger at Sully. "You've been upgrading him again, haven't you? Giving him more of your annoying habits. I suppose next he'll be insisting on a bedroom even though he doesn't sleep."

"I hadn't thought of that." Gully looked to the others. "Is that a possibility? My own room?"

Elliot said, "One step at a time. For now, you are right that you deserve for your voice to be heard. You are an essential part of this team and a great weapon against Yal-hara. Tell us, please, what do you think of Mr. Garcia joining us?"

"Oh, no need to say all that. I only wanted a chance to speak my mind."

"And?" Gram said.

"I agree with Teanna."

Sully chuckled into a cough. "Then it really is settled. Garcia stays."

"On a probationary period," Roni added, not quite sure how she had lost control of this decision.

Garcia seemed equally surprised as he bowed his head and wore a wide grin. "Thank you. Truly. Thank you. I wish my grandpa had lived to see this day."

Before the man could start blubbering in earnest, Roni took a closer look at the relic he held. To Elliot: "This box — what do you make of it?"

As Elliot approached, Garcia held out the relic box on his shaking hand. Elliot leaned over. "We have numerous books on languages in the Grand Library. They might help. But I can say that the design looks like something from Yal-hara's world."

"Why doesn't that surprise me?"

To Garcia, Elliot said, "You found this in Japan. How exactly? It seems unlikely that you simply stumbled upon it. Perhaps one of Yal-hara's representatives gave it to you."

Garcia shrugged. "It was pointed out to me at a junk shop."

"Pointed out? How?"

"I met a man through an online service of people searching for rare or unique artifacts. A lot of stolen and illegal items are there, but also collectors deal there and occasionally somebody like me. This man supposedly had an artifact related to another universe. I didn't expect much more than a conspiracy nut, but the more I messaged with him, the more convinced I became that he might be the real deal. We agreed to meet, and he brought me to a trinkets shop. As it turned out, it was his shop. The box was his proof that he spoke the truth. Cost me a grand, but he sold it to me. Now, I have a question."

"Oh? And that is?"

"Who is Yal-hara?"

Roni snorted a laugh.

CHAPTER 5

After Gram finished relaying her version of the Yal-hara story, one that provided all the pertinent facts yet avoided any of the ugly details, they started packing up. Roni could have interjected throughout the tale but chose to stay quiet. She knew Gram felt a lot of guilt over her part in allowing Yal-hara to swipe Roni's memories, and she knew Gram glossed over it with Garcia because the man didn't have the need, let alone the right, to know. Roni even agreed. Should they ever reach a point where Garcia required the information — if he even remained with the Society — then they could fill him in. Until that time, he only needed to understand that Yal-hara was a living relic who had made a deal to avoid being thrown into any old book, and most importantly, that she wanted to find a way to return to her own world. Understandable, of course, but impossible — unless they were to open all the books in the Caverns one by one, which would take more than one lifetime and would still, in all likelihood, fail.

"That's enough for one night," Roni said.

Garcia's crestfallen eyes darted toward Gram. "But I haven't even seen the Caverns. Or this famous bookstore that's your home."

"Plenty of time for that in the morning."

"Which it technically is."

Roni offered a placating smile. "In the morning. Go home now. Come back after nine. Elliot will give you the address, and I promise, you'll get a full tour."

The urge to argue flashed across his scholarly face, but he clearly thought better of it. Instead, he made a short bow. "Of course. I apologize. You must all be quite tired."

Gram adjusted her blouse as she stood. "It has been a long night. And getting Sully back to his apartment and into bed is no small feat for two old folks like Elliot and me."

"If I can help," Garcia said, pressing forward. Then: "I'm sorry again. My enthusiasm gets hold of me sometimes."

Tapping his cane on the floor, Elliot said, "Enthusiasm is a good thing to have. As long as you can control it with some common sense. Listen to Roni. We all need time to rest and absorb what has happened this evening. We'll see you in the morning."

"Trust us," Sully added. "All of our problems will still be waiting."

After a few more *goodbyes* and *goodnights,* the group dispersed. Before leaving, Roni asked Garcia if she could have the relic box. She wanted to look at it closer before going to sleep. He was happy to hand it over. "Anything the Society needs," he said.

That much was good. If he had refused, she would have been suspicious. Then again, perhaps he understood that, so he handed over the box to ease her concerns as he infiltrated the group. Or perhaps she was being paranoid. Or perhaps — sheesh, how did Gram or Sully deal with all the possibilities every new situation created?

Not much later, Roni and Teanna collapsed in their apartment. Roni flopped to the floor while Teanna slumped on the dingy couch. Though Teanna kept her own room neat and orderly, Roni's level of upkeep dominated the rest of the place. It had been hers alone until Teanna arrived, and without a word, both women knew it wouldn't change much. Besides, Roni suspected her roommate enjoyed a little disorder in her life. Sure. That had to be true.

Pushing aside an old pizza box, Roni set the relic on the floor. "I thought you might be able to find something out if you could look this over without everybody staring at you."

Teanna moaned as she sat up. "I could really use some sleep."

"Just a quick look. I won't be able to close my eyes until I know something about this. Is Elliot right? Is this really connected to Yalhara?"

"That's not exactly what he said."

"Are you going to argue semantics or take a look at the damn thing?"

"Okay, okay. Don't get all huffy."

Roni snickered. Whenever Teanna used a truly Earthbound phrase, it sounded so earnest and out of place. For a month, Teanna had latched onto *5 by 5* and a few weeks earlier, she couldn't stop finding reasons to say *Hasta la vista, baby.*

She picked up the relic box and turned it over a few times. She ran her finger over the carved symbols. She sniffed it.

"Anything?" Roni asked.

"What is wrong that you are so impatient?" Teanna placed the box back on the floor. "Is it because of Garcia? Why are so threatened by him?"

"What? No." Roni got on her feet and went to the kitchenette to stare into the refrigerator. "I just didn't want Garcia joining up with us because we don't know anything about him. A little caution seems prudent from your leader, don't you think?"

"It's more than that. What's bothering you?"

She glanced at the relic box. "Nothing. Just the pressures of keeping this team together, I suppose. But then, seeing that thing and knowing it comes from Yal-hara — okay, it's only connected to her — well, it reminds me that she's still out there. We've followed every lead we could to find her and no luck. Then, suddenly, this falls in our laps. Seems too easy. I don't like it."

With a chuckle, Teanna said, "You are so foolish."

"Gee, thanks."

"You don't think I know all that already? Or Gram? Or Elliot? We see you each day, and we know that you want to get rid of Yal-hara."

"You do, too. That was your requirement to stay here and work with us — to get rid of all the relics in our world. That includes Yal-hara."

"I only mean that we understand your focus, and as you often point out, you are our leader. So, we pay attention to such things."

Closing the fridge door, Roni said, "Then why did you all go against me about Garcia?"

"Because of what I just said. Your focus is Yal-hara, and here we have a man who brings us a relic that might be connected to Yal-hara. Gram and Elliot understood before I did, but I caught on fast enough. That's why I suggested the probation period."

Roni paused as she replayed the art gallery meeting in her head. Then: "You're saying that you all wanted to keep Garcia around because if he is actually working for Yal-hara, then at least we can watch him and maybe learn what she's up to. Something like that?"

"And if he isn't on her side, if he is exactly what he says he is, then he will be a true asset to the Parallel Society."

Weighing out the idea, Roni gestured to the relic box. "What do you think about that thing?"

"It has a very unique signature — um, would *aura* be the right word?"

"Probably. Can you track where it came from?"

"In Japan?"

"I was hoping for something a little closer. If this did come from Yal-hara, and if she is nearby, then maybe you can find her. If she's not, we know that she has people working for her around here — her main man, Kenneth Bay, for one. Any trail that relic could lead us to would be worthwhile."

Teanna picked up the box. "I'm going to bed. I will study this more."

"That's it?"

"We are both exhausted. But I promise you — if there is any hint of anything that I can track off this relic, we can head out right away."

Though Roni had intended to wake by seven, her blurred vision made out 9:12 in the matchstick green lights of her clock. She heard Teanna messing about the kitchen but didn't smell anything. That was good. Teanna was a horrible cook. She could fry eggs — she had eggs of a sort in her world — but she experimented with flavors by adding in anything she found. Eggs mixed with a dash of wine, leftover lo mein, and coffee grounds had been one of the more horrid combinations. And that was when things went well. Roni didn't want to deal with another smoking pan, burnt toast, or the fire alarm blaring away.

She threw on some jeans and a sleeveless tank top — hot summer weather threatened to come early this year — and cleaned up before urging Teanna to get ready. They were going to be late. Teanna already wore her usual — sweats. She said they gave her an ease of movement best for fighting. Plus, they made concealing her hatchets simple — she wore a leather holster underneath that kept them strapped to her back. But Roni suspected it was more basic than that. Teanna probably liked the soft feel of the fabric. Her world sounded like it had been a lot coarser.

By the time they reached *In The Bind*, Garcia waited outside on the sidewalk. The bookstore was five stories high and endless stories underneath, yet it appeared like any other building in the Philadelphia suburb. A little taller than most, but nothing out of the ordinary.

Roni unlocked the door and welcomed Garcia. Gram, Elliot, and Sully lived in two apartments on the fifth floor and would be joining soon enough. Setting the keys on the front counter, Roni called upstairs on an old telecom to make sure.

Garcia stood at the front door and gazed across at the hollow room. What had once been filled with high bookshelves, each stuffed with old hardcovers and paperbacks on every imaginable subject, now looked like a dance studio without the mirrors — an empty floor. The walls, ceiling, floor, and storefront window had all been repaired or replaced — damage caused by their last excursion into the Caverns — and Gram had only recently ordered new shelving. They were in no rush, she had explained, and as long as they could fulfill their true purpose as the Parallel Society, the bookstore's operations were not that important.

"All bookstores are important," Garcia said. "Especially the old ones."

Teanna scoffed. "In my world, books are for anyone learned enough to read them. The idea that you'd sell them is absurd."

"I think I might like your world."

"I'm not sure you'd survive for very long."

Roni snickered.

With his head indicating the oversized wood table that dominated a section of the floor near the right wall, Garcia said, "Is that an artifact, er, relic, too?"

"That's just a table," Roni said.

From the back, metal clanging announced the arrival of the old elevator. Gram slid aside the accordion gate, and Elliot pushed Sully out. A large staircase offered a manual way of going to the other floors, but Sully would never use stairs again.

"I apologize if I'm gawking," Garcia said, "but this is like stepping into Heaven."

Gram laughed. "I certainly expect the Lord has better accommodations for us than this old place. But come on in."

Garcia moved forward one step before pausing. "Where's your golem? Gully?"

"He usually patrols floor to floor all night. If he's not doing that, he'll be in Sully's old workshop. It's where he was created. Now, get in here already. Roni will give you a tour."

"No," Roni said. "The boys can do the tour."

"Oh?" Elliot said as he situated Sully at the big table.

"Don't be silly." Gram took Garcia by the arm and escorted him to the others. "Mr. Garcia deserves —"

"Please, just Garcia."

"Okay. Garcia deserves to be shown around by our leader."

Gritting her teeth, Roni said, "Your leader is very busy today. The boys will do it."

"We are happy to do so." Elliot caught a sharp glare from Gram. "Of course, it will be difficult to maneuver Sully's wheelchair in the Caverns. The rest of the building is no issue, but —"

"Fine." Roni stomped to the elevator. "C'mon, Garcia, let's go."

She led the way through the basement, into Gram's private collection room, and then across the jagged hole in the back wall opening to the Caverns. The entire time, Garcia jittered and gawked. An awed smile locked his face with joy. So different from Roni's first experience.

She had been confused. She had been terrified. In discovering the Caverns, her reality flipped. But for Garcia — why should he get a gratifying experience? It wasn't fair. Of course, she could hear Gram saying that life was never fair and to trust in the Lord. But Roni wanted to trust in having Garcia open a book into an underwater world.

"It's incredible," he said with such reverence that Roni swiped away her ugly thoughts. He went on, "For so many years, people mocked my grandpa. In my travels, I heard the snickers behind my back. But it's all true."

"I'd have thought the giant centipede would have been enough."

"Yes, but this — it's really here."

Roni gazed at the books chained to the walls and smelled the cool, cavern stone. Through Garcia's eyes, she saw it all anew. "I'm sorry," she said. "I'm not trying to be rude, but I'm responsible for the team, for the Society. You understand it's not personal."

"Yes, yes, of course."

Taking him back to the main floor, she wondered if she had spoken the truth. There was no time to worry, though. "Elliot, you and Sully and Gully can show Garcia the rest of the building. Gram's coming with Teanna and me. We've got a job to do." All attention perked onto Roni. "Not that kind of job. Not yet, anyway."

It was totally that kind of job, and Roni knew it from the start. But if she said otherwise, Elliot or Gully — heck, even Sully — might try to tag along. Of course, she appreciated their help and advice, but she still felt like she was learning the rules of how to lead. Allowing them to constantly influence her decisions only interfered with that process.

At least, that was what she told herself as she drove southward on I-95. From the first turn onto the highway, Roni assumed Gram knew the truth, but thankfully, nothing was said. They stayed quiet, allowing Teanna to guide them, doing her job of tracking the relic both by her keen eyes and her powerful senses. Magical, really — as long as she used her powers for the good of the Society.

Roni wondered if Gram had ever been tempted to offer team membership to Yal-hara. That would certainly have solved the problem of her existing in this universe, and it would have negated all the troubles Yal-hara had created since then. But it would have required Gram to swallow the bitterness caused by Yal-hara's actions toward Roni. Still, the thought continued to pop in her head — perhaps Gram had been tempted a little.

"That exit," Teanna said, pointing to a sign for Exit 67 — White Marsh.

"We're near Baltimore," Gram said, as if that held special meaning.

Off the exit, Teanna gave frequent directions *left here, go one block over, right over there* forcing them to weave through the smaller streets. They double-backed a few times as she tried to lock onto the scent or sensation or whatever it was that told Teanna where a relic could be found. Roni had yet to ask. It seemed too personal a question.

From the backseat, Gram said, "Teanna, can you tell me why my granddaughter feels so threatened by Garcia?"

Teanna grunted.

"Leave her alone," Roni said. "She needs to concentrate."

"Of course, of course. I only wondered if perhaps you were attracted to Garcia."

"What? No. Not in the least. He's in his forties."

"I didn't think a little age difference would matter to you."

"What's that mean?"

Teanna pointed to the upcoming traffic light. "Turn left up there."

"It means, dear, that you have avoided any serious love life. I assumed a lot of that distancing was from the problems with your Lost Time. After all, how were you going to explain that if you became close and intimate with a man?"

Driving onto a side street with weeds poking through cracked concrete sidewalks and graffiti painting the walls of abandoned buildings, Roni finally noticed they had snaked their way south, away from White Marsh and into the edges of Baltimore. A bad neighborhood, too. She checked the door locks. "I don't want to talk about my love life with you."

"That's good because it'd be a short conversation."

Teanna snorted as she gazed down an alleyway.

Gram went on, "You've got friends now. That's good. Teanna and Gully are loyal and worthy of your time, but neither will bring you the warmth of a loving man. There's a reason the Lord gave us the capacity to feel such a wonderful emotion. He wants us to fall in love, wants us to marry and procreate."

"Gram, please stop."

"What? There's nothing dirty about it. And now that your Lost Time has been restored, there's no excuse for sitting around becoming an old maid."

"Who the hell is sitting around?"

"Language."

"Then who the heck is sitting around? I'm working hard every day to save the universe. Just like you."

"I found time to marry your grandfather and have my children. You should do it, too."

Teanna pointed to a figure crossing the road at the end of the block. "There. That man is connected to this relic."

As they drove on, Roni saw that the man wore a fine suit — far too fine for this area — and he used a black cane with silver tips. She knew long before they passed by to inspect his face — this was Kenneth Bay, Yal-hara's attorney.

Of course.

Chapter 6

Keeping pace in a car looked suspicious no matter how one drove. If Kenneth Bay glanced back at any moment, he would spot Roni. How could he possibly miss the woman vibrating nervous energy behind the steering wheel of the only slow-moving car on the street? There might as well have been a spotlight on her with sparkling pinwheels spinning behind and a giant neon arrow pointing from above.

Gram scooted forward. "Isn't that —"

"Yal-hara's lackey? Yup."

Pushing back and crossing her arms, she said, "He looks quite a bit like his father. And his grandfather, for that matter."

"Protecting scum is in the family genes, I guess."

"We have our family business, they have theirs."

Roni wanted to chuckle — Gram did not often make jokes — but the well-dressed man strolling ahead dominated her attention. This wouldn't work. If traffic were heavier or he had earbuds in or something else distracting, then maybe she could pull off trailing him by car. This way — no. They were going to get made.

Roni sped up and passed Bay before turning right at the corner ahead. She pulled to the curb and watched her rearview mirror. When he came into view, he went left, away from the car. Perfect.

"I'm going to follow him on foot," she said, wondering how much training a person actually needed before they could successfully tail another. "The two of you swing the car around to keep tabs on him without having to be on top of him."

"Then what?" Gram said. To the untrained ear, she sounded pleasant, curious, and ready to help. To Roni, who had grown up under Gram's rule, the sound betrayed an accusation of *you haven't really thought this through, as usual.*

"Depends on what he does. Right now, we're simply gathering information. Where he goes, who he talks to, anything that will clue us into why he had Yal-hara's relic box and what she intends to do."

"That's a lot considering we don't even know if the box truly belongs to Yal-hara."

Teanna said, "I cannot say who the box belongs to, but I know that man has handled it."

"See," Roni said.

Gram huffed. "Well, then, if any of us is going to follow this man, it should be Teanna. She's the one with the gift for tracking."

"That's why she's going with you. I can follow Bay fine, and she can make sure you both end up wherever I end up. But if she's the one out there, then how are you and I going to find her?"

"I only meant that you need to carefully think through matters. This doesn't seem well considered."

"Are you going to drive or are you going to pick at me this whole time? Teanna doesn't have a license, but I'm sure she'd relish the chance to get behind the wheel."

Teanna perked up. "I can drive."

"No, no," Gram said, a sudden rush of accommodation painting her voice. "Happy to help."

Roni jumped out and headed after Bay. As the car pulled back into the street, she picked up her pace, afraid her spat with Gram had let the man get too far a lead. But with his cane and his cocky attitude, he did not bother with speed. Even in this slum of a neighborhood, he walked as if he had no fear. Nobody would dare mug him. Nobody would dare look at him side-eyed. He was a boss. Like a mafioso. Heck, like the leader of a street gang.

He strolled a bit further before crossing the road, then cut by the Wawa convenience store and gas station on the corner. Down a street lined with boarded storefronts, a dive bar, an old phone booth minus the phone, and a dank pool hall. Another turn. About halfway up this next block, he reached a door with muddy red paint. A faded blue awning bore TRUMBLE TAILORING AND MEN'S WARE in gold script that clung to a former glory which probably never existed in this section of town. Pausing to peer up and down the walk, Kenneth Bay entered the establishment with more than a hint of suspicion surrounding him.

Roni's excitement and trepidation battled to claim her racing pulse as she crossed the street and approached the tailor's shop. She had never seen Kenneth Bay anywhere but the cruddy diner they agreed on for meetings. To see him in this new context and to know that each step he took might bring her closer to Yal-hara thrilled her.

But those same thoughts petrified her bones. Seeing Bay outside of their regular environment gave his every movement a dangerous, unpredictable nature. And knowing Yal-hara stood at the end of whatever path they were on meant finally confronting her — confronting the Devil that had crawled over her at eight-years-old and swiped her memories with psychotic glee.

She wanted to burst into that store and swing an accusing finger at him. Catch him in some act of evil that proved everything she believed and justified every bit of vengeance she had imagined. This man and his predecessors had made a living off protecting Yal-hara from paying for her crimes. Roni had no doubt that more people besides herself had been hurt by the living relic. There had to be a reckoning.

No. She pushed those thoughts aside. Focusing on the wrong thing at the wrong time would only result in failure. Yal-hara paying for what she did, how she ruined much of Roni's life — that would come in time. If she concentrated on her job now.

From the outside, the tailor's shop looked too small for Roni to enter unnoticed. She peered down the alleyway. Maybe she could enter through the back door. As long as the tailor was busy with Kenneth Bay, he or she would never know somebody had slipped inside. Unless the shop had more than one person working there — doubtful, but possible. Unless the tailor had invested in a security alarm triggered by the alley door opening — not only possible, but given the neighborhood, quite likely.

Kenneth Bay took the decision out of her hands. The alley door opened and he stepped out. Roni sprang back from view. Pressing against the brick wall, her heart hammering, she counted to five before peeking around the corner. Bay continued his stroll, gingerly avoiding the stagnant water puddles and the errant trash as he headed away.

Roni followed. She kept near the wall — not that a wall in an alley would magically protect her from being seen, but it felt like the right move and offered a strange touch of security. When the alley broke into the next major street, he paused at the mouth. Roni ducked behind a dumpster. She pressed her face against the coarse brick and tried to peer down the narrow crack between dumpster and wall. The stench of sour milk and old beer wafted over her. Being a spy — not nearly as glamorous as the movies made it seem.

Bay checked his watch, but he didn't look around as if expecting anybody. Several people walked by as well as several more cars, yet nothing struck Roni as out of place. Nothing but Bay.

When he set off again, she jolted to her feet, gasped for the somewhat cleaner air further along the alley, and rushed to catch up. Once she reached the street, she spotted him entering another store — this one had the windows soaped over and the words FOR RENT drawn in. No contact name. No phone number.

Breathing in, she was greeted with the pleasant aroma of pizza and calzones — far better than a dumpster. A door with a jangling bell opened up ahead, and a young couple exited with two grease-stained bags. PAPA's PLACE had been painted on the glass of the door in swirling letters. A simple, everyday occurrence — people having lunch — yet this moment of familiarity helped center Roni's thoughts and ease her mounting nerves.

As she approached the empty store, she made sure to check the alley for another backdoor exit, but Bay never left. She tried to see through the soap streaks on the window yet only managed to catch glimpses of shadow and light playing against an off-white wall. From what she could tell, the place looked empty — no shelves, no tables, no counters, nothing but floorspace awaiting a new purpose.

She snatched a view of the street — no sign of Gram and Teanna. Another peek down the alley — still vacant. If she waited, he might leave. If she went in, she did so alone.

"Crap," she whispered. Then she opened the door.

Gently. Slowly. Easing it outward before wheeling in so as to get her back to the wall and her eyes scanning as much of the open room as possible.

No attack came. But no sign of Bay, either.

The room had a gray, dusty feel to it. The soaped window dimmed the light and the hollow space echoed every tiny noise. Even her breathing bounced back at her.

Keeping against the wall, she slid sideways, working toward the corner end of the room and then along the back wall. A plain, white door stood halfway along — probably to an office or a storage area. Not outside to the alley, though. That would have been a metal security door.

As she maneuvered, she noticed an object in the center of the room — small with a top like a sarcophagus. Another relic box. This one had been painted the same gray as the dusty floor and dimmed room. It was nearly invisible until she moved.

She stepped toward it, careful to keep her footsteps as quiet as possible. A quick check at the back door, then the front. When she reached the relic box, she crouched but held back from picking the thing up.

When Garcia had triggered his relic box, it released a glowing centipede creature. Roni had no interest in fighting another such monstrosity. But surely there had to be a method for holding the relic. And assuming that Kenneth Bay had set the box down, then not only did he know how to carry it, but he placed it here for a reason.

"Double crap," she said as she straightened. It had been a lure, and she fell for it. He knew she had followed him the entire time. Of course, he did. Only an idiot would have missed their car slowly rolling behind. He led her here and set the relic down to entice and distract her. Biting her lip, she raised her hands. "I'm unarmed."

Apparently, I'm also a lousy spy.

Two rough hands patted her down with what she regarded as an expert, impersonal touch. Not that she had much experience with pat-downs, but the man didn't cop a feel nor did he linger upon any other parts of her anatomy. All that professionalism flew away when he spun her around and gut punched her.

Roni buckled over, dropping to her knees as she coughed and gasped. She gazed up at a thick brute in blue sweats and a Temple University hoodie — more fat than muscle, but either way, he still hit hard. He kicked her, landing on the thigh, and she fell to her side. Her eyes watered, and she saw the blurry mustached-image of Kenneth Bay walking into view, his cane tapping as he approached.

"If you truly intend to combat the being Yal-hara, might I suggest you learn a little about tactics and a lot about subtlety." He spoke with exacting pronunciation, and his impatient tinge sprinkled upon each syllable.

Though her own voice sounded as strained as her aching body felt, she said, "Might I suggest you kiss my ass."

"Spoken like the very kind of lady you are." He made a tutting sound. "It is such a shame. All of this suffering is your fault — yours and the Parallel Society. What you have wrought against my client —"

"You can spare me the performance. Back when we were on the same side, back when I thought of you as Kenneth, I might have cared. But all your rambling about Yal-hara's tragic history — I don't believe much of it anymore. Not when you neglected to mention that she was the cause of my Lost Time."

"Surely, now that you've had a year to digest that knowledge, you've come to understand that she had little choice in the matter."

"I was only eight, but I can still recall the gleam in her eye. She enjoyed it."

"Maybe so. I cannot speak to what a being like her might feel. I am as human as you."

"That's debatable." She rubbed her thigh.

Bay turned toward the big man, and Roni braced for another punch or kick. Tapping the man's shoulder with his cane, Bay said, "This man is one to be considered more Neanderthal than *homo sapien.*" The man did not acknowledge the insult. Back to Roni, Bay said, "Yal-hara only wants what she has ever wanted — the freedom to go home."

Growling the words, Roni said, "I don't care."

"You should rethink your position."

"She raped my mind. She deserves her punishment. If anything, it's not enough."

Squatting so his face came closer to her, he said, "This attitude is bringing matters to a head, and if you'd only listen, you'd see that all the violence which will follow isn't necessary. Nor the heartbreak, the disappointment, perhaps even the betrayal."

Finally having the strength to swing her leg around so she could sit, Roni said, "How about this — you tell me where I can find Yal-hara, and I'll make sure she gets her freedom."

He offered a malicious chuckle. "Sending her into any old book is not the freedom she seeks."

"How about freedom from the mortal realm?"

With a sigh that presented more pity than exasperation, he stood. "At least, I can tell her that I honestly tried. You see that now, yes? I used that little box to bring you out here."

"You could've called me. I would still have met you at the diner."

"We wanted to see how skilled your newest member of the team was."

Roni came close to asking how he knew about Garcia, but then realized Bay referred to Teanna. "I'm sure she'll be thrilled to know she passed your test. Was that it? See what she can do and threaten me a bit?"

"I'm afraid not. There's more."

"There always is." She rolled her eyes towards the big man. "Don't you get tired of his yammering away with all that snobbishness?"

Though the big man stared back cold and firm, she thought she detected a slight tremor at the corner of his mouth — a desire to grin. She considered prodding the man's ego some more when she felt a sharp thwack on the head.

"Pay attention," Bay said, raising his cane for another strike. Instead, he lowered it and walked toward the back door. "Yal-hara has now learned about the Pages of Glass."

"Never heard of them."

"I am not surprised. You seem bent on making your career one of ill-informed bumbling. I suggest you ask the others in the Parallel Society. Because if you simply deliver the book containing the Pages of Glass to me, so that I may bring it to Yal-hara, then all the pain will end." He nodded, and the big man smacked the back of Roni's head. She bent forward, her brain shaking in her skull. Over his shoulder, Bay said, "It's entirely up to you. Deliver the book and all this wasteful and useless aggression will be over. Deny Yal-hara what she has always sought, and things will get much worse." He glanced back. "Yal-hara will wait no longer."

He left, and the big man followed.

Crawling toward the wall, Roni focused on breathing. Too shallow and her head grew light. Too deep and she could feel her lungs scraping against her ribs. When she reached the wall, she rolled over and rested. Sweat mixed with blood in her mouth like a bitter cocktail. She closed her eyes.

But before she managed a single, restful thought Gram and Teanna burst through the back door. Seeing the state of her granddaughter, Gram rushed over. Teanna checked the front door and dashed out the back exit. When she returned, a simple shake of the head answered all the obvious questions.

"Lord, please watch over Roni and see to her a rapid recovery," Gram said. Then: "We'll have Elliot to help the Lord along when we get back. Can you stand?"

"Give me a minute," Roni said, wrenching her arm free from Gram's grasp.

"Sorry, I didn't mean to hurt you." She looked up at Teanna. "Was it Bay after all?" To Roni: "What was he up to? This place is empty."

Roni gestured to the relic box. "Not entirely. But that wasn't why he was here. He wanted to deliver a message — Yal-hara's coming. And she wants the Pages of Glass." She caught the change on Gram's face. Anybody could have seen it. The old woman's drooping skin lowered to the floor along with her shoulders and her chin. She melted with despair. Roni reached out toward Gram. "What? What are these Pages?"

Gram's frightened figure shivered. "Something that was meant to always be a myth, but is too real. And too dangerous."

CHAPTER 7

No matter what tactic Roni employed, Gram refused to answer any questions regarding the Pages of Glass during the drive home. She had taken the passenger seat and strategically spent most of the time staring out the window with her arms crossed. Twice, Roni caught Gram kissing her crucifix and muttering prayers.

"I'm not trying to be an obstacle," Gram said after Roni, once again, attempted to get some information. "But this is a matter for the entire Parallel Society, and I'm probably not the best one to explain any of it. Have a little patience."

Though she stopped there, Roni could hear the unspoken words seeping from the passenger seat — be understanding, be quiet, be more like Teanna. Indeed, Teanna sat in the backseat, observing the world around her. Serene. Not a sound.

But Roni was not fooled. She had spent enough time with Teanna to know that the woman did not sit idly — ever. More likely, Teanna held still so she could hear every subtle sound between Roni and Gram. She could hear not only the words but the subtext, the emotions, maybe even the heartbeats pulsing out the disguised truths like a secret code.

"This is ridiculous." Roni had to be mindful of her driving or she would inadvertently speed up. "I am trying to become a good leader, I'm trying to look out for my team, but crucial information is being withheld. Yet again. You haven't changed at all."

"I am not withholding information. I'm postponing it. And you'll have to forgive me, but there are a lot of details, a lot of stories and incidents and histories that have built up after decades of living. I forget some of it."

"I find it hard to believe you would forget anything about Yal-hara."

"I don't mean that I can't remember these things. I only mean that if you want to know every little detail which Elliot and Sully and I have experienced in the Society, it would take years to tell you. One of the reasons I had you start off down in the Grand Library was so that you would read many of those books and journals and diaries. You would learn from the those who preceded us, learn about their lives and the kinds of things they had encountered. If you think that you're going to reach a point where you know everything about the Society and no surprises could come your way, you are sadly mistaken. Lord help us, that kind of thinking can get people killed."

"Perfect. Now I'm a threat to you all."

"Quit being so dramatic. We'll be home soon enough, and then we can all gather and you will learn everything you want to know about the Pages of Glass. Well, everything that we know. Until then, perhaps it's best we not talk with each other for a bit."

When they arrived at the bookstore, they found the main floor empty except for Gully. The golem stood in the middle of the room, his strong arms folded, his chest puffed, his eyes wide and alert — a sentry on-duty. Before Roni could even ask, he jutted his thumb back toward the elevator. "They're in the workshop."

"Thank you," Gram said.

She must have shared Roni's odd expression at Gully's behavior because the golem thrust his hands high with a fed-up shake of the head. "Why should anybody care what a bunch of stone and clay wants? Far be it from me to claim rights to any room in this building. I'm not human. I don't need to sleep. You all need your bedrooms for sleep and kitchens for food and bathrooms for those other gross human functions. What does poor Gully need? Nothing but a job to do."

Roni did not like this. Not because the golem complained — he did that often enough — and not because he had been kicked out of the workshop he considered his domain. Rather, Roni disliked the other implications the move suggested. Once the ladies clambered into the elevator and rode up to Sully's workshop, Roni's fears solidified. Elliot and Garcia had already begun moving tables and bookshelves around.

Elliot caught her eye. "It's very good you are here. We've decided that this should become Garcia's laboratory. A fitting shift from the hard work of one great golem maker to one potentially great potion maker."

"Don't let him get a big head," Sully said.

Garcia laughed as he wiped down a worktable situated under a wide window looking out onto the street. He had removed his professor's jacket and rolled his sleeves up. He moved to a low bookshelf. "A little help, please," he said.

Teanna strode toward him and gave a firm nod before picking up the other side. Garcia chuckled, and Roni fought the urge to snap out any comment that might undercut the man's joy. After all, this had clearly been a dream of his, and it was coming true. She had been thrust into the Society unwittingly with no desire to upend her life. But Garcia — he had sought this out.

Well, he is going to get a lot more than he bargained for.

She walked over to Sully's wheelchair and rested her hand on his arm. Softly, she said, "Are you sure about this?"

He nodded.

"But this is your workshop. And Gully's home. I don't know — it feels like you're giving up."

"Just accepting reality."

"Don't give me that *I'm not going to live forever* crap. You have a responsibility to the Society and to the universe and to me. You don't give up — ever. The end will come when it comes, but you don't hasten it. Understood?"

He gave her hand a pat. "I love you, too."

Elliot's deep voice cut through the air. "I see." His tone grabbed Roni's attention. She looked up to find Gram conversing with him near the entrance way.

Off the quick glance from Elliot, Roni knew he had been informed about their experiences in Baltimore. Grabbing one of the lab stools, she said. "I think we've waited enough. Start explaining."

"Explaining what?" Garcia asked.

Snapping her fingers at another stool, she said, "Sit. Listen. Don't ask stupid questions."

Elliot took several meandering steps toward the center of the room, his head low, as he thought out what to say. Before he could speak, however, Teanna said, "Shouldn't Gully be up here, too? He'll need to understand all of this."

Elliot said, "If Sully has not already put this information into Gully's instructions, he will make sure it is done at the next update. For now, I need all of you to listen closely. It appears that Yal-hara has come to believe that the myth of the Pages of Glass is no myth at all. Unfortunately, she is right."

Garcia folded his arms as his brow crinkled. "The Pages of Glass? That's never come up in my research."

Roni said, "Let the man talk and maybe we can all learn."

"Yes, yes, of course." Garcia reddened. "My apologies. Please continue."

Clearing his throat, Elliot went on, "What we had hoped would remain nothing but an old story has now become a real problem." He looked straight at Roni. "A serious threat to us all and our mission."

Roni reached in deep to find any smidgen of patience still remaining. "You've set all of us in this room to take heed of your words. And you've got Garcia bouncing like a five-year-old birthday boy. Please, for the love of all that is holy amongst every religion you all believe in, tell us what these Pages are."

As Elliot cleared his throat again, Roni shifted on the stool which sent a flare up her bruised leg. She winced. Raising an eyebrow, he watched her as he moved in closer.

"I got a little roughed up," she said under his scrutiny.

"Why didn't you say anything? I could have taken care of that right away."

Without further discussion on the matter, Elliot raised his gnarled cane and turned it horizontal. He rolled it forward and back, forward and back. Quite fast, a soothing warmth filled her leg and radiated over the rest of her body, seeking out and relaxing the pains in her gut as well.

She wanted to stop him, keep him focused on talking about the Pages of Glass, but she had to admit that his healing spells always felt good — like going to an ER in severe pain and receiving a controlled morphine drip. In an instant, all the anguish left the body and only a gentle buzz remained.

After a moment, he set the cane back on the floor. "That should do for now. How do you feel?"

Roni's head bobbed about, and she couldn't stop a soft, goofy smile from rising.

"Good. In the future, tell me of injuries immediately. It gets harder to heal the longer you wait."

Her smile faltered. *In the future*. Elliot — Sully — Gram — how much future did they have? The thought caused a hot poke through her chest, piercing her lungs and heart.

"Wow," Garcia said, the word echoing both from his volume as well as the gobsmacked delivery. "I mean I've seen things already, traveling the world and all, but that was, well, I mean it's one thing to read about the Society and what you all can do, but to see it firsthand."

"You are a potion maker," Teanna said from the back of the room. She loved to perch away from the group. Roni guessed so she could keep an eye on everybody. "You have seen magic before. Why should this astonish you?"

"Are you joking? This — this is unlike anything the rest of the world experiences. People who dabble in potions and relics and all these mysteries of the universe, well, they have no better success than trying to light a fire by striking flint in a tornado. They might get a spark or two, but that's it. But here — most of the people I've encountered could never dream of such a feat as Elliot pulled off with barely a thought. And those I interviewed who had direct dealings with you, they never expressed it in a way that made me feel what I'm feeling right now."

"Enough," Roni said. "Please. Everybody needs to stop interrupting and changing subjects and all of it. We're here to listen to Elliot explain about the Pages. All other discussions, debates, and tangents can wait until later."

Gram snickered. "Now you know why most people hate office meetings. It's what the term *herding cats* was made for."

"Not another word from anybody except Elliot." Roni gestured to Elliot.

His wrinkled lips pulled in before he finally spoke. "The origin of the Pages is murky at best, but I can share with you what I believe to be as close to the truth as we know. In 1712, near a village on the French coast, a fisherman pulled a thick book out of the river. The book had two thick glass pages in it — dark emerald glass. Of course, we know that the book slipped out of another universe and into the waters of that river, but to the man, he had received a gift from the Lord above."

Gram waved her index finger. "Just because we can understand the mechanism which this man discovered the book, does not mean we can discount the possibility that the Almighty caused it to happen."

"True. However, that detail is unknown to us, and you and I have debated that point more times than we ever needed. But most significantly — it's a detail unimportant to Roni. What is of importance is the fact that he used the notoriety which came with the discovery to better his life. People traveled from all over, paying good money, in order to see this strange object."

Teanna said, "Why would they do that? A book with two glass pages is unusual — in my world as well — but hardly worth great expense to see."

"Some came because they felt it was a religious pilgrimage of sorts. Others were just curious. But a few knew what this relic actually was, and to them, it was far too dangerous to allow this fisherman access. Late one night while deep asleep, a group of cloaked figures entered the fisherman's home and slaughtered him, his wife, and his two children. They stole nothing but the book. Then, in 1743 —"

Sully poked Elliot's leg. "This isn't helping. She wants the current situation."

"I merely thought some background — but I can see I am mistaken. Very well, then. The Pages have the unique property of being able to see rifts and where they go. Take the Pages and look through it at one of the Cavern books, and you can see what world that book opens into."

Roni's shoulders drooped as she let out a long sigh. "That's all? You've been building this thing up — I thought it was some kind of death ray or it'd turn us all into zombies or I don't know. But this doesn't sound so bad."

"Then you are not grasping the full implications. This book, these Pages, are the most dangerous relic in existence."

"And that's because?"

"Imagine you were the chief of a nefarious organization, perhaps barbaric even. You've learned about the multiverse and you have the Pages. Now you can pick and choose which books to open. You'll now know which worlds are rife for plunder, and which to avoid because they have horrible creatures, terrifying storms, or perhaps an emptiness that would have sucked you in and crushed your lungs should you have been foolish enough to open their books. The uncertainty, the grave risks — that keeps universe marauders back."

"Okay, I can see that."

"Then there are those who are worse than such takers — the conquerors. They would be able to study a world's defenses and identify the weakest. In no time, you would have empires built that stretch from one universe to another."

"That's bad, too."

"It's more, though. In the wrong hands, these Pages could be analyzed, reverse engineered, and then recreated. One set of the Pages is dangerous enough. But multiple sets would upend life in every universe. Crimes of all sizes could be committed with impunity when the criminal can escape safely to another universe. But it's not just crimes. Passions and lusts will also be unleashed. Look at the pain I caused when I fell in love with a woman from another universe. On top of it all, mankind has shown itself to be ingenious at taking a simple tool and finding greater uses then ever predicted. I'm sure there are other species out in the multiverse every bit as intelligent and creative, if not more."

Gram said, "I shudder to think what would happen if those Pages were let loose."

"We've done a good job over the centuries turning the Pages into a myth. A fancy dream for those who knew of the Caverns. Then we locked the Pages away where, we hope, no one can get ahold of them."

With a churn in her gut not caused by her earlier assault, Roni said, "And Yal-hara has found out that these Pages of Glass are real."

Thumping his cane against the floor, Elliot said, "She must never get the Pages. It could be the ruin of our world. It would definitely be the ruin of many other worlds. She puts on the act of a creature pining to get back home, but she is ruthless, vicious, lacking remorse, and as you learned when you were eight, without conscience."

Roni let those words settle in the air as she digested it all. At length: "You said that we have the Pages, that they've been locked away somewhere by the Society. Do we know where?"

"We do."

"Then show me."

CHAPTER 8

Elliot led the way down to the basement, through Gram's private office, along her collection of valuable books, across the open mouth at the back wall, and into the Caverns. As he walked, Roni stayed close behind and Gully brought up the rear. Thankfully, Garcia had not asked to come along.

He must have known better. Roni would have flat out refused — he had his taste of the Caverns and didn't need to know where these Pages were hidden. That might have sparked another squabble within the team. Responsibility fell on her to keep everyone working together as a unified group, but that didn't mean everybody got the same opportunities. Besides, she needed a little breathing room from the Eddie Garcia situation.

On the other hand: "Shouldn't Teanna have come with us, too? In case we run into trouble."

Elliot shook his head. "We'll be fine. The fewer who know where the Pages are, the fewer that can divulge that information — either willfully or otherwise." At least, they agreed on that point. "At this moment Sully, Gram, and I are the only ones with that knowledge. Soon, you will. Gully, as well. That is already too many. But this period of transition is a necessary evil. Once us old folks pass away, then you can share this information with the others."

"Don't talk like that. I know you're not immortal, but you all don't have to walk around acting like you're going to drop dead at any moment."

The Cavern's twisting conglomerations of stalactites and stalagmites cast various shadows depending on which decade of lighting equipment illuminated a given area. Bookshelves had been carved into the walls, each one housing numerous chained books, each book a portal to another universe. Other chained books hung from the ceiling while still more had been bolted into the stone walls high above. Surrounding the entrance to the bookstore basement, well-worn paths led off for the nearby locations. But the further one traveled, the rougher these paths became. Eventually, there would be nothing at all to guide an explorer.

Though Roni had spent many hours in the Grand Library digging up every description, sketch, or clue as to what the Caverns looked like, the large map she had developed still held many incomplete sections. She hung it on the back wall of the library, and whenever she studied it, she thought about all the gaps, all the places that must exist somewhere beneath the bookstore which she may never encounter. And now, she knew that whatever hole her map had which should denote the Pages of Glass location could never be filled. If anything, she would have to draw in a lie — a boring lie, at that — to dissuade future Society members from exploring that area.

At least, it can't be far. She had been on excursions with Elliot before which required days of provisions as well as hefty amounts of gear. This time, they simply walked in. Wherever he led them, he could not expect it to take too long.

They branched off several main pathways until Roni no longer recognized her surroundings. The chained books carried layers of dust, and the usual echoes of dripping water or dislodged stones faded into a sharp silence. It reminded Roni of the controlled quiet found in a recording studio — a lack of sound that she experienced during an elementary school visit to the local radio station. One of the kids' mothers had worked there.

"Isn't it amazing," the teacher had said. "The way the walls stop the sound in an instant."

At the time, Roni found it creepy. Now, she still found it creepy, but in this case, she had better reasons to be unnerved.

"We'll arrive shortly," Elliot said. "There is still time to reconsider."

Roni answered with an eyebrow. Nothing more.

Minutes later, after sidestepping through a narrow section of rock with streams of water cascading down the walls, they entered an unassuming junction between three passageways. An alcove pushed into the far wall — deep enough that the back could only be seen as a gray mass. But Elliot led them to this section, and it quickly became clear that the gray was not the alcove wall but rather a metal door.

The door only came up to Roni's chest. No hinges were visible nor handles. Rust had formed at the edges, and the surrounding limestone had encroached over the top corners. There were several dents near the bottom as if an angry giant had attempted to kick its way in. And in the center, Roni saw a circle — a keyhole.

Elliot gestured ahead. "The book is beyond that door. Take note, and in your head, mark where you are. I will not bring you here again. Now, let us return."

"Hold on." Roni crossed her arms, knowing she mimicked Gram too well. "You didn't really think I'd leave without looking in there, did you?"

"An old man can still have hopes."

"The key, please."

"I don't have it."

Roni's anger flashed, but she managed to cool it back down almost as quickly. Part of her self-training in leadership was to gain control of that reaction — especially when leadership in the Society meant not having control of so many things. CEOs of multi-billion-dollar conglomerates had it easy.

With a placating wave of his hands, Elliot said, "You misunderstand. I did not forget the key — there simply never was one created. The only way to open that lock is either through somebody who can cast a spell or somebody who can mold an object into the keyhole."

"I take it you can cast the spell."

"I never learned. Never tried. I never had to do so."

Roni's attention turned toward Gully. "I get it. A golem is often made out of clay. You never learned to cast a spell because Sully could always make a golem to open the door."

"Exactly."

"How about it, Gully? Ready to do your part?"

Shuffling forward Gully lowered his head. "Of course. Happy to help. Nobody ever talks to me unless they want something, but that's okay. Gully do this, Gully do that. Never *how are you feeling today, Gully?* Or *would you like to join us for breakfast, Gully?* I suppose I can't expect much more from humans."

Roni did not bother to respond. She knew enough from dealing with the golem's creator that such complaints were not meant to be answered. Not directly, anyway.

Gully crouched over the keyhole and gazed in. He put his ear to the door and knocked on its metal. Roni came close to interrupting, to pointing out that they were not asking him to crack a safe, but Gully raised his index finger to stop her. Then, with a dramatic flourish of his arm, he set his finger against the keyhole and pushed inward.

Elliot chuckled. "It's a good thing Sully is still around. When we get back, he'll be happy to reform your finger into its original shape."

"That's okay," Gully said as he maneuvered his hand clockwise then counterclockwise. "Whenever he can get around to it. I wouldn't want to bother."

A single, metallic clank and the door opened. Gully backed away with a slight stoop as if he did not deserve the honor of entering first. Roni made a mental note to ask Sully if he had started programming cowardice into the golem's instructions.

As if reading her mind, Gully said, "The real threat's behind."

Roni had stepped into many chambers within the Caverns before, but nothing prepared her for this one. Eight columns ran down the length of the chamber, four to a side in parallel lines. Each column had been carved into a grotesque creature — multi-limbed, jagged-toothed, guardians of the room. Some glowered at those who might pass below. Others appeared more interested in their own problems. Each column also held a torch, and each torch burned an unnatural pale-green flame.

As they entered, Elliot said, "I've never seen those flames go out. Whatever magic created them has certainly been long-lasting."

The flickering lights heightened the horrific visages on the columns and danced shadows on the stone flooring — flooring that had been set by skilled hands. Arches of painted wood braced the ceiling with gentle curves. With her head tilted back, Roni noticed a mural on the ceiling.

"This is like a church."

"Not exactly," Elliot said, gesturing to the side.

Roni followed his arms toward the dark walls. She spotted bones. A lot of bones.

A terrible thought struck her. Pointing to the columns, she said, "Are those things golems?"

"No, but I can see why you thought so. They are rather menacing. But they are not golems. When we first learned of this chamber, Sully spent plenty of time making sure."

"Do I want to ask what left all those bones?"

"We've never figured that out. However, this chamber had a purpose before the Society commandeered it. My guess has been that this room was not a church but rather a holy site originally used for sacrifices."

"Great. Just what I wanted to hear."

Gully said, "Not what I wanted to hear. And, you know, you could have asked me about the golems. I can recognize my own kind."

"Sorry. Didn't mean any offense."

"I'm not offended. I'm only trying to point out that I have uses you don't seem to recognize."

"I'll make a note for the future."

"Please do."

At the end of the columns, situated between the final two, a stone platform had been placed. Above the platform, four chains secured an enormous book like a victim being quartered. It hovered in the air, unable to move because the taut chains locked it still. Light from the flickering green flames bounced around the room enough to highlight the book yet somehow never quite spotlight it.

Roni said, "It looks like Gram really wanted to be sure with this thing."

"Indeed." Elliot turned to face her. "But that is not the book. Not exactly. That is the book which holds the universe in which the book with the Pages of Glass exists."

Roni paused. "Are you telling me you hid the Pages of Glass book in another book?"

"That is exactly what I'm telling you."

Doing her best not to shiver, Roni said, "Okay, then — let's go in."

Elliot's mouth dropped open. "Absolutely not."

"I am the leader, and I need to see —"

"No. Those chains are not to be removed. The spell around must not be broken. No one can know where inside that book the Pages of Glass actually reside."

"But —"

"This is not a debate. These are the rules. I, too, have never been in that book. "

Stepping onto the platform, Roni could feel heat pulsing off the cover. "You mean you've never actually been in there? You've never seen these Pages of Glass?"

"Of course not. Nobody has. Not since this whole thing was constructed to protect the book."

"You said Gram put on those chains. So, she knows where it is, right? She's seen the Pages?"

"None of us have. When Gram took over the Society, she was

brought here and shown this room. Instead of chains, the book had been tied by frayed ropes — the best that the weakening leader at the time could do. Gram made these chains to fix that error."

Roni eased away from the platform. Her stomach felt a little sick, and her pulse quickened. "If none of you have seen the Pages, how do you know they're in there? Or if they exist at all?"

"For me, Gram, and Sully, it's been a matter of faith. I know that answer won't help you, so I suggest you look at the more practical evidence."

"Which is?"

"In the Grand Library, you'll find plenty of accounts of people and creatures that have attempted to steal those Pages. You'll also find accounts by Society members who have actually seen the Pages. If you can have faith in the overall mission, you can certainly trust them. In particular, you may want to look up the journals of The Tiger."

"The Tiger?"

"There was a short period when the Society members thought codenames would be a better way to handle their personal lives. Or perhaps it was a superhero fetish. Regardless, that was the codename this particular man used — The Tiger."

They stared at the book for a few minutes until finally, Gully said, "If the two of you wish to remain here, I'm happy to keep guard. However, this does not seem like the safest part of the Caverns for us to be. I'm only pointing it out. Not making any judgments."

Roni bit back her laughter — Gully had feelings of a sort — and they headed back. Elliot led the way, and Roni did her best to remember each turn and pathway they followed. When they reached the bookstore basement, they found Teanna sitting at the bottom of the stairs.

"Finally," she said, jumping to her feet. "I tried to call you on your phone, but the Caverns don't get good reception."

"Parts don't. What's wrong?" Roni asked.

"Three little gifts were dropped off at the front door — more relic boxes."

Chapter 9

The three carved boxes had been placed on the big table in the main room of the bookstore. One had been made from mahogany, one of marble, and the last mere sandstone. The writing that spiraled from the lid to the base matched that of the first relic box they had dealt with — a language connected to Yal-hara.

Gram and Sully sat at the far end of the table. Sully slumped in his wheelchair, his pasty skin looking worse every day as if he were flaking off into nothing. Gram stroked his arm. While Roni knew the man was still cogent, watching him stare at these boxes with vacancy in his eyes broke her heart.

Garcia stood with his back against the wall, his arms crossed, his face screwed up in concentration. Teanna walked over and joined him on the wall. Either he didn't pick up on her signals that standing against the wall was her position or he didn't care. Even her repeated glowers in his direction could not make him budge.

When Roni approached, Gram's eyes flicked her way — a short acknowledgment that Roni now knew the secret of the Pages of Glass. *Or maybe I'm reading too much into it.* Everything about those Pages left Roni dizzy in her attempts to keep up with the truth. Easier to focus on the more solid problems facing them on the table.

"Who found them?" she asked.

With one hand patting her crucifix, Gram raised the other. "We were all upstairs chatting — getting to know Garcia better. Delightful man. The doorbell rang. I came down and answered it. I thought it was one of our old customers — they still come by every few weeks hoping we've reopened. Instead, I found these three relics sitting on the sidewalk in front of our door."

Without looking up, Garcia said, "She called for me and asked that I take a look. I presume because I had found the previous one."

"I'm not one to turn down any level of expertise."

Roni tried to convince herself that Gram meant exactly what she said, that there wasn't a thinly veiled insult directed her way. No, no, no. She had to put all that aside. The relic boxes mattered at the moment. All else had to be put off for another day.

Garcia said, "We carefully moved them in here and set them on this table. That's when Teanna ran out the door."

Teanna nodded. "I went around the block, but I could not find anybody who looked suspicious. Of course, whoever left these boxes may have come by car and then drove off."

"Doesn't matter," Roni said. "We know who they're from."

Pulling out one of her hatchets, Teanna said, "We also know what creatures reside within."

"I agree with the sentiment, but I suspect small axes won't do the job."

"They worked find before."

"There's no reason to assume these all hold centipede beasts you can handle."

"I don't intend to find out. If I smash the boxes —"

Garcia said, "I wouldn't advise that. These are not normal boxes — obviously — and they won't appreciate being assaulted by an axe. At best, you'll probably do nothing significant. Worst — you'll piss off whatever's inside and make it come out."

Roni bent closer to the marble box. "Anybody know how to destroy these things?"

Pushing off the wall, Garcia tapped a finger in the air. "Don't be so hasty. These can be dangerous, true, but remember — I carried one around for well over a year before it went off. We should take the time to study these boxes, analyze them. We could learn a lot about our enemy from understanding what they sent us."

"Garcia?"

"Yes?"

"Shut up."

Gram smacked the table. "There's no need for rudeness."

"Okay, then. Let me put it this way. Garcia, you are here as our guest and as a potential member of the team. Nothing more. Besides, why would Yal-hara have her people set these on our doorstep if not to cause us harm? Do you really think she wants us to analyze her relic boxes so that we can perhaps find out more information about her?

Discover a weakness, maybe? Does that make any sense?"

"While I agree with you," Elliot chimed in, "I would also say that Garcia's suggestion is not without merit. Perhaps we should take these boxes up to the new lab and see what happens."

"What happens? That doesn't sound a bit reckless?"

"Naturally, I would create a protective barrier around the laboratory to ensure that, should there be a problem, it remains contained."

Sully said, "With you in it? That's not using your noggin. I agree with Roni. We can't allow that."

With a placating chuckle, Garcia placed his fingertips on the table and leaned forward as if he might kiss one of the relics. "You're all overreacting. Worse, if you try to destroy these now, you'll squander a great opportunity to advance the Society's knowledge. If you don't want me doing it, I completely understand. But don't let any distrust towards me ruin the chance you have right here."

"It's not distrust," Teanna said. "Just caution."

Roni said, "We don't even know what triggered the first box to open. Maybe if they're picked up so many times, or maybe it's body heat, or maybe they are remotely detonated and we have to be concerned about Kenneth Bay or one of his people spying on us right now."

"All of that is possible," Garcia said. He pointed toward Teanna's hatchet. "I can guarantee this much, though. Striking it with that is not going to help. You want to destroy them, but you have no idea how to do so safely."

Teanna put her hatchet away. "We don't have to actually destroy them. We can handle this the same way we handle any relic. Gram will make a book, and we will throw the boxes into the book and into an empty void of a universe."

"Excuse me." Gully raised two fingers. "First, Roni is our leader. It falls onto her to decide."

Great. Now they want me to decide.

"And second, I need my finger fixed."

While the golem walked over to Sully to have his finger expertly reshaped, the room grew quiet. Roni walked over to the sales counter and looked outside the storefront window. She could feel the eyes of her team on her back and knew they would wait for her answer — but only for so long. Like it or not, Gully was right — she had to make the decision.

Of course, Teanna was right, too. In fact, one of Roni's first thoughts had been to use a book and simply get rid of these relics. But making books required physical exertion. Gram did not just spew them out with each breath. They needed effort on her part — and though Roni did not like to admit it, Gram was getting old.

Glancing over her shoulder, Roni saw the way Gram sat at the far end of the table. Her fingers had a slight shudder to them. Not from fear. Roni doubted Gram even noticed. But that shudder was there.

The lingering truth — Roni assumed that using their abilities put great strain on their bodies. The Old Gang needed to last as long as possible. Not only because Roni loved them and wanted them around, but because the Parallel Society needed them. Without Gram, they had no way to manufacture books at all. Without Elliot, they had limited protection and would have to heal the natural way. Even as Sully had abdicated his role to the golem, he had yet to completely update Gully's instructions with all of his thoughts, memories, and knowledge.

No way would Roni demand Gram go to an early grave simply to make a few books of convenience.

But at the same time, it was the responsibility of the Parallel Society's leader to put the safety of the universe ahead of her own personal desires. It wasn't just that the decision was hers to make — she would have to atone for any mistakes, too.

This wasn't simply trying to thread a needle. Rather, Roni felt like the spool of thread whirring through the twists and turns of a sewing machine, and she had no way to slow it down.

In the end, she knew what all leaders came to know — there was no right decision. She would have to go with her best guess and present it with complete certainty and utter conviction. Good leaders were often good liars. Or at least, good at faking surety.

Summoning her inner-poker player, she turned back to the group and hoped they didn't know how bad she was at cards.

"Here's what we're going to do — Elliot and Garcia will take the relic boxes up to the new lab. See what you can learn and figure out the safest way to destroy those things. Gram, I want you to take Sully back to his apartment. Then, both of you get some rest. Before you argue, recognize that if Elliot and Garcia fail, we're going to need you to make some books. I won't ask that of you unless I have to. So, rest up and be ready. Gully, you are to stay down here and stand guard. Whoever dropped off these boxes knows where we live. And we also know that Kenneth Bay knows the Caverns are beneath this bookstore — or has anybody forgotten about my disastrous date with the infamous Darin?"

To answer Teanna and Garcia's shared confusion, Roni added, "A guy who faked interest in me but really wanted to steal a chained book on behalf of Yal-hara. Teanna and I are going down to the Grand Library. We'll figure out what language is written on those relics. Maybe it can clue us into more about our enemy or at least what triggers these things off. Questions?"

Nobody spoke. In fact, Roni thought she saw the assurance of a team ready to follow orders. She would never admit it, but she even saw a glimmer of satisfaction cross Gram's mouth.

"Okay then. Let's get to work."

CHAPTER 10

The Grand Library had finally taken shape after several years of hard labor. Most of the books had been shelved properly, and those yet to find a home had been set aside in organized boxes. The worktables had been cleaned off, repaired, or removed depending on their condition. Roni had even been able to save the office desk for the librarian. Best of all, with some help from Elliot, she had put up walls to formalize a space for her Cavern mapping project — a glass window let her look across the library from inside or check on the map from the office desk.

For Roni, this section of the world belonged to her. Part sanctuary, part reservoir of knowledge — the Grand Library existed as both an integral secret floor of the bookstore and an extension of the Cavern. At least, that was how she thought of it.

Emerging from the elevator, she pointed to the nearest worktable. "Set up over there."

Teanna did so, but her stiff movements betrayed her discomfort. Roni did not press. She knew Teanna well enough now — the woman would not hide for long.

"This is strange," Teanna said after only a few seconds.

As Roni walked over to her desk, she said, "Relic boxes are new to me, too, but hardly that strange compared to all the other things we've dealt with."

"I meant *this* — having me down here. I'm not an academic. I should be upstairs with Gully, guarding the store. Or maybe I should be on the streets, searching for any sign I could use to track our adversaries."

"True." Roni opened the bottom drawer and pulled out a bottle of vodka. "But then you wouldn't be able to share a drink with me."

Teanna fought back a grin. "While I am always happy to do so, it doesn't seem wise at this moment. I need to be alert."

"Also true." She set two tumblers on the desk. "However, I am the one who gives the orders."

"Are you ordering me to drink?"

"I'm asking you to recognize that what has happened with these relics won't be the end. I've been through enough of these situations, and I know that whatever is going on will only get worse. That being the case, it seems to me that we should have a little drink to relieve a little tension so that we are at our best when necessary."

Teanna gave Roni's words a second of thought. Then she flopped in the chair and gestured for a glass. "You are the leader, after all."

Sitting at the worktable, Roni poured two tumblers of vodka and knocked hers back too fast. It burned down her throat. She winced. As the sensation eased into a warmth around her belly, she said, "Not anywhere close to top shelf, but it does its job."

After sipping on her vodka, Teanna said, "We also have a job. Not that I know how to do it, but shouldn't we get started?"

Roni wanted to order her teammate to sit and drink and not worry about the world above them. Or the one below. She had enough experience with the Caverns to know that all those problems would not run off while they drank. A short repose would not harm matters. But then, she also had enough experience to know that sometimes matters did get harmed. Sometimes procrastination damaged relationships.

She paused. A thought hovered within her, desperate to be heard but also hiding from her like a shy girl clawing the hem of her mother's skirt as a shield. Yet the moment Roni noticed the thought, all ability for her subconscious to conceal it evaporated. The thought would take shape into words, and she had only one way to thwart it.

"You're right," she said. "Let's get to work."

She directed Teanna to the *Foreign Languages* section which housed books covering the seventy-four different languages and over a hundred related dialects discovered since the inception of the Society. Many of the books were the lifetime work of Inez Pritchard. Elliot once said that nobody before or since Ms. Pritchard had come close in ability with language. It probably helped that, long before joining the Society, the woman spoke close to forty-two homegrown languages.

While Teanna got started on that project, Roni drifted several aisles over into the personal journals and diaries. She could have used the computer system to locate the book, but taking the time to find it herself meant postponing the inevitable for a few extra minutes. Besides, the database had yet to be fully updated. She would have remembered coming across a codename like *The Tiger*. Or any codename. Since she did not, the books from that era were either already shelved or tucked away in the boxes yet to be uncovered. Either way, it helped her push off whatever awaited them in the coming days.

The books, however, did not wish to be so helpful. Before she reached the end of the first aisle, she found *The Journal of the Tiger*. Damn. *In four volumes*. Crap.

She returned to the worktable and settled in a chair, wiggling to get comfortable — this would take time. Not a bad thing, of course, but a tedious one. Opening the first volume, Roni scanned through each page, seeking any keywords like Pages of Glass or Yal-hara that would suggest she had reached the correct point in the Tiger's life. While she searched, Teanna returned with an armful of texts to also sift through. A few too many. But Roni said nothing — she didn't want to detract from Teanna's clear efforts.

"You haven't asked me about the Pages," Roni said.

Teanna did not look up from her books. "Not my place to ask."

"Aren't you curious?"

"Of course. But you are the one that chooses what the rest of us need to know. We have to trust that you'll share with us anything important."

The same could be said of the Tiger. He had tried to join the Society in 1922 but was kept from being an official member. *Associate* was the word they gave him. He dubbed himself the Tiger and acted as if he were a full member.

> *It is understandable that the other members want to keep their ranks small. Secrecy is the prime operative of any secret society, and with one as vital to the safety of all mankind, the secrecy for this particular society is of the utmost importance. That does not, however, make their treatment of me any less infuriating. I'm alone, walking through the woods, angry, frustrated, and hungry to prove myself. Thus, I am the Tiger.*

He went on about his special circumstances and how undervalued he was. The more Roni read, the more she comprehended why the Society had sidelined the Tiger. He was annoying and arrogant. He wanted recognition — not a good thing in a group that must remain unnoticed.

Pouring more vodka in their glasses, Roni said, "Elliot told me that eventually I should show you the Pages, but not until the Old Gang has passed on."

"It's a good strategy," Teanna said.

"But is it right? Keeping secrets to protect secrets. Seems a bit backwards since you are my teammate — and my roommate, for that matter."

Teanna pushed aside the book she had been studying. "There was a time once, when I was little, that I went out on my own, behind my house, to spend the day tracking a *foosh*. It's a little creature like an oversized squirrel. I couldn't wait to learn how to track properly, so I decided to do it on my own. I followed the marks on the ground, the little trails dug in from repeated use, the scat that the *foosh* left behind, and in the end, I found the little creature's home. Feeling quite proud of myself, I looked up to discover that I had no idea where I was. It would be nearly nighttime when my father found me. Once the worry that I was dead had passed, he grew furious."

"I would've thought he'd be proud. You took the initiative at such a young age."

"I also showed impatience — not a good trait for a tracker. In my world, a child's education is carefully crafted for the best results in the profession the child was born into. I had destroyed those plans by teaching myself some basic tracking skills."

"And that's bad?"

"It can be. If I teach myself wrong." Teanna pulled her book back.

Roni said, "That's it?"

"You want to hear about my punishment? Why? The point of the story is already made."

"It is? What does it have to do with keeping secrets?"

"I thought it was clear." Teanna frowned. Then: "Perhaps there are cultural mistranslations."

She returned to her work and Roni did so, too. Skipping ahead several pages, she discovered that the Tiger had grown more and more of a painful thorn to the Society. He knew they wanted him to give up and leave. But he refused to abandon this opportunity — especially because doing so meant weakening the universe's protection. After all, as he saw it, the Society did not yet appreciate the value he would bring to their mission.

In an effort to placate the man, or perhaps a softening of their attitude towards him, the Society members invited the Tiger to join in an evening celebration. From what Roni could tell, there was no particular reason for the party, but in the Roaring 20s, there rarely needed to be a reason. As long as somebody provided the booze, the party happened.

> *Because the rest of us couldn't play a single instrument, Bluewing ended up spending the entire night at the piano. Diamond (who could play the tuba, but nobody wanted that) loved to sing and dance, and I made an effort to hit the floor with her. She seemed more interested in Silverblade, but then again, she hardly knows me. I thought that way for most of the night until things quieted down and she offered to show me the Caverns. I couldn't wait. I had been wanting to see these Caverns since I first heard of the Society.*

Roni suspected the Tiger had something else on his mind as well. Half-drunk, half-horny, and full of excitement, he followed Diamond through the winding passageways until he reached the chamber of carved pillars. The book which held the book which held the Pages of Glass had been tied with a special rope — the very one Gram would later have to replace with her chains.

Whether Diamond had lured the Tiger there out of malice or true desire, the Tiger did not tell. Perhaps he could never figure it out. But she explained what awaited anybody bold enough, brave enough, strong enough to enter that book.

> *I knew the challenge had been made. This was not a slap in the face sort of challenge, though. This was the Society's last test. Succeed here and I would finally be allowed to join them. I would finally be allowed to fulfill my destiny.*

As Roni read on, the world slipped away around her. She forgot about the Library, Teanna, the relic boxes, the Old Gang — all of it became a faint whisper. The Tiger had woven a masterful work, and — but no. She did not believe that. To do so was to allow her mind to create a lie that protected her from the truth. And the truth? She wanted to step inside that book herself. She had felt the desire when Elliot refused to let her go in, and she felt it now as Tiger took his first steps. The book, the Pages, held such promise that any sane person could not help but want to take a peek. Even if only for a second. Catch a glimpse of something powerful enough to change not only one world, but all worlds.

> *It was horrible. In all the time I have spent with the Society, I have never gone inside a book since this, and I never will. When I first entered, I dropped several feet to the floor. It was soft like walking on dry sand, but it looked the pink color and craggy surface of a tongue. In fact, as I turned in a circle to take in my surroundings, everything brought to mind a giant mouth. The long throat of a tunnel, the strands of mucous stretching off the roof, the pinks and reds and crimsons, and the rows of porcelain stones like teeth. The stench of rotting meat permeated the air and I doubled over to purge all that alcohol sitting in my stomach. That's when I heard the high-low, deep echoing pitches like a whale song. I knew at that moment what was going on. Somehow, through some magic of the universe in that book, some force had reached into my brain and pulled out my own personal childhood horror. It came from when my mother first read to me the tale of Jonah and the Whale. The idea of being trapped inside a giant whale terrified me as a boy, yet as I grew older, the old fear stayed with me. And here I was now, in that very position of Jonah.*

Roni closed the journal, keeping her index finger between the pages as a bookmark, and once more, thought about Elliot's response in the Caverns. As usual with the Old Gang, what they told her did not cover the full story. Since Elliot had pointed her to the Tiger's journal, it made sense that he had read it himself. That meant he knew what could happen if she had entered the book. He was protecting her every bit as much as he was protecting the Pages.

If that world reached into her mind, it would find numerous horrors to choose from. But she knew which it would pick — the worst one, of course. Yal-hara. Creeping along Roni's bed on spindly legs, crawling over her eight-year-old body, snatching her little girl memories. Even thinking of it now, Roni could feel how petrified she had been, unable to move, unable to do anything but watch and listen to this bizarre creature as it ruined her life.

Elliot, Sully, Gram, Teanna, Garcia — each one of them would have their own private terrors which that universe would draw from. A horrid experience meant to keep the person from moving forward towards the Pages. But what about Gully? He wasn't human. He didn't really have a brain with memories. For that matter, he was barely two years old. Not much could have happened to traumatize him. Perhaps he could withstand what that book might throw at him.

"What do you think of Gully?" Roni asked.

With an impatient shove of her book, Teanna said, "Why does that matter?"

"Do you consider him a living being? Or is he more like a robot? Something more like a tool."

"He's Gully. That's all."

"But should a golem be afforded the same rights as us? I mean, if he's only a piece of equipment — granted, he's a charming one and we project our humanness onto him — but he's not really alive. He doesn't have a heart or a brain. Yet we all agree that he deserves a vote when we all vote. We treat him like his opinion matters."

"Then you have your answer."

"I'm not so sure."

Closing all her books and stacking them up, Teanna flicked her tongue against her top lip. She sighed. "I will try one more time. Listen closely, and maybe you'll understand. Most every day of my life I trained to become a tracker. I was born for it. Any time my parents spent with me was spent preparing for the possibility that I might be called upon to fill this crucial role for my people. According to my father, one night he heard me crying and came to my bedside to ask what was wrong. I have no memory of this, but he would never lie to me, so I am sure it happened. Through my halting tears and gasps and carrying on, I told him that I worried I would never — *measure up?* Is that the right phrase?"

"You wouldn't be as good as you thought you needed to be, or as good as others required of you."

"Yes, exactly. Measure up. He patted my head when he heard this and laughed. As he walked away, he said that I shouldn't worry for I am also his daughter."

From the way Teanna stopped, Roni realized the story had ended. "Thank you," she said, baffled at how this connected with her talk of Gully.

Before Roni could open her book again, a loud bang echoed from above. One look at Teanna and all thoughts of a massive thunderstorm vanished, all chances that somebody had dropped a heavy piece of furniture disappeared.

Teanna popped to her feet. "Shotgun fire."

Chapter 11

Tearing up the stairs, Roni followed Teanna toward the main floor. When they burst into the room, they found Gully standing in the middle, holding a shotgun, and aiming it toward the back stairs that led to the upper floors. Teanna had her hatchets out, her feet spread in a wide stance, and her eyes roving the area. Roni thought she looked like a ninja, and right then, having a ninja on the team sounded like a great idea.

Trying to force her jackhammering pulse to slow, Roni strode over to Gully. "What's happened?" She half-hoped he would say that he opened fire on a cockroach — an intruder in his mind. But she knew he was smarter than that.

"A creature dropped in from above," Gully said. "I think Elliot and Garcia have accidentally opened one of the relic boxes."

She bit back a slew of curses and sarcastic comments that would do nothing to help matters. But she could not stop one question from escaping her lips: "Where did you get a shotgun?"

"Gram, of course. She put it under the front counter for me."

"For you? Specifically?"

"Because Sully had to sacrifice some of my strength in order for my mind to function at a higher level than most golems, Gram thought this would be a sensible solution."

As Roni tried to swallow this development, she heard a deep grunt from the back stairs. Her muscles tensed. Turning to look at the creature descending to the main floor, she felt each heavy stomp on the stairs as much as saw them.

At first, she thought she stared at an enormous gorilla. It had the hair and musculature of a large primate. But its face was all wrong. More like a lizard with long strands of hair flowing off its snout. Where its forearms should have been, Roni saw metallic posts — at least, they looked metallic.

The monstrosity reached the bottom landing with a powerful movement. It knew it had strength. No need to rush forward.

Snorting like a bull, it cocked its head to the right — toward Teanna — and the left at Gully and Roni. Appraising its opponents.

Where were Elliot and Garcia? Roni pushed down that thought, that terrible thought, because she could do nothing to help Elliot if he lay upstairs bleeding. Not until this beast no longer posed a threat.

She opened her mouth and started to utter an order to attack, but the creature beat her to it. Launching off its metallic forearms, it shot forward, kicking out at Teanna. Its speed startled everyone as it tore across the room.

Teanna dove into a forward roll while the creature landed on the spot she had just occupied. Gully swung the shotgun over and opened fire. The noise shook the room as the scattered pellets ripped up the wall to the right of the beast.

Roni understood now why Gram had chosen a shotgun for a weapon. Gully had terrible aim. With a weapon that spread its damage in wide patterns, aim held less importance. Except when their teammate was in the way.

Teanna flattened to the floorboards as Gully blasted a second shot into the air. This time, he clipped the beast, but that only made the thing angrier. It trampled the back of Teanna's leg, pivoted and kicked her in the side. With each attack, it grunted and snorted like mechanical pistons releasing pressure. Then it scooped Teanna up as if she weighed no more than a twirling leaf and hurled her against the wall.

"Watch where you shoot that thing," Roni said, shoving the shotgun barrel down. "You're going to hit Teanna." She pulled the gun away — Gully did not resist — and looked it over. She had never shot this kind of thing before.

Bellowing a raged cry, Teanna burst into the air. She hit the beast, dragging her hatchets down its flank as she dropped to the ground. It roared. Green-brown liquid sprayed out as it twisted away from those deadly weapons.

Roni struggled to pump the shotgun — it resisted more than she expected — but once she succeeded, the used shell popped out with a hollow sound and the next round clacked into place. She walked straight towards the creature. It loomed over Teanna, its back to Roni, and she held the momentary illusion that this would turn out to be easy.

But the creature planted its posts hard onto the floor, lifted its hindquarters into the air, and kicked back. One foot knocked the shotgun upward — the ear-splitting report followed by pieces of the ceiling raining down. The other foot caught Roni in the chest, thrusting her backwards. When she fell, the shotgun skidded out of her hands.

Roni's head felt loose. Rattled, she managed to rise onto her elbows — long enough to see Gully race across the room. As Teanna swept her hatchets back and forth, keeping the beast distracted, Gully swiped the shotgun off the ground, pumped in a fresh shell, and charged. He made no effort at stealth, and when he caught the beast's attention, Teanna made it pay for the mistake.

She hacked into its arm, cutting deep enough that the muscles went dead and the limb became useless, dragging with the odd, musical tone of a metal pipe. Confused and angry, unsure which threat to address, the creature tried to back away. But Gully planted the muzzle of his weapon against the beast's belly and squeezed the trigger.

A flash and smoke and a loud crack. The horrid creature flailed backwards.

When the echoes died in her ears, Roni clambered to her feet and joined her team. They all stared at the creature, apprehensive and waiting — but it did not rise again.

"Everyone okay?" she asked.

Teanna rolled her shoulder before holstering her blades. "A little bruised, but I'm fine."

"Gully?"

"I'm unharmed. And thank you for asking."

Roni surveyed the damage to the bookstore. Shotgun pellets had ripped up the walls, ceiling, and floor. The foul-smelling innards of the creature painted lines where it had sprayed out. A slight dent where Teanna had been tossed into the wall. Otherwise, not too bad.

"I hope Garcia knows how to shove this huge thing back into that little box. If not, I'm assigning him the job of cutting it up into little bits and spreading it in dumpsters across Philly. Teanna, you and I deserve another drink."

A thud against the ceiling stopped Roni. They all glanced upwards. The sound of glass shattering. A throaty yell.

Teanna reached back for her hatchets. "This is not over."

CHAPTER 12

Between the overall quiet of the last year and her regular outings at the clubs, Roni could feel how out-of-shape she had become. Dashing up two flights of stairs to the new lab left her winded, her legs sore, and her blood pounding through her veins. She wanted to bend over, hands on knees, and do nothing but breathe, but the creature attempting to kill Elliot and Garcia changed her mind.

Garcia crouched over the table set up by the window, frantically mixing liquids and powders into a glass. Elliot stood tall with his cane held vertical, moving in a steady pattern as if he churned butter. A shimmering amber dome protected them while the creature perched atop and smashed its fists downward — all six of them. Elliot winced at each blow as if he felt some of the force his shield withstood.

Looking straight at Roni, the creature paused. It had light, tan skin dappled with white specks and a lean physique. Still strong, though. More like a martial artist than the brute they had fought downstairs. No hair, either. Its numerous arms grew oddly — two out of the shoulders like normal, but two from the hips, and one out of each thigh. Three sharp horns formed a line down the center of its bald head. With a row of seven beady eyes like black marbles, the monster appeared to shift its gaze to Teanna and then Gully before returning to its attempts at entering the shield.

Gully raised the shotgun, but Roni said, "No. Too many people in this room."

"But Elliot and Garcia are protected, and we are standing behind the blast."

Fair point. Except Roni could see the sweat on Elliot's cheek. It was difficult to maintain a shield. She had seen him last far longer than this, though. Perhaps it was age getting the better of him. "Do not shoot that gun," she said. Then: "Teanna?"

Narrowing her dark eyes forward, Teanna twirled her hatchets. "No problem."

Like a nimble gymnast, albeit one with a few injuries, she sprang forward and vaulted onto the table. The creature whirled around to follow her movements. The instant her feet touched the surface, she bounded off with her hatchets leading the way. The creature covered its head using two arms, but the sharp weapons cut right to the bone. It screeched, and a satisfied smirk rose on Teanna's face.

That didn't last long.

The creature's four other arms punched upward. Teanna hurled to the ceiling and crashed onto the protection dome. Straining for air, she slid to the floor. But the creature had her in its mind now. It hopped down, grabbed Teanna's ankle, and swung her toward the doorway. A gasp escaped her as she met the floor with her face.

With a victorious bark, the creature lumbered toward her. Elliot dropped the shield, leaned heavily on his cane, sweat soaking his collar, and he coughed hard. Gully rushed to his side just as Sully would have done years earlier.

Before joining them, Roni glanced over at Teanna. That brave woman wobbled back on her feet and swiped at the creature. A few more attacks and she was dancing around it — hobbling a bit, though. While it attempted to catch hold of any part of her, she continued to take little chunks of flesh as payment. The thing did not seem too bright — no matter how many times Teanna evaded, it continued with the same tactic.

Roni hastened to Garcia. "I'm rethinking this idea of keeping the boxes around for analysis."

"We don't know what happened."

"Sure we do. Two of those boxes opened because you messed with them."

"We barely touched them." As he spoke, he swirled the contents of his potion, checking its color or clarity or something — Roni only knew that it took the man too long.

A loud grunt caught all of their attention. The creature had finally landed a blow on Teanna. She stumbled against the wall before regaining her composure. When the creature tried to follow up with another punch, she roared — teeth bared, eyes blazing — and swung one hatchet upward. The sharp blade cleaved the creature's fist, showering the floor in yellow-red liquid. Probably blood. It smelled like rotten grapefruit.

Gully helped Elliot settle on a lab stool. To Roni, he said, "Should I use the shotgun now?"

"No," Garcia said.

"I'm in charge here," Roni said. Then: "Gully, no."

"Look, because we've taken the time to examine these boxes, and because I happen to know a bit about what I'm doing, I have the answer right here." He raised the glass, the solution inside had become clear.

"Great," Roni said. "We'll all die waiting for you, but at least you got to announce how smart you are."

Scowling, he pointed towards the fight. "Just get me the boxes."

Roni looked over at Teanna and the creature. The two open boxes — the mahogany one and the sandstone one — were on the floor. Directly beneath the creature. It even knocked one aside as it dodged Teanna's incoming attack.

"Crap." Roni stomped over to Gully and grabbed the shotgun.

The golem startled. "But you said we can't shoot with all these people around."

"I'm not going to shoot."

Clutching the barrel, she heaved the stock over her shoulder and rushed into the fight. The creature faced off with Teanna, its focus centered on her. Swinging the shotgun like a baseball bat, Roni smacked the beast on the side. It howled, and she swore she heard a few bones crack. When it spun to face her, Teanna took advantage, lunging forward and slashing one, two, three times along its spine. It tried to punch Roni, but the pain and damage slowed its actions. She avoided the attack with ease.

When she wound up for another bashing, the creature whirled onto Teanna — perhaps hoping to surprise the nimble tracker. But Teanna not only dashed out of the way, she managed to get another strike on one of its lower-arms.

Breathing hard and hoarse, the beast backed up toward the corner. Roni could see that it still had plenty of fight. It merely needed a moment to regroup, get some air, and figure out how to deal with both women.

Roni made that part easy. She swiped the relic boxes off the floor and darted away from the fight. She thrust the boxes over to Garcia, her eyes wide as she peeked back at Teanna. They had slowed the creature, disoriented it, but how much longer could Teanna last?

"Hurry up," she said.

Garcia ignored her, having already placed the boxes on the worktable and positioned the potion-filled glass above. Elliot perked up enough to turn his head and watch closely. Behind him, Roni noticed that Gully kept his attention on the creature. Though he held still, she knew to her bones that he would jump in to help Teanna the second it looked necessary — regardless of Roni's commands.

The creature stood taller, puffing out its chest. While its upper arms hung limp, the others flexed their muscles. Blood dribbled along the curves highlighting the creature's strength, and even the chunks of flesh that Teanna had hacked out managed to convey a greater threat than before.

Garcia tilted the glass. The clear liquid poured out in a slow, gloopy strand like an egg yolk. With a pen, Garcia broke off the goo, saving a little less than half in the glass.

Fed up with waiting, Teanna attempted to take the offensive. But the creature had renewed its focus. In the corner, it didn't need to think about attacks at its flanks or from behind. It only paid attention to Teanna.

She jabbed at its leg. Ducking two fists, she twirled for a strike higher up when a third caught her on the shoulder. She tumbled to the floor, let out a high-pitched groan, and scurried to her feet — but slower than before, less steady.

The monster stepped forward. It opened its jaw, and with a large inhale, it let out a mighty — nothing.

It froze.

Its face wrinkled in confusion.

Roni looked to the table. The wooden relic box sizzled. Wisps of gray-blue smoke rose from it as the potion bubbled wherever it made contact.

Holding her shoulder, Teanna limped back toward the doorway. The monster moved after her, but its weakening legs shuffled a few inches before stopping. Gray-blue smoke seeped out of its wounds. It clutched its stomach. With a terrified gaze at Roni and a helpless expression as if it would cry out for its mother, the creature dissolved at an increasing rate until nothing remained. Nothing but the smoke which dissipated as it rose to the ceiling.

Roni expected some kind of odor — perhaps acrid like burnt plastic, perhaps disturbing like a finely cooked steak. However, she smelled nothing. Not even rotten grapefruit. Perhaps a faint hint of mold, but that could have been the bookstore itself.

"It worked," Elliot said with great satisfaction.

Garcia poured the remaining contents onto the second box. "Of course." Though he sounded confident, Roni thought he looked a bit surprised, exhausted, and shaken.

She scrutinized every member of the team, checking that they had survived with minimal injury — at least, nothing that needed immediate, serious attention. Though Teanna had taken the most punishment, each passing minute appeared to revive her. Satisfied, Roni walked over to the final relic box. Made of marble, it weighed more. She couldn't help but shudder at that extra heft coupled with the cold of the stone. When she set it on the table, the solid thud seemed to echo far too long in her ears.

"Destroy this one, too," she said, trusting the warnings her body had given.

Garcia's condescending tone irritated her long before she actual heard his words. "No, no, no, you don't want to do that. It's the only one we have left. We've got to study it more."

"Did you miss everything that just happened? We are not waiting for round three."

"Even if I wanted to destroy it, I can't. I don't have any more of the potion."

"Then make some." The growl in Roni's voice pushed Garcia back a step.

"Perhaps you're right." He got to work.

To Elliot, she said, "Are you okay?"

"I'll be fine. Just a little embarrassed."

"You have nothing to be embarrassed about."

"A few years ago, I could have held that shield up for hours. I've protected you on several occasions with exactly the same shield. But now — let me tell you this: getting old is no fun."

As they chatted, Teanna inched closer to the table. She never looked away from the relic box, and Roni worried Teanna had picked up on some nuanced movement — that the creature inside had already escaped, was now invisible, and stalked them like prey. Back before Roni had heard of the Parallel Society, the idea would have seemed far-fetched. But after all she had experienced, it was far too possible.

An eager grin spread on Teanna's lips. "Do not destroy this one until I return. Please."

"Where are you going?"

"Down to the Grand Library. Each relic box had different writing on it — different languages or maybe just different dialects. I couldn't match any of them. But this box has changed."

Elliot and Garcia both said, "Changed?"

"These symbols are not the same as those I wrote down earlier. But I think I recognize these new ones." Hustling out the door, she added, "Don't touch that box again. And please, don't destroy it. Not yet."

While they waited, everyone gazed at the relic box like visitors at a zoo waiting for a sleeping lion to wake. Roni kept expecting the writing to alter before her eyes — perhaps the others thought the same — but nothing happened. Though the fighting had ended, her adrenaline pumped hard. Until this third box was destroyed, she guessed that her nerves would remain on edge.

Hoping to minimize the tremble in her voice, she spoke in a low, soft tone. "Mr. Garcia, would you please work on that potion."

Garcia nodded, yet as he turned to his supplies, he kept snatching glances back. This bit of movement snapped the others out of their shared trance. Gully stepped toward the doorway to stand guard, while Elliot rested his chin on his cane as he considered the marble box.

"The shifting words must be like a security code that changes each day," Elliot said. "Or perhaps it's the trigger — some kind of spell that acts like a countdown."

"The words keep changing until they reach the right combination to open? Something like that?"

"Perhaps." He straightened with a stretch. "I'm an old man, but no matter how much I've seen, there are too many universes to see it all. I could be completely wrong. For all I know, the writing is mere decoration."

"I doubt that."

"Me, too, but almost anything is possible."

Several minutes later, Teanna entered the lab carrying a thick, dusty volume. She plunked it down next to the relic box and started leafing through pages. Snapping her fingers, she waved over a pen and paper. Roni had never seen Teanna show such vigorous interest in non-violent work, so she let the tracker have her space.

Gully continued his guarding of the lab, and Elliot watched Teanna like a proud grandfather. Roni did not want to disturb either of them. She turned to Garcia.

As he measured out a gray powder, she sidled next to him and rested her elbow on the table. "How long does a potion take?"

"Longer if you interrupt me."

She winced. "I know things are rough between us, but I wanted to thank you for making this potion — both before and now."

"It's what I'm here to do — how I hope to help the Society."

"I never even knew potions were a thing until you showed up. My introduction to the Society was rather abrupt and unplanned. I didn't have mentors to guide me along for years."

Garcia glanced over at Elliot. "He seems like a good mentor."

"Oh, he is. All of them have helped me get caught up, but they didn't tell me about any of this for over thirty years." She thought about her Lost Time and Yal-hara crawling over her paralyzed body. "There were other issues in the way. But the point is —"

"I got the point." With a terse motion, he dumped the powder back into its container and started measuring again. "You are the leader. You don't know enough about what the Society does, but for some reason, they trust you to run things. I have no choice but to accept this, if I'm to be a part of this team — which, according to you, is questionable. Does that sum it up okay?"

Roni pushed off the table and adjusted her shirt. "I was trying to be friendly. Sorry for the mistake."

Closing his eyes, Garcia said, "Making a potion is not easy. It's not throwing a bunch of ingredients together, stirring it in water, and you suddenly have magic. It takes precision, intention, concentration, and will."

"I get it. I'll leave you alone."

"That's not what I'm saying."

"Just focus on your potion."

Roni walked off toward the doorway. But Gully was there, and she did not want to deal with the golem at that moment. She stopped in the center of the room. Nowhere to go.

A black telephone mounted to the wall next to the doorway rang. Everybody jumped. Eager for anything to do, Roni hustled over. She had never noticed it before — simply part of the background — but the crisp paint around the edges and the dust accumulating on top promised it had been there for ages.

When she put the receiver to her ear, part of her braced for the voice of Kenneth Bay. Instead, she heard Gram. "Is everyone okay down there? We could hear the commotion, but I didn't want to leave Sully alone."

Roni laughed — more from relief than anything humorous. "We've got it all under control."

"What happened, dear?"

"Two of the relic boxes opened. I'll tell you everything tonight. There's still a loose end to tie up down here."

Slamming her book closed, Teanna said, "I think I've got it."

"Gotta go." Roni hung up the phone and rushed back to the table. "What's it say?"

From her paper, she read: "By the great Oslight and Her servant, Yal-hara, the command is given. Break free, find the Pages of Glass, and return." She pointed to a double-line on the box. "That's the end there. Then it starts over. Every time you see those two lines, the phrase repeats."

At the head of the box, instead of starting the phrase once more, the double-line was followed by an indented dot. "What's that," Roni said, running her finger over the surface.

When her skin touched the dot, all of the writing on the box glowed like the bizarre luminescent fish from the depths of the ocean. Roni jumped back as Teanna wielded her hatchets. Garcia slid to the end of the table, continuing his preparations. At the other end, Elliot stepped away, rolling his neck with a crackle as he summoned whatever energy he had remaining.

With a brave face, Gully walked right up to the box. He pointed the shotgun at it and held still. "Is this okay?" he asked Roni.

"Absolutely. Just try not to shoot any of us."

Roni felt a shiver run along her leg. Her chest ached and tightened around her heart. A sharp needling pain pressed between the ribs on her left side. Too much adrenaline. Too much fighting. She needed to be in better shape. Was this the start of a heart attack?

"Don't worry," Gully said to the group. "If that box opens, I promise I will —"

Smoke hissed out the seams of the box like a malfunctioning tea kettle. The noise rose in pitch. Then the top exploded off, blasting a wave of hot air across the room followed by a sulfur stench. The group fell backwards, the foul air punching them across the entire body at once. Garcia's potion shattered on the floor, forming a dark cherry stain.

Back on her feet, Roni froze as steam lifted out of the open box. And a hand reached up to clasp the edge.

Chapter 13

A woman emerged from the box. She faced the wall, her back to Roni. It was a smooth back. A flawless back. A promise and a seduction. The kind of skin which drove men to behave stupidly and women to hiss enviously.

When she turned, head down and dark hair hanging, she revealed a body that fulfilled the promise. Nude, she stood in full immaculate display. Stunning proportions that boggled the mind and boiled the blood. Roni had never desired other women, but seeing this one, she understood how that desire could exist. The woman astonished.

Until she raised her head.

Until Roni saw that she had no face.

What should have been a pert nose of perfection, symmetrical eyes of mesmerizing jade, and a supple mouth holding the dreams of lovers and romantics, lacked anything one could call human. Instead, a mass of small brown cones undulated like thousands of worms packed together, each with one end stuck to the surface and the other end stretching outward into the air. And like the woman herself, the aroma floating off her mixed beauty and horror — a gentle perfume of flowers and wine offered to lull in afternoon bliss; however, a note of dreck hung underneath like a sweet child that messed in her pants but won't admit it.

Roni's stomach contents shoved up her throat, stopped before spewing onto the floor, and retreated, leaving behind an acrid burn and a nasty taste in the back of her mouth. The faceless woman stood on the table, her legs taking a wide stance straddling the relic box, and she moved her head, somehow seeing each person in the room despite having no eyes. Again, Roni thought she might vomit but managed to keep it down. There was no time for disgust. The previous boxes told the story well enough — this woman had to be dangerous.

Indeed, Teanna must have gone through a similar experience because she only now placed one foot behind and settled in for a fight. Gully nestled the shotgun into a steady position against his shoulder as he kept his aim tight. The rest of the team watched the woman and waited.

A wet, popping noise — Roni could not tell where on the woman it came from — and she lunged at Gully. Moving like a flash of light, she knocked the shotgun upward and Gully downward. Elliot received a backhand to the side of his head. She soared across the table, nicked Garcia in the chin, before coming around on Roni with a sharp kick to the ribs. Only Teanna managed an attack, but the woman — the creature — evaded the hatchets and threw a dizzying series of punches as Teanna thumped into the wall.

As Roni dropped to one knee, she caught her breath. The woman paused and turned her ear toward the ceiling. Gram must have heard the resumed fighting and took action. She was repositioning Sully, probably trying to build a defensible position. The sounds vibrated across the creature's undulating face. With a quick turn, she dashed out of the room and up the stairs.

Pointing to the door, Elliot said, "Stall her." He then twirled his cane to begin casting a spell.

"Teanna, Gully — with me," Roni said. She snapped her fingers at Garcia. "Finish that potion."

They bolted out of the lab. As fast as the creature could move, such speed took its toll. She had halted halfway up to the fourth floor to recoup. The fact that she waited until she had been out of sight of her enemies suggested more cunning than her predecessors possessed.

Teanna did not stop her charge. With a metallic ring, she scraped one hatchet over the other. The creature snapped her head back, saw Teanna and the others, and dashed upward.

As Roni followed up the stairs, she decided that it was now confirmed — she was, indeed, without doubt, in desperate need of regular exercise. Her endurance had gone to the dump. The burn in her lungs, the sweat dancing on her skin, even the tingle in her fingers and toes from poor circulation — with an occupation best described as *saving the universe,* she had done a pitiful job of being prepared.

The woman without a face reached the fourth-floor landing and raced down the corridor. Roni heard a hatchet hack into the walls and the grunts of two fighters trading blows. Leading with the shotgun,

Gully swung into the hallway but stopped short.

As Roni passed behind him, she saw the creature smash her shoulder into Teanna's chest. Teanna flailed backward toward Gully. Before he could open fire, the creature stormed ahead, held Teanna off the ground like a shield and rushed.

Gully retreated. Roni grabbed his shoulder and pivoted him so they stepped backwards up the stairs. If she had not done so, he would have smashed right into the bannister and might have dropped his weapon. He was only clay and stone, after all.

The woman tossed Teanna at Roni. Gully — for once not trying to shoot in narrow confines — swung the shotgun as Roni had done before. The woman jumped back a few steps. Enough for Roni to help Teanna back to her feet.

"I'm tired of being thrown around," Teanna said.

Roni yanked her up a few more steps as the creature lunged for another attack. Sweat sprayed off the creature's exquisite skin with every rapid motion.

"Behind you." Gram's voice.

Roni sidestepped as Gram pushed by. Teanna and Gully fumbled their way onto the fifth floor while Gram blocked passage to the creature. In her hands, she held a large chained book. She clutched it to her chest so that the cover faced the creature.

Gram said, "You don't belong in this world."

The wriggling cones that made up the creature's face vibrated as if mocking Gram's bold words. It pounced forward, and Gram flipped open the book. The creature raised its hands, expecting something terrible to happen. But nothing did.

From behind, Roni saw Gram struggling with the book. The chain had caught on the bottom corner, stopping it from opening properly. Teanna jumped down to help as Roni did the same, but the creature also spotted the problem. She wheeled onto Gram, and with a daring swipe of her hand, knocked the book loose. It tumbled down the stairs, each thump like a cracking rib.

Staring at the creature, Gram flicked her wrists and two chains dropped from her sleeves. Teanna raised her hatchets. With a ripple of her cones, the creature jabbed at Gram — perhaps guessing the older woman was the easier target. Big mistake.

Gram rolled to the side. As the creature's arm passed harmlessly across, Teanna hacked at her back. Gram whipped one chain over the attacking forearm, cutting into the skin as it wrapped around the muscle several times.

Watching from the landing, Roni gestured towards the golem. "Protect Sully."

He rushed off to do as ordered. Gram yanked the creature down the stairs, but the thing had the strength to bring Gram with her. Teanna tried to take advantage. The narrow confines made it near impossible. The three brawled more than skillfully fought, and Roni couldn't tell who was winning.

From down the fifth-floor hall, the elevator doors opened. Elliot stepped out, moving his cane in a complex pattern, concentrating more on his spell and less on where he was — he nearly walked straight into the wall. Garcia emerged, holding a glass of liquid, and nudged Elliot toward the apartment door.

To Roni, Garcia said, "We're almost ready. Didn't want to waste time, so we started up now."

As the men entered the apartment, Roni shouted down the stairs. "Keep at her. We've almost got the potion."

The creature backhanded Gram, but Teanna hewed her weapon into the gut. Ichor dripped down her thighs and over the stairs. Despite her clear exhaustion and numerous injuries, the woman with the horrid face still managed to hold off two attackers and find the power to fight back.

Roni remained at the top of the stairs. She had to get to the apartment, but her legs refused to move. In her head, she knew what needed to be done for the safety of the world, but leaving Gram and Teanna to fight alone — no matter how tough either woman could be, it felt wrong.

Gram must have seen the dilemma on her face. Or perhaps the old woman had further abilities than Roni ever realized. However she knew, she knew.

While grappling with the creature, she managed a stark look right into Roni. A look of fear and acceptance. "Go," Gram groaned. "We can hold this beast off a bit longer."

Roni's eyes welled. Her fingers trembled. A little girl's voice peeped out of her. "Gram?"

"Go!"

Ripping down the hall, tears streaming, Roni burst into the apartment. Elliot worked his protection barrier a few feet from the entrance. She could feel the pressure against her skin as she stepped through it.

With his cane planted firm on the floor and his head bowed in concentration, Elliot still managed to put a hand out to her. "She'll be okay," he said.

"No," Roni said. Then nothing more. She didn't trust her voice to hold.

Several feet away, kneeling on the floor of the main room, Garcia put the finishing touches into his mixture. Roni glanced to the right. In the bedroom, she saw Sully sitting in his wheelchair, tucked in the back between the bed and wall — a framed photo of the Old Gang in their youth hung above him, staring out full of hope and promise. And Gully stood firm at the corner of the bed like a bouncer. A bouncer with a shotgun.

"Ready," Garcia said. "Hand me the box."

Roni looked to Elliot, but he focused only on his spell. She crouched next to Garcia, and with a fierce whisper, she said, "You didn't bring the box up here?"

"I thought you did. I didn't see it when we left."

"Crap."

"We need it —"

"I know we need it. I'm not an idiot."

"I meant that we need it fast. The potion I made before was able to eat through wood and sandstone, but this last relic box is marble. I had to make a different combination of ingredients for this potion, and it won't hold its power for long."

With a slew of curses that would have given Gram palpitations if not an outright heart attack, Roni stormed off. "I'll get the box. You be ready."

When she entered the hall, Gram slammed into Roni's side and both fell. Teanna came soaring across the air with an impressive flying sidekick. The creature took the hit in the shoulder — hard enough that she bounced against the wall and stuttered back a few steps. The joyful grin on Teanna's face lasted a mere second before her calculating aggression returned.

Roni jumped to her feet and helped Gram up. "That moron left the box back in the lab. Can you still fight?"

With her hair displaced and her chest heaving, Gram said, "This is nothing. Besides, Teanna's doing most of the work." She spun out another chain. "But don't dawdle."

Roni hopped into the elevator, slammed the gate closed, and headed for the lab. As it lowered, she saw the creature spring across the hall.

Gram whipped her chain at the vile thing, but then the floor blocked Roni's view.

Two floors. That's all the elevator had to travel, yet it rattled and vibrated and plodded along as if nothing important occurred above. Stupid elevator. How could it not feel a sense of urgency? The sounds of violent struggle echoed through the elevator shaft, and Roni cringed at the thought of that creature hurting those she loved.

Before the elevator stopped moving, she wrenched open the gate and jumped to the floor. She rushed down the hall and into the lab. The marble relic box sat on the worktable — exactly where they had left it.

The report of a shotgun snapped Roni back into action. Snatching the relic box, she bolted for the elevator. Before she closed the gate, though, she thought better of it and raced to the stairs.

Hang in there. Help is coming.

As she ran by the fourth floor, she heard a crash and a scream — Gram? Teanna? Maybe Garcia.

Her mouth had dried up along with her tears. She wanted to cry out, bawl at the mere thought of what might be happening up there, yet her body only produced an unsettling shiver. A dark question poked at the fears within her — *why had this creature gone upstairs instead of down into the Caverns?*

Reaching the end of the stairs, the answer hit her. The creature didn't know. Perhaps these relic box monstrosities behaved like a golem — they only could think as far as their limited instructions provided. Yal-hara had directed this particular creature to find the Pages of Glass. The creature had no idea where to start.

Gasping and sweating her way down the hall, Roni saw how the creature had simply gone after the first noises it heard, or perhaps it had enough intelligence to go after Sully for the location. After all, as far as Yal-hara knew, Sully was still the team leader.

She threw open the door. Gram and Teanna both roiled on the living room floor — alive but in bad condition. A shotgun blast had left its burnt pattern in the wall near the kitchen. And on the opposite side, the naked beast stood in the bedroom, looming toward Elliot and Garcia, as they backed up. Elliot's shield flickered.

Roni had it wrong. If this creature succeeded in capturing Sully, what then? How could it interrogate an old man, when it lacked a mouth to ask questions with? And there were two other beasts before this one. Yal-hara's plan was far simpler — kill the entire Parallel

Society. Then she would have unfettered access into the Caverns. She could find the Pages on her own.

As the thoughts stormed over her, Roni must have uttered a sound — the creature snapped a look over its shoulder. Its cone-covered face ungulated.

"You are really ugly," Roni said as she heaved the relic box toward Garcia.

The combination of her sudden appearance, an insult, and an object flying forward, confused the creature into a basic reaction. She flinched. The box hit the carpet and tumbled behind the wavering protection shield.

Garcia did not hesitate. He dropped to his knees and poured the potion over the box. Gray smoke rose in the air. The hard marble cracked. Bits flaked to the floor while most of it turned to ash — right along with the creature. It took only seconds. The vicious beast never reacted beyond a startled shake. Then it collapsed and sizzled.

As the muddy smell of burnt stone dissipated, Roni checked back on Gram and Teanna. Both women sat on the living room sofa, their heads lolled back as they breathed heavily. From what Roni could see, they were bruised and spent, but both had survived in relatively good condition.

Gram patted her chest. "Lord, help me, I pray we don't have to fight another one of those things ever again."

Roni started to smile, but Elliot cried out. "Help. Everybody help."

She rushed into the bedroom. The wheelchair lay on its side. Elliot cradled Sully on the floor while Garcia and Gully gawked like helpless children afraid of the horror they witnessed. Sully — poor Sully — he convulsed in Elliot's arms, spittle dotting his lips while his eyes rolled upward.

CHAPTER 14

Everything stopped. Roni's blood no longer pulsed through her body. Her lungs no longer inhaled the air. She heard no sounds, and her touch went numb. Only her eyes worked to any degree — and they only saw Sully.

He floated in darkness. A statue photographed upon an empty backdrop. He became a frozen moment. A searing image branded into her memory.

His glasses sat askew on his nose, the lenses reflecting light from the room as his head jittered in one direction than another. Little flashes punctuated by his wide eyes staring in loss. Then little flashes again. That slight piece of movement brought reality back into focus. With the power of a cyclone, all of Roni's senses returned. She became acutely aware of the sharp pain in her chest as her lungs inflated. She could feel every artery and vein flowing with blood once more. If the world had stopped spinning, she had somehow remained grounded. And when Gram stepped into the bedroom and barked out orders, each syllable rang in Roni's ears like gunshots at the side of her head.

"Gully, Garcia, get him on the bed. Gently." Gram put an arm around Roni and squeezed her shoulder. Then: "Elliot, stop acting like he's dead. It hasn't happened yet. Pick up your cane and do what you were meant to do. Heal."

Elliot lifted his tear-stained face. "You know I'm not capable of healing something this terrible. Heart attacks and strokes and aneurysms are difficult enough — but these kinds of things —"

"You can take care of that leg, can't you?"

As Elliot gazed down Sully's body, so did Roni. They had both panicked at the sight of Sully convulsing that neither had noticed the man's right leg had shortened, his foot had been grotesquely pulled to the right, and a jagged bone poked out of the side of his thigh. Blood saturated the carpet beneath him and now pooled out around his leg.

Garcia and Gully stood over the two men. Elliot said, "Wait. Don't move him. That's his femur. If we move him, we could cause more damage."

Sully's moaning ceased as he passed out. Teanna swayed into the room. She must have been hit a lot harder than Roni realized.

"Should we hold him down or move him or what?" Garcia asked.

Gully shrugged. "Why are you asking me? I'm a golem."

"You have his brain. He's got to know something about this kind of thing."

"First, I don't have his brain. His brain is in his head. I have the parts of his mind that he wanted to share with me. That's all. And second —"

"Be quiet," Teanna said, her words coming out short and unsteady. She staggered forward. "This is what we do. Garcia, pull two slats from the bedframe. Gram, get me a belt. Gully, find some ropes or rip up a shirt."

Gram opened a dresser and pulled out one of Sully's belts. Teanna secured it around the top of Sully's thigh and pulled tight until she staunched the flow of blood. She then used the bed slats and strips of shirt to make a splint around the leg.

"Looks like he broke the big leg bone."

"Femur," Roni said.

"Possibly multiple places. The muscles in the thigh are like giant rubber bands held taut between the hip and the knee. When the bone broke, the muscles snapped loose — that's what shortened his leg and twisted his foot. At least, that's how it is with the people in my world. Your physiology seems the same. Close enough, anyway."

"How do you know all this?"

"As a matter of necessity, all of my people are raised with a basic understanding of survival skills."

"And Sully — is he going to be okay?"

Teanna shrugged. "He's stable, for now. Gully, Garcia, get him on the bed — slowly and gently — and Elliot can take over with his healing spells."

"What can I do?" Roni asked.

With her hand still gripping Roni's shoulder, Gram ushered them back a few steps. "Right now, we stay out of the way."

Though his posture and expression lacked all confidence, Elliot rose to his feet after Sully was placed on the bed. He picked up his cane and held it over Sully's trembling body. As he traced patterns in the air, he closed his eyes. Tears still managed to seep through, but Roni saw the desperate hope infusing every motion. At least, he had something to do that might make a difference.

Roni shivered. "Should we call 911?"

"No, dear." Gram leaned her head against Roni's. "If we did that, the EMTs who arrived would see all the floors shot up, the holes in the walls from the fighting, the weird lab. And even if they somehow ignored it all or we had managed to cover it up before they got here, there would still be a lot of basic questions asked. Ones we would have to lie about. Look around you — do you think the seven of us could get our stories straight this moment?"

Under Teanna's supervision, Sully's fit eased into a restless sleep. Though he twitched and moaned, he no longer appeared to be a physical danger to himself. Elliot moved closer, waving his cane from Sully's head to toe and back again like a giant windshield wiper trying to clean the drops of sickness. Everybody watched in silence. Too exhausted for anything more.

As the day wore on, the unsettling plague of having nothing to do but wait bore down upon the team. Only Elliot had a task, and the strain visible on his tight brow left Roni filled with worry. Usually, his magic could heal a wound within a few hours. But Sully's injuries looked no better than when they had settled him on the bed.

"It's not easy," Elliot snapped when Roni inquired if he needed anything. "I'm trying to manage the loss of blood, the bone damage, replenish the blood, and keep the shock to his system at a minimal."

Roni sent Teanna home. She had taken the brunt of the abuse during the fight, and Roni wanted her rested as well as possible should they encounter any more trouble. Teanna did not argue.

When she left the bookstore, that bit of movement allowed the others to act. Garcia mumbled something about healing tinctures as he meandered closer. He gazed at Roni, his chin quivering. At length, he sniffled.

"I'll gather my things," he said, his voice hollow.

"Huh? Where are you going?"

"I suppose back to Guatemala. At first. Visit my grandpa's grave. He'll be disappointed."

Roni had no time for cryptic nonsense. She had too much of the real thing to worry about. "How's any of that going to help?"

Garcia looked more confused than Roni felt. He said, "I assumed — that is — well, this is my fault. I was too slow making the potion, and I brought the first box into your life. I can't see how I could fail my probationary time any worse."

Holding back a tirade of swears, she settled on, "Shut up."

"But I —"

"Not another word. Get back to your lab and start working. Figure out how to be faster for next time." To answer his stunned expression, she added, "I'm not losing any members of this team."

Garcia sniffled again — less mournful and more determined. She worried he would blubber his relief or thanks, but he only smacked his hands against his legs and hastened off to his lab.

His lab? Roni marveled at how fast the brain could adapt to change. Perhaps that was one reason she loved Gully so much. He reloaded the shotgun and stood guard at the fifth-floor landing. No matter what else — Gully did not change. Gully was Gully.

Roni entered the kitchen and smiled at a half-empty bottle of white wine in the fridge. Elliot and Sully were always full of surprises, but when it came to wine, books, and the occasional guilt trip, they were predictable as ever. She dug out a small glass, poured herself some chilled pinot grigio, and stepped out onto the narrow balcony overlooking the street below.

A few cars rolled by. An old man with heavy whiskers walked his terrier. Otherwise, the streets were empty.

Gram stepped up to the balcony and leaned over on her elbows, her crucifix pendant dangling off her neck. "You did well today."

Roni snorted her doubt. "Praise for me? I might be the one to have a heart attack."

Gram stayed quiet, and that silence turned Roni's sarcastic comment into an ugly thought. Roni shook her head. Only Gram had the power to twist her words with such skill — even through silence. More than once, Roni felt like she circled a drain, unable to find the phrase that could latch her to the side, that could save her.

But from what?

As a girl, Gram scared her. She was the child and Gram was the adult. To defy that authority either by design or by misspoken word terrified her. Gram could do anything as an adult — punish her, ground her, even throw her out of the house. Not that she thought

Gram would ever do such a thing, but she had seen it done to other kids. She had been aware that the possibility existed.

But now — now she was an adult. Gram couldn't punish her. At least, not through the traditional methods. However, when Roni had frozen, when Gram and Teanna had to take over giving orders to save Sully, that may have changed things. At the least, it showed Roni and the others that Gram still had power even if not the official leader.

With a bitter chuckle, Roni said, "You can still do this to me."

"What's that? What did I do now?"

"Even without saying a word, you get my brain spiraling from one terrible thought to another."

"I'm sorry to tell you this, dear, but that's all on you. If you ever want to know how to stop that, how to find peace within yourself, you know the answer."

"Are you trying to preach to me?"

Gram laughed. "Perish the thought."

Roni turned her back on the old man and the dog, her elbows resting on the balcony railing. She peered into the apartment, knowing that just a few walls over one of her dear friends struggled to survive. "There was a point during that fight — I really thought I might lose you. I thought you might die."

"I did, too."

"This is all Yal-hara's fault. It's been her from the beginning. From when I was eight years old."

Gram made an odd noise — a cross between a huff and a grunt. "You know, there is a point where you've got to accept responsibility for yourself and stop blaming others for the misfortunes of your life."

"Excuse me? This is all somehow my fault?"

"That's not what I'm saying."

"Well, you better start explaining quickly because it sure sounds like that's what you're saying."

With enough sharpness in her voice to warn Roni back, Gram said, "We've just been through a traumatic day, so I'll forgive your impertinence. But as the leader of this group, you need to pull yourself together. I know you hate Yal-hara. I know you blame her for all the misery in your life. And she is responsible for setting in motion your Lost Time. However, you cannot use that as an excuse for everything."

"But —"

"If Yal-hara had never existed, if instead your mother or your father beat you, abused you, then you would be in the same position. It would not give you the right to harm others."

"That's your advice — suck it up?"

Gram sighed. "Of course not. But I see it in you, I hear it in you — you don't want to simply solve the problem which Yal-hara presents. You want payback. You want Yal-hara to hurt. That's hatred in action. If you would read your Bible, you'd know that the path which you're walking on will only lead to self-destruction. It always does." She placed her hand on top of Roni's. "I love you too much to see that happen."

The air chilled as the sun descended over the horizon. Roni's stomach grumbled, and that gave her an idea. She pulled out her phone.

"Okay, fine. You think this can all be done nicely, that we can somehow solve this problem without hurting Yal-hara? We'll give that a try."

"Who are you calling?"

"Kenneth Bay, of course."

Chapter 15

The Olburg Diner. A small place, usually packed, overflowing with the rich stain of coffee in the air. Hard-working men and women started and finished their days with the diner's food. Nothing fancy. Just eggs and toast and other typical breakfast items or burgers, fries, and other sandwiches for lunch. For dinner, they offered a few more substantial meals like fried pork chops or fried chicken. Like any self-respecting diner, all the meals could be ordered at any time. They never closed, and they understood that their third-shift customers had different needs than their first-shift customers. The Olburg Diner aimed to satisfy everyone. Well, everyone local.

Roni could not recall whether the diner had first been her idea or Bay's, but it had become the only place he would willfully meet with her. Settling into a booth near the back corner, she noted that she had a usual spot to meet a mysterious stranger. She snickered — a bitter sound.

From her seat, Roni could see out the large wall of windows on her left. Overlooking the cracked pavement of the parking lot and the buildings across the street, the view offered little to inspire and plenty to break the spirit. The stores and apartments stepped out of decades long dead. The cars and sidewalks and even the people out for a late-night stroll all looked damaged. This was not an affluent town of up-and-comers. Olburg was the end for most people caught in a steady, laborious life.

Part of Roni wished that could be her life. Blue collar, straight forward, no complications. All the stresses would be normal — bills, men, maybe a simple vice or two. Depressing, true, but compared to the things she had dealt with only earlier that day, working an assembly line or packing boxes in a warehouse sounded wonderful. Sleeping with the wrong guy or drinking too much sounded easy to manage.

The waitress delivered a mug of coffee with a tired look on her middle-aged face. Her top lip curled at one spot exuding disdain for her customers, her job, and her life. When Roni explained she was waiting for someone, the waitress gave a grumpy roll of the eyes and headed to the next table.

Roni glanced over at the counter which ran along the right side. A television hung in the corner with ESPN detailing the latest controversy over some star baseball player's downfall. Beneath the television, Gram and Teanna sat with two men in coveralls between them. Gram nursed her own mug of coffee while Teanna scarfed down scrambled eggs, bacon, and hashbrowns.

Gram caught Roni's attention and grinned. Roni smiled back. Though Teanna was supposed to be observing the diner, she had only been awake for a short while — after only a short rest — so Roni thought it best to let the woman eat. There would be plenty of time for playing bodyguard soon enough.

The door chime sounded and Roni's head popped up. Two men wearing matching red *Philly's Finest Plumbing* t-shirts — one hefty and middle-aged, the other thin and young — grabbed the nearest booth. As Roni looked back to her coffee, a man at the counter tossed some cash down, waved at the cook, and left. Gram shifted stools to be closer to Teanna. Seconds later, the door chimed again. This time, Kenneth Bay entered the diner.

As usual, he wore a fine suit and used his cane more than necessary. Two thick-muscled men entered with him. They both wore dark suits with dark shirts underneath — clearly his protection; clearly more competent than the bozo from their last encounter. That gave Roni a bit of warmth. In all their previous diner meetings, Bay had shown up alone. The fact that he brought these men suggested he knew the trouble he had caused and possibly the threat Roni and her team posed.

A swift hand gesture and Bay's protection stood at either side of the entrance. The plumbers noticed this as did the waitress. Nobody said a word. Probably thought these men belonged to organized crime. Indeed, as Kenneth Bay limped by, the plumbers lowered their heads, only snatching peeks at the man who they assumed must be the boss.

Roni watched Bay approach. She would not look away. Though she did notice Teanna reaching back for her hatchets and Gram putting out a hand to stop it.

When Bay slid into the bench opposite, Roni gestured to the coffee mug. Bay shook his head, so she waved off the waitress who looked pleased to avoid the table now that an old-time gangster had arrived.

"I realize this sort of place is not what you're accustomed to for dining," Roni said, "but you should make a little effort. I mean, considering how often our meetings are held here, you could order something now-and-then to make up for us hogging the booth."

He tilted his head in thought. Then: "I doubt we'll meet ever again after this."

"What a shame. I always thought we had a good relationship. Maybe I'm flattering myself, but I got the impression you enjoyed our little get-togethers."

Bay bristled. "Did you call me here so you could play games or is there a real purpose?"

"See what I mean? You're full of joyful vigor." She sipped her coffee.

"Very well." Keeping his eyes locked on her, he raised his hand and wiggled his fingers. "Oh waitress."

He sang the words, garnering uneasy glances from the plumbers as well as an elderly gentleman who had walked in and sat at the counter. When she arrived, the waitress had aged another ten years. She held her lips tight to keep them from trembling. Roni could see every animal instinct in this woman raging fire — *run* they screamed, but all her societal training kept her for doing anything more than pull out her notepad.

"You want something?" she said, the words stilted and cold.

Speaking with sharp precision as he maintained his focus on Roni, Bay said, "Apparently I've been remiss in not trying your grand cuisine. I would like to have one of your finest hamburgers with whatever passes for cheese in this establishment, and I suppose some French-fried potatoes as well."

"Something to drink with that?"

"Whatever you pretend is coffee will be suitable."

The waitress didn't dare make a face at the insults. She rushed back to the grill to put in the order.

"Happy now?" Bay asked.

Roni sat back and folded her arms. "I always knew you were a prick, but you outdid yourself with that."

"From the way you're speaking to me, I can only assume that you agree this will be our last civil discourse."

Roni straightened as she pointed at him. In a barely controlled whisper, she hissed out, "You're damn right. You and your pathetic boss crossed the line by attacking us. When you think of all the crap that we let slide — starting with what she did to me when I was a kid and going all the way up to you arranging a man to date me so he could access the Caverns — you should be amazed we put the line so far back. Not my doing, I assure you."

"No, that would be Gram and Elliot and Sully's doing. I would never think of attributing such kindness to you."

"Wasn't kindness from them, either. Just guilt. But I'm sure there were plenty of other details between your side and the Parallel Society long before I ever knew about any of it. Not only that, but you lured me into this ridiculous arrangement supposedly so that I could get back my Lost Time. But you always knew Yal-hara was the cause."

"You mention our arrangement. Funny, but you forgot the part where you broke that deal."

"That was not my fault. But even if it had been, you negotiated the whole thing in bad faith. Now you're pursuing this ridiculous myth that you want to be real — the Pages of Glass. Does that even make sense? How can pages be made out of glass?"

"I do not expect them to be literal pages."

"You should not expect them to be literally anything. After you so graciously shared the information with me, I brought it to Gram and the others. You knew I would."

"I take it they denied everything."

"Not at all. They had heard the same stories. But they said they didn't know where the Pages were. So, I did what I had been trained to do. I went into our library and did the research."

The waitress arrived and set the food down, the plates rattling from the tremors in her hand. She poured coffee into Bay's empty mug and topped off Roni's mug before scurrying away. Bay slid the food and his coffee to the side. He would not be touching it.

Roni went on, "I spent hours looking through the journals of long ago, sifting through story after story, until I finally found the diary of Mr. Henry Billings Drake — a member from back when the Society was located in England. Would you like to know what I found out?"

"You clearly intend to tell me."

Roni took a slow sip of coffee. She had not planned this much of the conversation — there hadn't been time for plans — yet she saw the interest sparking his eye. He tried to hide it. He tried to act droll and bemused, but she knew that look, that hunger for information. As long as she did not fumble her words, he might believe her.

"I don't have the time, and I certainly don't have the desire, to go into heavy detail on everything."

"Thank goodness."

"But suffice it to say that Sir Drake admits in his journal that he proposed the idea of creating a book — a directory — which would list every world they discovered and its location in the Caverns. Simple enough idea. But the logistical complexity of the task and the limited resources they had prevented it from happening. However, the idea stuck around. In fact, about forty years later, another Society member — Florence McElderry — came to believe that this directory actually existed. That it had been compiled and then lost to the decades. The next step in the evolution of this story came when the Society moved to America."

Making a show of checking his watch, Bay said, "I'm certainly glad you're avoiding the full story. This gripping yarn is as pointless as calling this eatery clean."

"Go on and keep interrupting me. It's only prolonging the tale." She then stared at him in silence.

At length, he relented. "My apologies. You were saying that the Society moved to America."

"Yes, and a lot of details were lost in the transition, a lot of books and a lot of personnel information. In the end, Callum Murray wrote about a book in the Caverns that, when opened, would reveal the location of any world they wanted to know about. Over time, that idea of the book grew in its power until eventually it became the Pages in the book that could reveal all the secrets the multiverse has to offer. I'm sure you can see how embellishment upon embellishment turned those pages into something unique — Pages of Glass. I'm sorry to disappoint you, but that's the truth. It's all a tall tale born from an idea that had some merit long ago, but which never existed. There are no Pages of Glass."

"Yal-hara disagrees."

Roni searched Bay's face for any sign of doubt. She had made up a lot of that story, but Drake did exist, and he did propose such a directory would be of value. He just also happened to have the Pages of Glass and wanted to use them for his purposes. Later, in America, Callum Murray used the Pages to discover what he termed the *Book of Nightmares* — the same book Elliot had taken Roni to see, the same book Murray chose to house the book with the Pages of Glass. In his journal, he wrote that when he returned, the nightmares came with him. He could not stop seeing all the strange creatures, and terrible visions plagued him — even in his sleep. Eventually, it drove him mad.

But Kenneth Bay didn't need to know all of that, and Roni doubted that Yal-hara would care about a slight bit of insanity if it got her to those Pages.

Roni reached over and snatched a French fry off the plate. "I know you think you are in control — well, that Yal-hara is in control — but the truth is that this is our world. Not hers. Something I've learned over my short time with the Society, something you probably have yet to figure out because you are, after all, just the lawyer: it's like in sports — home-court advantage means everything. This is our world, no matter how much power she might accumulate or how much sway she might think she holds, there will always be advantages we have over her. We will always fight harder and feel everything stronger. You need to explain that to her. Make her see that she is on a dangerous path, and if she continues this way, continues pushing against us, things are going to get terribly ugly."

"Haven't they already?"

She swiped another fry. "You think this is ugly? You have no idea what I'm capable of when I get truly angry." She hoped her words sounded half as cool and threatening as she thought they did. After all, she'd already bluffed her way through the Pages of Glass myth. Why not pretend she's some sort of badass as well?

When she reached for a third fry, he slapped her hand. Teanna jumped to her feet as Bay's bodyguards stepped forward. She moved too fast for Roni to catch the details while also dealing with Bay, but one man ended on his knees, gasping for air, and the other had a hand in his jacket. But he didn't pull out a gun. Not with Teanna holding a hatchet at his neck.

Bay raised a hand and both men cautiously eased back to the doorway. Teanna waited until they posed no further threat. Then she hopped onto her stool and snatched a bite of toast. But all the diners, all the staff, held still and silent.

Running his fingers over his mustache, cooling the glower from his face, Bay said, "You draw quite a vivid picture. If you will, allow me to set you straight on a few matters."

She tried to hold her head up and look defiant, but the cowering schoolgirl side of her won more of that argument.

He went on, "Until now, Yal-hara has shown the greatest patience.

Her history with the Parallel Society has been fraught with broken promises on both sides. She has paid for her mistakes, stuck here in this world like a prisoner. Well, her patience has emptied. She no longer will accept her imprisonment. If I may belabor the metaphor — now is the time for her parole, if not her outright release. And while you have been bold with your innuendo of threats, let me be very direct. We know that the Pages are real, and we know that they will help Yal-hara locate the book to take her home. Turn over the Pages and allow her the freedom she deserves. If not, then she will leave by force."

A phone rang — a shrill old-style ring from the early 1900s. The sound pierced the air causing everyone to flinch. Kenneth Bay, his men, Gram and Teanna, even the waitress and the old man and the plumbers — everyone's primal side felt the tension. Everyone's primal side waited to see how this new element — the ringing phone — might change things.

Clearing her throat, Gram reddened. As she pulled her phone from a pocket, she looked to Roni with an apology on her lips. She listened, her brow drawing down, and then she gestured to Roni — the call was for her.

Roni nodded, and Gram scooted off the diner stool. She walked the phone over, her eyes darting between Roni and Bay, the threatening men, and even the innocent bystanders. She handed the phone over. Roni glanced at the screen — Elliot.

As she raised it to her ear, Bay wagged his index finger. She put it on speaker.

"What's wrong?" she asked.

"He is not doing well," Elliot said.

Roni snapped off the speaker and put the phone to her ear. "Just a second." She stared hard at Bay. "Now would be a good time for you to leave."

With a slight incline of the head, Kenneth Bay slid out of the booth. He set his cane on the ground with a sharp tap and headed toward the exit. Never looking back, he said, "You're still a novice at this game. I sincerely wish you would rethink your position. You're going to get yourself and a lot of others hurt."

Roni watched as Bay departed, fuming but unwilling to delay him with the final word. She had more important people to talk with.

"Okay, Elliot. I'm here. How bad is he?"

"I'm doing everything I can but there's too much damage. It's like juggling ten balls at once."

"Then we suck it up and call 911. We'll deal with whatever happens after Sully's taken care of."

"It's too late for that. It's too late for anything."

"Don't say that. Don't give up."

"Sully asked me to make this call. He wants everyone back at the bookstore. He wants to speak with you. Please, come home now."

The finality in his voice, the pain cracking through his words — Roni did not have to see Sully to know that Elliot spoke the truth. When she cut the call and looked up at her teammates, they knew it, too. Without having heard a word, Gram and Teanna's faces betrayed their understanding.

Gram gave Roni a long hug. She sniffled. "Come now, dear. Let's go say goodbye."

CHAPTER 16

Driving back to the bookstore, parking on the street, storming up the sidewalk, and riding the elevator, Roni tried to work through the problem. Her pulse throbbed in her head while her chest ached with any thought of Sully holding on in agony. She choked back on the image. Stay focused. Worrying wouldn't solve anything. If they could find out everyone's blood type, perhaps they could set up a transfusion — if anybody knew how to do that. Maybe Teanna's survival first-aid training could be utilized. If not the blood idea, then some other way. There had to be something, anything, that the team could think up to save Sully.

But when they arrived at the apartment, when she saw Elliot standing alone in the living room, his face drained of all hope, she knew the gut-wrenching answer. Too many complications and not enough time. Still, she shook her head.

"I know you're tired," she said as the others filed in behind her, "but you need to start working on a spell again. Pick one of the many things that are wrong with him and fix it. Where's Garcia?"

Mixing a glass of reddish liquid, Garcia stepped in from the kitchen. "Right here."

"Is that potion going to help?"

"This is cranberry juice with a little gin. I suppose it might help relax him, but I made it for myself."

Snatching the glass from his hand, Roni swigged half the drink. "Whatever potions you've got ready, administer them right away."

Elliot stepped forward and wrapped his long arms around her. She tried to push out of his grip, but he would not let go. His body shuddered as tears fell.

"No," she said, the word both belligerent and mournful.

"He asked me to use all I could in one spell, to give him enough energy so that he would live long enough for this moment. He wants to speak with you. Don't deny him this."

No, no, no. This wasn't fair. This wasn't how things were meant to happen. But looking from Elliot to Gram to Teanna and Gully, she felt the weight of expectations upon her. They wanted her to do as Sully had asked. They needed it.

Dabbing at her eyes, Roni stifled the moan that had crept up her throat and approached the bedroom door. She raised her fist to knock but recalled what Elliot had just said — Sully had needed a spell to maintain his strength. She shouldn't bother him with formalities at this time. She reached down and opened the door.

The bedroom had been tidied up a little — the wheelchair set back properly, the broken bits of wall and ceiling swept away — but it did little to change the gloom hovering over the bed. Propped up on pillows, Sully sat with his fingers laced over his belly. His legs had been covered with a blanket, and though the damage could not be seen, the shapes poking up like a bizarre mountain range betrayed the fiction. Even if it had been perfect, Sully could not hide the pale pallor of his skin, the non-stop tremors of his chin, or the hateful stench of death twisting around him.

He squinted as if unable to tell who had entered the room, but then his mouth turned upward in a weak smile. "Finally. Come, sit down."

He spoke with gusto. She shouldn't have been surprised — Elliot had said the spell would strengthen Sully in his final moments. Roni walked over, sat at his side with care, and placed her hand atop his. She opened her mouth to speak but snapped it shut. She would have to speak eventually, but she needed a little time before she could trust herself to utter a word that did not devolve into gushing tears.

"It's okay," he said. "I've lived a good life. A long life. Thanks to Elliot, longer than I should have lived. It's time now."

"I — no — you were going to teach me — you were —"

"You don't need me. I am confident that you are perfect to lead. It's time for you to believe it, too. You are stubborn yet thoughtful. That combination alone will make you an effective leader. And with what lies ahead, you will need it. The whole team will need it of you. Gram and Elliot — they're going to be sad when I'm gone. Of course, that's to be expected. I'm a pretty wonderful guy, after all. More than ever before, they're going to need a strong leader to guide them through these coming days. You're going to have to be that."

"How can I when I still barely know anything about the Caverns or the Society or any of it?"

"You know far more than you realize. Besides, you have Gully. I've given him a lot more of myself than you know, than anybody here knows. Trust him."

Sully coughed hard. The sound like coarse sandpaper running over gravel. And wet. Little bubbles broke through all the harsh clicks. Roni guessed that meant blood in the lungs. Even if she was wrong, she knew it meant something bad.

Breathing heavy from the exertion, Sully leaned his head back against the pillows and closed his eyes. For a moment, she thought that was it. It was over. Except his chest continued to heave up and down.

He raised one hand and made little circles as if signaling it was time to wrap things up. "You must prepare. Yal-hara will come again for the Pages. Things have changed with her. She won't give up. She won't back down anymore. She's done waiting. Everything else you need to learn, you'll figure out."

"I don't know if I can —"

"One last thing," he said, pointing to his nightstand. "Open that drawer."

Roni obeyed. Inside, she found a small, leather notebook. She handed it over, but he shook his head.

"That's for you."

"Me? What's in it."

"Take a look."

She opened the cover. "Your journal."

"You are still our librarian. I have nothing left to write in there. So, when the time comes, please make sure that finds its rightful place with all the Society members of the past."

"Stop talking like that."

He closed his eyes and rested his head back. "Now, please, call in my dearest loves."

A small voice inside Roni told her not to obey. That with some magical thinking, she could prevent the inevitable by simply refusing to let anybody come in.

Perhaps reading her thoughts on her face, perhaps simply knowing how little time he had left, Sully reached out and clasped her hand. "Please," he said in his weakest voice yet.

Moments later, Elliot and Gram stood by the bed. Elliot took Sully's hand, leaned over, and kissed the man's cheek. Gram wrapped her arms around Sully until he coughed. As she backed off, a cry burst from her lips and her tears flowed.

But nobody spoke.

Roni understood. They had no need. They could look into each other's eyes and hear all the words that never had to be uttered. His dearest loves, indeed.

Elliot lowered to his knees so that he could look straight on at Sully. He kissed Sully's hand and held it tight. With a gentle touch on Roni's shoulder, Gram indicated that Sully wanted her closer.

"He has more to say," Gram said.

Swallowing down the tightness in her throat, Roni scooted along the bed until she could bring her ear next to Sully. He smelled worse than before. He smelled of cold earth.

"To lead in this job," he said, skimming the surface of a whisper, "requires you to give your heart to the team, to the world, to the universe. You have that kind of heart. You have one big enough for all of that and more. You can do this. You can …"

His words trailed off. His head drifted to the side. And that was it.

If Roni had any doubts, the soft gasp from Gram confirmed it. Elliot pressed his head to the bed, and his body bucked up and down as he silently wept. Roni thought about holding him. Or maybe she should let Gram sit on the bed next. Or maybe they expected her to say something important. Sully's final words echoed in her mind, layering upon every thought she had, every instinct she felt, leaving her lost as to which act was correct.

She stood. The others needed to know what had happened, and maybe Elliot and Gram would prefer time alone with their departed friend. As she quietly walked away, she heard Gram sit on the bed and shaking breaths that grew into sobs.

Roni wanted to stop in the doorway, collapse to the floor, and howl her tears. But she was the leader. Wasn't that the real point of Sully's final talk? He knew he had no more time, and he chose to use it telling Roni — insisting — that she was the leader. Not simply in name but in her bones and in the bones of the Society. That meant she had lost the luxury of crying from her depths until exhaustion put her to sleep. Maybe later — days? weeks? — at some point when she was alone and all the threats were gone. Maybe then she would be allowed to suffer her loss.

Stepping into the living room, Roni saw Garcia, Teanna, and Gully jump to their feet. They watched her and knew. She did not have to break the news. It was clear enough to all. Even Gully could figure it out.

She waited a moment. Teanna had known Sully for only a short time. She would be sad but not devastated. Garcia didn't know Sully at all. He would be somber out of respect to the others. Gully — well, Roni had no clue if Gully could feel the loss or how deeply. Sully was his father and mother. His creator. She would have to discuss that with the golem another day.

For now, she ushered the group into the kitchen to give the mourners privacy. Then: "We'll let the Old Gang grieve, but we have work to do. Yal-hara is not going to back off, and she might get it in her head to strike while we're down. I didn't fully understand it, but Sully's made everything quite clear."

"And that is?" Garcia asked.

"We need to prepare. We're at war."

CHAPTER 17

Channeling intense grief into furious determination, Roni stood at the front counter of the bookstore's main floor. With her hands clasped behind like a veteran military officer, she directed activities as she thought through the plan. Gully waited at her side — an aide de camp.

Yal-hara was done testing the waters. She had dived in. But she also had acted rash. Her attack lacked any serious preparations. With all the years she had to plan her assault, she opted for relic boxes. That spoke of blind fury and acting out. And that gave the Society a slight advantage — depending on how badly rashness clouded the thinking of Yal-hara's species.

While Roni worked Teanna and Garcia from the start, eventually Gram and Elliot made their way downstairs to join the group. Roni wasted no time setting them tasks. Having something to do, something necessary and valuable, might help them cope. If not, at least it would help the rest of the team prepare.

She placed Gram in the *Specials* room on the second floor where all the costly items were stored. Gram would make books. Each one a portal into an unknown universe. It was quiet on the second floor, so Gram could concentrate. It was also private, so she could cry more, if she wanted.

The only disturbance would be Teanna — Roni had her collecting the finished books and distributing them strategically around the bookstore. Shotguns and hatchets were good weapons but nothing equaled the power of opening a book into another universe.

From the previous attack, Garcia had shown that creating potions took time. Well, they had time now. Roni ordered him back to the lab to produce whatever potions he thought would be useful. It was easier than listing the things she thought they needed and having him say that he didn't know this, didn't know that, could only produce this much, could produce more but only with certain ingredients. Better to let the artist do what he trained for. Plus, Roni didn't like to micromanage. She never understood the point. Why have a team if not to use their skills?

When it came to Elliot, however, Roni decided to wait. He simply wasn't ready. While he did come down with Gram, he did not appear aware of his surroundings. He stood by the big table, holding his cane in both hands as if it were a baby. His blank stare and hunched form radiated despair.

When she found the opportunity, she walked over to him. "Go back up to Sully."

"I'm needed here. Everybody's doing their part, and so will I."

"I doubt Yal-hara will attack tonight. Spend some more time with him. Rest or cry or be angry or whatever else you need to do. Then, be ready in the morning. I have an important assignment for you."

"I will. But first I must help —"

"You must listen to me. I'm giving you an order."

With a grim but grateful nod, Elliot shuffled toward the elevator. He paused. "He would be proud of you."

The last words choked in Elliot's throat. He bowed his head and sobbed. Roni rushed to his side and placed her arm around his waist. Escorting him to the elevator, she allowed her heart to show her sorrow — but only in that short distance. Once she closed the gate and sent him toward the fifth floor, she inhaled sharply and recomposed her body. A quick wipe at her face with her sleeve and she returned to the job.

For the next few hours, the team worked diligently — mostly placing books, extra hatchets, and ammunition throughout the building. Roni helped Gully relocate one of the waist-high bookcases from the Grand Library to the main floor. They positioned it parallel with the entrance, pressing one end against the wall, not far from the side stairwell. This would make a small barricade and a great place to stash weapons.

Teanna suggested a water bucket would be useful there, too, as well as buckets in a few other locations. "Sometimes creatures make fire."

After they set out the water, Roni told everyone to get rested and meet up in the morning. Back at the apartment, Teanna insisted that she do the same.

Roni chuckled. Already Teanna understood that it would be difficult for the leader to sleep well that night.

When Roni stepped into the bookstore the next morning, Gully reported all of the night's occurrences. Basically, nothing happened. Although it took him ten minutes of detailing every little noise he heard, every car that passed by, and how he double-checked the placement of all the previous night's work. Annoying to listen to most of the time, but on this morning, Roni found a strange comfort in the golem's steadfast behavior.

She had managed some sleep overnight; however, the bulk of her hours had been devoted to searching for a more solid plan. When Yal-hara made her next move, it would be with greater precision. As far as Roni could tell, these relic boxes had never been used before. Like working with the golem, instructing the creatures that emerged from the boxes brought unexpected difficulties. The mistakes made would not be made again. No matter how angry Yal-hara might have become, no matter how rash, she would learn from her previous errors. Next time, those creatures would not get bogged down trying to hurt the individual members of the Society or seek to capture one of them to extract information. Next time, Roni expected Yal-hara to send her creatures straight into the Caverns.

"She probably doesn't think they'll be successful finding the Pages — this time." Roni stood at the head of the big table while the entire Parallel Society sat around. "At least, that's what I would think in her shoes. But it's possible she doesn't think like a human being or that she might already know more than we realize. Either way, those creatures are headed to the Caverns. But I have an idea."

Two ways to get to the Caverns — the elevator and the stairs. She decided to have Gully destroy the stairs.

"But we've just had them rebuilt," Gram said.

"It'll be hard enough defending one way down."

"Then shut off the elevator."

"Which means that our enemy takes the stairs through the Grand Library to get to the Caverns. I am not having anybody destroy that Library after all the work I've put into it. Gully, do your best to preserve as much of the wood as possible. We're going to have to rebuild the stairs again."

Roni still had Gram hide some books near the top of the stairs. Just in case. While the drop would hurt a human — break the legs, at least, if not outright kill — she could not be sure the creatures would be injured as well. They might simply jump down the shaft and be on their way.

While Gully became a demolitionist, Roni had Gram and Teanna posting books and weapons in the basement, leading the way to the Caverns. They had to have their contingencies.

The night before, Garcia had mixed together several batches of his acidic brew that destroyed the boxes. Now, he started making the equivalent of smoke bombs and other disruptive potions. A few times during the day, Roni checked on his work and asked about other possibilities — sleeping gas, ways to protect from infectious diseases picked up in other universes, and more. While he made it clear that he could not provide any such things right away, with the proper lab and given the right ingredients, he promised a few miracles.

That left Elliot.

While nobody expected him to be bright and cheery the morning after Sully's passing, Elliot managed to arrive ready to serve the Society and the world. The bags under his eyes told more of how his night had gone then his stoic demeanor. Roni had never seen Elliot look so cold before. Perhaps, like her, he had squeezed all of his sorrow into anger. If so, Yal-hara didn't stand a chance.

"You will be our last line of defense," Roni said. "If we can't stop them, then you have to keep them from getting on that elevator. I want you to make a shield. The best you've ever made. The kind of thing that will take them hours if not days to puncture through. Can you do that?"

"I'll summon a steel wall if I have to. Whatever it takes."

"Good," she said, but she could see the trembling in his hands. He had yet to recuperate from the last few nights of spellcasting. "That leaves only one thing, but we won't do that until we're ready. Let's get to work."

Over the course of several hours, the Parallel Society implemented Roni's plan. She walked from one floor to the next, from one area to another. She checked on each member of the team, helping them where necessary, staying out of their way when that seemed prudent.

No one appeared at their best. Not even Gully. Gram and Elliot suffered the worst — not only sleep deprived but struggling to compartmentalize their pain. Still, by three in the afternoon, everyone had completed their tasks as much as possible. Garcia had several potions which required a final step that could not be done until they needed to be used. Likewise, Elliot had done all the prep work for his spell, but would not be able to set it in motion until needed. Otherwise, he would be stuck holding the spell in action all day.

Roni sent Teanna and Garcia to pick up some pizza while the rest relaxed. Even Gully looked tired when he rode the elevator back to the main floor. He had a little grin, though.

"Why are you smiling?" Roni asked.

"I thought up a special surprise, if our enemy makes it to the Caverns." He would say no more.

The pizzas arrived. They ate, and Roni knew the time had come.

She walked to the front counter and pulled out her phone. She called Kenneth Bay.

Without so much as a greeting, he answered, "I told you there would be no more meetings. We are through with you."

"I simply want you to relay a message."

"I am not your —"

"We're going to destroy the Pages of Glass." She heard his hesitant breath. Good. "Elliot worked out a spell that should do the trick in conjunction with a potion made by our newest member, Garcia — he's the one who destroyed your relic boxes."

"I – I don't believe you."

"You've given me no choice. You've made it clear that Yal-hara will not be satisfied unless she gets what she wants. I figure that if we take the Pages off the gameboard, there is no game left to play. Face it, by this time tomorrow morning, the Pages of Glass really will be a myth."

Kenneth Bay stayed quiet. Twice he uttered sounds as if about to speak. Finally, he said, "You're bluffing. Destroying the Pages serves no purpose. And that won't stop Yal-hara. If she can't destroy you to get the Pages, she'll destroy you to get access to the Caverns. She will not sit back anymore."

"I know."

Another long silence. "Then why are you calling? Why tell me any of this? Why do it at all?"

Roni lowered her voice. "Because I want her to worry. I want her to suffer." She cut the call. With an amused grin, she looked at her team. "I think that should do it. Yal-hara will order Kenneth Bay to lead an attack on us tonight. She'll be mad as Hell — sorry, Gram — and she won't be thinking clearly. But she will order the attack. And we're ready for it."

CHAPTER 18

Waiting. And waiting. And waiting.

The moment the phone call had ended, time became a sloth. All the hubbub of activity prepping the bookstore had been completed, the pizza had been eaten, and there was nothing left to do but wait.

And think.

Roni could not turn off her brain. She ran through the plan, picturing possible scenarios and how each one might change the needs of their setup, yet always she came to the conclusion that they had set things the best that could be done. She walked through the bookstore, checking on everything once again. Nothing had moved, of course. She stopped to share a few words with each member of the team, but by the third time around, they all made it clear that she was getting on their nerves. She wondered if this was how soldiers felt knowing an invasion was imminent yet unable to predict exactly when the call to action would arrive.

Garcia played gin rummy with Teanna. He tried teaching her, anyway. From the hushed chuckles between them, they clearly spent more time making nervous jokes than playing cards. Good. A little friendship could go far under the violence that promised to come.

A few times, Roni caught Gram or Elliot shedding tears. She wanted to join them. More than that, she wanted to scream and howl and bawl until her throat tightened up and her eyes dried out. Sully had helped to raise her. He was more than a family friend. More than an uncle. He was a father, a mentor, a pain in the butt, and an inspiration. Plus, he saved her life on several occasions.

But he would want her to hold all of that inside for now. She was the leader, and Sully would want her to lead. The time to mourn would come later.

As the hours dragged on, Roni caught herself watching Gully more than once. She wondered about him — about how he felt regarding Sully. Or about her, for that matter. Did he trust her because Sully had instructed him to do so? Or was he like the others — following along, waiting to decide whether she could hack it or not.

That wasn't fair, though. Not to Gully or the rest of the team. No evidence suggested that they judged her so harshly. That was in her head. She hoped.

Another circuit through the bookstore cleared her bouncing thoughts — a little. But it was only four in the afternoon, and Roni had figured all along that any response would happen later in the night. No chance of it coming any sooner. Yal-hara and Kenneth Bay required several hours, at least, to put together a plan of attack that might succeed. Plus, in Roni's experience, most things like spells, magic boxes, and the like took significant time to ready. And yet, as dusk gave way to the moonlit dark, she still felt the shock of surprise when an old but well-maintained Cadillac pulled up to the curb in front of the bookstore and out stepped Kenneth Bay.

He stood alone on the concrete, leaning his cane at an angle and staring at the bookstore with menace in his eyes. He did not move at first. Waited until the car that dropped him off drove away, revving the engine like an angry bear. Strange. Bay clearly wanted them to see that he was alone, that no other vehicle stood waiting with bodyguards ready to jump out, yet he created an image that bred distrust and threat.

He strode to the door and entered the bookstore with a firm gait. Roni and the Society sat around the big table, watching as he moved with a touch of bravado. It seemed like he couldn't decide whether to be intimidating or a bit contrite.

Roni crossed her arms, holding them at the elbows as she stood. She did not want Bay to spot her confusion. Whatever plan he and Yal-hara had fabricated, Roni could not see any of it. Her gut tightened and twisted.

When she stood, her entire team stood, too. That felt good. She even noticed the corner of her mouth twitching upward. And when she stepped into the center of the room to meet Bay, her entire team spread out behind her. They all knew the jobs they had to do. She trusted they would do them well.

Kenneth Bay paused as his head made a half-circle — taking in the layout of the main floor. He observed the front counter to the right of the entrance, the open main floor, the big table near the right wall, the low bookshelf sticking out as a clear obstacle, the gaping hole where stairs should have been, and the elevator in the back. When his eyes finally settled on Roni, he tipped his hat and made a slight incline. "Against the advice of counsel, my client, the esteemed Yal-hara, still hopes that we can avoid further unpleasantness. There is a non-violent solution to this disagreement, if we are all willing."

Roni snorted a laugh and glanced back. She spotted Elliot leaning against the elevator door. Perfect. He made small motions with his cane. To an untrained eye, he looked as if he fiddled absently while pondering the conversation. But, of course, Roni knew better — he had begun casting the barrier spell.

"I promise you," Bay said, "Yal-hara is not joking."

"Well, you and I both know that ship has not only sailed, but it's crossed half the ocean, ran into a squall, and was sunk."

"It does not have to be —"

"You killed Sully."

The coldness in the declaration, the rampaging anger rippling underneath the words, guaranteed that Kenneth Bay said nothing more for a moment. He took off his hat, pressed it against his chest, and lowered his head. Finally, in a soft voice, he said, "I am truly sorry to hear that. I liked the old man. You have my condolences."

"Don't want them. Don't want anything from you. Except for you to leave and never return. That would be nice."

Bay glanced back at the door as if he truly considered the possibility. "I'm afraid I can't do that. But if it is any consolation, when Yal-hara learns of this, she will feel like I do."

"You can both go to Hell," Gram said. Her face shook flushed red. Her hands had curled into tight fists and her arms vibrated from the tension.

Roni swallowed her shock at Gram's words. Then to Bay: "I think that says it all. You are not getting the Pages. They're going to be destroyed."

Kenneth Bay spread his fingers across his mustache and pulled his lips inward. "Even after all these years, not one of you truly understands who you are dealing with."

"She's a monster in the truest sense. We don't need to know any more than that."

"Oh, I agree. But before you cross her any further, you should understand just how much of a monster she is. Because you're not ready for what you face." He gazed as if deciding how much to say.

"You know, I never wanted to be a lawyer. My father did, and my grandfather as well — they embraced working for her and all the benefits that came with it. But I had no interest in continuing the family tradition."

"Yet here you are."

"I wanted to be a chemist. Or some kind of scientist. I never really had the chance to explore what avenue interested me most. When I turned fifteen, it was made clear to me that I had no choice. Either I joined with the family or Yal-hara would find new representation. *So what?* I thought. What do I care if she takes her business elsewhere? We had made so many millions that it wasn't going to hurt us. We had more than enough to live out the rest of our lives without ever suffering. That was my first lesson in how little I knew about Yal-hara. You see, if ever my family stops representing her, if ever she grows displeased with us and chooses to change representation, then it is important to her that there are no — to borrow a euphemism — loose ends."

Gram said in a low growl, "Can't have anybody out there knowing she exists."

"I'm afraid so. If my family no longer represents her, my family no longer lives. She would see to the destruction of every single member going out to second or third cousins. Possibly further. Anybody we might have had contact with and might have told would be killed. That was it. That was the choice I had — join the family firm or be the reason for the deaths of hundreds. I went to law school."

"Do you think we care about any of this?" Roni said.

"I had hoped that might convince you of how ruthless she can be. Allow me one more small story. Perhaps then you will understand who you are dealing with."

Teanna thrust her hands in the air. "This is ridiculous. Are we going to really stand here and listen to this fool go on and on?"

Roni was inclined to agree — except for the somberness in Kenneth Bay's eye. Like a man on the gallows knowing no alternative existed. He did not want to be standing in that bookstore. He did not want to be sharing these stories. He most certainly did not want to fulfill whatever plan Yal-hara had developed. But as had been his experience since he was fifteen, he had no choice.

"Give the man a moment," Roni said. "Then we'll kick him out."

Bay showed no offense. He knew he stood in enemy territory, and clearly, he knew how to navigate his way through such a situation. He set his hat back on his head and kept his eyes away from direct contact with anyone. "The first day I went to officially take over for my father, I met Yal-hara. My father had warned me, but as those of you who have met her know, the human brain can't really process something it has no frame of reference for. I can't imagine something that never existed in our world. I can make up a chimera of sorts but nothing truly unknowable can be known. I tried to do my best to be stoic — that's what my father told me to do — but watching that creature with all those legs and her odd body — I still lack the words to explain what she is."

"No need," Roni said. "We're familiar."

"Yes, well, she looked me over and told me that I was to bring her a child — no older than seven. I had also been warned by my father not to ask questions unless they pertained to legal issues. I stayed quiet.

"I did not know what she wanted the child for, and I did not care. Always in the back of my mind was the fact that if I failed to please her, it would be the death of myself, my family, and my family's family. The next day, I arrived in her office with a six-year-old that I had lured away from an elementary school. She had the child escorted into another room. She thanked me. And then she told me to return the next day with another one.

"I did this for three days. On the fourth day, I arrived empty-handed. Not for lack of trying, but three missing children in three consecutive days tended to get a bit noticed. Yal-hara said she was not interested in my excuses. I told her she was wrong. I told her that threatening my life and the lives of those that I love would get her only so far. I refused to spend the rest of my terms of service destroying children for no reason at all. She said *Good.* She then told me my father provided five children before he stood up to her. For only a few seconds, I had a warm feeling. The satisfaction of pleasing my employer. Something like that, anyway. But it didn't last long."

Garcia had been leaning on the edge of the big table. He raised his hand. "I realize I'm new to all of this, but if I may — I don't see how this story is supposed to make us feel cooperative with you or Yal-hara. If anything, you're making yourself sound just as much of a monster as she is."

"I want you to understand. Not be sympathetic. Because in the minutes after I felt so proud of myself, Yal-hara had two of her bodyguards hold me down in a chair. They pulled off my shoes and my socks and Yal-hara stepped forward. She lifted one of her spiderlike legs and showed how the pincers at the end were terribly sharp. She then reached down and snipped off one of my toes. Then another. And another. She left me the big toe and my pinky toe. When I sat there, screaming in pain but making no effort to run away, she appeared satisfied. She told me that her two tests had proven that I was both ruthless and determined. The very qualities she sought in her representatives." He tapped his right shoe with his cane. "Ruthless and determined. Just like her. So, I ask you one final time — will you please hand over the Pages of Glass?"

Roni lowered her arms like a gunslinger facing off on a deserted Main Street. Glowering, she shook her head.

"I didn't think so." He looked genuinely saddened as if he truly believed there might have been a chance his speech would have worked. He turned toward the door and took two halting steps.

Roni could feel the concerned looks darting between everyone behind her. She felt the same concern. Why would Kenneth Bay have traveled all the way out here and given his pitch if he intended to simply walk away empty-handed? Despite her misgivings, a tiny ember of hope warmed up within her that perhaps the night was over. Perhaps the fight with Yal-hara would be postponed for another day.

But Kenneth Bay did not continue to the door. He held still. No — not exactly still. His shoulders wriggled, and as the thought hit Roni that he was digging through his inner-pockets, it was already too late.

Moving more nimbly than he should have been able, Kenneth Bay whipped around placing his back leg out, forcing his body to drop low. His right arm swung wide. Spreading out from his hands, he tossed seven relic boxes onto the floor in an arc between him and the Parallel Society.

Far from over, Roni now thought the night was going to be long. Terribly long.

CHAPTER 19

The top of the center relic box slid aside on its own, scratching like claws against stone. Smoke dribbled over the lip. The creature that rose looked more at home on an icy tundra than in a Philadelphia suburb — weight and muscle ready to face the brutal cold, an armor-plated carapace that belonged in a giant-insect horror movie, and woolly hair bushing out at all its joints. Roni thought of it as a cross between a yeti and an overgrown cockroach.

Pointing with his cane, Kenneth Bay looked at the box on his far left. And it began to open. Made from cheap pine, sickly green light pierced the cracks and nail holes. The top pounded upward but did not release. The banging continued with an urgent insistence as if somebody had awoken in a casket and tried to claw their way to freedom. Whatever existed inside that box would have to fight its way out.

Roni spread her hand flat at her side indicating to her team that she wanted them to hold. If they charged forward, they might trigger all of the boxes to open at once — they would instantly lose. More importantly, they had to give Elliot as much time as possible to create the strongest barrier he could.

As the yeti-roach stepped one foot out of its box, Bay's focus on the second box appeared to be straining along with the box's contents. His eye twitched, and the tip of his cane trembled. Roni stepped back, her mouth agape, as she understood.

This was how Yal-hara had solved her problem of limited instructions for the relic box creatures. She sent Kenneth Bay. He would cast the boxes open. He would control the beasts, giving them instructions as they went, making sure they didn't go off course, doing everything he could to bring about a victory for his boss. There was no trigger — except for Bay himself.

The top to the pine relic box splintered and a few sharp jabs knocked out large shards of wood. A rotting arm reached outward. Like a gas leak, a rotten-egg stench wafted across the room. The yeti-roach glanced across, wrinkled its nose before letting loose a loud roar, and stepped over to protect Bay.

No sense in holding back anymore. "Now," Roni said and launched forward.

Gully stomped ahead, lowered to one knee, and opened fire at the yeti-roach. The shotgun blast knocked the creature back a few steps. Roni had the passing thought that if the spread of pellets were wide enough, they might hit Kenneth Bay, and then the situation would end rather quickly. But Bay continued to work at releasing the foul-smelling creature from the pine box. Not a single pellet had struck him.

Teanna dashed across the room, pulling out her hatchets as she headed to the far side of the unopened boxes. With swift grace, she used one hatchet to bat a stone box toward Garcia.

"Got it," he said, swiping the box off the ground and rushing toward the back.

As he headed off to dissolve that relic with a potion, Teanna and Gully continued to press forward against the yeti-roach.

Roni snapped her fingers at Gram. "We take care of the other one." She would have rather gone after Bay, but they couldn't risk either of the creatures reaching Elliot. Or worse, they might find their way into the Caverns.

Gram released a chain as she hustled toward the waist-high bookshelf they had dragged up from the Grand Library. Roni crouched behind it, and pulled out one of Gram's books they had planted.

The putrid-smelling beast finally staggered from its box. Its skin mottled green and black with open sores and blisters spattered across its arms. No head, but its mouth comprised a huge portion of its torso — and that was mostly teeth.

While Gram twirled the chain at her side, Roni scanned the room to check on the rest of her team. Teanna stood before the yeti-roach and swung both axes into its thigh. A loud clink followed sparks where she made contact with its carapace. With the butt of his shotgun, Gully attempted to smack the creature from the back. Further in the room, smoke rose from where Garcia poured his thick concoction over the stolen relic box. And Elliot — he looked calm, serene — like a Buddhist monk seeking nirvana. But Roni also spotted the glisten of sweat running down the man's temple. They needed to end this fight fast. He could only hold out for so long.

She vaulted over the bookshelf and landed directly in front of the tooth-filled beast. Holding the book at her chest, she flung open the cover. She shouted as the change in pressure between universes lifted the creature off its feet and swallowed it whole.

Part of her wanted to simply turn and draw in all the other boxes along with the yeti-roach and Bay, too, but Gram had warned her against it. Not only would she risk pulling in more than just the sought targets — indeed, Teanna and Gully were in the direct line of fire — but the longer the book stayed open, the more chances the creature already in there could find its way out — or some other creature living in there. These relics were bad enough. They didn't need more crawling into their universe.

Roni slammed the book shut, and Gram jumped over, wrapping her chains around the cover.

"Get down," Garcia barked, lunging across the room. Roni and Gram dropped to the floor as a large snake head whipped above them. Garcia came sliding in and hurled a vial of red liquid toward the relic box newly opened. The three-headed snake with two small lizard legs at the back reared and hissed as the potion exploded bright light in front of it.

Gram shoved the chained book into Roni's hands, dropped a new chain, and lassoed it around one of the snake necks. A strong tug and she pulled the creature to the floor with a hard thump. Though its one head wobbled dazed, the other two appeared unharmed. One snapped at Gram. She flinched back, giving the creature enough slack to pull itself free of the chain.

Behind this, Gully swung the shotgun against the yeti-roach's legs. As the creature flopped onto its back, Teanna drove a hatchet through its neck. Blood gushed out and bubbles foamed around the edges of the gaping wound.

The snake creature turned all three heads toward the broken stairwell. With a rapid motion, it shot forward, bumping Garcia aside. Gram tried to lasso it again with a new chain, but she couldn't create it fast enough. It fell short.

"Teanna, the snake," Roni shouted.

The hatchet-wielding tracker hurtled over the dead yeti-roach and raced across the room. Roni scrambled in the opposite direction towards the big table. When Teanna cut off the snake's access to the stairwell, Roni reached the table and snatched Gram's book that had been stashed underneath.

As Roni headed back, clutching the book, she spotted Gully pointing his shotgun at Kenneth Bay. Too slow, however. The fourth relic box flew open, the granite top bashing the side of Gully's head. As the golem recovered, a monkey with eight arms — a real spider monkey — sprang out of the box and onto Gully's chest. The shotgun went off — a new hole formed in the ceiling. Roni looked from the snake creature to the spider monkey beast. Which one to attack? Who to help? Gully or Teanna?

"I've got the snake," Gram said. It was all that Roni needed.

She dashed over to Gully. The spider monkey had knocked him on his back and it pummeled him with its numerous legs. Like a pro-ball kicker, Roni did not slow, planted her foot firm and punted that creature straight off into the wall. As she set her foot down, she braced in a wide stance, positioned the book on her chest, and went to open it.

But the spider monkey flitted up the wall, across the ceiling, and propelled down upon her. The book tumbled onto the floor. The cover opened wide. A high-pitched whine of soaring winds screamed as this new universe attempted to drain all the air from the old. With a terrified screech, the spider monkey latched onto Roni as its torso was dragged toward the book, pulling its arms and Roni with it.

CHAPTER 20

A whirlpool of wind pulled everything within its reach to doom. Survival instincts locked into gear. Every living being in that room suspended the need to fight each other as they now fought for their own lives.

Squawking in manic fury, the spider monkey clutched Roni. With sheer bug-eyed terror ripping at its limited mind, it bared its teeth and yelped at the book. Oddly enough, if not for that conjured beast, Roni suspected she would have died. But with its added weight, her body slid across the floor at a slower pace. Slow enough for Gram to grow a long chain and throw it in Roni's direction.

Roni reached out, but could not quite touch it. Gram reeled it back in and threw a second time. It landed across Roni's hand and she clamped her grip, feeling the metal dig into her skin the instant the chain grew taut.

With the blistering wind whipping through the room, every loose object spun in the air — papers, books, wooden coasters, Sully's extra glasses, and even the pizza boxes lifted from the trash. Holding tight to the chain, Roni checked on all of her team — each one had found a way to secure against the walls. Kenneth Bay also had managed to lodge his cane at a deep angle into the floor, pressing his chest against it to keep from moving. The yeti-roach's head rolled until the vortex of the book took hold and spun it down into another universe. In the back, Elliot held still, the hurricane winds unable to penetrate his shield.

Garcia yelled something to Gram, but Gram shook her head *No*. He insisted again. Roni could not make out what the plan was, but nobody else appeared to have any plan, and the spider monkey clung to her like a baby, limiting any chance she had of useful movement.

Gram must have drawn the same conclusions because she finally relented. With a strong pull on the chain protecting Roni's life, Gram tied it around a nearby support beam. She then released a new length of chain and let it slither across the floor like the three-headed snake once did. The winds pushed it around but it lacked a shape conducive to going airborne. Garcia reached out while keeping one hand locked around the leg of the big table. When he snagged the chain, Gram let go.

As he wound in all of the long chain, Roni heard a rattle like stones against wood. She looked to her side and found the two remaining locked relic boxes rolling toward the front counter. She put out her free hand to try to catch one, but they were too far away and the spider monkey stopped her from stretching her full length. The swirling winds pushed them further. Were they lighter, the winds might have taken hold and pulled the boxes in, solving the rest of their problems. Gram had said putting more than one in a universe would be bad, but it couldn't be as bad as their current situation.

Garcia tied one end of the chain around his waist and the other around the big table leg. He swallowed hard. Narrowing his eyes on the book, he wiped his shaking hands against his pants and managed a bold sternness to go along with his tentative steps.

A gust instantly grabbed hold, knocking him to the floor and tumbling him across the room. Despite the howling screams of the maelstrom, Roni had no trouble discerning Garcia's roars of shock and fear. The chain snapped tight. He let out a sharp grunt as it stopped him several feet shy of Gram.

Getting on all fours, the gale flapping against his face, he crawled back toward the book. These winds never stopped threatening to send him tumbling once more, but he stuck out his right leg to brace himself. Lumbering inch by inch he made his way forward — always maintaining one foot or arm at a strange angle to keep from falling prey to the merciless wind.

With a last lurch forward, he reached out but missed the book cover. Roni wanted to bellow a torrent of swears. But her anger shifted to hope — she saw that he had not missed at all. He had not been trying for the book cover. Instead, he picked up the open relic box of the spider monkey. He then rolled on the ground straight toward the book.

And straight in.

The alarm on his face told Roni everything — this was not part of the plan. He must not have expected the pull of the universe to be so strong. *Idiot. It's a damn universe.* But Roni also noticed that the chain remained straight and firm. He was still attached to it.

The spider monkey shot its head up and shrieked. Whatever happened inside that book, that relic box had been destroyed. The spider monkey knew it, had to be able to feel it, because it let go of Roni and disintegrated mid-air. The book devoured its ashes.

Flipping onto her stomach, Roni grabbed her chain with both hands and climbed forward to get a secure position. When she glanced back, she saw Garcia's hand appear over the edge of the book. Using his chain, he climbed out, flopped onto his back, and with one hand threw the cover closed.

The storm ceased in an instant. Pens, paper clips, a wireless mouse, and the shattered pine relic box clattered to the floor. Pieces of the yeti-roach splatted blood across the wood and hit the walls, too. Gram hustled over to secure the book with her chains.

"Don't ever let me do that again," Garcia said.

Feeling as if her arms had been pulled from the sockets, Roni sat up and rubbed her shoulder. She lurched to her feet and faced Kenneth Bay. "It's over," she said.

But he did not respond. His attention, his energy, focused on the two remaining relic boxes.

Crap.

From the first box, which had been made of riveted metal, emerged a massive amoeba sludge. It spread across the floor like a slow mudslide with mustard-colored streaks pulsing through its body. The wet, sloshing sound balanced only by the moldy cheese odor.

Gully pumped a fresh shell into his shotgun and fired. Holes pelted the creature in a wide pattern, but it quickly absorbed the damage and smoothed over to continue moving. Gully pumped and shot again. A column of mud emerged from the beast's middle and wrapped around the barrel of the shotgun.

Teanna assaulted from the other side. Another mud column emerged. In seconds, Roni and Garcia also had to contend with this multi-limbed blob. Teanna hacked one limb apart, but it's destroyed liquid arm rained down on its body to be reabsorbed. And a new tentacle arose.

As the fight continued, Roni saw Kenneth Bay turning his attention to the last relic box. It was smaller than the others and made of sticks — twigs, really. The top popped open and a small bird fluttered into the air. It flew overhead, out of reach — not that the team had time to deal with it.

Gully wrenched his shotgun free as a mud tentacle wrapped around Roni's leg. She kicked at it. Four times. Hard. When it finally let go, she watched as the bird zipped across the room and into the stairwell. There was no way to stop it, and Roni knew to her core what the bird would do — fly to the Caverns and search for the Pages of Glass.

Turning toward Kenneth Bay, Roni tightened her fists. But the mud creature walloped her across the hips, sending her flat on her back. As its arm of liquid dirt moved through the air, one of Gram's chains wrapped around the creature and pulled it off course. Roni rolled in the opposite direction and managed to get back to her feet.

With all the relic boxes open and all of the Society busy contending with the mud amoeba, Kenneth Bay found no resistance as he walked towards the elevator. Teanna hacked, Gully shot, Gram whipped, Roni kicked, and Kenneth Bay tapped his cane on the floor with each calm step until he reached the barrier Elliot had raised.

Roni could stand back from the creature, let her teammates do the fighting, but every time she moved to help Elliot, the creature created a new arm or a new tentacle to bat her away. It must have been given instructions to keep all Society members busy. Nobody would stop Bay.

She watched as he poked the barrier with his cane. She could see the resistance, but she could also see Elliot weakening. The fact that he had enough strength to last this long impressed her. He simply had to hold out a little bit more. Just give them enough time to destroy this blob of mud and then they could rescue him.

But Kenneth Bay reached into his pocket and produced a small revolver. He pointed it at Elliot and shot. The muzzle flashed like lightning, and the gunshot blasted the air with a thunderous roar. The bullet pierced the barrier, but in doing so, it lost momentum and trajectory. It split the wood above Elliot's head.

"Roni, help," Teanna said, snapping Roni back to the monstrous goo assaulting her people.

She bolted over, grabbed a spare hatchet set up against the wall, and made a sloppy chop at the creature. Blades were not part of her skills, but she would try.

A second gunshot crack from near the elevator. A quick glance and Roni saw that the barrier had deflected the bullet once more. At least, she thought so because Elliot was still alive.

"This isn't working," she said. "Garcia, get around this thing and destroy its box."

"I'm on it." Garcia darted off to the left, but the amorphous blob shifted some of its body to block passage. He tried to pivot right and then scoot off left, but the creature was not deceived.

Seeing the problem, Roni said, "Everybody else concentrate attacks over here."

Gram and Gully joined, assaulting the opposite end of the creature. They hacked and whipped and shot. It fought back — jabbing out wet pillars, but the constant abuse slowed its reactions. Or perhaps, like Elliot, it had weakened.

Roni glanced back as another gunshot flashed near the elevator. Garcia had made it around and now bolted up to the front counter. He swung behind and snagged the flask stashed there earlier. Screwing off the top as he approached the metal box, he closed his eyes and mouthed a few words. Roni knew that look, that behavior — the man prayed.

He turned over the flask and his potion dripped out onto the metal relic box. It dissolved fast. Perhaps because the acidic nature of the potion hit metal differently or perhaps Garcia had made a more potent version — Roni didn't know. Didn't care much, either. Because another gunshot pulled her attention. This time, she saw Elliot fall.

His cane slapped the ground as the barrier followed him down. A blossoming splotch of blood marked where the bullet had struck his leg. Sweat blanketed the man, and he gulped air like a drowning victim.

Kenneth Bay stepped around Elliot and entered the elevator. He didn't bother with the gate or the door — just pressed the floor button and stood back as if he had no pressing engagements to bother him.

While it started its slow decent, Gram said, "Roni, go stop him. If he finds the Pages of Glass —"

"It could take that bird years to find it for him."

"No. These relic boxes make no sense unless they came from the universe that holds the book with the Pages."

Gram returned to the fight, but Roni nodded. She thought about the journal of Mr. Callum Murray. He had said that the nightmares came out of the *Book of Nightmares* with him. Grotesque creatures and monstrous visions wracked his brain incessantly. He wrote that he had to lock them away so they did not haunt him. It never occurred to Roni that he meant it literally. If Gram was right, that bird — like many birds — could easily find its way home.

Whether or not he knew it yet, Kenneth Bay might actually succeed in locating the Pages of Glass. Roni's stomach clenched and her mouth ran dry.

CHAPTER 21

Roni did not think her heart could beat any faster or her adrenaline pump any harder, but she was wrong. With a massive jolt shocking her into action, her system ignited. Her mind cleared. Her muscles tightened.

Like an army drill sergeant commanding new recruits, she barked out, "Gram, Garcia — take care of Elliot. If he needs it, don't hesitate to go to the hospital. Teanna — secure this bookstore and be ready for another attack. If anybody steps foot in this building that doesn't belong here, get them to leave. If they refuse, make them sorry they ever came in. Gully — here with me. We're going to stop Kenneth Bay."

She headed over to the stairs that Gully had destroyed earlier in the day. The others snapped into action, and Roni caught a prideful nod from Gram. Perhaps later — if she survived — Roni would remember that look and feel a sense of warmth or satisfaction, or perhaps she would wonder why Gram had thrown several knowing, prideful looks her way when the woman had barely patted her on the back for an entire lifetime. But at the moment, she could only think about how they might avert disaster.

When Gully arrived, Roni said, "We have to get to that elevator. Try to stop Bay before he reaches the Caverns. That means getting to the Grand Library now."

"No problem." Gully crouched low enough for Roni to climb aboard his back. "Get on. I'll bring you down safely." He reached into the bucket of water intended to stop fires and soaked his hands and feet.

"You sure about this?"

He shrugged. "It should work."

He had the same upwards lilt, the same casual attitude, the same dry humor — exactly like Sully. With tears creeping into Roni's eyes, she patted his shoulder. "I trust you. Let's go."

Reaching out into the open stairwell, Gully smashed his wet clay hand against the wall. He pressed hard until it deformed flat onto the surface. Next his foot, then another hand, and finally the last foot. With four points of contact, they stuck to the wall, suspended over the jagged leftovers of the stairs. But Roni could see Gully's clay limbs slipping. They did not lose their grip, yet they did not hold secure either.

"Hurry," Roni said, fighting the urge to click her tongue and give a kick. A golem was not a horse. Besides, she felt more like a glorified backpack than a skilled jockey.

Gully repositioned his hands before lowering down a few inches.

"Faster." She peered down to see how far of a drop it would be. Too far. "We have to beat an elevator."

"It's a slow elevator."

"Gully!"

"Okay, okay. Far be it from me to stop you from risking your life to catch an elevator."

Wriggling his body as if preparing to jump, Gully looked back at her and winked. "Hold tight."

Thankfully, he did not let go. But he did loosen his grip on the wall. Together, they whipped downwards. Clay streaks formed lines along the wall as they raced to the bottom. About seven feet above the end, Gully let out a groan and lost his hold. They fell the rest of the way.

Roni's feet slammed into the floor, reverberating through her bones all the way up to her head. Gully smacked the ground next to her with a horrible noise like a pile of rocks thrown from above.

"Are you okay?" she said, trying to help him up.

"Forget me. Get the elevator."

Roni peered across the Grand Library. On the wall to the left, she saw the bottom of the elevator come into view. Taking a few steps forward, she felt pain jolt up her leg. Hopefully, just heavy bruising from the fall and nothing broken. Her steps turned into a run — an uncomfortable run — as the elevator came into full view.

Over her shoulder, she said, "Can you still do your part?"

"I'm fine," Gully yelled. "Stop worrying about me and slow him down. I'll meet you at the book."

As the elevator lowered, Kenneth Bay's face paled in surprise. That brief shock gave Roni a moment of petulant joy. Then with an arrogant smirk, he rolled his fingers in a childish wave, and the elevator continued its decent. Roni dug deep and pushed her livid legs harder. She dove the last few lengths. Slid right into the elevator. Popping to her feet, she brought a punch with her, clocking Kenneth Bay in the jaw. Knocked that nasty grin right off his face.

A sharp, painful jolt lanced through her arm. She charged forward, planning to slam her elbow into Bay's chest and shove him back. But he pulled the top of the cane like a lever snapping out the bottom and catching her in the groin. She coughed out all the air in her lungs. Stumbled. Just one step. But it was enough.

The top of that cane with its silver head slammed across Roni's temple. The world brightened solid white. Her head clouded over, and when she could finally see again, she sat on the floor of the elevator. Jabbing the pointed end of his cane into her thigh, he deadening the muscle.

"Please," he said through heavy breaths. "Do not make me kill you. I don't want any of this. I certainly don't want to be a murderer. The Parallel Society has fought hard. There's no shame in losing. Your mission can continue. You can still be the ones that protect our universe."

"Just so long as we open up the rest of the universes to Yal-hara. That's what she wants, isn't it? Not to find her way home — nothing so innocent. No, she wants access to infinite worlds, with infinite children and all their memories."

"What happened to you was an anomaly."

The elevator came to rest. Roni noticed the middle finger on her right hand had gone numb. Great — she must have broken it when punching Kenneth Bay's jaw.

"You're in no condition to stop me, now," he said. "Don't try. I don't want to, but I will kill you. If you make me."

"I don't have to stop you. Most of the relics are dead, I've got a whole team here, and you don't know where you're going."

An expression passed his eyes that Roni could not read — surprise? anger? regret? Maybe all of them at once. Whatever it had been, it disappeared in a flash.

Returning a controlled, stern gaze, he said, "You forget who you are dealing with. Again. Ruthless and determined."

CHAPTER 22

Limping along the familiar paths of the Caverns, Roni cringed at the pain accompanying each footfall. Short grunts escaped her lips as she fought back the urge to scream — in vicious anger or grim defeat or both. One middle-aged man with a cane was all it had taken to get by her team. And she had six people working for her. When Gram led the Society, there were only three. Three elderly people, at that. Yet somehow Gram, Elliot, and Sully had managed to secure the universe for decades.

"I haven't managed even a year."

She pressed on. All was not lost yet. She knew that. But that didn't take away the sting. Kenneth Bay should never have gotten this far. Their contingency plans should never have had to come into use. Passing one of Gram's books and a hatchet, both hidden in a crevice, reminded her that they had other contingencies which never came into play. The degree of failure kept mounting.

She walked on.

Mixed in with the familiar echoes of water drips and her own footsteps in the Caverns, she heard the melodic notes of a bird. Stupid bird. She had prepared for so many possibilities, but never a bird.

And while Roni could comprehend that this bird honed in on its birth universe, how could it possibly communicate that to Kenneth Bay? Then again, she had witnessed paper golems returning to Sully with answers written inside on more than one occasion. Or perhaps Kenneth Bay could simply speak the language of birds from a nightmare universe.

Roni threw up her arms and let out an aggravated groan. She limped onward as fast as possible, but it would be up to Gully to slow down Bay.

As she wound through several of the twisting tunnels, after passing along the narrow walls and rock slick with cascading water, she discovered what Gully had meant when he said he had a surprise waiting — one that gave her hope. Splayed flat on the ground, Roni saw the remains of a rudimentary golem made of small rocks and a few twigs.

"Holy crap." The words came out fast, and she involuntarily glanced around to see if Gram had heard. She lowered to the golem's side. On his deathbed, Sully had said that Gully could do more than she realized. She didn't think he meant that Gully could create another golem. And while this one could not have been more than three feet high and lacked all but the most basic form, the fact that it existed astounded her.

She tried to pick up the dead form, tried to cradle it, but the rocks tumbled apart. Gully had done a great thing. Not only because he had created another life like himself, but he had done so for the mission. Clearly this little golem had been meant as an obstacle to Kenneth Bay. A way to delay his progress.

Some of the stones had little wet drops on them, yet it took Roni a few extra seconds to realize they were from her own tears. Her fingers shook. She tried to stand, but her bruised leg wobbled. Moaning loudly, she pushed harder until she finally stood. Her pained cries echoed off the cavern walls.

As the sound died out, she heard another. Footsteps. From behind.

"Roni? Are you hurt?" Garcia arrived.

Quickly patting her cheeks dry, she said, "I told you to help Gram."

"I did. Then she ordered me to help you. Gave me directions to get here and said I should —"

"I don't care what she said. You obey my commands."

Garcia shrugged. "She's scarier." He pulled a vial of murky liquid from his jacket. "Drink this."

"What is it?"

"Poison. I want you dead so I can take over the world."

Taking the vial, she gave it a sniff — like old coffee. "You don't have to be a smartass."

"Seems you all talk to each other like that. I thought —"

"Yeah, I get it. But bonding time comes later. What the heck is this for?"

"Pain. Drink and it'll let you move without the pain. Mostly."

"Mostly?"

"I'm still learning. But it'll at least dull the pain."

Roni drank the concoction in one swig. Puckering her face, she said, "Work on making it taste better."

From further down the tunnel, the distinct tones of an argument bounced towards them. Roni recognized the voices right away — Kenneth Bay and Gully. She cocked her ear in their direction.

"I've already dismantled your little friend," Bay said. "And you look in horrible condition. Out of my way or I'll do the same to you."

Roni clamped her jaw tight and rolled her fingers into fists. This wasn't over. Gully held his ground up ahead, willing to fight — for her. Because she told him to do so. Because she gave the order.

She would fight, too. For Gully. For Gram and Elliot. For Teanna and Garcia. For Sully. And for their world and universe. This was her job. Her purpose.

Despite her injuries, she strode ahead with her eyes locked forward. "Okay, Kenneth Bay. Let me show you how ruthless and determined I can be."

Garcia hurried behind.

CHAPTER 23

Gully stood in front of the platform where the *Book of Nightmares* hung above. He had his fists on his hips like a schoolmarm from a black-and-white movie.

Kenneth Bay pointed his cane at the golem. "Enough of this. I can chip you away into pieces, if I have to."

"Do what you must," Gully said, sounding more like his creator with every passing hour. "You can't truly hurt me."

"Then I'll have to destroy you."

Roni and Garcia listened to the exchange as they walked down the center aisle. Garcia tried to hide his awe. Roni would have been amused if not for the serious problems mounting before them. She moved a bit ahead.

The enormous, carved columns gazing upon her made her feel even smaller than before. The pale-green firelight flickering off the torches attested to the nightmare promised by the hanging book's title. From far above, the melodic chirping of the relic box bird drifted upon the room — it had perched on the enlarged nose of one of the carvings.

Looking beyond Bay, Gully spotted Roni. "He won't listen."

Bay turned slowly, his arrogant smirk back on his mouth. "It's over. I've won. You're hurt. Your team has been stopped, and I have made it this far. Please, don't continue fighting a lost cause. It'll only get more of the Parallel Society hurt."

Roni halted well out of range of his cane. She patted her leg. "Good as new, thanks to my potion maker."

"I doubt that."

Placing most of her weight on her good leg, she nodded toward the book. "You really don't want to go in there. It's called the *Book of Nightmares* for a reason. From our research, we're pretty sure that's where your little relic boxes came from. It's the reason the book with the Pages of Glass was locked away in there, too."

"I don't care." He swallowed hard and could not stop a trepidatious glance up at the book.

"You're stuck, aren't you? I understand. I know what it's like to be in a family business. The pressures, the expectations — it's more than a job. It's the lifeblood of the family. But there's a point where it goes too far. Where it takes over your life and doesn't allow you any free will. You never wanted to be a lawyer. You never wanted any of this. Do you really think sacrificing yourself is going to make a difference? Not to Yal-hara. She has no loyalty to you. How many times has she held over your head the idea that she could pitch your family aside for some other lawyers? You mean nothing to her."

"You don't know the first thing about her." A flash of rage overtook Bay, and he whipped around, slamming his cane against Gully's side.

Gully had not been prepared for the attack and staggered off the platform. Garcia rushed over to him, and the golem pushed back like an old man hiding his embarrassment. "I'm fine," Gully said. "Don't bother."

Bay hopped underneath the book, and with his cane, yanked loose several of the chains. They came apart with a hard tug or two — old, rusty things. Dust rained down into his face. He coughed and waved the air clear.

"Why would you sell out all of mankind?" Roni asked. "All of our universe?"

"That's the problem with you people — you're so melodramatic about everything. Do you really think your little old grandma and her two little friends have ever saved the universe? The entire universe? We are small and insignificant beings. Always have been."

"And Yal-hara isn't? Is that why you serve her? You want to be part of something bigger, something you think is special?"

"Not at all. She is every bit as insignificant as the rest of us."

"Then why do any of this?"

Pulling on the top edge of the book, he wrestled against the last chain. Gully approached him until Roni put out her hand. She could handle this.

Bay said, "I do this for the same reason I've done every atrocious request for Yal-hara. For the same reason I served up children to her way back at the beginning — if I don't, she'll kill me. She'll kill my family. And my family's family. It's that simple."

With a final sharp jerk, he freed the book from its prison. It hit the floor with a heavy *thunk*. A quick grin of success, and then he stared cold at the book. His throat shuddered. Gully walked over to Roni, and as he worked at the clay in his hand to reshape it, he said to Bay, "If you go in there, you will most likely die."

"If I don't go in, I will certainly die."

"That doesn't have to happen. Let us help you," Roni said.

Garcia added, "Listen to her. She's good at helping people."

Gully said, "You don't think they put her in charge because she's a selfish person."

Bay gazed up at Roni, and in his eyes, she witnessed all the terrifying pressure hounding him. His fine clothes, his pristine mustache, his cane and hat — the armor of a man who had spent a lifetime in fear of displeasing his boss. Because to displease meant to destroy so many he cared about.

Roni leaned against Gully for a moment. The throbbing in her leg had eased some thanks to Garcia, but not enough. "I know it's easy to think of each individual person in this world as pointless. And maybe we are throughout most of our lives, but there is usually some moment, even just a fleeting one, where our decisions and our actions matter. Sometimes we don't even know it. And those little moments can have massive effects on millions of people. On the entire world. You're at one of those moments. If you go in there, if you survive and take the Pages of Glass and give them to Yal-hara, you're dooming the lives of billions. Because let's be honest — she's not going to leave this world alone. You said this place was her prison. The Yal-hara I've known will not let that rest. There will be payback."

"Probably," Bay said, his voice lacking all its earlier cockiness.

"This is what I'm talking about. This is why my little old grandma and her little friends have actually saved the universe. Because there are moments where they have had the opportunity. You have it, too. Right now."

Kenneth Bay lowered his head to look at the book in his hands. His shoulders rose and he let out a long, slow sigh. With the reverence of a holy man, he removed the chain that kept the book closed. He let it snake to the floor, then passed his hand over the dusty volume. With a sharp inhale, he set the book down next to the chain. He stared at it like a man standing on a rooftop ledge. Then he opened it.

When he looked back at Roni, his cheeks were wet. But his sad brow tightened. "You're just standing there."

"I'm hoping you'll do the right thing."

"You're not going to try to stop me again?"

Roni rubbed the bridge of her nose as she shook her head. "Maybe once more, but not yet. You still don't believe me. You don't think you're important, that any of this matters. I'm not sure you even believe me about what's in that book. About why it's called the *Book of Nightmares.*"

"To be fair, you have lied to me a lot. You even denied the Pages of Glass where anything but a myth."

"If I get the chance to ask you again to stop, I hope you'll listen."

He shifted his body as if he wanted to say something more but only gazed down at the book. Holding a deep breath, he stepped in.

Roni, Gully, and Garcia held still, staring at the lectern. Garcia's face widened as he gestured to the book with both hands. "I didn't believe he'd really do that."

"He thinks he doesn't have a choice," Roni said.

Wiping his hands against each other, Gully said, "Well, if he cares about any members of his family, he probably doesn't."

"We always have a choice."

"But, but," Garcia said, unable to look away from the book, "that was suicide."

"Probably." Gully walked forward. "And I guess that's that. We should chain up this book and go check on the others."

"No." Roni rubbed her leg. "We stick to the plan."

"But I don't like this part of your plan."

"Like I said — everybody has a choice. I'm going in there."

"What?" Garcia said.

"I'm going to make sure this all ends tonight. If what I've read about this book is true, then I'll probably be assaulted by all kinds of crazy things. But Gully, you don't dream. Which means you don't have nightmares, either. You're the only one that can protect me. The only one that can make sure I get back here safely. I won't force you to come with me. I won't order you. The choice is yours."

Gully sighed. "That's a lousy choice."

"Still a choice."

Although she did not expect different, she could not stop the strong warmth that filled her when Gully walked right to her side. No hesitation. He picked up one of Gram's chains from the floor and tied one end around his waist. He handed the other to Roni and waited for her to do the same.

Before she stepped into the book, she turned back and gave him a hug. "I'm so glad you exist."

"I'm pretty happy about it, too."

"Wait." Garcia handed her another vial — this one amber like beer. "Throw this at him, if you have to. And don't look. It's really bright."

Roni accepted the vial with a strong nod. "Thank you."

She turned back. Holding Gully by the hand, she led the way into the book.

CHAPTER 24

Her first impression — the *Book of Nightmares* wasn't so bad. Certainly dark. Quite gloomy. Not the kind of place she wanted to spend much time. But from reading the journals of Callum Murray and from experiencing the creatures in the relic boxes, she had built up a horror so mind-boggling, so evil, that she could only be underwhelmed.

She walked through a dark forest. Thick with trees that blocked out most light and created strange, shadowed figures with what little light remained. There were odd noises and a sense of foreboding that thickened with every step.

Gully led the way, but the path only went straight. It had an artificial, metallic surface — a manufactured feel that grated against the naturalness of the forest. Nobody had to tell Roni not to leave the path. She had read Bradbury.

Of course, she knew it would be too good to last. It was a childish hope that naming the place the *Book of Nightmares* had only been a ruse to dissuade people from entering. Because now she saw glints in the distance on either side. Yellow and red and orange eyes staring back at her. Watching her movements. Her arms prickled.

She heard sounds — disquieting noises. Wet slobbering and perverted breathing. But being leered at and hounded by sexual deviants was a commonplace occurrence for most women. Uncomfortable, threatening, but not the stuff of legendary nightmares.

Yet as Gully continued on the path, the chain between them pulling her along, she had the sense that the book was only getting started. It tossed out these unnerving but hardly horrifying bits simply to throw her off. Get her looking over her shoulder. Set up her psyche so that when the real nightmares began, all the fear within her would become an inferno.

Could a universe feed off of fear?

She did not want to know.

With a sultry stab, a spindle-thin leg poked out of the darkness like an insect burlesque about to begin. Then another leg. And another. And when the fourth appeared, Roni's heart dropped. Despite having only four limbs, it moved like a spider the size of a small, eight-year-old girl. Its round torso and stalk-like neck curdled Roni's stomach. Her skin froze over and she whimpered.

Yal-hara crawled onto the path as she had first appeared upon Roni's bed. Roni stood still, petrified. Her eyes unblinking. Her mind transformed into a child woken one night by an abomination.

A mothering, soft voice spoke: "Don't be afraid. I'm only here to collect what your father has paid. A memory. You must give up a memory. I will take it from you, and I will take tonight away, too. You'll never have to be troubled by thoughts of me again."

Exactly what Yal-hara had said that first night. Word for word. As if swiped straight out Roni's horrified memory.

Roni tried to back away, but she could not move. And she could feel another presence — a joyful presence, that of a man she loved. Sully. She could not see him but he tugged her forward. She could hear him muttering about staying on the path. Never stop moving forward.

"I'm sure this is confusing," the creature said, "but you needn't worry. You don't have to understand. All you must do is pick a memory that you'll never miss. Something you don't care to remember ever again, and I'll take it from you. There will be no pain, I promise. Not a single ouchy. Surely, there's some nugget of time in your short life that you wish would go away?"

Roni wobbled a few steps forward. Tears raced down her cheeks. She could not think, could not feel beyond static horror.

"Remember me," Sully said. "Close your eyes and forget about whatever you see. Think about us."

Roni nodded like the little girl she felt she was. She closed her eyes. She remembered the breakfasts she would spend with Sully and Elliot in their little kitchen. But even as she tried to recall which of the two men liked to prance back and forth with eggs and bacon and toast like the happiest waiter alive, even as she tried to surround herself with the warmth of their company and the delight of their love, she heard the clicking of those sharp nails — Yal-hara was just around the corner. Roni looked toward the kitchen door. She started shaking. The fork in her hand clacked against the plate of eggs. Each clack tightened her throat, pressed against her lungs, banished all sane thought.

The door vanished and in crawled Yal-hara.

Roni lay in bed. She could not move. The horrid creature crept up her eight-year-old body. Soon, she would invite Roni to offer up a memory — something the little girl would be happy to forget. One of those spindle legs would reach up toward Roni's temple and tap her skull. Soon, Yal-hara would swipe too much of her life and destroy Roni's chances at a normal future.

That moment when Yal-hara finished, when Roni knew something more terrible had happened — it played over and over. Always with Yal-hara saying, "Oh, dear. That's unfortunate. Sorry, young one. I told you to focus on a single moment, but you children always have to mix things together. It's your own fault, really. Nothing to do about it now, though."

"Open your eyes," Sully said. "Stop believing that you are seeing what you see. It's an illusion. A nightmare drawn from your life. From your brain. From your memories."

"My memories?" But Yal-hara had stolen her memories.

Like the breaking of a fairytale spell, the incongruous ideas of Yal-hara stealing her memories and Sully telling her to draw upon her memories returned her to the *Book of Nightmares*. The path. The mission.

She was on her back, and Gully sat next to her, his hand on her chest trying to talk her back to consciousness.

"Gully?"

The golem nodded. "You must stand," he said, but his voice was entirely Sully. "Stand and follow me. Hold onto the chain."

A surge of energy brought on by hearing Sully's voice awoke her. With the golem's help, she climbed to her feet. "How do you sound like —"

"Follow the sound of Sully. Hold onto the chain. We're almost there. Keep moving. Anytime you see something disturbing, you listen to ol' Sully's voice. He'll protect you."

Roni heard the multilimbed steps of the creature keeping pace with her just off in the distance. In the dark. She could feel those steps pinprick in her skin. She shivered.

"Forget all of that and pay attention to me. Sully's got you. Keep hold of the chain and blot out everything else around you."

Roni nodded as she locked both hands around the chain at her waist.

The golem with Sully's voice offered a reaffirming squeeze on the shoulder. "There was a time when you were nine-years-old that Gram and Elliot had to go off on a mission. They left me behind to care for you. Now, understand, I wasn't opposed to the idea. I'm your Uncle Sully, and I was happy to spend the time with you. But I didn't have much experience with taking care of children. Never bothered with marriage. Never had much interest in being a father. But as your uncle? Absolutely happy to do it."

"How can you say any of this? Sully is dead."

"True, true," Gully said with his own voice. "I am only a facsimile of a sort. But he put many of his memories inside of me lest they be forgotten. He did this so that I could help you when you needed me."

The crying whine of metal scraping metal erupted off to her right. A flash of light — a car crash. Her parents. Except they never actually died in a car crash. That was a lie told to protect her from the truth. A lie that haunted her night after night. A lie which obscured what Yalhara had done.

Thinking the name awoke all those glowing eyes. They growled at her, ready to pounce should she take a misstep.

"Roni, stop losing focus. Listen to my story."

With a vigorous nod, she tightened her grip on the chain. *Continue walking and listen to Sully's voice.* She could do that. *Ignore that it came out of a clay-and-stone golem.* She had to do that.

"At first, you and I played with dolls and read books and took care of the store. Everything seemed fine. But Gram and Elliot were absent for a day-and-a-half, so by the time they got back, things had gone terribly wrong. We nearly burned down the store while cooking — not something I had much skill in back then. We spilled hot cocoa on your favorite shirt — nearly burned your skin. We tripped three circuit breakers — never did figure out how that happened. Pretty much, I didn't get anything right."

"I'm sure you were wonderful. I'm sorry I don't remember it."

"You were young. I barely remember anything before I was a teenager." Gully made a strange pitched moan. "Sorry. Obviously, I don't have the memories to say that. But it's what's in me that Sully wanted said."

Something wet and strong slapped Roni in the foot as they walked by. "Just keep the story going. Please."

"Of course. The thing was that you were very upset. You hadn't eaten well the entire time, your favorite shirt was ruined, and I didn't even mention that we went for a walk and a bird pooped on your shoulder. It's true. Sent you into a fit of tears. But here's the thing — when Gram and Elliot did come home, you said nothing. You told them that we had a great time and everything was perfect. I knew right then that your deep loyalty would be a great asset when you took over. Now, because I don't like lies, I later confessed the whole thing to Gram. She suspected as much. She said something about there being no way I could have handled a nine-year-old girl perfectly. We laughed, but she saw what I saw, too. I remember her saying how she knew someday the truth would come out, that someday you would be forced into dealing with the Parallel Society, and she prayed that I was right about you. That you were going to make a good and true leader. I hope you know that I died feeling justified in those beliefs."

The chain in her hands grew limp. Before she could raise a worried voice, Gully said in his own calm tone, "We've arrived."

She lifted her gaze and saw Kenneth Bay with his hand on the book that contained the Pages of Glass.

CHAPTER 25

The book had a greenish tint and it sat upon a wooden lectern. The lectern had been situated on the stage of an amphitheater as if awaiting a professor to arrive and teach eager university students. But the longer she stood on the theater stairs, as her eyes adjusted to the dreary gloom, the more she saw that this place was not an inviting structure designed for learning. Many of the seats were broken, and many more had been stained with blood. A beige, oily liquid streamed down the walls thick as syrup. Insects as big as Roni's hand had been trapped in this liquid, and they oozed downward in a slow-motion waterfall of corpses. Rabid dogs had been chained at the doorways — foaming at the mouth and barking in madness.

The entire place confused Roni until she looked closely at Kenneth Bay. Pale fear coated his skin in sweat. This was not her nightmare. This nightmare belonged to him.

Guiding her down the stairs, Gully said, "This is so different. The room must alter itself based on who threatens the Pages."

Roni said, "But the Pages aren't —"

"I hate you." Bay hardly moved his mouth when he spoke these words, yet they filled the theater as if he yelled in a microphone. The barking dogs whimpered and quelled.

He stepped away from the lectern, his pants had been torn by something with claws, and bloodied footprints painted the floor as he walked. In one hand, he held a hunting knife. Greenish ichor dripped from the blade.

With his head lowered and his eyes never leaving Roni, he continued moving. When he reached the bottom of the stairs, he stopped and glowered at her. "I hate you."

"Yeah, you mentioned that." The vibration in her voice betrayed her

— she was thinking Gully may have been right. Maybe they shouldn't have come here. Maybe her plan had not been so bright after all.

She rolled her shoulders and lifted her head. No. She would not let doubtful thoughts stop her now.

Though it clearly caused him pain, Kenneth Bay climbed several steps. "I had a good life until you came along. Yal-hara was a calm prisoner in our world. I did my job, served her well, and nothing happened. Day to day, my job was simple. Easy enough, anyway. Manage some shell corporations to hide her money, file the proper paperwork so that she paid her taxes and donated to charity and did all the proper things a human in her position would do. I made sure nobody bothered her, nobody inquired about her, nobody discovered what she really is. And you know what I did the rest of the time? You have any idea?" Slashing the knife around the air, he said, "Whatever I wanted. I had all the money I could spend, and I had access to a real power. It was a good life. With great benefits. But you upended all of that."

He climbed a few more steps. Roni held her ground.

"Yal-hara took a keen interest in you, and she would not let it go. I tried — I tried to dissuade her from that stupid plan. Have that fool, Darin, date you to gain access to the Caverns and steal a book? I tried to dissuade her from any outright attack against the Society. But you kept thwarting her, and she kept getting more and more obsessed. There's no stopping her now." He put out his arms, looked over the bloodied mess that he had become, and he laughed. "Need I say anything more? She had accepted her fate. This world would be her gilded cage, her home until death. But then comes you and all that evaporates. And with it, all of my good life."

As he spoke, he continued to draw closer and closer. Roni had become so absorbed in his ranting that she did not pay attention to this danger. Until he lifted that hunting knife overhead. Until he let out a phlegm-soaked cry.

Leaping over the last few steps he brought the knife down fast and hard. The madness in his eyes, the anger fueling his fury — there was no need for the book to create a nightmare around him. He was his own nightmare.

The knife never hit her. Instead, it pierced through Gully's arm as he jumped between them. With a gentle push, he sent Kenneth Bay flailing down the stairs. Then he pulled the knife out and tossed it aside.

Roni linked her arm through Gully's for support. Garcia's pain blocker had worn off. If they didn't finish this soon, Gully would have to carry her out of this universe. Before she spoke, she felt his hand patting hers much like Sully had done in the past. She turned her head and pressed her lips against his shoulder.

Then to Bay: "I'm not the one who destroyed your life. I'm not the one who asked Yal-hara to hurt an eight-year-old girl and warp your mind. I had no contact with you. Like you, I had a good life. I had a loving family and a stable upbringing. In one night, Yal-hara stole that from me. I spent more than twenty years lost, not knowing what was real or imagined of my past. I spent those decades being lied to under the guise of protecting me. When the truth finally came out, it just about destroyed me. Even after I restored my memories — no thanks to your boss, by the way — but even after then, I've wanted to lash out for everything that was done to me. Everything that was taken away. So, I want to thank you."

Kenneth Bay tripped over himself as he headed back toward the lectern. "Thank me? I'm trying to kill you and you want to thank me?"

"When I got my memories back, I felt such anger towards Yal-hara. Towards you. I've wanted to see you hurt and watch her be ruined. But you know what? You're not worth it." She chuckled. "It's really that simple. All this anger and hatred, this desire for revenge — it's exhausting. I've spent the last year thinking about nothing else. But I could have spent that time with my family. With Sully. And now — again thanks to you — it's too late. He's gone."

"Not entirely," Gully said.

"True. He's still got more to teach me." She kissed Gully's shoulder once more. "The chaos of my life was because of Yal-hara. But now, I'm whole. It's all that hate which could have destroyed me. And it's destroying you. You don't see it now because your down there, hurting, mourning all that's been taken from you. But trust me — it takes so much more energy to keep that hatred burning than to just let it go."

Kenneth Bay put his hand on the emerald green cover. "The fact that I stand here says you're wrong. In this book, the Pages of Glass will set Yal-hara free. And as she goes through universe after universe, as she enriches herself and gains unparalleled power, I will be by her side."

He picked up the book. Gully moved toward him, but Roni stayed still, her locking arm keeping the golem back.

"I forgive you," she said. "And Yal-hara. I told you I would offer you one more chance, and here it is. Put the book down and come with us. We'll go back home, and you will be free. If you fear retaliation from Yal-hara, the Parallel Society will protect you and all of your family."

He laughed. "You can't even protect your own. Go. Leave. I have the Pages of Glass now. I can find my way out of here to hundreds of worlds. Who knows? Perhaps I won't even need Yal-hara."

As he turned toward the book, Gully spun around and wrapped himself over Roni. She heard the wind blowing before she could peek beyond Gully's shoulder to see that Kenneth Bay held the cover wide open. But the vicious vortex of winds threatening to engulf everything around him never came. Rather the air moved in strong gusts like a lovely, sunny day perfect for sailing the ocean, flying a kite, or relaxing on the porch and watching the world breeze by. Despite the blood and bruises on his face, Roni saw Kenneth Bay smile as he gazed into the book.

"Stop!" Roni threw Garcia's potion and buried her head in Gully.

Even with her eyes closed, she saw the intense flash of light. But when she chanced to look at Bay once more, he still gazed into the book. Tears streamed and his skin appeared sunburned. He continued smiling, yet Roni had the sense he was blind.

Bay snarled. "It's over. I win."

Three thick vines dripping blood and gore shot out of the book and wrapped around his head. His muffled screams carried through the amphitheater. Two small creatures — knee-high, long-snouted, thin-limbed, and mostly hairless — crawled along the vines, looked him over, conversed in a rapid tongue, and hauled him in with eager excitement.

It happened in less than ten seconds.

Roni watched as a single vine crept out and pulled the book's cover closed. The wind ceased and the amphitheater disappeared. They stood in the cold forest once more.

"Come on," she said. "We have to hurry."

They rushed over to the book, and Roni removed the chain from her waist. She wrapped it around the cover and clamped it tight. Setting it back on the lectern, she took a moment before facing Gully. "I want to make a promise to you, and I hope you can make a promise to me."

"Of course."

"I will do my best never to let that kind of hatred take me over again. I promise you that. I'm going to lead the Parallel Society from a position of caring for others. Not trying to destroy them. I want you to promise me that should I ever falter from that path, you will do whatever you can to bring me back."

Gully pressed against his nose as if he wore glasses and raised his lips just like Sully smiling. "Haven't I already been doing that?"

"I suppose so." Brushing away a few tears, she said, "Let's get out of here."

Gully put out his hand. "It shouldn't be as bad leaving as coming in. The *Book of Nightmares* has no reason to fight you on this. Then again, it never did, yet it sure tried anyway. I think it's best if you hold onto me to be safe."

As they headed out, Gully added, "I wonder how bad Kenneth Bay's going to feel when he realizes he's in the wrong book?"

"I don't think we'll ever find out. But I'm sure he isn't half as angry as Yal-hara will be when she realizes what's happened."

Chapter 26

Once they left the *Book of Nightmares*, Roni and Gully joined Garcia. Together, they worked to lock it up again. Most of the chains had been too weak to reuse, but a few could secure the book for now. Roni would make sure Gram came back at a later date to properly do the job, and Garcia promised to make a potion that would strengthen the chains.

Heading through the Caverns, Roni patted Gully's back. "I'm not sure you'll ever understand how much we owe you for our success today."

"Stop, stop," Gully said, putting his hand across his eyes. "I did what needed to be done. That's all."

"It's not all. When we were preparing for this fight and I asked you to retrieve the Pages of Glass, I had hoped I was only being overcautious. But without you doing that, we would've lost. Yal-hara and Kenneth Bay would now have the Pages. Countless universes are in debt to you."

"It wasn't a big deal."

"Stop that. It was monumental."

Garcia said, "That's very true. Nobody else could have gone in and done that."

Roni frowned. "If you don't mind me asking — what did you see in there?"

Gully grew quiet. "I saw what everyone sees. My nightmares."

"What? The only reason I asked you to go in there was that you don't dream."

"Apparently, I do. But don't worry, I've only been alive a short time, and I don't have as much stored memory as humans. The *Book of Nightmares* did not have a rich source of material to draw from."

Pulling him in for a hug, she said, "You truly are the hero. I'm so sorry."

Before returning to the bookstore, they traveled a new path within the Caverns. After close to an hour, Roni ducked into an alcove lined with chained books up the side at least fifteen feet high. "What do you think?"

"It's perfect." Gully passed over the *Book of Nightmares*. He then made a step out of his hands and boosted Garcia up so that he could reach his highest and place the book on that shelf.

"Hiding in plain sight," Garcia said. "I like it."

After pushing the book flush with those around it, he tapped the spine. "I hope he doesn't suffer long."

Back at the bookstore, Roni sent Garcia onward but redirected Gully into the Grand Library. Before they joined with the others, they had one more thing to do.

"The book," she said.

Gully stuck his fingers into his chest and pulled it open as if he were a superhero revealing the costume of his true identity. But instead of a brightly colored spandex outfit, he opened a cavity within the clay and stone of his body. The book with the Pages of Glass rested inside him.

Roni gaped. "You had it there? I figured you'd leave it in this library or up at Sully's apartment somewhere. Did that hurt?"

"Not at all. But I wasn't sure how the *Book of Nightmares* would react or if the various creatures might know that the Pages of Glass had been taken away. This way, I figured if we had to go in, the Pages were technically still nearby." He removed the book and handed it to Roni. "Turned out I didn't need to be so cautious."

"I'm glad you were."

The book felt surprisingly light. She rested it on her desk. It was a plain book yet something miraculous surrounded it. An energy, perhaps.

"You told me the plan was to destroy this," Gully said. "Why are you standing there?"

"I'm not sure how to destroy it."

"Nonsense. It's glass. We shatter it."

Roni handed the book back. "Put that inside yourself again. We'll deal with it later."

Although the golem looked unsure, he did as commanded. Roni

helped him smooth over the gap after he closed up his chest. Then she said, "Good enough. Let's go upstairs and help everyone. I'm too tired to think anymore tonight."

CHAPTER 27

Sully's funeral had been a small and quiet gathering. No obituary had been posted, no announcement on social media. Nobody knew except the members of the Parallel Society. But Elliot assured everyone that Sully had no family anymore. He had either outlived them or put distance between them. Not out of bad blood or animosity, but rather, there came a point when Sully decided it was too dangerous to be a member of the Parallel Society and have his family. He protected his loved ones by protecting the universe.

The next day, Roni returned to the gravesite. She sat next to the temporary headstone — a more detailed and expensive one had been ordered and would take a while before it could be delivered — then she tried to remember as many moments in her life with Sully as possible. Happy memories, goofy memories, even times she fought with the old man. Every instance kept him alive in her heart for a little longer.

She looked over the fresh dirt and wondered how long it would take the grass to grow in. Perhaps all of Elliot's spells over the years, especially the spells that gave Sully such a long life, might have an effect on the land around him. She snickered. Maybe Sully was radioactive.

"You'd probably love that. You'd make some stupid jokes like *Now that I'm dead, I'm positively glowing.* Well, I hope you're glowing a little bit for me. Because of the work you did, the things you've taught me, I finally feel ready. I can lead this group. I can do my job and learn what I don't know. Because after everything we've been through, there's simply no other way. It's not for us to push the job on to someone else. We are the Parallel Society. Nothing simpler than that."

"Spoken like a true leader," Gram said.

Roni jumped. "You should know better than to sneak up on somebody in a cemetery."

"Lord, I'm sorry. It never occurred to me." Gram did not look sorry. In fact, she looked quite amused. "Did you mean it? Do you really feel like our leader now?"

"I'm certainly ready to take on the role. You know better than I do — how long did it take you until you truly felt like the leader?"

"I'm not sure I ever did. You just do the job the best you can and over time, whether you feel like it or not, you simply become the leader. Everybody recognizes you as the one in charge, and more importantly, they come to recognize that you really do know what you're talking about. Even when you don't."

Roni watched Gram in silence for a moment. Then barked out a rough laugh. "Was that supposed to help me or confuse me?"

Gram laughed, too. "I'm no longer the leader. I don't have to come up with the right thing to say anymore."

Less than a month later, Roni could see that she was not the only one who had returned from their fight with Kenneth Bay a bit different. Teanna, for one, no longer went out dancing. Partly because Roni no longer went out dancing. Being leader meant being vigilant, and she felt her clubbing days were behind her. Teanna said she did not like going alone, but Roni noticed that their axe-wielding tracker had started filling her time with workout routines. When she wasn't lifting weights or taking martial arts classes, she went jogging. And if that didn't suit her, she could be found in their apartment twisting her body in one yoga pose after another. Roni saw it for what it was — preparation. Teanna had fought well, but her internal harsh critic required more from her. She even once said to Roni, "Tracking relics is helpful, but when it comes to fighting, I'm the best we've got. I need to be better. For all of us."

Garcia dove into his strength, too, by attacking his new laboratory — cleaning, organizing, reorganizing. He spent days traveling from one specialty shop to another seeking out odd roots, rare herbs, and strange plants. He then would get lost in his lab for hours, filling vial after vial with potions that either would be ready to go or only needed a single ingredient to react with. "We're never going to be caught waiting on me again," he said.

Roni grinned. "You're going to fit in real well."

"Does that mean I'm off probation?"

"Definitely. Welcome to the Parallel Society. Hope you weren't expecting a party."

"Don't need one. This lab, here with all of you — it's everything I've been wanting."

Roni left Garcia to his work and thought how proud his grandpa would have been. The old man certainly smiled upon them.

But Elliot, the other old man, did not thrive in the new arrangements.

He spent the first week in the apartment he had shared with Sully for so many years. Gram and Roni had been unsuccessful at getting him out, and they both worried terribly about his state of mind. Gully managed to get Elliot up a little — he required somebody who understood golems well enough to help him reform his body from all the abuse it had endured during the Kenneth Bay attack. Elliot spent several days working obsessively on Gully and this gave Roni hope. But when he finished, he shut away his apartment. Roni had to accept that she could only keep an eye on their dear friend and let him work through his grief however he saw fit.

Thankfully, Gram did not suffer the same depression. Instead, she played mother hen, flitting about the bookstore, always at the ready to help anybody in need. She also supervised the workmen who had been hired to fix the shotgun holes in the ceilings and walls as well as rebuild the stairs and several bookshelves. She was determined to make the bookstore, once again, a bookstore. Most of all, she made sure nobody asked questions.

The Parallel Society found a flow that worked. Roni thought everybody felt the hole left by Sully's absence, and she knew it would take more than a single month for them to find joy in their lives again. She wondered if the biggest threat to the Society was the waiting. No further attack had come. No other emergencies. And they all needed something to fill their time.

Even Roni.

When she summoned Gully down to the Grand Library, he did not act surprised at her request. The time had come.

"Are you positive?" he asked.

"I am. But before you start, we have one other thing to do."

"Oh?"

From her desk, Roni pulled out Sully's leather journal. "I thought you might wish to join me when I put this on the shelves."

Gully's head cocked to the side as he gazed down on the journal. "I would very much like that."

Without another word, Roni led the golem along the many stacks until they reached the space she had set aside for this journal. "I've already entered the book into the library system. This is all that's left to do. Would you like the honor?"

He reached out for the journal but pulled back. "No. This is your job."

Not for the last time, Roni wondered how much of what she saw in Gully was real emotion and how much she projected on him. She decided it didn't matter. Whatever the golem felt, he clearly felt something. She slid the journal onto the shelf and held still for a moment.

Wiping at her eyes, she turned away from the bookshelf. "As long as the Pages of Glass exist, we face a threat. I once told Kenneth Bay that they were myth. I'd like to make that a reality."

Gully nodded. He dug his fingers into his chest and pulled apart the clay, giving access to the Pages. Roni reached in — noticed the warmth of the clay — and removed the book. This time it felt heavy.

Gully said, "Do you plan to simply throw it on the ground and shatter it?"

"I was thinking about using fire. Melt it down."

"Have you considered that whatever power gives this Glass its unique properties might not be so easily destroyed?"

"Not until now."

They walked back to her desk and she set the book down. She placed her hand on the cover. It felt warm to her touch — like Gully's clay. Perhaps that came from being inside the golem, but she doubted it.

"Do you think it's possible that this is not a book at all? That it only looks like a book, and that it's really something else? Maybe something alive?"

"There's nothing inside the information Sully left with me to suggest that, but admittedly, he didn't know that much about it, either."

She ran her finger along the edge of the cover. Rough and uneven. Like hard-lived skin. "Perhaps we shouldn't destroy it, then. Not yet. Not until we know what it really is."

"Do you wish me to keep holding it?"

"It's probably for the best."

Yet rather than pick the book up, she lifted the cover. Inside, she saw an emerald-green, translucent sheet of paper. It was not part of the binding but rather sat in a slight indent within the book. She lifted it up.

It had more weight than she expected yet a strange, flimsy feel. She gazed through it.

Like looking into a gel used to color stage lights, the Page changed all she saw to green. It would have been funny and a bit sad if the Pages did not actually do anything. If it had been no more than a prop. A myth, indeed.

But as she turned her body to view different parts of the Grand Library, her eyes fell upon something that grabbed her by the throat, twisted her stomach, and sent a shockwave through to her feet. In the back of the library, she saw glittering on the wall — the back wall — the wall where she had mounted her detailed map of the Caverns.

She rushed across the library with Gully following close behind. Once in front of the map, she saw all different parts of it coming to life through the green lens of the Page. Her heart hammered. Her eyes stung from not blinking.

"Are you seeing this?" she asked.

"It seems the Pages interact very well with anything related to the Caverns."

She stumbled back and flopped into a chair. Placing the Page of Glass carefully on the worktable, Roni rubbed her eyes. "We have to be cautious with this. But we're going to use it."

"We are?" Gully said, his voice not exactly hiding concern.

"The best way I can think to fix the Yal-hara problem, to stop her from continually trying to attack us, and to stop her from destroying other worlds is with this."

"You'll have to forgive me and my slow golem brain. But how is that going to help?"

"The Parallel Society is going to figure out how the Page works. Then, we're going to use my map to locate the book that holds Yal-hara's world. And when we have it, we'll give it to her."

"Give her the book she wanted all along?"

"Kenneth Bay was right about one thing — Yal-hara has served her sentence here. If she truly wants to go home, then we will let her. If she wants something else — if she wants to conquer other worlds — well, we won't allow that. But one way or another, we're going to see that she gets back to where she belongs."

THE BOLD WARRIOR

THE PARALLEL SOCIETY BOOK 6

STUART JAFFE

Chapter 1

Turbulence shuddered through the cabin, and Roni held her breath. She didn't mind flying under normal conditions, but this recent job in Nebraska had left her nerves on edge. Teanna had located a relic near a large farm outside of Callaway. Rather than sending the whole team, Roni and Elliot opted to go together. Teanna had been feeling sick lately, Gram stayed back to mind the bookstore, Gully had difficulty passing for human in the tight spaces of an airline, and Garcia would have joined, but Roni thought it better that he remain to work on his potions. After all, this wasn't a living relic. Just an object that needed to be locked inside one of Gram's books and sent away from the universe.

Except that didn't happen.

She glanced over at Elliot. The old man sat in the aisle seat with one of his long legs stretching out as far as he could manage without disturbing the passenger in front of him. With his gnarled cane angled between the floor and the armrest, he couldn't bring down his tray table. Instead, he folded his hand across his belly and stared ahead with glazed eyes that seemed as unsettled as Roni felt.

Part of her wanted to sleep. Leave her old friend alone. He would talk to her, if he wanted. But sleep would never come. Not when the jock in the seat on her left snored heavily with his head leaning against the window and his mouth locked open. Not even the constant engine noise could overcome that. Besides, leadership did not end simply because she felt tired. And neither did friendship.

"I should have insisted on bringing the whole team with us," she said.

With a soft shrug, Elliot said in his deep voice, "We managed. And we succeeded."

"Still, it must've put more of a strain on you."

She could still see the sweat pouring down his face when they had realized the relic was more than an odd-shaped table — three cylindrical legs holding up a triangle top, the whole thing coated in heavy, black lacquer. As they approached it in the middle of a plowed cornfield, the table moved away. A living relic — a creature from another universe trapped in this one.

No matter what Elliot said, Roni knew from the relic's first halting steps that she had made a serious miscalculation. They lacked their potion-maker. They lacked their chain-wielding book-maker. They lacked their all-purpose golem and their battle-ready tracker. Between the two of them, all they had was Roni's bravado and Elliot's spell-making abilities. The latter took time and were better used for healing and shielding than fighting. The former served to get Roni in more trouble than out.

Rolling his neck to release a few loud crackles, Elliot bent over the armrest and said, "You don't need to worry about me. I've faced far worse than a tough piece of furniture."

"I know that. I've been with you for a few of those times. But we usually are together as the whole Parallel Society. I shouldn't have let us go off on our own."

"We had no reason to suspect this was anything more than picking up a non-living object."

"That's not the point."

"Nor is what you should or should not have done. You're asking me about all of this because you're worried that I might be shaken by the experience. I am not. Encounters like today's are a big part of the thrill in what we do. I cannot imagine ever feeling anything but exhilaration after a successful mission."

Exhilaration — not the word Roni would have used to describe being hit by that table once it got scared. It lashed out by scrunching down on its legs and bursting forward, popping off the ground and shooting like a malformed bullet. Roni dodged the first few attacks, but when it finally hit her in the shoulder, she fell back into the plowed earth, dropped her shoulder bag, and found using her arm difficult for a few moments.

But Elliot needed time to put together a spell to either contain or slow this violent thing. No, not violent. Not in the dangerous sense. It was merely scared.

Roni figured there had to be times when animals from Earth slipped into some other universe. Those poor creatures would be terrified. And if they happened to be a lioness, a bear, or a wolf, the results might be equally violent.

In the end, Elliot had to abandon his spell. This creature moved too fast, and Roni was the only other target available. Instead, they spread out, taking the frightened creature's attacks in stride, until Roni could get to her bag, dig out the emergency book Gram always provided her with, and lure the creature into a final assault. When it blasted across the field at her, Roni opened the book and it soared straight in.

Painful. Exhausting. A bit nerve-wracking. But exhilarating?

She looked at his eyes again — wearing facemasks on the plane made it difficult to gauge his expression, but she didn't buy the idea that he was elated with the high of a successful job. Staring at him, knowing he could see her in the corner of his eye, she waited.

"I promise you, fighting that living relic did not bother me."

"Something's bothering you, and I can't run an effective team if I don't know what problems you're dealing with. Is it Sully? Are you still in mourning?"

Elliot's eyes drifted down. "He's always in my mind, and I will always mourn his loss, but no. That's not troubling me."

"Is it Yal-hara?" Just mentioning that name filled Roni with enough dread to fuel all her fears for a century. The spindle-legged creature had been a trapped living relic for all of Roni's life. When she was eight, Yal-hara swiped some of her memories — important ones of her mother and father — creating Roni's Lost Time. But more than that, Yal-hara was both a guest and a prisoner on Earth, and recently, she made it clear that she intended to leave, to rule other universes, to swipe other memories of other children. Yet since their last confrontation, she had grown quiet. The loss of her lawyer, her main human representation in this world, must have caused her plans a major setback. At least, Roni hoped so.

But Elliot shook his head. "I have no illusions that Yal-hara has given up, yet I also try not to spend time worrying over things until they happen. Preventative measures, of course, but nervous fretting does no good."

"Then what are you sitting there thinking about?"

"I actually was thinking about our mission, about how brave you were dealing with that odd relic, and about how much — well, I suppose the word is *fun* — how much fun I was having. Hold on, I can see you getting heated. You know I would never lie to you."

"But you'll bend and twist the truth as far as you can. You and

Gram did it to me for years."

"I know I've done that in the past, but in this case, I'm not." That was an improvement. Hearing Elliot accept his part in hiding the truth of Yal-hara from Roni warmed her. She wasn't angry about it anymore, but she appreciated that he did not argue the point.

Over the speakers, the pilot came on to say that they were approaching Philadelphia International Airport and would be landing in twenty minutes. "You better hurry," Roni said.

Elliot's laced fingers tightened. "I was thinking about how much I will miss fieldwork and making our universe a little bit safer."

"Don't you start now. Gram talks about dying way too much. I don't need you mulling over that you're old and time is running out."

"I am and it is. However, I'm not referring to my death. Rather, I've been contemplating moving on to something new." He sighed. "There. I have said it out loud."

"Retirement? You can't retire. It's not possible."

"I assure you it is. But I wouldn't call it *retirement*."

"This isn't a job with a 401k or a pension or anything like that. It's not something you can walk away from. This is more than a job. It's a way of life."

"I thought much the same when I was young. Devoted myself to that exact idea. Decisions on family, on friendships, opportunities, and even love — all of it played second to the needs of the Parallel Society. Looking back now, I'm not so sure that was the right way to think about things."

Two flight attendants walked along the aisle. They gathered trash, asked people to sit upright and put away their tray tables. Passengers who had been sleeping groaned and stretched as they straightened in their seats — including the snorer. The time to talk was over.

But Roni inched closer to Elliot and whispered, "Your request to retire is denied. I won't allow it." Then she sat back, folded her arms, and glowered out the window as the clouds passed by.

They did not speak for the remainder of the flight. Roni wanted to talk, wanted to let Elliot voice his troubles, wanted to hear what needed fixing so she could fix it. Losing another team member would not help the Society — especially one who held so many years of knowledge and experience. Of course, she understood that eventually Gram and Elliot would no longer be around, but until the natural order of the universe took them from her, she had no intention of saying goodbye.

After landing and departing the plane, they walked through the terminal — part of which was under construction. The Philly airport was eternally under construction. With the crowds filing in and out of various gates, rushing to the restrooms, or dashing ahead with a sense of urgent purpose, Roni held back from talking further of Elliot's retirement. She never liked overhearing when people had important conversations in public places and figured she should do her part not to add to the problem. She especially hated it when she was forced to have such conversations in public. This one with Elliot would have to wait until they returned to the bookstore.

Saving her from further thoughts on the subject, her phone chimed — Gram.

"We're still making our way through the airport," Roni said after a short greeting. "Everything went fine, though. All taken care of."

"That's good to hear." Gram's tone stopped Roni mid-step. Elliot stuttered a few steps further, then looked back with a deep frown. Gram went on, "You both need to get home as fast as you can."

"Why? What's happened?"

"It's Teanna. Lord help us, she's missing."

CHAPTER 2

During the drive back to *In the Bind,* the family bookstore, Roni tried to swallow the idea of Elliot retiring from the Parallel Society. No matter what he wanted to call it, that's what he would be doing — retiring. They had barely adapted to the loss of Sully, but his loss had been final. He was gone from the world. Period.

If Elliot no longer worked with them, he would still be breathing. He would still be living on the fifth floor, still be around for breakfast, still be available for a spell or two when needed. Or would he? When a person left the Society, did they keep their abilities?

It didn't matter. He simply could not be allowed to leave. They needed his experience and wisdom.

They?

Fine. *She* needed his experience and his wisdom. She needed him.

But as she pulled off the highway and into the town of Olburg, she amended these thoughts. True, she did need Elliot in her life, but the Society required him. And Gram. And Gully and Teanna. And even Garcia. They were charged with protecting the universe from other universes that slipped into this one, and that enormous task could only be accomplished by working as a unified whole. She had seen that fact proven numerous times since becoming a member of the Society. And right now, the team had become more disunified than ever.

As they turned toward the bookstore, Elliot said, "I know you're upset at what I said earlier, and I do understand —"

"There's nothing to discuss."

"I'm not —"

"Teanna is missing, so your grand plan to abandon the universe will have to wait."

"I've served the universe and the Society for most of my life. You know I will do everything I can to help find Teanna, but —"

"Good. Teanna needs us."

"But after that is done —"

"After that, you'll get back to work."

"Stop interrupting. Just because you are the leader of the Society does not grant you the right to be rude."

Feeling grains of the little girl inside, she lowered her voice. "Sorry."

He said nothing more, and moments later, they parked on the street a block up from the store. Roni carried their bags as Elliot leaned heavier on his cane than in the past. The air had grown crisper, and she wondered if they would get any snow this year. Autumn had come and gone with little fanfare. The leaves had changed color, of course, but the temperatures had fluctuated wildly. As much as people pointed to climate change, part of her wondered if their collisions with other universes could be partially responsible, too.

In The Bind had been open for several months since their latest remodeling — a charming way to say they had to rebuild after destroying the place in a fight. Though there were still some empty shelves on the main floor, it brought Roni small bits of joy to see the store as it had once been. As she remembered it from growing up.

The Big Table still dominated an open area near the right wall, and she could still see the staircase and elevator in the back from the front counter, but most of the floorspace now had aisles of bookshelves. They were different heights — Gram had gathered them from garage sales, antique shops, and even a friend who worked at the city dump — but they were enough to hold treasures upon treasures. The worn, leatherbound editions of classic fiction, the bent and abused modern paperbacks, the textbooks from graduated college students, and the reference material left behind by ex-hobbyists — all found their way to the bookstore in search of a new home.

The air smelled of old paper and binding glue. Roni loved it. Whether the store was crowded with customers or empty at the end of the day, the restoration of the place gave Roni a surge of hope whenever she entered and breathed in its delicious aroma.

This was the home of the Parallel Society. Had been for decades. The floors above housed Gram and Elliot as well as a lab for Garcia to make his potions. And below — the Grand Library containing all the journals, diaries, notes, and maps of every previous member of the Society. Further below that — the basement, Gram's private office, and a hole in the wall that attached to another universe. A cavern that housed all the chained books leading to other universes and those books made to imprison the dangerous creatures with no home.

"Finally," Gram said from behind the wood counter off the right of the entrance. "I was beginning to pray for you both. Did something happen?"

"We're fine," Roni said as Elliot worked his way toward the table. "Some traffic, that's all. What's going on with Teanna? You said she was missing. Have you checked the MMA studio? She loves to have a workout there."

"Garcia is looking at all of her usual spots — the MMA studio, the diner she likes for pancakes, even the bowling alley. When he gets back, we'll know more and I'll tell you what I can."

"Tell me now."

"I don't know enough yet. Only that Teanna never showed up this morning, never showed up for lunch, and I doubt she'll be here for dinner. Though I pray I'm wrong. Basically, she's not been heard from since last night. That's not like her."

"It's not? Since when does she come here for regular meals?"

Gram's rotund body jiggled but Roni did not think the laugh bore any amusement. Gram said, "You've got to pay more attention to your team."

"That's all I ever think about."

"Well, you think about our schedules and how we can best use our abilities against relics. You've made sure that we're getting exercise and taking care of our health. That's all good and a part of leading the Society, but there's more to it. You have to observe our behaviors, so you can tell when something is off."

"And something's off with Teanna?"

"I certainly hope not." Gram patted the gold cross sitting on her large chest.

Walking right by the table, Elliot continued to the elevator. "I'll be upstairs."

Roni said, "We could use your help."

Elliot paused to lift his cane overhead and give it a shake. Then he stepped onto the elevator and closed the gate. Roni had to hope that meant he would cast a spell to search for their missing teammate.

With a raised eyebrow, Gram glanced at Roni. "You two have an argument?"

"Why would you say that?" Roni glanced to the side. "Where's Gully?"

"Just where you put him — downstairs guarding the Cavern entrance. Now out with it. Lord knows it does no good to bottle up your problems, and the tension between you and Elliot is obvious. So?"

Roni waited until the elevator began its labored and noisy rise toward the fifth floor. Then: "Did you know that Elliot's considering retirement?"

"No, but good for him."

"Maybe for him but not for the Society. We've barely come together and he's going to leave?"

"I never thought he would quit, but there's no law saying he can't. Perhaps he thinks you've shown yourself more than capable of handling things. Perhaps he feels confident that he can retire without detriment to the Society. You should take it as compliment."

"I don't need that kind of compliment." Roni collapsed in a chair at the Big Table. "Things are hard enough without him defecting from us."

"Don't be so dramatic. It's not like he'll never talk to us or help us out. Besides, there will come a time when I'm gone, too."

Roni smacked her forehead. "That didn't long."

"If you don't like me talking about my mortality, then you simply have to accept it. But you refuse to acknowledge that I'm an old lady who does dangerous things for a living. At some point, either through accident or nature, my life will end. As the leader, you have to prepare for that."

"I prefer Elliot's method — I'll deal with problems when they happen and not spend my time worrying over it all."

"Nonsense. He can say that because he's not the one who has to deal with the problems. He's not in charge. You are. You don't get that luxury."

"Can we skip the lecture tonight and focus on Teanna?"

Before Gram could start another discourse, Garcia opened the front door. Roni had never been so pleased to see the middle-aged man who had once revered the Society with fanboy glee and still maintained a wide-eyed delight at having joined the group. Although, he lacked all sense of pleasure as he strode across the room.

"Nothing," he said. "I can't find any trace of her."

Roni sat up, and Gram's hand went to her pendant. An unsettling quiet surrounded them. The time to worry had arrived.

As Garcia pulled out a chair at the table, Roni noted that he had stopped standing against the wall during meetings. Teanna still did that — always with her eyes roving the entry points, always ready for action — but Garcia had finally felt comfortable enough to sit. Sometimes little actions revealed true progress.

Gully entered from the side stairs. Fashioned out of clay and stone, it amazed Roni how much he resembled Sully, his maker. The golem even had the ability to express emotion — at least, Roni thought she saw concern as he made his way to the table.

"I heard Garcia return," Gully said, his accent not as strong as Sully's had been but distinctly that of an old, Jewish man. "Have we located Teanna? I knew we shouldn't have let her go alone."

"Everybody quiet." Roni pointed at Garcia. "You, tell me what's going on, what we know, and what we think we know. Right now."

Scratching his beard, Garcia nodded. "For a while, Teanna has been finding excuses to act on her own. She claims to be feeling sick or has to do research or whatever will get her out of doing whatever task you want her to do."

"That I want her to do? She only has to find relics. Isn't that why she chose to stay with us? She could've returned to her world long ago."

"But you also have her scheduled to do regular physical training."

"She's one of our best fighters. We need her in peak condition."

"And she's complained that all the studying is a waste of her time."

"Studying? She came to me. She said that learning a little about the languages found on Yal-hara's relic boxes had stirred an interest in her. I only started her education in that stuff because she wanted it."

Gram put out her hand, letting it rest open on the table. "Not everybody wants to dig deep into an interest the way you do, dear."

"Then she could have said something. And all of you — you knew about this?"

"I knew she was frustrated. I guessed that she made up some of her excuses. I assumed she hunted relics to feel useful in the way she understood, to stay sharp for the moment when serious trouble presented itself. She must have assumed the minor relics did not require her."

Roni pounded her fist on the table with one hard stroke. "Elliot and I could have died today. That minor relic we found turned out to be a living relic that tried to kill us. Teanna should have been there." She bit back any further expression of anger. Her team needed her to keep calm and in control. To lead. "If she's not hunting relics — which is clearly the case because she would have joined us in Nebraska if that were true — and if she's not staying sharp — which again would have had her helping in Nebraska — then what the hell is she doing?"

"There's no call for foul language," Gram said, sitting back as if a minor curse word had left a stench in the air.

"I want an answer. None of us are to be going on missions alone. So, one of you had to be with her. What's she up to?"

Gully stepped forward. "I tried to follow your orders each time Teanna left by herself. I did my best to follow her. But she always escaped me. Apparently, my raincoat, sunglasses, and fishing hat are not enough to disguise me from her."

Shaking her head as she thought, Roni said, "Then all we know is that she's been going off on her own and … that's it? No idea where or for what purpose? Nothing? And nobody thought to tell me any of this until now, until there's a serious situation."

"We don't know it's serious," Gram said. "Maybe she met a man and is indisposed. You've done that a time or two."

Roni shouted down all the thoughts rising on the tide of those words — especially the screaming voice wondering how Gram knew about any of her past wild behavior. Instead, she stood, tapped her fingers on the table, and gave herself a calm breath. Then: "Gram, give Elliot an hour, two at the most, to complete his searching spell or whatever spell he better be casting. Then call up for the results. Good or bad, you text me the answers immediately. Gully, you stay up here and guard the store. If Teanna is truly missing, if something bad has happened, then we need to be alert for attack. Garcia, you're coming with me. We'll start at the apartment and try to retrace her steps. Questions? No? Fine. Let's go."

CHAPTER 3

For those first steps, Roni entered the apartment she shared with Teanna like she imagined the police would walk into a crime scene — a stranger's dwelling where something terrible had happened. But unlike the police, Roni knew this location. She recognized all the furniture, all the books, all the decorations — everything down to the forks and knives in the kitchenette drawer on the far left.

She held still and looked over the rundown but welcoming place. She noticed the old beanbag chair which Teanna thought impractical until Roni bought it. One try and Teanna said it was a marvel of comfort — like being hugged by a chair. Only now, staring at it with a detective's eyes, she recalled that Teanna rarely sat in the thing. When had she started lying to Roni? Was the beanbag chair the first time? When had the laughter and the late-night talks and the drinking and dancing disappeared?

"You want to start in the living room?" Garcia asked as he closed the door behind.

Roni gestured to Teanna's door. "If she's got anything to hide, it'll be in her room."

"That's a harsh way to put it."

"She willfully deceived me. Apparently, numerous times. Whatever she's been doing was not something she thought I would approve of. So, yeah, she's got things to hide."

"I only meant, well, you see, that maybe you shouldn't be so hard on her until we know what's what. There might be a very good reason she's behaved this way."

In a quiet voice, she said, "The Parallel Society shoulders an enormous burden. The only way we can possibly succeed is if we can trust each other without fail. We have to be united, a cohesive whole.

Not running off on our own. We can't go missing."

"I agree. Shouldn't we then trust Teanna?"

"You're too new. You don't understand." Roni licked her lips, amused and horrified by the thoughts that came to mind. "I was like you. Eager to learn everything, determined to prove myself, somehow always making mistakes. But then we had this job in Ireland. An old abbey where — well, it doesn't matter. The thing is that the only reason I'm standing here, the only reason Gram and Elliot are even alive, is because we all worked together as a single group. That's what this new version of the Society needs." She gestured to Teanna's room again. "Obviously."

Garcia frowned. "You think I always make mistakes?"

She patted his back. "Get to work. I'll be with you in a minute."

As Garcia entered Teanna's room with a troubled brow, Roni walked down the short hall and into her bedroom. She closed the door, careful to keep it quiet, and turned the lock slowly. Then she backed up, stepping over the crumpled clothing and the empty soda bottle, and dropped to the edge of her bed. Her heart raced as her ribs clenched together. She covered her face with her hands.

From deep within, a wailing shriek rose up. She slapped a hand over her mouth and scrunched her eyes shut. In silence, she rocked. Back and forth, hearing only the mattress springs, until the burning in her lungs forced a gulp for air.

Two long shuddering breaths tamped down the rising gorge in her throat. No tears came. No gasping cries. Thank goodness for that much.

Lifting her head, she looked over the bed to the framed photo on the side table — Gram, Elliot, Sully, and her sitting at the Big Table. Gram had insisted they take the photo after that harrowing experience at the Abbey. Roni never gave it much thought, but now she wondered if Gram had intended it to mark the moment Roni truly became a member of the Society.

She picked up the photo and passed her fingers over Sully. "I could really use your advice," she whispered. "You've been gone such a short time and now everybody's trying to do their own thing rather than listen to me, but I'm responsible for them all, and I've screwed the whole thing up. You said I was ready, but the evidence strongly suggests I'm not. I don't suppose you left any instructions with Gully to let him run the Society? Or maybe we should go back to Gram?" She pictured Gram in charge again. "No. Not that. Definitely not that."

Setting the photo back on the side table, Roni groaned. She rolled onto her back and closed her eyes. Calmly, this time. Not at peace but allowing her body and mind a chance to release the tension. A sort of meditation. At least, that was what she hoped she would accomplish.

But Garcia's voice broke the seconds of silence. "Roni, come here."

With a quick check in the mirror to make sure no tears had fallen to stain her cheeks, she straightened her shirt and tucked an errant strand of hair. The walk to Teanna's room transformed her back into the Parallel Society's leader. She rolled her shoulders and raised her chin as she entered.

"What did you find?" she asked.

Teanna kept her room sparse as if it belonged to a military cadet. Impersonal but functional. Roni figured she could white-glove the room and not a speck of dust would appear.

Sitting at the basic desk in the corner, Garcia looked up from Teanna's laptop. "She's been researching all these strange cases of family attacks and abductions."

"Huh?"

Roni peered over Garcia's shoulder. Several file folders on the computer desktop marked different case names. As Garcia opened one after the other, they each held local newspaper articles, photographs, bookmarked online forum pages, and in a few instances, copies of police reports.

"It'll take time to sift through it all," Garcia said, "but check this out."

He clicked on a folder labeled *Interviews*. Roni expected clippings or video of news interviews with victims. No video files, however. All text. All conducted by Teanna.

"What is all this about?" Roni said.

"I think every time she feigned being sick or gave you any excuse for not helping out, she was talking with these people."

"I meant *why*. What about these people got her interest? And why did she keep it secret from us? From me?"

"At least, we have an idea of where she might have gone. I'm guessing she finally interviewed the wrong person."

"Or maybe she found the right one — the one that led her to the psycho committing these crimes."

Garcia sat back, folding his arms. "She's tough. Capable. One crazy is not going to stop her."

"Maybe it's a gang. Is there anything else in there?"

He opened the single desk drawer. "She kept receipts — gas, diners, that kind of thing. Like she planned to turn them in for reimbursement."

Roni picked up the stack of paper and studied the dates. She pocketed the ones for the last week. "Can you see where she went for the last interview?"

He clicked on a calendar program and it opened to one labeled *Crimes.* Teanna had marked the dates of each incident. They filled the calendar, becoming more frequent the closer to the current day.

At the top, Garcia clicked on a second tab named *Interviews.* Teanna had conducted quite a lot of them in the last month. Roni had him cut-and-paste the names, addresses, and contact info for the three most recent.

"Send those to my phone," she said.

"I take it we're going on a road trip."

"Definitely."

CHAPTER 4

Pennsylvania was a deceptively large state — a fact Roni often forgot until she had to travel through it. Heading northwest into the mountains became one long series of steep rock cutaways and tall pines mixed with glimpses of overcast skies. She did not talk much with Garcia. Her concerns for Teanna and the team dominated her thoughts, and she had no clue what Garcia pondered.

Eventually, they reached *Honest John's Mobile Park* tucked between two sharp-pointed mountains and within earshot of the highway. Fourteen trailers lined the area in five rows. Three of the homes looked new. The rest comprised a hodgepodge of rust, dust, and damage. When they reached the trailer of Mrs. Heidi Schmidt — not one of the newer homes — they parked and approached the door.

Roni put out her hand to stop Garcia from getting too close. "This woman lost her husband and child. Let me do the talking."

The face that answered Roni's knocking barely looked alive — sunken eyes stared off, scraggly hair poked out of a blue bandana, dead leather skin, boney fingers, and clothes that hung loose as if Mrs. Schmidt wasted away inside. The only bit of life to her was the burning end of a cigarette dangling from half-open lips.

"What you want?" she said, her voice filled with scratches and clicks.

With her most placating timbre, Roni said, "We're looking for our colleague and according to her notes, she recently visited you."

"Don't know any *colleague* and don't care. Go away."

"We can't do that. This is too important. She's missing. Have you seen anything strange in the last few months?"

Mrs. Schmidt coughed hard and it may also have been an unamused laugh. "Are you an idiot? You come here and you don't know what's what about me?"

"I only meant —"

"Are you two some kind of religious cult going up and down the park knocking on doors? Is that it? Because I ain't got no interest in your version of Jesus, and I got things to do."

"Please, ma'am, we don't want to add more pain to what you've been through, but —"

"What do you know about nothing? Get the hell away from me or I'll call the cops."

Garcia elbowed his way forward before the woman could close the door. "Wait, wait. You would have met her yesterday or earlier today. A young, black woman."

Mrs. Schmidt paused. "The agency girl? Why didn't you say so? Is there news on my settlement already? That's fast. I mean I'm not complaining, but I ain't ever expecting the government to do right so quick. No offense." Though her voice sounded more animated, the rest of her remained a walking corpse.

Putting out his hand, Garcia said. "I'm Eddie Garcia. Teanna, the woman you met before, is an associate of ours."

"Nice to meet you." She did not shake his hand, and she blew smoke in Roni's direction. "You have a check or something? How does this work?"

"Like we said, the woman you met before has gone missing."

"Right. Of course, she has. I should've known. You're all full of shit. All the time I spent answering her stupid questions and you're here to tell me I won't get nothing for my losses. Is that it?"

"No, not at all."

"Just be honest. I get it. You're like an insurance company. You do everything you can to pay as little as possible. If you're going to screw me, at least have the decency to tell me the truth."

"I promise you, we're not trying to lower your payment. In fact, much of the information regarding your case was transmitted to our computers before all this happened. So, you'll be fine."

Roni said nothing, partly because she knew to stay quiet, partly out of shock. The lies rolled out of Garcia with such ease. She had struggled — still struggled — to do the same when interacting with civilians, yet he had no trouble at all. Then again, he had spent years trying to find the Society which meant years trying to get information from people who would never believe in the Society. He probably learned his verbal skills early on.

Mrs. Schmidt tipped her head back. "If everything's all fine, then why are you here? And where's my money?"

"Payment will be forthcoming, but according to the information we got from the earlier interview, you might be entitled to a larger sum than the original estimate."

That got a raised eyebrow. "Larger?"

"Yes, but like you said, no company wants to give away money, if they don't have to."

"How much larger?"

"That'll depend. We need to go over the previous information, and we have a few follow up questions. From that we can determine the exact amount and get you paid this week. If you have time now, we'd appreciate it. Shouldn't take too long."

Stepping back, Mrs. Schmidt waved them in. As Roni entered, the woman stabbed her cigarette and said, "You should pay attention to your partner. He knows how to talk to people."

Chapter 5

The trailer felt like a morgue. Cold. Clinical. Dead. All the furnishings were in place, yet it lacked any touch of a home. It was a staging used to sell the idea of what one could create in such a space, but all of the personal had been removed.

Mrs. Schmidt kept the trailer clean. Near spotless. In fact, only an overflowing ashtray marred the perfection of housekeeping she maintained.

Gesturing to a couch lining the backend of the trailer, Mrs. Schmidt waited for Roni and Garcia to sit. She then sauntered down the narrow hall to the bedroom on the other end. When she returned, fresh cigarette in hand, she pulled over a tall stool from the kitchen area and plunked it down in front of the coffee table across from the couch. All done in silence.

Like dealing cards, she tossed photographs along the table. Each one stopped in front of either Roni or Garcia.

These first photos showed a brawny man with a thick beard and an infectious smile. Here he stood in a small boat with a massive lake trout he had caught. There he held a beer, laughing in the midst of a group while celebrating a birthday. Here he held Mrs. Schmidt with both hands around the waist while planting a crushing kiss upon her. There he twirled with a young boy sitting on his shoulders.

"Neal." Mrs. Schmidt stared at the photos, taking long drags on her cigarette but never cracking even a hint of joy at the memories.

Roni took a chance. "He seems like a wonderful man."

"He was a bastard. The man in those pictures — that was the man the world saw. Everybody loved him. Life of the party, always there to help a friend, a thoughtful and charming man. People respected him. Tough, too. Somebody got too drunk or out of line at the bar, and

Neal was there to rescue the girl and punt the drunk's ass right out onto the street. The King of the Poor. A real hero."

Roni held back on her reactions. This woman spoke with such emptiness that it grated, but at least she was talking. The desire to rush through and get to Teanna had to be tempered. If Roni pushed, she guessed Mrs. Schmidt would shut down completely — no matter what magical lies Garcia could conjure.

"A lot of stress being King," Mrs. Schmidt continued. "Lot of pressure to be a certain thing whenever people saw you. Especially when you're not any of that."

She dealt out a few more photographs. These were stark pictures of a woman's arms, legs, and torso covered in angry bruises. The last photo showed her neck with the distinct impressions of fingers grasping.

Garcia covered one of the photos with his hand as if he were comforting the woman in the picture. "I'm sorry this happened to you."

"I ain't showing you this for your pity."

Another two photos slid in front of Roni. A school picture of a young curly-haired boy with a wide smile missing two teeth. Next — that same boy as a curly-haired toddler playing in the dirt with a toy dump truck.

"This is your son?" Roni asked.

"Nick. Spoiled brat. I suppose it ain't his fault. He had a bastard for his father. And I tried everything I knew to get that boy to listen to me, but he ain't got nothing but wanting to be with his daddy. He learned quick that Neal was the King of the Poor, and Nick figured that'd make him the prince. Didn't take long for him to start treating me bad, too. Not hitting me — I'd have sent him into next week if he tried. But he ordered me around like I was the help or some such."

She collected the photos, and as she squared them up and put them back in a drawer, Roni swore she caught a glimmer of emotion twinkle from behind those cold eyes. The next instant, however, the woman returned, puffed away for a little, and then pointed at Garcia with the cigarette locked between her fingers. "I want that money, but I ain't going to lie about them. My husband was no good, and he was raising my son to be the same. I can't honestly say I'm sad to see them gone."

"Don't worry, ma'am," Garcia said, but he sounded less confident — only for a breath. "When it comes to the terms laid out by our associate in your previous interview, nothing will change."

"Except I get more money, now, right?"

"Hopefully. You've yet to tell us what exactly happened."

Mrs. Schmidt stared back as if about to scold one of her family. "You people." Turning back to the kitchen, she pulled down a bottle of Wild Turkey from an overhead cabinet. "What does it matter?"

"I'm sorry. I'm sure it's upsetting to go through it again, but we really must."

She poured half a paper cup and knocked it back in one swig, never losing control of the cigarette. "I don't hate my husband or my son. I know what I said, and I know what I've prayed for, but I never wanted what happened to them to happen. Never."

"And that is?" Roni said.

"Have a little patience, woman. A little respect, too, would be nice." She poured another cupful of Wild Turkey and downed it with a wince. A calm, dead tone set in. "They always tell you to be afraid of the dark alley or the forest at night or whatever. But that man came to us in broad daylight. Eleven in the morning. On a Saturday. Can you believe that? A damn Saturday."

Roni started to ask about the man, but Garcia put his hand on her arm. He nodded toward Mrs. Schmidt. That was all, but Roni got the message. They waited.

After a moment, Mrs. Schmidt decided to put the alcohol away. She turned back to them but lowered her gaze to the floor. "Nick sat in front of the coffee table, playing video games on an old PS3. Neal had picked it up somewhere instead of bringing home groceries one night. We fought hard about that, but now we had the damn thing and Nick loved it. Okay, I sometimes played a game or two on it whenever I was alone. Anyway, Neal, was stretched on the couch — half-awake and still a bit drunk from the night before. I was at the counter, cutting up carrots. That's when this man knocked on our door.

"He was young. Looked straight out of college. And he wore nice clothes. Nothing fancy or expensive, but a nice pair of slacks and a white button shirt. I thought he was a Jehovah's Witness or some other religious group trying to convert me. They always come round trying to sucker poor folks. Oh, and he was bald. Pale and bald. Give him pink eyes and I'd have thought he was an albino."

"Did he say anything?" Garcia asked. "I mean … before."

The grim line of her mouth curled downward. "He pushed me back and stepped in. Neal had a good radar for trouble, and he was on his feet right away. Even Nick knew when things were wrong. I remember him turning off the video game and moving behind his father. And there was a second there when I thought that this must be some tough guy that works for a crime boss or something, that Neal had gotten into some kind of big stupid crap and this guy had come to rough him up or make him pay or maybe even haul him out to meet the boss. But that ended faster than I could think it. The man jumped across the trailer, slammed Neal back against Nick and the two of them against the wall. Neal's a strong guy and he tried to fight back, but this man was stronger. Didn't look it at all, but he was."

She paused to check Garcia again.

"It's okay," he said. "What you say won't jeopardize you getting paid. I promise."

Mrs. Schmidt held still. Her eyes glazed worse than before as the unattended ash on her cigarette lengthened.

A sickening lump fell in Roni's chest. "It's not the money, is it? You can tell us what you saw, what happened, and we will believe you. Our job is to deal with things that are difficult to understand."

Whether those words helped, Roni didn't know. But something clicked inside Mrs. Schmidt. Enough, anyway, to resume her talking.

"This man," she said, "this wild beast — he puckered his mouth like for a really big kiss, but then … it changed. It turned hard and sharp. Like a bird's beak but it also had these hard edges. Made me think of a kid's drawing of a bird. And it pushed Neal further back, crushing Nick a bit, and I couldn't move. I just stood there watching.

"It bit him. It shoved its beak forward and latched onto Neal's neck. And Neal, he was punching the thing in the ribs, but each punch became weaker and weaker until after a while, his hands went limp. I thought he was dead. But when the pale man stepped back, Neal stood straight and loose. Drool fell off his lips.

"Then the thing went after Nick. Just plucked the boy right off the floor and chomped down on his shoulder. Nick screamed and kicked but just like his daddy, he went all limp. When the pale man set him back on the floor, Nick stood by Neal, holding his daddy's hand, but something looked wrong in his eyes. Like he wasn't really there anymore." The ash dropped to the floor as she lifted her gaze toward Roni. "I'm not a bad person. Not even a bad mother. I'm not saying I should win an award or nothing, but I never treated my kid horrible. Even when he treated me wrong."

"We're not judging you. That thing you saw — most people never come close to such an experience. We're never taught how to react, how to deal with that kind of thing. Whatever you did or didn't do, nobody can tell you that you were wrong about it."

"Maybe. Or maybe this was some kind of demon from Hell, and I'm paying for my sins. I certainly ain't never been an angel. I got sins to pay for. And I'm telling you, when that thing turned toward me, when I saw its eyes — lizardy eyes — I was sure I was about to die. It leaped onto me, knocked me down, and bit into my arm. My skin burned, and I didn't even think. I just did what I did. Still had the kitchen knife in my hand from cutting carrots. I stabbed the man. Straight into his back.

"He jumped off, screeching like a pissed off hawk or something, and he ran away. Then, I'm on the floor trying to catch my breath, when I watch it happen." Despite her cold stare, tears cut a path down her cheeks. "Both of them, both my men, they walked right out the door. I guess I was in shock. I didn't say a word. I watched them go, and I couldn't move, I couldn't speak, I couldn't really think.

"That's it. I called the cops, but I knew I couldn't tell them an albino with a bird beak took my family away. They'd have locked me up in the looney house. So, I told them we got attacked, and I got knocked out, and when I came to, my men were gone. You know, I keep waiting for them to come back, but they ain't coming."

Roni wanted to offer a word of comfort, but the woman looked so dead that any words would fall flat in the air. Instead, she asked, "If the official report you gave never mentioned any of the stranger parts of your story, why are you telling us different?"

Lighting up a fresh cigarette, Mrs. Schmidt said, "I used the same story I told the cops with your friend, but she knew I was lying. She knew enough of the truth on her own. Said I wasn't the first she'd come across who lost people to this pale man. It's not right. Not fair. And I keep seeing him, too. Everywhere. I hear him and see him. Can't sleep without him being there. It's a non-stop nightmare. I figure if I'm ever going to be rid of this, I got to tell somebody the truth. So, I told her like I told you. Maybe you can do something about it. If not, at least I might get some money." She glanced from Roni to Garcia. Her shoulders slumped. "There ain't no money, is there?"

"I'm sorry," Roni said. "No. We're not insurance adjusters or working for a government bailout or whatever Teanna told you. We're a group of people who hunt down things like the one that attacked your family. We find them, and we make sure they won't ever hurt people again."

"What? Like prison?"

"Sometimes. It depends."

"Well, if you find that beak-faced piece of crap, you kill it. Nothing else will do." Mrs. Schmidt paused, holding her cigarette before her mouth, staring off into nothing. Then: "I guess that's it. You should go now."

Garcia stood and offered a short bow. Just a slight tip of the body disarmed with a gentle smile. "Thank you for your time. You've been more helpful than you know."

"Yeah, sure, whatever. Do me a favor and don't ever come back."

At the door, Roni paused. "There is one last thing. I'm sorry, but it could be important."

"Really? After all this, you still want more from me?"

"It'll take a second." She pulled out her phone. "Please, if you don't mind, I'd like to take a picture of the bite on your arm."

CHAPTER 6

Roni drove back toward the highway. Near the on-ramp, she pulled over and idled. Swiping through her phone, she checked for messages before looking over the pictures she had taken of Mrs. Schmidt's bite.

Two Vs mirroring each other formed a diamond shape below her elbow. Two rows of teeth marks — small punctures like dotted lines. However, the oddest part was the larger marks near the center of the diamond. One from the top and one from the bottom. This beak had two prongs that broke the skin of its victims … and did what? While the teeth marks left behind little bits of blood, these prong marks had a greenish tint surrounding them. The wound did not appear infected, but to Roni's untrained eye, it sure seemed like the creature had injected something into its victim.

"I don't suppose you can reverse engineer a substance?" she said. "Like deconstructing a potion?"

Garcia studied the photo. "If we had a sample, I would try. But I've never done it before."

"Well, I doubt Mrs. Schmidt will let us draw her blood, so that's out."

With a few taps, Roni called the bookstore. Gram answered, and Roni jumped right to work. "I never got a text from you. What's happened with Elliot? Did he find Teanna?"

"Hold on, now," Gram said. "We're not as spry as we once were. Give the man a chance to join us."

Roni waited a full two minutes for Elliot to be standing next to Gram. His deep voice rumbled, and Roni swore he sounded as if casting this latest spell had aged him an extra few years.

"I'm afraid I have failed," he said. "But then, please understand, that my location spell has never been too good. When it works, it works perfectly. Otherwise, it utterly fails."

"That's true," Gram said. "Remember that time in Cambodia when you thought you had found that lost puppy? Well, Roni dear, it wasn't really a puppy at all. It was a living relic, but we thought of it as a puppy."

Roni tried to hide her annoyance. "Okay, Elliot. Thanks for trying." She then explained the results of their chat with Mrs. Schmidt. "I'm sending you the photos we took. It should get to you any second. See how that works? Phones are near-instantaneous. You can text me and I'll get the message right away."

"Don't be sassy." A moment later: "We got the picture." Then: "Sorry, dear, but we've never seen this kind of a bite before."

Elliot said, "There are books in the Grand Library that catalog all the wounds, footprints, burn marks, and such things that the Society has encountered. We should most likely have one compiling bitemarks."

"Why are you looking at me? Roni's the one that spent the last couple years down there putting everything in order."

Roni said, "I've seen so many titles, I can't recall a specific one like that. And there are still sections of the Library that need serious attention. But if there is a bitemark book, you've got a ninety-nine percent chance it'll be in the computer catalog."

"I'll get to it right away," Gram said.

"No. Have Elliot do it, and have him report any findings immediately."

"I can do all that."

"I want Elliot to do it."

"Oh? Why?"

"Because he's the only one who follows orders." She cut the call. In the silence that descended, she could feel Garcia's eyes upon her. "You have something to say?"

With a quiet exhale, Garcia scratched the back of his arm. "I don't see how that helps unite us."

"You have something *useful* to say?"

She regretted the comment as it left her lips. Partly because it was mean and unnecessary. Mostly because he was right.

"Sorry," she said.

"Not a problem. Working with family is never easy."

Roni snorted a laugh. "You have no idea."

Wagging his phone by his chin, Garcia said, "This might make you feel a little better. While you were creating the next thing you'll be apologizing to Gram for, I did a search on Teanna's diner receipt."

"And?"

"It's one sort-of-town over."

"What does that mean?"

"A few miles up, there's a collection of buildings and roads that looks large enough to be considered a town, but none of the online maps can give it a name."

Roni pulled onto the road. "Sounds like our kind of thing."

The nameless town proved even more remote than the trailer park. No signs marked the turnoff, nobody could see it from the highway, and nobody would know it existed without prior knowledge or a specific search of a map. Having a smart and enthusiastic potion maker holding a receipt with an address to look up online, however, gave Roni the advantage.

Driving up the classically named Main Street, the buildings looked well-kept and ready for use. Storefronts boasted sales for a smoke shop, a computer repair center, and a cell phone company. A bar had the lights off for the day while a martial arts studio was brightly lit up for classes. The only thing missing — the people. And the animals. And life of any kind. The place reminded Roni of an empty movie set dressed like a Hollywood version of small-town America.

"At least this isn't weird and spooky," Garcia said, pressing against the passenger window. "I mean, I swear I keep catching shadows in some of those windows."

"The people have got to be somewhere."

"Yeah, but why would they be hiding in the back watching us?"

"I didn't say it had to make sense. But somebody turned the lights on."

The center of town had a large traffic circle with a statue in the middle — some Revolutionary War figure judging by the sculpted clothing and the musket perched at the side. Beautifully maintained flowerbeds surrounded the statue, and a plaque stood in front that must have been cleaned recently — not a splotch of bird droppings to be seen. They drove the circle and found the diner situated on the far end half-a-block down from where the road exited.

Garcia pointed to the people packing in the joint to eat, and in a deadpan, he said, "Oh, good. We found everybody. They're getting a bite. Maybe the whole town. Not strange at all."

"Could be a town meeting. If we're lucky."

"You really think we'll be that lucky?"

"No, but we can hope."

She parked at the curb, and they headed back up the sidewalk to the diner. The concrete looked newly poured, and someone had taken the time to sweep the walk clean. When they entered, ringing a string of jingle bells overhead, they discovered a scene both strange and familiar.

The familiar — a busy crowd chomping down a variety of meals. The counter lined with hardworking folk, each hunched over a plate of food or a mug of coffee. The booths filled with families or friends digesting the day so far and that to come. Busy waitresses in pink polyester uniforms from the 1950s rushed to take orders, deliver hot grub, and chitchat for tips. The sizzle from the kitchen in the back as three men in stained white rushed to fulfill orders. And at the cash register, a squat, heavyset man, wearing wrinkled pants, a thin tie, and a greedy smile — the owner.

The strange — the quiet. All these people, yet it sounded as if they sat in church. The subtle sounds of a shifting body, a stifled cough, a sniffle. The soft clink of forks and knives made a gentle, tinkling music. In fact, Roni realized that all the sounds existed except voices. One child slurped the last of her soda through a straw while a man blew his nose like a new instrument for the horn section. The register rang a sale and the cash drawer made its distinct rolling sound as it opened. All of it could be heard, but nobody spoke. Not a single word.

A waitress approached Roni and Garcia as she grabbed two menus from a box hanging off the register counter. She motioned with her head for them to follow. No smile, no greeting. Nothing but a dead-eyed stoicism as she led them to a booth mid-way along the diner windows. She placed the menus on the table, dropped two sets of silverware wrapped in napkins, turned up the two coffee mugs already waiting, and left.

As Roni sat on one side and Garcia the other, a few customers glanced in their direction. Each face Roni met held the same emptiness.

Garcia leaned forward. Though he whispered, Roni thought his voice sounded amplified through a megaphone. "Is it me or are these people just like Mrs. Schmidt?"

"Might be worse. We need to take this slow and careful. Just observe what's going on, try to figure it out before we take any action. Understand?"

The waitress returned with a pot of coffee. After she filled the two mugs, she set the pot on the table, pulled a pen from behind her ear and held up her order pad. Then she chewed gum and stared at them.

Roni guessed the only way to order without a word was to point on the menu. But before she could do anything, Garcia set his down, flashed a smile at the waitress, and in a full voice that ripped into the silence, he said, "Hi there. We were wondering if you could help us out. We're looking for a friend that might've come through here."

Chapter 7

Roni wanted to leap across the table and bash Garcia in the jaw. She could see it happening. One hand pressing down as her body flew upward in slow motion. Her hair fluttered behind — somehow longer in her mind than in reality — and like a superhero, she soared in perfect form. It was a fleeting image — couldn't have lasted more than a second or two — yet she felt as if it had taken longer. Especially since the waitress stared back with her stony glare.

"Food?" she asked, her voice low and cracking.

Garcia sat back with a frustrated scowl. "Just the coffee for me."

The waitress looked at Roni as if to say, *Don't make me speak again.*

Roni started to point to the entry for a bacon cheeseburger but hesitated. With everything so odd in this diner, in this town, perhaps she shouldn't be eating their food. "The coffee's fine for now. Thank you."

Slapping her order pad down at her side, the waitress curled her top lip, looked Roni up and down, then shook her head, and walked away. The customers resumed their quiet meals making Roni notice that they had stopped in the first place. She listened to the bizarre orchestration of the diner. The little noises of eating and breathing and cooking and paying — all of it had a rhythm, a beat.

"Well, that didn't work," Garcia whispered.

Clutching her coffee mug with both hands to stop from forming a fist and actually hurdling over the table in a sloppy version of her imagined heroics, Roni blazed a glower at him. In a tight, low voice, she said, "You deliberately disobeyed me. We don't know what's going on here, I told you to take things slow, and you went charging in anyway. I should throw you out of the Society right now."

"We needed to see her reaction, and in my life, I've learned that the best way is to get a person right up front before they have a chance to prep an answer."

"That's not the point."

"That's everything of the point. We want to find Teanna, and that means gathering as much information as we can get. If you've ever watched a single crime show, you'd know that the first forty-eight hours are the most crucial in any missing persons case. We don't have time to gently coax answers from these people."

"Just because you don't agree with my approach doesn't give you the right to go off on your own and do it your way."

"What should I have done? Filed the proper requisition form?"

"Excuse me?"

Pushing in closer, his body pressing against the edge of the table, he said, "Ever since I joined up with the Society, you've pranced about trying to make it damn clear that you're in charge, you're the leader, the boss. That much is fine. Every group needs somebody at the top. But you want to control all of us. You don't trust us to do our jobs properly."

"Because you haven't done them properly. You're all disjointed. We need to come together as a single force, yet everybody has their own agenda. Look at you and me. We're out here because Teanna wouldn't go along with the team. If you would all listen to me like you're supposed to do, we might have a chance at running smoothly."

"Oh, just do whatever you say."

"Not like that. The rules I've tried to get you to follow are intended to make us better at communicating. So we know what to focus on. So we're not taken unaware like we have been in the past."

"I see. Better communication. How's that going?"

"That's the point here." She wanted to smash the mug down on the table. Instead, she clenched her teeth. "None of you have given my way a chance."

"Right. Because you know better than all of us. We should all follow your way without question."

"That's not what I said."

Garcia leaned back and rubbed his face. Glancing around the diner, Roni noticed a few people standing at the front, waiting for a seat. She looked out the window. Empty streets. Either these new arrivals had been masters of stealth or she had lost focus by arguing with Garcia. The latter seemed the most reasonable explanation. But as Garcia set his elbows on the table and laced his fingers together, Roni knew they were about to begin round two. This time, she would have to pay more attention to the crowd. Maybe do what Garcia said — look for a reaction.

"I'm not trying to piss you off," he said, his voice even softer than before. "I feel the same as you — I want this team to work, to be the best it can."

"Then why won't you all give me a chance? Why won't you listen to my ideas?"

"Because you won't let us breathe." She pulled back, and he must have noticed because he quickly said, "Think of it like we're teens. The more rules you impose, the more you try to force us to behave a certain way, the more we're going to rebel."

"But you're not a bunch of rebellious teens. You're all adults."

"And adults hate to be micromanaged."

"That's not what I do."

"It is entirely the way you run things. Hell, you've even tried to tell me the best times for potion making."

"You were exhausted, staying up all night, practicing at one potion or another, and I only mentioned that a more structured practice schedule has proven to work wonders for people."

"Can't you hear how belittling that sounds?"

Roni paused — partly to regroup her thoughts, partly to scan the crowd once again. She had not counted the customers, but it felt as if more had slipped into the diner. They went about their routine and silently ate their food. Yet little moments froze like snapshots as her focus crossed the room — a surreptitious glance from a trucker drinking coffee at the counter, a wary eye from a mother peeking over her menu, a threatening glower from a young man swiping at his phone. For a bunch of dead-eyed freaks, these folks sure could get under her skin.

She had missed the last bit of Garcia's speech, but apparently, the message had not changed. He went on, "We've tried to be understanding. This is a big undertaking and there are bound to be bumps in the road."

Roni snickered. "Did Gram tell you that one?"

"Well, um, yeah. And she's not wrong."

"She rarely is."

"Then why not listen to her? Or Elliot? Or me? Why not try giving us a little freedom?"

"*Freedom?* You feel like prisoners? Listen, I apologize if the delivery of my advice has come off as belittling or overbearing or whatever, but the fault is not all on my shoulders. None of you have given me a real chance. I mean, sure, when Sully was alive, when he was the official leader, you all would follow my orders because I was only the temporary leader. You knew that at some point, no matter what happened with me in charge, Sully would take back control. I was like the substitute teacher. Only now Sully is gone, and you still treat me that way."

Garcia lowered his eyes and winced. "You're not hearing me. There's a big difference between being a strict leader and being a dictator. You wonder why Teanna started going off on her own missions? You want to understand why we're sitting in this weird diner in this weird town?"

"So, this is all my fault?"

The waitress walked over to their booth carrying a large round tray with two plates on it. Moving as if half-asleep, she took the time to stare at Roni, then Garcia. The silence surrounding them managed to become even quieter. She set the plates down — two burgers with fries — and the sound of the meals hitting the table echoed as if they stood at the mouth of a huge cave.

"This isn't ours," Garcia said. "We didn't order any food."

The waitress opened her mouth but held back her response. Instead, she let her lips curl into a twisted, forced grin. Backing up, she bumped the table behind her before she stumbled back to the crowd.

Roni saw all of that, but it only happened in the periphery. Because when the waitress had set the plates onto the table, when Roni looked to see what the food was, she caught sight of something that froze her breath and electrified her nerves. A bitemark. A sharp, diamond shaped bitemark on the inside of the wrist.

She surveyed the diner once more. This time, however, she noticed the other marks. Poking out the collar of a shirt, sneaking a view from the end of a cuff, hidden beneath the long hair of a lowered head. Every single one of them. The entire diner. They all had bitemarks.

"Roni? You okay?"

Trying to control her voice, she said, "I think we're in trouble."

CHAPTER 8

Throughout her time with the Parallel Society, Roni had been involved with numerous physical altercations. However, these fights confronted creatures of varying cognitive ability — many acting on pure instinct. Rarely did she have to battle other human beings.

But as the diner patrons stood from their stools, chairs, and booths, as they moved in unison like a conducted orchestra, as they turned their hollow eyes upon her, Roni wondered if she could hurt these people. After all, the evidence suggested they had no control over their actions. Whatever had entered their systems through those bitemarks turned them, and they were not responsible for the fact that they shuffled closer and closer. Then again, survival seemed like a good idea, too.

Garcia jumped to his feet and yanked Roni out of the booth. He swiped a semi-sharp dinner knife off the table. Holding it low, ready to stab straight outward, he backed up. As they passed the next booth, Roni grabbed another knife and held it out. Her eyes roved from one threat to the next.

The customers and staff had formed an arc. Whatever possessed them to these actions had not been able to overcome their instincts of self-preservation. They clearly wanted to swarm in and cause damage — maybe bite, maybe kill — but none of them wanted to be first. That poor fool would get stabbed. No question.

But that would be the end. One stab. Maybe two. The rest of the diners would crash over Roni and Garcia. A flood of violence would slam against them, crush them, leave nothing but blood and bone behind.

With her back pressing against Garcia and her pulse twitching on her neck, Roni said, "You didn't want me to micromanage, so here's your chance. Get us out of this."

"Thanks so much," he said, his breathing ragged, his arm trembling enough that she could feel it through their backs. "We can't get to the entrance. Too many of them to cut through. You see any exits on your side?"

"Nothing. The backdoor is probably through the kitchen."

"I have my emergency potion but —"

"This is an emergency, don't you think?"

Garcia reached into his coat pocket and brought out a glass vial with a cork stopper. A quick glance and Roni saw a muddy liquid sloshing around inside.

He held it above his head and with a full voice that cracked the oppressive silence like thunder in a monastery, he said, "All of you back up. You don't want to mess with this. I toss this, and it'll be like Vietnam in here. Fire like Napalm. Understand? You let us through or this'll burn you all dead."

Nobody moved.

A glimmering, hopeful light brightened within Roni. They were going to walk out of that diner, regroup, and figure out how to find Teanna. Deal with everything one simple step after one simple step. That was the way to handle complicated matters. Break it down into baby steps. Easy to manage. And despite all the trouble getting her team to follow her without question, she suspected that after this incident, she would have their support. In fact —

A burly man pushed through, forcing others to start moving forward, and the momentum spread across the crowd. Though they still refused to speak, the sounds of shoes scuffing the old linoleum tiles stacked upon each other, building into a horrid, phlegm-soaked noise like a large animal straining to breathe. They moved in closer.

"Were you bluffing?" she asked Garcia.

"Yes. No. It's not Napalm. It's like a flash-bang grenade but in potion form."

"Then throw it already."

Garcia hurled the vial toward the kitchen. He dropped to the floor and Roni followed. They curled over, covering their ears and clenching their eyes shut. Still, Roni heard the concussive explosion. She saw light play against her eyelids.

A tap on her shoulder and she hurdled back on her feet. A slight ringing in her ear. All around her, the diner patrons rolled on the floor. Some pressed their palms against their eyes. Others plugged their fingers in their ears.

"Won't last long," Garcia said.

She nodded and took a step toward the entrance. He grabbed her by the elbow. Shaking his head, he gestured to the two men entering the diner — two men who had not been inside when the potion went off.

Back to where they started — stuck inside the diner with the main exit blocked. Dashing for the kitchen was out. They would have had to stand on people in order to reach the swinging door, and by the looks of the two new men — young and muscular, soulless in the eyes — Roni and Garcia would be lucky to reach the door at all.

"Watch out," Garcia said, moving off to the side.

At first, Roni thought the burly man might have lunged at them or perhaps the waitress wielded a sharp pencil overhead. But Garcia shoved a small table out of the way, grabbed a chair, and heaved it over the booth and through the big window. Glass blasted outward onto the sidewalk. The clashing notes of numerous shards clinking into each other lasted mere seconds before they shattered into hundreds of tiny pieces, glittering on the ground like a 70s light show.

Garcia stepped onto the booth bench, then the table, and with one foot on the lip of the window ledge, he reached back for Roni. "Come on."

Many of the customers had returned to their feet, and only the shock of the shattered window halted them. But that wouldn't last much longer. As with the flash-bang potion, those in the back of the diner had the least reaction. If not for the thick crowd making movement difficult, some of those men and women would have attacked. Roni had no doubt. They'd probably try to bite her. Well, no way would she let that happen.

Taking Garcia's hand, she climbed out of the diner. The crunch of glass as she landed on the sidewalk pounded through the air like a siren. Her heart pounded, too. The ghost town silence surrounding them could not have been louder.

Still clutching hands, Roni and Garcia bolted for the car. But they only managed three steps. The glass door to the diner swung outward as all the patrons poured into the street.

From behind, Roni heard the same crunch of glass. She whirled around to find the waitress had jumped through the window. Several others followed her.

"You got another flash-bang in that coat?" Roni said.

Backing away into the street, Garcia said, "Ever since I joined the

Society, I've kept some basic potions in my coats. All the time. One to heal wounds. One that makes light. That kind of thing. And one flash-bang."

"Next time make it two."

"Noted."

From homes on the opposite side of the street, two doors opened. A family of four walked out of one while an elderly couple emerged from the other. They did not hesitate to join the townsfolk closing in on Roni and Garcia.

"You wouldn't happen to have a teleport potion?"

"If such a thing exists, I haven't found it, yet."

Roni wanted to run, but she thought that might ignite the growing crowd into a frenzy. For the moment, these shambling lost souls remained calm. Threatening, sure. But nobody had raced forward in an attempt to tackle, maim, or bite. They acted like a pack of rabid dogs who silently approached and never barked.

Until that same burly man shoved aside a pregnant woman and opened his mouth. "Take them!"

The shredded voice — withered and weak — still managed to ripple across the townsfolk. Heads that lolled to one side or another popped straight with sudden urgency. Dragging legs and stooped shoulders firmed up as the crowd transformed into a powerful new entity — a mob.

"Run," Garcia said as he tugged on Roni's arm.

With only one unobstructed route — back to the town circle — the choice of escape had already been made. They dashed along the street, heading toward the statue in the center. Arms reached out, but Garcia batted them away like a heroic adventurer hacking through jungle vines. In their wake, the crowd filled the street, growing angrier, pounding fists against hands and chests.

When Roni felt the cool stone of the statue against her back, she exhaled a breath of relief. She knew it was false. They had succeeded in reaching the center of town, but that did not make them any safer. Just free of the first bad situation. And a wriggling thought in the back of her mind pointed out that they had not escaped to this location — rather, they had been herded to the statue.

"You're bleeding," Garcia said.

Roni looked down. The side of her shirt had a dark, crimson splotch. It grew wider. She pressed her hand against the spot sending fire up her flank. Hissing, she peeled up the shirt for a quick peek — a slice just above her hip. Not too deep and closing up now that she had started putting pressure on the wound. Lowering her shirt, she pushed harder against it.

Garcia held a baseball bat in his hand. She had no idea where he had acquired it — probably some kid recently left it on the grass — but she was glad he had it. Taking wild swings, he kept the nearest townsfolk from getting too close.

"We can't stay here," she said. "They'll kill us."

"I don't think that's their plan."

"Strange way to show it."

"They could've killed us easy enough already. We're more than outnumbered."

"Then what?"

"Just what the man said. They want to take us." Reaching into his pocket, he pulled out another glass vial. "Here. Drink this." He thrust the vial over. "Should work fast. It won't patch you up, but it'll take away the pain."

She downed the liquid in one swig. Bitter stuff. Like overripe melon. It did work fast, though. A pleasant warmth radiated from her stomach as if she had taken a double-shot of vodka. As this warmth spread, the pain in her side disappeared. Her sore muscles, her rapid heartbeat, her adrenaline-soaked system eased. She could think clearer. See clearer.

Bending down, she picked up a sharp rock. Not much of a weapon but better than nothing. "I suggest we don't get taken."

As an elderly man with white whisps of hair and a crooked back raised his walker, Roni wasn't sure she could fight back. Strike this old man too hard and she might kill him. Not hard enough, and he looked like he wanted to kill her — or at least, knock her unconscious so the mob could whisk her off somewhere.

To her right, three teenage boys cracked their knuckles, moving in on Garcia. Although they had the same empty gaze as the rest, Roni detected a gleam, a joy, at being allowed to cause harm. The first took the baseball bat in the thigh. He whined hard and limped away. The others paused.

"Come on," Garcia said. "You want to get hurt? Come get hurt."

Watching these events unfold, Roni missed the ten-year-old girl and her mother storming up on the left. They grabbed her arm with enough force to topple her. She angled back, determined to stay upright. With her rock, Roni struck at the mother's hand, gouged a chunk of flesh clean off, but the woman only pulled harder.

Roni lost her balance and crashed to the ground. The mother and the daughter fell, too, both rolling back into the roiling crowd. Roni's rock tumbled out of reach. She glanced up and saw the elderly man's walker racing down upon her. But Garcia took one step over, straddling her in a cross between a batter's stance and a swordsman's lunge. He swung his bat and cracked the elderly man's arm. The man careened sideways and flopped to the ground — probably broke a few bones when the walker clattered atop him.

Hoisting Roni to her feet, Garcia panted and sweat dribbled down his face. They couldn't last. Not against an entire town.

Tires screeched as a car engine roared down the street. The mob paused, all heads turning toward the sudden appearance of such a bombastic intrusion. Roni considered running, but the mother and daughter had returned. They growled and launched towards her — the mother aiming to tackle Roni by the shoulders, the daughter going for the legs. The three fell again.

Garcia swung his bat, knocking the mother unconscious with one powerful hit. He turned to the daughter but fell victim to the same dilemma that had plagued Roni against the old man. But Roni had learned the error of that thought — this was no innocent ten-year-old. Not anymore.

With a firm kick to the head, she dislodged the girl. Clambering up, and with the aid of Garcia batting anybody else who dared come close, Roni managed to get to her feet. Stuttering a few steps, she discovered the girl had been gnawing on her calves. Roni made two fists and prepared for the worst.

But the majority of the crowd focused to where those car sounds had come from. Over their heads, Roni could see tumultuous writhing. Bodies thrown off to the side. Short, painful cries. And then, a voice that raised her pulse.

"Roni?" Soft and strong. Just like the man who created him.

Gully punched and stomped his way through the crowd. Most backed away now, especially when they noticed the blood of their peers on stony fists. Or when they noticed that he wasn't human.

As she watched the dear golem bludgeon his way closer, she caught movement to her side. A quick glance — the burly man rushed towards her. He held a meat cleaver and he garbled a noise. He swung.

The heavy blade sliced downward and made contact. Not with Roni. It cut through part of Gully's arm. With a vicious snarl, Gully backhanded the burly man. He didn't bother to see where the man landed. Instead, he pulled the cleaver loose and offered Roni a grin.

"Ready to leave this town?" he asked. Turning to Garcia, he added, "Can you run?"

"Absolutely," Garcia said.

With a nod, Gully swept Roni up, holding her tight against his chest, and barreled back the way he had come. Garcia stayed close behind. Neither needed to fight, though they were clearly ready. But the boiling mob had reduced to a simmer, unsure of what they faced in this man constructed of clay and rock.

A car idled with the passenger door open. Gram sat in the driver's seat. Gully got in the back, carefully placing Roni down, while Garcia took the open door. Before any of them had settled, Gram gunned the gas and peeled out. In seconds, they were burning down the street heading out of town. Nobody spoke until they entered the highway and cruised along ten miles over the speed limit.

"Thank you," Roni finally said.

"Don't thank us," Gram said. "It was Elliot who sent us after you. Knew you'd be in trouble."

Garcia arched his back against the seat. "How'd you even find us?"

"The good Lord, of course. That and tracking the GPS on Roni's phone."

"Wait, wait," Roni said, sitting up and wincing at the movement. "If Elliot sent you, said we'd be in trouble, then does he know what's going on in that town?"

Gully pushed her back. "None of that now. You need rest and healing."

"Elliot will heal me when we get home."

Gram said, "And Elliot will tell you everything he knows, too. He has the answers for us. Until then, be patient."

Of course. Because everybody in the Society knew that patience was Roni's strong suit.

CHAPTER 9

On the drive back to Olburg, Roni gazed out the window while pressing her hand against her wounded side. Gully sat straight and stiff, never speaking a word but patting Roni's leg from time to time. Up front, Garcia snored — his adrenaline crash finally catching up with him. And Gram kept focused on the road. They all had questions but knew to wait until they reached the bookstore.

That moment arrived soon enough.

Elliot stood by the Big Table, cane in hand, ready to administer his healing spells. He had closed the bookstore early — no doubt to a few grumbling customers — and made sure to clear the table completely. Fresh-brewed coffee spread a rich aroma throughout the store.

Despite her protests, Roni gratefully allowed Gully to carry her in and rest her across the Big Table. Elliot's cane passed overhead, back and forth, and her body responded well before the magic engaged. She had experienced this spell enough times. Her body knew what would be coming, and the healing warmth covered her skin in anticipation.

Twenty minutes later, Roni got to her feet, her injured side and damaged calves like new even if her sore muscles still complained. Elliot then turned his attention to Garcia.

But as the man took a seat near Elliot's side, Roni said, "Gram told us that you have answers. Something that could help us find Teanna."

Without looking away from his patient, Elliot said, "One thing at a time. Once I have finished with Garcia, we can adjourn to the Grand Library, and I promise I will tell you all that I know."

"You want to wait? Teanna is out there —"

"I promise you, we can afford a few moments to recoup."

"Come with me, dear," Gram said. "We've got a little time, and I have something I want to tell you."

That didn't sound good. Pointing back at Elliot, Roni added, "The moment you're done healing, you call up to us. Understand? Then I want you both down in the Grand Library, and make sure you have everything you need to present whatever you want to show us. I don't to want to waste more time searching for some book or a piece of paper or anything. Call us once it's all ready. And please, don't take too long."

Elliot and Garcia shared a soft grin before starting the healing magic. Perhaps they thought she couldn't see. Part of her fumed at that look. She wanted to set them straight, make them understand that she cared deeply for the Society, have them see her intentions.

But Gram cleared her throat twice until Roni followed her to the elevator. Gully came, too. But Gram put her hand out like a crossing guard stopping oncoming traffic. "Not you. I need you to stand guard."

Gully slumped his shoulders. "Of course. That's what Gully's good for. Standing guard. He never tires. He's always willing to stand like a statue and watch, watch, watch." He continued muttering to himself as he sauntered back toward the front entrance.

Snickering, Gram reached over to the panel and pushed the button for the fourth floor.

Roni's arms prickled. "We're not going to your apartment on the fifth floor?"

"No."

With a slight bump, the elevator ascended. Roni stared at the glowing number four. "Why would we go there? It's just storage and where we keep the rare books, the ones that need climate control and — hold on. Isn't it?"

Gram did not answer, but one hand pressed her crucifix against her chest.

When the elevator stopped, when Gram opened the gate and stepped onto the fourth floor, Roni remained still. From the back, she could see a simple square room, richly carpeted and furnished with beautiful, old reading chairs. At least two on either side. Immense paintings filled up the walls — portraits and landscapes. But even from a distance, Roni could tell those images, those landscapes, did not exist anywhere in her universe.

"Whatever this is," she said, "we don't have time for it. Elliot will be done with Garcia soon, and we need to discuss what happened in that town, what Elliot's learned, and how we're going to find Teanna. The rest of this — it can all wait."

Gram turned back with a perplexed frown. "What you must think of me." That frown broke into shivering jowls and glistening eyes. "I know I've never been a good replacement for your mother. Elliot and Sully tried to make up for my deficiencies. We figured the three of us could match the one of her — or, at least, come close. But there simply is no replacing a parent. Even the bad ones, and your mother wasn't a bad one."

"You want to go through all of this again? Now?"

"Lord, help me, you really think I'm that selfish."

"I don't know what to think. I never do with you. My entire life was filled with lies from you."

"Half-truths."

"Some. And some outright lies."

"We're not here to discuss that. Forgive me or don't. I've made my peace with what I've done, and my mistakes have been brought to light. You can't fall back on them as an excuse anymore."

"Excuse for what?"

"For failing in your duty." Gram's eyes narrowed into a familiar sternness that tightened around Roni's heart. Taking one step closer, one step that seemed to raise Gram's head to the ceiling, she glared downward. "You and your teammate have been injured. Another is missing, at best, and possibly dead. I'm giving orders to Elliot and Gully in your absence. Sometimes in your very presence. Do you understand? You don't seem much in control right now."

"I've tried. But none of you — not one — even try to listen to me." Roni cringed at the sound of her own voice. She didn't want to listen to herself, either.

"Perhaps it's time to remedy that."

With a flick of her wrist, a small chain dropped from Gram's sleeve. At the end of it, Roni saw a large key.

"Come," Gram said as she turned away and headed deeper onto the fourth floor.

Roni reached for the elevator control panel. She could go back to the main floor, aid Elliot, get the information she needed, and with the help of Gully, maybe she could find Teanna. But as much as her trust in Gram wavered, she knew the matron of the Parallel Society would not willfully endanger any of its members. If she thought Roni had time for this, if she thought it necessary, then perhaps Roni should listen. Lowering her hand, swallowing against her dry throat, she stepped out of the elevator.

Walking across this glorified reading room, Roni gazed at the portraits of previous leaders — including a blank canvas with Gram's name underneath. Probably another duty for Roni to undertake at some point. The landscapes mesmerized. Primordial worlds brimming with potential and scarred wastelands at the end of their existence. Golden mornings reflecting on placid waters and violent nights erupting on fiery mountains. Roni wondered who had painted these works and if the artists had stood in those worlds or merely imagined them based on the journals of Society members past.

At the back, Gram turned to the left and pressed a recessed panel in the corner. A section of wall slid aside revealing a metal door. With her chained key, she opened the lock and slid the door aside.

"Nothing to be afraid of," she said, reaching into the dark room and flipping a light switch.

"Who's afraid?" Roni said, but the slight tremble in her voice gave her away.

They entered a room that comprised the rest of the floor. No carpeting, no wood walls, no portraits, no landscapes. Nothing but a metal folding chair sitting in the middle underneath a row of fluorescent lights. Not even any windows.

Gram paused, gazing upon the chair with a fond grin as if remembering a past love. "Every iteration of the Parallel Society throughout history has had a room like this. A version of it suited to its time. It is usually called *the leader's office,* and now, it belongs to you."

Roni cocked an eyebrow. "I don't mean to sound rude, but this place is empty. Am I expected to furnish it or something?"

"No. In fact, there is never meant to be anything more in here but the single chair."

Roni walked a few steps in, the click of her shoes bouncing back off the walls. "If this is the leader's office, how come I never saw you use it? Why do you have a second office in the basement?"

"Would you want to work in here?" Gram grinned, but when the joke did not land, her mouth returned to a slim line. "Calling this an office is a misnomer. This room serves a different and far more important purpose."

Turning in a small circle, Roni breathed in the emptiness of the place. "I figured out that this floor is not the storage area. That it probably never has been a storage area. But I don't understand. What's so important about an empty room?"

"You've done a decent job under terrible circumstances."

"You just told me I failed."

"You've done that, too. This room — it exists to help the beginning leader find their way."

"How?"

"I don't know. I never needed it."

"I guess you were a natural leader then. Good for you."

"Don't take that tone with me. I'm still your Gram. And no, I was not a natural leader. Nobody is. But I had advantages that you don't. When I became leader, the Society was already set with Elliot and Sully and myself. We knew each other well enough, and while there were always bumps in the road, I didn't have to convince strangers to follow me. When Sully took over, he didn't need this room because we were already a family who had gone through decades together. But you — you have two old folks who've known each other for longer than you've been alive and are pretty set in our ways. You have a young woman from another universe with her own agenda. You have a man obsessed with the Society who thinks he knows us better than we know ourselves. And you have a golem. Lord only knows how that thing actually thinks. You need help."

Roni nudged the metal folding chair with her foot. "This is going to help me?"

Gram shrugged. "It's helped others throughout the centuries. Can't hurt to try."

"What do I do?"

"I'm not sure. I suppose you sit and wait. Let the room do whatever it's meant to do." After a squeeze on the shoulder, Gram handed over the key, walked out, and closed the door behind her.

Roni stood alone. Watching that chair as if it were a rabid dog poised to attack at any moment, she imagined its bared teeth, its vicious bark, and the way it wanted to hurt her. Such lessons in life always hurt. Sometimes physically, most times mentally, but always in some way.

She turned back, reached for the door — Teanna needed her, needed the team, and this leadership exercise could wait. But she pulled back her hand. What kind of leader would allow herself to be defeated by a folding chair?

With tentative steps, she approached the metallic beast. Whatever Gram thought might happen, whatever benefits she hoped this would give Roni, it needed to happen now. The focus had to stay on Teanna.

Roni could hear Gram in her head — *but helping Teanna is why I brought you here.*

"Fine," Roni said and stomped over.

One final glance at the unassuming chair and she plunked herself down. Every part of her body that contacted the metal surface felt vibrations. Not painful, but not welcoming either. More like the growl of that rabid dog — the threat.

From behind, Roni heard a familiar voice. "It's about time we had this talk."

She popped to her feet, whirled around, and saw the misty shape of a person fade away. Gone. Leaving only the empty room and silence.

Roni stood still for a minute. Heart racing. Eyes searching. If the figure returned — but no. Not unless she sat in that chair again.

Thrusting her hands at her sides, she stormed out of the room. "No damn time for this." Teanna needed her and the Society. Simple as that.

CHAPTER 10

Despite her urgency, she had no control over magic. Elliot's healing spell would take the time it would take, and she could not force it to move any faster. The final few moments, however, managed to give Gram enough time to send a disapproving glare Roni's way.

When Elliot stepped back with an exhausted sigh and thumped his cane on the floor, Garcia swung his legs off the table and stood. Relief played across his brow as if, despite already having seen and experienced Elliot's magic, he thought that this time it might not work. Or perhaps he simply had the giddiness of a man who continued to be amazed at being a part of a world he had fantasized about for so long.

Roni gestured to the side stairs that led to the Grand Library. "Let's go."

"You boys better watch out," Gram said. "She's got no patience today."

"Why do you keep forgetting that Teanna is missing?" An idea struck and Roni looked right at Elliot. "Is there a spell on you all? Maybe something's been done to you without you knowing. Can you find out?"

"There is no spell," Elliot said, meandering toward the staircase. "We understand why you are anxious. Garcia is also feeling the same, even if he doesn't show it. But to both of you, I ask that you trust me. Gram trusts me. A little longer and you'll have your answers."

Gully cocked his head to the side. "I trust you, too." He then put both arms out like a game show host or a used car salesman promising honesty. "Even if I didn't know better, my maker, the great and wonderful Sully, trusted you with his life. I could do no less."

Wrestling down a thousand outraged comments, Roni said, "Can we please go downstairs and hear what you have to say? I trust you. I do.

So, if you think we have the time to waste here, then let's waste it. But can we get started wasting it faster, please?"

Elliot climbed down the stairs, chuckling. "I'm already on my way. What's your excuse?"

Holding tight to the railing, he waited for Gram to join him. Arm in arm they slowly worked their way to the Grand Library. Another three minutes were required for him to pull together several books which Roni suspected would never be opened but had been brought to underscore the research work he had done. He could have accomplished all of this two minutes faster, but he paused to look over the map on the back wall that Roni had been drawing and putting together for years — the map of the Caverns.

However, at length, the entire Parallel Society sat across two work tables, and all eyes focused on Elliot. To Roni's surprise, and obliterating her expectations, Elliot opened one of the books he had stacked and flipped through the pages. When he stopped, he looked over the book for a moment before turning it around and presenting it to the group.

"The first thing I want you to understand is that I am not mistaken." He pointed to the bottom right-hand page.

Roni and the others leaned forward. On the page, hand-drawn illustrations depicted different bitemark patterns. On the bottom right, Roni saw the distinct triangle markings that together made a rough diamond shape. Next to each marking, she read a creature's name as well as some basic information. Next to this now-familiar marking, she only saw two words — *the Scholar*.

"It's blank. We don't know anything about it?"

Pressing down with both hands, Elliot put all of his weight onto his cane. "Of course not. If that were the case, I would not have waited to bring everyone together to discuss this. The lack of information merely means that at the time the book in your hands was made, the Society knew little about the Scholar. But these other books and journals give us plenty of information. Because Roni's bouncing right leg and fidgeting fingers on the spine of the book tell us all that her impatience has gone into dangerous territories, I will skip a lot of how I discovered the information — I will trust that you believe I have exhausted all avenues of research."

"Yes, yes. We all agree." Roni knew she sounded as impatient as Elliot had described. After all, he wasn't wrong.

"Very well. Listen close. Despite its name, the Scholar is not a seeker of knowledge. Rather it is a creature that thrives on calculation. There is some dispute as to whether this creature evolved naturally in its world or if it was manufactured — perhaps a genetic experiment, perhaps a breeding one — but it is clear that the creature behaves like a living computer. It thrives on solving difficult, if not impossible, equations."

Roni's forehead wrinkled as she looked around, half-expecting to be told she's on some hidden camera show. "This thing is a glorified math geek?"

"As I read the evidence, I agree with those who believe this creature had been produced by intelligent hands. Just as in this world we have created computers to solve problems we could not handle on our own, this creature's world created it for the same purpose."

"I don't mean to question your research," Garcia said.

"Then don't."

He took the book out of Roni's hands and looked it over. "We were nearly killed by an entire town of insane people. All of them had this bite on them. What does any of that have to do with being a math whiz?"

Wagging his index finger, Elliot said, "Do you know how some computers in our world can solve massive equations — say, calculating a genome or solving biological, geometric problems? They often do it by harnessing the computational strength of other computers. As powerful as your phone is, or your laptop, it is weak compared to the requirements for the mathematical necessities of this world's most difficult problems. So, we chain these computers. Patch together the force of each one to make something greater than the sum of its parts."

"I don't like the way this is headed."

"You shouldn't. Because, yes, I believe the Scholar is able to hijack the brainpower of anybody it bites. It is using those people as a way to enhance its own computational abilities."

Roni said, "Then why did they all attack us? Why weren't they off with a pencil and paper writing down math problems?"

"I suspect the Scholar was protecting itself. Using some of them, at least, against you. There were most likely more people in that town than fit in the diner. Where were they?"

"I know," Gully said, raising his hand. "They were somewhere else calculating math problems."

"I think so, too."

"Okay," Roni said. "But then what about the lady we met in the trailer park?"

Garcia snapped his fingers. "That's right. Mrs. Schmidt was bitten but she didn't attack us. But she did say that she knifed the pale man — maybe he didn't bite her long enough."

After a pause, Elliot said, "Some think distance is a factor. The closer those infected by the Scholar's bite are to the Scholar, the more control it has over them."

"You don't sound like you know for sure."

"I don't. I only have the information I could find based on the Scholar being discovered here in the 1800s. That time, the Parallel Society successfully removed it from our universe. They wrote in their journals all they had learned about the creature, but the primary goal is always protecting our home, not researching these living relics."

"So, this pale man is the Scholar. At least, we've got a name now."

"No. The pale man is often seen in conjunction with the Scholar. He bites for the Scholar and is usually the first victim."

Folding her arms as her chin lowered, Gram asked, "So, why is it here? Why come back?"

"It's possible — even probable — that this is not the same Scholar as the one from long ago. Then again, we have no knowledge about how long these creatures live. So, I don't know. I think Teanna might. Or she was following something else that led her to the Scholar."

Roni bolted up straight. "That's how you know she's alive."

"Yes. The Scholar would not kill her. Just like it would not kill you and Garcia. It wants your brainpower. Think about it — you were attacked by fifty or more people. There's no way you could have survived unless they were holding back. Which they were. They wanted to stop you long enough to bring the Scholar in so that it could bite you."

"Or the pale man."

"Yes. Exactly."

"You think Teanna was bitten. And what? She's being held with the rest of the town to help calculate this math problem?"

"I suspect so."

Gram said, "We keep mention this problem it's trying to solve. What is it? You likened the Scholar to a computer linking with other computers. I imagine that we can link a handful together and work out astonishingly complex problems. But this creature is pulling together an entire town. What kind of equation does it need to solve that requires that much power?"

"That's a good question," Roni said, her fingers tensing. "It also makes me wonder how it got here. It's been here before — or one of its kind has. So how did it get back here?"

Gully placed one hand atop his head. "I hate to suggest this, but perhaps somebody brought it here on purpose. Perhaps to solve a problem that this somebody could not solve on their own."

Only one *somebody* fit that bill — Yal-hara. That hideous creature wanted her freedom. Even assaulted the bookstore and failed in her attempt.

Before Roni could utter the name, Gram put out her hand. "We shouldn't go assuming anything. What Gully is alluding to is a possibility, but we have no evidence to suggest it is the truth." To Roni, she said, "I see you boiling up at the mere thought of her. Please, keep yourself open to all the angles. That's part of your job."

Jumping to her feet, Roni said, "Gather up whatever you need. We're going back to that town tonight. We'll find out what's happening there, and more importantly, we're getting Teanna out."

CHAPTER 11

A few hours later, after the sun had descended for the night, Roni perched on the side of the western mountains overlooking this forgotten town. She had her phone, a pair of binoculars, and a thermos full of Gram's hot cocoa. Looking up and down the empty streets, she waited. The stores were lit up. Many of the houses, too. In some of the dark ones, the blue of a television set flickered out the windows. But, of course, even with the aid of binoculars, Roni found it difficult to spot a single person.

After setting the binoculars down, she pulled out her phone and tapped on the camera. A few passes over the town and she captured the basic layout in photos. She then did a video pass. Finally, she focused on smaller sections, zooming in to get the finer details. When she finished, she pocketed the phone and took a sip of hot cocoa.

Roni sat back against the trunk of a large maple. The cocoa warmed her, of course, but it did not bring the comfort she had hoped. All the time squandered to get to this point — it ate away at her. Elliot had promised Teanna was alive but that did not mean she was safe. That did not mean she was unharmed. And all of it had been unnecessary.

Even if Garcia had been right, even if Roni managed with too heavy a touch, surely Teanna would still have come to her. Roni thought they were like sisters. They lived together, they celebrated together, they shared their private lives far beyond the daily grind of working for the Society. Surely, Teanna would have confided in her sister.

Making barely a sound as he approached, Gully crouched next to her. "All set up. Now don't be expecting the miracles of my predecessor and maker. I'm not claiming to approach anything like his genius."

The corner of Roni's mouth lifted. "You are literally made in his image. You even have some of his mind in you."

"All I can promise you is that I did my best."

"What more could we ask for?"

As Roni scanned the streets, Gully pointed toward the town's edge where the ground sloped upward at the base of the mountain. She lowered her view and saw them — three little golems. One made of sticks and mud while the other two looked more like haphazard collections of rocks. Clearly, Gully had been practicing.

"They look good," she said.

"They're still too small. I can't construct anything more than two feet high without it falling apart."

"In this case, that's a good thing. It'll make them harder to see."

"The instructions aren't enough yet. I don't know how Sully managed to fit all he required on those little slips of paper. Even with me, he had to put in pages of information at the cost of some of my strength and overall powerfulness."

"Powerfulness?"

"You know — the things that make a golem a golem."

Roni gave Gully's back a gentle rub. "Don't worry. You are every bit the golem as any other. More, in fact. None of the others were ever as smart as you."

"I appreciate you saying that, but it is what it is and I am what I am. There is no changing that."

"Stop it. You are all the things that we need you to be and more. In fact, you're the only golem I've ever met that can create other golems. That alone makes you better than all the rest."

Gully seemed satisfied with the answer. Or, at least, he decided there was no point in furthering the discussion. After all, the three little golems he constructed had reached the town.

Through the binoculars, Roni watched as they spread out to cover more ground. Each one had the same goal — locate Teanna. Assuming the Scholar had taken Teanna much like it had taken all of the town, and assuming Elliot was correct that the Scholar's influence over his victims waned the further away they were from him, and assuming it wasn't too late, then these little golems were their best chance to find Teanna undetected. It required a lot of assuming.

As the two stone golems worked their way through back alleys and along fence lines, the one made of sticks and mud climbed up the side of a modular house. When it swung atop, it started hopping from roof to roof, crossing distances impossible for a human being.

"You've certainly learned how to make them stronger," Roni said.

"Are you talking about Sticky? Is he jumping well?"

"He's doing a fantastic job."

Gully clasped his hands together and arched back with a smile. With a full-throated cheer, he said, "That is wonderful news."

"I'm glad you're happy, but keep it down. Sound travels. The whole point of using your golems is that there's no heartbeat, no blood flow, no humanness for the Scholar to notice. We don't want to blow it by you shouting about your success."

In a heavy whisper, Gully said, "Of course, of course. Sorry."

Roni didn't want to think about her leadership issues anymore that day, but she couldn't help herself from making a comment. "At least you didn't bite my head off for trying to order you to be quiet."

She returned to the binoculars, hoping to let some silence steal away her thoughts. However, watching the golems work brought its own stresses.

Based on their movement, Roni guessed that they searched the town in a grid pattern. They had crossed about a third of the residential area and a small amount of the commercial. As they scurried along, peeking in windows or jumping from rooftop to rooftop, she realized her mistake — she should have told Gully that they needed to focus on large buildings. If the majority of the town congregated in one location, they would need something big enough to accommodate them. These small homes would not suffice. The golems were wasting more time.

Too late now. Better to let the operation continue than attempt to recall them and start over. Besides, she had an important question to ask.

"Before he died," she began, "Sully told me that he left a lot of information inside of you — more things than I realized at the time or would understand. I don't suppose you have any advice for me from him on how to fix this team?"

Gully closed his eyes and held still like a Guru in meditation. At length, he turned to face Roni. "Perhaps this story will help. A long time ago, when you were little —"

"Hey, that wasn't so long ago."

"Well, back when you were little, and Gram was raising you, she felt the emptiness of your parents not being around."

"I know. I felt it, too."

"It will help if you don't interrupt me." He waited and when she did not speak further, he nodded. "She felt the loss of her own daughter, and she feared the loss of her granddaughter. It was a difficult time for her. Before you say anything, the answer is yes — she harbored a lot of guilt over everything that happened back then. So, she decided that it was her job to make sure your life was as fulfilling as possible. Overcompensation, you understand. She spent the next week signing you up for dance classes and tae kwon do and swimming and the local soccer team and a pottery class and piano lessons. Possibly more, but those were the only activities Sully was aware of. Basically, she wanted every single moment you experienced to have some purpose that would ultimately bring joy to your life and perhaps fill the emptiness left behind."

Roni squinted as several thoughts bounced through her head. "I'm sorry, but that's not right. None of that happened. At least, I don't recall it ever happening."

"That's because it didn't. Sully and Elliot stopped her. They intervened so that you could discover the things you wanted to find joy out of and not have it dictated to you by Gram."

"I see." Roni checked on the golems progress — they had reached the traffic circle at the center of town. She lowered the binoculars fast. No need to remember that. "I get the point. I do. But this is different. Gram was acting through a combination of guilt and mourning, and in doing so, she tried to control my life so that I would become what she wanted. I'm not trying to control everybody. I only want to show them how effective they can be together. I see their great potential, and I'm trying to get them to see it, too. I guess I come off as a bit harsh, but isn't that what a drill instructor does — all to prepare the troops so they don't die in battle? That's what I have to do. That's the seriousness of the stakes we face. Look what's going on right now. Teanna is out there, and if we don't do things right, she might die."

One stone golem scampered along the far edge of the town at the base of the opposite mountain. Near one of three churches dotting the town, the golem had taken great interest in a small utility shed off to the side. Roni had no clue how they communicated, but the other two golems hustled over to join the first. Gully rose to his knees.

"What did they find?" she asked.

"I'm not sure, but look over there."

Swinging the binoculars where Gully had indicated, Roni spotted four townsfolk moving with great urgency toward the church.

She got to her feet, her grip tightening on the binoculars, pressing them harder against her eyes. Two of the approaching townsfolk split off to come around the opposite side of the others. Roni wondered if they had decided on that tactic themselves or if the Scholar controlled such decisions rendering these people as mere puppets.

"Don't worry," Gully said, standing close enough that his arm brushed her shoulder. "I gave them instructions to search for Teanna. But I also gave them instructions on what to do if they were caught."

"Is Teanna there, then? Did they find her in that shed?"

"I don't know if she's there or not, but I guarantee we'll find her connected to that spot."

"Great. Now we've got to figure out how to get there."

Two of the golems tried to open the locked door while the third walked in circles around the shed. This one — the one called Sticky — came around the back into view, and Roni saw it spot two of the townsfolk. Hastening around front, Sticky gestured to its comrades.

And they collapsed.

More than that. Roni saw that they had disassembled. The townsfolk rushed in, drawn by motion and sound, expecting to find an intruder — possibly Roni and Garcia again. Instead, they found nothing. An odd pile of rocks and sticks and nothing more.

Gully sniffled. "They were my best creations yet."

Roni scanned the faces of these four townsfolk, searching for signs of confusion or frustration or anger. She saw only the cold, dead gaze she had become familiar with. Until one of them looked directly at her. His brow tightened as if he could see across the town, up the mountain, through the trees, straight into Roni.

"I think we better get out of here," she whispered. "Fast."

CHAPTER 12

Ten minutes up the highway, one town over, Roni pulled into the parking lot of a small motel — the *Mountainside Inn.* The place lacked all amenities beyond the most basic — a bed, a sink, a toilet, and a shower of questionable hygienics. However, for the Parallel Society, the motel offered privacy, anonymity, and vacancy.

Gram, Elliot, and Garcia had already purchased three adjoining rooms. By the time Roni and Gully entered, basecamp had been well established.

The nearest room remained as purchased — a rundown motel room featuring two queen beds and an odd, dark splatter stain on the corner wallpaper. The middle room had been cleared, the beds stacked against one wall. Tables from all three rooms had been brought in. This would be for main operations. The back room chiefly served Garcia as an *ad hoc* potions workshop.

When Roni and Gully entered the main operations room, all eyes turned their way. Gully thrust his hands overhead. "We've had great success. You should be proud of us."

"We are always proud of you," Elliot said.

Roni caught a strange look from him. She turned her head to the side and opened her hands. *What?*

His hesitancy only made her want to speak the question aloud, but before she could embarrass herself and him, he nodded toward the front room. Turning to Gully, she handed over her phone. "Since you think we did such a great job, here are all the pictures I took. Fill in Gram and Garcia on everything that happened. I want a plan for how to get to that shed when I get back."

"Where are you going?" Gully asked.

"Just the other room. I need to speak with Elliot."

She could feel Gully puffing up with his new responsibilities, and she held back an amused smile. Even if she had allowed her lips to curl upward, the moment she turned toward the bedroom door, the smile would have vanished.

She stepped into the room, closed the door behind her, and leaned back. Elliot lowered to the corner of one queen bed, and with his cane, he tapped the other. Crossing her arms, Roni sat where he wanted and braced herself for something bad.

"I want you to know that I believe Sully would be very proud with the way you are taking to your new position of leadership." The words came out stilted and unsteady.

"I appreciate that, but I've had enough with the subject for a while." Roni looked him over carefully. Then: "I don't think that's really what you want to talk about."

His fingers tightened around his cane. "No, it's not. Not exactly. You see, Sully had no time at all to learn the ropes of running the Society. And then, he was out of time entirely. But that did not deter him from doing the best he could in that short moment, from finding pleasure in the process. That was his way. He embraced change and newness. If he had an idea or if an opportunity arose that interested him, he jumped right in. I have always been more cautious — well, not always — but certainly in my latter years. I fear I don't have many left."

Roni's jaw jutted out. Her hands gripped her arms tighter. "What is it with you and Gram? The two of you love to think about your deaths. I'm not going to indulge that. I won't. It's morbid and unnecessary. You'll die when it happens and there's nothing we can do about that. Why dwell on it?"

"I am trying to say that it is clear to me you will be able to lead on your own."

"Great. You've managed to combine the two subjects I really don't want to talk about — the struggles of being a leader and your mortality. Wonderful. Glad we had this private talk about it. Can't wait for more."

With a smirk, he said, "You still need to work on not being so rash. Not everything is an attack."

"I know that." She relaxed her arms and rubbed the back of her neck. Softer, she said, "These things you want to talk about — it's hard to juggle them when my focus should be on Teanna."

"I'm not being clear." Frustration passed his face and behind it came a look that scared Roni — a sad look, a look of loneliness. She dismissed the idea. She was reading too much into what she saw. But then he said, "Perhaps I should have saved this conversation for later. It's just that I fear there won't be time. Not ever. Not for this."

The darkest thought rose in her mind. "No. I sympathize with you. I truly do. The loss of Sully hurts, and I'm sure it has hurt you most of all. But you do not get to call it in early. I'm sure taking your own life is a sin in any religion. Besides, Sully wouldn't want that, and neither do I."

Elliot thumped his cane on the floor. "I am not suicidal."

"You're not? Well, good. Don't scare me like that."

"You should know me better than to even think such a thing."

"Sorry. Then what is all this about?"

A pause. Then: "It's nothing. It's an old man trying to express himself and doing a poor job of it. Please, forget this. You are right — our focus should be entirely on Teanna. My old man thoughts can wait another day."

"You sure?"

"Quite sure."

"Okay." Roni walked over to the door leading out. "Tell the others I needed a moment. I'll be back in short order." She did not wait for a response.

Outside, the mountain air filled her lungs with a clean scent of pines and earth. An old urge clawed up from deep within — cigarettes and a bottle of vodka. That would be perfect. But she shut that down fast. It would ease her stress, of course. It would also muddle her thinking, and she needed a clear mind.

The motel building ran a straight line parallel with the main road. At the far end, a sliver of a placard poked out with the word *OFFICE* written upon it. Standing beneath the sign, a pudgy man with a mop of curly hair stared at her. When their eyes met, he motioned with his head into the office. As he entered the building with his hands in his pockets, Roni shuddered similar to the way she had done whenever in trouble as a child.

"Crap," she muttered as she headed down the walkway. This was the kind of establishment that was willing to rent rooms by the hour. What could they possibly be upset about that required a visit to the office?

When she crossed under the sign, hot air and cigarette smoke hit her. Old green carpeting and wood panel walls only added to the stifling sensation. A tall counter blocked the front, and a metal desk could be seen several feet behind. Off to the side, an old television set complete with rabbit ears served mainly as a table for long forgotten pieces of paper.

The large man lowered behind the desk, and Roni now saw that he wore a name tag — Bill. A tuna fish sandwich with three bites sat on a paper plate in front of him. A can of soda, two letters with the words *Final Notice*, a letter opener, and a corded phone. Nothing else.

Donning a smile she hoped did not look as plastic as it felt, Roni said, "Hi, there. I take it you're the manager."

"No, ma'am, I am not. I'm Bill, the assistant manager. That's why I have the night shift. See how that works? I'm just the assistant, so I get the lousy hours and less pay."

"I'm sorry to hear that."

"Yeah, well, the thing is, this is my mealtime. I'm trying to eat in peace and let all of you sleep through the night. But that's not what's happening. So now, I have to interrupt my mail and my food to deal with you and by the time we're done, I'll be back on the clock and unable to finish."

"I can't imagine what we've done that's a problem, but I'm sure we can fix it. As for your meal, it's not like anybody's going to be watching you. We certainly won't tell on you. Go ahead and finish your sandwich."

"It's not that simple. I've heard you breaking up those rooms. I don't know what you got going on in there, and I don't want to know. What I want is for the rooms to be back the way they're supposed to be and for you all to leave. But, somehow, I don't think you're going to be cooperative. I've dealt with your kind before and it never turns out well."

"My kind? What are you talking about?"

Rising to his feet, Bill said, "I'm not going to argue with you. I brought you in here as a courtesy to politely ask you to leave. Don't make me call the police."

As Roni struggled to find some way to calm the situation, Bill stepped forward and spread his arms wide with his fingers flat on the countertop. That's when Roni saw the edges of a bitemark on his forearm.

Double crap.

In a move that lacked speed but made up for it in strength, Bill shot out his arm, attempting to grab Roni across the counter. She stumbled back. He came around, blocking the exit, and breathed heavily as he loomed in. What she saw on his face, in his eyes, surprised her — fear. Not the dead-eyed glaze of his peers.

"Please," he said, his voice cracking across the word. "I don't want to hurt you. Any of you. Just leave."

Inching away, Roni said, "You're like Mrs. Schmidt, aren't you? The further away you are from the Scholar, the less control it has over you."

"You need to leave."

"I can't. You're blocking the way."

Even as Bill glanced over his shoulder at the exit, his body kept moving forward. The wood paneling pressed against Roni's back. She had some mace in her purse, but the purse was back in the room. Snatching a glance at the counter, she saw a pen but it was too far out of reach. The letter opener, too — but it waited for her all the way on the metal desk.

With honest regret in his eyes, Bill said, "If you survive this, please leave. I've always tried to be a peaceful man. So, please, leave and don't ever come back."

He punched her. A short hit rolling up from her stomach into her sternum. The air whooshed from her lungs as a burn ripped along her skin. While she fought back her stomach's urge to empty onto the floor, her legs wobbled and she tottered to the side. Her arm caught the counter and kept her from dropping to her knees.

Bill shifted his position and pulled back his fist for another strike. Reacting more than thinking, Roni propelled her entire body forward. Her shoulder caught him right below the ribs, and the combination of momentum and surprise powered him back a few steps.

She glimpsed the exit. The room swirled as she tried to clear her head, regain some balance, and escape. But it was too much. She thought she had managed a step or two in the right direction when Bill's arms wrapped around her from behind, lifted her off the floor, and tossed her over the counter.

Slamming onto the desk, feeling the smudge of a tuna fish sandwich on her elbow, she rolled off and flopped onto the thin, green carpet. Bill came around, his steps measured, his expression woeful. "I am so sorry. I really am. This wasn't the way I wanted things. I just wanted to be left alone. A quiet job in a quiet town. I didn't want to be part of any of this."

Roni tried to focus on the words Bill said but they came to her with an echo that made meaning difficult to decipher. She scooted back and managed to get on all fours in hopes of eventually standing. A sharp kick to her side sent her back down.

Lying on the floor, she saw this man hulking towards her and had one thought that might save her. "You can't kill me. Right? The Scholar wants all the brainpower. It wants the pale man to bite me."

Bill halted. For a moment, Roni felt an ember glowing in her belly — hope. But then Bill turned to the desk and wrapped his fingers around the sharp letter opener.

"It wants to bite you, yes. But it doesn't want to battle you. Not over and over." Bill wielded the letter opener overhead. "Trust me. It's better to die now, quickly, than live with this thing in your head."

Roni kicked out but came short of Bill's shins. She forced herself to sit up and scoot back against the wall. "You come any closer to me, and I'll scream. I'll fight. I won't make this easy for you."

"Please, don't. I don't want to hurt you."

He took a step forward. Roni kicked out again. Her foot grazed his shin. Not enough to do any damage.

Then she saw it. The shaking in his eyes. The sweat glistening on his lips. The shriek building in his chest, desperate to get out but held back by a voice in his head that would not go away.

Moving cautiously, Roni got to her feet. She had her hands out, ready to block or grapple or claw if necessary.

"You can fight this thing," she said. "I can see it happening in you right now. Just fight harder."

Like an amusement park animatronic, Bill moved his head from side to side. "It's not like that. How do you stop the voice in your head when it's your own voice?"

"It's not you. It's the Scholar. You know that. Don't let it win."

He raised the weapon higher, trying to strike but holding back, locked in a tug-of-war over his own muscles. "I'm so tired of that voice telling me to go to the town. I'm so tired of thinking about equations I don't even understand. I can't sleep. I can barely eat. It's still going on right now. Velocities and orbital trajectories and triangulations and calculus — I don't even know how to do any of those things. I barely passed algebra in school."

The letter opener struck down, but Bill had not moved any closer. It swished through the air, and Roni flinched even though she could not be hit. Not yet. It would only take Bill stepping forward once more to close the distance.

"You need to get by me," he said, raising the weapon overhead again. "You need to get out of here, grab your friends, and leave.

Because they're coming. The Scholar's people. They'll be here and you won't be able to stop them."

"You want me out of here? Well, I want to go. I want to do as you say. But I can't until you put that down."

Scrunching his eyes tight, Bill said, "I can't take another night of this. When they get here, when they take you to the Scholar and it bites you, this will only get worse. They'll bring me back with you. Once I'm at that town, there won't be any break. It'll just be math over and over and over. Square roots and gravitational computations and mathematical simulations. I won't do it. I can't take it. No more."

Bill's eyes snapped wide open. He inhaled deep and strong, lifting the weapon tighter overhead, and he bellowed his pain. A roar of anguish and rage. But he never stepped forward. He plunged that letter opener into his own neck. As blood spewed out the wound and painted the metal desk, he looked straight at Roni.

And he smiled.

That twisted spark in his eyes, dotted with specks of his own blood across his face, snapped out. His head wobbled. His body slouched to the side. And he crumpled to the floor.

Roni plopped back against the wall, one hand covering her open mouth. She had seen death before. She had watched vicious creatures die, and she had killed a few by her own hand. She had witnessed the terrified shock as both man and monster were consumed by other creatures, and she had seen the shock of a living being pulled unwillingly into another universe. While she never took those things lightly, this suicide — this willful, self-inflicted death — did not wear the same face as the others. No expression of pain or regret, of loss or fear. This had been a welcome release.

Roni closed her eyes. She had to push away that image. No other choice. No time. She rolled her shoulders back, stood straight, looked forward, and lowered her hands. Shaking the nervousness out, she stepped over Bill and exited the office without even a glance back.

The fresh mountain air tasted stale now. As if it knew things had changed.

Opening the door to the operations room, she found the whole gang bent over a table filled with ketchup packets, plastic cutlery, pencils and pens, papers and books — all spread out in rough approximation of the town's layout. Gram held Roni's phone and compared their efforts with the photos.

"We're ready," she said as Roni stepped forward.

"With what?"

"You said we were to come up with a plan by the time you came back. We've got one."

Gully gestured to the table. "It's not the greatest plan. If we had more time, we could come up with something less risky. But I think we've done a good job."

Stepping toward the adjoining workshop, Garcia said, "I already have one potion on hand. It'll take me a half-hour to make another flash-bang and some other necessities."

"No," Roni said. "We're leaving. Now."

"We are?" Elliot asked.

Gram locked eyes with Roni, and whatever Roni's face portrayed provided enough. "You heard her," Gram said, clapping her hands to get everybody moving. "Break all this down, pack it up, we've got to get going." Looking back at Roni: "How long do we have?"

"They're already on the way."

CHAPTER 13

As Roni led her team back toward the hidden town, she wondered how many of the Scholar's drones passed by going the other way. When she and Garcia were attacked in the town, the Scholar had thrown a large number of people at them, but that did not mean it would sacrifice so much computational power on a faraway threat. She took the exit and parked as close to the town as she dared — the rooftops of the first buildings barely visible in the distance.

As the group met between their cars, she could see the worried expressions and hoped that fear was of the Scholar and not her leadership. They all stood still. Waiting.

"Well?" Roni said. "Let me hear this great plan of yours."

Gram exchanged a look with Elliot before speaking. "Shouldn't we go back to the bookstore?"

"No time. Whatever your plan is, we're using it."

"But we haven't had a chance to really think it through."

Elliot said, "Perhaps we should —"

"No," Roni said. "Right now, as we stand here, the Scholar has sent a bunch of its people to that motel to capture us. That means there are less people in the town. But that won't last. We won't get this opportunity again. That thing likes to reach out its influence, to control everything around it. I have no doubt that it's got part of its brain trying to control the people on their way to the motel. If we wait, it will just bring them all back into the town and be that much more difficult for us to fight."

"In that case," Garcia said, strolling toward the trunk of his car, "I better get started on the rest of these potions."

Gram jabbed her head up. "Okay. You heard her. Everybody knows what they're supposed to do. Go get prepared while I fill in Roni." She gestured for Roni to come close. "If that's okay with you."

Roni nodded.

Gram launched into her explanation, but Roni only half-listened. The plan was simple enough to grasp. Also, given the limited time the team had to formulate their strategy coupled with the limited reconnaissance Roni and Gully had been able to perform, any plan they came up with could only bring the team as far as the shed.

Roni watched Gully gathering sticks and rocks to create a new golem. Working out of the car trunk, Garcia measured solutions and added powders for whatever potions he thought necessary. Sitting on the curb with his legs folded and his cane held firmly in front, Elliot worked on a spell.

But Roni could feel the doubt. See the worry. This was not a machine working in perfect time. Rather, they were separate parts, confident in their own space but unsure of each other's success.

Part of her wanted to shout at them. You all know each other. You have all fought together before. There is no reason for you to doubt. No reason for you to worry. We can do this. But another part of her thought of football teams, baseball teams, and basketball teams. These groups of people who worked together year after year yet watched their success rise and fall the same way — their confidence shaken by a losing streak or a change in management.

Roni stepped back from Gram. "Maybe — maybe you should lead this one."

"Lord help me, no. For one thing, my part in this is to drive the getaway car. For another, you'll never get where you want to be if you give up your position so quickly."

"I'm not the coach of a sporting team."

"What?"

"Nothing, nothing. Just … if this doesn't go well —"

"It'll be fine."

"You don't know that."

"If you're looking for certainty, you've got the wrong job. And if you require complete cohesion in the group at all times, you've got the wrong job. Do you think that Sully and Elliot and I worked together at our best when you were added to the mix? It threw everything off. You had to carve out your own section of the bookstore and your own space within the team's function. It was a major change, an upheaval to what had always worked for us in the past, and it took a while before we could operate well together. But that didn't mean we couldn't do our jobs. That didn't mean we couldn't succeed at our missions." She put her arm around Roni and gestured to the team hard at work. "They all know what they're doing. They all know their part in this. All of us have the same goal — to get Teanna back."

Roni knew Gram meant well, and she wanted to believe. Unfortunately, she had to face a simple fact. "You've forgotten something important — I have no powers. You need to be with the group because you make the chains and you make the books."

"You don't need my chains. You're plenty strong on your own. And I've made two books for you to carry along, just in case. Besides, it's too late to restructure the plan. Everybody's ready. We all know our parts, and we're going to succeed."

Gully clapped his hands as his new golem rose from the ground. Still only a couple feet tall, but this one looked bulky, stronger, with sticks and vines lacing through rock like tendon around muscle.

Garcia closed the trunk as he slipped several vials into his coat pocket. His forehead had reddened a little, and Roni wondered what concoction he had created for that result. But he smiled with the satisfaction of a job well done.

As Elliot stood, the familiar haze of a protective dome formed over him. But then another coating of light spread from the top downward. As it descended, it washed out Elliot's appearance. If Roni looked closely, she could make out the edges of the dome, but otherwise, it blended in with the surroundings.

She walked a circle around where Elliot had been standing. Whatever angle she looked at, the dome changed its appearance to fit the trees and hills — even showed her Garcia standing behind it.

She raised an eyebrow at Gram. "This might work after all."

CHAPTER 14

Huddled around Elliot, the group shuffled down the town's central street. It felt awkward and silly to walk as if shackled together, but nobody complained. Roni figured that Elliot would have made a bigger dome if possible. After all, he had done so in the past — she knew he was capable — but either the camouflage technique made it unfeasible or Elliot's aging body could no longer handle the strain. She worried that the former might cause the entire dome to collapse prematurely, and she did not want to think about the latter.

Unlike the previous visits to this town, there were people on the streets. Not many. But enough to make it clear that the Scholar had changed its security strategy. The townspeople on the sidewalks looked through the dome, clearly unaware of the team's presence. However, that did not ease the nerves.

Feeling the heat of Garcia's breath on the back of her neck failed to stop a shiver from rolling up Roni's bones. She fought to control her breath. A sneeze, a cough, tripping on a crack in the pavement — any little sound might give them away.

With his cane held firm, his eyes closed, and one hand resting on Gully's shoulder, Elliot continued forward. They led him like a blind man. Roni thought he might have the best idea — not seeing the townspeople would certainly make it easier to walk the street with confidence.

Her calves burned from the short steps they were forced to take. Sweat trickled down her back. Next time, she would have to tell Elliot to put in some ventilation.

When they reached the center of town and navigated their way around the circle, Roni couldn't help but watch for a growing crowd. Perhaps it was her imagination, but she swore she could feel Garcia's breath quicken. Off to the side, she spotted the diner.

The shattered window still littered the sidewalk, and Roni's car was still parked a bit further down the street. She liked that car. Probably wouldn't ever get to drive it again.

A clutch of five women exited the diner and stopped with their shoes grinding the glass. They all had that sickening, empty gaze. Roni's skin prickled. But as her tension mounted, Elliot turned them onto a side road, heading for the eastern edge of town. Putting distance between them, the diner, and the center of town lessened that tension, but another form replaced it — they were closing in on their target.

As the road narrowed, they had to be more careful. If the dome bumped into a parked car or one of the passing townsfolk, their ruse would be over. Thankfully, the Scholar did not bother with his townspeople driving. Probably too difficult — especially when it had to either trust or control those heading to the motel. Whatever the Scholar's issues, the result meant that Roni and her team did not have to deal with traffic.

Gully pointed ahead on the right. The ground sloped upward, and sitting atop that gentle hill, the church could be seen. The sign out front read: *Cornerstone Family Church.* Below, on a message board: *When nothing is left, you best be right. Trust in Jesus.*

They climbed the hill and reached the main parking on the side. Off to the right, sitting in the grass, Roni spied the shed. Two young men stood guard at the front of it. Otherwise, Roni did not see anyone close by. The group halted, and she shifted to face Gully.

Speaking low and soft, she said, "Where's your golem?"

"Give her a minute."

Her? Roni tucked that away for another day. She did not have time to consider golem genders at the moment.

She checked the rooftops and peered in the alleyways but found no sign of Gully's golem. Elliot let out a shuddering breath — exhaustion taking hold faster than Roni would have expected. Even Garcia's nerves shifted into a new gear as he bounced from one foot to the other. Only Gully appeared confident in his golem. It would have to be enough.

At length, when the new golem approached from down the mountainside, Gully pointed to his creation with pride. "I had her parallel us up there so that she wouldn't get seen by any of the people, and I didn't want her to use the same routes the other golems had used in case the Scholar figured that out. Smart, huh?"

Roni gave Gully a peck on the cheek. "Very smart."

The tough little golem hopped off a large rock and onto the back grass of the church. She crossed the open field swiftly, reaching the shed with hardly a sound. At that point, crouching on the opposite side from the guards, she paused. No need for a breath or to rest sore muscles — Roni wondered what was going on.

"She's listening," Gully said. "Making sure the guards did not hear her. Not yet."

As if in answer, the little golem picked a small pebble from her belly and threw it down the hill toward town. As it made a few noises, the two guards perked up, their attention pulled momentarily in that direction. Not for long, but enough for the golem to swing around the shed and dash between the two men. She tapped them both on the back and continued sprinting downhill.

Roni imagined they must have felt duped and angry. Perhaps those strong emotions could override the Scholar's desire to keep them guarding the shed. Perhaps the Scholar wanted them to follow this golem, to learn where she came from and who controlled her. Regardless, the golem tore up the nearest street and the two guards pursued.

Gully said, "She can run a long time but she's not a great tactician. They're going to catch her. Maybe quicker than we'd like."

"Then let's go." Roni stepped through Elliot's barrier and marched toward the shed.

As the others followed, she heard Elliot release his spell — the magic sizzling away like static in the air. Then, she heard Elliot slump his weight onto his cane with a long sigh. Best he took the rest while he could. He had earned it.

When she reached the door — no surprise — a padlock secured it shut. Kicking the door down would have opened it with ease, but it would also create a lot of noise. Too much. Therefore, the plan had always been for Garcia to handle it.

Before he reached Roni, he had removed a vial of amber liquid from his coat. He motioned for everyone to back up a couple of steps as he dumped the contents onto the lock. The metal hissed as it dissolved. Within seconds, a white trail of smoke snaked upward. Raising one hand for the rest of the team to see, Garcia counted down from five. When he hit one, the padlock dropped to the ground.

"Teanna?" Roni said as she pushed forward.

With a few hand motions, she ordered Garcia and Gully to stand guard as she entered the shed. Filled with rakes and shovels, shears and trowels, bags of grass seed and cans of paint, the shed had much to be expected but no light. Using the flashlight app on her phone, Roni looked throughout. When she reached the back, her skin bristled. An old work sink stood there with two pipes running up from the back toward the roof. A pair of handcuffs dangled from each pipe.

"She was here," Roni said.

Garcia peeked in. "They could not have taken her far. The time for you and Gully to meet us at the motel, everything that happened there, and for us to get back here — not enough to get far at all. Only if they had acted instantly would I be worried that she could be anywhere."

"Because the Scholar probably took a few moments to think about it. This isn't a math problem. Maybe the Scholar's not as good a thinker when the variables are so flexible."

Gully said, "So where did they take her?"

Roni stepped from the shed and observed the town spread out before her. It would have to be someplace close by. A short drive, at most — if they could drive. Otherwise, the Scholar would be pushing its control far beyond its reach. And it didn't want to be messing with any of this in the first place — probably. It came here, or was brought here, to solve a problem. That's what all this was about — probably. Which suggested that the Scholar would have the majority of townspeople together in close proximity — a supercomputer of human minds that it could control the strongest. Probably.

"Some kind of gathering place. A town hall," she said and looked over to her right. "Or the church."

Bolting across the field and parking lot, Roni blasted toward the church. The banging of the doors echoed throughout the high ceilings as she darted down the center aisle, skidding a few steps shy of the front stage. She looked back at the empty church. Not a single member of the congregation. Not even a priest or reverend or minister or whatever denomination this church belonged to.

Garcia, Elliot, and Gully hurried in. She put out her hand — not only to stop them, but to ask for their silence. And she listened.

If there were people, even a small amount, surely she would hear them.

"Wait here." Not giving them time to answer, she dashed through the side door.

She entered a hallway that led to offices as well as stairs going down. Skipping every other step, she raced to a basement and looked around.

It was a large area, low-ceiling, finished off to be used for potluck dinners, AA meetings, and numerous other community gatherings. But no people. Not a soul.

Moments later, the rest of her team came down the stairs. She looked to them. "Is there a town hall? A courthouse? They have to be someplace big enough to handle all of the town."

"I agree," Elliot said. "But from what I could tell in your pictures as well as walking through this place, the church is the biggest building for such a purpose. This one, in particular, is larger than the other two churches."

Ignoring the fact that Elliot somehow could see while having his eyes closed during their entire walk through the town, Roni turned to Garcia. "You have anything?"

He put out his hand as if serving up an idea with the caution of a novice waiter. "Perhaps there's a school?"

"A school. That's good. Where are the schools here?"

"Hold on." Garcia pulled out his phone and started tapping. Moments later: "There's a small elementary school on the west side of the town, but I don't think it's any larger than this church. Probably smaller."

Gully said, "Give me a few minutes, and I'll make a small golem that can check it out for us."

Roni nodded. "Do that. I don't think we'll find anything, but it's better to be sure. Garcia, what else is there?"

"A few miles north of town, there's a regional high school. Serves all the teenagers for five surrounding areas. It's big."

He turned his phone toward Roni and when she saw the pictures, she snapped her fingers. "That's it. She's there."

"We don't know that," Elliot said. "Let Gully —"

"Yes, yes. Gully can create his golem to double-check. But we don't have time to wait. We're heading to this high school. Besides, it's going to take us enough time just to get out of here safely. I'm sure Gully's golem can figure it out by that point."

Roni waited for further objections, and when none came, she nodded for Gully to get working. As he headed off, she placed an arm around Elliot. "Do you think you can cast another spell? Or do we have to figure a different way to get out of here?"

Chapter 15

The original plan had been to find Teanna in the shed, grab her, and call Gram to barrel the getaway car through the town for a rescue. But without Teanna, calling in Gram would alert the Scholar to their presence, to the fact that they had found the shed empty, and that they were closing in. By the time they reached the high school, the Scholar would most likely be gone. And Teanna, too.

Roni could see that Elliot needed more time to recoup which nixed walking out the same way they had entered — huddled under his camouflaged dome. While Gully and Garcia might be able to hop from rooftop to rooftop, Elliot would never be up to the task, and Roni did not trust her own legs for such a feat. Besides, the noise they would make clumping along would catch somebody's attention.

They needed to leave quietly. But also quickly.

"Why not go out the same way my golem came in?" Gully said as he looked toward the back of the church — toward the mountains.

"Good idea," Roni said, "but I don't think Elliot can manage that."

Stomping his foot, Elliot said, "Of course, I can."

"That spell took a lot out of you. We all see it on your face. I mean, come on, you're still sweating."

"I have endured far worse than a little exhaustion in my life."

"You were a young man then."

"Would you rather we spend another hour sitting around here?"

She had no response. After a moment, it became clear that she had no other ideas. Pointing at him, she said, "I'll be watching you the whole time. You give me any reason to think the hike is too much for you, I'll stop us wherever we are. Understand?"

"I understand. Now, if you don't mind a suggestion, I think we should get going immediately. The longer we stay here, the greater our chance of being caught — and the faster we'll have to move across that mountain."

Roni gestured to the stairs, and the team left in silence. In order to keep her promise/threat, she brought up the rear, always paying attention to Elliot's gait, his breathing, his posture — everything that might indicate he pushed too hard. As they exited the back of the church and headed straight to the foot of the mountain, she saw Garcia offer a potion to Elliot. The old man patted Garcia on the shoulder, mumbled something, and then with a grateful smile, he downed the liquid. From that moment on, he acted nimble and spry. Whatever specific boost the potion provided, it did the trick. They swept across the mountainside like ghosts. Even startled Gram when they appeared at the car doors.

"Where's Teanna?" she asked as the group clambered in.

"Garcia, give her the address." Roni spotted the little golem making her way to the car. "Gully, see if she found anything."

Gully rushed out as Gram started the engine. After a few exchanges, Gully hugged his creation and kissed the top her head. He walked back to the car, and she disassembled behind him.

Taking his seat, he said, "The elementary school was closed and empty."

Roni reached over to clasp his hand. "I hope you thanked her for us. She did a great job tonight."

"I think she knew."

Gram pulled onto the road and drove off. As Roni settled back, she noticed that Elliot was fast asleep.

It did not take long to reach the high school — a huge, single-story building surrounded by athletic fields. All brick with long rows of windows, the facility had the utilitarian design of many American high schools built in the 1970s. Most importantly, the lights were on and people could be spotted mulling about inside. A lot of people.

"Looks like the right place," Roni said, avoiding any gloat in her voice.

Gram parked and shut off the car. "Is there a plan?"

Surveying her team, Roni came to a few rapid conclusions — they were tired, stressed, and eager to be done. But they would not stop until they rescued Teanna. The way each member looked back at her with determination flushed her chest with pride.

"We'll keep this simple and safe. Elliot, you need to rest as long as possible. Gully, I want you watching over Elliot. Gram, I've still got the books you gave me, so you keep the job of driver tonight. Garcia and I will go in. Once we find Teanna, we'll hopefully be able to get her out, back to the car, and we drive home. If we can't, we'll call you for whatever we need."

"Not bad for an instant plan," Gram said. "But I have one request."

"Oh?"

"Do you mind if we all join hands and have a little prayer?"

Roni fought back a hard laugh. "Might as well get all the help we can."

For a short time, the Parallel Society held hands in a rough circle while Gram thanked the Lord for all He had done, asked for His protection as they embarked upon a dangerous mission, and praised all His wisdom and benevolence. When she finally said *amen*, the team continued holding hands. They grasped at that moment of peace — though tinged with fear — until Roni finally broke the circle.

"We have to go," she said.

Garcia grunted agreement and stepped out of the car. As Roni went to follow, Gram clutched her hand and pulled her into a strong embrace.

"Don't be a hero," Gram said.

"I never try to be."

"You know what I mean. Promise me that you'll call the moment you find her. Let us help. You don't have to keep trying to prove yourself to us. We're with you already."

Roni wanted to say that she wasn't trying to prove anything, but the words stuck. Partially because she didn't believe them. Partially because she did.

She kissed Gram and left the car.

Maneuvering around the school turned out to be easy. Roni and Garcia kept to the unlit fields, allowing them to run without notice. The clatter of their movement might travel back to those inside, but for somebody to discern such noises from that of an entire town trudging about the tiled school floors would be incredible. For that same somebody to then conclude the noises came from intruders outside on the perimeter would be impossible.

When they reached the back, Roni noticed several entrances. Two led to the gymnasium, two opened into halls on either side of the building, one set of double-doors connected to the main hall splitting the building down the middle, and one lone door had been tucked away in a darkened corner with the dumpsters — the janitor's door. Perfect.

"You got more of that lock dissolver?" she asked Garcia as they crouched behind the dumpsters.

"I'm not an idiot."

"That's debatable."

She had meant it as a joke, a light ribbing to ease nerves, but his mouth twitched as he produced another vial from his coat. Showing a greater degree of professionalism, he refrained from further comment. Instead, he got to work on the door.

The familiar hiss and white trail of smoke arrived. Seconds later, he eased the janitor's door open, trying to avoid any rusty squeals. They crept inside, closing the door every bit as slowly behind.

They entered a long cinderblock hall lined with rolling trash collection receptacles, stacks of fertilizer, rakes and shovels. The lights were off, but the main hall at the end provided enough to guide them. When they reached the corner, Roni poked her phone out at floor level and took pictures in both directions. Scooting back a few inches, she and Garcia looked at the results — empty.

As Roni started for the hall, Garcia tugged her back. To answer her scowl, he held up his phone. He had gone to the high school's website and tapped on a map of the building. She gave him a nod — *good work* — as they leaned over his phone.

Only two locations made sense for the Scholar to congregate all of the people — the gymnasium and the auditorium. The former was to the left, the latter to the right. Motioning with his hands, Garcia suggested they split and check out both locations at once, but Roni shook her head. No way would she split a group of two. That would be suicide. Thankfully, the need to be quiet kept Garcia from arguing.

Which left the decision with her.

Gymnasiums were big, cavernous blocks that bounced sound around with terrible acoustics. No matter how quiet the townspeople could be, the simple act of walking would create a thunderous ripple when compounded by their numbers. Not to mention the squeaks of sneakers on the waxed floor. If they were in the gymnasium, Roni thought the echoes would have been heard through much of the school. Hard to miss.

She pointed to the auditorium, and Garcia nodded. With a quick glance at the map to make sure she knew the route, she headed off to the right. Garcia followed close behind.

Hugging the walls, they hastened to the end, peeked around the corner, and continued onward. The closer they came to the auditorium the more Roni heard the small sounds of activity she had expected. There were others around — there had to be — but she never saw them. Perhaps if she had picked the gymnasium, they would have run into those tasked by the Scholar for things other than helping his brain, but this was the right way to go.

Roni and Garcia dashed down a short flight of stairs and along the hall that ran one side of the auditorium. At the far end, she spotted the music room. On her left, she found what she sought — entrance to the stage wings.

She reached for the door when Garcia stopped her. "Isn't it likely the Scholar will be on the stage? If that's the case, then it would have guards set up right on the other side of that door."

"The only other way in is through the back. We go that way and we've got to walk the entire auditorium just to reach the stage."

"No, we don't. We only have to go as far as it takes us to find Teanna."

Roni licked her lips. "You're absolutely right. We go around the other way."

They backtracked until they reached the lobby. This time when Roni reached for the door, Garcia stood behind her at the ready. For a man that resembled a bookish college professor, he sure could find his inner-warrior when needed.

She pulled on the door. No locks. No resistance.

They slipped to the side, staying pressed against the wall. The place smelled like a locker room — too many bodies, too much sweat. The majority of the town stood at attention in front of every seat with their dead-eye gaze facing the stage. Thin tubes ran from the base of their skulls into the aisles and down to that same stage. Tiny, bright sparks fluttered through the tubes in both directions.

The house lights were out in the auditorium as if they all watched a play. The stage had been illuminated which provided enough spill that Roni could see the faces of all the people standing at their chairs. Moving down the left wall, she scanned row after row, searching for that one familiar face.

She tried to avoid seeing the stage itself — tried to avoid hearing the gurgles coming from that direction — but she failed. Pausing, she turned her head and saw clearly the two relics sitting there. One was a stone with carvings along the base which reminded Roni of Yal-hara's relic boxes. All the sparking tubes twined together into one thick mass and connected at the top of this large rock. But, of course, it was the other relic — the living relic — that consumed her focus.

The Scholar.

It was a bulbous creature. Soft, dark skin — an odd shade of blue. Like murky water. Its body spread out like a puddle, and four limbs rose from the center. Roni could not tell where eyes or mouth or other sensory organs were situated and part of her didn't want to know. A single, thick tube ran from the relic stone into the Scholar — no doubt connecting its brain with all the others. And it barely moved. In fact, the longer Roni watched the creature, the more convinced she became that it was dormant in some way. Perhaps not sleeping. Perhaps lost in the quiet of its massive calculations.

Garcia tapped her shoulder. "They're not seeing anything. The townspeople. If they could, we would've been spotted by now."

"I don't think the Scholar's seeing much either."

"Should we risk being more direct in finding Teanna?"

Roni weighed out the possibility. "We'll take it slow. Test the waters before we jump all in. Understand?"

"No problem."

"I meant it. Slow and quiet."

"Okay, okay."

Moving up and down the aisle, they checked the faces on the end. None of them were Teanna, and none of them responded to Roni's or Garcia's presence. Nearly all brain function appeared to be consumed by whatever problems the Scholar wanted to solve.

Snapping his fingers, Garcia pointed down the middle row. As Roni worked her way toward him, she saw — Teanna. Standing firm, dark skin glistening sweat, muscles taut as if she wanted nothing more than to burst out and fight. Beneath her braided hair, a sparking tube snaked out and joined the others.

Roni stiffened at the sound of doors opening. The shock tilted through her system as her focus locked on the back of the auditorium. Emerging from the dark, the burly bald man from the diner stepped forward.

CHAPTER 16

At first, Roni could not move. Her mind blanked at this unsightly man. He snorted hard and cracked his knuckles, and Roni wondered if he performed these intimidations on his own or if the Scholar controlled every muscle.

Careful not to make sudden movements, she eased her head to the side and gazed over at the Scholar. If that thing paid any attention to her, Garcia, or the brute, it made no indication. Not even a twitch of the fingers or the simple rise and fall of breathing. It was a pile of malformed goo, yet Roni trembled at the danger such a weak-looking thing presented.

With an eager lick of the lips, the burly man swaggered down the center aisle. Roni reached over and gave Teanna a shake. She had the slim hope that a simple jerk might wake up her friend. No such luck.

"Garcia, I'm sorry to do this, but will you please deal with that man?"

Scratching his jaw and using a wink to tamp down his fear, he said, "No need to ask. You're the boss."

He reached into his coat pocket and pulled out a vial of dark golden liquid. Pushing the top off with his thumb he did not hesitate to down the whole thing.

"What potion is that?"

"Whiskey."

He rushed up the side and picked a row close to the back. He crossed in front of the people there, knocking them down into their seats while yelling. Roni could not make out the words — pretty sure she heard Spanish. Whatever he said did not matter. The burly man took the bait.

After all, the Scholar would not like having its precious brain supply disrupted. For the time being, Garcia posed a threat greater than Roni. As the man tried to head off Garcia, she tried to change that view.

Keep moving, Garcia. Keep moving.

Stepping directly in front of Teanna, Roni reached for the tube behind her neck. It felt warm to the touch and whenever it sent another bolt of energy along, Roni felt a tingling vibration roll up from her fingers. Not unpleasant, but not something she wanted to endure for too long.

Where the tube met Teanna's skin, smooth tape had been applied — perhaps drugstore bandages. Roni pulled back. She had both thought and hoped that the tube would be connected like a plug — something she could pull loose without risk to Teanna. She couldn't be sure without taking a direct look, but she swore she felt stitching.

That couldn't be. That was crazy. When would the Scholar have had time to stitch in all those tubes? For that matter, when did it have the opportunity to put these tubes in at all?

"Come over here, big boy," Garcia said as he hopped over two more rows. "No comments on how that sounded."

Looking into Teanna's eyes, Roni said, "I know you're in there, and I know you're fighting. You would never stop. So, keep fighting. Please. Oh, and if you happen to know a safe way to get you out of this thing, I wouldn't mind you sharing that information."

Roni grabbed Teanna's wrist, hoping that a human touch might wake her. Strange jagged ridges under Roni's thumb pulled her attention down, and she saw the scabbed bitemark. With her head lowered, her focus then shifted to the floor — to Teanna's hatchets.

"There's the perfect thing to bring you back."

She picked up one of the hatchets and placed it in Teanna's hand. It slipped loose from her limp fingers and clattered to the floor. Roni bent down, picked it up, and placed it back in her hand again. Like before, it slipped right out and banged on the floor.

"What's that?" a harsh voice called out from the stage.

Roni shot to attention, part of her thinking she could blend in with the others standing straight and looking forward. With any luck this newcomer would assume the sounds came from Garcia trampling over chair after chair, person after person.

From the stage left wing, a tall Slavic-looking woman stepped out. She wore a slick apron covered in splashes of blood. In her hand, she carried some kind of mechanical device with a wire connecting to special glasses that had a greenish light around the rims. She pushed the glasses up on her head. Probably the one responsible for attaching all the tubes. She certainly looked exhausted with heavy, deep-set eyes.

With her left foot bouncing, Roni stood shoulder to shoulder with Teanna trying to observe everything yet look as if she saw nothing. The woman on stage watched Garcia and the burly man for a moment, long enough to let Roni think she might get away with the ruse. But then the woman pointed directly at Roni.

"Hey. What you doing over there?"

The woman in the bloody apron stepped down the stage left stairs. With her focus lasered on Roni, she strolled forward methodical and patient. Strange. Why didn't the woman run? Why didn't she attack with real fight?

The answer struck fast. It was the Scholar.

At the diner, the customers did not blitz forward and overwhelm them. At the town circle, the townspeople pressed in but never attacked with conviction. It was the Scholar. That creature could only devote so much energy to controlling these people's actions. Getting them to move, especially fast, must tax the Scholar's brain too much.

Which meant Roni had time. Not much — the auditorium wasn't that big — but enough. It had to be.

She gave Teanna a hard shake. "Come on. Wake up."

Nothing.

She chanced a look at Garcia. He had scrambled to the far end of the audience. The burly man never stopped closing in.

Back to Teanna. Roni picked up a hatchet and held it in front of Teanna's face. "You know this. It's part of you. Just reach out. Break free of that stupid relic and grab it."

Cringing, Roni slapped Teanna's cheek. "Come on, come on, come on."

She could hear the woman with the bloody apron walking up the incline.

"You can't wake her," the woman said. "But you can join her." Widening her eyes, she shouted, "Hey, Manny."

From the stage wings, a man emerged. A well-dressed man. Thin. Frail. A man that, should his eyes have been pink, would have been considered an albino. The pale man.

He stopped at the edge of the stage and opened his mouth. As he revealed his jagged teeth, the shape of his mouth contorted into the rigid angles of a diamond. He hissed.

An outburst from the back. Garcia had run out of chairs and

flopped to the floor. He scrambled to his feet but now stood in the corner. With the burly man sauntering closer, Garcia had no escape. If he had another potion to help, he wasn't thinking about it.

"Please, wake up. Come on, Teanna. Fight."

"The Scholar won't let her go." The woman's voice sounded so clear. A few more steps and it would all be over. "I connected your friend to the Scholar, and once I've connected a person, they don't want to leave."

Roni glowered over her shoulder. "Like hell."

She windmilled her arm, bringing the hatchet down hard on the sparking tube that linked Teanna and the others with the Scholar.

CHAPTER 17

Stabs of heat pierced Roni's bones as a bright flash lit up the entire auditorium. The woman in the bloody apron brought up her hands as if defending a physical attack. Flailing back, she dropped and hit her head against the floor. Roni managed to stay standing, but she clenched her eyes shut and found it difficult to convince herself she could open them again.

But more than anything, Roni heard the screaming.

It came from the stage.

The Scholar had awoken.

Unable to move, Roni's body rippled as if her muscles continued to be stimulated with jolts of energy. She might have stayed that way for hours — jittering with her eyes stuck closed — if not for the voice of her dear friend.

"Roni?"

Her eyes snapped open, and she put out her arms in time to catch Teanna's tumbling body.

"I don't care that I'm sounding like Gram," Roni said, "thank the Lord. Are you okay? Do you know what's been happening?"

Using Roni for support, Teanna tried to stand on shaky legs. "I've been aware of everything. Just unable to control my own body. And you slapped me."

A quick laugh, and only then did Roni hear the tears in her voice. Dashing at her wet cheeks, she said, "You can get back at me when we're sitting safe at home. Let's get out of here."

The Scholar let out another high screech, and Manny, the pale man, bounced around the relics with hisses and jerky movements. Teanna pushed away from Roni. She stepped out into the center aisle, already regaining much of her strength. While the Scholar's arms thrashed about in rage, Roni noticed several of the tubes flashing and then going dark — like lightbulbs popping out. Several people throughout the auditorium began to shake their heads, move their arms, come into themselves.

The woman in the apron rubbed her back as she stood. "Round up those trying to get free. Beat them if you have to. None get out alive."

Other than Manny or the burly man, Roni had no clue who the woman commanded, but she clearly commanded somebody. Roni spun back. "Garcia! Run!"

Like a rabbit spotting an opportunity to get by a distracted dog, Garcia bolted for the exit. He sprinted right behind the burly man, but his enemy did not pursue. Too many of the audience had started to cry or yell or scream as they discovered they were still connected to the tubes. Those close to the burly man turned on him, and he raised his fists to punch his way through.

As if a valve had shushed closed, the Scholar's screams dissipated. Its arms regained control. Manny ceased his chaotic dancing about. Before Roni had the chance to utter the thought *This ain't good,* all of the townspeople still under the Scholar's control in that auditorium turned to face her and Teanna.

"Okay," Teanna said, her neck crackling as she rolled it. "What's the plan?"

"Um … we didn't think this far ahead."

"Well, that's disappointing."

Jaw set and body alert, Teanna stepped in front of Roni. She shoved the townspeople directly before her, and as they floundered back, she took her hatchet to the twined tubes on the floor. The auditorium erupted in a fresh blinding flash, but the Scholar muted its own screams this time.

Shaking her head, Teanna reached back and pulled Roni several steps forward. "Stay behind me and stay close. I'll get us out."

Seeing Teanna acting like Teanna sent a deep freeze throughout Roni's bones. "These people. They're innocent in all this." She thought of the little girl back at the town, the one that gnawed on Roni's calve. Roni had kicked that girl in the head. Or the old man with the walker that tried to bash Roni's head in. Garcia had used a baseball bat on that man. She wanted to throw up. She had seen them as monsters but now thought they were victims. "Don't kill any of them."

"I know about them far better than you. Trust me."

Teanna spun her hatchets so that the blunt flatbacks led the way.

Getting hit by one of those would still be painful, even damaging, but not likely to kill. Not unless she struck the same person multiple times.

She led Roni clambering over those newly freed people in the row and when they stepped out into the aisle, the woman with the apron charged Teanna. Despite all she had been through, Teanna's muscle memory had no problem handling the situation. She ducked the woman's grasping arms, pivoted to the side, and struck the woman with the back of her hatchets — one in the chest, one on the forehead. The woman never stood a chance. She collapsed. Unconscious.

Manny cried out. Two sharp yelps before he returned to fawning over the Scholar.

Spinning around, Teanna pointed up the aisle. But when Roni turned, she saw only a thickening crowd that reminded her too much of her diner experience. "We can't get out that way."

"Then we go to the stage."

But as Roni stepped forward, thick hands grabbed her shoulders. They yanked her against a large man — a burly man. She did not have to look to know. His muscular arms reached down, locking her head, and hauling her back. Roni opened her mouth to yell for help but no sound came. She could barely get any air.

Instinct drove her fingers up, attempting to pull the man's arm free of her neck. When that failed, she dug her nails into his skin. A sharp squeak slipped through her lips causing Teanna to turn back.

Snarling as she evaluated the threat, Teanna pointed with one hatchet. "Let her go."

Roni could feel the man's chest rumble as he spoke. "Give yourself back to the Scholar. It's your only choice."

Not the only one. Teanna rushed forward. Against such a seasoned fighter, the Scholar was no match. She easily dodged the townspeople's lackluster attempts to grab her, and in several steps she was within striking range of the burly man.

Though he still held Roni in a headlock, he loosened his grip to let her breathe. Probably thought he needed her alive as a shield. That was his mistake.

Teanna did not stop her attack. She slid in low and slammed the backs of her hatchets against his calves. His body arched backwards giving Roni a chance at freedom. She stomped on his foot and when he let go completely, she jumped forward.

Whirling back, she saw Teanna pop to her feet and club the burly man on the back of the head. Down he went. Teanna jumped over his wilting body and plowed a clear path toward the stage.

Though several of the townspeople blocked the aisle, they were no match for Teanna's well-placed beatings. The few on the end either found the internal strength to override the Scholar's commands or the Scholar thought better of sacrificing more of its brainpower. They stepped aside.

Climbing the side stairs onto the wood stage, Roni could not be sure whether they were leading the charge or being corralled to the slaughter. However, when they finally stepped upon the boards and she saw the situation spread out, her confidence rose that the Scholar had underestimated them.

There were no guards. And all of the Scholar's work — papers with mathematic symbols as well as scribblings in symbols that Roni did not recognize, three laptops providing further assistance, and a rat's nest of sparking tubes all spiraling into the top of the relic stone — it looked like the floor of a mad professor's study. Hardly the setup of a brilliant mind filled with malicious intent.

At the opposite end of the stage, the burly man stumbled up the stairs. Blood dribbled down the back of his neck and onto his shoulder. Manny rushed to attend the burly man but was swatted away.

Teanna curled her lip at the blob of the Scholar in the center of the stage. Then to Roni: "Take care of that." She raised her hatchets and lunged after the burly man.

Standing on that stage, watching as Teanna barreled into a fight, a blast brighter than any axed tubing could emit shocked through Roni's system. Like phosphorous bursting from her sternum and ribs, a sensation of anger and pride amplified within.

She was better than this. She had faced truly dangerous monsters, creatures of terrifying physical ability, and she had taken on those that operated in the realm of the mind, too. Yet she had become frozen inside. Her responsibilities demanded so much of her, leaving her feeling like she danced the tightrope without a net.

Yet Teanna simply leapt into the fight.

Having been taken down by her, the burly man treated her with greater respect — both fists raised to protect his head, a boxer's stance, cautious but ready to throw a punch the moment he spotted an opening. Teanna danced around the man, feigning and fighting, always searching for a chance to attack. They traded savage blows.

She never forgot who she was, what she was. She knew her purpose and no matter the situation, she acted. Well, Roni could do that, too.

Manny slithered across the back of the stage. Roni saw him and as he hissed, she swiped one of the yellowed papers off the floor. She pulled out a lighter. Manny wanted to attack, but he held back. She flicked on the flame, waving it below the page, just out of reach. "Stop this now or I'll burn all your work."

Nothing changed. Roni wasn't even sure the Scholar could hear her. But if it could, it ignored her. Several townspeople in the front row shambled toward the stage stairs.

"I'll do it," Roni said, shaking the paper. "I swear."

Still nothing.

The people crowded onto the stairs, some falling off as the others pushed ahead. They moved mindless and foolish. Still a threat, though. Manny circled her, showing off his teeth as he crouched ready to lunge whenever he saw the opportunity.

Teanna roared as she swung her hatchets only to be blocked and countered. Dodging that attack, she whipped around to strike again. With both combatants in bad shape at the start, they had become evenly matched.

And Roni — standing there with her lighter and a piece of paper. Damn. She could do better.

She walked over to the Scholar, raised her foot, and stomped down. Before she could make contact, one of the Scholar's arms slashed out, deflecting her off balance. She wagged her arms trying to stay upright, and the Scholar's eager hands ready to take hold and rip her apart.

Uttering a groan, she righted herself and jumped away from the creature. Along the ridge of its body, a thin strip of flesh separating the top and bottom halves, Roni noticed small black dots — eyes. The thing could see, after all.

Pocketing the paper and lighter, she pulled out one of Gram's books. Not the oversized version, but a simple pocket-sized book that could handle the job.

"You know what this is?" she said, satisfaction following at the way the creature withered from the book. Manny retreated. "You both do. Good. Because either you set this town free, or I'm sending you to a new universe. An empty hell that you'll die in."

Raising one hand, the Scholar pointed to the relic stone with all the tubes. The next instant, all the people on the stairs ceased moving. The burly man jumped back out of Teanna's attack range and stopped his aggressive assault. Only those townsfolk who had been cut free of the Scholar moved about, and they were mostly crying in shock, unsure of anything and unable to remove the loose end of tube attached to their skulls.

Roni understood the threat — open the book and the Scholar would cause torment to all of the town. It had complete control over them. It could make good on that promise. And what did Roni know about these tubes anyway? If the Scholar ended up in another universe, perhaps the tubes would keep functioning fine. Or they might act like ones already severed — flashing bright and causing anguish.

Her finger caressed the edge of the book's cover. Just open it and be done. It seemed simple enough.

But the Parallel Society did not exist to hurt those who were meant to live in this world. They protected the universe from other universes. She knew that sometimes such protection meant that people got harmed, but that did not give her the right to harm everybody as a matter of convenience.

She put the book away.

Teanna must have understood, too. But she took the Scholar's message differently. With a frightening yell, she surged forward and brought her hatchets down into the relic stone. Clearly, she wanted to sever all the tubes in one giant stroke. Instead, her weapons bounced back with a metallic clang.

The Scholar's flesh fluttered. Roni thought it was laughing.

The doors in the back of the auditorium banged open, drawing the attention of over a hundred people. Garcia stepped forward with Elliot and Gully close behind. After pointing to the stage, Garcia ducked back into the lobby. Roni thought this strange until Elliot's spell went off.

A mustard-yellow mist spread from Elliot's cane all the way to the stage. It moved like lightning, and as it hit Roni, the world flipped on her. The edges of her vision grew fuzzy, and she found standing straight difficult. Her balance had upended. Yet even as she dropped to the stage floor — or perhaps the stage floor lifted to meet her — she noticed all of the townspeople having similar difficulties.

Only one figure stood unaffected — Gully.

The golem blitzed down the center aisle towards the stage. At least, Roni thought that was what she witnessed. It all clouded around her head, swirling moments and images like the mist that brought the confusion with it. For one moment, she saw Gully leap onto the stage. Another moment, she floated in the air, reaching back toward the Scholar, wishing she could understand the creature, communicate with the creature, stop the creature. And then Teanna walked by her side. Only they weren't walking. They flew. Legs out, arms wide, laughing at the ridiculousness of it all. Below her, the stage disappeared and she was soaring above the audience. Not high, though. A few feet, maybe. A flash of clarity hit — Gully had tossed her over one shoulder and Teanna over the other. And clarity dissipated into the fogginess surrounding them.

"Take them to the car," Elliot said. "I'll finish up here."

Once in the lobby, once fresh air filled her lungs, Roni's head cleared fast. "Put me down," she said.

Gully set them both on the floor. "Gram is right outside waiting for us. Garcia should be with her, too."

Backing out of the auditorium with his cane held out, Elliot closed the door. "We have a few minutes before that spell's effects end. We need to go. Now."

While the others headed out, Roni hesitated. "We can't leave the Scholar here. Or Manny. They don't belong in our universe. It's our job — we need to get rid of them. And what about all those people?"

"That's not why we're here."

"But that creature —"

"Is *not why we're here*. We came to save Teanna. We should go home, take our win, and then we'll figure out what to do about the Scholar and his lackey and the people. Only with a well-thought plan."

Elliot's deep, soothing voice pushed away at the screaming banshee within that faulted her for not opening that book. *You had the chance. It'll never be that easy again.*

"I know it's hard," Elliot said, "but you can't win every fight all at once. Wars are made up of smaller battles."

Roni watched the auditorium door as she listened to her team get into the car. Pressing down the urge to run back in, to race through the aisles, vault onto the stage, and finish the Scholar, Roni turned away. Elliot stood right behind her.

"Sully would've been proud." He pulled her close and kissed the top of her head. "I'm proud."

Dabbing at her eyes, Roni said, "Let's go home."

Chapter 18

By the time the Society returned to the bookstore, everyone agreed they needed rest. As much as Roni wanted to question Teanna, learn all of what happened, and formulate a plan for stopping the Scholar, she recognized that nobody had the mental stamina to keep going that night. Besides, even if the others had wanted to do so, Teanna did not. She had shut down since entering the car. Elliot had performed a gentle healing spell while they drove — enough to remove the bitemark and offer some protection from the Scholar trying to control her again, but she stared out the window almost as dead-eyed as before. She spoke once, insisting that the bond between her and the Scholar had been broken, but Elliot continued healing, and Teanna did not argue further.

The next morning, Roni woke in her apartment and performed a task she had not done in years. She cleaned. Not much, but she picked up some of the thrown about clothes, washed the dishes that had been piling in the sink, and cleared much of the clutter from the coffee table. Even if she had the time to dust, that wasn't going to happen. There were limits, after all. Still, having Teanna back home flushed Roni with joy, and she wanted to make her friend feel welcomed.

As the sun cracked over the horizon, Elliot called. He asked about Teanna and made sure Roni was okay, too. Then he inquired if perhaps Roni wouldn't mind coming over to his apartment — he had a matter to discuss.

Roni didn't like the sound of that. But Teanna often slept in, and after all of that had happened, Roni guessed Teanna might sleep through the afternoon. Well, she deserved the rest. So, Roni quietly left, and shortly after, thinking of the aborted conversation at the motel, she knocked on Elliot's door.

When he let her in, he moved like a man who spent days crossing a desert and had only begun to restore himself. She guessed her team all looked like that. Limping exhausted through the morning, unable to accomplish much more than a cup of coffee. And even that might be too much. But then she saw the apartment and revised her previous assumptions. He had been more like her — busy, indeed.

The entire place had been packed up, ready to move. Carefully marked boxes lined the back wall of the living room with words like — *Dishes, Summer Clothes,* and *Bedding*. From where she stood, Roni spotted a wardrobe box in the bedroom. Most of the furniture was gone, too. Just a mattress on the bedroom floor, a chair in the living room, and a coffee table with a flatscreen sitting on it.

"What's going on here?" she asked.

Elliot chuckled. "I should think that's obvious."

"You can't move. You've always lived here. Well, I know not *always*, but you've lived here as long as I've been alive."

He surveyed the near-empty room, his gaze lingering on the patched holes in the walls, the stains outlining where paintings and photos once hung, the various points throughout the room where a million memories flashed by. "I can't live here without Sully."

"I'm sure it's hard, but —"

"You have no idea what it's like."

"I only meant —"

"No. You've spent your life pushing people away. When those you know die, it's an inconvenience. It doesn't rip your soul out of your chest."

That hit scored, but Roni tried to let it flow away. He was hurting and lashing out. Even if he did so on purpose, she could be understanding. After all, she loved Sully, too. She missed the old man. Not as strongly as Elliot or Gram, but then, she had not fought by Sully's side more than half her life. Still, she comprehended the idea. Should she and Teanna manage to live a full life, and decades in the future Teanna were to die first, Roni could see how devastating it would be.

"Sorry," she said. "You're family to me, and I hate to see you leave the bookstore. That's all."

Cooling, he put out his hand. When she walked over, he held her and kissed the back of her fingers. "I didn't mean to yell at you."

"That was hardly yelling."

"This isn't easy for me. I love the bookstore, too. But it is necessary."

"You've obviously been getting ready for a while. Part of your retirement, I guess."

"I have never said —"

"Not that I'm going to allow that to happen." Roni gestured to the empty room. "I don't know how I missed it."

"I knew it would upset you, so I made sure to have the furniture removed when you were out of town working."

"You must have a place picked out. Where are you moving to? I mean it can't be that far from here. You don't drive much, or do you plan to spend some nights at the bookstore?" Roni knew how foolish she sounded, but she refused to let him get comfortable with other possibilities.

"I haven't decided where to go, yet."

"But all of your stuff."

"I'll find my way. Don't worry. However, this isn't why I asked you here. Not entirely." With his cane he pointed to one box marked *Books*. "That is for the Grand Library. I trust you'll see them properly indexed and shelved."

"Of course."

"Please get the book that's on the top."

She opened the box, and sitting on the pile of others, a book covered in black leather waited. No title. Just a symbol similar to an Egyptian hieroglyph.

"This one?" She held it up.

"Yes. Bring it here." He opened the book. Its pages were thin and the print miniscule. "In the kitchen, you'll find a magnifying glass next to the sink. Please get it for me."

When Roni returned from the kitchen, Elliot had spread the book on his lap and leaned in close. Her curiosity blended with an unusual tension. Trying to stay calm and patient, she waited as Elliot used the magnifying glass, moving his head across one line after another, mumbling to himself as he read. At length, he stabbed a finger at one particular section and handed the glass to Roni.

"Take a look," he said.

She bent closer to the book, bringing the glass in and out until she found the proper focal length. "Oh," she said. Before she had a read a word, she saw the symbol — a triangle over a circle with three dots in the center.

From her pocket, she pulled out the yellowed paper taken from the

Scholar. The same triangle symbol appeared numerous times on the page.

"What's it mean?" she asked.

He shrugged. "I only thought to look in Sully's books this morning. When I saw this, I called you first thing. But I suspect that if you let me work with that paper, I can decode some of it. Perhaps enough to help us."

Roni shoved down the swelling in her chest. "So, then, you're staying? I mean I know you're going to leave this apartment, but you'll still work for the Parallel Society, right?"

"That was never in doubt."

She refrained from saying *It was to me.* Yet despite Elliot's implied promise that he would always be working with her, she sensed that he held back something. Declarations and emotions trembled on his lips but were never released. She could hound him into opening up. She knew how, and with his fragile state regarding Sully, it would be easier than normal. But part of her reined in the idea — after all, did she really want to know?

Instead, she wrapped him into a hug and kissed his cheek. "Okay. Good." She handed over the paper. "You translate this. See if you can find anything useful. I'm going to do the same from the only other angle we have open."

"Which is?"

"Teanna. She's got to know something."

"True," he said with a thoughtful turn of his brow. "Be careful with her. Gentle. She's been through a traumatic experience and she's from another world. We have no idea how she will react to her situation."

"I'm not a monster."

"I am not suggesting you are. I merely want you to check your enthusiasm. Make sure she's ready to talk. And then listen. That's the most important. Listen to what she tells you so that she never has to tell it again."

"I'll be careful. But she's tougher than you're giving her credit for."

"I have no doubt. But I also know —"

"You worry too much." Roni started out the door. "I guess that's part of why I love you. Call me if you find anything important in that paper."

Chapter 19

When Roni returned to the apartment, Teanna had awoken, straightened her bed, showered, and stared out the window in their small living/dining/everything room. Maintaining the peaceful quiet, Roni started the coffee machine and took a rag to things already clean to be cleaned again. When the enticing aroma of the brewed coffee wafted throughout the apartment, she poured two mugs and offered one to Teanna. Then she sat next to her friend and shared a look at the town of Olburg as it awakened for another day.

"I just met with Elliot," she said, keeping her voice soft. "He might be able to figure out that paper I brought back."

She didn't expect Teanna to answer, yet she still experienced a drop when only silence filled her friend's gap in the conversation.

"Anyway, it'll take time, and everybody seems pretty shook up over last night, so I thought maybe you and I could go out for the day."

Teanna turned her head slightly — interest or anger, Roni couldn't tell.

"Don't worry. We're not forgetting the Scholar. But we're in no shape to fight that thing yet. We need to understand our enemy better anyway. Elliot's taking care of that. But we also need you in good shape, and you are not — understandably, of course. Come on. Let's go catch an early movie and grab lunch after."

With several long sips of coffee, Teanna finally nodded. Roni didn't think it would be that easy, but she also knew how to take a win when it came. She quickly swished her finger along her phone until she found a movie playing at 10:30 am, and they headed out. Without a word, they drove to the theater, parked the car, walked in, and settled in their seats. As the lights doused, it occurred to Roni that Teanna had only agreed to this because it was a silent activity. For the next two hours, she could have her peace. Well, for Roni, it went both ways. She craved a little peace, too — from the stress of trying to pull Teanna back, from knowing that when the movie ended and lunch began, she would have to try harder.

Time sped up, devouring two hours in minutes, and before either woman felt ready, they had left the theater. Hunger pushed them to the Italian place on the corner — Maria's Pizza. They ordered cheesesteaks and waited in yet more silence. When the red plastic baskets arrived, they tucked into the food, happily gorging in order to avoid speaking. But even that did not last long enough.

Stifling a belch, Roni watched Teanna for any sign she would be heard. Teanna, however, could have been a mannequin posed to annoy Roni with a defiant glower. The thing that got under Roni's skin most — that she recognized herself. Teanna behaved much like Roni had in the past. Cold, stoic, belligerent, unresponsive — all rolled up. A childish response to those looking from the outside, but from the inside, Roni knew it was sound strategy. At least, sound to someone struggling to make sense of a tormenting situation.

Luckily, Roni also had the history of how Gram, Elliot, and Sully had reacted to her. She could take an approach based on what had worked and what had failed. Which led her to searching her past, looking for a memory that would help.

Without preamble, she launched into speaking, allowing the sudden sound to startle Teanna into paying attention. "I don't know how much Gram has told you of my past, but there's a story I've heard her repeat at parties and such, so it's possible you've heard this one before. Anyway, when I was a kid — maybe nine or ten — I was invited to a birthday. Gram was very excited for me, and I'm pretty sure I was excited, too. This was after my Lost Time, so Gram lived with a lot of guilt, and I think she wanted me to have a wonderful time, some splash of normalcy.

"I don't remember who was the birthday boy or girl, but I certainly remember the party — it was at the Philly Zoo. All the kids met at the birthday kid's house, and we went to the zoo in a bus, and while several complained in an effort to sound older or cooler, most of us were on board with the idea. I certainly was. The Philly Zoo was a blast with all of us digging the usual suspects — the elephants and giraffes and chimpanzees and such. Even the kids trying to be cool got into it. The zoo had a special picnic area for us to eat cake and watch the presents being opened. Afterward, they brought a pony out, and anybody who wanted to ride got to ride. You better believe I was right in that line."

Roni sipped her cola. Partly because she was thirsty. Mostly because she needed a moment. The opening of her tale had been stretched as far as she dared, and now she had to get to the center of it all. If this didn't work, if Teanna refused to open up, what then? Elliot moves out and Teanna becomes some rogue actor. Doubtful that Garcia would stick around after the others left. Gram would remain. Gully, too. But neither would have much faith left in Roni. As far as she could see, that was the optimistic outcome.

Setting her cola back on the table, Roni wiped her mouth. Teanna waited. Not impatiently — perhaps even with a spark of interest.

Roni continued, "I had to watch a few kids go before me. They got in the saddle, and one of the zoo staff walked the pony around a large circle. Finally, I got my chance. I hopped up and got comfy. I'm sure I was beaming.

"But then one of the parents helping run the party had some question for the lady controlling the pony. I wasn't listening. I was imagining being on a full-sized horse, taking the reins in hand, guiding the animal whichever way I wanted. They're off chatting, I'm off dreaming, and I don't know if it was my fault — maybe I accidentally acted out my imagination. Or it may have had nothing to do with me — maybe another kid or a sound or something spooked the pony. Whatever got it going, that animal took off at a full gallop. I grabbed hold of the pony's mane and held on for dear life.

"Looking back as an adult, I'm sure we didn't go far before other zoo staff jumped in and calmed the pony. I doubt it lasted long at all. But for me, it felt horrifying and seemed to last forever. The worst of it — at that moment — was knowing I had no idea how to stop this animal. I didn't think of it as a sentient creature that would avoid smashing through a fence or that it would get tired or anything like that. To me, it was a machine gone crazy, and I was helpless to stop it. Oh, and I screamed. Full-on, high-pitched screaming.

"When it was over, when I got back to safety, I cried and I probably ruined that party. I mean everybody was nice about it. They all tried to console me, and the parents tried to get the party back on track. But all the nice things they said, all the attempts to be helpful, just upset me more."

Teanna dropped her head to one side and gestured to herself.

"This is different," Roni said. "The fate of a universe-saving group did not rest on me. Not back then. Just listen, I'm almost done.

Because I didn't say anything for almost a week. Gram and Elliot and Sully — they all tried to get me to talk, but I wasn't having it. One night, I overheard them in discussion about me. Gram was concerned that I had suffered such trauma that I might need a shrink. Elliot said that no, I was fine. Just angry and scared and full of doubt. Even Sully said that the whole experience had been too painful and frightening to talk about. But they were all wrong.

"Once I got over the initial fear, once I was safe again and back home, I didn't care about any of that. The reason I didn't talk, didn't want to see my friends, didn't want any contact was simple — I was humiliated."

Teanna's hand flopped down causing the forks and knives to jangle. "You think I was humiliated?" Her voice cut across the table.

"I don't know. How could I? This is the most you've said since we got back. But I'll tell you this — it helped me to talk with Elliot and Sully about my problems."

"I am not a little nine-year-old girl afraid of a pony."

"I didn't mean to imply —"

"I'm angry. You understand that? I left my world to join the Parallel Society because I believe in its mission. But since Sully died, the whole thing has fallen apart."

"I'm trying my best."

"You're not. You're that same little girl afraid of looking bad. So much so that you can't function the way you should. Because of you, nobody knows what to expect of anybody. We're all just going along like we've always done, and that worked fine at first, but cracks form when you let things go." Teanna gripped the sides of the table. "You think I wanted to go off on my own all those times? You think that was fun for me? I went because nobody would make the call otherwise. Nobody would stand up and find those relics, form a plan —"

"Like hell." Roni scowled as she made a fist. "You just didn't like my plans because they weren't what you wanted to do. All of you have treated me like that, like I'm a surrogate leader and you're waiting for the real one to take over."

"You want credit without earning it."

"I have earned it. For years before you came along. If anything, you should be proving yourself to me."

Teanna stood, still locked onto the table, her dark skin turning pale as she tightened her hold. "I'm not the one trying to be in charge. You want the position? You have to earn it over and over again. That's part of the deal. That's how you get us all to respect your views, your plans, your judgment."

Roni popped to her feet, pointing right into Teanna's face. "I can't earn anything because you've already decided that I'm not worth it."

"Oh, you are such a fool. I give you chance after chance after chance. Even now, I'm waiting for you to do the right thing, but instead, you want to argue and whine."

"What magical right thing is that? Praise you for going off on your own, nearly getting killed, and nearly killing the rest of us in trying to rescue you?"

With a sharp motion, Teanna lifted the table an inch and slammed it down. "The right thing would be to stop worrying about me, trust that you know me to be tough enough to handle myself, and ask me to share what I learned about the Scholar."

"Hey," a chubby man with thick, black hair stepped from behind the front counter. "Both of you get out of here before I call the cops."

Roni looked around — several customers stared back, food halfway to mouths, eyes bulging in shock. "I'm sorry," she said. "We didn't mean to get so loud."

"Well, you did and I don't want that in my restaurant. Get out."

Thankfully, Teanna did not protest. Roni walked back to the car, unsure if Teanna would get in. But when she put her hand on the car door, Roni relaxed. A little.

"I didn't ask you about anything yet because I was trying to give you the space to process what happened to you."

Teanna said, "You should know me better."

"Fine. Since you're all okay, let's hear it — what do you know about the Scholar?"

Getting into the car, Teanna grinned. "Everything."

CHAPTER 20

Teanna refused to elaborate until the entire Society sat together. She made it clear she did not intend to be cruel or punish Roni, but rather, she wanted everyone to hear the same information at the same time to avoid confusion.

"I think we've had enough of that," she said, and her tone told Roni these words were not said in spite, just in truth. That was comforting. It suggested that Teanna did not hate her or feel betrayed by her or had given up on her. Roni thought she had a chance to salvage their friendship.

When they entered *In the Bind*, several customers perused the shelves. Gram sat up front by the register. Upon seeing them, she hurried around the counter and swept Teanna into a big hug.

"There wasn't time to give you a proper welcome last night. I prayed that you weren't harmed by all that happened, and I can see the Lord provided. You look strong."

"I feel strong."

Roni said, "We need to have the whole group together. Teanna has some important things to share."

"I'll close the store," Gram said. Then she rolled her eyes toward the ceiling. "Garcia and Gully are in the workshop. They've been arguing for at least twenty minutes."

"About what?"

"I didn't ask. I heard the shouting, told them to make sure the customers didn't hear it, and got back here to work."

Roni let out a frustrated sigh. "I'll take care of it. When you're done with the store, please get Elliot and meet us up there."

A quick ride on the elevator and Roni entered the workshop. Teanna opted to help Gram — a choice Roni had no intention of disputing.

Garcia leaned against one wall with his arms folded and his scowl directed across the room. Gully stood on the receiving end, his fists planted at his sides, his jaw locked in defiance. The simmering argument rolled between them, giving Roni the clear sense that it would take little to spark up the yelling again.

She walked into the center of the room. "You only have a few minutes until everyone is here for Teanna's report. I don't care which one of you explains the problem, but it better be done calmly."

"Easy for me," Gully said. "Him, not so much."

Garcia pushed off the wall. "Hey, I'm not the one who wants to change everything after I've spent months getting this space perfectly situated."

"I'm not asking for everything to change."

"You certainly don't care about my contribution to the Society."

"All I said was that I have seniority."

"Quiet," Roni said, struggling not to yell herself. "Both of you." Once they settled back — still pouting and glaring — she pointed to Gully. "What is it you want changed?"

Laying on a thicker Sully-like accent, Gully said, "You've seen what I've done in the field — made my own golems. I want to continue that work. The better I get at it, the better I can help you and the Society. So, I merely asked Garcia if I might have some of Sully's old workspace. That's all."

Garcia shook his fist in the air. "You told me I should get out and let you redo the workshop."

"Is that true?" Roni asked.

With a guilty bounce to his head, Gully said, "I may have over-expressed myself. I didn't mean it to sound so cruel. But he doesn't need all of the workshop to mix ingredients. A table in the corner should suffice."

"A table! For my potions, I've got to have —"

"You've seen Sully make incredible golems. That takes a lot of room. If I bring in a six-foot slab of clay, where am I going to put it?"

Roni put up her hand to silence both. She then turned to Garcia. "Calmly, now, please tell me your side of this."

"I think my side is obvious. Elliot gave me Sully's workshop so that I could become the potion-maker all of you need me to be. That requires space for ingredient storage, space for my books, space for preparation, and of course, the space involved in creating these delicate concoctions. But Gully thinks he can barge in and demand that I rework my entire design to accommodate him because he has a new hobby."

Gully said, "It's not a hobby. I have a new skill for the Society that could be far greater than your potions."

"I highly doubt that."

"Why? Because I'm a golem? That's racist."

"Golems aren't a race. You aren't even human."

"Then it's prejudice."

"Doesn't matter. You can make your clay toys anywhere. I need a controlled environment for my potions."

"You were making them out of the car trunk last night."

"Which could have ended terribly for us all."

"I'm only asking for a small section of the workshop."

"Sure, now that Roni is here. Before, you wanted me out completely."

"Then we should have her decide. She's the leader, anyway. She's the one who should say which of us gets the workshop."

Putting out both hands, Roni said, "Enough. I'm sick of it. You all want me to give orders, make these decisions, yet if I do just that, then you all get angry and tell me why I'm wrong. No more of that. Garcia, you're an adult. Act like it. Gully, you've got the mind of an adult. You can act like it, too. The both of you work this out and do so fast. We have the Scholar to deal with — a real problem — so I don't need to be worrying about this bull."

Both man and golem had the sense to look ashamed. Garcia said, "What about Elliot's apartment? Gully could use that?"

"No," Roni said with enough force to brook no argument.

Garcia finally lifted his head. "We'll talk later."

Gully nodded. "I'm sure there's a solution."

"Good," Roni said. "Now clear a space for a meeting. Gram, Elliot, and Teanna will be here any minute."

Like sullen children, Garcia and Gully cleaned up the workshop. Roni couldn't decide if she had handled things the best way, but it certainly satisfied. When Gram entered, she shot a quizzical look at Roni, but otherwise, she said nothing. Elliot and Teanna soon followed, and as they took time to watch Garcia and Gully, Roni stepped forward.

"Teanna is going to run this meeting," she said and sat.

There was a short moment of uncomfortable stillness. They all must have expected her to keep rambling on, but Roni had no interest in playing that game. Whether they liked it or not, her focus had always been on the Society's mission — protecting the universe. Being the star of a business meeting meant nothing. Probably meant nothing in any organization, but in the Society, that went doubly so.

Teanna exchanged a nod with Roni before standing in front the group. With her braids tied back, she looked more serious and more in control than usual. Roni wondered if Teanna knew the effect she had created.

"I'm not a speechmaker, so forgive me if I don't say things the right way."

Gram tilted forward and touched Teanna's arm. "There is no right way or wrong way for this kind of talk. You just tell us what you need to, dear."

"I guess the first thing to know, then, is that when I was under the Scholar's control, I was also aware. All the time, I could feel what my body did, could hear what was said around me, and understand how stuck I was. I want to thank all of you for freeing me from that. To somebody like me, it was a nightmare."

Garcia said, "I'd think it would be a nightmare for anybody."

"That's wrong. I thought the same, but when you are connected to the Scholar, you are also connected to the others, too. The whole town thought like one collective, but also, I could hear the individuals. As much as it disgusted me, I could hear and feel how some of them found the experience comforting."

"That's crazy."

Elliot said, "Not at all. Many people — most, in fact — prefer to have somebody else run things. We love to complain about our government or our bosses or even the coach of our sports team, but most people have no desire to do those jobs. After all, it's easy to point out how wrong things are. It's so much harder to fix them."

"Right or wrong," Teanna said, "I could feel that's the way many in the town thought. And we should be glad for it because it made them complacent — which eased the Scholar's vigilance over us. That creature saw how plenty of the brains it used were content to be used, so it did not take much notice when I did what I could."

Gully chuckled. "I should've known you wouldn't let any opportunity go to waste. You're a good soldier that way. Other ways too, of course. So, tell us — what trick did you manage to pull off?"

"Simple enough — I noticed that in order for the Scholar to

command us, it needed feedback. Communication had to go in both directions between us. Since it was consumed with its calculations, I suspected I could poke around its other thoughts undetected. I tried, anyway, and I had some good luck."

Garcia stepped up next to Gully, and the two shared a joyful smile. "I like the way this is sounding."

Roni ignored their sudden change in attitude. If she had pointed it out, their fight might have resumed. Instead, she asked Teanna, "What did you learn from that blob with hands?"

"For one thing, that's just the baby," Teanna said.

Garcia's smile dropped. "I don't like the way *that's* sounding."

"It's still growing. That's part of why it needs the townspeople. Its own brain can't handle the computations on its own. Even when it's fully formed, it'll still need some extra brainpower, but not as much."

Elliot said, "When will it be fully formed?"

"Not long. A few days, maybe less. But we're getting the story all out of joint."

Not so easy, Roni thought, but she said, "Please, everybody, just let her talk."

"This all begins with Yal-hara." Teanna put up a hand to silence anybody who wanted to interrupt — especially Roni.

Though Roni kept her mouth closed, she seethed at the thought of that spindle-legged creature being the root of this plagued tree. Yal-hara had done more harm than any other living relic this incarnation of the Parallel Society had ever faced. And the harm she had done to Roni — the terror, the Lost Time, the deceit, the betrayal, and the death of Sully — all of it and more rested at the creature's numerous feet.

Teanna continued, "After she attacked the bookstore and failed, she did not give up. We never thought she would, and we were right. What we missed was the fact that she had not used all her relic boxes then. She still had one left. She held it back from the fight because she believed it contained an embryo for the Scholar, or a Scholar. I'm not too sure if there is more than one because it's not too sure.

"But for Yal-hara, she had no way to know unless she opened the box. If she was wrong, she might have unleashed another violent creature — one she would have to deal with herself. But after all that happened, she had little choice. That was how she saw things. Once she made her initial moves against us, there was no going back to the peaceful prison the Society had constructed around her. She wanted her freedom. She still wants it.

"So, she opened the box. Luckily, for her, the box did contain the beginnings of the Scholar. She's spent much of the time since helping it grow and strengthen. The initial attacks on the town — Yal-hara led those. Helped the Scholar convert people until it could function on its own, too. Of course, the pale man pitched in. In fact, eventually the Scholar will use the pale man, absorb him, until he has taken his form. Then it'll be able to move on legs and have a more substantial body. Until then, it relies on its allies — especially Yal-hara. And now, she's ready to use the Scholar."

Gram locked eyes with Elliot. "She's trying to find another way out of our universe. One that doesn't require the Caverns or my books."

"Such as what?" Elliot said. "The only other openings are the rifts we capture, and those are unpredictable."

Teanna said, "Only unpredictable to most. That's the other reason the Scholar needs so many brains working for it — the task is immense. Yal-hara wants the Scholar to calculate the intersection of specific universes with ours. She's trying to find one that is suitable to her, then time its location and appearance perfectly so she can walk through the rift when it arrives — before the Parallel Society can reach it to stop her."

"I have a question," Garcia said, scratching his beard. "I know she's bad and I've helped you all fight against her, but wouldn't it be better for us to just take her to the Caverns and let her go? It's our job to get her out of our universe, and that's what she wants, too."

Speaking harsher than she probably wanted, Gram said, "Yal-hara is a vicious and dangerous beast. She has caused a great amount of damage here and must pay for it. We continue to confine her to this world as part of that punishment, but also, as a necessary protection of other universes. Because she doesn't wish to simply leave. She has always sought other worlds she could dominate. So, no, we will not get rid of our disease by sluffing her out to infect another world. That would be sinful."

Elliot said, "That paper Roni acquired during Teanna's rescue — it must be part of this complex calculation. If we're lucky, it could be a vital part. I still cannot figure it out, but that may not be important. The fact that the Scholar does not have it could set back Yal-hara's plans."

"If she misses her opportunity, then dear Lord, the Scholar would have to start all over again."

"No," Teanna said. "Anything on paper has long since been put into the machinery of those brains. And the Scholar's own memory is deep and enormous. That paper is now nothing more than scribbles touched by a living relic."

Gully snickered. "I suppose that makes the paper a bit of a relic, too."

The words shot through Roni and she sprang to her feet. An idea raced around her head, but to do it would mean having to reveal things to the group that might undercut her leadership. No, not *might*. It would definitely undercut her. Then again, she didn't have much leadership at the moment. Unless …

"What is it, dear?" Gram finally said.

Roni lifted her head to see the entire room watching her. But they weren't eager eyes. They weren't the eyes of soldiers looking to their general, expecting an answer to how they'll deal with a tough enemy. That would be asking too much. For Roni, the eyes that fell upon her fell with wariness. They waited with tentativeness, with caution, even a little fear.

"This can't go on," she said, not meaning for the words to come out. But before anybody could question her, she answered for herself. "I have something I must do. I want everybody to get ready. We'll be dealing with Yal-hara soon enough. Garcia, make all the potions you need. Gram and Elliot, we'll be meeting down in Gram's basement study. Please get it ready and pull out the most detailed map we have of Pennsylvania. Teanna, sharpen those hatchets."

Roni headed to the door when Gully said, "What should I do?"

She stopped and turned back. "You need to start doing what you were built to do. Stay by my side and protect me."

"Always."

Chapter 21

The elevator doors closed leaving Roni and Gully standing on the fourth floor. She glanced into the reading room with its simple square of carpet and two chairs. A tremble vibrated across her shoulders.

"I need you to stay here," she said.

"No, no. I should be with you. Like you said — I'm to be by your side, protecting you."

"I know. But I don't think the room will function if you're in there."

"I don't understand that. How does this room function?"

"Not this one. The next room — the leader's office." She forced a grin. "I'll be fine. Throughout the history of the Parallel Society, leaders have used this special room to help them."

"Did Sully use it?"

"He never had the chance."

"Then Gram did. We can ask her about it."

"She never used it, either."

Gully frowned. "None of this is convincing me to let you go in there alone."

She placed a hand on his cheek. "I don't have to convince you. I'm ordering you to stay here. Make sure nobody disturbs me. And don't come in unless I call for you." She glanced in the direction of the office. Then: "Or if I scream. If I'm screaming, you can come in."

As she turned away, Gully said, "I'm sorry. About before. I should not have fought with Garcia. It was not helpful to the cohesion of the team, and I suppose I've failed in protecting you from these problems by making them worse. Well, no more. I promise I will fix the situation with Garcia, and you won't be bothered by it. You have my word."

Roni strolled across the reading room, her attention on the hidden door in the back. The landscapes of strange worlds in other universes became background noise to her. The portraits of previous leaders, the blank canvas set aside for Gram, and the quiet way her feet shushed across the carpeting — it ceased to weigh on her. Not because she felt strong enough to bear it. Rather, it simply didn't match the overwhelming burden of knowing Yal-hara had been behind their current problems.

As Roni turned to the left and pressed the recessed panel in the corner, as the wall opened upon the metal door, her mind teetered back and forth over that evil creature. She wanted to rip Yal-hara into pieces, yet she also wanted to hide. Her anger prodded her while her memories yanked her back. That was the worst. In one breath, Roni could be a fearless, aggressive leader of the Society, confident that she knew how to deal with their nemesis. In that same breath, she could be an eight-year-old girl watching the twisted living relic crawl over her, ready to swipe her memories.

When Roni used Gram's key, the door opened and she entered the utterly plain, mostly empty office. Only a few fluorescent light bars and that single metal chair. And Roni's nerves, too.

She approached the chair with prudence — slow, careful steps as if worried she might frighten an animal. But the chair did not move. She laughed at herself. Of course, it didn't. It was a damn chair.

She glanced back at the door. A simple call for Gully and he would arrive in seconds. She could skip over this part and join the others in the basement.

But then she thought of all the Society leaders who came before her. Gram had said many of them sat in their office chairs. None had died from the experience. At least, she never found record of any such deaths in the Grand Library. Besides, Gram would never have shown it to Roni if it could cause harm.

"I'm stalling," she said, the words coming out like a jingle.

She walked back to the door. Her feet itched to run, to sprint back to the elevator, wrench Gully in and be done with this room. But she closed the door instead.

One thing above all turned her back to face that chair — Yal-hara. If she listened to her frightened heart, if she grabbed Gully and left, if she went ahead with the plan formulating in the back of her mind, if she did all of that and failed, then forever she would know she could have done more. She would know that Yal-hara had won, had escaped, because she refused to live up to her responsibilities — to her family, to her friends, to the Society, to the world, to the universe.

Slumping her way to the chair once more, she allowed her horrible memories of Yal-hara to play out. They wrenched her insides around, at first. But then, as she neared the chair, those images set fire within her.

"Whatever it takes," she said, looking at the chair.

And she sat.

The tingling in her legs started and the vibrations radiated throughout her body. Lifting her chin, she tried to look confident and prepared as if she expected everything that might happen. But when she heard the voice behind her, she flinched and all that faux-attitude dribbled away.

"You came back," the voice said.

Roni wanted to rise from the chair, but the last time she had done so, the person disappeared. She needed to have patience, to let this play out however it was intended to. Quelling her nerves with a hard swallow, she said, "The Society is counting on me. I have to try everything I can."

"That sounds about right." Steady footsteps sounded off as the person walked into view. "I hope you're ready for this."

A young woman stepped in front of Roni — a woman Roni recognized immediately. How could she not? She saw that face every single day when she looked in the mirror.

"What are you?" Roni asked, bending down to peek under the chair. "Is this some kind of illusion?"

"You won't find any machinery or projectors or anything like that," her double said. "Before you ask, I'm not a sophisticated golem, either. I really am you."

Too confused to be scared, Roni said, "How? Are you from a parallel universe?"

"No, but the room and the chair are part of the Caverns, so it's possible we're standing in another universe — but not parallel. Think of it this way — just like the connection to the Caverns has been relocated from one version of the Parallel Society to another over the centuries, this room and chair are also relocated. And just like the caverns have a long history, so does all of this. In each iteration, the room looks like an empty space that belongs to whatever time period it exists within. Now, the chair changes, too. It is more of a manifestation based on the needs of the leader."

"So, if Gram had ever bothered to come in here, she would've had a different chair?"

"Absolutely."

"And mine is a damn metal folding chair?"

"Practical, sturdy, foundational — that seems about right."

Roni shook her head. "Basic. That's what it is. Why aren't you insulted? Or does parallel me not care about how she's seen?"

"Not parallel. Pay attention. And I do care, but not in the same way. See, I'm part of you but I'm also my own being. I have my own history, my own desires, my own life."

"Isn't that the definition of a parallel universe? You exist as a copy of me. One that had experienced a life with different choices."

"Except I didn't exist until you sat down. When you stand, I'll cease to exist."

"Not entirely. You remembered me when I came back."

"Of course, I did. I told you that I'm part you."

"How?"

"It doesn't matter, and frankly, I don't understand it anyway. We're here to work on you. That's the whole purpose of this."

With a bitter laugh, Roni said, "Hope you have a lot of time."

Her double laughed right back. "Oh, don't worry about that. Time doesn't exist here. Or, at least, not in the same way. You'd have to be here for years before it would matter to your world." Crouching down so they were level, she added, "You ready to begin?"

"I don't know." Roni started to get up, but her double pushed her back.

"If you get off that chair, this room shuts down. I'll disappear."

Sitting back, Roni folded her arms. "Fine. Let's see what you got. What do I call you? I'm Roni. You can't be Roni, too."

"You're welcome to it. I've always preferred our full name — Veronica."

"How can you say you've *always preferred?* According to you, you only came into existence a few minutes ago."

"And yet, I have a preference. Go figure. Do you want to hang out here and try to solve the mysteries of how the rifts operate, how the Cavern exists at all, and how it connects up here? Or do you want to get down to your purpose in sitting in that chair?"

"Okay, okay. No need to be bitchy about it."

"Insult me and you're insulting yourself."

Roni rolled her eyes. "Wonderful. This is going to be so much fun."

Veronica walked a slow circle in the room, tying her hair back in the process. When she finished, she stood in front of Roni looking far too familiar.

"I think the first thing you've forgotten is that you can lead. You already know how."

"Gee, thanks for stating the obvious. My problem isn't that I don't know how to lead. The problem is that my team no longer trusts me enough to follow."

"Strange," Veronica said in such a patronizing way, Roni wanted to stand if only to make her double vanish. But she waited until Veronica made a show of thoughtful consideration. Then Veronica said, "You've led this team before. Several times. What do you think changed?"

"How should I know? Isn't that why I'm here?"

"You'll do better if you think of me less like an answer machine and more like your therapist."

"In that case, I'm leaving. I don't need therapy."

Veronica snorted a laugh. "Honey, everybody needs therapy. Now quit acting like a baby and start thinking."

"That's not how a therapist should talk."

"First, I don't think you've ever been to therapy, so you wouldn't know. Second, I said to think of me *like your therapist.* I never claimed to have a license or anything. Okay? Are we done with your stalling? You do love to stall."

Roni squirmed in the chair. If only she could stand and pace — or punch. But all she had available was to clasp her elbows tight and cross her legs. And scowl. She could scowl hard.

In response, Veronica smirked. But before that reaction could provoke Roni into further bluster, Veronica said, "Something must have changed. Lately, you've been acting cold and distant to everybody. And you try to control them — harshly sometimes."

"I do not. And if I do, I've been given plenty of reason not to trust that they'll follow my original orders."

"Sure. Okay. But you weren't always at odds with them. So, what changed?"

"Garcia joined the group. That's been the biggest change recently. Maybe having him involved was a mistake. Maybe that's what's broken the unity of the group."

As if considering the idea, Veronica bounced her head in thought. "Perhaps. But really, he's been nothing but supportive."

"Are you kidding? He argues with me all the time."

"Challenging, true, but didn't you do the same to Gram when you first joined?"

"That was different."

"In some ways. Then again, anybody joining a tight-knit group like the Society is going to have a hard time finding how they fit in. Do you still argue with him all the time?"

Roni considered it. "I guess not. Not as much. He has been a great help with his potions. I mean, he clearly wants us to succeed."

"Do you think he wants *you* to succeed?"

"Absolutely. Why wouldn't he?"

"Well, what about the others — Gram, Elliot, Teanna, Gully? Do you think they want you to succeed?"

"Of course." Roni couldn't believe she was getting angry at herself, but then everything about this conversation irritated her. Not only because it was so bizarre, but also because Veronica knew exactly where she led the conversation but wouldn't just come out and say it. And Roni understood — she had to figure it out; otherwise, the lesson would not truly be learned. That's the way human beings operated. Doesn't matter that Gram had warned the stove was hot. Roni still had to touch it to learn.

"Then your entire team wants you to succeed, and the addition of Garcia is not enough to warrant the change you've seen. What else has changed?"

"Nothing really."

Veronica released a teenager's groan. "Lying to me is lying to yourself, and that's never a good thing to do. Come on, now. Stop hiding and admit what we both know. What else changed?"

Roni shrugged.

"Don't give me that crap. You know. Say it."

"Say what?"

"His name. Let's start there. Say his name."

Clenching her fists, she said, "Fine. Sully. You happy? Sully died and that changed everything. I'm not going to keep sitting here and be psychoanalyzed by myself."

"I'm not going to do that. You wouldn't, so I wouldn't. But you haven't actually dealt with this loss, yet. Sully died. He broke up the team, and you have gone right into his job."

"I was expected to. It wasn't by choice."

"You stepped up."

"I did. And now Gram and Elliot resent me for it. They don't ever say it, but they don't really think of me as a leader. Teanna? She was starting to love the old man, and now her roomie and friend is also her boss. How's that supposed to work? Garcia has his own trouble fitting into a position held by a beloved man for so long. Everything is screwed up, so how could I possibly expect it to be otherwise?" The words babbled out in an exhaled rush that left Roni breathing hard.

"All of that is true, but none of it matters."

"What? Isn't that the whole point of us talking? I want to find the problem and fix it. Clearly, you think — or I think to tell myself — that the problem is losing Sully."

"Almost." Veronica knelt by Roni's side. "Everything you've pointed out — those are your team's individual problems. But you left somebody out."

"Gully? He's still directly connected through Sully's instructions. Always will be. Plus, he's a golem. He's only as real as Sully made him."

Veronica placed a hand on Roni's knee. "No, not Gully."

"That's everybody on the team. Unless you mean me."

"Bingo." She stood and walked behind Roni. "It's time for you to say goodbye."

When Veronica returned, she walked with an old man on her arm. A slightly bent, bespectacled old man. Roni's throat lumped. She lurched to the edge of the chair — almost stood — before she recalled that doing so would make the whole thing disappear. Sully was too real at the moment to allow that.

"Is it you?" she asked, feeling foolish as the words left her.

Sully put up his hands. "Who's to say? I feel real to me. But I know I'm dead, too, so perhaps I'm not real, after all. I couldn't tell you."

A laugh escaped her lips and a cry caught in her mouth. "I miss you."

"And I you."

"I've made a mess of everything."

"Oh, it's not so bad. Squish over. Let an old man sit with you."

Roni inched aside, and when this version of Sully settled next to her, she could smell the mixture of age and a glass of wine.

He let out a breath as if winded. "That's better."

She pulled him into a long embrace, her body shaking with tears. When she tried to speak, an anguished moan came out of her. That sound sent her into a convulsion of sorrow. She could feel him patting her arm, and that seemed to be enough. Veronica and Sully did not rush her. They simply waited as Roni cried out months of bottled tears.

CHAPTER 22

Closing the office door behind her, Roni stood in the reading room as the real world returned to her. She didn't know if mourning Sully would change much, but the act had cleared her head — at least, for the moment. Veronica had reminded Roni that she had led this group successfully in the past. She could do it again.

She checked the time on her phone. Three minutes since she had gone in. Not hours. Yet she knew she had spent hours with Sully. After the cries had petered out, she sat there with him and discussed Gram and Elliot. He told her about some of their early exploits — things she had heard many times before but always enjoyed hearing. She supposed he could only tell her things she already knew since he was a manifestation borne from within her. At least, she chose to believe that.

Still, she kissed the tips of her fingers and brushed them against the door. "Rest in peace."

Walking back to the elevator, her steps a bit stronger, she had to admit that chair, that room, did not provide an action plan to fix everything, but it had helped. If nothing else, she felt a surge of confidence that had been lacking of late. When considering what she intended to do, she needed all the strength she could get.

Gully lifted his head slightly as she approached. "That was fast."

"Not for me." She pulled back the elevator gate and paused. Might as well get started right away. "I need the Pages of Glass."

"I hardly think we're that desperate yet."

"It's not up to you to decide."

He tightened his mouth. "It sort of is. You entrusted me with holding these dangerous things. I wanted to destroy them, but you insisted I keep them safe. I've done that."

"A good job of it, too."

"I think part of that job is to make sure they aren't used unless absolutely necessary. The last possible act. That form of desperate."

"They're not bombs. And if what I think is right, they're going to stop Yal-hara before she can cause immense harm to countless worlds."

"I'm sure you believe that—"

Roni put out her hand, palm up. "Gully, enough. I'm ordering you to turn over the Pages of Glass. But I shouldn't have to. You should trust me."

"One thing — will you promise that when we are done with them this time, promise me that we'll destroy them."

"You have my word."

With a defeated sigh, Gully pressed against his chest and pulled the clay open. If the act caused pain, he did not show it, but Roni could see it wasn't a pleasant experience either. When he finished, he reached in and removed two paper-thin, emerald glass pages. He placed them into her open hand.

"Thank you." Roni stepped onto the elevator. "Let's go join the others."

"Um, one last thing."

"What?"

"Will you please help patch me back up? I don't want the rest of the Society to see me like this."

Roni swelled as she stepped back into the reading room. "Of course."

Completing the job of golem reconstruction took longer than Roni intended, but as they descended in the elevator, she could see the pleasure it gave Gully to be whole again. When they reached the basement, they weaved through the maze of old boxes containing older magazines and copies of books once popular enough to sell thousands and thousands of copies but now cluttered up the floorspace. Gram's office sat behind a large door that often was blocked by yet more boxes. But Roni rarely thought of this space as Gram's. Rather, it was the conduit to the Caverns that began at the gash in the back wall.

"Good," Gram said, waving them over. "We were starting to worry."

"Only you were," Roni said and gave Gram a short squeeze on the arm. "What do we have?"

On a small table, Elliot had opened flat an atlas. Teanna and Garcia stood next to each other as they looked over a map of the Pennsylvania Catskills.

Elliot pointed to several black felt-tip marks on the map. "We've plotted out where the town is — the one you and Garcia were in."

"I was there, too," Teanna said.

"Yes. Likewise, you all were inside the high school which we've marked right here."

Roni said, "What are the red marks?"

"Those are where we have had various encounters with Yal-hara or her representatives."

Loaded with an energetic rush, Garcia sped along, "If you think about how brazen the Scholar has been, taking over an entire town, it suggests to us that the Scholar expects this rift to open soon. Or that Yal-hara is impatient and is pushing the Scholar to locate a satisfactory rift as fast as possible. Because if not, then it would make more sense to gather the brain power over a longer period of time from a variety of sources so as not to ping the attention of anybody."

Gram said, "In the past, Yal-hara has always shown great patience. She could wait for years between moments of causing trouble. Until recently."

"Exactly. She's escalated. It speaks of desperation. Add to that the fact that both her and the Scholar cannot travel easily — I mean, neither of them looks remotely human — and from what I've been told, Yal-hara likes her comfort. Put all that together and it makes sense that she would want a rift nearby. No more than a few hours."

Teanna traced a large circle drawn on the map. "This is the area she'll be working within."

"Excellent work, everybody," Roni said.

Looking over the map, she thought about each dot and the horror they represented. A short moment later, she noticed the room had grown quiet. When she lifted her head, she found the entire team staring back at her.

"What?" she asked.

Gram snickered. "We're glad you like what we did."

Though Roni wanted to defend herself, she decided to let it go. Better to focus on the problems at hand rather than search for new ones. "Elliot, let me see the Scholar's paper, please."

When he handed it over, she pulled out the Pages of Glass. She could feel Gram tense and heard a sharp inhale from Garcia. Passing one of the Pages over the paper, she peered in and saw nothing. The same squiggles and symbols.

"Damn," she whispered.

"Language," Gram said.

"Sorry, but I really thought this would work." She set the Pages and the paper down.

Teanna pointed to the map. "What's that?"

Part of the Page rested atop the map, and a clear, bright dot could be seen like a twinkling star. Roni quickly positioned the Pages side by side to cover the entire atlas, but only one of the Pages of Glass lit up with a half-dozen dots.

"Why doesn't the one Page work?" Teanna asked.

Pushing closer, Garcia said, "Take the blank one and use it on the Scholar's paper first. It might work like some potions — some ingredients need to contact others first before they are capable of producing the results I want."

Roni thought it sounded dubious — great for potions, but this wasn't the same — yet she didn't want to undercut whatever goodwill she was feeling. She picked up the dormant Page and held it over the Scholar's work. Nothing happened. Yet when she placed it back on the map, four more dots appeared.

"I have to admit," Roni said, "I didn't think that would work."

Elliot said, "I did not, either. But we do know that the Pages react with other relics, and since the Scholar's paper was created by its hand, perhaps that is enough."

Perhaps. But Roni wondered if the Pages were more like the Leader's Office. Something greater than a relic. Something still connected to the Caverns.

Gram said, "It may be my old eyes, but I think those dots are different sizes."

"No, ma'am," Garcia said. "Your eyes are fine. They do vary in size."

A thrilling jolt hit Roni. "We know the Pages of Glass exist for one purpose — to find universes. That's why Yal-hara wanted them. She could use the Pages to explore all the captured rifts in the Caverns and pick out the ones she wanted to conquer. I also discovered that the Pages reacted to my map of the Caverns in the Grand Library."

Teanna's eyes widened, and Roni braced for a tirade about how irresponsible she had been for not sharing the information. Instead,

Teanna said, "If each one of these dots is a universe that the Pages can see, then these must be the places the Scholar is trying to calculate the locations for."

Gram said, "So what do the different sizes mean? Bigger universes? Larger rifts?"

Roni smiled as she locked eyes with Teanna. "We don't know, but it doesn't matter. Not yet." She pointed to the map. "Because there's only one dot within the active range we think Yal-hara can go. Birchville, Virginia."

Teanna's hand lowered to one of her hatchets. "We know where they're going to be."

CHAPTER 23

Despite everyone's desire to get moving immediately, Roni insisted they get some rest. It would be a long drive, and they would do better to leave in the early hours before sunrise. Though Teanna and Elliot disagreed, Gram backed Roni up as did Garcia and Gully. The astonishment that ripped through Roni left her dumbfounded. Not only had most of her team stuck by her, but the two dissenting voices accepted the decision.

It didn't make sense to her that simply acknowledging Sully's death, letting her sorrow loose, could have somehow regained the respect of her team — especially considering none of them knew any of it had happened. Something else had to be at play. The possibilities bounced around her head as she tried to catch a little sleep, but before she could think too long, her phone alarm went off. The team reassembled at the bookstore and with the sun an hour away from rising, they headed out.

Driving down into Virginia, they used two cars — Roni, Teanna, and Gully in one; Gram, Elliot, and Garcia in the other. After three hours through Pennsylvania to get to Route 81 and then south for another hour to get through bits of Maryland and West Virginia, they finally entered the target state, tired and anxious. The morning sun cast stunning golds across the sky as they sped along the highway.

"This is a beautiful land," Teanna said. "I don't think the people in your world have much appreciation for how lucky you all are."

Roni said, "That's a common theme with my world. Those of us who have things generally don't respect our good fortune. It's a perspective issue, and our brains are not adept at dealing with it."

"Is that why you've had such trouble with Sully's passing? Maybe your brain assumed he would always be around, so you never took the time to appreciate what you had with him. When he died, you could only be angry and upset at that loss."

Roni focused on her driving. Anything else would bring strange thoughts into her head. After all, nobody knew what happened in that office chair. Teanna could not possibly have known. Yet she spoke as if continuing a conversation started in that office. It made no sense.

At length, she asked, "Why are you bringing this up?"

But Teanna's face shifted as she pointed to an upcoming sign. "Isn't that our exit?"

Roni turned off the highway and checked her phone for the proper directions. As they drove further west, deeper into the Virginia mountains, as traffic thinned, she peeked over at Teanna on occasion. Despite the tenuous nature of their previous conversation, it pleased Roni that her friend had started chatting again — regardless of the reasons behind it. A sign, perhaps, that the old Teanna remained intact and could bloom once more in full. One day.

But the look on her face as she watched the thickening trees pass by — it scared Roni. The word *grim* came to mind. *Hunting*, too. Teanna looked like she paced through those woods, searching out her prey, ready to take it down mercilessly. It was more than all of that, though. At length, Roni finally uncovered the word she sought for Teanna's countenance — *vengeance*.

"Not much of a town," Teanna said as they drove along a road with a smattering of buildings on either side.

"We're not here for a vacation."

"Not at all."

Roni wanted to follow up on that comment, make sure Teanna would be able to handle facing the Scholar again, but her next turn came along and then Gram flashed her lights — she needed to stop at the gas station coming up. They pulled up to the pumps. Garcia took care of one car and Teanna offered to take care of the other. Roni went inside. She wanted a bottle of water — actually, a bottle of Jack Daniels sounded even better — and a little space.

"I thought you'd been fishing this morning," the hefty man at the register said.

A scruffy man leaning on the counter gave a tiny salute. "Wanted to, but the police got the whole park blocked off. Can't get in to do anything — and not just the lake. Some private thing going on, I guess. They were tight-lipped about it all."

"Must be a celebrity wedding."

Scruffy laughed. "What the hell you talking about? What famous person is going to have their wedding out here?"

"I'm just sayin'. It's got to be somebody important or rich or something if they can close down the entire park."

When she got back to the cars, she informed the team what she overheard.

Gram said, "Sounds like we were right."

"I don't know," Garcia said. "Probably we're right, but it could be anything."

"We're right," Roni said. Then to Garcia: "We're going to go check, anyway. We'll find out."

Following her phone's map, she led the group up to the main gate of the Cold Shell Park. A gate house sat in the middle of the road with a metal arm blocking the way. On the opposite side, a police car sat.

As they pulled up to the gate, a police officer got out of the car and walked over. He looked too young to wear a badge — probably earned it only months ago which led to this crappy assignment. None of the seasoned officers would want to spend the day dealing with the occasional parkgoer.

Roni lowered her window, but the officer had no interest in talking. He waved them off, trying to use a commanding voice that came out more loose than in control. Still, Roni had no intention of causing trouble for the young man. She waved and turned the car back — Gram's car followed.

Once they were no longer visible to the gatehouse, Roni slowed. A tall, chain-link fence ran along their side, and she didn't want to miss a turn as she trailed the park's perimeter. The sun rose higher, but the park still appeared shrouded in shadow.

"Pull over," Teanna said. "I'll sneak in and take care of everything."

"Absolutely not. We went through a lot to get you back. I'm not letting you go off alone. I know it's been hard on you lately, but we're never going to get this group working well, if everybody goes off on their own."

"I've been doing it all on my own just fine."

"Really? You were captured and turned into a brainpower battery. The only reason you're sitting here contemplating ways to slice open Yal-hara is because your team saved you."

"And the only reason you're here with any chance of stopping Yal-hara is because I took the initiative to go out and found her. I got caught. That happens when you take risks, but that's how you get results, too. Or would you have preferred that I sit around the bookstore like an obedient child while Yal-hara vanished from our universe to run havoc over the others?"

"You know that's not what I mean."

"If we don't act, that's what will happen. She may even go after my home universe."

Roni froze. She hadn't considered the personal dangers for Teanna. "We won't let that happen. Trust me. I'm only asking that in the future you accept —"

"Not until these living relics are taken care of." Teanna opened the car door and rolled out.

By the time Roni braked, pulled over, and stood in the grass with the others, Teanna was gone. A large hole had been chopped in the fence.

"What happened?" Gram asked.

Gully flapped his arms at the hole. "What does it look like?"

"I meant *Why?*"

"It doesn't matter. We've got to —"

"Gully," Roni said, "you were quiet throughout the entire argument, please continue that." A blind woman could have seen the anxiety on all the faces looking at her. "Everybody relax. I have a plan." Well, half-a-plan. "First thing we need is to see what's going on in that park. That's what Teanna is doing right now. She was just a bit too enthusiastic to wait for the car to stop. Now, gather what you need, and let's get moving."

Moments later, Roni stood by the fence, holding the hole open as wide as possible, and helped the team step into the park.

CHAPTER 24

Roni clenched her teeth as she stomped through the woods. If Teanna had been there, Roni would have unleashed a verbal assault strong enough to cut through mountains. She understood Teanna's frame of mind, but that did nothing to fix the potential harm caused by her going rogue. Again. At least, the rest of the team followed her plan — what she had of one.

For the moment, it was simple and direct. They spread out in groups of two — Gram and Gully, Elliot and Garcia. Roni should have been teamed with Teanna, but that clearly couldn't happen. They stayed within view of each other but kept plenty of distance — no clumping targets, plus they could cover more ground.

When they broke from the woods, they saw a large group of people forming a wide circle like an audience surrounding a stage in the round. Roni had no doubts about the makeup of this audience — most or all had to be the Pennsylvania townspeople. There hadn't been enough time for the Scholar to rampage through another town.

But from what Roni could see of this circle, there was no stage in the center. Of course not. Yal-hara and the Scholar had no need. They stood on a patch of ground that would be unimportant any other day, and after she stepped through the rift that would soon open, it would be unimportant again.

Moving to the edge of the audience, Roni could not get a good look at the center. As if responding to her thoughts, several of the townspeople stepped aside and backwards, gently absorbing her into the mass of people. Scanning across the heads, she thought she spotted Gram and then Elliot. They had entered the audience, too.

The ground felt soft and slick with morning dew — at least, Roni hoped it was morning dew — as she gently pushed her way forward.

Those around her grunted and swayed like a cult lost in a group trance. Some breathed heavily. Others stamped their feet in place like impatient children. But none turned toward Roni with anger. Not one attempted to grab her. No harm came.

Yet when Roni tried to turn around, to slip back the way she had come, they closed ranks around her becoming a wall of people unwilling to bend. When she shoved, they did not move. They did not strike back, but she would have had an easier time pushing marble statues.

"Gram! Elliot!" She hoped they would hear her call.

"Roni!" Garcia yelled back.

"Can anybody move?"

"We're stuck," Gully said. "I might be able to climb on top of them, but I suspect they'll find a way to drop me back to the ground."

Elliot said, "Are you okay?"

"I'm fine," Roni said.

Before she could say more, the people in front of her parted. Then, more parted. And more. And like a rippling sea, they moved to one side or the other forming a long aisle toward the center.

While Roni knew in the back of her mind that eventually this day would bring her in contact with Yal-hara, she still felt a surprise jolt when she found the spidery creature standing at the end of the aisle. Her bone-thin legs shot upward and back down like a twisted, four-legged spider. Roni could still feel those horrid things crawling over her as Yal-hara moved in to destroy the life of an eight-year-old girl. Yet this time, Roni did not shake with fear. The disgust roiled in her belly, yes, but the terror did not manifest.

Instead, she noticed how aged Yal-hara's face looked. Gram and Elliot were old, of course, and they had wrinkled skin, gray hair, and such. But they never seemed old. They never acted old. Though well into their seventies, they gave the impression of people a decade younger or more.

Not Yal-hara.

Her skin hung limp as if it wanted to drip away from her bones. Blood trailed lines beneath the surface across her neck and torso, and as Roni walked closer toward the center, she saw the blood also filled Yal-hara's yellowed eyes. All the most frightening pieces of her had paled over the years. She looked ill.

But Roni would not be fooled. Old? Yes. Perhaps ancient. Sickly? Most certainly. Harmless? Never. Even if Yal-hara had lost all her limbs and breathed her last, Roni would approach with the same caution as walking toward a venomous snake.

The center of this bizarre gathering formed a circle. Yal-hara standing to face Roni, but now that Roni drew closer, she noticed the Scholar a few feet in the back. Teanna had said the creature would be growing, changing, and indeed, it no longer resembled a pulsating blob with arms. If anything, the Scholar had taken on the shape of an over-sized Sumo wrestler — around seven feet tall, four arms, and enough mass that it could defeat several of Japan's best at the same time. It sat in the field, bald head bowed, four hands laced over its gargantuan belly as it concentrated.

"I can't seem to get rid of you," Yal-hara said, a sibilant hiss underlying her words.

Roni raised her arms and shrugged. "I feel the same way about you. I mean, do you understand that all of this is your fault?"

"Ah. Still crying about your Lost Time. You know I was doing that because I had to."

"You did it because you enjoyed it."

Yal-hara's slim smile turned grotesque as she licked her lips. "Nothing wrong in finding pleasure with what must be done."

"Well, I think there's plenty of wrong with what you've been doing."

"I am shocked." She pressed one of her boney limbs against her cheek. "After all, the Parallel Society has treated me so fairly all these years."

"You came here —"

"I did not choose to be here."

"But you chose to hurt people — including me. The Society at the time would have been justified in locking you away in one of Gram's books, but they exhibited mercy."

"They did no such thing. They had me trade one prison for another." Yal-hara's eyes flared, and Roni tried to retreat. But the wall of people had closed in behind her. She had no choice but to step into the circle.

"They had to protect the people of this world."

"From me? I abided by the rules set out. I left all of you alone. The Parallel Society simply had to leave me alone, too. Let me live quietly, unseen, and then provide me an exit. But you never provided."

"Because you don't want to go to your home. You want to go to some weaker world where you can attempt to rule them."

"My ambitions have nothing to do with you."

Roni scoffed. "It's our job."

"No. You're supposed to protect your universe. Not all the others."

"I know you have a low opinion of humans, but we can be better than a bunch of selfish animals. I'm not so sure the same can be said for your kind."

"I am hardly selfish."

"You turned an entire town of people into zombies with no free will all so you could solve a difficult math problem, all so you could get out of here and harm others in other universes. That practically defines *selfish.* If you're so much better than humankind, then set them free. You know the rift is coming here. You don't need the Scholar anymore which means it doesn't need these people."

Yal-hara tittered. "You're pathetic. Here I am, the one who scrambled your brain, the one who made you betray those you care about, the one who destroyed your life, I stand right in front of you, and all you do is talk. You should hate me. You should want to see me torn apart. Yet from you — nothing. And why? Because you think you can talk me out of my plans?" She paused, her head cocking at an odd angle. "Or is it — yes, I think you are hoping that by freeing these people, your Society can get close enough to help you. Is that why you talk so much?"

The grunting of the crowd continued but it took on a more rhythmic sound as if each person had noticed the others and started synchronizing with them. Roni didn't know what to think about that, but she was sure it wouldn't be good. She tried to remain placid and expressionless. Yal-hara couldn't be allowed to know how Roni felt or thought. Especially because Roni had no idea what she planned to do next.

"You're waiting on your lady of the ax," Yal-hara said. "How sweet to think that she has any care for you left after you abandoned her."

"We did not, and she knows it."

"Ah, but you are hoping she'll arrive, mow down a path through these innocent people, and kill me — since you're unable to do it yourself."

Yal-hara had started pacing, and at first, Roni took it as a point of power — she can pace while Roni must stand still. But the longer the pacing continued, the more agitated it felt. The grunting had become a single, unified chant and with it Yal-hara's nerves appeared to rise.

It's coming. The rift will open soon.

"I just had a sumptuous idea." Yal-hara halted long enough to push her face close in on Roni. "After I become a great Queen of a new world, I'll come back here at take everything from you all over again. Perhaps I'll start with your Gram."

A bomb went off inside Roni, a raging inferno that had been held back by a small door — and Yal-hara had just thrown it open. Roni's hands thrust upward and clamped upon Yal-hara's neck.

"You want to see how much I hate you? How about you feel it?"

CHAPTER 25

At another point in time, Roni would have felt guilty. She would have shunned the joy at seeing another living creature suffer under her actions. She would have remonstrated against the very idea that anybody deserved pain as a punishment. But this was Yal-hara and such a point in time did not exist for her.

With her bloodshot, yellowed eyes bulging out and her mouth agape, Yal-hara batted at Roni's grip. But only for a few seconds. Then her eyes settled back, her mouth curved into a hungry grin, and her limbs set firm on the ground. She did not struggle nor did she show any concern.

Roni clenched her fingers tighter. "I'll kill you."

"Doubtful."

Two of Yal-hara's legs shot forward, dug in under Roni's ribcage and thrust upward. As she rose off the ground, her lungs expelled all her air in a painful lump. Yal-hara tossed her across the open circle. Roni hit the ground and rolled to the edge where several people stood over her, repeating their wordless chant, ever faster.

Back on her feet, she rushed toward Yal-hara like an enraged bull. All the years between them flooded her system, blotting out her surroundings, her duties, her life. Her racing heart pumped hot blood. Her racing mind burned to cause harm.

All knowledge of fighting flew away from her, and for that instant of contact, she reacted as a pure animal. Grappling, punching, kicking, growling. The ferocity of Roni's assault made up for the lack in skillful technique.

Yal-hara was forced to dance back, pivot to the side, and finally climb over her combatant in order to return to the center. She widened her back legs and planted the front ones firm into the ground. All her playful amusement vanished.

"I allowed you into this circle as a sign of respect," Yal-hara said, snarling as spit flew from her mouth. "Yet you disgrace yourself with this pitiful display. I shouldn't have expected anything more from one of the Parallel Society. You all are spoiled meat."

Roni's rage fired again. She stormed forward, screaming hatred, unwilling and unable to stop her fury. But when she reached the center, Yal-hara whipped her body around to slam Roni into the ground.

The hard hit left Roni wobbling on all fours. Yal-hara raised one leg and stomped down. Roni's face smashed into the grass and dirt. Her back blasted pain from the point of impact outward like the radius of a bomb. From the corner of her eye, she saw Yal-hara reposition at her flank. The creature leaned on her forward legs and mule-kicked Roni in the side. Roni toppled, rolling all the way to the circle's edge.

Yal-hara moved in for another strike. "I will not be stopped again. You do not have the right to steal any more of my life."

Her face flared with a maddened fury, and Roni saw her own reflection in that raging visage. Her own hatred drained away. Clutching her wounded side, she tried to stand, but Yal-hara swung another hard blow.

"No more," Yal-hara said. "I've lost too many years to such a worthless adversary."

As she pulled back for another hit, a voice called out, "Maybe I can change that."

A round ball landed flat in the circle. From the ground, Roni saw Teanna standing proud with both of her hatchets at the ready and a line of bodies trailing behind her. Not dead, though. Unconscious. And that ball — the pale man's head.

Rapt in anger, Yal-hara galloped across the grass, leaping into a vicious assault. Teanna met fury with fury. Sharpened hatchet with hardened limb. They swiped and dodged, lunged and deflected. Teanna's brazen attacks slowed as did Yal-hara's more calculated strikes. They fast realized that neither would win a rapid victory and settled into a longer, more strategic bout.

The battle consumed them, and neither noticed Roni laboring to her feet. She scanned the crowd, searching for signs of her team. The people's chanting had increased its tempo and the movements of their bodies had become larger and more forceful. Roni's people were stuck in that swaying mass, and it was growing dangerous.

"Give up," Yal-hara said, breathing hard as she circled off with

Teanna. "You are not ready for a fight with me."

Teanna's brash voice matched her sneering chuckle. "Because I'm young and strong? Skillful and agile? Well-trained and brutal? I think it's your old, creaking body that's not ready."

"It's your arrogance." Yal-hara flew forward. "And my ruthlessness."

They plunged into another run of attacks and parries. Amongst the clanging metal and effortful grunts, Roni heard something else — something strange, off. A crackling that made her look for the sparking of a fire. Instead, she spotted the air near the Scholar ripping open like roughly sliced skin. The tattered edges glowed green and red while the center swirled the air around it.

Yal-hara paused to look back at the open rift. A smile twisted on her lips. But Teanna landed a blow on the shoulder, and Yal-hara flung back into a pummeling assault, batting one limb out after another, overwhelming Teanna with the sudden ferocity. She finished with a mule-kick Roni knew too well and sent Teanna flailing back into the crowd. Without waiting to see the results, Yal-hara whirled about and dashed toward the rift.

But after a few strides, the ground shook beneath. A fiery ball rose from within the crowd. Roni had no doubt for the source — Garcia. A shimmering dome of energy formed nearby — Elliot. Then off to the left, an angry shout could be heard as the crowd pulled away in all directions. The jingle of chains whipping outward — Gram. Taking advantage of the confusion, knocking aside bodies, Gully plowed toward the center.

But none of that help would arrive in time. With Yal-hara barreling toward the rift and the crowd engulfing Teanna, there was only one option Roni could live with. She stepped in front of the rift, planted her feet in a strong stance, and raised her fists.

"Never," Yal-hara growled, thundering ahead.

Roni screamed as she threw her punch, letting her body follow through, hurling herself into a calculated crash. But the brutal collision she winced against did not come. She heard the galloping feet cease, and when Roni got a clear look, she saw that Yal-hara had leapt over her. The creature landed behind and continued on into the rift.

Faster than the click of a tongue, Yal-hara was gone.

"No!" Roni shot forward, her eyes locked on that sizzling cut in the air, her legs pumping harder with each step. The Scholar lifted its malformed head. At first, Roni thought it moved in front to block her way, but then she saw that the Scholar grew larger, becoming an obstacle without moving its legs.

When she reached the bulbous creature, she discovered another horrible truth — it had become strong. Fast, too. Its arms snapped out and grabbed her. Other arms slugged her in the sides and head. Still other arms pulled at her limbs. It seemed arms continued to grow and reshape in order to pummel her again and again. Then, without warning, it tossed her aside — a baby no longer interested in its toy.

Roni's head throbbed and one eye swelled over. She could barely see but managed to catch a glimpse of Gully blazing forward, head down, as he threw the first of many punches at the Scholar. Moments later, Teanna soared across the air, digging her hatchets into the Scholar's shoulder. The creature arched its head back and howled. A ripple of energy swept out from him and through the crowd. Roni felt it more than saw it, wasn't sure it had happened or if it had been a misfiring in her bruised head, yet in seconds, the truth became evident.

The entire crowd of townspeople had been released. Angry screams and terrified weeping flooded the air. People collapsed. People ran off to escape. People stood dazed.

Garcia reached Roni first. "Open your mouth." He poured a foul-smelling liquid down her throat. "That'll help keep you together until Elliot can properly heal you."

"No," Elliot's heavy voice said before she could see him. "Use your best potions to heal her. It's your job now."

Despite the pain, Roni's eyes opened wide as she sat straight. "What?"

Elliot knelt beside her. Teanna and Gully fighting with the Scholar drifted away. The fraught townspeople reacting with rage, confusion, terror, and tears vanished. Gram and Garcia's efforts to protect Roni from the violence around them disappeared. Only Elliot remained.

His gentle grin weighed heavy. "I've been trying to tell you for a while now. You kept saying I was retiring or worried about dying. But I've been waiting for a new way to serve the Society. I wait no longer."

"Can't it hold until we're done here?"

"No. Because I'm going in that rift. I'll stop Yal-hara."

"You can't."

"You think I'm too old? Don't be foolish. You should know by this point that you're never too old in the Parallel Society."

"But how will you —"

"There's no time." He leaned in and kissed her forehead. "I love you as if you were my daughter."

"Don't do this."

"Goodbye, Roni. Take care of your team."

The world crashed back in violent reality as Elliot walked away. The chaos around them did not touch him. Using his cane, he kept a steady pace, weaving around the battle with the Scholar and pausing to let two distraught townspeople sprint by. Then, much like Yal-hara, he stepped into the rift and was gone.

With a thundering boom, the rift closed up — a rarity for such things. So rare, Roni had to believe the Scholar and Yal-hara had picked this rift for that purpose. After all, going through a rift that remained opened would have left Yal-hara vulnerable. The Society could have locked that rift into a book. Yal-hara would have her universe, but it would also have become a new prison. Instead, she was free.

Gully flopped to the ground where the rift had just been. Seeing him brought Roni back to the moment — to the fact that the Scholar remained.

"Gram, Garcia, get in there and help our team."

Chapter 26

While Gram launched into the fray, Garcia remained behind to administer another potion upon Roni. The liquid tasted worse than the first one, but Roni's head did clear more and she noticed the throbbing pains all over her body lessened. Enough for her to look across the field at the ongoing fight with the Scholar.

Teanna spun with her blades out. One dug into the Scholar's torso. The other never got the chance. Even as Gully came in, the Scholar punched Teanna away. It then took Gully with three of its arms and tossed him aside. Gram slung her chains around two arms on the left, but it grew numerous others to clamp down on the chain and tug Gram closer.

"We're getting destroyed," Garcia said.

But Roni grinned. She had seen this before. When she wasn't the leader. When she was part of the team and trying to stand out, to do her own thing. That's what she saw now. Each one thinking they worked together but only focusing on themselves. Not selfish. Directionless.

"That's my job," she whispered.

"What?"

She turned her swollen and bruised face toward Garcia. "Do you trust me?"

"I can try."

Not the answer she wanted, but it would have to do. "Stop worrying about my injuries and cause a distraction. A major one."

Something in her voice changed his expression. A bright smile came over his face. "I've got the perfect thing."

Running toward the Scholar, he pulled out a vial of liquid with a pinkish hue. As he pulled back his arm to throw, Roni cupped her mouth and yelled, "Gully, be ready to run to me!"

Garcia chucked the vial forward, and it broke open on the ground in front of the Scholar. Pink foam bubbled out of it. A high-pitched squeal spit into the air as a burning light flew up from the vial — pink foam trailed behind it. Like a drunken pixie, the bright light swirled loops around the Scholar and the pink foam held firm in the air for seconds before flaking off toward the ground.

The Scholar tried to catch the screeching light, using most of its hands in a continually failing effort. Gully took advantage and raced back to Roni.

As he neared, she said, "Make golems. Small ones. Lots of them. Have them attack."

"What should they look like?"

"I'm giving you the order. You figure out the details. Get to it."

Gully nodded and started grabbing rocks. In moments, he had a squad of golems heading toward the Scholar. They were made of a couple stones and a stick. Little things that flopped as they tried to roll. They wouldn't accomplish much damage, but they would be numerous, annoying, and perfect.

Shouting over the wailing crowd, Roni said, "Teanna, knock it out!"

As the foam light finished its run, Gully's ever-growing army started to bump into the Scholar. Other golems rolled up the initial ones, climbing higher like a mound of ants. The Scholar gazed down, and Teanna struck. She concentrated three blows on the back of the Scholar's head. Enough to daze the creature.

"Gram, lock it down."

Chains lassoed around the creature's neck. Gram swung a chain over to Teanna who stretched it off to the right. As Gram pulled her end to the left, Garcia got behind and helped secure the chain to the ground. Gully had finished with the golems and hustled over to help Teanna.

When Roni saw that they had secured the Scholar, she forced her body up. Blood rushed to her head, stars flushed her eyes, but she did not collapse. Three strong breaths and she started to move. Limping toward them all, she pulled out the small book Gram had made earlier — felt like years earlier. "Everybody behind me," she said. They all listened.

Once they were safely in back of her, Roni opened the book.

Chapter 27

Several months had passed before Roni could open the door to Elliot and Sully's apartment. She stepped into its echoing emptiness and saw Elliot's intentions written on every blank wall, every stacked box, every mote of settled dust. Since Virginia, she had tried hard not to feel betrayed. He knew all along he would leave — even told her so — but he managed to avoid telling the full truth.

"Because you knew I'd do all I could to stop you."

Her voice bounced back at her. The hollow room seemed appropriate. After all, she could not mourn Elliot's death for he could very well be alive. But she could not think of him as alive for his absence reminded her of the treacherous path he had chosen and he could very well be dead. If she wasn't careful, she'd lose it going in mental circles.

At least she had managed to keep the Society together this time. When they had returned home and chained the Scholar's book into the Caverns, Gram suggested holding a ceremony for Elliot. Not a memorial, she had insisted, but an acknowledgement that wherever he now journeyed, he could use all of the Society's faith and support — even if only in spirit. Roni agreed.

That alone had been enough to firm up the team's solidarity, but then Roni suggested they resume Teanna's original reason for staying in this world — to hunt down relics. That mission gave them all focus. Together, they drew upon their collective knowledge and skills, and for a while it became easy to get lost in the job.

Days of tracking, capturing, and disposing of strange objects from other universes filled the hours. Garcia continued his self-education in potions and Gully worked at his golem making — they managed to split the workshop in peace. Fulfilling her promise, Roni gave the Pages of Glass to Gully with permission to destroy them. But he had found that task far more difficult to accomplish. He even enlisted Garcia's help, but so far — whether through force, potions, or fire — they had yet to succeed.

And so, the team carried on.

Roni didn't think she had been avoiding thoughts of Elliot. This wasn't the same as when she buried her loss of Sully. But she eventually admitted to herself that she had not dealt with his absence, either. So, she stood in the middle of the empty apartment.

"I've come up here a few times, too," Teanna said from the doorway.

Though she startled a little, Roni did not turn around. "I thought I would feel something stronger. A profound sadness, maybe."

"But you only feel the void."

"Exactly."

Teanna walked up beside her. "That is because Elliot is not dead. Your body can sense it. Not in blind hope, but in truth. I feel it, too. He is out there. And so is she."

"Yal-hara."

"I think if she were destroyed, we would sense that as well."

"You know, he was really proud of you." Roni had no idea why she spoke those words. Nor did she expect Teanna's response.

"And you."

Letting her instincts guide her, Roni turned toward Teanna and put out her hand. Teanna took hold and swept Roni forward into a strong embrace. They remained still a moment before Teanna concluded with a few rather masculine thumps on the back. Then she left Roni standing alone in the apartment once more.

With a lightness lifting her chest, Roni strolled into the kitchen. Perhaps she should move in here. Seemed like a waste to let it remain empty. She would save a lot on rent. Teanna could move in too, of course, if she wanted.

As Roni envisioned what the place might look like and what living above the Caverns might feel like, her eyes rested upon a piece of paper set on the small, round table where she had eaten numerous breakfasts. It had Elliot's handwriting — she could tell without moving — and an odd dread chilled her.

"No being a coward now," she said, and walked over to snatch up the paper.

Much of the writing had been half-finished words and crossed-out phrases, but it looked clear enough. Elliot had lied. He had decoded the Scholar's page. At least, some of it. Most importantly, near the bottom, Elliot had circled three words.

Just as Teanna said they would sense if Elliot had died, Roni knew these words told her exactly where Yal-hara had gone, and thus, where Elliot would chase after her. Roni looked over the paper again. Okay. Time to get the team together. Her finger traced Elliot's clear handwriting — *City of Infinity*

CITY OF INFINITY

THE PARALLEL SOCIETY BOOK 7

Chapter 1

Standing guard outside a large home nestled behind a winding, gravel driveway, Roni shivered. Though the afternoon sun spread copious warmth upon her, she could not stop the nerves chilling her skin. It wasn't a feeling of being watched — shrouded in trees, nobody could easily see them from the street. Rather, she continually considered what they would find when they entered that house. Yal-hara's house.

Garcia hunched over the lock, dissolving it with one of his potions, while Teanna stood aside Roni. They scanned the light traffic and handful of pedestrians, searching for possible threats. If anybody dared to glance their way — but nobody paid any attention. If anything, it seemed as if some of those strolling with their children to the park or rushing to reach the bus stop actively looked away from the house. As if their core, animal instincts warned them off.

"I'm starting to think Yal-hara fostered a bad reputation in this neighborhood," Roni said in a low voice — just in case her talking might attract attention.

"She would benefit from as few visits as possible. If she let people fear the house, then she had a good strategy in that regard." Teanna jutted her chin as she surveyed the area. Her trim physique continued to add definition from a strict regimen of healthy eating, intense exercise, and solid rest.

The shift from party girl to vigilant warrior had happened fast. Part of it came from discovering that black skin did not fare well in America. Most of it came from a desire to be prepared for the next time they crossed with Yal-hara.

And there would be a next time. Roni was determined to see that happen. They all were.

Because of Elliot.

When Yal-hara escaped this world by cutting a hole into another universe, Elliot had jumped in after her. For the many months that followed, his absence, his loss, numbed the rest of the Parallel Society. They went through the motions of closing up the rips to other universes, locking them away in Gram's special books, and fighting the creatures that slipped through in the process, but the heart of their efforts did not beat. They did the work because it had to be done and no more.

Until Roni came upon a piece of paper in Elliot's old apartment. It contained his attempts at decoding a page of math and symbols they had taken from the Scholar — the creature responsible for opening the path Yal-hara and Elliot had jumped through. On that paper, Elliot had written the words *City of Infinity,* and Roni knew right away this was where they would find him. Since then, the entire team had become single-minded in their attempt to uncover the location of the City. Find the City, and they would find Elliot. They all believed it. They all hoped it would prove true.

"We're in," Garcia said, but the clang of the doorknob dropping to the entranceway had already told them as much. "Ready?"

Roni paused. That was a good question. So far, everything had gone as expected. After spending a few months systematically sifting through the Grand Library for any information on the City, Roni decided they should track down Yal-hara's old home in hopes of finding information she may have left behind. Gram and Gully remained in the library, combing through the remaining books while the others hit the pavement.

They started with the only address they had — the original house Gram, Sully, and Elliot had put Yal-hara in decades ago. But Yal-hara had left that building soon after. Though kept prisoner in this world, she had no intention of being under constant scrutiny. She knew the Society could not watch her and protect the universe at all times, so she had little trouble escaping. Roni clung to the hope that Yal-hara maintained a residence somewhat nearby — considering the number of interactions they had with her over the years, it was not an unreasonable guess.

After numerous avenues resulted in dead ends, they finally located Mr. Kemper — Yal-hara's latest lawyer, representing her even after she escaped this world. He refused to hand over any information about the creature, even the closely guarded secrets that no longer held value. The firm's reputation, any lawyer's reputation, was built upon keeping their client's secrets — valuable or not. However, after a surprising amount of persuasion, mostly from the threatening hands of Teanna, Mr. Kemper grudgingly provided them with the address of Yal-hara's former home.

Roni peered into the dark opening, the stinging scent of Garcia's potion hovering in the doorway, and tamped down the rising knot in her chest. Before her mind could convince her of some reasonable excuse to close the door and walk away, she entered the house. A pressure of vile hatred wafted against her skin. It hung in the air as if it had been floating in the foyer, waiting for somebody to enter.

It was Yal-hara. Her hatred. Her vileness. It permeated the wood and glass, the carpets and mirrors, the membranes and —

Membranes?

Roni tapped on her phone's light. The foyer had been designed to mimic wealthier homes — white marble floors with a Turkish carpet dominating the center, a stunning cherry stand in the center with an abstract sculpture sitting upon it, an upholstered bench to the side where nobody had ever bothered to sit. But the archways leading deeper into the house had a green residue growing in patches of viny mold.

With her own light on, Teanna stepped forward. She peered through the opening into the next room before waving the others over. "It's everywhere."

Roni followed into a wide room dwarfed by a baby grand piano. But neither the immaculate instrument nor the beautiful bookshelves nor even the stunning oil paintings on the walls could draw their attention. Not when the strange mold stretched along every corner of the room. Floor and ceiling, wherever the walls connected, the green fur could be seen. Like a weird, pulsing caulk with a hard rib down the middle, it filled in the crevices of the house, lending each space the sensation of being surrounded.

Garcia had an empty vial in one hand. "You think it's safe to take a sample?"

"It came from Yal-hara, or at least, her house." Roni raised an eyebrow. "What do you think?"

After a short internal debate, Garcia returned the vial to his pocket.

They passed through a formal dining room and into the kitchen. It would have been an impressive tour, if not for this alien fungus. Roni fought down the temptation to open the large refrigerator. Considering the house had no electricity, whatever waited in there had probably become a wall of its own mold by now.

The entire house felt frozen. Locked in the moment Yal-hara had left, yet new life had formed as well. The creature that had terrorized Roni left behind a dusty, dying museum for her to explore, yet she wanted nothing more than to leave. Because she could feel Yal-hara the same way she could feel the bedsheets of her eight-year-old self that night when her memories had been taken and her Lost Time began.

"I found her study," Garcia called out.

Roni followed his voice into a room far less human and far more Yal-hara. Though cluttered with old books and stacked documents, the room contained a pristine order — an exacting choice made for each object from the extra-wide office desk to the crystal figurines on the bookshelves to the circular table only large enough for a crystal decanter. The same exacting way Yal-hara's numerous, spindle legs moved — picking out each placement before setting down. Just as she had walked over Roni, the footfalls creeping over her eight-year-old legs and stomach and chest.

Damn. Roni thought she had finally gotten over dealing with all of that. Would she ever? Does anybody truly get over the terrible things that happened in life?

As if in answer, her eyes fell upon an old box sitting open on one shelf. Palm-sized with an ornate, swirling design built from two different shades of wood, her skin prickled at the sight. Not just any box — a relic box. Meant for trapping creatures from other universes, the box would have symbols surrounding it which acted as instructions — orders, really — that forced the creature into certain behaviors. Under Yal-hara's control, that usually meant violence. And this box was open.

Before her racing heart could spin her around, she heard Teanna's voice, soft at her side, "It's okay. There is no writing on this one."

"But it's open. There's a creature loose in here."

"No. This box has yet to hold anything."

"How can you know that?"

"Remember when she sent her old lawyer to attack us with all those boxes? Not a single one remained unscathed when they were opened. The creatures inside are prisoners both in mind and body. When they are released, they are furious. A wood box like this one would never have survived."

Roni looked closer. Teanna was right. The box looked pristine.

With an embarrassed chuckle and feeling warmth flush her cheeks,

Roni turned away from the shelves. Her heart still pounded against her chest, but a few slow breaths helped calm her pulse despite the foul mold stench. A thought hit her that perhaps the mold was a creature from a relic box, but even if true, the stuff clearly presented no immediate threat. Unless …

"We should all be wearing masks. Thick ones. Like biohazard masks. We have no idea what that gunk could do to our lungs."

Garcia fluttered a piece of paper from the desk. "This looks like some kind of expense summary."

"How does that help us?" Teanna said.

He shrugged. "I'm just reporting what I've found."

"Perhaps you should focus on —"

The air pressure in the room displaced with enough force to pop Roni's ears. The walls shuddered as if a train sped by from the kitchen. With an odd *whoosh,* the spicy-sweet aroma of coriander spread across.

Nobody moved.

Roni listened but heard nothing. "Any idea what the heck that was?"

Teanna said, "Possibly Yal-hara has set up some kind of alarm. We should be careful."

"And encouraged," Garcia said. "An alarm suggests there's something worth protecting here."

A thick rumble mixed with a higher-toned hum came next. Then the deep whine of a heavy foot pushing down on old wood boards. The sounds grew louder. Something alive roamed this house. And it was coming their way.

CHAPTER 2

The nature of her job with the Parallel Society meant that Roni had witnessed numerous creatures from numerous universes. Some were friendly, comforting beings. Some were nasty, monstrous revulsions. But nothing prepared her for what entered the study.

It had a massive, lizard-skinned head, beady-eyes, and a long snout with jagged teeth clearly evolved for tearing flesh. But that was not particularly strange. Terrifying, sure, but not strange. What bothered Roni, what shocked her, was that this head sat upon a seven-foot, humanoid body that — as best as Roni could think of it — looked as if somebody had removed the flesh much like removing the hair on a poodle. Rings of lizard skin remained at all the joints, but in between, Roni saw only bone. And while a poodle had a cute aspect to it, this creature forced bile up Roni's throat. Its bits of flesh were not fluffy, puff balls. Rather, they hung from the bone like shredded fabric.

She struggled to understand how its organs could function. With no esophagus, no abdomen, no thighs or forearms — how could this creature exist? It made no sense to her brain, but she could not deny her eyes.

Nor could she deny its full-throated screech as it stood in the doorway sizing them up.

"Heck of an alarm system," Garcia said. "How could that have been hiding in this house and we didn't hear it?"

Teanna pulled out her two hatchets. "Doesn't matter. It's to be dealt with now."

Issuing another screech, the creature burst forward several steps, and Roni noticed that running up the thing's leg — along the back, barely visible — was a thin, vine-like line of mold. The deeper it stepped into the room, the more she smelled that sour odor. It combated the warm coriander. Sickening. Before Roni could point out her observations, Teanna matched the creature's vocals with a screech of her own. With this battle cry, she charged ahead, holding one hatchet overhead to attack and the other close in to protect.

Though the creature did not appear intelligent, it fought back hard — whether through hidden smarts or classic instincts, Roni couldn't tell. But she watched the beast evade Teanna's strikes. When it could not get out of the way, it successfully blocked the attacks. Then it counterstruck.

Caught up in her own assault and the fact that the creature had done nothing but block, Teanna missed the shift. The creature's blow came in a clumsy arc, but it glanced off the side of Teanna's head. She wobbled to the wall.

Garcia jumped right in before the monstrous thing could follow through against Teanna. He had an open vial and splashed the contents onto bone and skin. With a double hiss — one from the burning liquid, one from the burned creature — it stumbled back toward the doorway.

All of these attacks gave Roni enough time to dig out the small emergency book Gram always provided. Handheld with a short chain attached to the spine, the book could pull in a single enemy and hold it for a brief time. Long enough to get the thing back to the bookstore where Gram could permanently dispatch it into a larger, more stable book.

As Roni braced her body with a wide-legged stance, she raised the book toward the creature. But Teanna burst in between, her vicious yell louder than before, angrier. Blood ran down her face while she threw one punishing blow after another, her hatchets spitting bone into the air like woodchips. The creature raised a forearm to block, but Teanna cut through, leaving a jagged stump behind.

With a ferocious swing, she buried one hatchet into the beast's shoulder. Muscle memory had her follow up by slashing the other hatchet across the belly, but this thing had no belly. The weapon breezed through emptiness, and the lack of resistance stumbled Teanna's rhythm. She twisted too far, and the creature took advantage. Using the forearm Teanna had cut apart, it sunk its sharp bone through her shoulder blade. She bellowed and clunked to her knees.

Garcia sprayed more of his acids upon the enemy, sending gray smoke into the air. Roni tried to ignore the conflicting scents, but her stomach curdled anyway. It wasn't the stench, anyway. It was fright. Because she couldn't open the book with Teanna and Garcia in the way — not unless she was willing to have them vacuumed into the book along with the creature.

But before she had to deal with the fact that such a contemplation even entered her head, she noticed a dark line on the floor. A vine. Stretching from the baseboards all the way towards the creature.

"It's a puppet," she said.

"What?" Garcia looked across at her, and the creature backhanded him for losing focus.

Roni dashed forward. With its forearm still grinding into Teanna and its attention divided on Garcia, it never noticed. Running right by, Roni grabbed Teanna's hatchet. Her mind raced, making sure she had drawn the right conclusions but knowing the time for second-guessing had long since gone. She raised the hatchet high and brought it down into the floor. Hard. Fast. Slicing through the vine.

The creature's next screech cut off and it collapsed into a heap. Roni wanted to do the same. Instead, she eased to the floor while she caught her breath.

"Good … work," Teanna gasped out.

Roni nodded. Dabbing at the sweat on her face, she said, "Garcia, do what you can."

He hurried over to Teanna, took a fast look at her wounds, and rushed out. Returning with cloth napkins from the kitchen, he created a compress for her shoulder. He also applied pressure to the head wound which appeared worse from all the blood, but quickly revealed itself as a long but shallow cut. "She'll be fine when we get back. I can mix up an excellent restorative in my workshop."

"Then let's get going. I don't want to be here any longer than —"

Roni froze, staring at the bookshelves.

"What is it?" Garcia asked, helping Teanna to her feet.

"That relic box."

"You think that monster came from there?"

"No. But it changed. The box, I mean. It was wood." She walked over and lifted the box off the shelf. Made of orange and blue plastic, it looked like a child's toy.

"Maybe that's a different one. Maybe the wood one got knocked down in the fight."

She glanced around the floor for any sign of the wood relic box. Or the remnants of one. But she knew she would find nothing. Because this plastic box was the same one.

With a frown, she closed the lid and slipped it into her coat pocket.

The tension in her chest screwed tighter as she felt its weight against her side — greater than that of the plastic she had held. More like she expected a wooden box to feel.

Her phone rang the *Halloween* theme — Gram.

Swallowing down the startled yelp that had come too close to escaping her lips, Roni managed a deep breath before answering. She hovered her finger over the phone while Garcia escorted Teanna back toward the kitchen. Roni followed. They were going to drive to the bookstore. Gram would be there. Perhaps she could wait to talk until then. That would give Roni a little time to recompose.

In the distance, police sirens whined. Garcia peeked back over his shoulder. "Maybe we shouldn't go out the front door."

Scooting ahead while she put her phone away, Roni said, "I'll scout us a back exit. As long as Teanna can handle the walk, we'll go a block up and over. That way we'll come to our car from the opposite direction."

"I can handle it," Teanna said, wincing with each jostled step.

Roni had her doubts, but if the police sirens were for them — and given the noise they had made in a wealthy neighborhood, who else would the police be coming for? — they needed to move. Thankfully, the house conformed to the build of most luxury homes. Numerous doors.

Five minutes later, they limped along the street, trying to be inconspicuous. Five minutes after that, they had reached the far end of the block, crossed over, and headed toward their car. When they finally drove off, a single patrol car slowed in front of the house and flashed a spotlight across the large property, settling on the front door. Roni didn't wait to see if the officer chose to investigate any further.

While Garcia tended Teanna in the backseat, Roni stayed focused on the road. She could feel that plastic box in her coat. Feel it pressing against her, heavier and heavier.

With a shake of her head, she fished out her phone. Gram had left a message.

"Hello, it's Gram. I hope you're having good luck and not in any trouble. I'm praying on it. But that's not why I called."

Roni chuckled. Voicemail was not a method of communication that Gram had ever become comfortable with. In fact, leaving messages was one of the few times Roni ever heard Gram ramble self-consciously.

"Anyway, I wanted you to know that I've continued my search in the library, and I may have found something. I mean not *may,* I did find something. A journal that mentions the City of Infinity. Oh, I don't know how long I can make this message, so hurry up and come home."

A few thumb strokes, a few rings, and when Gram answered, Roni simply said, "We're on our way."

Chapter 3

By the time they reached the bookstore, *In the Bind,* Teanna's bleeding had been brought under control. Nevertheless, Garcia rushed to the elevator in the back, promising to return with a potion that would speed her body's natural healing. Roni and Teanna plopped down in chairs at the Big Table which dominated the only section of the main floor not broken into long stacks of old, used books.

They had no worries about customers. Ever since Elliot chased after Yal-hara, an unspoken agreement had been made to keep the bookstore closed. Nobody had the energy within to mind the front counter, deal with customer demands, and re-stock the shelves at the end of the day. But Roni knew that eventually — sooner than she wanted — they would have to reopen. If for no other reason than to keep up appearances.

Huffing along and with more waddle to her walk than Roni remembered, Gram approached Teanna. "You'll be fine, dear." She patted Teanna's shoulder and continued on to the head of the table. When she sat, she kissed the cross around her neck, closed her eyes and muttered to herself. A prayer, no doubt. Even as the thought hit Roni, her grandmother lifted her head, crossed her body with one hand, opened her eyes, and smiled at the group. "We'll wait for the others."

The elevator dinged, but instead of Garcia exiting, Roni saw Gully — the last golem Sully had ever made, the one with part of Sully within him. She smiled at the living mass of clay and rock. He gave a short wave as he approached, wiping his hands on the heavy apron he wore.

His face took on a concerned look as he spotted Teanna. "You have to be more careful. What would we do without you?"

Teanna grinned. "At least, I'll be missed."

"That's not funny," Gram said. To Gully: "I'm sure she'll be fine. Roni's got Garcia taking care of her."

As they continued to comment about Teanna's condition and wait for Garcia's return, Roni's hand reached for the relic box. She wanted to bring it out, show it to Gram, let them all examine it together, but her instincts told her to hold back. For now. Trusting her instincts had been an on-again off-again experience — part of her growth in commanding this odd group — but she listened this time. They were here to learn about Gram's discovery. There would be plenty of time later to worry over an unused relic box that changed its form.

Garcia hastened back to the table with a glass of steaming liquid — thick and dirty. It looked as appetizing as a fresh cow patty. Teanna curled a lip when she sniffed it. She winced as she downed the drink in three large gulps. "That's disgusting."

"I never said it would taste good. Just that it'll heal."

"Start learning how to flavor your potions. That was the most horrible thing I've ever had, and I've eaten mud grondoes. Trust me. In my homeworld, you eat a mud grondo, you'd never forget it."

Clearing her throat, Roni said, "Time to focus. Gram, we're all here. What have you got?"

The room grew quiet. Gram set a leatherbound book on the table. It smelled of deeply engrained oils and even deeper age.

"Well over a hundred years ago, in 1902, there was a member of the Parallel Society known for taking great risks. He went by the name of Hayle — presumably, his last name — but I can't find his first name anywhere. The other team members all called him Hayle and wrote about him as such. A few days after Halloween, Hayle and two others were given the job of closing a rift not far from here — just over into New Jersey."

As Gram spoke, her fingers flattened against the journal. After a moment, she clenched her hands together, but that only sent the nerves up her arms. It wasn't much, Roni suspected nobody else had noticed, but she saw clearly that Gram did not like this story.

"Something bad happened," Gram went on. "Hayle doesn't explain and the other references to this rift gloss over the entire thing, but here's what I can tell you — whatever they faced, they succeeded in locking the rift into a book, and in the process, Hayle fell into the rift as well."

Garcia said, "Why does that sound like somebody pushed him in?"

"I thought so, too. If this had been a murder, if the lack of reference to it is an indication of a cover up, the whole thing was doomed right away. Hayle survived. He kept his journal during the seven years he spent in an underground world he called *Angel's Haven*. And he found his way back."

Roni said, "This place — Angel's Haven — you think that's really the City of Infinity?"

But Gram shook her head. "Patience. You'll see. Now, during those seven years, he lived with a people called the Coana. He doesn't describe them other than that he thought they were beautiful. Presumably, the angels of the haven. He learned their language, befriended them, and all the time, he searched for a way back home. Once he could communicate effectively with them, he explained about the Parallel Society, and in time, he helped them found their own version. But really, and this is me reading between the lines, he needed them to aid in his search."

Raising his hand, Gully said, "Hold on, hold on. I know I'm only a ball of clay, so my brain doesn't work as well as yours —"

"Hey," Roni said. "None of that kind of talk."

"Sorry, but I can only think as I was made to think. I can't help the guilt I feel when I'm suggesting points that might contradict what you people think."

With a smile larger than necessary, one that perhaps released some of her tension, Gram said, "That guilt you feel is very much a part of the man who made you. You should embrace it."

"I don't know about that. Can't say I like the idea of walking around feeling guilty all the time. Then again, who am I to say?"

With an exasperated huff, Teanna said, "Please, ask your question. I'd like to get a little rest."

"Of course. Sorry. I'll be sure to feel guilty about the delay a little later." Gully faced Gram. "Why would Hayle be searching for a way back? He knows the rift is locked away in a book. There is no going back."

Gram said, "A good question. First, he didn't know for sure that the rift had been contained. So, there was a slim chance he could simply find an opening home. But he held little hope for that. However, in any world, there are other rifts. Those rifts don't disappear simply because the doorway to our universe has been locked away."

Roni said, "If he could find one that led anywhere else, he could start traveling, looking for a world not already chained in the Caverns, and maybe — with a lot of luck — he would find a path that led him here."

"That was his plan. But it was a foolish one because the books and the rifts don't work that way."

"Except he did get back, right? I mean, we have his journal."

"That brings us to the most important part, the part he made sure to write down but also made sure not to share with anybody — the *Vestu Books*."

Crossing his arms while bending over slightly, looking far too much like his maker, Gully said, "I would like to go on the record to say that I do not like the sound of this. Also, there is no guilt about me stating this fact."

"Nobody should like the sound of this. According to Hayle, there are ten books that bind all the universes together. Sort of like super-strong versions of the books we use. Hayle believed that if he could find those books, he could use them to get back here."

"And he did," Garcia said.

"I don't know."

"But the journal."

"We do have it. Yet according to the journals of his teammates, he never returned."

"But if he also found the Vestu Books, then —"

Gram raised her hand and waited for Garcia to sit back with a deep frown furrowing his brow. Then: "First, it's not clear that he ever found the Vestu Books. Second, it's even less clear how this journal came to be in our possession. So, I don't have any answers for you yet. But there's a little more to the story, and then I think you'll all understand why I thought it important enough to call you back here."

"I only meant that —"

"Let her finish," Roni said.

"Thank you." Gram paused, her loose chin wobbling as she pulled her final thoughts together. Roni wondered why Gram looked just as itchy as she felt. She reached into her pocket, but before she could plunk that plastic relic box onto the table, Gram continued. "Hayle built trust with the Coana, they told him of the Vestu Books, and they eventually showed him their most-prized book — an artifact that had never been opened for they believed it to be a conduit to the afterlife. Hayle, however, knew with one look that this book contained a rift. The very next night, he crept into the room that held this book and went inside. That is when he found the City of Infinity. His initial entries at that point describe a city that stretched as far as he could see, the whole thing an equally infinite cavern, filled with bits of every imaginable world. He was sure he had reached the center of the Caverns, a place that connected everything. If the Vestu Books are real, he was convinced they would be found in the City."

"Did he find them?" Garcia asked.

Gram turned one hand upward. "Maybe. His meticulous journal becomes sporadic. He spent a long time there — twenty years according to him — and his writings are more like ramblings. In a few cases, he's delusional claiming that talking cockroaches saved his life."

Teanna grunted — less from pain, more from frustration. "Why tell us all of this if his journal can't help us? He doesn't share anything useful about the City."

"This is the first solid proof we have that the City is real. That Elliot's note wasn't a mistaken translation." Gram's voice tightened. "That Elliot might be alive."

Roni's heart swelled as she stood, all thoughts of the relic box whisking away. Until Gram had spoken the words out loud, Roni had not realized how much she longed to hear them, to hear some confirmation that her hopes could be true. Tears welled in her eyes.

"Are you okay?" Gully asked.

With a broad smile, she said, "Elliot is alive. Better than that, we know how to find him."

"We do?"

"Hayle wrote clear directions. We go to Angel's Haven and find the book they have with the rift that leads to the City of Infinity."

All grew quiet. Roni could feel the shocked eyes upon her. But before the obvious questions could be asked, before a single voice of dissent or incredulity at the task could be uttered, Gram thumped her hand against the journal and offered her own infectious grin.

"Looks like we've got a lot work to do. Let's get to it."

CHAPTER 4

While everyone jumped into the research, the size of the Grand Library promised the job would not be accomplished in a matter of hours. After several days, Gully suggested his time would be better spent in his part of the workshop and Garcia split his time between potion studies and this daunting research. Teanna broke away to exercise but always returned. Both Gram and Roni stayed with the books, searching and searching, escaping the clutches of the Grand Library only for the necessities of the body — food, sleep, relief. Roni assumed Gram would go to church on Sunday, but they had a few days before that happened. Considering the lack of progress, she thought it highly possible they would be digging through these books for years.

It was a matter of scale and terminology. Hayle only referenced the Coana's world as *Angel's Haven.* Any other mention of it from any other journal, especially from before Hayle's time with the Society, could use a different name. And while they had started their work around the years of Hayle's membership, the answer for finding the book that contained the Angel's Haven rift could be anywhere. The place may have been discovered a hundred years earlier. Or if they missed the references to the world from early on, it was possible that at any point after Hayle's time, somebody may have written about the book, the world, or Hayle. Which meant that every book in the Library could potentially hold the answer.

Rubbing her dry eyes, Roni leaned back. Her chair squeaked, and Gram lifted her head, a gleam of hope in her eye. Roni shook her head and marked the book off the current list to check through. She wanted to slam it shut, hurl it across the room, and shred the current list, but she merely sighed. Then her stomach let out a loud whine.

Gram lowered her reading glasses — a simple chain wrapped

around her neck kept them from falling, and the frame rested upon her hefty chest. Roni prepared for a short lecture on the importance of keeping fed, but Gram slid her book aside, folded her hands, and stared forward. Roni cringed inwardly. Gram was building up to something, had been for the last two days.

"Roni, dear," she began, the tone promising an uncomfortable talk. "I have something to say."

"Hold that thought." Roni stood and headed toward the stairs. She needed some lunch — a three martini lunch sounded about right — and any talk this serious required her to be in the right frame of mind. Hunger would not be conducive to hearing Gram fairly. "Let me eat first. We'll chat later," she added over her shoulder.

They would. She knew it. She had no choice. Not because Gram was Gram, but because the Parallel Society was the Parallel Society.

Roni did not have the luxury of hiding. Nor did she want it. The old Roni would have used every excuse to postpone the conversation. The old Roni would have never addressed the concerns of others.

But that Roni knew nothing about rifts to other universes, underground caverns with chained books, and the monsters that came with it all. That Roni had dark gaps in her memory which plagued her with a false sense of incompleteness. That Roni had been a child no matter her age.

This version of Roni, this leader of the Parallel Society, understood that she needed to let Gram speak about whatever concerned her. But Roni also understood that dealing with Gram in a proper light was equally important. Gram needed to be heard — not just listened to — and that meant getting some food first.

But before she reached the main floor, Gully came rushing down the stairs. "I'm glad you're already on your way up. I wanted to talk."

"Sheesh, everybody wants to talk today. I need to eat."

Roni assumed everyone would understand she should first have some food and then deal with their various problems. She was wrong. Gram and Gully followed her to the main floor and into the kitchen. They even sat with her as she scarfed down a microwave burrito and chugged store brand cola.

As she wiped her mouth, Gully said, "You're done? Come with me to my workshop. You must see what I've accomplished."

Roni raised an eyebrow at Gram who only grinned back. Good. At least Gram could be patient. Or perhaps that grin was amusement at Gully. Either way, they followed Gully to the third floor where he and

Garcia split the space into two separate workshops. One — a clean, organized area dedicated to the study and creation of potions. The other — a messy, cluttered studio where golems could be constructed from clay, dirt, stone, wax, and any other materials at hand.

As they passed through Garcia's part of the workshop, he pointed at them as way of acknowledgement, never lifting his head from the flask of bluish liquid he tinkered over. Gully waved them further in. Once on his side of the room — a series of tall bookshelves acted as a wall between — Gully bounced about like a child eager to impress his parents.

No need to ask what he wanted to show them. A seven-and-a-half-foot golem dominated the center of the room. It stood dormant. Though lacking beyond the most basic facial features — two holes for eyes, a straight line for a mouth — its muscular sculpting proved a step forwards compared to Gully's previous attempts. He made sure to give this golem thick biceps, well-defined abdominals, and powerful quads. For Roni, it brought to mind the many vicious creatures they had fought in the past.

"What do you think?" he asked.

"It's lovely," Gram said. "Does it live?"

Taking on a tone like a professor — also like Sully — he said, "Not an *it,* but a *she.* Her name is Betty. Because she is meant to be there for Roni."

Roni noted the Archie Comics on a nearby desk. "I'm hardly a Veronica."

"It's just a name. She's nothing like the Betty from those stories. My Betty was built for strength. The next time we face a powerful enemy, we'll have her muscle on our side."

Gram said, "That's smart of you. Lord knows we can always use extra muscle."

"Since I had to sacrifice strength for brains, I figured why not go the other way, too."

Roni said, "I hope she's smart enough to tell the good guys from the bad guys."

"Don't worry about that. Like any golem, it's all in the instructions I write down and place within her. She'll be fine."

Offering an honest smile, she said, "You've done a great job."

Gully rushed toward the bookshelf barrier and raised his head along with his voice. "You see? You thought I was wasting my time, but Roni loves Betty. I don't think she'll be as excited about your potions."

After a few more minutes, Roni and Gram extracted themselves from Gully's exuberance. When they reached the elevator, they had to wait — Teanna must have called for it earlier. Roni glanced back at Gully's golem and chuckled.

"He's getting better at that," she said, pushing the elevator button again. "Pretty soon he'll be a full replacement for Sully."

Gram cocked her head. "I think that's the first time you've said such a thing without it sounding like you were reliving Sully's passing all over again."

"I guess I'm getting comfortable with the idea."

"Perhaps you should get comfortable with the idea that Elliot might not come back, too." She spoke the words with such trepidation that Roni knew this had been the talk Gram wanted all along.

Setting her jaw as the elevator arrived, Roni said, "I'm not giving up on Elliot."

"Of course not. We shouldn't. But we can't focus solely on him, either. Since I found that journal, we have done nothing else."

"Gully made a golem."

Gram led the way onto the elevator and pushed for the Grand Library. "He made her for the purpose of greater fighting strength for when we go after Elliot. You could see that in everything he said and did."

"Betty is for everything we do, not just rescuing Elliot."

"That's exactly my point. We have so much more we should be doing. The rifts didn't just stop because we lost one of our team. We have a core job to accomplish."

When Roni turned towards Gram, she tried to pull back on her intensity. She wanted Gram to see that she had a clear direction and solid control. In the past, she would have whined like a petulant child — *this is how I want to do things, so that's what we're going to do* — but that wasn't the case now.

Keeping her voice calm, she said, "The Parallel Society, my team, can only function its best when we are whole. We'll never be good at our core job until we are complete. That's why Teanna had to drink Garcia's awful potion, that's why I'm pleased to see Gully getting better at making golems, and that's why we need to get Elliot back. We can only protect our universe by protecting the team. Keeping this group together as a unit is the foundation of everything we do. On top of that — we don't give up on our own."

Gram's expression gave away little. Perhaps a bit of shock. Maybe a tinge of pride — but Roni refused to read that much into it. With a hesitant stammer, Gram started to say, "I-I should tell you —"

But the elevator door opened and Teanna stood in front of them. "I think I know how to find Angel's Haven."

Ten minutes later, the entire group gathered in the Grand Library. The beautiful wood work reaching back through ages of styles, the stacks thick with every journal, diary, and publication produced by The Parallel Society over its long lifespan, the modern touches of laptops and wi-fi, even the Cavern map Roni had taped up in the back — all of it coalesced into a sanctuary for her. Her private temple of knowledge. The unvarnished truth about the universe. Seemed fitting to her that Teanna's answer would be presented here.

Standing before the team, Teanna looked healthy. Garcia's potion mixed with the warrior's vitality must have worked well. Yet she held still, smile twitching, and Roni wondered if the poor woman had a touch of stage fright.

But that didn't track with the spirit Roni knew lived within. Teanna faced her fears. It was part of what made her such an asset to the Society. And as a friend. When Teanna glanced at Roni, however, the anticipation did not look like one of eager friendship. Rather, it made Roni think the warrior awaited orders. Of course.

Clearing her throat, Roni gestured to Teanna. "Whenever you're ready."

Teanna gave a firm nod and relaxed as she launched into her talk. "The answer is Mexico."

Not much of a talk. "You'll have to be a little more specific. How do you know the book to Angel's Haven is in Mexico?"

"I've seen in your movies and television programs depictions of Mexico that match many of the stories Garcia has shared with us."

Garcia said, "My dad's family is from Honduras, not Mexico."

"Yet the stories are similar. Small towns, distant from any other, centered around a church usually. But sometimes —"

"Centered around an old artifact." Garcia sat straighter. "Something significant to the town's history. Or superstitions."

"A book that leads to another universe would be significant, yes?"

"Without a doubt."

Teanna widened her stance as if to affirm her successful logic. "I used your computer system to start searching for mentions of Hayle.

When that produced nothing new, I looked for mentions of Central and South America. A little bit ago, I found this."

She pointed to a book as everyone crowded around. Roni saw the cover — *Daily Journal of Samantha Orlon.* After flipping to a bookmarked page, Teanna pointed to one paragraph and waited for the rest to read it.

> *The decision to leave this book with the people of Cieloguro is not taken lightly. If anything goes wrong, I will blame myself and carry the weight of any harm that comes to these good people. But after facing down the beast that fell through a rift above their homes, a beast they assumed to be a real angel at first, and after watching them band together in the name their Lord and Savior to fight this so-called angel when it grew violent and became a demon to them, I cannot take the book away. It is more than a container of a rift. It is the thing that saved them. An object they will forever revere. A holy book every bit as important to their history and faith as the Bible itself. I pray that the rest of the Society can forgive me for keeping this secret, but to do otherwise would be a betrayal of all that has occurred here. I only tell of it here because some Society in the future must know where all the books are. To hide this from all would be a betrayal to the Society as well, and I cannot allow that.*

Teanna said, "This is the only mention of a book that we didn't have some other record of, correct?"

"Possibly," Gram said.

"And it is the only mention of creatures mistaken for angels, other than Hayle's journal?"

"Possibly. We have a lot more to go through to be sure."

Roni stepped back, a strong flutter in her stomach. When she raised her head, all eyes followed. That was to be expected. In fact, she felt a surge of excitement that she had not been shocked by the looks. They awaited her decision.

Patting Teanna on the back, Roni said, "We're going to Mexico."

CHAPTER 5

Driving from Pennsylvania through Texas to the US-Mexico border took twenty-nine hours. Rather than going in a few cars, Roni had the Society rent a van so they could ride together trading off drivers as they went. She hoped the decision would help bond the team more. They had been through enough that the group had its dynamics worked out mostly, but from the books she had been reading on leadership, management, and CEO strategies, she thought this long drive might get them over that final hurdle — make them into the single unit she remembered Gram, Elliot, and Sully being all of her life.

Plus, they had the problem of Gully.

They needed him along, and she had no intention of leaving anybody behind. Not only for the simple idea of keeping the team together. That mattered, but the full truth — she figured any rescue of Elliot would involve facing Yal-hara again. After all, he left them to stop her. And if the worst-case scenario proved to be reality, if they found Elliot was — well, *still missing* was as far as her brain would allow — then the Society would hunt down Yal-hara to finish this. Regardless of the outcome, Roni wanted every tactical option available to her — Gram's chains, Teanna's skills, Garcia's potions. And Gully — their jack of all trades.

But bringing Gully along meant they could not fly. He'd pass a cursory glance from a tired border patrol agent on a hot day while lined up with hundreds of other vehicles, but no way would Gully get through airport security. Not to mention all the crowds and the tight confines of a plane. Somebody would notice along the way that Gully did not look quite human enough. While many would dismiss their own eyes, find ways to justify what stood before them, it would only take one person to cock it all up.

Now, Roni watched Mexico rolling by while Garcia guided the van off the paved roads onto dusty dirt pathways, taking them further and further away from civilization. The sun burned hotter, it seemed, and even the van's air conditioning sounded as if it worked harder. Teanna and Gram rested. Good. They would need all their strength later. Gully sat on the back bench with a content expression. Or perhaps Roni projected that onto him because she wanted it to be true — he had been quite upset when she refused to let Betty come with them.

"With some disguise, I think we'll get you across the border," she had said, "but a nearly eight-foot golem that lacks the facial sculpting Sully gave you? I'm sorry, but she'll get caught."

"Would that be such a bad thing? Maybe the world would be safer knowing golems existed and can help them. We shouldn't be forced the hide our existence. We should —"

In the end, Roni placated her friend by suggesting Betty guard the bookstore. It would be a good first step in testing her abilities, and Gully agreed. Enthusiastically, too. As if any success of his golem would change the situation in the future.

Looking at the road ahead, Roni wondered if he might be right.

"Should be just a few minutes," Garcia said, checking the map on his phone.

His voice cut through the quiet, startling Teanna awake. Gram opened her eyes slower, but soon the whole team sat at the ready.

For a second, Roni wondered if they had driven through a rift. Cieloguro looked out of place, out of time. A swath of land that had broken free of their universe, froze at that moment, and never reconnected.

Centered around an adobe church, the town had only a handful of buildings to support the few farming homes spread out beyond. A circular fountain before the church acted as a lovely piece of art, a celebration of their religion, and a necessary source of water. The few buildings had flat roofs, some apparently thatched, and a quiet haze filled the air.

Several townspeople stood about. The town may not have changed since the 1800s but the people certainly had. Jeans, t-shirts, a few suits, sneakers, a sundress — yet not a car in sight. Only a donkey pulling a cart with baskets of fruit.

"What is this place?" Teanna said.

A portly woman leaned over a boy, whispered something, and the boy dashed away. She then started closing up her food stall selling fruits and vegetables. Others in the area lit cigarettes, leaned against walls, and folded their arms — watching the show that broke up the long, sweltering day.

Emerging from the church, a man in black with a white priest's collar approached. He had thin hair and a thinner mustache, but a prominent belly suggested he did not have to scrounge for food. He waved at them. Garcia pulled around the fountain and stopped before the church. Two burly locals — one wearing a sombrero, one bald — stood behind the priest. They did not act nearly as friendly.

Roni stepped from the van and waved. Cumin and garlic soaked the air as if the town sweated the aromas. She forced a smile, trying to appear both friendly and official. Gram had suggested their cover story, and Roni thought it made the most sense considering the odd assortment of people sitting in the van. She glanced back to see Gully sinking in his seat — his hat and sunglasses trying to cover his face.

"Hello," she said to the priest. "We're aid workers, here to help."

Garcia had argued against this lie. He thought they should be honest with the town. "They know about the book, after all."

Except in Gram's experience, most people did not accept the reality of such a book that came into their possession. Treating it like a holy relic would not make them open to handing it over to some strangers claiming to be from the same group that brought the book over a century ago. Garcia tried to argue further, but Roni made the final decision.

Standing in the hot town center, Garcia paused. Roni wondered if he would break from the plan, admit the truth right from the start. Instead, he translated her welcome and their cover story.

The priest halted him with a hand. "I speak English," the man said, with an affable chuckle. "I'm sorry to inform you, but you have come to the wrong place. We did not ask for aid workers. There are many small villages throughout this country. It is easy to get lost."

"This is Cieloguro, isn't it?" Roni said.

"It is."

"Then we came to the right place."

"I doubt that."

Widening her ridiculous smile, she said, "My apologies. We're not trying to offend you." She put out her hand. "I'm Veronica. You can call me Roni."

Though he clearly didn't want to touch her, he also didn't want to be impolite. At least, not when there were other people around to witness. He shook her hand. "I'm Father Perry. You can call me Father Perry."

Before the priest could launch into further protest, Garcia said, "Please, your holiness, we do not wish to cause you any harm. In fact, just the opposite." He pulled out a vial of the same thick healing potion he had given Teanna. "We bring you this. A special medicine that will help any ills in the village."

The boy who had run off now returned along with several strong and sweat-stained men. They held tools – hammers, saws, and machetes. All good weapons, too. Teanna left the van, stepping behind Roni.

The priest plucked the vial from Garcia and sniffed it. When he reared back, Garcia said, "Not a pleasant odor, but it is effective at clearing up small matters and even a few serious ones."

The blazing day pressed on the top of Roni's head, yet she focused on the priest and tried to stay still. She could feel the town's eyes upon her — worse than the heat. But as she scanned the area, she saw that the priest held their attention. They were ready to welcome or attack or any other reaction. It all depended upon the priest. Roni had the urge to swallow but her mouth was dry.

Father Perry motioned to the bald man who then hastened off behind the church. Handing the vial to the other man — the one with the sombrero — Father Perry smoothed down his thin mustache.

"Un momento, por favor," he said, his attention on the corner of the church the bald man had left by.

All held still. Roni kept thinking of things to say but held back. Elliot had taught her that there were times when the best course of action was no action at all. Sully would say, *Patience can be the most difficult form of patience there is.* Picturing those men brought two tears into her eyes. Thankfully, they blended with the beading sweat on her face.

At length, the bald man returned. With him, he assisted an elderly woman who leaned in heavily on a cane. She had white hair, bright against her dark brown skin, and her body trembled even when standing still. Her jaw never stopped moving side to side. Despite her ailment, she struggled through crossing herself before mumbling something to the priest.

Garcia listened close and whispered back to Roni and the team, "He's asking how she is feeling. She says everything hurts but the Lord keeps her going, so she will keep going. Now, he's explaining who we are and about the medicine I offered."

The old woman glanced at them, complete understanding overtaking her. She reached out and Father Perry took her hand. Garcia shook his head, unable to hear what they said, but when they pulled apart, Father Perry nodded at the man holding the potion. With a sorrowful step, he offered the vial to the old woman. She snatched it — probably the fastest motion she had made in years — and downed the liquid as if taking a shot of tequila.

The waiting began again.

But not as long as before. Not long enough for Roni's mind to wander into melancholy thoughts. Garcia knew his craft well, and the old woman's shaking body held still. Even her jaw stopped its metronome movement.

Her face brightened with a genuine smile. She muttered *Gracias* before shuffling back home. The bald man went to assist her but she waved him away. And she giggled. That sound sliced across the onlooking townspeople, breaking their walls and releasing a torrent of joy. Conversations erupted. Laughter, too. Several folks rushed toward Garcia, begging for more of the medicine.

"A miracle," Father Perry said.

"It's not forever," Garcia said. "Not for a woman of her age with her problems. But the medicine will offer relief."

Spreading his arms wide, Father Perry said, "Welcome."

Chapter 6

The people of Cieloguro turned out to be warm and full of joy. Over the next hour, in an open-air building meant for events and large gatherings, most of the town arrived. Each family brought food and drinks. Several pulled out instruments and started playing music. Roni and her team were placed in the middle of the festivities — except for Gully. While he wanted to partake, Roni insisted that he remain back. Seeing a living golem would probably turn the town against them rather quickly. Gully sulked in the van, but he seemed to understand.

The food tasted phenomenal and the drink proved strong. Garcia continued to act as translator until he found a young woman willing to dance and dance and dance. Teanna kept a cautious eye, but Roni noticed a part of the warrior reawaken — the same woman who enjoyed clubbing not so long ago. For Gram, the mixture of great respect for the elderly and for their faith bathed her in a sense of belonging she could not hide. Roni had never seen the woman with such a peaceful grin.

Eventually, the night won out. People drifted home. Some stumbled.

Father Perry had some lumpy pillows and woven blankets brought out. "You may sleep here. Should be a clear night."

With that, the Society was left alone. They agreed to get some rest while they waited for the town to fall asleep. Gully joined the group and promised to waken them in a few hours.

"I can be a good alarm clock," he said, not hiding his bitterness.

Roni patted his shoulder. "I am sorry about all this. But remember why we're here. This is about finding Elliot. That's it."

"Sure seems you're having a lot more fun finding him than I am."

She had no answer — at least, none that could simply be accepted.

And she needed rest, too. Patting him once more, Roni grabbed a blanket and settled in. Gram already snored. Garcia and Teanna had claimed their spaces to sleep, and Gully stood guard — keeping to the shadows lest he be spotted by a curious, late-night insomniac.

A good start. All they had to do now was rest, find the book, and go save Elliot. She tried not to remind herself that staring at the enormity of a mountain made it no easier to climb. Pay attention to the path in front and don't worry about the whole journey.

"Not a bad first step," she muttered to herself and closed her eyes.

Roni managed a little sleep but not much. Enough to know she needed more. But her whirling mind refused to stop bouncing thoughts around. Most centered on Elliot — concerns about his well-being, concerns about him facing down Yal-hara alone, concerns that they may never find him. But she also pondered her recent conversation with Gram.

It happened every few weeks. Gram would find some way to corner Roni and pester her about the Society's job and the possibility that they would have to continue on without Elliot. At first, Roni didn't understand how Gram could give up on her dear friend so fast. But soon she saw the darker truth underneath. These talks were less about Elliot and more about Gram herself. After all, for several years, Gram had been drilling the idea that age was catching up, that someday sooner than expected she would pass. Sully had died. Elliot had left. Gram stood alone, feeling the cold grip of Death on her shoulder.

Maybe it had to do with age. Maybe Roni lacked the years to accept such pragmatic appreciation of the end of life. No matter the reasoning, Roni had no interest in entertaining thoughts of Gram's demise. The Society needed her. Roni needed her. She wasn't allowed to die. Simple as that.

"Time to go," Gram whispered, and Roni jolted to her feet.

Everybody stood ready, waiting on their leader. Roni kept her face firm as she inhaled several breaths of the cool night air. Her heart hammered from the startle as well as her maddening thoughts. She gave her head a shake and strode forward.

"Keep quiet until we're inside," she said. "Once we start the search, keep even more quiet."

Teanna led the way, moving with smooth, silent steps. The rest followed like a group of incompetent ninjas, making plenty of noise as they scampered across the empty town center and toward the side of the church. Garcia's vials chimed softly from inside his pockets. Gully had little practice at stealth while also wearing a disguise. His coat flapped about as he ran. And Gram tried to keep pace with the others, but she ended up several steps behind, breathing heavy, and working hard at betraying nothing on her face. Each sound amplified in the night's stillness, and Roni cringed as she brought up the rear. Not a good start.

Once she reached the team, she saw Garcia already worked at dissolving the door lock. With a snicker, he stood back and opened the door. No locks. As Gram muttered a prayer of thanks, they filed in.

Dimly lit by one candle alone on the front lectern, the church looked plain and practical. This was not an architectural wonder like Notre Dame or a great artistic achievement like the Sistine Chapel ceiling. This was a place of worship for a sincere people. A handful of pews stretched back into the dark beyond the candle's reach — each one a backless, wooden bench. The front had a few basic adornments to make the place special — plastic garland spiraling along a railing, a simple carving of the crucifixion decorating the lectern, and a table off to the side that held a Bible and several items probably used during various ceremonies. Gram would know. Roni should have known, but she never paid close attention to church when little and ignored religion as an adult.

"Spread out," she said. "Try to be thorough, but don't damage anything. Unless we have to."

"That won't be necessary," a stern voice said as the electric lights snapped on.

Father Perry stood in the back with a row of armed men including the bald man and the one who had worn the sombrero. All of their welcoming charm had vanished.

"We opened our doors to you," Father Perry said. "We gave you food and shelter, yet you attempt to steal from us."

"You don't understand," Roni began, but the bald man lifted his rifle.

Father Perry took a few proud steps forward. "Do you think you are the first thieves to come here for the book? Do you think your lies tricked us? We knew the moment you arrived that you were not to be trusted."

"You welcomed us anyway?"

"We gave you a chance. You could have enjoyed your evening and left untouched. That would have been a better choice."

Roni could feel Teanna inching a hand toward her hatchets. She knew Garcia would toss out a potion that created a smokescreen or caused dizziness or some other disruption to the enemy. Gram could drop her chains in seconds and whip them around to disarm, injure, or tie up these men. And Gully could not be killed by gunshots, so he would walk straight at them, sending terror through their ranks as he knocked several men unconscious. It would all happen in minutes, maybe seconds, but Roni wanted none of it.

"Please, listen," she said. "I did not lie."

"You are not aid workers."

"We did come to bring aid. In fact, we are the only ones who can. That book —"

"So you did come for the book."

"Not to steal it. To use it."

Father Perry's shoulders grew rigid. "You have no right to use it."

"We have every right. We're the ones who created the book in the first place. Not us specifically, but our group. We're the current version of the Parallel Society."

Roni thought this might get a startled reaction, a shocked gasp, or even a reversal of attitude. Instead, Father Perry laughed. His men remained quiet.

"I do not know how you learned that name," he said and sat on a pew bench. He wiped his forehead, chuckled, and looked at his hands. "You have put me in a terrible position. I am a man of the Lord. It is wrong for me to take a life, and ordering these men do so on my behalf would be no better. Yet, I cannot allow you to say and do the things you wish."

Glancing back at her team, Roni searched for an answer. All but Gram kept their focus on the armed men in the room. As a surge of pride rushed through Roni, she noticed that Gram studied the priest. So, when Gram stepped forward, when she ignored the rifles lifting to a tighter aim, when she walked up to the pew next to Father Perry and settled with a groaning sigh, Roni knew not to interfere.

"Father," Gram said, the title reverberating with respect. "I am a faithful woman, and I would never lie to a man of the cloth. Please, believe me, believe my granddaughter — we are the Parallel Society. It is vital that we see the book entrusted to your town so long ago."

Even from several feet away, Roni could see the hope in the priest's eyes, the desire to have faith in this old woman before him. Yet he lowered his chin and shook his head.

"If you go now," he said, "I can promise no harm will come to you."

Gram rested her hands on his. "But we can't go until we complete our mission."

The shake of his head grew stronger. He tossed down Gram's hands as he stood. "Enough lies. You are not the Society. They would never have come in secret to us."

Roni said, "Your town, whatever happened here, has been lost to us for decades. We only found out about you now because the book you have relates to a bigger problem. So, yes, we lied about who we were. That was my call, and I apologize. We didn't know if we could trust you."

"And we still don't know if we can trust you."

"Garcia gave you a potion to help that old woman."

"That is hardly proof of anything. Except maybe bribery."

Pushing aside Roni with one hand, Gully stepped forward, removing his hat. "Perhaps if you saw me, you would believe us. I am not human. I am a —"

"Golem," Father Perry whispered. His mouth dropped open and the men behind him lowered their weapons. "I never thought I would see another."

"Another?" Gram said.

With his face opening into true joy, he said, "You really are the Society. After so long, you've finally returned. I — I have to admit that some nights I doubted. I thought the whole thing might be a story made to keep us faithful. But then there was always the golem."

"You have a golem?"

He nodded. "Come. We'll show you."

Just as the town had shifted from welcoming to threatening, it now shifted into something akin to reverence. The crowd of armed men parted, and as Roni followed Father Perry through, she could feel the eyes track her — not warily but with awe. Yet when she looked at these men, their focus was not on her. Of course not. They wanted to glimpse the golem.

Exiting the church, Roni's arms prickled. The temperature had dropped a few more degrees. Some of the women had started a large fire, and many onlookers gathered around to stay warm. Flames whipped the air and crackled against the night's silence. The orange light cast moving shadows across the small clutch of buildings transforming this town locked in time into a new entity — one that nobody appeared too comfortable with.

When they reached the edge of town, when they entered a graveyard, Roni couldn't stop the chill spreading down her spine. Father Perry halted before one particular grave and motioned to several men. They had shovels and started digging.

He then pointed to the expensive headstone with a beautiful statue of a busty, muscular woman, armored and wielding a sword. "Our golem," he said. Seeing their confusion, he added, "She hasn't moved in more than one lifetime. But everyone in the town has been told the tales of Camilla, of how she patrolled the town day and night, protecting us and her charge — the book."

"What happened that she is like this?" Gully asked. More than curiosity in his voice, Roni sensed a tinge of fear.

Father Perry stroked Camilla's arm with familiarity. "My grandmother told the story of bandits who came to raid the town. Camilla and several men fought them off, but the bandits nearly got away with the book. They only took an interest in it when they realized the town coveted it. Camilla decided to bury the book and stand guard right here. That way, nobody would be tempted."

Teanna said, "If she is here to guard it, why does she remain a statue?"

"I had hoped seeing one of her kind alive and well would have changed that. I'm afraid I cannot deny the truth, though — she has died."

Gram moved closer to the statue. "Standing here motionless for so long must have done something to her. Whoever made her had an artistic gift far greater than Sully ever had, but look here." She pointed to a small hole in the belly. "This must be where the instruction spell went."

Pushing forward, Gully peered into the hole. "Empty. She could have stood still forever and jumped back into action when needed as long as she had her paper inside."

"This golem is beautifully sculpted but poorly designed. Our Sully made sure the papers were always closed off and secure."

Roni pictured Camilla holding her endless vigil at the head of this grave for years, decades, without a problem. Then — what? — a bird came by and pecked the paper loose. Or perhaps the townspeople bore another side they had yet to show. Perhaps they had removed the paper out of fear of the creature.

But the sound of shovels hitting metal drove away those suspicions. The men hauled a small box from the dug grave and handed it to Father Perry. He brushed off the dirt and dialed in the proper sequence on a combination lock. With a slight hesitation, maybe a prayer, he opened the lid.

Removing a dusty, hard-covered volume, he said, “None in this town, living or dead, has ever opened the book. We have protected it all this time because your people convinced us of its great power and purpose. I trust the Lord has brought you here too fulfill that purpose.”

He handed the book to Roni. She did not offer speeches or waste time acting mesmerized by the grandeur of the moment. Elliot needed them. And they needed him.

She placed the book on the ground and opened it. The townspeople gasped and startled back. Nothing happened beyond a slight hiss as if breaking the seal on a bottle of soda. No whirling decompression, nothing attempting to escape. A portal to another universe that matched this one close enough — while not new, it still struck Roni as unusual.

To her team, she said, “Gather our things.” To Father Perry: “Once we go in there, you must continue to protect this book.”

“Always,” he said.

A few minutes later, her team stood over the open book. No further words, though. They all had the same goal. One by one, they entered the book with determination and grit, and after each one, Roni’s smile grew a little more.

CHAPTER 7

Roni flopped onto a stone floor. Like falling out of bed, it hurt more from the surprise than any actual injury. The rest of the Society had rolled out from underneath the open gash hovering in the air, and helped each other stand. Roni glanced back at the passage leading through the book.

Father Perry and several men gazed down upon her, their faces struck with awe. None had ever dared open the book, and now they witnessed an event that would solidify every religious belief they harbored. Church would be packed a generation of Sundays to come in that village.

"We're okay," Roni said to the men watching.

Acting as if he could not hear her, Father Perry motioned for his men to back away. Roni did not need to see what transpired next. She knew. The dark frown on his face, the frightened obedience of his men — these were cold decisions made out of ignorance. She felt no shock, then, as the book closed, probably to be buried again in the graveyard. The once-golem from so long ago would keep its vigil for them, and maybe they would be able to sleep.

As the opening in the air winked out and a sharp sizzle died on soft echoes, Roni took several long breaths to settle her stomach. Entering other universes could jumble her gut. She glanced around their surroundings.

A lecture hall? Sort of. A theater? Maybe a general use auditorium. Built out of rock — a cave, perhaps. No. The ceiling stretched so far above, the end could not be seen — so a cavern. Still, this section had been carved with a purpose. A courtroom, then, or a governmental chamber or such. Dimly lit from an unseen source. And that smell — fresh, outdoors kind of air. Like hiking through a forest after a morning rain had swept through.

She sat in the center — a smooth, flat circle. Eight stone tiers arced around half the circle while the other half opened to a curved stage. Perhaps more of an auditorium. No stairway up the tiers. Rather, a gently sloped section following the curve of the room. One arched exit visible to the left. She could make it out because of the soft light glowing off the walls — phosphorescent fungus or rocks?

"These are seats," Garcia said, examining one of the tiers. "I think."

Roni got to her feet and joined the others. Along the tier, round bowls had been carved into the stone. In the bottom, she could make out four lumps like hand holds.

"Look here," Teanna said, pointing to writing that had been set in the stone. Short strings of characters in front of each bowl.

Gram bent down and ran a finger over the writing. "Name tags?" She then waved Garcia over to give her a hand back up. She chuckled. "Oh, my Lord, I am not a spring chicken anymore."

Two creatures hurried in through the archway. Roni and Gully spun at the noise. Teanna had her hatchets out and stood ready. The creatures reared back, nearly fell over.

Pale gray, rocky like the cavern walls, and about the same height as Roni, their bodies were composed of two distinct segments. The top half looked the most humanoid — one head, two eyes, two ears, nose, mouth, slender torso, two arms. But two extra appendages protruded from the ribs beneath the arms as if another pair of arms had been stunted at the elbow. The bottom half looked like a ball gown from centuries ago — a large, hooped dress that flowed as if a gentle breeze blew around them in the still air.

The lead creature had its arms out and emitted a repetitive clicking noise. Roni thought of a bicycle wheel with a card in the spokes. She could not discern a pattern, inflection, or rhythm to the clicking, but her gut told her that this was an attempt at communication. More than that, she could see the creature's eyes and mouth form a familiar shape — worry.

Roni motioned for Teanna to lower the hatchets. The creature may have eased a bit, but it still looked concerned. Its eyes darted to the walls and ceiling. Roni glanced about but saw nothing. Still, in a low voice, she said to her team, "Keep your eyes open."

The rapid clicking ceased. The creature rubbed its head, and with visible effort, its mouth opened. The lips formed shapes, and the sounds that came out all had an undercurrent of that clicking noise.

"You … from … Hayle."

Roni's face lifted into a bright grin, and the creatures reacted with a flush of excitement. "Yes. Sort of." She paused, ready to put together some story. Except Mexico would have gone much better had they been upfront at the start. "We are with the Parallel Society. The same group Hayle came from. But he has been gone for a long time."

The creatures exchanged a look. Then: "Go."

"We can't go. Our way back is closed. For now."

"Must … go."

Glancing at Gram, Roni said, "You ever come across these things before?"

"Dear, I would have spoken up already, if I knew anything."

"Then I guess we have to start at the beginning." She moved closer to the lead creature and pointed to her chest. "My name is Roni. Me. I'm Roni."

The creature's mouth struggled to form the necessary shapes, but once it figured out what it wanted to do, it said, "Botolu."

"Nice to meet you, Botolu." She put out her hand. "We're not here to harm you. We want to be friends."

Botolu's eyes snapped upwards. When it looked back, Roni saw panic. It grabbed her by the wrist and yanked toward the door. "Must go."

As Roni pulled back, Teanna jumped forward. With one hand she twisted Botolu's grip free while the other hand wielded a hatchet, ready to defend any further aggressions. Especially when Botolu's companion slid forward.

This one had more muscle in the arms, and its two protrusions angled forward. Roni had no desire to learn what defense mechanism Mother Nature had given those things.

Again, Botolu's urgent eyes snatched a peek upward. Roni followed the gaze. She heard them before she could see their shapes descend from the darkness of the cavern. A wisping and fluttering. Like parachutes unfolding on a windy day.

Botolu inched back, its body drooping forward. The companion with the muscles did the same. That got Roni's heart pumping even harder.

Seven figures floated down — the pale-colored skin and the round, dress-like bottoms of more creatures. Watching from underneath, Roni saw numerous undulating appendages — legs, perhaps, of a sort — which reacted to the unseen currents they floated upon. They drifted downward, their hooped-shaped halves catching the air, flapping and ballooning, easing them to the ground with graceful precision.

All of the creatures wore a blue sash crossing from shoulder to waist. The centermost creature had a thicker torso than the others, and this one moved with a commanding presence. It emitted clicks much like Botolu had earlier, and the others stood straighter. Behind her, Roni felt Botolu and its companion also straighten.

Once satisfied with their obedience, the creature stopped clicking and smoothly approached Roni. It placed one hand on its shoulder and closed its eyes — a formal greeting? — and then, in a most-human gesture, it put out its hand.

With a voice that held plenty of clicks, and a smile that held plenty of threat, the creature said, "I am Rakmo, and I lead my people."

Roni shook the hand and returned a smile. But she knew they were in trouble.

CHAPTER 8

Rakmo had several of its compatriots escort Roni and her team to a "welcome room" — a seven-minute trek along numerous ramps reaching upward. There they were told they could relax while waiting for official business to conclude. Rakmo promised that when it returned, it would greet them properly and help them in any way it could.

The room turned out to be a strange combination of natural cave and designed dwelling. The floor had been flattened and smoothed while the walls remained uneven and craggy. Stalactites hung like planned ornaments but the outline of the room had an organic unplanned layout. No furniture that anybody could discern, although Gram suggested that the glassy bowl shapes divoting the floor were probably more seats — they certainly matched the shapes found in the chamber they first fell into. Moss grew around cracks in the ceiling and filled the air with their fresh fragrance.

"Look at this view," Garcia said, pressing against an enormous glass wall which curved to match the natural structure around it.

Roni peered out to see a massive open column. Landings and balconies endlessly dotted up and down the sides. Ramps connected many of the levels, but all the creatures used them for upwards travel only. The empty central area held a constant flow of billowing hoopskirted creatures descending through the air with the grace of a ballet.

Glancing over Roni's shoulder, Teanna snorted. "Very pretty for a prison."

"This is hardly a prison," Garcia said. "You're looking at a thriving city."

"Maybe so, but not for us. Just try leaving this room and you'll find out."

Roni looked to the only exit. Two creatures stood on either side — mostly out of view, but the edges of their bulky flanks visible. "Guards?"

"They were escorts," Garcia said. "I know everyone likes to be cautious, and you all have more experience than I do with this sort of thing, but do we really start off assuming the worst in our hosts every time?"

Sitting her back against the wall, Teanna gestured across at the guards. "They're not experienced. If they wanted to be seen, they would be standing on the opposite wall of the corridor, staring in at us. Since the idea is not to be seen, they clearly don't have a good sense of what they're doing. I've also watched them shifting around — trained guards know how to hold position. Doesn't appear to be any others but those two, though, so if given the order, I think we can break free without too much trouble."

"I don't believe this. We've entered a new universe — another *universe* — and you want act like we're all enemies from the start."

Gram said, "Teanna makes some good observations, and as you've pointed out, we've been to other universes before. You haven't."

"Ah. Telling me I should be quiet. Okay, I will, but perhaps your expertise is blinding you to new possibilities. I'm not saying Teanna's entirely wrong, but not entirely right, either. Maybe we are being guarded, watched, and if I try to leave, forcibly kept here. But perhaps I can walk out that door and they'll simply follow me. Make sure I don't go anywhere they don't want me going. In medieval Japan, those in power often kept the loved ones as honored 'guests' who had free but limited movement within the castle."

Teanna said, "We all work out of the same bookstore. Congratulations that you've finally found the books on medieval Japan. Except in those cases, the *guests* were hostages being held to force certain behaviors from a rival. Who could we possibly be hostage for?"

"Then maybe this is nothing more than the same caution we might have with a sentient being from another universe falling onto the Big Table some morning. Maybe they're simply trying to figure out how to safely approach us while also insuring the protection of their own people."

"Those first people to welcome us didn't seem so comfortable when these blue-sashed ones arrived."

Gully said, "Please, stop with the arguing. It's of no use to us."

"The golem's right," Gram said. "The two of you can debate this out when we get home."

With his mouth open as if slapped, Garcia said, "You were chiming in just a minute ago. Now, suddenly, debate is a bad idea? Is this what always happens when you go to a new universe? Everybody loses their composure?"

Teanna said, "We're not the ones trying to convince the rest that everything is fine."

"And I've let you ramble plenty," Gully said. "I only spoke up now because you both seem to be running in circles. Not very helpful."

As the bickering increased, Gram paused to stare at Roni. She raised her hand to silence the others, and when that did not suffice, she raised her voice and said, "Garcia's right."

That got everyone's attention. Including Roni.

"He is?" Gully said.

Even Garcia looked confused. "I am?"

Gram patted the middle-aged man on the head. "Not about much, but you are correct that we are not behaving in an organized manner, not like we should when we enter another universe."

"I said that?"

"More or less." She gestured towards Roni. "The Parallel Society chooses a single leader for many reasons, and one of them is exactly this — to guide us into working together on a unified front. So, Roni, what do you want to do?"

Pinching her top lip between her teeth, Roni watched the endless waterfall of creatures descending through the air. Blue sashes stood on small platforms sticking out periodically, and each one of those creatures bore the cockiness of authority. When she turned back to the team, she tried to exude confidence but fought against any hint of that cockiness.

"I'm thinking about Botolu — the first creature we encountered. It clearly thought we might know Hayle. To me, that suggests these creatures live a very long time. Enough that they don't think it strange for another creature to live centuries. Working back from that, it's possible that Botolu has actually met Hayle. After all, these creatures know English. Not French or Russian or Swahili. Their exposure to human beings was with a person or people that spoke English."

Teanna said, "I hope that means they know how to feed us. I'm starving."

"That," Garcia said, "we can finally agree on."

Gully waved his hand in the air. "Would you like me to ask our guards for some food?"

Roni barely heard them. "Botolu also seemed worried about these blue sashes. Maybe … " She shook her head. "Maybe they're political rivals. Maybe they're religious leaders from different groups. Maybe they don't have either concept and are simply factions caught in a physical conflict. Maybe none of these are true. There's too much we don't know."

Gram said, "Perhaps we should —"

But the guards shifted sideways, both making loud clicks, and pulled everyone's attention. Three blue sashed creatures entered the chamber — Rakmo leading the way. The two that followed had loose, wrinkled skin and appeared thinner than the others Roni had seen so far. If these things behaved like any animal back home, she had to assume the two were old, nearing the ends of their lives.

"I hope you have been comfortable," Rakmo said.

Roni opened her mouth, but Garcia jumped in. "Yes, very much. Thank you for your hospitality."

Teanna added, "Are we free to leave?"

Rakmo's eyes widened even as its mouth turned down. Confusion? It spoke English with ease and not much of an accent, yet Roni guessed that it had not enjoyed many opportunities to practice. Hearing rapid speech from overeager and over-cautious individuals might be overwhelming.

Opting for a slow, calming approach, she stepped forward. "We have been comfortable. Are you the leader here?"

Rakmo wiggled its fingers at the sides of its head. "Yes, yes, yes. Forgive our not being ready. There are many who thought you were all a myth. Those that still live from when Hayle visited are not trusted by all." It indicated the other two creatures. "But I never doubted. Welcome."

"Thank you."

"Please, come with me and we will talk about why you have returned." Rakmo gestured to the entrance. As the team all stood, it raised its hands over its head. "No, no, no." It pointed at Roni. "Just you."

Chapter 9

Sandwiched between two bulky guards, Roni followed Rakmo through a series of twisting, moss-veined corridors. Without warning, they reached a dead end, but Rakmo merely pushed through the wall and it gave way. Roni could not spot hinges or any kind of mechanism, but clearly part of the wall moved with assisted ease.

They stepped onto the outer-edge of the column. Cool air blew against Roni's skin, and she pressed back against the cold stone. There was no guardrail, no handhold, nothing to keep her from falling but her balance. She prickled some from the air but mostly from standing so high up without the natural parachute these creatures had evolved.

Rakmo proceeded across a bridgeway linking two columns together. It looked to be made of stone and had been crafted with care. Though as wide as an average hallway, each step filled Roni with the certainty that she would tumble over the side at any moment. She kept her eyes locked on Rakmo's back and made sure not to slow down. If the guards behind her decided to give a shove, she would scream, lose her balance, and plummet to her death.

And it was over.

While her fingers still jittered with adrenaline, her feet found solid ground as they stepped onto a new column and entered an archway. She shuddered at the comfort of the cavern walls surrounding her. A thin line of green-white moss ran along the side like a handrail, and indeed, Roni noticed Rakmo using it as such. It led them up another series of ramps until they finally entered a room that had to be its office.

Like all the rooms Roni had experienced, this one was mostly empty. It did have the seating divots in the floor, of course, as well as a massive window overlooking the great drop downward. But this room also had three oversized blue sashes on one wall like an official seal. Several long shelves of stone hung beneath it, and an abundance of light suggested the phosphorous stones were a sign of wealth or power. Or both. On the wall opposite, an artistic series of lines and curves had been carved into the stone.

Rakmo settled in the centermost divot. "When I was a boy," he said, and no other words could have pulled her attention more.

He's a male, Roni thought. Rakmo paused, a questioning expression on his brow — perhaps. She couldn't be sure she read their expressions correctly.

He continued, "Your man, Hayle, arrived and shocked our world. He truly changed everything merely by his existence. From the moment he appeared, our world split in time. There was only life before and life after this special arrival." Rakmo erupted in a series of rapid clicks. Then: "He was lucky we were never a violent people. Most of us anyway. We flocked to him as a curiosity. At first. He tried to speak our language, but your voices cannot produce the correct sounds."

Roni snorted a laugh. "He wrote in his journal — he lied — that he learned your language."

"Perhaps you misinterpreted his meaning. It is easy to do for the less intelligent. When he taught many of us to speak English, there were some that could not grasp the concepts of speaking your way no matter how it was presented to them."

"You speak very well. Especially since you haven't had a chance to use it for over a century."

"We live long. We forget little. Hayle was not a great teacher, but many of us are patient and smart. Once the first of us learned, that one taught the others of us. After we could communicate, he told us that he struggled to get back to his homeworld, that he was here by accident, and then he described your world and its many wonders."

Roni sat in a nearby divot — not comfortable but then it hadn't been designed for a human — and she listened. More than his story, though, she heard the way he spoke. He puffed as the words flowed from him — pride in his ability to speak English, perhaps. But she also picked up a sense of arrogance. He thought himself better than her, better than all of them. In fact, while the words did not directly say it, Roni felt that this story was meant to relate how Hayle could never have succeeded without Rakmo.

Pushing those impressions down, Roni refocused. She had to remember that these creatures might not even think in terms of pride, arrogance, superiority, and such. All the body language and tone of voice could not be trusted to convey the same information as a human being. Not yet, anyway.

Folding his hands across his belly, Rakmo said, "The more he explained about your world, the more incredible his tales became. But it seems that any people who achieve a basic level of intelligence also become easily swayed. Many of our people flowed to him as if he were a prophet. Many others wanted him gone. They saw that he was a disruptive, destructive influence on our peaceful ways. We had a wonderful home here, and he threatened to change it all, turn it into something ugly — something human."

"That's not the way we are. Not anymore. The world that Hayle came from believed in pushing others to be like us. But our world has changed. The Parallel Society has changed, too. We are not like Hayle."

"But I am."

Rakmo knocked a fist on the floor twice. As if they were actors waiting in the wings for this cue, the guards entered carrying Botolu between them. From the look of the beaten creature, one guard would have been enough. Indeed, after depositing their prisoner on the floor in an unceremonious clump, only one guard remained. The other hastened out, but then returned with a thick, wooden post. The base had been designed to sit perfectly in an open divot, and once placed, the guards proceeded to tie Botolu to the post in a standing position.

After they retreated out of the office, Rakmo stared at Roni with a defiant scowl. At least, Roni interpreted the look as such. Enough so that she blurted out, "You don't have to do this. He's not with us. He only happened to be where we appeared. It was chance."

"No." Rakmo rose to his feet and moved toward Botolu. "*She* leads those bent on destroying all that the Blue have built in the name of the great Hayle."

"But you said —"

Rakmo backhanded Botolu across the face. Her head snapped to the side before lolling forward. "I said that Master Hayle was a danger and he was. I watched him manipulate my people, and I saw how powerful he became in such a short time. If he could do so without any understanding of our language, our culture, our history, then I knew I could do so much better."

He smacked Botolu again. Roni flinched as if she had been struck, too.

"Stop," she said, holding still, trying not to betray any emotions that would anger Rakmo — both for her own and for Botolu's well-being.

"Hayle's approach promised upheaval, a destruction of all we held sacred. But that was a result of his ignorance." A strike to the stomach this time. "With careful, cautious, measured control, the Blue has allowed our world to grow into something so much more than we were destined to be. That is the great gift of Master Hayle."

Roni clenched her fists and bolted to her feet. Before she could speak, however, Botolu raised her head and clicked loudly. The mocking sound — Roni had no doubt to that — pulled Rakmo's attention.

In a scratched and strained voice, Botolu said, "You nothing but same. The Blue be old, cling to yesterday. The past ways fail in front of you yet you blind."

Rakmo shook his head. "This is the stupidity we have to handle. Her little group wants nothing more than to destroy all we have built. And why? Because some of our traditional ways of doing things no longer work with the way this younger generation thinks." He leaned towards Roni. "I fully admit that our world is not perfect, but they seem to think they know better than our centuries of accumulated wisdom."

"We peaceful before Hayle. We can again."

Keeping Roni's attention, Rakmo whipped his arm behind and slapped Botolu once more. Roni stormed in between the two. "Enough," she said, still holding her tone down. "I don't want to interfere, but I can't allow this abuse to go on."

"Do you hear her?" Rakmo flailed his arms at Botolu. "You see how they say that the Blue are locked into the past and yet they also want to return to our days before Master Hayle. They make no sense. The world we built, the one influenced by Master Hayle, is worth preserving. It has brought great prosperity to us."

"Not all," Botolu said.

Rakmo winced at the words. "Master Hayle taught that there would always be those that prosper and those that suffer when a society changes. That is an unfortunate yet necessary outcome."

The idea of being a diplomat soured Roni's stomach, but she had to salvage the situation for her team. Locking her face into a blank expression, watching her tone, she said, "I appreciate what you are trying to show me here. I'm sure that Hayle would be proud of all you have accomplished. I want to assure you that for myself and the Parallel Society, we only are here because we are following Hayle's travels in search of a friend."

Pulling his head back, Rakmo's hands gripped his chest as if they were the lapels of a vest. "No other humans have ever arrived."

"We know. But Hayle did not stay here. Eventually, he found a way to leave for another world. That was most likely through a book. If you will show us that book, we will leave and no longer disrupt your lives."

At mention of the book, Rakmo and Botolu shared an odd look. Roni felt a twist inside, a concerned note that she had screwed up. Both creatures seemed surprised, but she had no clue what could be said to patch over things.

With a flourish of his hands, Rakmo whirled toward the wall with carved art. Only now, Roni saw that the lines could be construed as a face. An old face. The artist's interpretation of a human face.

"Forgive me, Master Hayle," Rakmo said to the wall. "You promised the return would happen and that it would be difficult, yet I convinced myself that we merely had to show the weakness of our enemies and your people would understand."

"Oh crap," Roni whispered.

Turning back, Rakmo went on, "Master Hayle promised that if we followed his way, that we would grow strong as a people, that we would bring order to our world, that those who mattered would discover wealth. And he delivered. When he left us, he knew other humans would arrive one day. He promised it would happen. And he delivered. He said your arrival would be a sign of greater riches to come for your world has so much to give. And here you are."

"That's right," Roni said, looking for any out she could find. "The Parallel Society has returned. Hayle made it back home, and he wrote of you all and so we came to see for ourselves."

Rakmo pressed a small section of the wall and a tiny panel slid upward. He reached in and grabbed a small object. Returning to Roni, he placed it in her hand. A pocket watch. Silver. The chain long gone but the inscription still legible — *For my dear Hayle.*

"He left this with me. He said that if all of our efforts to prove our control fail, it would prove to you that I am the leader. For only a great mind can unlock the grand knowledge within it, and only a true leader can hold onto it. I present it to you so that you know beyond doubt I am worth listening to, that our enemies are weak, and that I should handle our trade."

"Trade?"

"Your riches for our riches. I learned well from Master Hayle. When we exchange what we value for what you value, we prosper. When we prosper, the Blue will gain greater strength in our world so that none will ever have to fear, starve, worry, again."

Roni glanced at Botolu's limp form. She held up the watch. "This is nothing special. It's just a machine to tell time. If Hayle made you think he had some divine knowledge, he lied."

"All he said has occurred. I have learned what I could about these trade deals, and I understand it is in your interest to make the powerful side appear less so, but I assure you, we are prepared to work hard for all of us. There is no need for games."

"I'm sorry, but we are not here to trade with your world. The truth is that Hayle would have said anything to get ahold of the passage out of here. He did not care about any of you."

She had not meant to be so blunt, but her neck burned as her muscles clenched in anger. She wanted to dig Hayle out of the grave and throttle him to death. How dare he. To abuse his position, to enslave generations of these creatures to a false belief in humans, all for what? The book? A raw rift? He would have found it eventually. No need to destroy an entire culture for it. But none of her thoughts would help, and now that she had opened her mouth, Roni feared she may have ruined matters for Botolu and possibly her team, too.

With a deep breath, she tried to relax. She lowered her shoulders from their tense position and forced a placating smile. "Perhaps I have misspoke."

"Misspoke?"

"Or maybe I misunderstood your words. It is clear that you have worked hard to maintain fluency in English, but maybe we are not speaking as clearly with each other as we would like." She didn't think this approach would work, but she had to try.

Except Rakmo paused. She could see him replaying the entire conversation, trying to figure out where things had gone wrong. But as he considered, Roni felt the air pressure in the room shift hard — popping her ears. Loose rocks tumbled off the walls. And that odd *whoosh* flowed around them, leaving a spicy-sweet aroma of coriander in its wake.

Watching her closely, Rakmo's body tensed for the first time of the entire meeting. "What trade trick is this?"

Roni glanced down at the watch in her hand. No longer silver, it now appeared to be plastic — orange and blue. She lifted her eyes to Rakmo. "Something bad is coming."

Chapter 10

Moving faster than Roni had seen before, Rakmo rushed to the window and gazed down upon his city. He pressed against the stone edge. The silence that followed thickened, promising a break of sound that would hurt regardless of the words that might accompany it. When Rakmo finally turned back, his grim countenance cut even worse.

"You come to my world," he said, loud and venomous. "You claim Master Hayle lies to us when all he has ever said has been true. Now, much as he said would be, you attempt to swindle us."

"No," she said. "I have nothing to do with this."

"We know plenty about these trade deceptions. Master Hayle taught us well."

"This is not about trade. This is an attack."

Rakmo faced Hayle's portrait again. "An attack? You threaten us without even bargaining in good faith."

"We are not the ones attacking."

"Then who?"

"I don't know."

"Of course not. You can only promise that we are in danger. I suppose you hold the answer to our survival and we should agree to whatever deal you want in order to be protected."

"I don't care about your stupid trade."

"Yet the only aggressors to have stepped into these caves in decades is you. I do not understand why you would be so against Master Hayle, but I do know when I hear lies."

A harried Coana burst into the office, and realizing its rudeness, dropped to a bow. It began clicking rapidly.

"In English," Rakmo said with impatience. "This human needs to understand that we see through her deceit."

The messenger peeked at Roni. "Um, yes. I report, um, attacks from walls."

"What does that mean? Speak clearer."

"Attacks, um, from animals, yes, grow from walls."

Another entered, saw the situation, and dropped next to the first messenger. It started to click when the first shoved it and clicked harshly.

"Sorry," the new arrival said. "Column North and Column Twice say they are being attacked by the moss."

Roni said, "Please. Let me get to my team."

"Be silent," Rakmo said, sweeping his arm in the air. He then pointed to the two bowing messengers. "You are to show me this moss. Guards, enter and take these prisoners back to the holding room."

"Listen to me," Roni said.

"Speak to me again and Botolu will be executed."

As the guard removed Botolu from the post, Roni backed up several steps and closed her mouth. Rakmo's sudden shift betrayed his growing fear — and possibly, a deeper uncertainty in his own abilities. It was easy to lead when everything went as expected, when only success and prosperity followed. When faced with a real challenge, however, a breaking of the norms, the true nature of a leader shined – or darkened.

Rakmo clicked to the messengers, and the three of them hastened out of the office. The two guards grunted and clicked at each other until one finally left. The other gazed over Roni and Botolu with a look that read as disdain in any culture.

"Go," he said, motioning to the exit.

Though Roni had no idea how to get back to her team, she knew to keep moving. Botolu followed and the guard brought up the rear. At times, he would grunt the words *that way* or *no, other way* or *down*. Roni obeyed.

Even if she wanted to rebel, the growing chaos in the column kept her following directions. Screams of surprise and pain echoed up from below. Clashes of stone and feral growls came next.

"Thank you for trying to help me," Botolu said. "I greatly appreciate it."

With a furrowed brow, Roni glanced back. "You're suddenly speaking well." She noticed that Botolu stood straight and walked firmly. "And you're not hurt."

"The pain was real, but not as bad as I made it look. We learned long ago that the Blue believe us to be weak and stupid. The more we play into that belief, the better for us."

"But he was going to torture you."

"It is especially important to act weak when they want to hurt us. Rakmo would refuse to admit the truth, but violence is not deep within our people. Just the opposite. There is a part of him, a part of them all, that cannot feel right about abusing someone already suffering."

"Not a big enough part, though."

"Sadly."

The guard ordered them through an archway on the right, and they entered a major intersection of numerous paths. Coana rushed from all directions, weaving around each other, hurrying from one archway and through another. Their clicking voices, rustling bodies, and slapping feet overflowed the room with sound bouncing off the walls and ceiling.

Until a loud bark — a thick guttural noise mixed with a higher-toned hum — came from one tunnel. Everyone halted. All the clicking ceased. Each face turned to the archway opening into that tunnel.

Another bark, and a hideous monstrosity burst forth. Roni expected this beast yet still had held hope she would be wrong. The oversized, lizard-skinned head and jutting snout with vicious teeth confirmed it all. Unlike the vile beast she had faced back at Yal-hara's old home, this bone creature's joints were covered in thick furry moss. Roni checked the ground for a puppet string vine controlling the beast but spotted nothing. Raising her head, she saw why — a thick, fibrous strand stretched from the moss clinging to the ceiling all the way into the creature.

As panic washed over the crowd, this predator grabbed at those foolishly rushing by. The guard abandoned his duty in seconds. He tore down one tunnel, leaving Roni and Botolu staring at each other.

"Do you know how to get to my team?" Roni asked.

"Follow me."

Botolu raced off to the left with Roni close behind. Pain-wracked cries of Coana kept pace with them, but Roni never asked Botolu to slow down. Part of her screamed to turn back and help. But there were more than one of these beasts — the numerous growls and barks attested to the fact. Roni and Botolu could not do much alone.

"This attack," Botolu said as she ran, "it is truly not your doing?"

"I don't know what it is exactly, but it might be connected with one of our enemies."

"Then maybe we'll find luck and Rakmo will be killed today."

Roni hid her surprise even as she wondered if Botolu spoke seriously or simply expressed her desire to be rid of a problem. Before she could think on it further, they rushed across a bridge, dropped a few more levels down, and reached the holding room. The two guards had kept their stations on either side of the entrance, their muscular chests pushing out their blue sashes.

As Roni and Botolu approached, both guards stiffened. The echoes of violence surrounding them, however, caused enough uncertainty that they were slow to react. Roni barreled right by and into the room. Her team jumped to their feet.

"Teanna, Gully, take care of these guards." Roni noticed the pleasure in Teanna's eyes as the warrior cracked her knuckles. To Garcia: "Check over Botolu and give her one of your healing potions." When Garcia hopped into action, Roni turned to Gram and showed her the watch. "Twice now. What does this mean?"

While Gram looked over this new evidence, Roni glanced back at the entrance. Gully dragged an unconscious guard into the room while Teanna stood astride the other one and pummeled him senseless. Closer in, Botolu held an empty vial and appeared to be reacting well to the elixir. Garcia watched her bruising closely, monitoring the healing effects and making sure the differences with human biology did not cause a poor reaction.

"I'm sorry, dear, but I've never seen this before. What struck you back at Yal-hara's has definitely followed us."

"Or could something be happening across more than one universe?"

"Possibly. All the more reason for us to leave this world and find the City of Infinity."

Pocketing the watch, Roni marched over to Botolu. "When I mentioned Hayle using a book, you and Rakmo both reacted. You clearly know about the book. Can you take us to it?"

"Of course," Botolu said with such ease that Roni stuttered a step.

Teanna and Gully joined the group, and the golem said, "So quick to help. You make things suspicious."

With her hatchets retrieved from the guards, Teanna added, "We are not in the mood for your world anymore."

"It's okay," Roni said. "I appreciate your caution, but I can vouch for her. She's proven herself."

Knocking her head from one speaker to the next, Botolu said, "It is no secret. Everyone knows of the Great Book. It is that very past which the Blue hold onto. They follow their traditions based on Hayle's power, and that all stretches back to the Great Book."

Gram said, "Then you've seen Hayle use the book?"

"Oh, yes. I will tell you, but if you want to see, we should leave. It is at the top of Mountain Pillar, and that is not an easy climb." She gestured to the pile of two guards. "Also, we should not be here when they awake."

Roni nodded. "Lead the way."

The group turned toward the exit when a lone moss-beast appeared in the archway. It leaned its massive lizard head back and barked its horrible noise.

"I've got it," Teanna said as she stormed forward, hatchets singing as they slid against each other.

The beast lunged towards her, but Teanna pivoted to the side, kicked off the wall, and landed behind. Before her enemy had a chance to turn around, she swung the hatched overhead, hacking through the mossy cord connecting the beast to the ceiling. A loud cry and the beast stumbled to its knees.

But then another moss-covered line shot out from the beast and reconnected to the ceiling. The beast rose, ready to fight again.

CHAPTER 11

Gully rushed behind the beast and locked it in a bearhug. While unable to move, it roared its anger. Teanna sliced above its head, severing this new moss line.

But the beast was ready this time. Even as the hatchet cut through the line, a new line flew out of the moss ringing the beast's neck. Teanna slashed at this one, but another spat out for the ceiling.

Botolu shivered at Roni's side. "What a fascinating and terrifying creature. Is this because we wish to go to the Great Book?"

Garcia knelt nearby, hastily pouring together a fresh concoction, while Gram formed a new book to dispose of the beast.

"There are many myths surrounding the Great Book," Botolu went on, "and I always considered them to be ways of keeping people from trying to open its power."

Flexing its arms outward, the beast broke free of Gully's grasp. The golem tumbled backward, knocking Garcia's vial to the floor and spilling its contents. The beast thrust both fists forward, catching Teanna in the hip. She stumbled, regained her footing, and snarled.

"Even more so, the myths were ways for Rakmo to keep his grasp on the people. Though, I suppose he has lived his lies for so long, he must believe them."

As the mossy monstrosity stomped ahead, several new control lines emerged from his neck to string up to the ceiling. Gram's book was ready, but she ran into the same problem Roni had experienced back home — no way to catch the moss-beast without also pulling in her own teammates.

"Rakmo is blind to the world we wish to bring about. A better, more peaceful world. He talks of holding onto the past, but he wants a past that never existed. A fantasy conjured by Hayle instead of the true world we all came from."

Roni tried to listen while making sure that Botolu remained safe – they needed her to find the Great Book. But Roni also needed to focus on the battle. The team often worked better when a leader coordinated their attacks — and she was that leader now. More importantly, she saw the answer.

"Gully, wrap around that thing's neck. Don't let it make another connection. Teanna, cut them all down."

She didn't have to say another word. Gully dashed across the room, jumped into the air, and tackled the beast to the floor. Both arms locked around the mossy neck as he pressed his clay muscles tight. At the same time, Teanna rushed up, standing one foot on the beast's bone chest, and utilized both hatchets to slice through all the moss lines.

The beast thrashed about as it strained to push a fresh line through the golem. But to no avail. Its legs kicked straight, its torso wracked to one side, yet it could not break free. When the motions slowed, Teanna dismounted but kept her hatchets up for another strike. Finally, the body fell apart, bones clattering against each other.

"Thank you," Botolu said. "I don't believe I could have stopped that animal."

Roni bit back a storm of remarks and simply said, "Take us to the Great Book. Now."

They left the carnage of the holding room, and Botolu led them through the crowds. She guided them up several ramps. The higher they went, the less populace the column became. In panic, most of the Coana headed downward, a large number opting to float their way to supposed safety.

"When Hayle left us," Botolu said, taking yet another ramp upward, "he made sure that we would never open the Great Book. He said it was a portal to deadly powers, that the greater beings of the universe would use the book to enter and destroy our world. They would subjugate our people and lay waste to all we cherished. If any other had said such a thing, we would have ignored him. At that moment, though, the majority had fallen under Hayle's influence and would believe any nonsense he stated. Even those who did not follow him still had the understanding that he could be a powerful being himself."

Gully said, "In all the years since, am I right that none of you has ever opened the book?"

They crossed a bridgeway to a new column — one that started this high up and continued higher, eclipsing all the others. It had a less polished design, more natural, and a bright light could be seen shining up top. A chilling breeze passed over.

Botolu gazed up. "This is Mountain Pillar. At the top is where we'll find the Great Book. It is a difficult climb, to go so high, and few have ever had the courage to attempt it. Those that did, never returned. So, yes to your question, Mr. Gully. Nobody alive has ever opened the Book. And if those that went up there did so, they never were able to tell about it."

Gram said, "Then why are you helping us get up there?"

"Because I don't believe the Great Book is so dangerous. At least, not in the way people have been taught. If it were this deadly, terrible thing, then why did Hayle step into it? That man was not brave. He was selfish. It never made sense to me that such a person would risk his life like that."

A two-toned beeping rose from the columns below. Botolu's face tightened. "That's an alarm. They must know you have left their custody."

"Then we better go," Roni said, peering up the narrow pathway that spiraled around the pillar. To her team, she said, "There won't be any railings. Judging from the cold, it might get icy, too. Be careful and stay focused."

"Wait," Gram said. With a flick of her wrist, a long chain streamed down to the ground.

"Good idea." Roni grabbed one end and handed it to Gully. "You're the anchor."

As the golem tied the end around his waist, he shrugged. "Of course. Whenever you need me, I'm there. It'd be nice for a little appreciation once-in-a-while, but I'm fine with the hard end of the work. Always."

Roni played out the chain several feet before handing it to Garcia. After he looped it around, she moved on to Teanna, then Gram, and finally herself. Botolu stared in shock. "You do have power."

"Some. Use this for protection."

"No need. I'm quite capable." She led the way up.

As they trekked onward, Roni glanced back at everyone. Gram crossed herself and kissed her pendant. Teanna and Garcia looked ahead with firm, determined stares. Gully's eyes brightened and he waved at Roni. She turned away to hide her chuckling.

Trudging along the steep path, a rhythmic silence overcame them.

Silent in that nobody spoke. Rhythmic in that a steady beat of grunts, stomps, and breaths filled the emptiness. The rattle of the chain between them provided a melody of sorts, and it, too, seemed to fall into the same rhythm.

The cold air sharpened as the wind picked up. No longer a chilled breeze, it now blew with a bite. Snow dusted the ground as flakes danced on the wind in a sparse display.

Eventually, Roni called for the team to rest. Nobody argued. The chain had been digging into their skin, and they each wriggled out of the oppressive line. They pressed their backs against the craggy wall, sitting down and rubbing their sore waists. Roni thought they had covered half the distance to the top and guessed the second half would be far more difficult — the bitter cold, if nothing else.

The light at the top had brightened and grown. It seemed to halo the peak, but Roni still couldn't tell the source. She guessed the Blue had some guards stationed up there and they had several large fires burning for warmth. Except the light looked pale instead of amber. Then again, she had no idea what they burned, so the fire could have been purple for all she knew. Its intense light sent a bright glow outward while also reflecting off the cavern ceiling – that much she could tell.

Less than five minutes later, Botolu peered over the edge. "Rakmo's here."

Taking the chain in one hand, Roni crawled over to gaze down the sheer drop. She made out a handful of splotches moving along the pathway. "How can you tell that's Rakmo?"

"Human eyesight is weak. You must trust me. We should go."

Roni pushed up to her feet. She faced the group. "Time to move. Rakmo and several blue sashes are starting after us."

She gestured below as a wind gust poured down the pillar like a dumped bucket of water. It slammed into Roni and shoved her. When her foot reached back for balance, she found only air.

As she tumbled into open space, she heard Gram yelling her name.

CHAPTER 12

Roni's stomach flipped with her body. Bits of snow pelted her face as the long drop below and the cold light above swapped places over and again. Sweat rippled along her skin, sliding her grip on the chain. She heard screaming. Only her burning throat suggested the sound came from her.

A vicious tug and the chain stopped giving line. The sudden jolt jacked her arms, threatening to pull them from the sockets. The chain ripped the skin of her hands and she shredded down to the end.

Her grip locked tight — all instinct, no thought. She no longer flipped, but her momentum sent her spinning clockwise like a figure skater increasing speed. Roni stuck out her foot, hoping to scrape the pillar and slow down. Though she hit nothing, her spinning did lessen.

"I've got you," Gully said.

"Everyone on the chain," Gram yelled.

Roni glanced up, managing to see that Gully had never removed the chain and still remained the anchor. The others wrapped their arms around the taut chain, risking their lives should any of them fall. They heaved back, lifting Roni a short distance. But when they reached forward to grab more chain, she dropped a bit. Not as far as she rose, though.

Her biceps trembled. Her fingers cramped. She wanted to snake her leg around the chain, but the end did not reach far enough down. Taking controlled, slow breaths, she focused on maintaining her grip. From above, she heard the groans as they heaved back to gain another short distance.

Three more times, she felt the chain pull her higher. Twice, they slipped and she fell back some. The hard blowing winds froze down her back and into her sides. She closed her eyes, trying to remove her mind from the agony in her muscles.

But she saw Yal-hara. She could feel that awful monster crawling along her body, its spindle legs poking into her as it found purchase enough to lean in close. Roni tried to banish the image, the thoughts, but instead, she conjured Yal-hara's crackling, hissing voice.

Give up, Yal-hara said. *Let go and be done with it. All your problems will be over and you can finally rest.*

It sounded exactly like the horrid creature. But why would her weary brain say such a thing? Surely, she knew herself well enough by now — she would never consider suicide a legitimate answer to any problem.

A new set of shivers shook her body.

Could that voice actually be Yal-hara? Perhaps the same force with which she had stolen Roni's memories so long ago also kept them connected. If true, then Yal-hara might be able to infiltrate Roni's mind and make such vile suggestions. Yet to do so must also require a lot of energy or time or both. If it had been cheap and easy, Yal-hara would have been bouncing through Roni's mind every day. But this was the first time contact had been made.

Roni snickered. *Yal-hara must be scared,* she thought. She held her breath and reconsidered the idea that Yal-hara's words might not be from her own head but rather planted there. Or possibly communicated from another universe. *Or I'm losing my marbles.* She laughed. Hard. And lost her hold on the chain.

"No!" Gram shrieked.

Roni reached out as if she could find the chain again, even as she saw Gram recede into the dark. Her heart jumped gears, pounding hard enough to cause chest pain. Her fingers still bent as if clutching the lost chain, and she wondered if it would be better to watch the ground approach or simply stare above and wait. Tears soaked her eyes.

Until she spotted an alabaster movement — Botolu jumping off the side. The Coana held her body in tight, bulleting down through the air. Roni's chest tingled deep within and she worried she might be having a heart attack. Botolu swished right by, the air flowing in her wake, and Roni flipped over to watch this strange creature.

Facing the ground, the wind resistance of falling smashed against her, drying up her eyes and mashing back her cheeks. She had to squint in order to see, and Botolu had become so small that she blended in with the snowflakes. For a held breath, Roni understood that Botolu had given up. With the leader of the Parallel Society plummeting to her death, the creature had lost whatever opportunities she saw in helping.

Best to escape, regroup, and fight another day.

Except in the next inhalation, Roni saw a white circle expand below. An instant later, she dropped into Botolu's arms — the creature's bottom half ballooning outward filling with air.

Roni gripped Botolu with all the strength she could muster. "Thank you," she whispered.

"We're not safe yet."

They were still falling — with nothing like the gentle grace Roni had witnessed of the Coana in the past. Of course not. With Roni's added weight, they dropped faster.

"Do not worry much. I can guide us back to the pillar. But the landing will be rough."

Roni looked to the large slab of rock bulging upward. It grew larger as they drifted in, and every instinct in her promised they approached too fast. Her body tensed as she lowered her chin to protect her throat.

They flew over the pathway and crashed into the rocky side. Both of them shouted until the force of hitting the wall robbed them of the air needed to make sound. Roni toppled end over end, bruising up her shoulders and back, rear and legs. She curled tight, trying to cover everything vital, until she banged against the steep pathway and spewed out the last of the air in her lungs.

Inhaling sharply, coughing back hard, she eased her legs out. Botolu drifted to the path and settled with ease. Roni wanted to laugh but she ended up coughing more. The cold air felt like a gentle blanket after all her stressed sweating.

"Thank you," she managed to whisper out.

"You're welcome. But I'd be lying if I said it was done purely to help you." Botolu turned her head down the pathway, then up, then glanced over the edge. "I need to get you and your friends to the Great Book. I need you to use it and show the world that Rakmo is full of lies."

"We'll get there." Roni sat up. "And I'll try not to fall off the pillar ever again."

"That would be helpful."

Brushing off her pants as she stood, Roni pushed away the negative thoughts plaguing her mind, thoughts that discouraged her from hiking up once more, retreading the same pathway, burning more energy, tiring her exhausted muscles. None of that mattered. Because at the end, she would be one step closer to finding Elliot, closer to bringing him home.

"Stop!" Botolu said.

Roni stared at her — confused and a little shaken by the firmness in Botolu's voice. But then she heard the sounds of movement behind. When she turned around, Rakmo approached with four burly, blue-sashed Coana accompanying him.

Botolu pushed by Roni. The protrusions that looked like stunted arms flexed forward. The tips glistened, and Roni wondered if they spit out some type of poison. Whatever they did, it was enough to make Rakmo and his cohorts freeze.

"Turn back," Botolu said. "There is nothing for you up here. Nothing but death."

CHAPTER 13

Standing on a pathway ledge far above the populated columns, feeling the frigid winds whipping around the cylindrical Mountain Pillar as her drained pulse throbbed onward, part of Roni wanted to slump over and sleep. But that was the same part that mimicked Yal-hara only moments before, that old defeatist that questioned everything and everyone, the whiny brat that she had fought against all her life. Rolling her shoulders back, she lifted her chin. Joining the Parallel Society and experiencing all that came with it had tamed that part of her. She refused to let it loose once again.

Keeping her tone firm despite her jittering nerves, she said, "We did not come here to fight. We simply want to leave."

Rakmo did not move or speak or even click, yet his guards reacted as if given an order — all four raised their dangerous arm protrusions. A pause, and Rakmo clicked with what sounded like patronizing disappointment. To Botolu, he said, "Look at how quickly you have thrown away your principles. You profess to embrace our ancient, peaceful ways yet threaten violence at the first challenge."

"I am not threatening you. Merely stating a fact of our situation."

"Ah. I knew you could speak." With a casual motion, as if having a friendly debate with an old colleague, Rakmo linked his hands over his belly. "This hardly seems like the time for wordplay — in their language or ours." He clicked something fast, and Botolu bristled.

"You have abused the trust and authority our people have bestowed upon you. You seek to stop these humans for what it might do to your hold on power, not what is best for our lives. If you continue this way, I will fight." She took one step closer. "Even the most peaceful should not be afraid to battle for justice and the rightful futures afforded us all."

"Hold on," Roni said, nauseous at the idea of a brawl on this narrow path. Easy for them, of course — if they fell, they could puff out their bottom half and float to safety. Roni had nosedived to her near death once already. That was enough. "I realize our arrival here has stirred up hard, deep troubles between your groups. I'm sorry for that. But —"

"If you want to debate our issues," Rakmo said, barely taking an eye off Botolu, "then return to the room we provided you, let us finish dealing with the strange animals you brought into our world, and stop trying to undermine all the good Master Hayle has taught us."

"Thank the Lord you're okay." Gram hustled toward Roni, tears rolling down her round face.

The rest of the team followed, and Roni noted the relief in each members' eyes. She wanted to smile at them and offer a nod of thanks, but she needed to stay focused. Especially when the blue sashes stepped close behind Rakmo and filled up the pathway.

"Be careful," she said to Rakmo. "The Parallel Society are seasoned warriors who have battled far deadlier things than you. And unlike Botolu, we have no moral qualms with necessary violence." She nudged Botolu to the side and walked straight up to Rakmo. "Don't make it necessary."

"Now, now," Gram said with a nervous laugh, "there's no need for all this behavior."

Roni swallowed down the urge to yell at Gram, but Rakmo appeared taken by surprise.

Gram continued, "Am I correct that your followers are not as fluent in English?"

"Yes," Rakmo said, eyeing his guards.

"Then please forgive us for putting you in such a difficult position. My granddaughter did not mean to back you into a corner — that's an expression of ours. It means that she got you to a point of limited decisions."

Glancing back, Roni mouthed, *What are you doing?*

"Don't mistake me. She's absolutely correct that we are far better at fighting than you, and we will defeat you with ease. But I am older, I've been around longer, and I have seen the way people like you react when threatened in front of their followers."

Crap. Roni was so riled by nearly dying and then facing Rakmo that she hadn't considered his situation. If he allowed Roni to get away with all of her threats, he would lose power over his guards. Even if they couldn't understand the words spoken, they certainly understood the standoff. Rakmo couldn't back down.

Bowing her head slightly, Roni said, "I apologize. It was not my intention to —"

"Apologize?" Botolu spit the word as if it were poison. "To the one who would gladly kill all who oppose him if given enough shadows to do it in? No. I will not let any of you betray my people."

Rakmo spat out several fast clicks before saying, "You have no right to speak that way of me. I have served our world well. Brought so many a better life."

"Only those you think worthy. The rest of us are subjected to poverty and abuse."

Waving her hands high in the air, Gram said, "Stop this. There's no reason to act like spoiled children. The solution to all of this has not changed. We do not belong here. The sooner we leave, the sooner you can return to your lives. Mr. Rakmo, you will find it much simpler to control how people perceive what has happened when we are not around. In our world, we call that *spin.* You can turn the story into whatever you want. But only if we are gone. If we remain, then we can speak as well. You've seen a little of our strength. Believe me, believe Roni, believe the same powers that brought you Hayle — you do not want us to flex our muscles."

Stunned silence overcame them all. Only the soft patter of snowflakes against the pillar could be heard. Roni reached over and clutched Gram's hand. Gazing beyond, she noticed that both Teanna and Garcia had readied for battle — hatchets and potions in hand, feet set apart for sturdy balance. For his part, Gully held the chain taut between his hands.

Rakmo held stone still, the snow accumulating on his shoulders. The way he locked eyes with Roni made her think they were in a game of chicken. Until he finally brushed off the snow and relaxed his body. He motioned to his guards, and they inched closer to him.

After a round of clicks, he said, "Your grandmother is a wise person. I see how being rid of you will make our problems easier to handle."

Gram nodded, unable to hide the blush in her cheeks. "Then we'll get going, and we will pray that you find good fortune for your world."

"But," Rakmo said, and there was no mistaking his tone — this was not over, "you do not understand the Great Book. You think it is a tool, and perhaps it can be, but it is far more than that. It is a transit to the deep powers of the universe, the divinity that binds us, that keeps our world from tearing apart into nothing but the smoke and vapor rippling off a flame. Master Hayle brought us profound knowledge that changed our world forever. He also taught us of the way existence always attempts to maintain balance."

As Rakmo continued on, Roni's fists rolled tight. She did not like the idea of a physical confrontation in these narrow confines — she didn't like the idea of a fight at all — but each word out of Rakmo's mouth confirmed what she already knew. He was a zealot. And there was no negotiating with a zealot.

"You see now? We continue to prosper only because we have listened and obeyed Master Hayle's instructions. He warned us against opening the Great Book without specific procedures — special magic, some call it. To do so could be disastrous to all. Not just destructive but deadly."

A slight movement caught Roni's attention. Gully. He had slipped toward the front, scooting along the wall until he stood by her side. Though Rakmo took no notice – caught up in his own revery, he barely saw those he lectured in front of — his guards certainly reacted. They clumped even closer to their leader, crowding against each other like a Roman phalanx without the shields.

"So, while I pity the unfortunate position you are in, I cannot condone your solution. You will not be allowed to the summit, and you will not be allowed to open the Great Book."

Roni eased one foot back and to the side. Teanna had taught them all the basics of good fighting, and it always started with a strong stance. While taking a fighter's stance earlier might have provoked a bad reaction, Roni saw no other choice now. Rakmo acted determined to escalate things.

She glanced at Botolu one last time, hoping for an answer there. Nothing. A complete blank. Probably, events had moved too fast for Botolu to keep up. Especially after Gram had pointed out the benefits to Rakmo of the Parallel Society leaving. Roni leaned closer, ready to promise that they would not abandon these people. But she held back. She didn't want to lie, and while her intentions would be true, that amounted to little when faced with numerous forms of subjugation.

It turned out not to matter. Gully attacked.

Shocking every living being on that pathway, Gully launched forward, rushing the guards with his arms out wide. He barreled into the group, letting out a deep growl unlike anything Roni had ever heard from the golem. Three guards toppled off the ledge.

"What are you doing?" Rakmo said, whirling around, searching for a safe direction to move.

The remaining guard plowed into Gully. Its protrusions rammed forward like pistons. They jabbed into Gully's clay chest, leaving behind numerous holes, each one oozing poison. But golems did not have blood, and the poison dribbled down — useless and ineffective.

Stepping back perplexed, the guard watched the poison as if able to make it flow back into the enemy. But Gully did not hesitate. He planted his hands on the blue sash and propelled the guard straight off the pillar.

Rakmo pointed at Botolu, his hatred reddening his pale form. "I thought we could find common ground, but you make allies with these animals. You should —"

Botolu grabbed Rakmo's outstretched hand and twisted it hard. Rakmo emitted high-pitched clicking as he tried to pull his hand free. Botolu shoved forward — not too hard, Roni thought, but enough to send the off-balance creature into the air to join his guards.

Looking back, Roni saw Teanna shrugging. Garcia and Gram were equally surprised. Gully had moved so fast, they never had chance to help.

"They won't die that way," Gully said, standing on the lip of the path and watching the decent of Rakmo and his guards.

"Of course not," Botolu said. "But they will have to climb again to catch us."

Roni clapped Gully on the shoulder before picking up the chain. As she looped the front end around her waist and handed the rest to Gram, she said, "Then we should get going."

CHAPTER 14

The air around them continued to smell fresher the higher they trudged Mountain Pillar's steep path. But Roni could taste the urgency and concern of her team. Like coffee — smelled wonderful, tasted bitter. The chain dug into her hip as she pushed harder. Gram huffed with each step as did the others. It could be damaging to keep this pace, but nobody suggested a rest. Rakmo and the Blue were behind them — angry and humiliated. They would not be slowing down.

After they passed the point where Roni had fallen, she continually checked and rechecked the chain. Botolu kept several feet ahead, leading the way (though there was no other way to go) and scouting ahead (though there had been no sign of anything living on this cold rock). Nobody spoke. The silence did not embrace them. Rather it weighed heavy. Forcing them to think about the threat closing in from below.

At least, Roni took the silence that way. For all she knew, Garcia designed new potion possibilities based on this world's version of snow and stone while Teanna happily played out scenarios in which she disemboweled Rakmo.

Still, Roni decided a little conversation would help distract everyone. Plus, perhaps more importantly, she wanted a specific answer. "Gully, thank you for getting us free and on our way."

"It's all part of my golem services," he said, his Yiddish accent growing thicker each day.

"But why did you do it?"

"You told me to. I would never have done such a thing without your command."

"I never said a word."

"Wasn't that the look you gave me? When you turned back, you looked at me and nodded."

"I didn't."

"You gave a look."

"I swear I didn't."

"I may only be clay and stone but I know a look when I see one and you gave me a look."

She heard muffled snickering from the others. Good. That had to be worth at least another fifteen minutes of hiking.

More silence. Only this did not feel so oppressive.

While the temperature continued to drop, Roni found her breathing did not strain any greater. The air had not thinned. Perhaps they really were underground. The heights they climbed only brought them closer to the surface. She had imagined that while closed up like a cavern, the world they were in might have been enclosed everywhere with no surface to reach. Not so much a cavern as a world locked in stone. Now she considered that the truth might be simpler.

"Hold up!" Garcia called out.

The wind howled as it whirled around the pillar, and for a moment, nobody could say a word or move an inch. They had to stand still and endure. Roni spit out the snow that accumulated on her lips before finally turning back.

"What's the problem?" she yelled.

He waved her over. As the rest of team huddled, he crouched to the ground. Roni approached with overly-cautious steps. Climbing upward had been easy to keep a strong pace — she always had one hand on the chain and one against the wall. As long as she never stopped touching the wall, she would not end up too close to the edge. But the circle around Garcia made such a safety measure difficult to maintain. She refused to be on the lip of the pathway, but she didn't want to push anybody else away from the wall.

"Come here, dear," Gram said, turning sideways to make room. Though a full step in the wrong direction, Roni braved taking the spot. It helped that Gram placed a secure arm around her shoulder. Roni wouldn't even have minded if Gram muttered a prayer or two.

Teanna gestured at Garcia. "You stopped everything for a pile of rocks?"

Indeed, Garcia squatted next to a fissure in the wall spotted with various sized rocks at the base.

Gully said, "I appreciate you thinking of me, but it will take too long to make a golem big enough to handle all five of our enemies."

"They're not really enemies," Gram said. "Not to any of us but

Botolu."

Before the two could digress further, Roni flapped a hand at Garcia. "What's special about these rocks?"

He gave a grateful nod. "It's not the rocks. It's the crack in the wall that made them. Give me a moment, make sure they don't catch us, and I can block up this road. Stop Rakmo completely."

"Quit wasting time and get to it. Gully, Teanna — stand guard for Garcia. Warn us if you see Rakmo or the Blue."

As they moved into position, Garcia swung open his bag and began mixing ingredients. Gram pulled Botolu aside, and Roni could hear her explaining what to expect. For her part, Botolu backed the idea fully — even wondered if perhaps Rakmo could be killed in the process. Roni wasn't sure if Botolu wanted Rakmo dead or expressed concern about such an outcome. It wouldn't be the first time that a peace-loving soul discovered the vicious animal within.

Roni had learned that about herself long ago. She had never sought the violence of her life — fighting monsters, banishing them into empty universes, hunting down those that didn't belong in her universe and sometimes destroying them. All of it had been thrust upon her when she joined the Society. Before that, she had been an average woman. Boring, even. Did that mean she condoned the violence? Did that mean she had betrayed her peaceful ways?

She hoped not. Because she believed in the ultimate goal of the Society — to protect their universe from others. If they did their job right, the violence would be controlled and limited. The peaceful days would be far greater. At least, peaceful from other universes. She had no control over the destruction mankind wrought upon itself.

"Ready." Garcia shook a vial of black liquid.

Roni snapped her focus to the man and gestured for him to start. After snatching a peek down the path, Garcia dribbled the thick liquid into the wall fissure. He continued pouring until some of it pooled at the base, winding between the rock debris. Scooting over the newly formed black puddle, Garcia dumped the remainder of the vial.

"I see them," Teanna said.

Waving at her, Garcia said, "Get over here. We're all set."

Teanna and Gully hustled up the path until they were above the liquid. From his bag, Garcia produced a lighter and sparked it alive. He placed a thin string down — one end in the liquid, one end stretching several feet away. With the flame held in one hand, he pointed at the group to move further up.

Breathing hard, Rakmo's voice preceded him. "We are finished with diplomacy. You will all be punished for what you have done."

Roni held off covering her ears, but she expected a ground-shaking experience. Instead, when Garcia lit the makeshift fuse and scurried back toward them, when he crouched with his head bowed against the wall, when Rakmo and the Blue appeared at the turn in the pathway, she heard a soft pop and saw smoke puff out of the wall. A line of rocks spewed across the path, several going far enough to slip over the edge, but that was it. Easy to walk over.

"Well, shit." Roni hoped nobody far below would be struck by the falling debris.

"Language," Gram said.

Rakmo faltered when the rocks tumbled out, but then his amused clicking could be heard — Roni recognized the specific sound now. Soon, the blue-sashed guards joined in. They all continued to close the gap.

She was about to whirl around, yell for her team to run, and hope they could find some way to regain the distance advantage they had squandered. But then she saw Garcia — still crouching, still tucking his head, still pressing against the wall. Teanna and Gram understood. Or perhaps they felt the rumble vibrating against their feet. Because they turned their backs to the rocks and dropped down. Gully followed. The rumble strengthened like an earthquake reaching further and further from its epicenter. Roni had just enough seconds to grab Botolu's hand and yank her to the ground.

Though she saw a bright flash — brighter due to the general dark of the underground world — and glimpsed part of the wall burst into the air, Roni managed to get her head down and protected fast enough that she heard the explosion more than witnessed it. A thunder of mythic proportions shattered all other sounds. Obliterated all sense of noise. This was more than the cracking of hard, ancient stone. It roared like the birthing of Zeus and the death of a Titan.

Roni covered her ears while balled up with her back toward the cavern ceiling. She felt small stones pelt her as they rained down. They plunked upon the pathway like hail while echoes of the shocking explosion rolled into the distance.

When it finished, she lifted her head. A massive pile of rock and dirt blocked the pathway. Garcia jumped up and danced in front of the ten-foot wall. He wore a great smile and pumped a fist in the air.

As the others clambered to their feet, Botolu stared at the debris wall with petrified awe. "You really have godly power."

"No, dear." Gram cleaned the stone dust off her sleeves. "Just a long history of war in our world."

Roni said, "Great job. But we're not done yet. Chain up and let's go. That'll slow them down, but they might be able to climb over."

With a few congratulatory slaps on Garcia's back, the team lined up with the chain and resumed the final push toward the top of Mountain Pillar. They moved with more confidence and more urgency. Plowing through the thickening snow, sweating despite the cold, they stomped step after step until finally the darkness blasted away under a bright sun splashing through an enormous opening in the ceiling. Roni's foot came down upon a flat surface. The path had ended. They had reached the top.

Flat and snow-covered, the plateau of the pillar looked smaller than Roni had expected. The opening gap above, however, was large enough to contain a circus, a football team, and probably an entire Broadway musical cast combined. Sitting in the center, Roni saw a wooden podium. Strange how many of the worlds, despite their vast differences, used the same structure to hold a book — a simple podium.

They all crossed the short distance and huddled around the book. No chain. No lock. No protection at all. Then again, the taboo of opening it kept most from daring to come here, and the rest would have to make a treacherous climb.

Placing her hand on the cover, Gram said, "I can still feel its energy. Such an old book, and yet it still vibrates like it was formed days ago."

"Why shouldn't it?" Gully said. "Don't your books last as long? Don't all the books in the caverns?"

"This is different. The caverns of our bookstore exist to hold those chained books. Outside of that place — you never know. The books at the Abbey in Ireland had to be replaced regularly. Part of me wondered if we would find an open rift up here alongside a deteriorated book."

Teanna glanced at the pathway. "We don't have forever. Can you open it or not?"

Gram lifted the cover. A warm firelight flickered up from deep within. Thankfully, no depressurization winds blew either in or out of the book.

Roni took Botolu by the shoulders. "Thank you for your help. I know we're leaving your world a bit worse than when we got here. That's not the way we're supposed to do things, but I promise we will return to help you."

Botolu shrugged loose. "My people have been hurt by such promises."

"I am not Hayle."

"And I am not stupid. While I have come to believe your intentions are honorable, none who have gone through that book have ever returned. Why should you be any different?"

"Because we understand where we're headed." A half-truth since she had no clue if the book would get them directly to their goal, but at least she could keep her face stern and true.

"That may also be so, but only if I go with you can I guarantee you will make every effort to come back and help fix this world."

"It's not that simple."

Garcia said, "Stop arguing. Rakmo is coming and we've got to go."

Botolu gestured to the book, though her eyes narrowed on it — a bit more fearful than she probably wanted Roni to see. She said, "Would you leave me here to face Rakmo alone?"

Now it was Roni's turn to look at the book unsure. "We are most likely going into a fight against a violent, horrible creature. You won't last long as a pacifist."

"That is my problem to face. Do not forget that you would have fallen to your death without me. Perhaps I'm good to have on your team."

Teanna shoved Roni's shoulder. "Talking time is over. I can hear them coming. Everybody into the book."

A gust of wind ripped over from the surface above. Snow waterfalled down, hit the flat where they stood and spread out in all directions. As it wafted into the open air and began its long decent, Roni considered grabbing the book and finding a way to climb further up. If they could reach the surface — a part of this world that the Coana had clearly not explored — then perhaps they could help Botolu now.

Roni shook off the thought. That was guilt speaking. She hated leaving this world to Rakmo knowing he would do as Gram had described — spin any story he wanted about them. But Elliot had to come first. Without being whole, they would never succeed against their foes. Especially Yal-hara.

"I will go first," Gully said.

Gram said, "We might need you to defend as the rest of us enter."

"But if something dangerous is on the other side, I am more capable of facing it. I should be the one —"

Teanna pushed him. "Just go already."

More than anything, the strain of her voice awoke Roni. She could hear Rakmo and the Blue approaching. They grunted and huffed, making no attempt at stealth.

"Hurry," Roni said. "Everyone in."

At her command, the team finally responded. Gully poked his head in. He pulled back, and set the book open on the ground. "It's a drop again. Not too bad. Not too good, either. Be careful. But it looks like a comfy room. I recommend holding onto the book's edge first. I will demonstrate."

"If you don't get in there," Teanna said, "I'll demonstrate how to hack off a golem's arm."

Shaking his head, Gully stepped into the book, holding onto the edge as he lowered down. "I understand the situation, but it won't do any good if one of us breaks a leg falling in here." He dangled by his hands for a second, his voice dim as it traveled to them from another universe, and then he let go.

Garcia did not hesitate to go next. Gram followed. Then Roni pointed to Botolu. "Your turn."

"Is there any special way to do it? Should I hold on like Mr. Gully?"

"You've got your lower-half to slow you down. You can just jump in."

"But the Book is small. How did the others fit? How will I?"

"Trust the book. It'll make it work."

With apprehension trembling through every motion, Botolu approached the book. Roni offered a warm tilt of her head as if to say that she understood but everything would be okay. After all, she did comprehend that this was more than travel for Botolu. To her, this was the *Great Book*. This was the path that those who never returned had taken. This was a religious experience.

Yet despite all her fears — both real and imagined — Botolu stood at the book, closed her eyes, and very much like Gram, paused as her lips moved in silence. A prayer. Then she jumped in.

"Stop!" Rakmo yelled. "You will bring evil onto us all!"

Roni pushed Teanna. "Your turn."

She could see that Teanna wanted to go last, to be a line of defense for the others, but Roni also saw the disciplined warrior. Her leader had given an order. This was not the time to argue.

With a single nod, Teanna dropped into the book. Rakmo and the

Blue stood at the end of the pathway. Shock paled his already pale skin. Too late, and he knew it. Snow swirled from above, and he gazed upward as if seeing the divine.

Roni moved to the book. She stared directly at Rakmo as a thought struck her. "Be careful what you tell this world. Because unlike Hayle, we will return. And if Botolu's people suffer more, you will answer for it. All of you will."

She didn't wait for a response. Instead, she grabbed the book's cover and closed it behind her as she entered a new universe.

Dropping down, she flopped onto a soft rug covering a hardwood floor. Dark brown beams crossed overhead and darker trim outlined plaster walls. A hefty fire crackled in a fireplace, blazing warmth throughout the book-filled room.

A study. Old human style. Electric lights but they were placed inside lanterns to maintain the throwback effect, and thick wooden shutters blocked the windows as if preparing for the Dust Bowl.

Roni gazed up at her team. All stared beyond her, jaws open as wide as their eyes. Her heart sank. Her shoulders slumped. Couldn't they catch a break just once? However, before she turned around to face this new threat, she heard a deep, rich, familiar voice and knew that they had indeed caught their break.

"At last," Elliot said, "my dear friends have arrived. Welcome to the City of Infinity."

Chapter 15

All of the Parallel Society rushed upon Elliot with tears and hugs and exuberance. He laughed – a smile wide and full. They gathered together like a family reunited after a soldier's lengthy deployment. Roni saw how Elliot made sure to touch each one of them, make eye contact, and assure them all that he was healthy, in good spirits, and most importantly, still on mission, still fighting for their world.

But he also looked older, grayer, more wrinkled. Whatever hardships he had endured, they had taken more than a toll upon him. He leaned heavier on his cane, trembled in his fingers, and had the far-away gaze of a man who had survived war. Yet he still commanded the room. He still had a spark to his eye. Perhaps it was seeing his treasured friends again — at least, in part — but Roni suspected he simply loved the action, the purpose, the value behind the Parallel Society.

Using his cane, he pointed across at a creature with an insect body and a young man's head. "This is Otaur. He is a member of his world's Parallel Society, but he's also a great asset to us and an even greater friend."

Otaur placed one of his multiple arms over his chest. "I am indeed honored to have the gracious opportunity of making your acquaintance. So much over these years has been conferred and transpired that one might say I have grown accustomed to you long before this precise moment."

"Years?" Teanna said.

Elliot scratched his back as he winced. "Yes, well, as we have suspected for longer than I was ever part of the Society, time moves at different paces in different universes."

Placing a loving hand on his arm, Gram said, "It's been several months since you left."

"Many years here. But no matter. I never gave up that you would come for me, and I have had plenty to deal with just keeping this world together."

"Yal-hara?" Roni said.

"Naturally." Elliot pulled a well-used handkerchief from his back pocket and patted his brow. "Otaur, would you please get the phone." He finally looked beyond the group. "And who is this?"

Botolu stepped forward. "I suppose I am the founding member of my world's Parallel Society."

Grinning, Roni said, "A lot has happened on our way to finding you."

"A pleasure to meet you." Elliot made a slight bow over his cane. To Roni: "A lot has been happening here, too. A war is building as Yal-hara gains more and more control. I have helped form a resistance, but I've learned that I truly need all of you. It is too difficult alone."

Otaur walked over, his hard-shell body clacking a steady rhythm. "Your phone."

Elliot flipped open an unusual device. Similar in shape to the phone in Roni's pocket, this one had loose fringe on the edges that moved in a haphazard manner — as if the phone were alive.

"It's finally happened," Elliot said after tapping at it and putting it to his ear. "Yes, I'm serious. I have them here right now. Follow our procedure and make your calls. Close up and head to the meeting point. There's no need for the waiting areas anymore."

Garcia warmed his hands by the fire. Roni had to admit that after the bitter cold of Mountain Pillar, this cozy room welcomed them more than she could have hoped for. Minus the repeated feeling of being watched by Otaur. She couldn't tell if he was merely curious about her or suspicious. Probably both.

Elliot pressed a button on the phone, and the weird fringe curled inward. He snapped it shut and handed it back to Otaur. "There is a lot I must tell you all, but first, we have to close this house and join the others."

As the old man moved to lock the window shutters, his insect partner doused the fire. Garcia shuddered as if surged with sudden chills. Roni clamped her mouth — she had far too many questions, but it looked like the answers would be coming, if she could be patient.

Gram, on the other hand, had no patience. Her eyes widened as she moved to help her dear friend. "You are clever."

"I am nothing special."

"I'll be the judge of that."

They spoke with a rhythm of familiar banter, and not only did Elliot smile, but so did Gram — both in a way that Roni had not seen before. Then again, she had not seen them separated by a time-shifting universe before. Thinking on it more, she saw in Gram's face the same strong desire that had pushed Roni from the start. Despite her earlier protests, Gram had wanted to find Elliot just as badly as Roni had. Perhaps more.

Gram said, "You've been waiting for us all this time, but you didn't know where we would appear or when."

"It was a problem. However, I had the help of Otaur and several others from other universes. Together we pinpointed the seven most logical entries you would use, depending upon which books would bring you here, and we purchased those properties."

"Like we did in Egypt back in '83."

Elliot chuckled. "There is a similarity, I suppose."

Gully said, "I don't have any of my creator's memories about Egypt. What happened there?"

But before Elliot or Gram could respond, Otaur said, "I am most sorry to interrupt, but it is eminently certain that Yal-hara is also cognizant of this auspicious arrival and has deployed at least a full squad of her soldiers."

With a grim brow, Elliot said, "You're right. We must go."

"Soldiers?" Teanna pushed off the back wall where she had been leaning, quietly observing.

"Not to worry. Come along."

Hobbling with his cane, he opened the one door in the place. It led to a long, metallic hall. Dirt and rust lined the edges. Several other doors dotted the walls and, at the far end, a large, riveted gate waited.

When they reached the end, Otaur yanked open the gate — it slid to the right along a track. A wooden fence gate was revealed, and through this, they all could see a freight elevator about the size of a bedroom. It had a metal bench opposite them and large, clear sides. A single light had been mounted on the center of the ceiling. Otaur shoved the second gate upward, and they entered.

Roni placed her hand against the clear wall. It didn't feel like glass — too soft, too thin. But it was too clear to be plastic.

Garcia appeared to be pondering the same question, his fingers dancing across the surface. "We really are in yet another universe."

Roni couldn't tell if these words were meant for her or if he merely spoke to himself, so she did not respond.

"This is not a fast elevator," Elliot said. "If you wish to sit, we'll be a few minutes."

He then pulled back a panel that revealed the buttons for floor selection — seventy-four of them — as well as a brass knob. Pressing for the first floor, he then turned the knob halfway and leaned back, holding his cane close in. A quick nod over and Otaur closed the vertical gate. A mechanical whine echoed around them, the mounted light shut off, and the elevator lurched to life.

They descended in the dark at a gentle pace. Roni wondered why make clear walls when there was nothing to see. But then the elevator emerged from the housing around it, and they continued down the side of the building — with a full, clear view of the City of Infinity.

"Oh, Lord," Gram said.

CHAPTER 16

Growing up near Philadelphia, Roni thought she had seen a big city. But once, for her birthday, Gram, Elliot, and Sully took her to New York City for a weekend to catch a Broadway show, visit Chinatown and Little Italy, climb the Statue of Liberty, and even experience the subways. It was a whirlwind visit, and when she returned home, she found that Philadelphia suddenly seemed quaint — a city still, but in miniature. Yet now, looking at a mass of streets stretching beyond what the eye could discern, housed in the largest cavern she had ever witnessed, Roni marveled at the idea that she ever found New York City big enough to approach the word *vast*.

The City of Infinity defined vast.

In all directions, buildings upon buildings pressed against each other, scrounging for every inch of space. Lights of red and blue, yellow and orange, green and pink twinkled like starlight as the elevator descended. Though the buildings stretched upward, only a few dappled the sky with the height of the one they currently rode. Even fewer surpassed it.

After dropping several more floors, Roni noticed that for every few blocks of city, the architectural styles changed. Some were different periods in Earth history — Victorian, 1950s America, modern Japan. Other blocks had been designed for cultures and creatures from other universes — shapes like mud mounds or jagged glass, entrances high up for those who could climb the walls, others with no visible doors at all. There were buildings with branching arms that gathered flocks of birdlike creatures, and Roni could not tell if they were simply birds looking for a rest or citizens of the city going about their day.

She wondered if she would see flying cars or other fanciful dreams of the past. A surge of relief hit her when she realized the answer was *no.* Thank goodness. Humans had enough trouble driving on flat roads. She always thought it would be insane to let most people have to deal with up and down as well.

"It's amazing," Botolu said.

Gram clutched her cross. "And beautiful."

With a long sigh, Elliot said, "I only hope we can keep it this way."

"Yal-hara?" Roni asked.

"Indeed. When I followed her through the rift that she had created with the Scholar, things did not go as anticipated."

Shaking his head, Gully said, "Things rarely do."

"While the rift did bring us both here to this city, it did not deposit us in the same location. As a result, we've ended up on two very different paths over these years. Of course, we had very different goals, as well, but she began her life here better off than I did. I suppose I should explain how this city operates first. Then it all will make more sense."

Roni noticed they had only gone down about ten floors. "Looks like we have plenty of time." She sat on the bench, and Botolu joined her. The Coana's eyes darted between Elliot and the mesmerizing city stretching outward. Her bottom half rustled as if anxious to jump off the elevator and float down to the city streets like a bird embracing the world's unique air.

"Get talking," Teanna said.

Otaur snickered. "Speak with caution. To begin Elliot speaking is to invite him never to cease."

"Now, now." Elliot chuckled as well. "I may have picked up a habit of talking too much, but it is only because I no longer had all of my family around to fill in the silent spaces." He paused, and Roni wondered if he had been stalling. But then, he thumped his cane in place as if to give more stability on the vibrating elevator and possibly more strength to speak. "Think of this city as a massive circle, forever spreading out in all directions. But there is a center. Much like a universe. Now, this circle has been divided into eight pie-slice sections and a ninth section is the central circle like a bull's-eye. That is where the city is run from. Each section has a representative there on the Center Council, and like all governments, they decide the things necessary to making any society exist without eating itself alive."

Folding his arms, Garcia said, "Which means, like all governments, that they are where the corruption, the greed, and the power-hungry work."

Otaur said, "You should not judge all other species in the universes, and particularly within this one, with similar motivations of that which you have emerged from. We do not all subscribe to the base emotions and ambitions that your kind falls prey to."

Roni glanced out at the city. The lower they dropped, the more detail she could see. The homes, the people, the vehicles — all had seemed like carved models but gradually took on a greater sense of reality. Like watching from a plane landing at an airport, even the ground became sturdier as they descended. And along with all of that solidity followed the weight of their situation. All of Elliot's words led to the same dark and dangerous end — Yal-hara.

Before Garcia could start bickering with Otaur, another thump of Elliot's cane silenced them. He lifted his chin slightly and continued. "The City of Infinity operates like any city and government, but there is more. Things that make it different."

Gully said, "Does it really matter how the trash is picked up or elections are run or any of that?"

"This city is what keeps the universes from destroying each other, so yes, it matters quite a lot."

Otaur said, "Once more, my friend here has failed to expose the vital information of his tale — that Yal-hara runs our city and continues to acquire great leagues of power."

"Is that true?" Roni asked, not from doubt but from a need to give her heart a moment's respite. It beat ferociously in her chest.

"Of course," Elliot said. "When we arrived here, I thought she might right away begin sneaking into homes and stealing memories from children like she had done to you. But all that time locked on our world had turned her from a bitter, brutal creature into one that relishes the evil she creates. We always expected her to seek out a universe to dominate. She's always hungered for power. Yet I never imagined that her goal would be to rule over all universes, to take seat at the center of all power. And she had a great advantage from the start — her mental abilities."

Otaur tapped one leg against his hard shell. "It is rather obvious that she has utilized these mental abilities to manipulate otherwise sensible individuals."

"We don't know the specifics, she's worked hard to hide that information, but we do know that she quickly found influential people who decided to help her with money, property, and eventually power."

Throughout the ride downward, Gram had kept most of her

attention on Elliot. She had a sunken, pained expression, and when she finally spoke, her voice cracked as if she had not used it in months. "What about you? You said that the two of you followed different paths. What happened exactly?"

Elliot rose to his feet, cane at his side and a stern expression like a Bible prophet. Except he did not look upon Roni and her team as potential disciples. Nor did he see them as a congregation gathered to hear his words. Rather, he squinted beyond them, out the window, to three white blobs moving fast along the building walls.

"What are those?" Garcia asked.

Elliot walked across the elevator until his nose pressed against the window. "Skullers. Soldiers for Yal-hara."

Jolting upright, Teanna checked the window. Below her, Botolu continued to stare out at the City. If she shared Teanna's alarm, she showed nothing.

"They can be like hound dogs on a scent," Elliot continued. "Yal-hara only started using them in the last few months, and I had assumed she had become fed up with the little bit of trouble we had caused her. She wanted me gone for good. But now I think she was searching for all of you."

Roni saw them becoming clearer as they lowered floor by floor. No surprises there — only a horribly twisted mind like Yal-hara's could have conjured these beasts. They were multi-limbed creatures with a central, bulbous body. Pale white skin like bones dug up from the grave covered its limbs. As she caught more detail, Roni saw that body was an actual skull — a moldy, moss-covered skull with a determined expression. Its eight limbs moved with the graceful fluidity of an octopus. Roni first thought of the creatures as skull-octopi, but then Elliot's word sank in — *skullers.* It fit.

Elliot snapped his fingers at Otaur. "What floor are we at?"

Otaur rushed to the control console. "Forty-one."

"We must go faster."

"The precision with which this device was constructed is outdated. Furthermore, its current condition is far from enviable. I cannot in good conscience put all of our lives at risk simply to expedite our journey."

When Elliot turned away from the window, Roni witnessed something she had rarely seen, and certainly not to this intense degree — anger. He stormed across the elevator and shoved Otaur aside. With one hand, he spun the control knob to the right. With the other, he held his cane out and moved it in a simple, repeating motion. Creating a shield, perhaps. Roni wasn't sure — she never had the chance to learn what different cane motions went with what spells.

The elevator picked up speed, and Roni's stomach lurched at the sudden shift. The sound of the wheels complaining down rusty metal tracks matched the walls whining as they twisted against the changing forces of wind. Metal banging surrounded them. Roni thought Otaur may have been right. The elevator seemed like it could fall apart any second.

Out the window, the skullers soared across the building faces. As the elevator rushed by, one skuller bound into the air and smacked right into the elevator's side. Gram and Otaur both cried out in shock. Teanna backed up, hatchets in hand. While Elliot continued his spell, Gully moved to protect Roni, but she pointed to Botolu and the golem shifted his position to comply.

Little suction cups lined the length of the skuller's long arms. Roni thought it might try to squeeze the window into shattering. She had no idea if such a thing were possible, but that didn't stop her from fearing it might happen.

Instead, the skuller arched back and drove its hard bone head forward. The first hit created a sharp crack. It pulled back and hammered a second time. More cracks developed while the first deepened.

"What floor?" Elliot asked, his tone both stern and unwavering.

Otaur checked the control console, his chitinous body clicks added to the elevator's horrendous shrieks. "Twenty-two."

"Not fast enough."

The skuller's next strike sent thick shards onto the metal bench. The window had some type of safety built into it to prevent the whole thing from collapsing, but the shards were dangerous enough. Sharp, deadly — they forced the team to the other side of the elevator to avoid getting sliced open.

But Teanna charged forward. To avoid getting her hatchet stuck in the window, she smashed the backside against the hole the skuller had made. Acting like a bat, the hatchet broke more of it away, sending it outward — at the skuller. The creature swung wide to avoid most of the sharp edges, suctioning to the elevator with two arms, then slapped back and made a snorting growl. It was not pleased.

It battered the window with its head, widening the hole. Teanna swung both hatchets again. She used the blade-side this time and managed to dig one into the side of the skuller's neck — at least, that was what Roni thought to call the muscles and bone connecting the head to the body of tentacles.

Roaring, Teanna yanked hard and wrested the skuller free. With its limbs flailing, she slammed it onto the elevator floor. The team circled around her, ready to assist. But when Teanna pulled back her hatchet for another attack, the skuller kipped into the air and thrust its eight limbs outward. It caught all of them.

Roni fell back against the window. Teanna by her side. The skuller spread the others against the walls of the elevator. Wind howled at their speeding descent as cold air swirled around them. Gully clamped his hands around the tentacle pressing his chest. Garcia strained to reach his potion bag — he must have dropped it when the skuller struck. Elliot held onto his cane but his spell had been broken.

The skuller smelled of decay. When it turned to face Roni, she learned its breath smelled no better. The limb holding her readjusted towards her neck.

Gram had been shoved against the doorway. Roni squirmed at the shift of the skuller's grip, and Gram's worried face darkened. Her lip curled into a sneer.

With a harshness in her tone Roni had never heard before, Gram said, "Gully, catch this."

She flicked her wrist and a chain dropped from her sleeve. Grunting, she whipped the chain in a wide arc around the skuller and reached Gully.

"Got it," he yelled.

"Then pull already!"

Gram and Gully both tugged back on their ends of chain. The metal links snapped back, locking around the skuller's neck. Garcia reached over with one hand to help Gully, and Otaur did the same with Gram.

Though made of bone, Roni swore she could see surprise in the skuller's eye sockets. They wrenched it back. Its horrid growling became a wispy cry for air. The tentacles let go in order to clutch at the chain, but Elliot stabbed his cane into the back of the skuller's head, pressing against the force of the chain, tightening it, cutting off even more air. Roni thought they would choke the thing to death, but Teanna — now free — had no intention of waiting that long. Double-striking with both hatchets, she cleaved through its skull. Pale bone and gray goo spattered the floor.

The elevator dinged their arrival.

As the gates opened, Gram released a new chain and twirled it, ready to attack. Teanna freed her hatchets while Garcia grabbed his bag.

But instead of another skuller, a short insect creature stood. The right side of its face had been crushed long ago and poorly healed. Otaur rushed to greet his friend and Elliot's tense shoulders drooped.

"One of ours?" Roni said.

Elliot nodded. "This is Lop."

Making a slight bow, Lop said, "A true honor for this meeting, and while I would wish to be regaled by the stories of your journey, we must proceed with haste. Yal-hara's servants are after you."

"We know." Elliot gestured to the dead skuller.

"Only the start, I fear. Come, I shall lead the way."

As they filed out, Roni overheard Gram lean close to Elliot and whisper, "Lord knows, my dear friend, you are never dull."

Chapter 17

Following a child-sized insect through streets mixing eras of human history while being chased by freakish skull-octopi had never been on Roni's bucket list — never been near any list — yet no part of her questioned the reality of it. A version of Roni that existed a decade ago would have checked into the nearest hospital — possibly asking for the mental ward. A version of Roni from a few years back would have grabbed a fifth of vodka and assumed she had already drunk too much so she might as well keep going until she could banish herself into darkness. But the now-Roni? None of it fazed her. Her team seemed equally accepting of the situation. Their guest, on the other hand —

"Botolu, are you okay? This can be a lot to take in."

"I am … it is … um …"

"Overwhelming?" Gram said from behind them.

Botolu looked back with fearful innocence. "The city is a marvel. But the dangers ..."

"Wishing you hadn't come along?"

With a fierce shake, her determination reignited. Botolu moved faster. "I will go anywhere I must. My people are counting on our return."

"Quick now," Lop said, edging toward a long row of terraced houses straight out of 1940s England.

The group entered one building, walked down a narrow hall, and into a small sitting room. Roni could not hide her relief at being off the streets — out of the skullers' easy view. Some of the others looked equally relieved. Without asking, Gully took up a guard post at the front entrance, and Teanna's eyes never stopped roving the room's windows and doorways.

Elliot stepped into an adjoining room to confer with his insect friends. Roni forced down the urge to barge in on them. If Elliot thought it best to discuss something away from the Parallel Society, she would have to trust his judgment.

With a sigh, Botolu slumped into an uncomfortable looking loveseat as exhausted concern washed across her face. Roni sympathized. To volley from her claustrophobic world to an endless expanse reminded her of discovering the Society for the first time. Everything she had grown up believing spun away, and she had to learn new rules for what had once been the simplest truths — like the fact that her grandmother no longer just baked delicious sugar cookies but also had magic powers and saved the universe from time-to-time. For Botolu, she not only found that there were worlds unimaginable only a day ago, but that she had jumped into it without a safety net, without a trusted guide, without any connection to her home.

"There's no way back, is there?" Botolu said.

"To your world?" Gram said.

"Those that climbed Mountain Pillar before me, those brave enough to reach the top, they must have stepped into the book. They would have come to this incredible city. But not one ever came back. Some would have decided to explore this place forever, yet surely at least one would have wanted to return, to tell us all what they had found, to be a hero to us all. Only none ever returned. There must be no way."

"Oh, there is always a way. After all, Hayle found a book to your world, and so did we."

In a comforting tone — at least, comforting for a human — Roni said, "And those things don't end. We trap the rifts in books because we don't know how to close them. So, when we return to our world, we can take you to the book we used, and you'll have no trouble reuniting with your world."

Botolu sat up with a sprinkle of hope, only to slump again. "How can you be sure we'll be able to get to your world?"

"Because others have done so," Elliot said, resting his side against a waist-high piece of furniture – a serving table, Roni thought. He coughed a moment, the exertions on the elevator catching up with him. Then: "Books don't change the universe they connect to."

Gram said, "That's right, and we know Hayle found a path back to our world. Well, his journal did, at least. But that means there is a path back, and that means we can get you back to your world, too."

With a grunt, Teanna said, "Not if we don't live through this."

"True." Elliot gestured to his insect friends. "The present is far more important than the future. For now. Otaur and Lop have volunteered to be decoys so that we may escape to our meeting site."

Roni said, "No. We can't ask that of them."

"We didn't. That's what volunteering is about. Don't worry, though. They have the best chances of any of us."

"Quite true," Otaur said. "Our plan is to acquire the interest of Yalhara's scouts and lure them away. When they latch upon our trail, we shall evade them with ease by slipping through cracks in the walls or foundations of the various structures within this sector of the city. After all, while you humans have proven to be quite resourceful and rather creative, your older construction methods leave much to be desired."

Not waiting for permission or further protest, Otaur and Lop scurried out of the building. Elliot edged near a window looking onto the street. Peeking from the side, he watched in silence. When satisfied — Roni assumed that meant his insect friends had safely moved beyond his view — he turned back to the team.

"We must wait a few minutes before leaving through the backdoor. That should give them enough time to succeed in their mission." He checked his watch. Then to Gram: "Before we were interrupted, you asked what had happened to me. Would you like to hear that now?"

Roni understood right away that Elliot hoped to distract from the threats surrounding them. Part of her, however, craved the rest of his story. The way Gram snatched glances at the window and clutched her cross, Roni suspected she felt the same way. Observing the others in the room, she saw similar comprehension and desire clashing about. All except Gully and Botolu. Roni couldn't read their faces — the golem lacked many expressions and the Coana's expressions were not guaranteed to translate to the human variety.

Seizing one final glimpse outside, Elliot wrinkled his brow and sighed. He hunched forward over his cane as if formulating his words, remembering all that had happened, caused him pain. "When I first stepped into this world, things did not go well for me. I had no idea where I was or what the rules of this place were, but I had been in new universes before. The Society had prepared me. Unfortunately, in order to make this city exist and run, a universal money had been established. The few dollars in my pocket were useless — a lesson I learned when trying to buy an apple from a street vendor. Worse, there were no exchanges."

"Why not?" Gram said. "If you're going to create a new currency, you have to be able to trade it with other forms."

"Only if you want to encourage contact with other universes — or worse, tourism. Not here. Not in the City of Infinity. This is the hub that keeps the wheel together. The money used here is only for here, and the people who live here are only for here. Unsanctioned travel to other universes is not only illegal, it is watched closely."

"Is that why those creatures are after us?" Roni asked. "Are they like the Rift Police or something?"

"Not the skullers. They are new. But I suspect Yal-hara ordered them after us because she's worried the rift allowed you and the rest of the Society to enter the City." He rechecked his watch. Again, that pained frown. "You see, without any money, I had to survive homeless for over a year. Most people could tell with ease that I did not belong. Nobody wanted to get into trouble for aiding me. I lived on scraps thrown away, wore the same clothes for months, and had to steal a shower whenever I could."

Roni cringed. Elliot had always been the tidiest of them all. Forced to live such an unkempt life must have been more than disgusting, more than distressing — it had been demoralizing.

Even without knowing Elliot, Botolu seemed to understand. Crossing her arms, she said, "I like this Yal-hara less and less."

"Oh, I agree with you completely." Elliot's old finger clenched under the strain of memory. "Anytime I tried to settle down, Yal-hara's goons would appear – all kinds of creatures that had joined her. The only advantage I had was that this city is infinitely huge. Makes it much easier to hide. Which is what I did until a strange insect creature crossed my path. That turned out to be Otaur. He had been leading a fight against Yal-hara, but it had not gone well."

Patting her chest, Gram said, "And you had to take it on yourself to join his fight."

"I would have under most circumstances, yes, but in this case, his fight is our fight. All of us. It's not simply against the being that stole Roni's memories, but it is against the being that wishes to use the power of this city to dominate all universes. How could I turn away from that?"

"You couldn't," Gully said. "And we wouldn't want you to."

Teanna's knee bounced as she stared towards the window. "How much longer do we have to sit here doing nothing?"

Elliot checked his watch a third time. "Otaur should have called by now."

"Then if your plan has failed, we need to come up with something new. Right, Roni?"

Roni felt a lump tighten in her gut. This world appeared to have a steep learning curve and they stood near the bottom. Each word out of Elliot's mouth helped them along, but she knew far too little to start hatching escape plans. Of course, they rarely had enough information when they had to do such things. It was the nature of the job. She simply had to lead as best as she could with whatever the situation presented. After all, she had the full team together now. And they had a target.

"Stopping Yal-hara must be the priority," she said, rising to her feet. "Where is this meeting you keep talking about?"

Elliot said, "That's part of what we're waiting for. When Otaur found me, when we realized that we both had come from our world's versions of the Parallel Society, he helped me become a shadow that Yal-hara could not find. Wherever she placed light to look, like a shadow I disappeared. Once she gave up — well, backed off to a degree — I helped Otaur reach out to the other Parallel Society groups throughout the city. Few talked with each other, suspicious of moving beyond their districts."

"Why?" Garcia asked.

"Politics, xenophobia, a variety of reasons. But we eventually built a new Parallel Society — one just for the City. Our focus is simple — get the City's residents to recognize the threat in Yal-hara and then stop her."

Botolu spoke, and her voice startled the others. "Since this creature is still active, it would seem you have yet to succeed."

"Sadly, that's true. We've become a thorn in her side and nothing more. But I knew the rest of you would come eventually. So, we've waited and prepared."

Elliot's phone rang like a bird chirping underwater. He pulled out the odd thing and its bizarre feelers opened outward. He tapped at it a moment, then let it close before putting it in his pocket.

When he scrunched his brow but said nothing, Teanna jumped to her feet. "Well?"

"It is time to go."

"But?" Gram said.

"Otaur managed to pull away the other two skullers, however, he said there are many more patrolling the area. Yal-hara knows you've arrived and the danger that poses for her."

Teanna again: "But we have an address for the meeting, right?"

"We do."

"Then let's go."

Roni crossed the room and put her hand on Elliot's arm. "What's the matter? What aren't you telling us?"

His wrinkled face quivered. "This will be difficult."

CHAPTER 18

At first, Roni wondered why Elliot acted so fearful. Of course, she knew that the skullers were out there, and so she felt agitated, too. But when they left via the back exit, keeping off the main roads by skirting along the alleyways and side streets, and eventually walked out of the human section of the city, nothing had happened. No freakish skull creatures had accosted them. If anything, Roni's team were the freaks — a long line of strangers hustling between buildings, trying not to be seen. Yet the residents they passed never bothered to even look at them.

In this new city section, Elliot changed tactics and guided them up a populated road, staying close to where the sidewalk met the buildings. Roni stayed quiet, observing the unusual world they had entered. She could hear the surprised silence of her team behind her.

She felt as if she had stepped into a cartoon. The colors were bright — the walls, the cars, the clothes, even the food displayed in the store windows. Bulbous vehicles rolled down bubbled cobblestone streets. Lampposts as thick as old trees stood with globes atop. The buildings bulged. Not a straight line anywhere. Extra-wide doorways allowed easy access for the sphere-shaped customers. Yet despite the largeness of everything, none of it carried any extra weight. People moved with ease as if light and airy. Cars zipped along as if they were finely-tuned racing machines and the driving surface newly smoothed asphalt. Even breathing felt fresh and joyous.

For the few blocks they remained on this street, Roni even caught herself marveling at the City, forgetting for a moment that their lives were threatened. Worse, part of her imagined stopping. Settling into this little section and spending the rest of her days in a cartoonish world where happiness bounced off the walls and sumptuous smells of fresh bread, hot soup, and charring steaks rolled across the air. She noticed that the cars whisking by did not disrupt the lovely aromas with exhaust. And did she hear singing, too? Beautiful singing.

"Stay focused," Elliot said. "Parts of the City can act like a trap. They don't intend to be so — at least, I have found no evidence of malice, but streets like this one lure and lull those from other worlds. They play upon our minds and can confuse you."

Garcia said, "Like how some people go camping for the first time and never want to return to civilization?"

"Yes. Except stronger."

They continued onward, and Roni managed to ignore the enticing calls upon her senses. Mostly. Twice she caught herself drifting toward the doorway of a bakery — so many bakeries — but the steady tapping of Elliot's cane reminded her of where she belonged.

Turning a corner, they walked along a street with all the same colors and scents of where they had just been, only this one had emptied of the populace. The closer Roni looked, the more she spotted signs of decay — a few empty storefronts, a few broken windows on higher floors, garbage piling up.

Ahead, a large metal gate blocked the road. Chipped black paint covered rusting iron spikes along the arched top. Reaching three stories high, it did more than simply mark a clear border, it warned against trespassing.

"I take it we're going in there," Roni said.

Elliot moved to the sidewalk and approached the small doorway for foot traffic. The solid metal door had three peepholes at different levels, but he did not bother waiting to be seen. With his cane, he pushed the door open. It whined in pain and stopped halfway, but it was enough.

Before entering, he faced the group. "Be careful."

Stepping through the old gate, Roni tried to ignore the dread hanging aloft as if it watched every move made beneath it. The transformation from one section of city to the next brought with it even more discomfort than just the air. The place had died long ago and been left to rot. It reminded Roni of bombed-out Europe from World War II. Piles of broken brick, twisted iron, and other rubble dotted the decrepit streets where the last people living here had attempted to rebuild. But they were all gone now.

"Well," Roni said, her voice dying in the stillness, "this isn't ominous at all."

Elliot glanced back. "It is the fastest route. If we don't take the subway, we would have to travel days in order to reach the meeting."

"The nearest station is in here? Doesn't look like anything operates."

"There are many subway systems throughout the City. Not all connect with each other. The one we seek is only used by the Society, and as far as most others know, it is not used at all."

Garcia snickered. "A secret subway for a secret society. That's poetic."

"I have a question," Gully said from the rear. "How come this place is abandoned? I should think a prime piece of real estate would be easy to sell."

Elliot paused and turned around. "The City of Infinity may actually be what the name implies — infinite. No way to know for sure. But when sections of it die, and there are more than just this one, it is usually cheaper and easier to continue building outward. Most new sections come from new groups discovering the City. They wouldn't know what to do with the architecture of another universe's creatures and would have to raze the entire thing just to rebuild. It is fortunate for us, though. The Society has taken control of many of these abandoned areas. It has become our territory."

As he started down the street once more, Gram folded her arms. "So, you hold territory now?"

He increased his stride. "I don't know why you are mad at me, but please set it aside until our lives are no longer threatened."

Nobody spoke for a while. Roni knew they all reacted the same as she did — scanning the cracked and missing windows, checking the dark alcoves and grey shadows, searching for any sign of a living soul amongst these ghosts. If danger planned to attack, the Parallel Society made sure it would not surprise them.

The brick buildings had iron strapping on the corners and lining the edge to the roof. Geometric designs etched in the metal popped up at uniform points along each structure. Street names, perhaps? Or store signs? Roni wondered what kind of creatures had lived here. When their section of city resembled human construction, how close were they to human?

Something moved. Her skin prickled, and she heard the others stiffen. But Elliot trudged onward. Whatever was out there, animal or enemy, Elliot had the right idea — keep moving, don't stop, get out of here as fast as possible.

"There it is." Elliot rushed through a junction with a dead traffic light strung overhead. On the far corner, next to half of a destroyed building, metal fencing surrounded a stairway leading underground.

A breath escaped Roni's lips, but it was enough for everyone. The team hustled across the street, clearly as eager and anxious as their leader. They clumped around the entrance and gazed down into its dark maw.

Elliot lifted his cane and pressed it against his shoulder. Roni had never seen this before and wondered what helpful spell he intended to cast. His free hand reached into his pocket and produced a small penlight. Then he lowered the cane back down. Roni held back an embarrassed laugh.

Turning the head of the penlight until it came on, Elliot smiled. "Watch where you step. This station is in better condition than many others on the line, but it is still falling apart."

"Great," Teanna said. "If Yal-hara doesn't get us, the city can just fall on our heads."

The stairs went down to a landing, turned back and down, another landing, and once more back and down until ending at a stone platform. Iron pillars lined the middle, with rusting beams across the top. Rat-like vermin chittered as they sped along above.

"Amazing," Botolu said. "A city beneath a city."

Gram pointed to cracks in the beams. "Will these hold?"

"Long enough," Elliot said. "But I wouldn't encourage testing their strength." Keeping the penlight pointed upward, he created enough diffused amber glow for everyone to see. "At the end, we'll jump onto the tracks and —"

The swift attacking skuller blasted right between Gram and Elliot, knocking both aside. It slid near Teanna, whisking its front three arms in various directions — both a threat and a distraction. As Teanna focused on these arms, the skuller plowed a fourth straight into her belly.

Before the warrior fell, the skuller leaped towards Roni. She had enough time to see that the creature avoided staying in one position too long. Against seven opponents, to stop moving meant death.

Roni reached for the nearest arm, hoping to detain the skuller enough for the others to help. No such luck. Spinning its body, it lurched Roni off her feet and whipped her into an iron support.

The flaking metal punched her shoulder, spine, and hip. When she dropped to the stone platform, sharp fire raced along her side. Anguish swept over her face as she struggled to sit up.

Keeping on the offensive, the skuller dashed from Garcia to Gully, swiping at Gram and Elliot as they tried to get to their feet, dodging Teanna's double-hatchet strike, before climbing to the crossbeams. One beam lurched under the skuller's weight. The creature jumped off and landed in front of Roni. It's skull smile opened wide.

It leaned on its back arms, ready to lunge forward, but it never got the chance. Gully rose behind it and slammed down, clamping the skuller's arms in a golem-tight bear hug.

"A little help would be appreciated," Gully said.

Botolu rushed forward, the protrusions under her arms evidence of her anger. "You do not harm Roni," she said, as she plunged her bodily weapons into the creature's head.

The skuller's flailing arms straightened at odd angles before the whole creature lolled forward. Gully let it slither to the floor. Its body moved like a limp drunk.

"Did you kill it?" Garcia asked as he approached with a vial of brown sludge.

"I could never," Botolu said.

"Well, I can." He poured the potion onto the skuller, his eyes wide, his mouth a determined line.

The sludge dribbled over the skuller's bone head, seeping into the cracks, dribbling into the hollow eye sockets, slipping between the teeth. A stench of old kitchen trash wafted over Roni. Whether from the potion or the victim, she could not tell, but she wrinkled her nose and resorted to shallow breaths.

Seconds later, the skuller ceased all movement. Its boney frame visibly dried as if all its body's moisture had drained away. The skull grew whiter. Its eight arms sucked inward. The whole creature looked brittle. The drying continued, and like a parched desert, cracks formed over all the creature's surface. Small pieces of bone loosened and fell. One arm broke off, sending dust particles into the air. Soon, the rest of the skuller followed — deteriorating piece by piece until only dust remained.

Roni kept expecting for the creature to cry out, but it never made a sound. Botolu had seen to that. Though lacking the tormented shouts and seizures of a body in crisis, this silent death weighed greater. Not only for Roni. She could see the horrified looks on the team's faces. Perhaps worse on Botolu and Garcia.

Groaning, she stood. "Anybody hurt bad? Anybody need healing?"

A few shaking heads. No other response.

Kicking the dust pile, Roni clapped her hands twice. Eyes snapped onto her. "Let's hope we don't have to do that again."

Garcia said, "I had no idea the potion would act so strongly."

"It's okay. You saved our lives. Nothing to be upset about."

"I did not intend for it to be so cruel."

Roni glanced back at the dust. "It's Yal-hara's fault. Remember that. Because she isn't done with us, and we may have to use that potion again. You have more, right?"

He closed his eyes and a dark look replaced his shock. "I'll save one for her."

"I wouldn't mind seeing that." Lifting her voice, she pointed to Elliot. "Can we get on the subway now? I'd like to leave this place."

CHAPTER 19

The old subway train, a metallic monster that squealed even when travelling straight, had been rattling through the dark tunnels beneath the city for nearly an hour. Roni rested her head back but could not find a comfortable position. Teanna and Garcia had no such troubles — they both stretched out on the floor near the back of the car. Gully stood guard at the side door, now and then watching the front and rear doors as well. Sometimes Roni wanted to hug Gully hard enough that she might leave her imprint on his chest.

She listened to the echoes of the train in the dark. Dim lights flickered from recessed holes. Elliot said the train's momentum powered them. She shrugged. It didn't matter. Like most of the team, she kept her eyes closed. Not much to see anyway.

Now that they were in the tunnels, Botolu felt safer, more at home. The mesmerizing expanse of the city had left her confused as to how any of it was possible. Roni heard Botolu peppering Elliot with endless questions. Many of them centered around how the city functioned.

Elliot answered with a patience Roni had been listening to her entire life — tolerant of the questions provided she actually paid attention to the answers. He would have no problems with Botolu, though. She was not the brat Roni had been.

Elliot said, "We travel to other universes through books that capture rifts. I should think the possibilities would seem limitless to any of us."

Roni stifled the laugh welling in her chest. She nestled deeper in her uncomfortable seat, rolled her shoulders downward to ease the tension in her neck, and listened.

When Botolu pressed to know how so many people could be fed and how a single government could handle the needs, the policing, the operation of this place, Elliot said that he did not have all the answers. He had spent much of his time surviving, then building a coalition, then bolstering them into a resistance. Matters of public policy held little concern.

Yet he did know a few things. Food, for example, mostly came from other universes. Apparently, the Center Council had access to a universe with three fertile worlds. None of these worlds bore intelligent, sentient, civilized life, so the City claimed the worlds for farming and hunting. That universe provided nearly all the food required.

"But if the City is truly infinite," Botolu said, "then how do these worlds feed a people that never stops growing?"

"It is a constant problem, I'm sure." Elliot guessed the Council employed others to scout for new worlds in which to grow food for the City. Or perhaps there were other parts of the City, undeveloped parts, fertile enough to solve the problem.

The City existed as a universe unto itself. Like all universes, this one had no end that anyone had ever discovered. While physics could be different from one universe to another, some constants had proven true. One of those insisted that a universe, any universe, expanded in all directions. So, it seemed logical to Elliot that some expansion would include farmable land.

The same held true for other materials such as wood and metals. Raw materials were harvested, gathered, or mined in other universes and hauled to the City of Infinity. From there, lumber yards and smelting facilities and other factories made whatever the populace required.

"And what of all the waste?" Botolu asked.

An easier one, Elliot had said. All compostable waste went back to the farming worlds to be reused. Some trash ended up recycled — elsewhere in the City, large recycling plants churned garbage into reusable basics. But when it came to everything else, including natural waste, the Council had decided long ago to dump it all into an empty universe. Garbage gathering vehicles roamed the City at all hours, picking up the trash and delivering it to a large rift carefully maintained and constantly watched. Elliot thought it unnecessarily dangerous, but those that lived here took it for granted as the way things were done.

Botolu did not like this answer. "If all universes are always expanding, then how can you be sure the universe used for your trash is actually empty?"

"I have not lived here long enough to understand how the people rationalize these decisions. For many, I suspect, it is nothing more than habit." He paused. Then: "Perhaps we should have included Gully in this conversation. He seemed particularly eager to learn about trash management here."

She brought up a few other questions regarding the practicality of the City but Elliot finally pointed out that he casts spells with his cane, Gram creates chains and rift-containing books, and a golem guarded the train — certainly an endless city existing in a cavern that was an entire universe could handle the plumbing. Roni expected Botolu to balk at this. Instead, her face puckered as she wandered off to reconsider all she knew of existence.

Another twenty minutes passed. Another twenty minutes hoping for sleep and only achieving mild rest. Better than nothing, though.

Roni thought she had finally managed a true slumber because she heard little voices echoing around her — the beginnings of a dream, she hoped. But then she heard a sternness in the tone of one voice and recognized it as Gram. Opening one eye, she peeked along the train car. Gram and Elliot sat forward, their heads pressed close together.

"I don't know how I can apologize more," Elliot said, his low rumbling voice soothing in Roni's ear regardless of his words. "Had I the ability to reach across universes, I would have told you I was okay. I would have sent instructions on how to get here. But I could only sit back and hope you found a way. And you did."

"Lord, help me, you still think I'm upset about that? The moment you stepped through that rift I knew it would be up to me and Roni and the others to find you."

"Then what is it? Why are you acting this way?"

A pause. Roni kept her eyes closed, but she thought she heard Gram try to speak twice, her voice catching each time. Finally, Gram said, "You left us. You left me."

"What?"

"Not a thought given, you just went straight through a rift."

"I didn't think Yal-hara would go through a rift that led to a dangerous world or even one that had no world in it."

She slapped her thigh — Gram's way of striking out without actually hitting the person in front of her. "I don't care about Yal-hara or the risks you took. You're not hearing me. You left. All these decades, it was you and Sully and me. The three of us against everything the universes could throw at us. Sully died, but at least he tried to replace himself, tried to ease us into a future without him. But you … you just walked away."

"You know that is not what I was doing."

"It's what you did."

Roni heard a muffled sob. She slipped one eye open — she couldn't help it. Elliot held Gram as she cried into his shoulder. A strange jealousy fluttered through Roni. Not the common hateful, angry jealousy. Rather, she felt more a wishful jealousy. A hope that someday she could have a friend so close that their problems could be solved with a few words, a cathartic cry, and a knowing hug. She tried to picture Teanna or Garcia or even Gully holding her that way, but it felt false. Then again, none of them shared over fifty years together protecting the universe.

She closed her eyes once more, let the rhythm of the train lull her, and in the quiet that followed, without realizing it had happened, she finally fell asleep.

A hard lurch woke her. The train had stopped. As Roni sat up, she found Teanna back-to-back with Gully, her hatchets out, her eyes searching for threats.

But Elliot waved her down. "No, no. Nothing is wrong. We've arrived."

He walked to the far end of the train car and slid open the back door. Like every other rusty piece of the train, the door cried on its slim tracks.

Gesturing for the others to follow, he said, "Just a short walk. Then you can finally meet the group I have put together here. My version of the Parallel Society."

CHAPTER 20

After hours knocking along the dark tunnels of the City, the cool air rushing down from the surface refreshed and invigorated. Even more so, the brightness of the sun. If there was a sun.

If the day had begun, then they had entered this world near the end of night. Or they had traveled on the subway far longer than Roni realized. Yet either way, she would have expected more of a dawn than the full light of early day. Then again, she recalled that Elliot had said time acted differently in this universe. Maybe the day/night cycle progressed at a faster pace.

As they climbed the stairs to the surface, Roni peered up toward the cavern roof. Unlike the Coana's world, this roof looked solid. No gap letting in snow or sun. Yet darkness did not prevail. Light came from somewhere — bright and strong enough to provide a sense of day. Perhaps a bit overcast but bright enough.

She wanted to ask Elliot, only she remembered the way Botolu had bombarded him with one question after another regarding the functioning of the City. His ultimate answer probably applied here, too. Whatever powers existed to create this universe provided what it needed. Besides, she had more important matters to attend.

When they emerged from the subway, snow covered the street. Botolu let out a gleefully long set of clicks. More than the snow, Roni startled at the lack of buildings. Just an empty street on a hillside. The city blocks stretched in all directions below, but the beginnings looked to be miles away.

Garcia said, "Is this like Central Park? A massive oasis amongst the bustling city?"

"Poetic," Elliot said. "Perhaps true long ago. But this area is more like the one we came from. It is a dead, forgotten part of the City, rediscovered and used by us."

He led them around the snowy hill, following a well-worn, dirt path. A short distance and just as Roni had grown comfortable with the idea of a snow-covered hill in the middle of an endless city, they came upon a dilapidated wood cabin. Muted voices and sounds of splashing water drifted their way.

With three sharp motions, Elliot banged his cane on the wood planks of the cabin's porch. The sounds coming their way ceased. Two knocks replied, followed by two more. Elliot banged one last time before grinning at the team and waving them forward.

They cut around the cabin, and when they reached the back, they found four natural pools of steaming water. Shaped through erosion and land contours, the waters held an authentic beauty surrounded by neglect. They had refused to change even as the world around them changed. Except even the unmoving mountains moved with the plates beneath them. Universes did not remain still. Nothing truly did.

At that moment, the waters had no choice but to slosh about at the movement of several creatures and humans. They mingled and laughed and splashed as if gathered for a birthday party. For his part, Elliot put his hands out wide to greet everyone as the host.

Teanna asked, "Why the coded knocking, if we simply walk around the building and enter?"

Waving to a few in the water, Elliot said, "Because they would have tried to kill us, otherwise."

"Good. I'm happy to be around sensible fighters again."

Elliot ushered his companions onto the cabin's back porch — a simple platform, raised on short stumps, covered with an angled wood awning that had warped with age. He stepped in front of the team and gestured to the lounging creatures behind him. "These are all descendants of various Parallel Society members throughout the universe. At least, the ones I could find." He turned to face these creatures. "And this is my Parallel Society."

Standing at the edge of one pool, a creature looking mostly like a human puffed up his chest. His face pushed outward — not as pointed as a rat yet not a snout like a dog. A thick trim of gray hair ran along his jaw matching the salt-and-pepper slicked back hair on his head. He wore a heavy, leather outfit — stifling under any circumstances but especially so standing over the hot springs.

He walked up to Teanna and put out his hand — smooth skin, four fingers, sharp claws. "It is an honor to meet the great leader of Elliot's

Society. I am Stak. And though we are small in numbers, I offer myself and my team to your capable service."

Elliot said, "You're mistaken. That's not —"

From the water, a creature that looked like a woman covered in fish scales said, "Of course he is. Stak is not as observant as he likes us to think. For a Parallel Society as great as Elliot has boasted, they would need more than sheer strength to succeed. They would need spells." She pointed at Garcia. "You are the one behind this group. Your bag smells full of potent and powerful items. I look forward to discussing the ingredients you use."

With an uneasy chuckle, Elliot said, "I'm sorry, but if you'll simply allow me —"

At the edge of the far-left pool, sitting cross-legged, a man wearing a bright chest plate and an intricately carved helmet laughed. "Forgive my colleagues. They assume all cultures are alike and akin to their own. But where they come from, wisdom and age do not necessarily go together." He bowed his head toward Gram. "I am Glissford, and it will be my honor to serve under your guidance."

Gram shook her head. Before she could speak, however, Elliot said, "Please, all of you, listen to me."

Roni had enough. A tinge of her old, insecure self scurried up and down her spine, angry and humiliated, ready to lash out. But the emotion only lasted seconds. A small burst. A last cry.

Projecting her voice with the strongest tone she could muster, she said, "I lead the Society."

Stak laughed — a thick, hearty sound that served to both mock her as well as put on a show for his peers. "You? You have no weapons, no satchel of magic, and certainly no wisdom of age. These strong, capable fighters follow you? I doubt it. Why would they? What power do you have?"

Roni gripped her pant leg to hide her trembling fingers. Her voice remained firm. "None."

Taking a few steps closer, enough so that she could smell the sweaty wet fur, Stak said, "Elliot promised us a great leader, someone who could show us the way to defeating Yal-hara and protecting all universes." He looked her over once more. Then: "You're nothing."

As he turned back to the pools, Roni spoke louder. "What have you done that's so special? Besides failure." Stak whirled back on her, and she continued, "Are you going to deny it? Please, show me all your great triumphs. Was it when you let Yal-hara rise through the ranks of your government? Was that your success? Or was it when you let her become the leader of this world and threatened to destroy everything we all care about? Perhaps that was the greatness which you think you've achieved. From what I can tell, all of you have been waiting for salvation from someone else. Elliot came along and told you of me and my wonderful team, he promised we would arrive despite the fact that nobody had arrived before to save you, and so you decided to wait more. Let Yal-hara continue with whatever she wanted to do. And now, you have the gall to question my ability? Any of us? While you were languishing in these soothing waters, we traveled through universes to get here. We fought for our lives to get here. You want to know what powers I have? I'm the one who led them through every damn bit of it."

Gram muttered, "Language."

Roni held her tongue to avoid laughing. Thankfully, Stak and the others appeared to take the silence as further condemnation.

Stepping forward, closing the distance to Stak, almost nose to snout, Roni said, "Tell me, where are all the people from your universe to help in this fight?"

For a heartbeat, then two, nobody moved. Trickles of water and tense breathing surrounded them all. If Stak behaved like most creatures, Roni expected two possible reactions — either he would act like this whole thing had been a test and laugh it off to save face, or he would fight for dominance. But she wagered that he had no interest in running this show.

At length, he took one step back. Looked as if settling into a fighting stance. Roni's heart sank and her muscles clenched. But he turned his head toward Elliot and wagged a finger.

"I guess you are right," he said. "She is brave, daring, and just might be a help." Yanking Roni into an embrace, he patted her back with two hard smacks. "Welcome to the Parallel Society of the City of Infinity."

All the tensions of this meeting disintegrated, vanquished by relief and joy and hope. The leaders sprang to their feet, climbed from the pools, opened their arms, and approached Roni's team as if the problem of Yal-hara had already been solved.

Stak shifted to Teanna, ushering her into the daylight to better inspect her hatchets. Glissford strode toward Gram, offered a respectful bow, and asked her to explain all about her world, her Parallel Society, and her grand exploits. The fish-scale woman introduced herself to Garcia — *call me Dyon* — and lured him to the pools where Botolu had already eased into the steaming waters. She chatted with a bald, burly woman named Eyopton, both equally fascinated by the other. Clumped together like nervous teens at a school dance, four muscular fighters with stick-like spikes along their spines disassembled and reassembled a handful of guns. Roni would later learn that their leader had a difficult to pronounce name and so went by Wex.

From the back porch, Roni watched her team undress and join this hodgepodge of creatures in the springs. Elliot stood by her side with an arm on her shoulder.

"We'll be safe for the moment," he said. "Let them relax their tired bones."

Roni had already reached those conclusions — if Teanna willingly set aside her hatchets, she had determined that no threat would touch them. Then again, Teanna made sure those hatchets were within reach.

Gully stood behind the pools, facing the cabin, and gazed upon the group. Made of clay, he couldn't go into the water. At least, Roni suspected as much. Perhaps he would be fine — after all, he had endured rainfall without damage. Still, something stopped him from joining.

"I suppose I should stand guard." He sighed and turned to look at the hillside approach. "Sure. Why not? Nobody cares if the golem can't have any fun."

As the new and old Society members continued to greet each other and learn what each had to offer, Elliot tapped Roni's elbow with his cane and jutted his head toward the cabin door. Nobody seemed bothered as they went into the building. If anything, she thought they relaxed more.

Inside, she found a gutted old place. One piece of furniture hid beneath a stained and dusty sheet. Nothing else. Just the outlines of where things once had been — one main room, a kitchen area, and one adjoining bedroom. Simple enough.

"I am sorry," Elliot said, resting his back against a central post. "Over the time I have spent here, I encountered many obstacles to keeping this version of the Society together. It became useful to boast about you, to encourage them and get them to believe in a savior of sorts."

Roni snickered. "If they only knew."

"I may have exaggerated, but you are more than you ever give yourself credit for. Still, my team was falling apart and I had to give them something to believe in. I chose you. I apologize for any problems that may cause you."

She kissed his cheek and hugged him. "I'm so thrilled to see you, I don't care about the circumstances. I know that's how the others feel, too."

"Teanna, probably. And certainly Gully. I doubt Garcia feels strongly one way or the other. And Gram … well …"

"Gram is Gram."

A warm grin rose on his lips. "Indeed, she is."

Taking a circuit around the old room, Roni said, "What is it you wanted to talk about? I know you didn't pull me in here just for the apology."

Elliot gazed down at his hands resting on his cane. Then: "Morale is low. Maybe it has ticked up with your arrival, but overall, things are bad. Yal-hara has managed to achieve greater success than I anticipated. I had hoped that when she joined the Center Council, experienced a few years of bureaucracy and the pettiness of politics, that her desires would shift. After all, becoming the leader of a world sounds wonderful until you realize that it makes you responsible for getting everything to run smoothly."

"I doubt she thinks about the welfare of anybody in any universe. She just wants the power."

"Like all dictators. If she dealt with any of the bickering on the Council, I never found out about it. But she also never got deterred from her goal. Moved faster than I had expected. Now, she's the Head Council, and I'm worried we don't have much time left. If we can't stop her, she'll take control of every last scrap of a universe she can find."

Roni stopped pacing and crossed her arms. "What have you done to fight back?"

"Not enough. We've attempted smear campaigns, education campaigns, and even an assassination. But we've been outmaneuvered every time."

"Assassination? That doesn't sound like you."

"Stak's plan. I was against it, but I was also outvoted." Lifting his eyes to meet hers, he said, "But you are here now, and you can stop her."

"Don't get too excited. It's one thing to brag about me to the others, but I'm no superhero. We both know I've had plenty of failings."

"The fact that you can admit as much says a great deal. But it's more than that. You have a unique connection to Yal-hara. When she swiped your memories, created your Lost Time, it began the events that have led us here."

"Great. So my personal trauma makes me qualified to take her on?"

"I believe that connection is more than an emotional one, more than abuser and abused. As much as she has peered into you, it is true that you have seen into her, too."

"That's a terrible idea." Roni shuddered, recalling her near-death on Mountain Pillar and the way Yal-hara's voice infiltrated her mind.

"It is also true. It will give you a great advantage over the rest of us. An insight into our enemy. That's why I boasted about you, set you to lead all of us, to become the Commander in our war against this evil power. And you've already won them over."

With a raised eyebrow, she said, "What? I stood up for myself and my team. That's all."

"I'm afraid they think otherwise. We'll put it to a formal vote later, but I can tell from their reactions — particularly from Stak — that they've already decided. You are to be the leader of them all. A sort of king of kings."

A merry burst rolled in from the pools, and Roni sauntered over to the sole window. Peering through the dirt and grime, she thought of all the hardship she went through to become a true leader of her Parallel Society — most of it an internal struggle, a fight against feeling incompetent and unworthy. It had taken her years to overcome all of that, to gain the trust of her team, and even after she had accepted her place, she still battled herself.

"They don't know me," she whispered.

"You think soldiers in an army ever know their commanders? The orders come from people far off the battlefield and the soldiers obey. Our soldiers are lucky enough to glimpse you, get a sense of you, and that is more than most ever receive."

Garcia said something that caused Teanna to splash him. Dyon joined in while Glissford watched on with an amused frown. Yet Gully stood guard, scanning the hillside, ever vigilant. And if she asked, Roni knew the entire group would leap to their feet and join Gully. They would stand dripping wet and hold their weapons at the ready.

"You said that Yal-hara and I are connected."

"I believe so."

"Then perhaps I shouldn't be our leader. What if that connection has grown something inside of me, something that would make me susceptible to her? Or to the same power-hungry corruption that consumes her? If that's true, then I should not be given this powerful position."

"The fact that you ask such a question and make such a point proves you belong in this role."

Other arguments popped into her brain, but she held off voicing them. She knew Elliot too well. Whatever she could think up, he had already prepared an answer for. This was all hitting her suddenly, but he had waited a long time for her arrival.

Closing her eyes, she inhaled and searched for that brash voice that had quelled Stak, that deep strength that had climbed Mountain Pillar, that confident conviction that had sought out Elliot in the first place. To her surprise, she did not have to search hard. She felt it on that first breath as if it had patiently stood next to her heart, knowing that at some point it would be called upon.

When she opened her eyes, she looked back at Elliot and nodded. Putting her hands in her pockets, she planned to say that they should take a dip in the waters, too. But she felt the two plastic objects, and she knew the respite had ended.

Pulling out the orange and blue relic box and watch, she gazed across the dust-strewn room. "Do you know what these are? How they connect to any of this? Or Yal-hara?"

Elliot shook his head. "But I can take you to a woman who will know the answer."

CHAPTER 21

Before they left, before Roni issued her orders to this new version of the Parallel Society, Otaur and Lop arrived. Muddy and drained, they lowered into the hot waters with gratitude. As far as Roni knew, most insects averted water, but then she reminded herself that most insects were not sentient beings that spoke English and exhibited enough courage to use themselves as decoys against vicious skullers.

They had nothing significant to report, though Wex demanded details of their harrowing escape and Stak backed him up. They indulged the group for a short time. Glissford informed them of the discussions surrounding Roni, and Otaur stretched three of his arms along the edge of the pool before he said, "We are well-acquainted with Miss Roni's impeccable qualifications and heartily endorse her leadership."

Roni hated to break up the joyful gathering. Seeing her people smiling and laughing without a hint of underlying fear had warmed her. They all relaxed, and they all had deserved it.

But Elliot said the time had come, the trip would take hours, and with a reluctant sigh, Roni agreed.

I never even got to dip a toe in, she thought as she started commanding the full team. She had to admit that it filled her with pride to see how the Society reacted to her — jumping into action, full faith, and nobody questioning her decisions. Maybe they'd have a chance against Yal-hara after all.

Gram and Teanna were to stay behind with the others. Their job — to investigate and understand all they could about these new Society members. What powers did they possess, what numbers did they represent, what experience did they have. Every bit of knowledge that would be vital to the functioning of this group. Then Roni wanted everybody reformed into the most useful combinations.

"We are no longer separate Societies working together. We are one Parallel Society. No more working side-by-side yet staying with your own kind. We will mix and match everybody, regardless of what universe you come from. We are one army now, and I need the best from everyone."

Not a single argument, objection, or even muttered comment.

She then ordered Gully and Garcia to join her and Elliot as they left for the subway. Otaur skittered out of the pool and insisted that he come along, too. Apparently, his devotion to Elliot ran far deeper than Roni had realized. So, they added him.

"Wait," Botolu said, hurrying to join.

Roni shook her head. "I need you to help Gram and Teanna."

"My job is to keep you alive so that we return to my universe."

Gully said, "Don't worry. I can take care of the *keeping Roni alive* part. I've been doing it for years."

"He's right," Roni said with the force of an order. "I have Garcia, too. And Elliot. He's been protecting me for the longest. My whole life, in fact."

"I cannot put my entire universe's well-being into that many other hands. I need to be with you."

Roni walked Botolu toward the far end of the porch. Softer, she said, "I know that for you, the mission is all about getting home with me intact. I appreciate that. But that's not my mission. I promised I would help you, and I will. For now, though, I must stop Yal-hara. Back in your universe, you've had to manage a lot of people with different skills that may or may not be immediately useful. You probably didn't know all these people right from the start. Well, that's the situation we're in, and that's why you are the perfect addition to Gram and Teanna's work here."

Though she did not like the decision, Botolu finally agreed. As they parted, she pointed at the others. "Mr. Gully, Mr. Elliot, and Mr. Garcia, I charge you with protecting Miss Roni better than any other person you have ever protected. If she is returned to us injured in any way, I will blame you."

That had been three hours ago.

The subway train lurched to a stop at another dead station. Roni wondered how much longer the train could continue to operate before it finally died. Considering the desolate sections of city this abandoned subway serviced, she guessed that somebody had to be maintaining the engine and at least a few of the cars. Still, she made a note to ask Elliot if a backup existed. Just in case.

Otaur led them up a flight of stairs that ended in a beaten metal door. "I shall be but a moment. Please comport yourselves as appropriate while you pass the time."

He then dropped to the floor and slipped under the doorway crack. Before Roni could form words in her head to ask Elliot about how such a large insect could manage this feat, Otaur returned.

"We have an abundance of access without detection," he said, and pushed open the door.

They entered another subway platform; however, this one bore the gleam of modernity in its white-tiled walls and digital information displays. People crowded on the far end to board an idling train. Moments later, the doors slid closed with a two-tone chime and the train whisked off without a single whine, groan, or shriek of rust and decay.

Following Otaur, they reached the surface and the sidewalk of a bustling, vibrant city. Sleek, mirrored buildings with white trim towered over them. Skybridges connected some buildings, and on a few occasions, large digital walls tossed commercials, music videos, and news reports into the air. While the majority of pedestrians resembled humans — albeit with a purplish tinge to the skin — enough other creature types peppered the crowd to make Otaur's presence unremarkable.

"We have only but a smattering few blocks to walk," Otaur said.

To go to the Everything Library. That was what Elliot had called it on the long ride. Of all the oddities they had witnessed, the mere name of this one left Roni filled with anticipation. Partly due to her involvement with restoring the Grand Library beneath the bookstore back home. Partly due to a general love and appreciation of books.

However, when they reached the wide marble steps leading toward the library entrance, all grandeur vanished. What may have once been an opulent and imposing testament to the enduring power of knowledge had deteriorated into a leftover from another era. An afterthought. The shining, reflective sides of other buildings had become dull and damaged here. The design — sharp shards pointing in haphazard directions like a jagged crown — must have once dominated the skyline. Only now, the surrounding buildings dwarfed the library.

"What happened?" Garcia asked.

"Time," Elliot said. "Time and politics."

Though people still used the library, Roni observed a building that acted as its own historical record. The remnants of the library it had once been shone with the energy of those who had sought to make it a great repository of information. Long rows of computers on one side — many of them clearly dead or missing parts — and longer rows of books on the other — many shelves with bare patches where great works once stood. A wide marble table sat between. Three librarians worked there with a presence and spirit that maintained the peaceful wonder all libraries held.

"This must have been a noble place," Roni said, not sure where the thought came from.

"It had hoped to be. But it never succeeded."

Garcia ran a finger through the thick dust on one table. "Oh?"

Whispering as he led them further in, Elliot pointed to a set of glowing blue spheres set apart on a dais. "Those each hold all the books, music, and personal interviews of at least ten worlds. They were the start of the Everything Library. It had originally been a massive project, an ambitious undertaking that required the support of the entire city. The goal was to create a central source for all knowledge ever recorded in any form — every bit as simple and complicated as it sounds. With the city residents representing all universes, the librarians would have access to all the cultures and civilizations throughout all universes. It would take lifetimes, centuries, but at some point, they hoped to have a full collection of the knowledge every species had discovered. Except no amount of time would ever be long enough to succeed."

They walked beyond the main floor to a back stairwell which only went downward. Roni swore she felt the librarians snatching surreptitious glances their way, but whenever she peeked back, the staff had their heads down in their work. Descending the stairs, Roni's stomach curdled. "What were the politics?"

"The same as anywhere — power and money. The project cost a lot, and after a few decades, grumbling about spending so much turned it into a regular problem. Politicians complained about the library or supported it depending on what direction they needed the public to go. Eventually, though, long before Yal-hara, those in charge realized the big mistake they had made in allowing the library to exist from the start."

With a bitter snort, Garcia said, "Educating the people."

"I'm afraid so. Governments always act supportive of education, but the truth is that an educated public is difficult to control. If you want to maintain power to do anything other than the best for the people, you need them to be unable to think critically. The less educated they are, the easier they are to bend into whatever stupid, sadistic, or wrong-headed ideas you have."

Roni said, "But the library is still here."

"Another rule of government — once a thing exists, it is near-impossible to make it un-exist. They cut funding to the overall project, but it would have been political suicide to demolish the beloved library. Even now, though barely used and clearly not given enough money to be properly maintained, public opinion of the library is high. It has become an institution. So, the barest funding is provided."

Climbing down floor after floor, the light grew dimmer and the walls filthier. At the rough, concrete bottom, the stench of forgotten, aged trash greeted them. Two cockroach-type bugs scurried away. Roni wondered what Otaur thought of such creatures.

"Something's wrong," Elliot said, pointing to a single, metal door that stood ajar. The area around the knob had been dented, and the jamb had been bent outward.

Gully pushed ahead to inspect the damage. "Looks like somebody used something like a crowbar to force this open."

With a hard sound to his voice, Elliot said, "Or a boney tentacle. Hurry!"

He bolted ahead with Otaur following fast. Garcia and Gully looked to Roni, and she wanted to hug them for that. Tilting her head down the hall, she led them on at a full run.

Not far up, Elliot slumped against the wall with his hand clutching his chest. Breathing hard and beading sweat, he slid to the floor. Roni stumbled to a stop by his side, but he waved her on. "I'll be okay. Go help the Master Librarian."

She wanted to argue, but Otaur settled in next to him. The insect placed a leg upon Elliot's wrist.

"Fear not," Otaur said. "This is no cardiac affliction, rather only an overexertion." Garcia and Gully raced ahead as Otaur went on, "I am a physician of some renown, and I shall reinvigorate this patient with such skill that even a facsimile of perfection in health could not be —"

"Just keep him alive," Roni said.

She dashed down the hall until she reached the only open door. Bursting in, she found an abandoned storage room decorated with a small cot in one corner, a hot plate nearby, and a table and chairs in the center.

Garcia stood to the left and Gully to the right. Both had their arms out and crouched forward as if trying to calm a frightened animal. Near the back wall, a creature stood that Roni had to assume was the Master Librarian.

Dressed like a dignified butler, her top half appeared human enough — ginger haired, round faced, and exuding a motherly warmth — but a mash of fibrous lengths stretching to the floor composed her bottom half like soft bristles on a baby's brush. She wore a monocle chained to her coat and had ink stains on her fingers. And fear — fear radiated from her.

Like the others, she held out her hands. Her eyes darted from Garcia to Gully and back. No one spoke, and Roni only heard her own heavy breathing.

"We're not going to hurt you," she said. "We came for your help."

The Master Librarian lifted her head towards the ceiling. The others followed her gaze. A scratching sound. One water-stained ceiling tile peeled back. As Roni's body tensed, as she prepared to fend off whatever dropped through that opening, the real attack came from the wall.

A skuller smashed through behind the Master Librarian and wrapped its eight arms around her chest. She screamed. The second one plunged from the ceiling onto the center table, kicking off papers and books.

Roni pointed to the Master Librarian. "Garcia, help her. Gully, with me."

As Garcia raced across the room, digging out vials from his pockets, the Master Librarian spun in panic. The skuller on the table snapped at her before launching toward the wall between Roni and Gully. The golem leapt onto the creature, trying to use his weight to flatten the skuller, but as Roni hurtled in, the skuller shoved upward and clonked Gully aside. It whipped out two legs, flinging Roni off balance. Keeping its eyes on its enemies, the creature crabwalked sideways toward the Master Librarian.

Despite her shrieks and thrashing about, Garcia had managed to get behind her. He clamped his hands upon the head of the skuller and pulled back. The poor woman's screams raised an octave.

"Use a potion," Roni said.

"Can't," Garcia grunted as he pulled harder. "Don't want to hurt the Master Librarian."

"You're doing that anyway."

Roni dove at the loose skuller, but it dashed away. She tumbled into the legs of a chair. When she came back to her feet, she lifted the chair and hurled it at the skuller. She had no hope of actually hitting it, but if she kept it busy, it would not be able to join the other one in attacking the Master Librarian.

"Allow me," Gully said and stomped over to Garcia.

The Master Librarian's throat had tightened and she subsided into gasped crying. Perhaps she figured out that these strangers were on her side because she tried to hold still, scrunching her face as if expecting a doctor to administer a painful shot.

Roni rushed over to grab the chair and bat it at the skuller. It skittered across the floor, trying to reach its partner — darting one direction then another. Roni held the center of the room now. She kept the chair out like a lion tamer. *I sure wouldn't mind a whip,* she thought.

"I'll not hurt you," Gully told the Master Librarian as he reached one hand beneath the gaps between the skuller's legs and pulled back. The sound of snapping bone crackled up Roni's spine. But since she did not hear agonizing screams, she assumed the broken bones belong to the skuller. Another snap. Then another.

Gully stepped back with the creature in his hand, two of its lengthy arms limp while the others flailed about. A gray tube extended from its underbelly into the Master Librarian's back like a horrifying umbilical cord. With a fluttering motion, Garcia opened a butterfly knife and slashed at the cord. It cut apart with ease, sluicing gray-yellow liquid to the floor. Gully smashed the beast in its own puddle. Garcia hurried to sprinkle the leftover contents of his vial onto the creature's head and let the potion do its job.

Elliot and Otaur arrived. Limping across the room toward the Master Librarian, Elliot still managed to convey strength and dignity. Whether from seeing its partner crumble away or from the addition of two more opponents, the remaining skuller clearly knew when to run. Moving faster than any skuller Roni had seen before, this one zipped up the wall and smashed through the ceiling tiles.

When Roni turned back to the group, she found the Master Librarian on the floor, face down, her coat in ribbons, her back bruised where the skuller had taken hold. A charred circle marking the center dribbled more of that gray-yellow liquid. Blood pooled. Elliot already stood over her, passing his cane back and forth. The healing spell created a glow around her wounds.

Chapter 22

For the next hour, Roni could do nothing but wait. She had witnessed Elliot's miraculous spellwork, she had benefitted from it many times, but the effort he put in this time far exceeded anything before. Thankfully, the Master Librarian had passed out right near the beginning. Roni didn't think the poor thing could have handled any of this. Garcia offered to help, too, and Elliot bent close to whisper his instructions. Roni guessed this was to prevent the Master Librarian from hearing too much should she have awoken.

Tired of sitting still — unable, really — Roni paced the hall to the stairwell like a captive panther. Everything had been moving so fast she barely had time to think of the next step in front of her, let alone plan against the bigger threats they faced. The original plan had been to find Elliot and return home — become the full-force Parallel Society once again. While part of her allowed room for the idea of dealing with Yal-hara first — Elliot did start all of this by chasing after the spindle-legged monster — Roni never anticipated Yal-hara's rise in political power, never planned for the various resistance groups to crown her as their leader, never thought she would be climbing icy pillars and fighting skeletal beasts.

That last part shouldn't have surprised her. She had been through enough weirdness in this job to know better.

The bug clicks of Otaur's approach grated along Roni's arms, the back of her neck, and into her ears, but she turned towards him with a pleasant smile. "Yes?"

"The Master Librarian has requested your presences. I've been dispatched to retrieve you by our mutual friend, Mr. Elliot. Please attend with me as I return to the main operation."

When Roni entered the storage room, Elliot sat at the table, hunched forward and patting sweat from his forehead. Standing behind him, Gully looked as if ready to fend off an attack from some invisible threat. The Master Librarian had been moved to her cot. She sat up, propped by a few rather flat-looking pillows, leaning away from the wall. Her eyes were closed. Her breathing fast and shallow. Squatting over the puddle of blood and muck, Garcia poked at it with a cotton swab.

"She's holding on, for now," Elliot said. "But the damage to her spine is too severe. I cannot heal her completely."

"What about you?" Roni asked Garcia.

He shook his head. "I have a few healing potions, of course, but Elliot told me not to bother."

Whirling back to Elliot, Roni said, "Why not?"

"Yal-hara's soldier injected a toxin into her," he said. "Garcia's working on an antidote."

Garcia rubbed his neck. "Cross your fingers and pray on that one. Without any knowledge of her anatomy, without a proper lab, and certainly without much time, it's not looking good."

"Do your best." Roni patted his shoulder as she drew a chair next to the cot. "I'm here," she said, unsure if the Master Librarian could hear her.

The woman lifted a weak hand and pinched the bridge of her nose. Rolling her head up, her neck crackling at the movement, she smiled at Roni. When she spoke, she had a firm voice, but an urgency, too. She knew her time slipped away.

"We've waited for so long to meet you," she said. "It's good to finally put a face to the idea of you."

"Idea?" Roni said. "Like it was foretold? I'm sorry, but I don't believe in prophecy."

"No prophecy. Though it's funny you should doubt such a thing considering you are sitting beneath a city that exists to keep all universes in harmony. In the face of that kind of power, why not prophecy, too? But no, in this case, no prophecy."

"Then what do mean — the *idea* of me?"

"I know history, and history dictates that whenever an evil rises, eventually good rises against it. Never seems to happen as fast as we want, evil often gets to play its horrible games for too long, but in the end, it never holds. Somebody always comes along who won't sit by and allow the evil to continue."

"You think I'm that *somebody?*"

"I know you are. Many things point to that conclusion, but the two most important are simple enough. First, you are still here when you could have grabbed Elliot and left."

"That's his doing."

"No. Had you ordered him to return to your world, he would have followed."

Roni didn't know how true that was, but at the same time, she could see Elliot begrudgingly obeying her commands. He would have done everything possible to dissuade her, and once back home, he would have pestered her until she agreed to return or help in some way. Yet the Master Librarian had hit close enough.

Sitting back, Roni said, "Your second point?"

"Yal-hara sent her vicious brutes to kill me. Why? She's known about me living down here for years. I have no contact with her. I'm not an essential part of Elliot's resistance. I merely sit in this room and continue the project — though, of course, it's a foolish thing to do. So, why suddenly attack me now? Obviously, the answer is you."

"Trust me on this one — Yal-hara is not afraid of me."

"Maybe not this very moment, but she is afraid of what you will do when you know."

"Know what?"

"How should I know?" The Master Librarian shrugged. "You're the one who sought me. Ask me what you came to ask me, and maybe we can figure everything out."

Roni hesitated. Up to this point, all that had been said constituted nothing but conjecture. The hypothesis of an educated, intelligent being — no doubt well-reasoned thoughts — but no hard evidence backed any of it up. Except the attack, but even that lacked proof of its purpose. For all Roni knew, the Master Librarian had a side hustle selling off rare antiquities, and the attack had been a warning from a competitor.

She shook off the silly thought. That was her brain trying to find a way out. What really gave her pause was simple — anything further that the Master Librarian shared would be the truth, would carry implications that Roni and the Society had to help, would prescribe a dangerous road ahead. Pretty much the usual.

In the wake of her recent adrenaline rush, she wondered how long a body could handle the repeated jolts to the system a Society lifestyle provided. Glancing at Elliot, she grinned. Quite a long time, apparently. With the help of a spell or potion, of course.

As she turned back to the Master Librarian, her eyes fell upon the fresh blood staining the dirty pillow casing. The woman's face had paled since the conversation began.

Roni pulled out the watch and relic box. She could feel Elliot, Otaur, and Gully crowd behind her. Garcia kept at his antidote, but from the corner of her eye, Roni spied him leaning closer to hear, too.

While the Master Librarian inspected the objects with shaking, weak hands, Elliot said, "I thought that if anybody would know what these are …"

She laughed. "Oh, Yal-hara is afraid indeed." To Roni: "What do you know of the Vestu Books?"

"Not much. There are ten of them, I think."

"The City of Infinity is divided into ten sections — slices coming out of the center."

Elliot said, "I've explained that to them."

"Then I will explain again. This is too important for me to rely on others." She licked her lips, and Roni noticed a gray film on her tongue. The Master Librarian squinted and her brow furrowed down. She groaned but put out a hand to stop any fussing. "I'll be okay. Well, I suppose I really won't. I am dying, after all. For now, though, just listen. Now, there are eight sections that comprise nearly all the city. The ninth section is the central hub — the inner-circle where most of the government operates. You've seen some of the city, so it should be obvious that every known universe is represented by, at the very least, a block or two on these streets. You understand so far?"

Roni said, "Eight sections, each with residents from different universes. The ninth is reserved for government."

"The ten Vestu Books link to the real universes corresponding to these representational blocks of city. Your world is in Section One. With the first Vestu Book, I could travel anywhere in your universe."

"And there are other universes in Section One."

"Precisely. It is these books — powered by the life energy of this city — that binds all existence in near-harmony. But nothing, not even the universe is perfect. There are times when universes collide, rifts form, and for that we have you and all the other versions of the Parallel Society."

Garcia's mouth gaped open. With an awed whisper, he said, "So, we're the tenth book."

The Master Librarian snorted into a hacking cough. "No. Without the ten Vestu Books, all that is, all the planets and stars, all the living creatures throughout, would become unstable. Rifts would occur daily as one universe spilled over another. Some would collide so hard they would destroy each other. Everything within them obliterated in an instant. The Books are the most important ever created, and they are the most protected, too. Locked with powerful spells and stored in a tenth City location, a place like the City that is a universe unto itself. It is said to be a place of great wealth and beauty. A golden city filled with people who only exist to serve the Head Council member in protecting the books. While many in our City travel to other universes, those in the Tenth have never known another world. They are born, live, and die only to serve the Vestu Books. There is only one access point to the Tenth, and it is known only by the Head Council member."

Swallowing down the bile racing up her throat, Roni said, "Right now, that's Yal-hara."

The Master Librarian looked over the plastic watch and relic box again. "These are trophies. Less awards and more like markers of a change, of a Vestu Book having been opened. The fact that both trophies occurred in proximity to you only furthers the proof of a deep and strong connection to Yal-hara."

"Two trophies means two books opened," Gully said.

Roni picked up the trophies. They felt heavier now, the edges sharper, the orange-blue colors darker. She sighed. This job would never get easier.

Looking directly at the Master Librarian, hoping the knot in her chest did not reflect in her eyes, Roni said, "We have to stop Yal-hara before she can open another book."

"That makes no sense," Garcia said. "If opening all ten destroys existence, what benefit is there for her?"

The Master Librarian raised one shivering finger. "She's too smart to keep them all open, keep them all unstable and vulnerable. There is also, admittedly, some educated guesswork to all I've said. After all, I've never been Head Council, so I've never seen the tenth location. But however she does it, once she has shown all the universes that she controls whether we exist or not —"

Elliot thumped his cane on the floor. "She can demand whatever she wants. She'll become the ultimate dictator."

"Then how do we stop her?" Gully asked.

"All of my sources say she disappeared quite some time ago. Left her underlings on the Council to manage the City. Couple that with Roni's trophies, and I think there is no doubt. She has gone to the tenth location."

Roni said, "And we haven't any idea where that is."

The Master Librarian sat straighter, her face twinkling to life with a sudden surge of energy. "Perhaps we do."

CHAPTER 23

The sparkle dimmed fast, but the Master Librarian had enough strength to point toward the exit. "Otaur and Gully. Please be kind enough to go upstairs and return with a book for us. Its spine number is 27-03158R. If you have any trouble, ask the nearest librarian. They love to help, and they are comfortable dealing with all manner of creature."

Otaur performed an insect bow — impressive since he lacked a waist to bend from. Though Gully did not offer such a grand gesture, he swelled at the responsibility. This dying woman had requested the book with good reason. A quick nod from Roni, and Gully ushered Otaur down the hall with urgency in his eyes. A moment later, she heard the golem running toward the stairs.

Elliot used his cane to poke Garcia in the back. "How much longer on that antidote?"

The potion-maker had dabbed a sample of the goo on the floor with a new mixture he had concocted, but his slumped shoulders gave the answer before he shook his head. "Even with a proper set up, this could take weeks or months or maybe never. I'm sorry."

"It's okay." The Master Librarian tented her fingers in her lap. "I have lived a long and fascinating life. Can't think of much I regret, and that is an accomplishment all should strive for. Oh, but there is one thing — ever since Elliot told me how your Grand Library contains all the life stories of your Society people, I have thought that I should do the same. I had intended to, yet somehow, I never got started. Now, it is too late."

It all sounded familiar. Roni had heard Gram and Elliot both talk about the end of their lives too often. She hated it. But this felt different. Perhaps because she had no close relationship with the Master Librarian.

No. Something more.

Roni tried to open her thoughts, her emotions, to the moment so that she might see clearer. She experienced a flash of Sully's death — a heart-wrenching stone in her chest. She thought about the sacrifices of her father in the Caverns — a loss close to dying with the same finality. This moment, watching the Master Librarian, crushed the air in a similar way.

The inevitability.

When Gram and Elliot spoke of the end of their lives, they saw it approaching — but in the distance. Sully, her father, and now the Master Librarian — there was no distance. Death coated the room. That was what pressed against her, made breathing a chore, gave the world its unique gloom.

The Master Librarian placed her unsteady hand on Roni's knee. "Don't be sad for me. Or anybody who has experienced a full life. Regrets or not. Success or failure. Doesn't matter. Lives are meant to end, and when they are full — long or short — it is a good thing. I have had both. A long, full life. Even if that were not true, with my final moments, I am going to make my entire existence worthwhile." She narrowed her eyes. "We are going to get you to Yal-hara."

Roni heard the words as both an excited declaration of hope and a vicious threat of danger. Gully burst into the room with a triumphant swagger as Otaur followed behind carrying a book far too large to easily hold. Plucking it from his insect hands, Gully handed the hefty tome to the Master Librarian.

"Thank you," she grunted as she half-lowered/half-dropped the book into her lap. "One last thing. Roni, would you please go to my table and open the drawer?"

Garcia moved aside to allow Roni by. She kept her face still, unsure what to expect, but hoping to find a pen for notes or a letter opener or something similar, something basic. No such luck.

Pulling open the drawer, she found what had once been a porcelain figurine — the kind of thing people collected back home. This one showed a Dutch boy peering down a well. But the porcelain had become plastic, and the expert paintjob had become a hodgepodge of orange and blue.

"Where did you get this?" Roni said as she set the figurine on the table.

Elliot stepped back as if the thing might come alive. "How?"

"It happened a few months ago," the Master Librarian said. "I'm not sure how that converts into time on your world — days, perhaps? — but that's when it happened. I received it from one of Yal-hara's people. As a warning, I suppose. Or a taunt."

"This means three Vestu Books have been opened," Garcia said.

"And that this one went unnoticed. It could have discolored and altered the way it has done so by being near Roni. Just as the others have behaved." She reached toward the table, waving a feeble hand until Roni finally walked the figurine over. "I suspect this was the first one. Yal-hara testing if her method to opening the Books was sound. Judging by the increased speed between each opening, she is getting better at it."

Tucking away that the Master Librarian did not admit she had a trophy until now, Roni pointed to the book Gully had brought. "What's special about that?"

The Master Librarian leafed through several pages until she finally placed it flat. The two-page spread displayed a map outlining a jagged area with numerous pieces cutaway or meandering off from the main section. Street grids marked some sections while others had languorous roads. Colored lines marked various points, and writing in another language with another alphabet labeled everything.

"This is the City of Infinity," she said. Heading off Roni's question, the Master Librarian went on, "It is forever expanding, yet it always retains this shape."

"I thought it was a circle."

"Not precisely, but it helps when trying to comprehend the City. This is its true shape, and somewhere in this place is the tenth location. We must find it."

"Oh, that's just perfect," Garcia said. "We've got three trinkets and a map of a city that never stops growing."

Roni snapped a harsh glare. "We have more than that. We have all the Parallel Societies of all the universes that have joined us. And we have us — here, now, thinking through the problem. So, let's think."

In the thick stillness that followed, Garcia paused, swallowed, and finally nodded. "I'm sorry."

She placed a hand on his shoulder and brought him closer to the map. "You're right that we don't have a lot to go on, but if we ask enough questions, bounce enough ideas, we'll get somewhere."

"I have a question," Gully said, raising his hand from the back. "How old is this map? If the City keeps growing, how do we get an accurate layout?"

The Master Librarian tapped the book. "These pages are the overview of the city's shape and structure. But the other pages in this book reflect all the changes that occur, and it self-updates every day. Elliot is not the only person capable of casting a spell or two."

Garcia picked up the plastic relic box. "Can this still work? Maybe we can trap Yal-hara inside it."

"No. It is only a toy now. Except …"

"Except what?"

The Master Librarian placed the plastic watch in her hand and cocked her head as she considered it. "The Vestu Books are believed to be the most powerful objects in all universes. It seems unlikely that such power could act upon anything without leaving something behind — even as minor as a residue." She raised her hand to stop everybody from speaking. "We know these linked to Roni, or at least they linked to the connection between Roni and Yal-hara. There must be something we can do with that information."

"No, that's not right." Roni's thoughts jumped in her head. "You said that each Book connected to the universes within the corresponding sections of the City. That's the link. The connection to me was probably a result of Yal-hara using the Book. If somebody else had used it, then I wouldn't be the one getting these trophies."

"Possibly."

Roni looked at all the confused faces. With a broad grin, she said, "The Books link with the City. That means the City also links back to the Books."

Elliot jolted upright. "Which links back to Yal-hara."

Slapping his hands on the edge of the cot, Garcia said, "These trophies are connected to you, and you are connected to Yal-hara. The Master Librarian has said that the trophies also retain some bit of the Books that created them. Right? You just called it a *residue*."

Despite her pain, The Master Librarian joined in the excitement. "Then the trophies can act like a link back to Yal-hara as well."

"It's worth a shot," Roni said. "But how do we do that?"

Otaur skittered up the side of the cot and sat on his back two legs. "I believe rudimentary mathematics would be a rather perfect solution to our quandary." When nobody continued with him, the insect sighed. "When attempting to discern the location of an unknown, if the searching party has at least three target points, they can utilize a common concept entitled *triangulation*. Because we have acquired three of these so-called trophies, we merely must extrapolate a location in the

City that parallels the location in each universe upon which the so-called trophy had been uncovered. Once all three are diligently mapped, we use mathematics and pinpoint the access link to the tenth location. Quite simple, really."

Shock rippled through the group until Garcia broke the silence in a stunned voice. "That kind of makes sense."

They got to work. After twenty minutes of reasoning out where to mark the possible locations for the trophies to be linked to the Books, a clear pattern emerged. Regardless of how they determined their answers, all the locations resulted with the same area at the center. Still, Otaur insisted on confirming it with math.

Once they had the district figured out, the Master Librarian flipped through her book of the City so they could look at a detail of the area. Even on the main map, the district looked daunting in size, but when she stopped and spread the book open, ice slid over Roni's skin.

The Master Librarian's shaking fingers tapped across the pages. "Somewhere in all these streets is the access point."

Looking at the district map, Roni's throat tightened.

"It's a big job," Gully said, "but at least it's not the whole city anymore."

Roni shook her head as she stabbed at a small raised-bed garden off a narrow alleyway. "It's there."

"How do you know that?" Garcia said.

Feeling stronger as the correctness settled in, she gestured to the entire page. "This map, this district, is the exact shape of the gaps in my map in the Grand Library. I've worked for years on that map. This has all the missing pieces."

CHAPTER 24

Organizing and maneuvering an entire army — even one that comprised less than fifty people — required time and patience. Roni had little of either. But to go from locating a position on a map to locating it physically, conveying that information through the ranks, and gathering all of Teanna's new Society groupings without alerting their enemy meant careful, quiet, and maddeningly slow progress.

At least, Roni and her team could snatch a little sleep. Except for Teanna — some even called her *General* now. She handled the groups, giving them specific routes to take to the garden and staggering the times they headed out. After seeing the odd paths being ordered, Roni pushed her to be more direct, but Teanna explained that approaching in different ways would reduce the chances of being discovered. More important, though — this offered each group their first opportunity to start working together, start acting like a team, start bonding.

"Okay," Roni said. "You know what you're doing."

Teanna spit out a laugh. "I've never led an army before. But I'll do my best."

Holding back her desire to comment, Roni offered a firm nod instead. She had noticed how each grouping comprised of a good balance. Some groups mixed Stak's and Glissford's people into a fighting unit. Dyon's Society had more healers and stealth movers, so they were sprinkled throughout each group as needed. Roni spotted only one unit of all healers. The insect units did not mingle much with the others, but Teanna explained that was not out of any prejudice. Rather, the insects could scale walls and infiltrate spaces that most other creatures could not. Best to keep them together.

The big surprise involved Wex's spike-backed warriors that used guns as their main weapon. Roni expected Teanna to scatter these men and women throughout the new groups. A little firepower for protection. Instead, Teanna kept them all together and added some of Dyon's people, too, creating an elite force. Though Teanna used the word *elite* loosely — none of Wex's team had ever shot their weapons beyond target practice.

The only misstep had been with Eyopton — the bald, burly woman Botolu had befriended at the hot springs. Roni could not blame Teanna for what happened, but she knew Teanna blamed herself.

"Botolu warned me," Teanna said. "I would have listened a few hours later, but it all occurred right at the start, right when I was trying to get everyone to accept my command."

Eyopton and her people refused to merge with other Society members. "We have always survived together, and we will always stay that way."

Teanna tried to reason that they were all one Society now, that they would only survive when the idea of *together* included all of them, but Eyopton would not listen. She had no interest in adapting to the new circumstances. Botolu entered the discussion, but nothing worked. In the end, Eyopton left to inform her people that they would not be part of a new Parallel Society.

"Besides," she said, "our old one works just fine."

A handful of individuals also backed out either from fear or, like Eyopton, a desire to cling tight to the way things had always been done before. Thankfully, the majority stayed, and with each new group collecting at the garden, Roni's sense of success grew stronger. She tried to ignore that they kept thinking of the new Society as an army when they totaled fewer than fifty.

Stak marched up and down the alleyway leading to the garden. His silver-gray hair rippled with each anxious motion. Glissford sat on a pile of loose bricks, sharpening his sword to ease his tension. Without looking, Roni knew Garcia would be checking over his potion inventory while Gram would find a quiet alcove to sit, hold her cross, close her eyes, and pray.

Gully arrived, pushing the Master Librarian in a wheelchair. The poison in her system had robbed her mobility and weakened all her muscles. Her hands rested atop the map book, barely keeping it from falling off the chair, while her head flopped with each bump in the road. But she wanted to witness this moment, and Gully thought it best to give a dying woman her last wish.

At length, Teanna reported to Roni that all were accounted for and ready to go. "Though, I have to admit, I still can't believe this is going to work." She gestured to the small square of raised beds barely sprouting. "Seems an odd place for it all."

Gram said, "I should think that is proof in itself. Have faith in our Lord. If you can't do that, at least have faith in Roni."

"Besides," Elliot said, "why does this seem any odder than a hole in the basement wall of a bookstore leading into the Caverns? In fact, this makes more sense to me. The Caverns are like tunnels between the universes. The chained books contain the rifts, which also makes the Cavern a massive library, but the tunnels themselves, if traveled long enough, would bring you to almost anywhere you could dream of going. That this wonderous place would connect to the tenth section of the City is, in a way, obvious."

Dyon approached the group, and in a hushed voice, she said, "My healers have checked their supplies seven times. Everyone is anxious to get started. They keep asking me what our orders are. They're starting to worry we don't have much of a plan."

Roni said, "Hard to plan when we know nothing about the battlefield on the other side."

"That won't sit well with my people, and I'm sure Stak's people will like it even less."

Gram squeezed Roni's arm. "Perhaps the troops need some words from their leader."

An ice bath could not have shocked Roni's system more. "That's a bad idea. I've never been good at speeches unless I'm really angry. Even then, I'm probably not that good, I simply don't know to shut up."

With a little extra force, Teanna ushered Roni aside. "Everyone here is nervous."

"Of course, they are. I'm nervous, too."

"But we've been in battle before. These people have spent most of their lives here in this city. The rifts open in their respective universes, but they are here. Safe. You understand? Every single one of these individuals is new to all of this. They need to hear from you."

Roni looked over Teanna's shoulder at their dismal army. What she had taken to be anxious nerves altered. Now, she saw the sweat, the shivering breaths, the clenching and unclenching hands. She saw the way Stak paced nonstop and aggressive, trying to stomp out all the bubbling self-doubt. The way Glissford gripped his sword white-knuckle tight. This army was not nervous — they were terrified.

Roni's heart sank low. "What could I possibly say that would change anything?"

"The truth. I hardly know them well, but I think the truth — no matter how ugly — is all they really want."

Stepping around Teanna and pointing at Elliot, she said, "Get started."

Lifting his cane, Elliot and Garcia took the three trophies and placed them together at the corner of the garden's first raised bed. Elliot waved his cane in a circle over the trophies. Motioning with her head, Roni had Gully bring the Master Librarian closer so she could see every last detail.

Then Roni walked in front of her little army. She had no clue what words would come out of her mouth but trusted Teanna. If they needed the truth, she could deliver that much.

As the murmuring subsided and all attention focused on her, Roni put one hand in her pocket and scratched the back of her head with the other.

"Teanna told me earlier that you all have basic assignments to your groups. When things get chaotic — and they will — remember those assignments. You'll probably end up doing more than that, but you can always fall back to what your main job is."

Every word out of her mouth sounded horrible to her ears. Peering back over her shoulder, she saw Gram with her hands clasped together and encouragement in her eyes. Teanna gestured forward for her to continue, and even Botolu looked eager to hear more.

Roni lowered her gaze to the ground, fighting off the urge to vomit. Then: "With the most skilled, veteran, well-trained fighters imaginable, going into this mission would still be hazardous. Deadly. Instead, most of you have no experience, and none of us has ever seen the place we're heading to. The fact that we are still going should tell you how important this mission is. And, unfortunately, how desperate. If we had the time to train you, to scout ahead, to work out the best plan of attack, then we would be doing those exact things right now. But Yal-hara has already opened three of the ten Vestu Books. That's three too many. If we don't stop her, she will rule all of us and destroy any who resist. Even if that means destroying an entire universe."

She glanced back once again, and Teanna held up her fingers to indicate the need for a tiny bit more. Trying not to huff, Roni lifted her head. "There will never be a greater fight in your life than this one. Everything you believe in — whether it's family, friends, lovers, gods and goddesses, community, politics, society, everything – it is all at stake. All that you value, all that you exist for, we're fighting for that. That's our one great strength. That is how desperation overcomes inexperience." She put out her hands. "That's all I have for you. Get yourselves ready. We're about to go."

No grand cheer followed. No pat on the back. But Roni saw the way these people found their groups like seeking out old friends, the way they held their heads up as if marching in a victory parade, the way they inspected their weapons already picturing the fall of their enemies. The terror had been transformed. The unsteady gazes and shaking hands had been replaced with determined eyes and clenched fists.

Before everyone could settle, the trophies pulsed a bright red. The light spread outward, painting the alleyway and garden, hushing all noise, pulling all focus. As Elliot continued moving his cane, the trophies also moved. Stuttering motions at first, but then they slid across the rough concrete as if skating on ice. Soon, they moved in a circle that followed Elliot's cane. He looked like a puppeteer and the trophies were his marionettes.

"What now?" Roni asked.

Elliot said, "I don't know. This is not some spell I've created. I'm merely gathering energy and sending it down into the trophies."

The red light intensified, and the Master Librarian whispered, "If you can stop, it'll be ready."

With a shrug, Elliot brought his cane down to his side. The trophies continued their circular dance.

"It works." The Master Librarian could not look away, and Roni knew straight through to her core that the old woman held to the last string of her life.

The trophies spun faster, creating a strong wind with a stronger howl. The Master Librarian howled back and laughed with childish glee. "Step in," she said. "Go on and do your job."

"Wait," Gram said, hurrying to Roni's side. "There's no guarantee this thing works the way we think. You even said that we don't know what's on the other side. You can't jump in there blind."

Gully walked closer. "She's right. I should go first. After all, I'm just a golem. If I die, it won't really matter." He paused. Then: "No, no, don't argue with that statement. I wouldn't want to think you actually cared about me."

The glowing red of the trophies looked angry, menacing. Enough so that Roni gave Gully's offer serious consideration. But only a fleeting thought. A breath of the human desire for self-preservation. Then she looked at her army once more.

They were loosely held together. Too many of them would gladly go home if they could do so without losing face. They needed more than somebody designated as a leader. More than somebody with a heroic history they only heard about but never experienced. She had to show them that she would be brave, too. For them. Or else they would never follow.

She walked straight to the circle of spinning trophies. A quiet figure appeared at her side — Botolu. They stared at each other, a silent argument flashing between them. In the end, Roni's shoulders lowered. She had impeded Botolu too many times, and there was no way the Coana woman would allow Roni through without being by her side.

Roni peeked back. Maybe it would help to see more than one person enter. Besides, the argument was over. She couldn't stop Botolu without causing a major fight, drawing blood, and undermining any goodwill she had acquired from the others. She gave a nod, and they joined hands.

They stepped in.

CHAPTER 25

Roni had expected the elevator-drop gut-punch of traveling to another universe, but the electric pulse jittering through her nervous system was entirely new. Botolu kept tapping her head as if trying to loosen water in her ear. Standing in the center of a city park, they shivered. A few tried to walk off the uneasy sensations. But then the others trickled in, and they needed help, too.

When the last of them had entered — Elliot, worrying Roni that he might have a heart attack — everyone broke off into their groups as if they had practiced the maneuver hundreds of times. Roni caught the prideful surge in Teanna before pulling the core group of leaders together. They huddled at the center as the others hopped about in whatever way helped get rid of the strangeness of travelling here.

A quick scan of the area gave Roni enough information to start. Things looked bad. The city of golden beauty did not tower over this little park nor did the park itself shine with an abundance of natural life. Instead, even from this distance, they could see that the buildings surrounded them with bleak and ominous darkness. The park looked burnt and dead.

Not a living sound, either. No people. No animals. No machines. Nothing but a gentle breeze and flashes of stark light off in the distance.

"Lightning?" Teanna said.

Gram said, "Not likely. We're still in the Caverns — even if not the same universe."

"I don't think I want you to explain that one."

Roni watched for more flashes. When they came, she made her decision. "That's where we're going. It's the only place anything's happening which means it's the place Yal-hara will be found."

Wex brought his head close to Teanna and muttered a few words. She then turned to the others. "Assuming the street layout is roughly a grid, he suggests we have two forces on side roads while the bulk of us go up the main road. I agree."

"Sounds good," Roni said. "Divide up the groups as you see fit. Let's get moving."

Teanna snapped to attention, and Roni feared she might salute. Perhaps sensing the discomfort, she merely nodded before heading off toward the teams. A few minutes later, they awaited the order to go.

As they hiked out of the park and into the city proper, two thoughts competed for Roni's attention. First, she wished they had thought ahead and brought along good communication equipment. Even a simple walkie-talkie would have been helpful. If people died because they couldn't coordinate their positions or call for help — but she refused to let such thoughts weigh on her. Not now. She had never commanded such a large group before and was bound to make some mistakes. If she lived through this, she could wallow in the guilt later.

She suspected she shared her second thought with her entire army — a mix of awe and apprehension as they finally caught a solid view of the city. It consisted of old-style buildings she knew from Philadelphia and New York. Practical brick structures with metal fire escapes and potted plants or herb gardens in a few open windows. Canvas awnings shaded storefronts at the street level.

But all of it — all the bricks, the plants, the windows, the doorways, the sidewalk — every visible surface had been lacquered a deep black. It painted the signposts and streetlights. Parked cars — models ranging from the familiar to the bizarre — trash cans and public benches also stood like obsidian statues.

Garcia approached a car and ran his finger along the side. Bits of soot crumbled away, but the machine beneath remained the same charred color. He sniffed the substance, scraped it off his finger and into an empty vial, then wiped his finger against his pant leg. In answer to Roni's questioning expression, he shrugged.

Leading the main group along the center of the street, their shoes crunching the gravelly surface like walking over sand on glass, Roni noted the lack of moving cars or people. To Elliot: "Is this another abandoned section like in the City? Just a failed area and we'll find the real city beyond?"

"Not if the Master Librarian is correct, and I see no reason to doubt her. The place she described is this one. But something terrible has happened here."

A block up the road, they encountered the first people. A woman holding the hand of a little girl while an older girl strolled by their side. They all wore light charming dresses styled from 1950s America and appeared to be out for a walk on a warm day.

Except they didn't move. They couldn't. They had become dark, stone statues.

Roni put out a hand to halt. She wondered what the flanking groups would do when they saw something like this. Knowing they had to operate independent of any central command, Teanna would have put the strongest minds on those teams. Wex led the group a block over on the left. Roni thought he would keep anybody from running off in fear. On the right side — one of Wex's trusted soldiers led that group. Would that be enough?

As she walked forward, she felt Teanna and Gully follow. They approached the horrid statues with cautious steps. Roni's pulse raced and her lips dried. Each face looked as if it might smile right at her. Each dress looked soft and airy. She could see the individual hairs — not only the strands breaking free from the older girl's ponytail but also the smaller ones on her arm. If they had been true statues, carved creations from a sculptor's mind, they would have been masterpieces.

Teanna braved reaching out to poke the mother's arm. Her finger came back dusted with black particles. "Hard and cold like stone," she said.

Roni walked around the statues, and when she reached the back, her gut twisted.

"Oh, Lord," Gram said.

Whirling around, shocked to hear Gram's voice, Roni found her grandmother, Garcia, and several others standing nearby. She couldn't let them see the alarm coursing through her. Not the newbies. To them, the horror of seeing the statues, of seeing the backs of their heads — it would be too much, if their leader broke down, too.

With her jaw locked tight, she turned back to the statues and braced her body not to react. All three — the mother and both girls — suffered from the same trauma. It looked as if their brains had burst outwards, leaving behind a hole frozen that same instant. Roni checked around her — no brain sculptures on the ground.

Garcia closed in, squinting as he tapped on his phone's flashlight. "Am I seeing this right?"

Roni knew he didn't need confirmation. He simply needed another person to experience something terrible so as not to be alone. Standing on her toes, she peered in the back of the mother's head.

Nothing. Empty. No brain. No skull. Hollowed out. If the woman had not been petrified, her head — presumably, her entire body — would have collapsed into a pile of mush. Before looking away, Roni caught sight of something low and to the side. Pulling Garcia's hand, she shined more light on it.

Moss. Mold and moss. With a strange, thin vine like a crack in the stone.

Roni stepped back. As others peeked inside, her eyes roved the dark windows. She saw shapes. More people. Frozen people. Further down the street, there were still more.

She heard the gasps and murmurs rippling through her army. How many would refuse to go further?

The answer could have been high, but Elliot spoke up. "This is what we are here to fight. Everyone must take a look at these unfortunate souls. I have no doubt what we are witnessing is the aftermath of Yal-hara opening the Vestu Books. This once great city, a place of enormous and vibrant beauty has been decimated, turned into — whatever this is."

One of Glissford's men, a fellow with a bushy mustache, said, "But their heads. The Books did that?"

"I believe we are seeing where all the skullers came from." A collective gulp from the group. Then Elliot said, "They did not appear until a few months ago. That lines up with when Roni began seeing the trophies — though it was only days in her universe. Before then, we'd never encountered a skuller. Yet ever since Yal-hara took over and managed to open only three of the Books, the skullers became a problem."

Roni rolled back her shoulders and raised her chin as she moved to the front of the group. "Elliot's right. I know this has shocked us all, but we must continue our mission. She cannot be allowed to open more. It's that simple. Whatever horrible things we see, that doesn't matter. She cannot be allowed to open more. Pull yourselves together, and when you feel doubt or fear, remind yourself of the mission — *she cannot be allowed to open more.*"

Turning to face the cold, empty city street, Roni trudged forward. For someone who did not feel qualified for giving speeches, she thought she had done a pretty good job. When the heavy steps of twenty-some men and women followed, she knew she had.

Before she could puff up with overwhelming pride, she heard scrabbling against hard stone. She didn't see any movement, though. Another block, and she heard it again. And she wasn't the only one.

Botolu came alongside. "I know I'm ignorant of a lot in this universe, but where I come from, I know this one thing well — we're being watched."

Gunfire erupted a block over on the right. Then a few shots popped from the left. Everyone around Roni lifted their swords and spears, chains and potions. Whatever weapons they had, they brought them to the ready. Elliot began work on a spell.

They held still. Listening.

As the clanking of steel and the echoes of weapons fire continued, Roni considered sending some of her team to support both side groups. But doing so would deplete the main force before they reached the target. Perhaps that was the enemy's intent. She needed more information.

"Scles, come up here," she called out.

Another one of Otaur's people skittered to the front. He had more of an insect face than the others, but he also looked less scared than most. "I am here to report of my presence at having been summoned."

She would send her runner to the righthand group since the gunshots started on that side. But as she gave her orders, a runner from the left side — their old friend, Lop — zipped in from an alleyway. He stayed on all six legs, low to the ground, racing towards them.

Instead of launching into a long-winded way of saying that he carried a message from that group, he sprang onto two legs and said only one word. "Ambush!"

CHAPTER 26

Before any member of the Society could react — most experiencing the word *Ambush* in its true context for the first time — the bone-white octopus-arms of a skuller extended from behind Lop and wrapped around his head and upper-arms. Lop had time to reach up to his attacker, but nothing more. The skuller squeezed until Lop's hard outer-shell cracked. Roni flinched at the horrible noise as green-yellow sludge oozed between the skuller's arms.

Despite all their planning and big talk, this moment, this first contact with real danger, scattered Roni's army like water splashing in all directions. They darted off, leaving Roni and her team alone. Those few who did not panic raced after the others, trying to corral them back. But Roni didn't have time to worry about all of them. A skuller stood ten feet away, dripping with the blood of her soldier.

She sidestepped, circling the skuller, forcing it to turn. "That's right, you little bastard. Pay attention to me." She kept talking, kept moving, and knew she didn't have to explain anything more.

The skuller reared back with a hiss. But as it launched at Roni, a chain whipped around it, taking it down like a wild pig. Gram tugged hard, tightening the chain around the thrashing skuller. Springing forward, Teanna rushed by, and with two sharp swings of her hatchets, she split a hole in the top of its head. Garcia came next — hustling over, dumping a vial of dark liquid in the hole, and running to Roni's side.

A soft pop and gray smoke curled out of the skuller.

No time to relax, though. Roni had too many things to do and didn't know what to deal with first. She wanted to thank her teammates for their professionalism, courage, and simply having her back. She wanted to admonish the rest of her army for falling apart, running off, and endangering everybody else. But she also wanted to find the words to encourage them, to reassemble the groups, and to find a way to make them fight. Unfortunately, she never had the opportunity to decide.

Five more skullers crawled from the windows of nearby buildings. Stak barked several orders and one of his new groups came running — perhaps over their initial fear or, having had a moment to think, simply more afraid of Stak. They stormed to join Roni.

But while the additional strength gave everyone a boost in confidence, Roni noticed little white splotches bobbing in many of the windows. Maybe all of them. Skullers from all the dead citizens in these blocks watched. If those cretins decided to swarm out and attack as one, Roni saw no way to survive.

Heavy thumps erupted from back the way they had traveled. As the noise grew louder, Roni could feel slight vibrations in her feet. The five skullers froze as they touched the street. They looked toward the growing beat and skittered back up the walls. When they ducked into their windows, Roni scanned for the other skullers. They all coward below the sills, hoping not be seen.

Swallowing against her drying mouth, she turned to face the far end of the street. Curiosity mixed with disbelief brought all the new Society into the open. They cautiously stepped out from their hiding spots, gazing down the street toward the park, and Roni realized she had been mistaken — they were not curious nor in disbelief. Whether they were conscious of it or not, their animal instincts had taken over, and those instincts understood that the sound of danger came from the same direction as the only exit.

"Form up your groups," Stak said, pointing at one set of people, waving at another.

Teanna jogged over to help reorganize. She clumped them into two larger teams. Roni approved. With any luck having more people around each individual would keep them in line.

As the approaching enemies lumbered into view, Roni had enough time to notice the lack of gunshots from either block over. Her flanking teams were probably dead.

When two skullers, two drastically different skullers, stepped into the middle of the street, Roni thought all her people were probably going to die, too. Bigger than an elephant, these creatures had visible muscle powering their many arms. Whatever animal they had birthed from, it gave them enormous heads with a mouth of teeth like a lion.

Or a T-rex. Roni thought her people deserved a pat on the back for not running away again.

"I'm sorry," Garcia said, "but there's no way I have enough potion left to petrify even one of them."

Keeping her eyes on the giant skullers, Roni said, "Go help Elliot. We'll need all the healing we can get." Motioning for Gully, Gram, and Botolu to follow her, she marched up to Dyon and Stak.

"Let me form a unit with just my people," Stak said. "We can handle one of them."

Dyon said, "Bravery's admirable, but we're going to need a lot more than that."

"We've got more." He snapped his fingers for his people to join him. With a devilish twinkle, he added, "I may have neglected to mention some aspects of my Society. You worry about the one on the left. We'll take care of the one on the right."

Teanna looked to Roni. Glancing back up the street where Yal-hara waited, where little flashes of light against the dark sky taunted her, Roni shook her head. This would never end well. She strained to hear Wex and his teams firing their guns — but the silence on the flanks remained. A dim hope, of course.

"Do it," she said.

As Teanna reorganized yet again, Roni swallowed down the ugliness rising in her throat. She wouldn't say it out loud, couldn't be sure she even understood, but that didn't matter. Roni knew. Deep to her bones. She had allowed Wex to run his teams separate because she hoped he could be a good diversion. And now, she allowed Stak to go off alone because either he would succeed and all would be well, or his group would be slaughtered but they would buy the rest a little time. That's all she could expect from these untrained teams. Too many of them would be fodder to gum up things. Nothing but a tactic to give the real Parallel Society time to fight Yal-hara.

How Gram knew what went on in Roni's head would forever be a mystery, but she walked over without being called. "Lord knows the decisions we make as leaders are not easy. Especially when we know those decisions will result in deaths. If it helps, though, I think you're doing the right thing."

The giant skullers mulled up the block, not showing any aggression, but the viny-mold webbing their bodies promised they were not in control. Soon, Roni knew it, soon they would charge. When that happened, fear would overtake many of her army.

"We can't play defense anymore," she whispered. Then to Teanna: "Take them down!"

Stak thrust his fist in the air, and his team of five sprinted off to the right. As they ran, they changed. Each furry body bulked up in muscle and bone. They grew taller and wider until they stood twice their height, brimming with strength, and baring their teeth.

By the time they vaulted into battle with the skuller, Teanna had the rest of the army roaring as they charged to the left. Roni wanted to run into the thick of it, let the rage burn through her bones, blinding out all else. But Gram placed a firm grip on her shoulder.

"You can't go in there," she said. "Leaders stay in the back."

"That's a modern thing," Roni said. "Leaders used to lead from the front — as in *lead the charge*."

But Roni stayed back with Gram at her side. And they watched.

On the right, Stak's group caused the skuller a lot of trouble. They bit and pummeled and jumped from one flailing limb to another. But whenever the skuller landed a blow, it sent Stak's people flying off into the nearest building or skidding on the hard street. Each time, the warrior would need a few extra seconds to recover before jumping back into the fray.

On the left, it was a slaughter.

The skuller swung its massive arms with speed and intent. It clobbered swaths of the army. Yet when those people floundered into the walls, they did not require a few extra seconds to recover. They never recovered. Crimson splotches marked where they hit, and their bodies folded on the ground below. Others never made it that far, dying when the skuller cracked open their heads. Blood splashed in the air and rained back down on the living.

"We have to stop this," Roni said. She pulled out one of Gram's books.

"That won't work, dear. They're too big."

"Bullshit. I've seen them work before."

Though Gram bristled at the vulgarity, she stayed on topic — that worried Roni even more. "Lord, I wish it weren't true, but the small books I've given you don't have the strength for something like that. Not here. The skullers were created by the Vestu Books. Look at this city, look what those Books did. My version of a book can't fight it, and if you go in there, you'll only end up getting yourself killed — or the others who will try to defend you."

"I can't just sit here."

"You shouldn't. I know we hoped to go after Yal-hara together, but that's not an option now. You go. Yourself. You can do it. I'll let Teanna know, and she'll do everything possible to keep this fight going, to give you all the time you can get."

"But —"

"Do you really want to waste all these lives? Go."

Roni turned toward the dark end of the street. The lightning flashes had brightened. Growing stronger. She felt — something. A tug. No. *A connection.* Just thinking about Yal-hara, looking off in her direction, and Roni knew that vicious soul was there.

"Okay," she said, cold and hard, as she headed away from the battle, from her army, and toward her end.

CHAPTER 27

With each step, Roni picked up speed. Her legs lifted her into a brisk walk, then a light jog, then an outright run, then a soaring sprint. She left the city and darted across a dark and open plain. Blackened dirt plumed beneath her feet, reflecting in the flashes of light. Blood pounding, lungs straining, sweat pouring – yet she pushed harder. Ahead, she saw a circular platform with ten pedestals, each a different height, each an ornate stand for one of the ten Vestu Books.

Careening to the steps that led onto the platform, she skidded to a stop. A wave of dark dust followed. In the center, a brazier burned, casting firelight and warmth around the circle. And, of course, standing between the brazier and the Books, Roni found Yal-hara.

Like a spider or a praying mantis or a scorpion or perhaps all of them, Yal-hara still horrified and threatened. Her four bone-thin legs moved with a shake now. The last time Roni had encountered this monster, she noticed the wrinkles and graying. Yal-hara had gotten old. Yet she looked rejuvenated. Not young but full of exhilaration.

She spider-stepped along the edge of a wooden beam that ran across all the pedestals. The walkway looked out of place until Roni realized — Yal-hara, all three feet of her, could not look into the Books from the ground. She must have had this beam nailed in. Indeed, the longer Roni observed the beam, the more she saw how clumsy it looked — hastily installed with no concerns other than to serve an immediate purpose.

Treading with care, Roni regained control of her racing breath and thrumming pulse. She could hear the fighting in the city streets, reminding her that she had to move fast, but she knew better than to blindly lunge forward. Yal-hara stood ready.

"So afraid," she said, her sibilant voice creeping up Roni's spine.

"So pathetic."

"We've stopped you before."

"Have you? Slowed me down, perhaps, but you have never truly stopped me. After all, I am right here. And you are exactly where I have wanted you."

Roni's foot froze over the last step. Trying to recover, she said, "If you wanted me here, you could have told me where you were from the beginning. You could have —"

"I sent my servants after you."

"To kill us."

Yal-hara tilted her shoulder and lifted upward. "No, not you. If your friends had happened to die, I would certainly not have been upset. But I gave orders to capture you and bring you here. But these servants aren't too bright."

"Capture me?"

Turning, Yal-hara gestured toward the Books. "After all, how am I going to open the tenth Book without you?"

Every line in Roni's face deepened as she scanned across the pedestals of Vestu Books. All but one lay open. Flashes of red, blue, green, and orange snapped out of their pages, reaching upward like lightning in reverse.

"You have all the Books open."

"All but one." Yal-hara pointed to the last. "Soon enough, though."

"But there were only three trophies."

"Trophies? Ah, you mean the artifacts that brought you here. Yes, each one is connected to three books. Every three books, when opened, created a single artifact. That gets you nine books."

One of the giant skullers bellowed. Roni snatched a glance at the city. It appeared that Teanna's teams had surrounded the skuller, but it still swung wildly, sending numerous bodies flopping through the air. On Stak's side, Roni counted only three fur-covered fighters. She hoped the other two were still alive.

"I thought to have so many Books open would cause chaos."

Yal-hara clicked her tongue. "Is that what they told you? And you believed them? After all the lies Elliot and your grandmother have punched down your throat, yet you still want to swallow the next one."

"Are you saying that you don't want to use the Books to control all the universes?"

"I'm saying that this is not the first time you have operated under a false premise."

"You're no better. You stole my memories and have lied to me more than they ever did."

"I have never lied to you. Think through all you know, and you'll see that while I may have refused to divulge all you wanted to know, while I may have misrepresented the meaning behind the facts, I never told you something that wasn't ultimately true."

None of this answered the question, but Roni knew not to ask again. Even if the words out of Yal-hara's mouth were truthful, they only served to waste more time evading an honest reply.

"It doesn't matter," Roni finally said as she dug into her jacket pocket. "I won't let you open that final book."

She pulled out one of the small books Gram had made and held it forward like a weapon. With a determined sneer, she reached and pulled back the cover. Bracing against the brutal winds that came when one universe depressurized into another, she tucked her head and planted her feet in a firm stance. But nothing happened.

Yal-hara tapped one taloned finger against another. The simple sound mocked Roni worse than applause. "Pathetic, indeed."

Roni turned the book around and gazed in at the emptiness of another universe. Part of her wanted to jump in, but she tossed the book aside. Gram had been right. The Vestu Books drained all the power or blocked it or something. Without an empty universe's vacuum pulling everything within the book's path, Roni could not force Yal-hara inside.

A croaking rattle came from the city. Roni hoped to see Teanna and her soldiers standing victorious upon the corpse of a giant skuller. Instead, she watched a man torn in half. As Glissford charged forward, his gleaming armor bright against the dark of the city, one of Gram's chains wiped over the back of the skuller. But it could not hold the beast in place, and Glissford was caught in the skuller's arms.

Yal-hara had continued — probably a gloating speech filled with insults — and Roni lifted a wry lip at the idea that she had missed it all. "But to finish this," Yal-hara was saying, "I've been stuck waiting for you."

"What?" Roni's attention drew again to the city battle. Stak held onto the skuller's head, and maybe it looked cracked — too far away to tell for sure — but no others of his team could be seen. Things on the left side did not appear any better. The giant skuller barreled through the lines, bowling down large swaths of soldiers. Roni had no clue how Teanna managed to keep them all fighting.

Yal-hara cocked her head and made that horrid sound which still echoed in Roni's nightmares — that monstrous laughter. "You have no idea what you are doing. Each new Head Council brings to the Vestu Books their own energy. Like a signature. That unique energy changes the nature of the locks upon the Books."

A snap of light and a burst of smoke erupted near one skuller. Perhaps a hasty potion from Garcia. Or a spell from Elliot. No – Roni spotted a green glow off to the side of the battle. Elliot must have shielded the wounded as Dyon's healers worked.

Yal-hara went on, "It has taken me years to break those locks, but as I toiled toward that goal, I learned, too. Especially about the tenth book. Because I knew that specific one would be different. Special. Eventually, I understood — to open it, I needed my full signature, my full energy."

Roni put a hand on the wooden beam to keep from falling. "No."

"The night I came to your room and stole your memories — that night was different than any other time I had taken a child's memory. Something strange happened. You and I, our energy, became connected."

"That's a lie."

"I wasn't thrilled to learn of it, either. But I know how the universes love to screw with us. So, yes, the truth is that I can only open this Book with you. If you wanted to stop all of this, you should never have come. You should have stayed home. Of course, I would have sought you, but you've made the whole thing far easier."

Roni fought down the screams scrabbling up her throat. Her muscles quaked. Arguments raced through her mind, but her body took over before she could form a clear thought. She stormed across the platform and belted Yal-hara in the jaw. Pulling back her fist, she howled her rage and unleashed a furious wrath. She struck again. And again.

For a moment, Roni thought Yal-hara's age had slowed the monster down. In the past, she would have evaded the punches, darted around, and attacked from behind. But other than hopping back a few steps, Yal-hara stood ready for another hit.

Fine with me, Roni's frenzied brain thought. She pulled back her fist and smashed forward once more.

But this time, Yal-hara moved to the side. With one hand, she snapped her spindle-fingers around Roni's wrist, yanking in the direction of the punch to take Roni off balance. Yal-hara's other hand pressed flat onto the cover of the tenth Book. Between the beats of her heart, Roni saw she had been tricked.

A surge ripped through her like the draining of blood from the head when standing too fast. The pedestals spun around her, their light dazing her dizzy mind. Yal-hara continued her disgusting laugh. A golden light blazed beneath Yal-hara's bony hand, and with a triumphant shout, she pulled back. The book, the tenth and final Vestu Book, flew open.

Roni dropped to her knees. Tears soaked her face while her body shuddered. The colorful flashes of lightning ceased as if the books bowed in respect for their newly awoken master.

And the ground shook.

CHAPTER 28

Rumbling from deep beneath the Cavern, something powerful rushed up, reaching for the surface. Yal-hara stepped off the wooden beam, backing away with ecstasy on her face. A spear of light thundered out of the tenth Book. It rose like a dragon and spread into a tidal wave that swelled toward the city.

Roni jumped to her feet. Standing side by side with Yal-hara, she watched the glittering wave smash into the obsidian buildings, tearing them down like sand castles. Scattering from the windows, skullers raced along the walls, trying to outrun the inevitable. The cries of Roni's army reached her ears as she watched the giant skullers topple over.

It all happened too fast.

One second, she fought with Yal-hara for the safety of all. One second later, all had been decimated. The wave of light hit the end of the city and broke apart as if it had never been. Only rubble and smoke and silence remained.

Roni stared at the dead ground before her. She wanted to weep over Gram and Elliot, Teanna and Gully, and even Garcia. She wanted to howl and curse and utter every sound of pain known to creatures throughout existence.

But she heard Yal-hara's vile laugh once more. She heard that bone-thin waste of breathing space expressing joy. And all of Roni's loss lumping in her chest set ablaze, burning her like a fever, blinding away all else but her enemy.

With a warrior cry, she launched into the air and tackled Yal-hara. If this hated creature fought back, Roni felt nothing. She bashed her fists down over and over, barely feeling each painful blow, never sure if the blood she saw was her own or Yal-hara's, never caring. She would punch until nothing moved beneath. She spit and screamed with each blow.

Something struck the side of her head — Yal-hara had found a bit of strength — and Roni fell over. Yal-hara swung atop and stabbed downward with her sharp, narrow claws. They pierced Roni's hands, nailing her to the ground.

Blood rushed out of Yal-hara's crushed face, yet still she smiled. "I win."

Shrieking, Roni wrenched her hand to the side, snapping Yal-hara's bone. With a sweeping strike, Roni impaled the bone sticking out of her hand into Yal-hara's cheek. The monstrous beast roared, and Roni thought that sickening noise would be the last sound in her ears. Yal-hara had won. At least, Roni knew that when she died, she might reunite with all those she loved.

"No!" a voice called out of the dark.

A pale streak shot onto the platform. A breath of life in a ballgown baring teeth with ferocious beauty. Not a gown but the billowing of a Coana — Botolu.

Yal-hara snapped her head to the disruption. She only had time to utter one word. "But —"

Botolu crashed into Yal-hara. Sinking her only weapons, the growths from beneath her arms, into her enemy, Botolu let loose a banshee cry. Yal-hara screamed, too — partially from pain, partially from surprise, but mostly from fear. Roni had never heard a more lovely sound.

Sitting up, she half-expected to see Botolu beating Yal-hara senseless. But as Roni's head cleared, she knew that would have been wrong for her friend. Instead, she found Botolu standing over the paralyzed monster, unsure of what to do now that the danger had subsided.

"Are you hurt bad?" she asked Roni without looking away from Yal-hara.

"I've been worse." Roni wasn't sure that was true, but the words came out anyway. She struggled to her feet and stumbled a few steps.

"What should we do with this thing?"

Roni's right hand trembled. Like poking a wound, she wanted to gaze back at the rubble of the city, the grave of those she loved. She wanted the rage to scorch her once again, surge through her with righteous hatred, give her the strength to leap upon Yal-hara's prone body and dismantle the evil beast.

But Botolu stood next to her. Breathing hard yet holding still. If Roni attacked, would Botolu stop her? Yet even as the question entered her mind, Roni knew the fight had ended. The bloodlust had washed out of her system. Her enemy lay helpless. They only had to make sure Yal-hara could never again cause such harm.

An idea struck. One that brought with it a poetic grin.

Groaning with each motion, Roni closed all the Vestu Books. As their light died, the amber glow of the brazier filled in. When she reached the tenth, she paused. What if she looked inside? How much of the story of the Vestu Books and all their power was a myth? Yal-hara certainly knew some of the truth.

Roni licked her lips and closed her eyes. That kind of power should never be in one hand. She closed the book.

With a few groans, she then dragged Yal-hara by a limp boney hand. Scanning the ground, she located what she needed a little way off the platform — Gram's book. No word or ceremony. She simply approached. Yal-hara's body banged down the short stairs and collected soot while heaved along the ground.

"Please," Roni said, "open the book."

Botolu hesitated. She looked hard at Roni, clearly weighing the morality of this action versus the violence of an execution. At length, she bent down and flipped open the cover.

Yal-hara lolled her head to one side. "No, no," she muttered. "Don't."

As Roni lugged the monster toward the book, Botolu said, "Perhaps we should reconsider."

But the words came out half-hearted. As Roni dumped Yal-hara into the book, she saw Botolu's uneasiness but willingness as well. And when Roni closed the book, Botolu said, "You have a second book, yes?"

Roni nodded. She pulled out the second of Gram's books and opened it. Without pause, Botolu tossed the first book inside. After Roni closed it, Botolu nodded. "Good."

"Not quite," Roni said, thinking of all the books locked away in the Caverns. "But good enough for now."

Gazing back at the platform, the pedestals, and the Vestu Books, Botolu said, "What next?"

Roni exhaled and a sharp burn ran along her side. She wanted to sleep for a month. Instead, she managed to face the city. "We bury our friends."

CHAPTER 29

With Gram's book tucked tight under Roni's arm, they shuffled through the soot, heading back to the city. As they drew closer, the weight of the destruction pressed upon them like mounds of dirt thrown upon their graves. Roni tried to numb her mind. If she thought about what lay before her, about the loss of all those she cared for, she feared she would fall to her knees and never stand again.

"How are you still alive?" she asked Botolu, hoping to fill her thoughts with anything but what her eyes witnessed.

"I vowed to stay by your side as much as possible. When you left the skuller battle and went after Yal-hara, I followed."

"But I never saw you, never heard you."

Botolu clicked an answer, and Roni did not ask for a translation. There was no need. She had been too focused, too preoccupied with Yal-hara to notice anybody following her. Botolu also made a point of taking a less visible route, hiking a long distance up the left or right side and coming in from behind the platform. It took more time, but at least she didn't arrive too late.

When they entered the city streets, they had to climb over huge debris piles like hills formed at a dumpsite. Roni worried they might get injured trying to locate bodies, let alone trying to find their way back to the park — if they could even recognize the park anymore. But once they had overcome the initial piles, they discovered the energy wave that had toppled everything did not waver in direction. Since the city had been built on a grid, the rubble conformed to that grid design. It would be easy enough to keep to the main road and reach where the battle had taken place.

"Do you hear a buzzing sound?" Botolu said.

Roni heard nothing. "Maybe something electrical."

Increasing her pace, Botolu started checking the smaller, more accessible piles of debris. "No. I hear a clear buzzing, something different than electricity. More like the sound around the books. Like … like …"

"A spell?" Roni perked up. She rushed from one pile to another, knocking over rocks and bricks. "I can't hear anything. Where is it coming from?"

"I'm trying to figure that out."

"Hold still and listen."

Roni didn't want to believe it. No, she wanted desperately to believe it, but her heart feared that if this turned out wrong, the great weights over her would finally crash down.

"There!" Botolu dashed down the street, climbed a mid-sized rubble pile, and pulled back a wide piece of wall.

Underneath, Roni glimpsed a soft glow. Digging like a mad dog, she thrust aside everything she could grasp until her heart lifted. She shouted and cried. There, under the dirt, Elliot stood with his cane out, quaking as he held together a shield dome. Garcia, Gully, and Otaur huddled near him. Gram and Teanna stood by his side, helping to keep him standing.

Roni stopped, frozen at the sight of her family staring back at her. Tears streamed and her body shook, but she could not bring words to her mouth. Everything felt thick and slow as emotions muddled through her. Only a loving smile from Gram broke into Roni's fogging mind.

"If you need to take time," Botolu said, removing another chunk of debris, "I can handle this myself."

Snapping back, Roni started digging again. "We're here," she said to Gram and the others. "We'll get you free."

They continued their work but found nobody else. The rest were all dead. Even the wounded under the shield had not survived the concussive impact. Dyon, too – sprawled over a body as if trying to protect it.

Roni scanned up and down the street. None of the new Society members would have known to seek Elliot for protection. Even if one of the others yelled to run for the old man, panic at the energy wave would have blinded most from sensible action.

By the time she and Botolu pulled away enough parts of buildings and streets that Elliot could release the shield, Roni had regained her composure. Her people had lived. The rest she would deal with, but at least, she did not have to bury anybody she loved. As the guilt from that thought coursed through her, Elliot dropped onto a large chunk of concrete and bowed his head. Gram rubbed his back, but Roni saw that her one arm hung limp at her side.

"Yal-hara?" Teanna asked.

Roni pulled out the book. "In another book inside this one."

Standing, Gram released a chain from her good arm and locked it around the book. "What about the other ones? The Vestu Books?"

"I closed them."

"Good," Elliot said through gasping breaths. "The Council will have the Books locked once more, and a new Head Council will be chosen."

"Can't really trust those people, can we?"

"Not at all. Which is why I will remain in the City of Infinity."

Gully said, "But we came all this way to bring you back."

"My time being a Society member is done. I have a few years left in me, I think, and I should like to do the best I can for all universes — not just ours. That is something I should do right here."

Roni's instincts told her to argue, but she held back. She could see in his eyes that he truly wanted it this way. It hurt her — maybe hurt him, too — but forcing him to return to their universe after having spent years in the wondrous City seemed cruel. Also impossible.

Elliot looked to Otaur. "Of course, I'll need a hand, a team. I can think of no better to begin with than you. That is, if you will help me."

The insect winced as he stood taller. "It would be my privilege and honor."

"Good. Because I think there's a chance we can make you Head Council."

"Me? What an absurd notion. To lead the central construction that maintains all our universes into a functional system requires great care and consideration, a logistical mind, as well as a devotion that far exceeds the capabilities of the most ordinary individuals."

"Which is why you'll be perfect."

Garcia coughed and spit out a gray glob of dirt. "I'm glad Elliot knows he wants to stay and play at politics, but I don't want to." His coat was soaked where the violent razing of the city had also smashed the vials he held. "Can the rest of us go home? Please?"

A loud grunt followed by the clatter of shifting stones pulled all attention down the street. Another section of rubble moved. Everyone hustled towards it, and when they reached the pile, the top piece — a door — burst aside. Stak stood with a lamppost in hand. He had one member of his team left alive.

Once retrieved, the rest of the Society searched for other possible survivors. One of Glissford's people and three of Dyon's had managed to find safety beneath a row of cars. The search continued, but no further good news came. Yet Roni felt a thrill that even those few had lived. Anything was better than the disgust thinking she had led every soul to their deaths.

After spending a short time bandaging the wounded, the group found their way to the park and the entry point. Stepping through the glowing opening, they returned to the raised-bed garden. Elliot brought up the end and closed the pathway behind him. He then stomped on the trophies, shattering them into plastic shards.

"Lord, no," Gram said, standing by the slumped body of the Master Librarian.

Roni curled over. That thrill from earlier vanished in an instant. Tears rolled up from deep in her chest as she saw the dead woman in the chair, as she pictured the dead group leaders — Glissford, Wex, Dyon, as she thought of the nameless dead who had fought despite their fears. Nameless only to Roni, though. All dead. All of them.

She crouched down, afraid to let her knees touch the ground, and wept. Soon, Botolu lowered next to her and cried as well. Between her own shaking breaths and harsh sniffs, Roni heard more crying — muffled, hidden tears. She did not have to look. It was Teanna and Garcia. And while the old guard did not weep — they had endured too many losses over a lifetime — they did hold the solemn silence expected from such veterans.

As they mourned, Stak whispered to Elliot, "Whenever you're ready to fight again, you can call on us."

"Rest up. It'll be sooner than you think."

Stak motioned with his head, and the few survivors followed him out of the alleyway. Even Otaur joined them, somehow sensing that Roni's people needed to be alone.

When the last tearful heave shuddered out, Roni stood and wiped her eyes. She looked at all the swollen, bruised faces. "Let's get out of here."

"That would be wonderful," Teanna said. "Does anybody know how?"

Gram patted her chest. "I'm sorry, but Hayle's journal never mentioned his return journey in detail."

Roni walked over to the Master Librarian and grabbed the map book in the old woman's lap. "This will have the answer. For us, at least." She turned to her beloved golem. "I'm sorry to ask, but I believe this is the final time. I need the Pages of Glass."

Gully peeked at Garcia. They had spent months trying to destroy the Pages.

"If you had succeeded, you would have told me," Roni said. "And I know where you keep them."

"Yes, yes. I have them." Gully turned his back to the group as he dug his fingers into his torso, pushing aside his clay until he reached the thin, green pages. When he handed them over, Roni noticed he had attempted to patch his body.

"You know we'll fix you up when we return."

"Of course. What good is a golem, if he's got lumps and holes?"

Garcia said, "I can heal all of us when I can get to the workshop again."

Agreeing, Roni set the book on the ground and flipped it until she found the two-page spread of the overall city layout. She then used the Pages of Glass to look upon the book. Through its green lens, she could see all the rifts and their locations. After marking each one, about twenty, she then found the close-up maps for each location. One by one, they combed through each spot, using the Pages to identify where those rifts led. When they found the eleventh rift — hidden in a coffee shop several miles away — they found their route home.

CHAPTER 30

Traveling back turned out to be both easier and harder than expected. Easier because the rift dropped them in a familiar part of the Caverns. Harder because the damage done by the Vestu Books collapsed many tunnels and left others in precarious condition.

Roni could never be sure if those Books would have dismantled everything in existence. Perhaps, like Yal-hara had said, much of what they thought was merely myth. But the damage was real. She had no doubt that since the Books caused that much of a problem, there would be a lot of rifts to lock away all over the Earth. The Parallel Society would have some busy years ahead of them.

Once they reached the opening to the bookstore, they found Gully's giant golem, Betty, holding it from collapse by wedging her body against the stone wall. She must have been like that for days — except time moved differently here.

"You are doing spectacular, my dear," Gully said. "Hold on a little longer, and I'll make you some helpers."

Everyone had work to do. Garcia hurried to concoct enough healing potions for the entire team. In a flurry of activity, Gully created a dozen small golems to relieve Betty, shore up the tunnels, and locate new structural problems. Teanna used a laptop to search recent news articles of unusual events that hinted at rift activity. She began a list. When they were ready to get back to work, there would be no wasted time. Botolu spent the first few days overwhelmed by the Philly suburbs, but as soon as she learned of the Grand Library, she delved into the many journals detailing the Society's full story.

Roni understood. Until they recovered completely, Botolu felt stuck here. Best to use that time and all the knowledge that surrounded her by seeking answers on how to deal with the problems awaiting her when she returned home.

Yet whenever the world around Roni settled into predictable moments — breakfast, lunch, and dinner; paperwork and books; meetings and decisions — part of her wanted to shed tears again. She saw the faces of those who had trusted her. It had yet to fade, yet to grow easier. And she wondered how awful she would feel when the day came that she didn't cry over their deaths.

She had all of that on her mind when she called a meeting at the Big Table with Teanna, Garcia, and Gully. Before anyone asked, Roni said, "Gram won't be joining. This is for us. The new Parallel Society."

"Another *New* Society," Gully said. "How many times can we use the word *new* before it's old?"

"I don't know. Maybe you can figure it out. But I'm using it again. Now. Because I need you all to take a moment and look at each other. This is it. Sully is gone, Elliot won't be returning, and someday, Gram will pass. The four of us — we are the Parallel Society. And like the team that came before us, we will be together for decades to come. The only way this will ever work is for us to go beyond mere leader and teammates. We have to be family. That's the strength Gram, Elliot, and Sully always had."

Teanna said, "Then we're in good shape. We already are a family."

"I think we're at the start. But we have a long way to go. I need you all to know that I'll be working hard to be there for each of you and that I see all your great contributions to the Society. Even when you're in the background, I know you're there. I could never have defeated Yal-hara without Teanna leading the fight against the skullers. I could never have reached the top of Mountain Pillar without Garcia creating obstacles for the Blue Sashes. I could never have made it through that first book in Mexico without Gully being recognized for the wonder that he is. All of you are vital. This universe — all universes — owe you a great debt. And, well, that's about as mushy as I can get."

With a sharp sniffle, Garcia stood. His eyes glistened. "I know I have only begun my journey with the Society, but you have my word that I will always be here for you. For all of you. We are family."

Gully stood, too. "I know I was created to stay here and help you whenever I could, but I think we can all agree that I am so much more. Not trying to boast, but I feel I can safely say that there is no other golem quite like me."

"That is very true."

"Thank you. That's probably the nicest thing you've ever said to me."

"Well, we are family now. Right?"

"Yes." Gully smiled wide. "We are family."

Teanna shrugged as she stood. "We've been family longer than we've known each other."

Putting her hand forward, Roni said, "Okay, then. To family."

Each member put their hand in like a sports team huddle, and to Roni's surprise, nobody made a joke about it. They stood there, hand upon hand, until finally Roni gave the whole effort a strong shake. The new Parallel Society broke off, returning to their work, but each member carried taller, walked firmer.

"Do you have a moment?" Gram said, snapping Roni back. "I'd like to chat."

Roni gestured to a chair at the Big Table.

"I want you to see something," Gram said. "Come."

They walked back to the elevator, rode up to the fifth floor, entered the stairwell, and climbed up to the roof. As one of Olburg's taller buildings, they could watch over most of the town. It offered a beautiful view for a sunrise or, as was the case at that moment, a sunset. Rose and crimson hues reached across the sky as the sun drifted behind the hills.

"It is pretty," Roni said, "but I've been up here before. I used to sneak up here to smoke cigarettes when I was teen."

Gram raised an eyebrow. "I was well aware."

The evening traffic rumbled along the street below. A car honked a few blocks over. If they could have seen through the hills, Roni knew that on the other side, she would get an amazing view of the Philadelphia skyline bumping the horizon.

"If this is about Botolu, I've already told her that we'll make arrangements to get to Mexico within the next couple weeks. By then, we should all be ready to head back to Coana and help her cause. But I won't leave here until I'm sure we can handle our job in this universe."

"And that falls on Teanna?"

"Garcia and Gully can support me. Especially since I have no intention of fighting Botolu's fight. She's got to get her own people to stand up. But I can bring proof that Hayle was not some deity or prophet or anything worthy of their praise. Teanna will do fine. Plus, Gully is making some golems to help her. And she'll have you, too."

Gram closed her eyes and let the last remnants of the sun wash over her. "I know Teanna can handle the job. She'll make a great leader one day. You'll train her well. That's what I want you to see, to hear. The way you handled the hardest, worst decisions you had to make on that battlefield — giving up all of our lives in order to stop Yal-hara — I have never been prouder. I knew then that all of the discussions I had over the years with Elliot and Sully proved that I had been wrong. I worried that you never would become who you are, but they insisted you had it in you."

She turned to Roni and took her hands. "I know that sounds terrible, but like a good leader, I need to be honest with you. I made a mistake back then. I know you were very aware that I had doubts. But this is what you never understood — it was never about doubts in you. I didn't realize that back then, but watching you take charge of the Society, save all the universes, do the job the best I've ever known it to be done, well, it hit me. All along I had feared that the Society might destroy you like it destroyed your parents. It would have been my failure again. I'm sorry I held you back."

Roni clamped down the swelling in her chest as she pulled Gram in for a hug. "It's okay," she said, her words muffled in Gram's shoulder.

"Hold still," Gram said. "This might hurt."

A sharp prick like getting a doctor's shot flared in Roni's back. She stepped away and tried to reach the spot. "What was that? What did you do?"

"What I should have done years ago. Relax, now. Stand straight and lower your hands to your sides."

Though wary, Roni obeyed.

"Good. Now, flick your wrist like this."

Gram demonstrated, and Roni did as instructed. A bizarre cascading sensation rushed down her arm like hot water. Her wrist burned a little. Then she heard it — the clinking of a chain spooling onto the rooftop.

She looked down. A thin, tiny chain trickled next to her shoe. When she raised her head, she could feel tears on her cheeks.

Gram smiled back. "You'll be able to make books, too. I'll show you how. You'll need to do so because I have no power now. I'm just an old lady living in her granddaughter's bookstore."

"What?"

She held out a piece of paper. "The deed. My powers and the deed to the bookstore. With those, you are as complete a leader of the Parallel Society as I could ever pray for. Now, don't worry. I'll still be around, and I'll teach you how to use those powers well. But I plan to be in the background. A voice for advice but no longer active. I've had my fill of adventure. And … well … I suppose that's it. I love you."

She kissed Roni's cheek as she handed over the deed. Then she walked back into the building.

"I love you, too," Roni said, but didn't know if Gram had heard.

The sun had nearly set, but the list of things to do the following day had increased enormously. She had powers now. She needed training, she needed to help Botolu, she needed to reorganize the team now that Gram would no longer be as involved.

She needed to recognize why Gram brought her to the rooftop.

With a deep breath, she tried to clear her mind. Find stillness. Peace. Watch the sunset. Take another breath. Tomorrow's problems were for tomorrow. Because if nothing else, Roni knew that moments of peace were fleeting, and the problems of the universe were infinite.

About the Author

Stuart Jaffe is the madman behind *The Max Porter Paranormal Mysteries,* the *Nathan K* thrillers, *The Parallel Society* series, *The Malja Chronicles, The Bluesman, Founders, Real Magic,* and so much more. His unique brand of old pulp adventure mixed with a contemporary sensibility brings out the best in a variety of SF/F sub-genres. He trained in martial arts for over a decade until a knee injury ended that practice. Now, he plays lead guitar in a local blues band, *The Bootleggers,* and enjoys life on a small farm in rural North Carolina. For those who continue to keep count, the animal list is as follows: one dog, two cats, two aquatic turtles, and fifteen chickens. The horse is now at a new pasture. She's having a wonderful time hanging with a herd of thirty other horses. Much better for her. As best as he's been able to manage, Stuart has made sure that the chickens do not live in the house.

For more information about Stuart and his books, please visit *www.stuartjaffe.com*

www.ingramcontent.com/pod-product-compliance
Lightning Source LLC
Chambersburg PA
CBHW020302030826
48979CB00027B/2007/J

* 9 7 8 1 9 6 3 5 1 7 1 6 3 *